A Question of Duty

Martin McDowell

A QUESTION OF DUTY
Copyright © Martin McDowell 2012

First Published in the UK by
Paul Mould Publishing
p.mould@yahoo.com

In association with
Empire Publishing Service www.ppeps.com
P.O. Box 1344, Studio City, CA 91614-0344

All rights reserved. No part of this file may be reproduced or transmitted in any form or by any means without the prior written permission of the author, except by a reviewer who may quote brief passages in a review printed in a newspaper, magazine, journal or online.

A CIP Catalogue record for this book is available from the British Library or from the US Library of Congress.

Simultaneously published in
Australia, Canada, Germany, UK, USA

Printed in Great Britain
First Printing 2012

UK ISBN 97809566239-2-8
USA ISBN 978158690-116-5

Dedication

To Doreen, my wife, Amy and Steven

Acknowledgement

The Trafalgar Companion –
A Guide to History's Most Famous Sea Battle and
the Life of Admiral Lord Nelson
by Mark Adkin

Patrick O'Brian for his Jack Aubrey Novels

Front cover taken from an original painting by David C Bell

Also available *Worth Their Colours*

Coming soon *First Encounters*

"Look at Troubridge! Tacking his ship into
action as though all the eyes of England
were upon him. And I wish to God they were!"

Admiral Jervis observing Captain Troubridge of
HMS Culloden leading the English Fleet
into action at the Battle of Cape St. Vincent
14th February 1797

Contents

Chapter One: A Crack Frigate...11

Chapter Two: By Their Deeds Shalt Thou Know Them...................29

Chapter Three: Affairs Ashore...81

Chapter Four: Sinead Malley..116

Chapter Five: La Pomone..156

Chapter Six: New Shipmates..189

Chapter Seven: Witness or Defendant?......................................229

Chapter Eight: A Question of Duty...273

Chapter Nine: Delivery...327

Chapter Ten: Praise and Recrimmination..................................380

Chapter Eleven : A Settling of Accounts....................................429

Chapter Twelve: A Life More Sedate..486

Chapter Thirteen: Just Conclusions...536

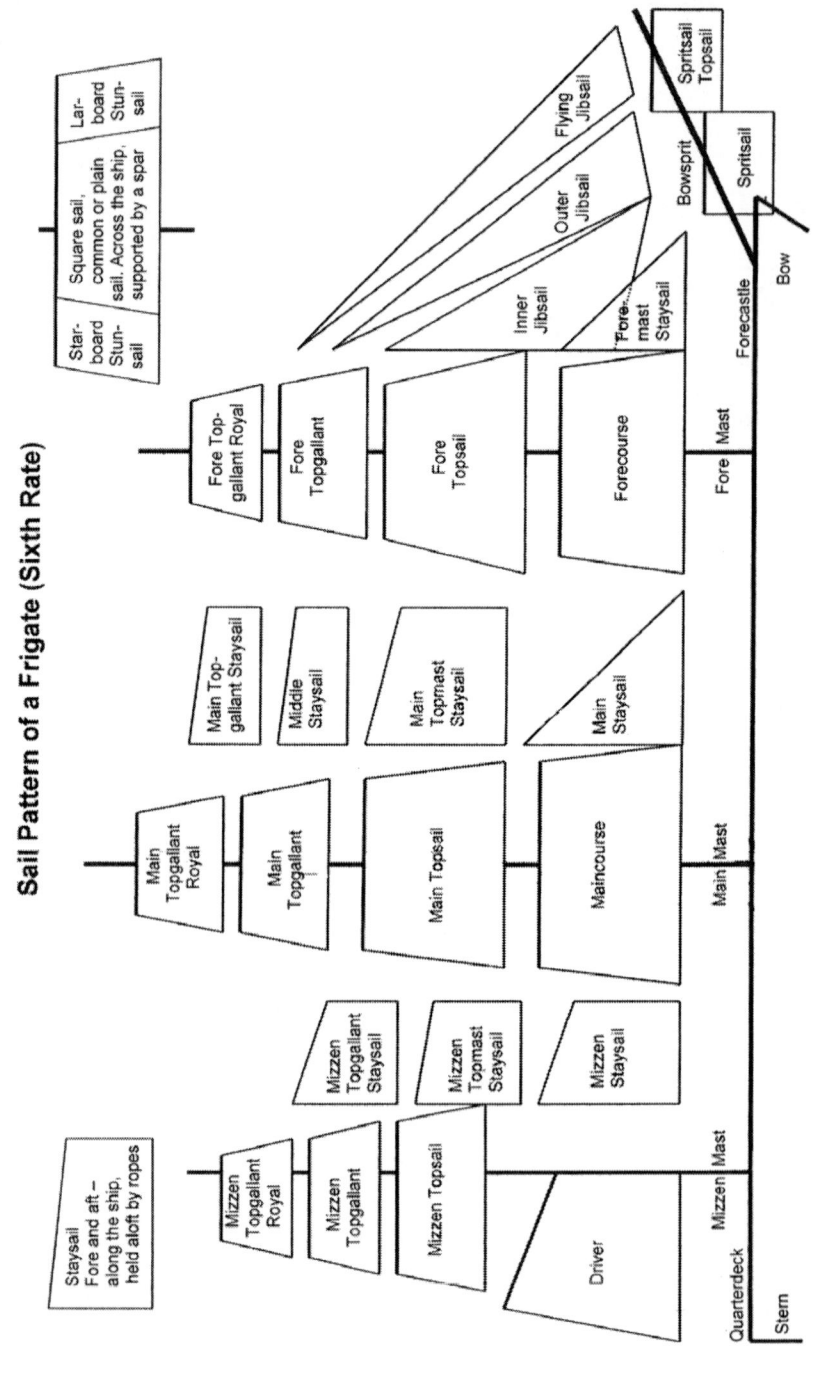

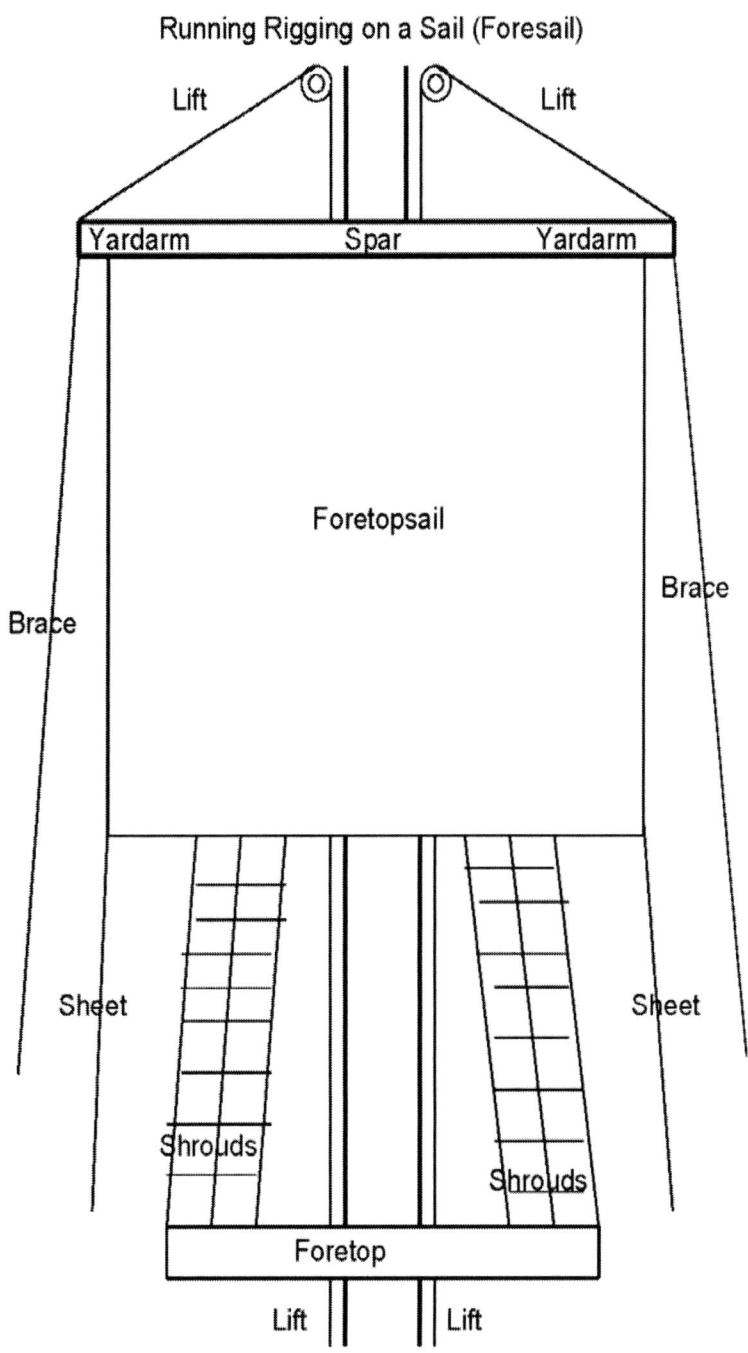

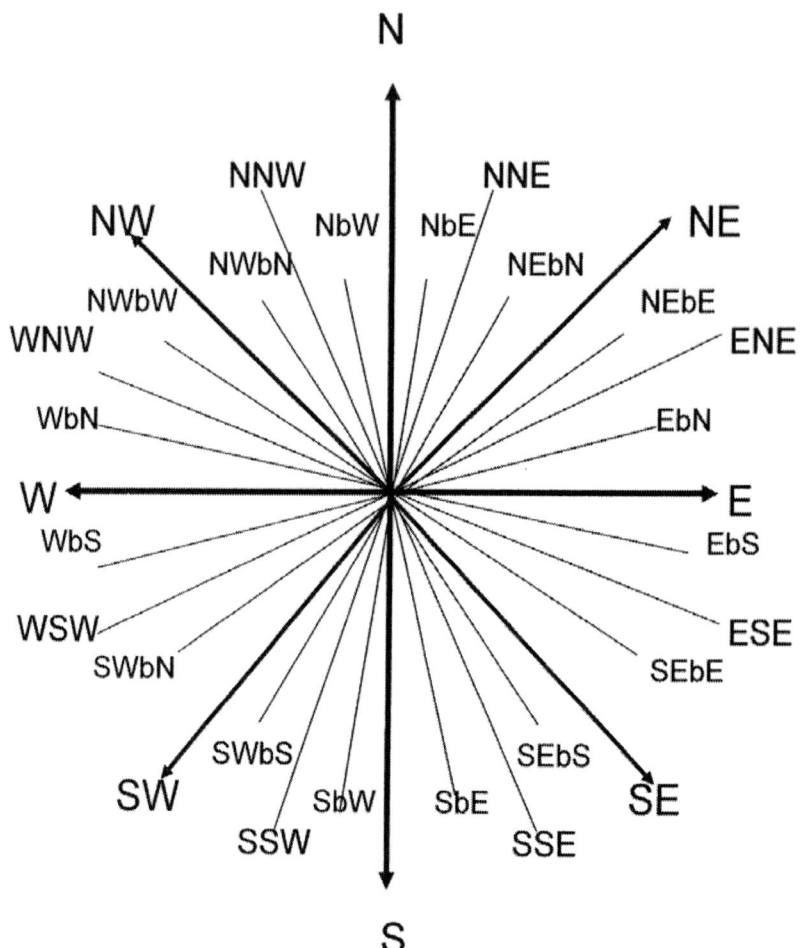

Chapter One

A Crack Frigate

Two tall ships, each stern and resolute and each much burdened by a tower of white sail, stood out bright against the contrasting pastel blues of a hurrying sea and shifting sky. Both were players in the high drama that had built between them throughout a flawless day in the high summer of 1809, their theatre being the Western Approaches, where the Atlantic and The Channel combine. On this day their stage was a benign, but busy ocean, stretching far out to meet a ruler-straight horizon that supported a backdrop of royal blue and this burnished sky continued the set by soaring upwards to hold scattered and wayward clouds, stragglers from an earlier, thicker day, all now sailing on to crowd the far distance. The azure sea added its colour; regular waves rolling hopelessly after the hurrying white billows above, leaving white horses to fall back from their crests as they quickly surrendered the unequal chase.

All was pushed on by a stiff Northeast wind that had cleared the skies of the unseasonable rain of the previous days and, harnessing that wind, bursting through the waves, the two vessels added their lazy beauty to the unblemished picture of an ocean in lively mood, their urgent passage marring its surface with a blue-white and far extending wake. Now, under a mile apart, each carried a full spread of sail in the muscular wind, for each was on their maximum canvas, both vessels on the edge of sailing prudence. One thing alone stood in clear contrast; the leader had her gunports picked out by a contrasting band, yellow on black, but those of the chaser, black on a dull reddish brown. These were clearly the colours of the different navies, perhaps of warring nations, and both were running full before the wind, receiving its power not quite perfectly over the stern, but just enough from their left to be termed over the larboard quarter. Both were steering South South West and neither had yet shown any colours, but clearly one was the pursuer, the other the pursued.

Captain Reuben Argent stood alone on his portion of the leading ship's quarterdeck, this being the weatherside, from where came the wind, this portion of the polished decking being his by right and tradition. He was tall, just turned 30, and on the lean side of muscular, but certainly of fair appearance, finely chiselled features under a shock of wayward chestnut brown hair. He gazed along the length of his ship, HMS Ariadne, his first command, but his dark blue eyes took in nothing of the ordered deck arranged before him. He could feel the strength of the wind against the left side of his face, but more importantly to him, he had his mind focused on what came to his left hand resting on a thick hawser, this rejoicing in the title of larboard mizzen royal backstay, a vital support which arched up to the highest spar of the mizzenmast. All his senses were turned towards the vibration that was carried down this immense cable that ran from the high mast to the deck, then for him to combine the message with what he sensed of the strength and constancy of the wind. His ship took a dip in the regular waves and, without thinking, he braced his left side against the gunwale; the thick bar of polished wood that topped the ship's side. Beneath, the sea hissed past and under his ship's counter, passing mere feet from where he stood, above the deep swell of her wake that angled away, out into the far distance. The big driver sail, lowest on the mizzen mast and angled hard out to starboard, rose straining above him; it now bellied full out, to add its weight to the enormous force that thrust his ship onward and through the easy swell.

All on the Quarterdeck showed calm, as though on a fleet review. Two steersmen stood at the wheel, occasionally studying the compass in the binnacle, more often studying the pennants at the mastheads that told of the wind's direction. Two Officers and a Midshipman had their telescopes permanently levelled back over the taffrail, focused on their pursuer. Their ship curtsied and slid to starboard and all on deck subconsciously leaned away from the movement beneath their feet. Whatever was being conveyed to Argent through the backstay had arrived in the affirmative and Argent looked up to the final two vacant spars at the very tops of his masts.

"Set Royals. Mizzen and main."

The Officer of the Watch, Second Lieutenant Lucius Bentley, had for sometime been standing closeby. Not close enough to be intrusive, but close enough to create no danger of missing any bidding from his Captain.

"Aye aye, Sir."

He hurried forward to the Quarterdeck rail, where the Captain's sanctum dropped down to the gundeck, and he leaned his protruding stomach and angular face over it.

"Mr. Ball."

A tall figure, thickset, which distorted the impression of his actual height, turned from studying the towering spread of straining canvas and then he, the First Bosun's Mate, lifted a lined, weatherbeaten face, framed in ginger whiskers, to the voice above him.

"Sir?"

"Set Mizzen and Main Royals."

Henry Ball couldn't keep the tone of enquiry from his voice, the canvas already set amounted to well over an acre, but it was soon banished by the acknowledgement of the order.

"Royals, Sir? Mizzen and Main. Aye aye Sir."

A blast on his silver call whistled across the deck, then his bellicose voice roused the Larboard Watch, idle but alert on the gangways and forecastle. His fellow Bosun's Mates, standing idle for just such as this, immediately joined in. The response was instant, the men swarmed up to the highest ratlines and the two sails fell and were sheeted home. Argent checked the set of the canvas and then trained his own glass back over the rail.

George Fraser, Ship's Bosun, never without a pained nor aggrieved expression on his face, looked up at the new sails now drawing hard at the very tops of their masts.

"Oh My Lord. He'll have the sticks out of her, see if he don't. Then where will we be? Wholly done for! Done and trussed."

He said this to no one in particular and none heard other than his good friend, offduty Quartermaster Zachary Short. They could have been brothers, years in the Navy had rendered both weatherbeaten, stocky, ill-tempered and scowling. Fraser pulled himself up over the gunwale, his oaken face matching the tone of the oiled wood.

"And I be feelin' for that cathead. This be dealin' more strain on him than any anchor ever could."

His narrowed eyes looked with maternal anxiety at the square, solid protrusion that came from the ship's side just behind the bows, it cradling the huge starboard anchor. His pained and uneasy expression intensified as he studied the straining cable leading down from this most solid block of timber, back to an invisible collection of submerged barrels that existed at the end of the cable, somewhere in the deep. He took himself over to the larboard bow and studied the same; here also an identical cable was bent around that cathead and it also arrowed down to a similar collection of barrels. Each batch of barrels, one each side, were severely cutting their speed, holding the ship back via his treasured catheads. He straightened himself back on deck, sighed, frowned, cursed under his breadth and looked back along the ship to the quarterdeck.

His Captain, Reuben Argent, was studying their pursuer. Through the fine lens of his good Dolland, a flickering red, white, and blue now showed as her ensign rippled in the wind behind the maze of rigging. This now confirmed her status, this being long assumed, that she was, indeed, a French cruiser. Details that had been blurred half an hour before were now more clear; the delicate timberwork below her bowsprit and also her figurehead, now showing as something birdlike. He saw his opponent set her own Royals that would maintain her continued gain on his own command. Her stunsails, on extensions to the larboard yardarms of each spar, widened the spread of canvas down her weather side. These had matched his own for some time. He snapped his glass shut, his mind making calculations. Seven bells in the forenoon watch; half an hour before midday, hours of daylight ahead. One hour more, he calculated, and she would be using her bowchaser guns, which his glass showed to be ready and run out.

He turned to his First Lieutenant, Henry Fentiman. This was not his Watch, but in the circumstances he could be in no place other than the quarterdeck. Fentiman could have been kin to his Captain, apart from dark brown hair, nearly black, perhaps more humour in his eyes, and a countenance perhaps more ready to laugh at any humour that offered itself.

"Have the men been fed?"

"They are carrying their rations to their messes now, Sir."

"After the Noon Sight, clear for action."

"Aye aye, Sir."

"And Mr Fentiman!"

"Sir?"

"Leave the ship's boats inboard. At least for now."

The Second Lieutenant had remained at his post. The Honourable Lucius Bentley had heard all and was puzzled. He looked at the ship's boats, secure on their cradles between the masts.

"And what of splinters, Sir? From shot hitting the boats?"

Argent re-opened his glass and returned it to his eye, pointing aft.

"Is it on this particular day of the year, Mr Bentley, that you are allowed to question my orders?"

Bentley's face alternated embarrassment and annoyance. Argent had not even deigned to look at him whilst delivering the rebuke, nor was he smiling. Bentley found it dismissive and negligent, but his face showed more sulk than simmer.

"No. Sir."

"Then please aid the First Lieutenant to carry out my orders, in the manner that I wish them. And Mr. Bentley."

"Sir?"

"You may run up The Colours."

Bentley's face remained set and grim.

"Aye aye, Sir."

* * *

The three Midshipmen sat cramped in their berth. The three were wholly unalike from each other, in as many points of comparison as could be imagined; height, build, age, intelligence, and social standing; save, perhaps, one point. Midshipmen William Bright and Daniel Berry could both be described as being of cheerful and optimistic temperament. Both were attending to their Journal to record their day so far aboard the warship; Berry writing, Bright drawing the joining of the foremast and foretopmast at the foretop. The third, The Honourable Jonathan Ffynes was looking on with both disdain and annoyance. Watery blue eyes looked down from a corpulent face from which jutted a nose pointed and a little too long. Lank blond hair hung down from the top of his head as gravity dictated his own Journal was days in arrears. His tone was both languid and sarcastic.

"I fail utterly to see the point of what you are doing. Come nightfall we could all be in irons, wet through in some French bilge, and all that you do now, thrown over the side. Or us dead; of course."

Bright looked up. His character matched his name. He was the shorter, but then also the youngest, 15 years of age. Clear, brown eyes shone from a face a little wide, but this was to the good; it gave enough room for a most disarming smile.

"You may be right, Jonathan, but I don't think so. This may be our first action since the Captain assumed command, but he's worked the ship hard at both gunnery and sail handling, and so I have faith. Perhaps so should you. What do you think, Daniel?"

Berry looked up, puzzlement spreading over his face. He was the tallest and eldest, now into his twenties, but not the Senior; The Honourable, him having served an odd two months more, these within his 20 years, held that informal position. Berry considered his answer; until then he had been coping well enough with recording his day. Now a question requiring balance and thought was upon him.

"It depends. Is she a lot bigger than us?

A pause.

"And who fires best and fastest."

Bright looked at Fynes, nodded, and grinned.

"There. He agrees. It's down to gunnery."

Ffynes was unconvinced, especially about their Captain.

"And what are those barrels all about, dragging us back?"

Bright came up with an immediate answer.

"Ah, on my Watch I heard the Captain discussing this with the First. He wants the Frenchman to think we are a poor sailer, slow, to tempt him up close, so that we can then cut the barrels loose and nip upwind, with a turn he can't match, him being too close to follow. He's trusting the ship; and us!"

Ffynes looked puzzled, but an intruding voice, that of an adult used to authority, shouted in through their door.

"Change of watch. Noon Sight. And we're clearing for action."

All three dropped whatever was in their hands and filled them instead with their sextants, almanacs and boards, then they hurried to the quarterdeck. The ceremonial fixing of the ship's position was upon them, a procedure almost religious in its ritual. The hand of the Quartermaster's Mate was about to turn the glass and ring eight bells, as the breathless Midshipmen stepped into the Captain's presence and, with their arrival, the glass was turned. The Ship's Master, Leviticus McArdle, tall, thin, sepulchral, and Scottish, was in his place, facing the direction of the sun. Whatever mood he was in, within the company of Midshipmen and apprentice Master's Mates, his face never failed to register wholesale disapproval. He raised his sextant, which signal required all others in the Noon Sight party to do the same, this solemnity being accompanied by the sound of hammering, as chocks were removed to disappear the wooden screens that divided the main gundeck into cabins, one of these being McArdle's own. All brought the sun down to the horizon in their mirrors and then considered their reading, then, after much awkward thumbing through their Almanacs, they each chalked their findings onto their board and waited. McArdle consulted his own sextant and Almanac, then allowed the heavy instrument to carry his simian-like arm down to his side. All his pupils held up their boards. All said a latitude reading between 49 degrees 15 minutes to 49 degrees 45 minutes. All save that of Daniel Berry. His read 48 degrees 25. McArdle's dour Scottish eyes moved up to Berry's face like an elevating gun.

"Mr Berry. On a longitude of 4 degrees 14, ye have placed us somewhere in the middle o' Brittany. Tomorrow your reading will agree with mine, or ye will spend some time at the masthead. Go forward now and practice. Ye need 49 degrees 20."

The chastened Berry hurried off, accompanied by Bright, whose reading had matched that of the Master perfectly, but, through friendship, he felt duty bound to try to help the inadequate Berry achieve the required improvement.

Two seamen and a Bosun's Mate had meanwhile been casting the log line. The sand in the log-glass ran out and the seaman set to watch its progress through the narrow neck called "stop". The Mate nipped the line and called the log.

"Eight knots, and a half, just over."

At that point two quick reports sounded from somewhere behind and two cannonballs skipped across the waves to sink, under 200 yards astern.

* * *

Argent had taken himself down to the gundeck and was sighting along the starboard of the two sternchaser guns. Ariadne, being 30 years old and Spanish built, was pierced for such guns, unlike more recently built frigates. Both crews stood obedient, awaiting his orders, their guns cleared and ready. The remains of Argent's greatcabin, the last of the big stern windows, was now disappearing past them. The Gun Captains were plainly identified in their blue jackets, which, over the past months, had become edged with white ribbon, this progressively becoming recognised as standard Gun Captain uniform throughout the ship. Argent looked, straightened up, and then bent to look again. Finally he gave his orders.

"You're doing this for show. If you can do her damage, get some through her rigging, but not too quick; make it a bit Indiaman, a good merchantman. Am I clear?"

All looked puzzled, but this was the Captain.

The starboard Gun Captain spoke his thoughts.

"Bar shot when the range falls, Sir?"

"She won't come within range of bar before we turn. Keep on with solid, and do what damage you can."

The puzzlement remained, but all raised a knuckle to their forehead to make their respects. Both Gun Captains, in unison, gave the answer for them all.

"Aye aye Sir."

Argent had one more order.

"And when it comes to broadsides, you're of no use here. I want you at the main battery, tailing on and helping where you can. Clear?"

Again from both Gun Captains.

"Aye aye, Sir."

Argent turned to view the long sweep of the now cleared gundeck. The 16 guns down each side, all 18 pounders of long Navy pattern, gave the Ariadne her class, a 32 gun frigate, 6th rate. The two sternchasers, plus two 24-pound stubby carronades on the Forecastle, and two of the same on the Quarterdeck completed her armament. Within his sight, through the subdued light from the battle lanterns, the last preparations were being made. The decks had been wetted and sanded, arms chests in place, drinking water alongside. The great guns had long since been cast loose and run back, their muzzles now awaiting their charges. Gun Captains stood behind each gun, checking their flints, quills and powder horns, whilst their Seconds checked the two cartridges in the saltbox by each gun. The crews examined shot for spherical, hammering off any flakes of rust.

Argent felt the need to tour the gundeck, to go up one side and back down the other, this would be their first action. He exchanged no words, other than to acknowledge the respect of each gun crew, them knuckling their forehead and speaking the single word "Captain".

Argent met the gaze of each Gun Captain, then simply spoke his name and nodded his head in greeting. Thus it went, a grave exchange down the line of black malignant shapes, with their now patient crews; East, Morrel, Simmonds, Baker, Fletcher, and so on. Samuel Morris, Gun Captain of No. 3, Starboard Battery, paid his respects as his Captain passed by and spoke his name. With Argent now passed on, two of his crew spoke almost in unison, fear plain in both their voices and faces. These being Matthew Wilmott and Thomas Bearman, both pressganged, but the latter taken out of a merchantman.

"What'll it be like, Sam?"

"Not no different from gundrill; much. All noise and smoke, with things leapin' about, till some of theirs comes inboard and then things gets a mite shameful. All you has to do is look lively and get this gun reloaded. The more we sends their way, the less they sends back to us. So, you follows orders and does what's needed, quick as lightnin'. Quicker would be better."

He resumed checking the flint on the gun's firelock. Bearman and Wilmott exchanged glances, not reassured. The two sternchasers began to answer the enemy closing astern, and at their sound, Wilmott placed his hands on the gun to steady himself, a yellow pool growing around his left foot.

Captain Argent took himself back to his quarterdeck and took his Dolland glass from the Marine Sergeant stood by the wheel. Again he studied his opponent. It was impossible to tell for certain but now he guessed that he was faced with a large frigate, probably a 42, but there could be no confirmation whilst she remained bows on. Two more puffs of smoke, a double report, and then the double fall of shot, one of them level with the stern taffrail but off to windward.

"All hands to wear ship! Starboard tack. Stunsails in. Helmsmen, when we draw, come up to due West."

The nearest gave the answer.

"Due West. Aye aye Sir."

However, one of them mumbled under his breath.

"When we draw! As if I didn't bloody know."

The orders were repeated along the deck and, once again, the hands climbed the ratlines to alter the sails, Argent was taking the ship across the wind. From taking the wind fine on the larboard quarter, she would move her stern around, to then take it over the starboard quarter, which required a major change in the angle of the sails. Whilst Fentiman hurried to the Quarterdeck rail to oversee the order being carried out, Argent hurried forward himself along the Larboard gangway to find the unmistakable figure of Ship's Bosun, George Fraser.

"Mr. Fraser!"

Fraser stopped and looked up amidst all the hurly burly of men running up from the gundeck and the already squealing blocks on the spars. His "Sir", was lost in the noise, but he had the sense to run back to meet his Captain.

"Sir."

"Cut loose our sea anchors Mr Fraser. Their business is done. Our Frenchman now has a full enough appreciation of us being a poor sailer."

Fraser's teeth showed in a broad grin within the leathern face as he knuckled his forehead and sped off, gaining an axe on the way. With great relish he chopped through the thick rope holding both clusters of barrels to watch them disappear in an instant. Fraser was certain that he felt the ship jump forward.

The sails had to be turned to meet the wind coming from the opposite side, a complex task involving all the important ropes known as the "running rigging": braces to the yardarms, and sheets to the sail corners. When the stunsails came in and the starboard braces were slackened to allow their yardarms to angle forward to the bows, the helmsmen made their turn. The hands were waiting on the larboard braces and began to haul back the yards on that side. The big mizzen driver swung over the quarterdeck and the ship heeled to larboard as the wind hit the canvas that was being swung around to meet it. The topmen came down alongside the lowered stunsails and all the crew took into their hands their allotted sheets and braces to now trim the sails to properly gather the wind from the new direction. Soon all ropes were coiled and neat. The whole had taken mere minutes.

Argent had ignored all that went on, he continued to study the Frenchman. She had pressed on South South West, perhaps taken by surprise. He could now see her side, she was indeed a 42. A broadside erupted from her, but to no effect, the shot fell short, someway off the starboard quarter. For some two minutes she made no response to the Ariadne's change of course, then her ratlines turned black with men as they raced to take in her own stunsails and trim their sails to make a course to follow that of Ariadne, whose smooth turn still showed on the intervening sea. Argent smiled as the minutes ticked by before the Frenchman achieved the required new course, Ariadne had gained almost a quarter of a mile. His crew were better.

* * *

Argent turned to the Duty Midshipman, in this case the only one remaining, The Honourable Jonathan Ffynes.

"Mr Ffynes."

"Sir."

"My compliments to Mr Fraser. Ask for his presence with me, here on the Quarterdeck. And when you've done that, my same to Mr Short. I'd be obliged if he'd take the wheel."

Ffynes began a run along to the starboard gangway to the Forecastle, but was immediately stopped by his Captain's arresting hand.

"Don't run, Mr Ffynes, it gives the men a poor impression. A purposeful walk will perfectly suffice."

"Yes, Sir. Aye Sir."

Bosun Fraser duly appeared.

"Sir?"

"Mr Fraser, we will progressively up helm. I'm going to take her as close to the wind as she'll lie. Let's see how far Mr Frenchmen can sail into the wind, because I think we can best him. Constant trimming is the answer. I count on you and your Mates to do a better job than that crew of Johnnies lubbering about over there."

Bosun Fraser rose to his full height, which brought him to Argent's chin. His expression deadly serious, he gave a full salute.

"Aye, aye, Sir."

"And Mr Fraser."

"Sir?"

"Have the remaining jibs and the lower staysails standing by, they may be needed. Check all forestays and add another preventer stay to the foremast."

The last caused the good Fraser some puzzlement.

"Extra preventer stay. Aye aye, Sir."

Argent gave Fraser time to gather his Mates and allocate men to the many stations that held the anchor points of the sheets and braces. Then he began the contest.

"Up helm. Come to Nor'west by West."

Quartermaster Short, now at his place, repeated the new course.

"Nor'west by West. Aye aye, Sir."

The bowsprit swung across the horizon as the ship answered the changing helm, moving her further into the wind, but just astern of beam on. Fraser saw the movement and called his orders. The wind was now hitting the ship almost directly onto her side, but the sheets and braces that controlled the angle of the yards and sails had been already loosened to make the adjustments needed. All was quickly done. The speed of the ship remained unaltered.

"Mr. McArdle. Throw the log."

Argent studied their opponent. She came up onto the new course competently enough, but the sail handling was neither quick nor smooth. Her mainmast set were slow to adjust, the sail edges shivering as the wind met the wrong side.

"Steady on that course, Mr Short."

"Nor'west by West. Aye aye, Sir."

Argent waited the few remaining seconds whilst the log was recorded. McArdle delivered the result.

"12 knots and a half. Sir."

Argent walked to the taffrail, without his glass. The Frenchman had held the distance, or perhaps she had surrendered a little more, but nothing of note. He allowed some time for the deck to become ordered from the recent changes.

"Up helm. Come to Nor'nor'west."

The helmsmen eased over the spokes.

"Nor'nor'west. Aye aye, Sir."

Again the bowsprit swung Northward, and Fraser set the men to their tasks. Ariadne was now "close hauled"; sailing as much against the wind as mariners considered a standard, and possible, course. Argent looked back to the Frenchman. No change of distance, this time she showed good sailhandling. It was now down to the qualities of the two vessels. He looked along the deck to his own crew. Adjustments were constant; the men, not just the Bosun and his Mates, were looking up to make their own judgment, pointing out their concerns and anticipating orders, then gathering around the required sheet or brace.

Argent waited a quarter of a glass. The sand ran through.

"Mr. McArdle. The log again, if you please."

He then went to the taffrail.

"Mr. Fraser. Ready all staysails."

Fraser saluted and made off, yelling in all directions.

McArdle had been waiting patiently until his Captain chose to give him his attention. He was reserving final judgment of his new Captain, but so far he was pleased with what he saw. Argent turned towards him to hear his report.

"11 knots, Sir. Plus a half."

Argent nodded.

"Thank you, Mr. McArdle."

Argent placed both hands on the Quarterdeck rail, watching preparations. He saw that all was ready. He spied Fraser and bellowed in his direction.

"Set staysails. Take in mizzentopsail, maincourse and topsail. Forecourse and foretopsail. All canvas below topgallants!"

Again he observed a highly animated Bosun, eager about his duties. He turned to the helmsmen.

"Mr Short. Come up another point."

"North by West. Aye aye Sir."

Ariadne's canvas was quickly changed and the larger, lower squaresails, rapidly disappeared. They would steal wind from the fore and aft staysails that were now needed and, quickly set, these began to draw strongly. The staysails ran down the line of the ship, not across it, as did the square sails on the spars of the masts and the wind hit the taut staysails full on. Fraser had the crew strain the yards of the remaining square topgallants and royals around their full extent and they continued to draw the wind. Argent put his glass to his eye, as did all other Officers possessed of the same. The Frenchman had copied the Ariadne, not as fast, but the fore and aft staysails that matched Ariadne's were now set and she was coming onto their course. One minute passed, then two, then her remaining square sails began to shiver, then the wind caught the wrong side of the maintopgllant, putting it aback and working against the other sails. The Frenchman's bow swung back over, to regain the wind or risk losing sails or even masts. She lost some distance whilst the sails were reset, then she tried again but with the same result.

She could not follow the Ariadne's course so far into the wind, she had to turn off to regain it. Why was impossible to say; hull design, the rake of the masts, how stiff each ship was with the wind pressing full from the side, sail trim; all could contribute. She could try on staysails alone, but, without the squaresails that Ariadne continued to carry, she would fall behind. The race was lost; not only was the Frenchman slower, but the distance between them was growing because of their divergent courses. Ariadne pulled away and Argent watched and waited for what he knew would come. They were drawing the Frenchman North to the English coast, on a chase she was unlikely to win, and soon it came. The Frenchman put her helm down and wore around to run South East towards her own waters. Argent closed his glass with a satisfactory snap.

"Congratulations, Gentlemen. We've won the weather gauge. Stand by to tack ship. We're going after her. Midshipman!"

Berry jumped to attention.

"My compliments to Mr Fraser. I would appreciate his attendance here. "

As Berry ran off, Argent turned to Lieutenant Bentley.

"Mr. Bentley. Please to send the ship's boats out astern."

* * *

The French ship was practically hove to, moving slowly South East, on topsails alone, all lower sails being furled up for the impending action. Her Captain was offering combat, this British frigate may be handy off the wind, and sharp with her sail handling, but five extra guns either side would count for something. To continue to run before this lesser vessel was out of the question. She was ready, guns run out.

Argent studied his opponent. French built, the classic high taffrail at the stern, slightly higher out of the water. She was a 42, but she had more lighter guns along her quarterdeck than he. Comparing their numbers of 18 pound guns, they were not so different, unless hers were 24's! He issued his orders to his Master Gunner, Joshua Tucker and Lieutenant Bentley, his Gunnery Officer

"Mr. Tucker, I want six chainshot issued to the starboard battery, each gun double shotted for three rounds. Larboard battery ready loaded, double solid shot. Mr. Bentley, when the guns are loaded, Larboard Watch on deck for sail handling. Starboard Watch remain at the guns. Make it so."

From both in unison, "Aye aye, Sir."

Bentley remained, but Tucker rumbled off, each side of his square frame moving forward to extend further his stubby legs. Each step of the companionway down to the gundeck was a significant descent. He was amongst the smallest in the crew.

Argent took a last look through his glass.

"Mr. Fentiman. Beat to Quarters."

Fentiman strode to the rail and leaned over to the waiting Marine Drummer. He yelled the repeat at the top of his voice. Most heard and responded before the drummer had lifted his sticks. The crew ran to their posts; guncrews, Officers, and topmen; these latter, the elite seamen, would be needed to alter the sails as the action may require. The three Midshipmen ran to their positions, each to command their section of guns; on the starboard side Fynes 1 to 8; Berry, 9 to 16. On the larboard side. Bright commanded 1 to 8, Bentley, the Gunnery Officer, 9 to 16. Ffynes and Berry arrived at their posts, but their anxiety grew with the lack of activity, they were merely required to watch the guns being loaded, a practice that the gun crews probably knew more about than they did. Ffynes, doing his best to sound warriorlike and inspirational, felt the need to encourage his men.

"Gun Captains. You know your orders."

One replied.

"Yes, Sir. Very clear, Sir."

"Now men, we're going to pay them out. Show them what it means to tangle with a ship of His Majesty's Navy."

Sam Morris, him that had replied, looked up from priming the flintlock. He made no effort to keep the indulgent tone from his voice.

"Yes Sir. Make 'em sorry they saw the sun rise this mornin'. Sir."

Ffynes took this as an encouraging response, his nervousness causing him to miss the ironic edge to Morris' voice, which most would recognise as showing anything but heightened battle fervour.

"Yes, yes, Morris. That's right. That's the spirit."

Morris himself grinned down the barrel of his gun and caught the eye of Joe Dedman, his Second. A veteran like himself, Dedman was sending the last ball of the last chainshot into the muzzle of the gun. This was nothing new to either, Dedman had been serving guns since he came onto his first ship as a Ship's Boy and was then required to be a Powder Monkey when the guns were in action.

The distance was closing rapidly, Ariadne was holding due South, moving at twice the speed of her opponent and coming up far astern of her, almost at right angles to the Frenchman's course. The Frenchman was content to let her come on, anticipating that Ariadne would turn sharp to larboard, then sail up from astern to trade broadsides. Argent stood his Quarterdeck, as was his place. All was calm, the ship's routine uninterrupted, a Master's Mate came forward at the urging of the emptying hourglass to ring the bell. The last grains fell through and he turned the glass and rang the six bells of the afternoon watch. McArdle was at the wheel, on the opposite side to Zachary Short. Lieutenants Fentiman and Sanders attended their Captain, Lieutenant Bentley was now on the gundeck, as was his place. Argent was choosing a long, in fact overlong, wide curve, to sweep up astern of their opponent. He was very far out, an experienced Commander may well have viewed it with suspicion, and judged it as being much further behind his ship than necessary. Sanders had been studying the French stern through this telescope.

"She's called "La Mouette", Sir."

"Hmmm. Anyone translate?"

"It means seagull, Sir."

"Thank you Mr. Sanders. Your command of French does you credit, but I trust you'll desist from any attempt at diverting us with thin humour about trimming feathers."

"Aye aye, Sir. Just so, Sir."

However all grinned just the same, but Fentiman saw an occasion for further jest.

"Perhaps not feathers, Sir, but maybe we'll trim her roaming ways instead and she'll end the day a polly in a cage! But perhaps not so much of a "pretty polly!"

Chuckles came from across the deck, including the gun crew on the quarterdeck starboard carronade. The tension brought laughter from even humour this thin.

"Time will tell, Mr. Fentiman, time will tell."

Ariadne was on a larboard tack, taking the wind over her larboard quarter, carrying all plain sail, bar highest Royals, far more than La Mouette. Argent judged that Ariadne had sailed up to the Frenchman's wake far enough; with no change her bows would soon cut through it.

"Up helm. Steer East South East."

"East Sou' East Sir. Aye aye, Sir."

The Ariadne was now close hauled into the wind and she curved round to larboard and, aloft, the topmen trimmed the sails, aided by the Ariadne's complement of two dozen Marines and the whole Larboard Watch stationed on the upper deck. Ariadne was coming up to engage. Her speed slackened but slightly, which brought her within range of La Mouette's two stern chasers. Smoke billowed from the guns and the balls had placed a hole in the foresail and parted some rigging before they heard the report, which defiant sound coincided with the dull hiss and buzz of both balls passing on and over. The distance was down to 300 yards, 250, 150, 100, less. La Mouette came up to East South East, to match Ariadne's course, anticipating to trade broadsides. Perfect! Argent chose his moment.

"Up helm. Fire as you bear."

The four helmsmen hauled on the spokes and the Ariadne turned fiercely into the wind, sails flapping as they lost its power. Fraser took his cue, he had every spare man grouped around the foremast and mainmast.

"Cast off fore and main sheets and braces! Haul larboard."

Ariadne turned like a Spanish dancer, immediately and fully answering her helm, especially with the big driver hauled back to fully catch the wind and quickly push around her stern. All within Fraser's command hauled on the larboard sheets and braces to haul the lower sails of the fore and mainmasts around, against and into the wind. The straining seamen stamped their way aft, hauling at their ropes until the sails slapped back against their mast. The forestays and the extra preventer groaned, but vitally held, against the enormous strain of the ship still moving forward into the wind. Ariadne came to a dead stop where Argent wanted, the backed sails working against the mizzen mast's driver, topsail, and topgallant; a dead stop immediately off La Mouette's larboard quarter.

On the gundeck all was quiet, to the crews came only the muffled noise of the stamping feet above and the indignant waves below slapping into Ariadne's hull as she made her turn into the wind. Each gun was trained as far forward as the gunport would allow, giving them the earliest possible sight of their target. Each man at his place; Officers stood back, Gun Captains crouching down awkwardly to sight along their gunbarrels, hands on the quoin handle should they need to change the elevation, the lanyard to the flintlock hanging slack in their left hands. The No. 2 of each and another guncrewman waited to lift the heavy gun casable with the thick woden handspikes, this bulbous at the rear, and resting on the quoin. All guncrews had their ears covered, to at least deaden the forthcoming noise. All was silent, tense, and still; as their ship came up into the wind, swinging round, and they waited to see their target through their gunports. The gunners of La Mouette remained viewing nothing but the empty ocean, they had been expecting the Britisher to come up, but she didn't arrive. The keyed up Ffynes couldn't cope with the unbearable tension.

"Remember men, mizzen and foremast first. Main if you have time."

Morris, as tense as anyone, anxious that the first shot should tell, mumbled, but still loud enough for most to hear.

"Why dohn 'ee shut up!"

However, by good fortune for Morris, this was drowned by the noise of the first gun being discharged. Morris saw the big driver of La Mouette and made no change, his anticipation of the elevation had been perfect, his gun was moving exactly onto the Frenchman's mizzentopsail. He allowed for the delay before the barrel came onto the target, then pulled the lanyard. The flintlock sparked and the gun leaped in after a fearsome crash, a plume of smoke issuing upwards from the touch-hole. All other guns back down astern began firing as they came onto target. Morris sprang forward to recharge the flintlock, his crew the same to reload the gun. There was not a wasted movement as the gun was made ready and run out again. Morris took his sight, called for his adjustments from his crew, and again the evil roar and the gun springing back on its squealing truck.

Argent was in the Mizzen top above the smoke, steadying himself on the rigging with one hand, a speaking trumpet in the other and his feet on the edge of the small platform. The rigging of La Mouette seemed alive from an invisible malignant hand. The shrouds, stays, and braces of her Mizzen mast jerked and twitched, her driver soon in rags, this soon made worse as its boom was cut one third down. The furled Mizzen sails above the driver were not spared, shreds of sail soon hanging down besides the limp and severed ropes. There came a pause before the second volley came, ragged, but this caused by each Gun Captain carefully laying his aim. The foremast received the same treatment, but this appeared even worse due to its more complex network of vital ropework. In seconds the forsail exploded into rags, followed by the two jibsails that stretched between the foremast and the bowsprit. The French Captain, was, in less than two minutes, denied the use of all sails on his Mizzen and Foremast.

Argent brought up his speaking trumpet and pointed it at Bosun Fraser.

"Out all jibsails. All foresails braced round for the larboard tack."

Then to the Quarterdeck.

"Down helm. Across her stern, Mr. Short."

Ariadne's jibsails, rooted on the bowsprit, appeared in seconds and were drawing in a minute. Facing the wind they quickly pushed her bows over to starboard. The angle was now narrowing for the third discharge, but all guns achieved a shot to inflict similar damage to the mainmast. La Mouette could no longer manoeuvre. Ariadne picked up speed and headed to cross the Frenchman's stern, at a range of something under 50 yards. On Ariadne's gundeck, all was shrouded in smoke, but at the third discharge the crews ran across to man the larboard battery. La Mouett's two stern chasers were the only guns firing as Ariadne closed. A crash came from somewhere forward, followed by screaming, but how many men were down could not be seen in the smoke and gloom. The screams subsided as the wounded were carried down to the Surgeon. Silence again. Bentley took his cue. Excitement hurried his speech, but the crews knew enough, his words were merely a reminder.

"Rake her down her starboard side, men. Remember, her starboard side. Leave the larboard untouched. Good and careful aim, now."

Again the Gun Captains crouched to sight their pieces. They were going to rake the Frenchman from her stern. The predicted gun elevation was obvious; horizontal; the Frenchman's guns and their crews were on the same level as themselves.

Argent was shinning down the ratlines to regain his quarterdeck. As he swung under the splinternet rigged over his deck, he heard Fentiman shouting orders for the driver sail to be let out far to starboard to regain the wind. It drew taut quickly and Ariadne picked up speed; the guns would soon bear. Argent looked to the stern of La Mouette, just yards off his larboard bow. The guncrews of the sternchasers were jumping through the windows into the sea, they knew what was coming and they knew that it was a death sentence to remain at their guns. La Mouette's crew were desperately trying to get some sail onto the Mizzen to swing their stern away from the fearful raking to come. The rudder moved, but not La Mouette.

As she was, Ariadne was picking up too much speed. Argent wanted to give his crews time for three shots, involving two reloads. He strode to the rail and again raised his speaking trumpet.

"Mr. Fraser. Start all sheets."

Fraser's men ran to obey what they had all heard. The sheets to the corners of all sails were loosened. The sails hung limp, curling in the wind, but giving no impetus to Ariadne, her own momentum now drifted her past the stern of her helpless opponent. The first gun fired. The double shot crashed through the woodwork below where the greatcabin windows were placed, as ordered, through the two starboard windows. The next gun followed, and the next, their shot entering through the gap. All guns fired, then a short pause before No. 1 repeated their earlier effort, followed by the rest of the battery. They fired once more, for the final time, and the two larboard great cabin windows were untouched. "Cease fire. Reload," came up from the now silent gundeck. There was silence everywhere aboard the Ariadne, but they were close enough to hear the result of their gunnery. Screaming came from within La Mouette's hull. The Ariadnies knew the affect of what had been done, the double shot had raked through the entire length of the ship, overturning guns, smashing men and guncarriages, wreaking havoc down the entire length. Argent broke the spell.

"Up helm. Bring her onto their broadside."

"Up helm. On her broadside. Aye aye Sir."

Again through the speaking trumpet.

"See to your trim, Mr. Fraser. Topsails, fore and main for the larboard tack."

Sheets were re-attached and, pushed by the driver and the two biggest sails braced round, Ariadne took herself opposite the wrecked battery of the La Mouette. Those on deck viewed her from over their ship's gunwale, whilst the guncrews, those that could see, looked through their own gunports. Four of La Mouette's guns protruded from their gun port, but at odd angles, which told their own story, their carriages obviously wrecked. Argent chose his moment.

"Back foretopsail, Mr. Fraser. Start topsail."

Fraser began the sailhandling that would halt the Ariadne, but by a miracle one gun on La Mouette had survived. It discharged with a roar and a cloud of white smoke, its shot smashing the gunwale along the larboard gangway, injuring three men on the foretopsail sheets with splinters. Bentley ran up the companionway from the gundeck.

"Did anyone see which gun?"

Sanders answered.

"Her number three."

Bentley disappeared and ran to the bow section.

"Two, three, four and five. On her number three."

The Gun Captains crouched down and motioned left or right to their two crewmates both ready either side of the carriage with their levers. The carriages were crudely levered around and all four Gun Captains raised their arm and called, "Ready."

"Fire."

The guns discharged and recoiled in. The crews set about an immediate reload as the smoke from the discharge blew back in through the ports.

Argent looked at the result. The gunport had two wounds, one on either side. The other two must have gone straight in. The gun did not reappear.

The Tricolour came down. The Captain had a choice; to try to bring guns across from his larboard battery under close enemy fire, or surrender. It would cause a hopeless loss of life. He surrendered. Argent saw the colour come down and turned to his Quarterdeck.

"Mr. Sanders. As you seem to have some command of French, please to take yourself across and accept their surrender."

Sanders grinned from ear to ear.

"Aye, aye, Sir."

As Sanders hurried off, Argent spoke to the remainder assembled there, traversing his eyes, so that his words would seem directed to all.

"Well, Gentlemen, I believe tomorrow to be the 1st July and I consider that terminates our patrol."

Chapter Two

By Their Deeds Shalt Thou Know Them

"It seems we've caused quite a stir. Or are we at the head of some kind of waterborne carnival?"

Argent sat in the stern of his barge in the company of his First Lieutenant, Jonathan Fentiman. As was his nature, Fentiman reacted easily to any humour, however ironic, and this was no exception, a wide grin spread immediately across his face. Each Officer held their swords stiffly vertical with their left hands, whilst Argent's right was placed custodially on the two books on the seat beside him, the Ship's Log and the Ship's Ledger. Oblivious to the activity within their own boat, each studied the crowd lining the quayside. The noise was growing, sourced from a three deep crowd atop the ancient walls; high enthusiasm highly apparent, clapping and cheering, all accompanied with the energetic waving of hats and handkerchiefs. Argent angled his head around to his helmsman above and behind.

"Whiting. Steer for the steps below The Tower."

"Aye aye, Sir."

Gabriel Whiting, Captain of the Foretop, made no change. He didn't need to be told where Captains landed on the quayside at Plymouth. He ran his hand down the smooth wood of the tiller, and then resumed his grip. The Captain's Barge remained on the course he'd already set. The four white oars, two each side, continued to dip into the calm water, in perfect rhythm, and perfectly parallel on the recovery as they came back above the surface for the next stroke. It was a faultless exhibition of barge handling.

Fentiman, unlike his Captain, who stared rigidly ahead, could not resist one look back astern. Just inside and to the West of Drake's Island, their own ship lay at anchor, with La Mouette one cable off, a White Ensign above the French Tricolour, identifying her as a French prize. He grinned again as the steps approached and Whiting took charge. All the barge crew were under his command back aboard Ariadne, because all were fellow foretopmen.

"Easy all. Toss oars."

With the oars vertical, the barge glided to the damp and weed-strewn platform that began the steps up to the quayside. Abel Jones, in the bows, lay his oar down flat within the barge and stood up from his place, the painter in his left hand. With practiced ease he jumped out from the slowing barge, threaded the rope through a large iron ring on the platform edge and took the strain to slow the boat. His fellow oarsmen had already thrown over the plaited rope fenders to prevent any damage to their precious vessel. He then seized the gunwale to steady the boat at the platform edge to afford his Captain and First a safe disembarkment. Fentiman rose in his place to step out first, followed by his Captain. As Argent's foot came onto the old and worn stonework, the cheering intensified. At the top there was a dense crowd. Whiting stepped out of the boat.

"Give us a second, Sir."

Whiting was not going to have his Captain buffeted about by a bunch of overwound landsmen. He motioned to his crew and they all disembarked. Whiting was immaculate in his Topcaptain's blue jacket with polished silver buttons and white duck trousers; his crew in blue-chequered shirts, with the same white ducks. Beneath a black-tarred hat, all sported a pigtail extending down between their shoulder blades, finishing with a red ribbon. A bright scarlet kerchief was tied about their necks and a silver earring shone in each right ear. The uniform was their own concoction; Argent had made no requirements. Leaving Jones to mind the boat, the crew mounted the steps, Whiting had the hefty Moses King at his shoulder, backed up by two more from the foretop, including the mighty Sam Fenwick.

"Make a way there, mate. Give us some room. Captain has business."

The cheering was unabated and drowned Whiting's speech, except to those who needed to hear, those nearest, and therefore most able to see that he would truck no failure to comply. He and his men leaned into the crowd and a way was made. Argent and Fentiman followed through to the top of the steps, smiling and nodding, trying to hide their embarrassment, trying to withstand the buffeting of their backs and shoulders from those who could reach through his bodyguard. Both Officers were grateful to find a closed carriage across their path, black but with an inviting open door, held open by a Marine Captain. They accelerated into its welcoming safety. The door closed, the Marine thumped the roof and they were moving.

Whiting, his Officers now safely through and on their way, returned to the top of the steps. They were required to remain, to await their Captain's convenience. So, why descend to the dank of the lower steps, why not remain above, especially when he found himself staring at a very comely face, framed in a maid's cap?

"Now then, lass, wouldn't you like to know how it all happened?"

* * *

The coach eased smoothly through the imposing gates of the Port Admiral's Official Residence, this incumbent being one Rear Admiral Sir Arthur Broke. Next door, but smaller, for overnight use only, was the place of residence that applied to Rear Admiral Septimus Grant,

Commander in Chief, Western Approaches, him being senior to all, including Broke, and in command of all Naval Ports West. This included Plymouth and the area of sea to their South and West known as the Western Channel; the "Chops" to those familiar.

Argent had never met either before. Rear Admiral Grant had held his command at the beginning of the Ariadne's commission, three months previously, but Flag Officers of such exalted rank did not come to see mere frigates on their way, whilst Sir Arthur Broke had replaced the Admiral that had given Argent his orders, that three months ago. The Marine Captain preceded them to the imposing front door; burnished brass, shiny black, double width, and immediately on their approach both wings opened in unison, propelled inwards by the hands of the two Marine sentries, both stationed outside. All three proceeded through and the Captain turned left and motioned them towards another set of imposing doors, ceiling high, equally black, brass equally burnished, and these he opened himself.

"Admirals Grant and Broke will see you immediately."

Argent and Fentiman entered a large, high-ceilinged room, ornate plaster decorating every corner, and below this confection hung a full collection of Naval disasters, departures and engagements, all painted in the same colours, in the same style, within the same heavy guilt frames. Both Argent and Fentiman halted when they perceived the two Flag Officers awaiting them, one standing, one sitting, this latter merely turning to observe their entrance. The atmosphere in the office was divided in two by the stony deadpan expression of the Officer sitting, and the beaming welcome of the one standing. This was added to by the fact that the one sitting sported his full Admiral's uniform, whilst he standing was in his shirtsleeves. There was a smell of pomade that seemed to emanate from the colder half of the room. Ariadne's two Principal Officers came to the attention and saluted, which was returned by the Admiral standing. He spoke first.

"Welcome. Welcome to you both. You don't know me, I'm Septimus Grant. This is Vice-Admiral Sir Arthur Broke, Port Admiral Plymouth."

Broke didn't change his position; he merely nodded, then thought of an addition.

"It looks like "Broke" where you see it on your orders, but pronounced "Brook". "Brook.""

He paused to look directly at Argent.

"Although I suspect that one of you already knows that!"

Argent felt his heart sink as he recognised Broke, a face distant in his past, but wholly familiar nonetheless. However, both Argent and Fentiman spoke their greetings and walked to the chairs that stood before a giant desk. Grant took his place behind the acres of green leather as both newcomers sat down.

"First, well done. Heartiest congratulations. You'll both take a glass of madeira?"

Grant stood up again and leaned well forward to fill the two glasses waiting on the far side of the desk, holding the bottle at the base to cover the last foot.

"A French 42, new built, if I'm any judge. There'll be a few Johnnies on the other side grinding their teeth at this one. Well done. Well done, indeed. You'd concur, Sir Arthur?"

"I would, but I'll hear the whole story first, before I swoon overboard."

The smile on Grant's face fell away, but he recovered, regained his previous good cheer and continued on.

"Yes, as you say. Now, Argent, you have your books?"

Argent placed the two imposing ledgers on the desk and slid them towards Grant. That done he took one of the, now filled, fine cut-glass goblets and handed one to Fentiman. He then took his own.

"Your engagement is detailed here?"

"Yes, Sir. Myself and Lieutenant Fentiman here worked together to provide as detailed an account as we were able."

"Excellent. Can't wait to read it. And your losses?"

"Five, Sir. Four wounded and one amputee. They're coming ashore now."

Grant's beaming face expanded even wider.

"Five! Did you hear that, Broke, five. They took a French 42 with no more casualties than you'd get in a Force Eight gale. What do you say now?"

Broke looked up, expression unchanged, just short of disapproving.

"As I say, when I've heard the story. Your own damage you repaired on the way home, I take it, Captain?"

"After a fashion, Sir. One shot hole and a shattered bulwark. My carpenter made temporary repairs, but a full repair remains to be undertaken. Sir."

"And this is your first command. How long?"

"Yes, Sir. Almost twelve months, Sir."

"And how did you find this 42? She'd lost her rudder or somesuch."

Broke's hostility was plain and Argent could see no justification. His own temperament stiffened, yet he held it within the necessary bounds.

"Why no, Sir. More to say, she found us. But we outsailed her, to use our guns when she couldn't."

He turned to Grant.

"May I recommend to you, Sir, my Bosun, George Fraser. And his Mates and also my Quartermaster. Their sail handling whilst we manoeuvred was of the highest order, Sir. It decided the whole action."

Grant grinned, but Broke spoke, now scowling.

"I'd like to see any damned Bosun that didn't jump to my orders!"

Grant ignored him, but now realised that their meeting was going to be neither friendly nor convivial.

"Just so, Argent, well spoken. Allow those men ashore and they'd do well to take themselves to The Benbow. There they'll be well looked after; at my expense."

Broke's head and shoulders jerked back. He plainly disapproved and Grant saw fit to cut short the interview.

"Make a list of your requirements for your next Commission and submit them to my Secretary, that being Captain Baker, who just showed you in. Now, give me a chance to study this, and then please return. I invite you both to dinner this evening, with myself, Broke here, and a few other guests, mostly Navy; no surprise there. Bring two other Officers from your ship. They'd be most welcome."

He stood up and Argent and Fentiman placed their half finished glasses on the desk, then they also stood. Argent replied.

"Thank you, Sir. We will both attend with pleasure. It's been a long time since we had anything other than ship's cooking."

Grant grinned and came around the desk, it was too far to reach over and he extended his hand to both.

"7.30 for 8.00. Until then."

Both saluted and left. Broke said nothing.

In the carriage, Argent sank back deep into the upholstery, then he gave vent to a deep sigh.

"It seems, Henry, that our fortunes may take, what could be, a turn for the worse."

"How so, Sir?"

Argent saw no reason to hold back from the truth.

"Our good Admiral Broke owns land above my Father's, and we've had two disputes with him. Since he bought that estate, he has not proven to be a good neighbour. Firstly, he cut off our water to create an ornamental lake, and secondly, he tried to deny us access to a drove. We were forced to take him to Court and he lost, both times; and expensively."

He paused, took an intake of breath, and looked at his First Officer.

"I hope that this has no adverse impact on your own career."

Fentiman stuck out his jaw and pursed his lips.

"So, nothing so serious as you scrumping his apples? Or having unwelcome designs upon his daughter?"

Argent gave a short laugh.

"No, to both."

"Well, that's all right then. And throughout it all, I was thinking that his adversity to us was because, perhaps at school, he was required to translate the story of Ariadne and Theseus from the Greek and made poor fist of it; and the memory still rankles. Whatever, it seems then, that we are not to be listed amongst our Port Admiral favourites. No-matter, at least not for now. Whom should we bring tonight?"

"I thought Bentley and Sanders."

"Yes. Yes, I agree, Sir."

The carriage had reached the quayside and both stepped out. Whiting and his crew sprang to attention, which interrupted the climax of Whiting's story to the serving girl of where he had swung aboard the Frenchman to disable her helmsman, fight off a French Marine and cut down her colours.

* * *

George Fraser and his Mates climbed out of the jollyboat that they had rowed over themselves, with Quartermaster Zachary Short at the tiller. Henry Ball was doing the necessary with the painter through the mooring ring and, when all were out, the boat was pulled along to clear the steps and sit idle on the dropping tide. All five climbed to the top and adjusted their finery, not least Fraser wearing his Bosun's hat with the large display plate above the brim showing the word "Ariadne" beneath the image of a fair maid very sparsely clothed. All others had their black-tarred hat circled by the ribbon with the single word. Each then set a fine pace to the only Inn on that quay, but the exact one they required. The sign showed the identifying image of Benbow, minus legs, sat upon the quarterdeck of his embattled flagship. The five piled through the door.

As each was fully aware, for all had frequented before, this was a haunt of sailors; civilians were but few, this was a drinking den of man o' war's men. Blue jackets, tarred hats, and tarred pigtails marked almost all there as such, at least all those standing. As they edged their way to the bar, the five received examining, curious looks from those who noticed their passing; not challenging, nor unfriendly but certainly inquisitive, "So let's have a good look at these Ariadnies, those what brought in that Frencher". Fraser reached the bar. The Landlord was familiar.

"Donaghue, you Irish pirate! We do hear tell that a special mess has been set up here, just for the likes of us. Compliments of the Admiral. Tell me that we ain't got it wrong."

Donaghue did not pause from polishing a glass.

"No, you have the right of it. Some rum and some vittles, beer included, the messenger said. So, find yourself a table and we'll see to you directly."

Fraser grinned and slapped his distorted hand on the bar.

"There, 'tis true. So, you Feinian wrecker, we'll have a drop of rum now, right now, afore we takes our seats."

Donaghue quickly obliged and soon each had a glass.

"Right lads; time to set up our mess."

No tables were wholly free, so they spread themselves over the ends of two, but nevertheless they were close enough. Fraser took charge.

"Now then, all of you. Fair's fair. The first is to our Captain, 'tis him that put us here. A fine sailor an' a fightin' sailor."

All lifted their glasses and drank. Soon their food arrived, deep trenchers full of some kind of stew, and a bucket of fresh bread. Fraser seized the potboys arm and examined the fare.

"Right, all looks sound enough. So lad, five quarts, at your best speed."

For the next ten minutes there was little conversation. Navy habits were too far ingrained, that of getting the food inside you, before you were called on deck to attend some "all hands" emergency. The beer arrived quickly and soon all were pushing an empty plate away and concentrating on their drinking. Zachary Short felt the need for conversation, talking across the gap between the two tables, him and Henry Ball together at one, Fraser and the other two Bosun's Mates at the other.

"So, George. What're your thoughts?"

"My first thoughts, now we'n safe back here, is the prize money. That 42 'll fetch a tidy sum, 'specially with so little hull damage. 'Tweren't not much damage done even to the knees on her gundeck, after the rakin' we gave her. The price of a 42 spread over a crew our size, I think we got summat to look forward to there. They'll have her renamed, crewed, and in service before no time."

Henry Ball saw his turn to speak up.

"I think he's talkin' about our berth, George, the ship we've fetched up in. We bin twelve months, nearly, with Argent on the Ariadne. What's to say about that, now we'n off her for the first time, for an hour or more."

The Salt that was Fraser, leaned back against the rear of his chair, whilst retaining hold on his quart mug.

"Well. I'll tell 'ee. Tell 'ee straight. When he first came aboard I thought we had a total pain in the arse. He warn't no flogger, not like that tripehound afore, I saw that early, but he did run I ragged, forever alterin' the rake of the masts, riggin' the yards further up or down and when I saw him being rowed out to take a look at her beam on, I knew what we'd be in for, shiftin' ballast down below, an' waitin' for his verdict, more up or less down."

He took a drink. All listened.

"But now he's got her straight, or how he likes, there's no complaint on that score. She's not new, we know that, but she's always been a good sailer, stiff on the wind and holds to windward, on any tack, and he seems to have got an extra knot or two out of her."

Short now spoke up.

"Ah, but it didn't end there. When he had it all fixed to his likin', then there came the sail handlin'. Does thee remember, first time out, we warn't no more than a mile off Rame Head than he had us takin' in, settin', trimmin' and all sorts?"

He took a pull from his quart, but the others remained silent, knowing there was more to come.

"And I remember that day when we sailed past The Lizard doin' circles, circles! Like some daft girl on a dance floor, tackin' and runnin' free, then haulin' our wind to tack back. I haven't served with the like, nor heard of anyone like 'im, neither."

He warmed to his theme. He sat forward, his face poised over his now empty tankard.

"And then there was that other time, when he had the starboard watch strike down and reset the whole of the fore topgallant mast and had the larboard do the same with the mizzen. Set up in competition, like."

Then he sat back, reflectively.

"But, there is one thing that we here've bin' spared an' that's all the gun practice. Both Watches, not only up an' down the masts, but in and out with the guns. Every damn day, sometimes twice. Throwin' the ship around or practicing gunnery. We must've busted up more barrels than a finicky cooper."

All grinned. Fraser stood up and yelled at Donaghue, now spied behind the bar. He had run out of Irish insults.

"Michael! Five more. And rums to chase it down."

The request was made clear by his waving his empty quart above his head, and pointing to each of his companions. Ball spoke up, as the pot boy removed the empties.

"Well, 'twere arduous, I grant you, but we'n all sat yer on the strength of what it put into us, prizemoney to come, that bein'. So, I can't bring myself to complain too much. And he's Cornish, like I be. I hear he has family down Falmouth way, so we b'ain't stuck with no London toff, nor Lord summat nor other. He was brought up near the sea, and knows seamen, so no complaint from me. 'Specially when that prizemoney starts to jingle in my pocket."

All yelled tipsy agreement as the next set of quarts arrived, then a tray of five glasses of rum. All was quiet as the rum disappeared, then came long pulls from the quart glasses. There were two sailors sat at the same table as Short and Ball and they looked across. The one sat beside Short spoke first.

"So you'm all off the Ariadne?"

The quart pots came down as one and then Ball and Fraser spoke in unison. Assume a challenge or an insult, until you know better.

"What of it?"

"Well, I've heard what you've been sayin'; complainin' some, and I can't hold my peace no more, but to tell 'ee that there wouldn't be a man on my ship as wouldn't swap places with any one off yourn."

The five listened, intent to hear more. This was gossip concerning another ship, probably in detail aplenty; too much there could not be, so the sailor had their full attention. Fraser leaned forward to see, Short sat back to give him view.

"Now what gives you cause to say that?"

The sailor looked past Short at Fraser. His face was scarred and his cuffs ragged.

"First, I wouldn't say no to a share of your good fortune."

Fraser knew exactly what he meant.

He stood and used his 'gale at sea" voice again.

"Michael, two more here. Rum. And quarts."

He lowered himself into his seat and the five looked to the scarred sailor to finish what he had started.

"Our Captain's a toff from up country, or somesuch. One Henry Cheveley. And I d'tell 'ee, all that matters to 'im is the shine on whatever can take a polish. We hardly ever fires the guns with shot, on account that the "true recoil", as 'ee calls it, rips up the deck; what we has to holystone twice a day.

He paused to drink, within the silence. He had their full attention.

'Tis rare we'm sent out on the King's business, other than our duty patrol to the Irish coast, which means The Fastnet Rock, then back, all completed at the best speed 'e can get out of her, to give most of our time in port. He uses any excuse for delay, an' all. Other than that, as 'ee sees it, there b'ain't much need of extra sailin', 'cos of the likes of you sittin' down in The Chops, and the lads out of The Nore keepin' the Frogs out and away from up there. 'Specially after Trafalgar."

The sacred subject had arisen and the sailor raised his glass, just arrived. They used the rum.

"Nelson."

All responded to the toast, which was spoke and drank to, but none of the five broke the ensuing silence. All were intent to hear more of the unsatisfactory doings aboard this rival ship.

"So, we spends most of our time, in harbour, preparin' for the next inspection, often as not from his good oppo, the Port Admiral."

Fraser's face set in deep puzzlement.

"But, from what you say, you'n the Plymouth picket, what does the coast, as far over as Ireland, and you stays out, re-supply and re-fit allowin'. That's her job. I served on one, as a topman. Up and down, weeks and months of it."

The seaman answered.

"Like I said, he's out, only when he 'as to, an' back, with all the rush he can muster, like a jack in the box. I can't answer for what the Lords of the Admiralty thinks we're doin', but we'n more like the Captain's yacht. He prefers us layin' at anchor. 'Tis rare that he sleeps aboard when we'n in harbour. If we takes her out between patrols, often as not it's to entertain some local ladies needin' some sea air. A trip out to look at the ocean, then a nice meal and a steady berth ashore."

Ball's face became pained. He tugged at his whiskers.

"What ship?"

"Herodotus."

"And how come you'n ashore?"

"We'n both Master's Mates. Come ashore to exam for our Master's Ticket."

"Well, mate, all I can say is that doing a bit of polishin', an' takin' ladies out for a jaunt, caught between a bit of there an' back sailin' don't strike me as too bad a berth. I'd swap that for battlin' back at gales and Frog 42's. That's a fact I would."

"Ah, mate, but I 'aven't told you half of it. Cheveley's a flogger. Four, five times a week, the cat's out. Any reason, no matter how small. A speck of dust here, a smear of summat there, gets a man two dozen. B'ain't hardly a man of the whole crew has hasn't felt the lash across his back. And here's the worst of it. I've served with floggers, and, as a crew, you cope, but the worst of the Herodotus is the Captain's toadies. You don't know who they are, but they goes off tellin' tales. That gets 'em off punishment; mostly, but even them gets the odd dozen, so I've heard, if they don't bring enough stories to his Mightiness. The lads can't speak out, like, even in their own mess, at least to share their thoughts about what's goin' on, a good moan together, like."

The Ariadnies looked at each other, distaste and disgust written on the face of each. "Toadies!". A ship could be no worse than one with Captain's spies amongst the crew. Fraser spoke up, but not with words of condemnation, such did not need voicing, the sad pall that had settled on the table told all. Instead, came the only consolation he could give.

"Let us buy you another."

* * *

The four stepped out of the same carriage as used earlier, into the evening yellow sunlight and approached the same double door, as had Argent and Fentiman, some hours earlier. Argent led, with Fentiman just behind his right shoulder, then Bentley and Sanders together, perfectly in step. The Marines open the doors and they stepped in. Candles were already burning, there being no windows in the hall and it contained no guests, merely the same Marine Captain Baker from their previous meeting. Argent thought that they may be too early, he had misheard the time, perhaps, but the anxiety disappeared as Baker hurried over.

"Captain Argent and Lieutenant Fentiman. Good evening. May I be informed of the names of your other two guests?"

Fentiman gave the reply.

"Lieutenants Bentley,"

Bentley bowed.

"And Sanders."

Sanders did the same.

Captain Baker made a note.

"You are the last to arrive. But still on time," he added hastily. "The others are in the drawing room. So, if you'd like to follow me?"

He led them down the hall and turned right at the last door, entered and held open the door for the four to pass through. His role nearly played out, finally he attracted the attention of Admiral Broke, he being the host, this being his residence. Broke began his approach, as his role as host required, and the Captain left. Sanders spoke their thanks.

Broke's mood had not improved or perhaps it changed for the worse at the sight of Argent and three of his Officers, for his face showed no welcome. However, proper society manners were paramount, but, subsequently as it proved, not those that applied to the Royal Navy. He started with Bentley.

"Lucius! Please to see you again. Have you heard from your people? I trust they are well?"

Bentley was somewhat taken aback by this snub to his Captain, but could do nothing other than make his reply.

"I believe so, Sir, we have only been ashore but hours, and I hope to see them tomorrow. That's about the earliest they could arrive, now they've been informed that we're safe in harbour."

"Yes, yes. Of course, but word travels fast."

The meaning of the last was lost on them all, but Broke did then turn to his other guests.

"Ah, Argent and Lieutenant Fentiman. I bid you both good evening. And your other Officer?"

Argent gave the reply, but his voice had a hard edge.

"Sir Arthur. Permit me to introduce Lieutenant Sanders. This has been his first voyage with us, and his first posting."

Broke took a hard look at Sanders, but then his face softened. He was as tall as Argent, perhaps better proportioned, certainly more muscled. Classic good looks, with a queue of shining dark hair. The upper echelons of society certainly; perhaps even aristocracy, he concluded.

"Pleased to meet you, young man. And what of your family?"

Sanders flushed and struggled for words.

"I, er, I'm afraid I, er, I have no family, Sir. I was taken out of an orphanage as a Ship's Boy. Then made a topman and then my Captain sponsored me as a Midshipman. I passed through and thus am I here. Sir."

Broke went pink then puce. He didn't know who to be angry with, Sanders for being what he was, or Argent for bringing such as this to such an occasion. His jaw clenched, but eventually he spoke, whilst extending an arm with a pointed finger.

"Sherry's over there."

He made no excuses, but turned and left and Argent looked at Fentiman and raised his eyebrows.

"Sherry would be welcome."

Fentiman nodded ancd Argent allowed his men to lead the way, then waited for Sanders to give him a re-assuring pat, twice, on his shoulder. They obtained their drinks, took a sip, and looked around. The company was almost wholly Naval, gold epaulettes on all, indicating that all were at least a Post Captain of more than three years. Argent alone wore but one, his promotion being less than three years old, whilst all his Lieutenants stood with empty shoulders. One Post Captain stood out, he was large and loud and the cut of this uniform was of the finest and up to the limits of possible ostentation, edged cuffs and lapels, and long tails with their own set of gold buttons. It plainly came from the best military tailor that could be found. There were five Ladies, all of late middle age, all dressed modestly but the quality of what they wore was very evident. One was being led his way, by Admiral Grant and both were smiling, their eyes fixed on Argent, who now hoped for a marked improvement in the evening so far. Grant made the introductions.

"Captain Argent. Permit me to introduce Lady Constance Willoughby. Lady Willoughby, this is Captain Reuben Argent, of His Majesty's Frigate Ariadne."

Argent took the proffered hand and bowed deeply over it.

"An honour, Lady Constance."

He straightened up.

"Lady Constance, permit me to introduce three of my Officers. Lieutenants, Fentiman, Bentley, and Sanders."

Each bowed in turn, to be acknowledged by a gracious nod of the Lady's head. This done, she turned to Argent.

"I wanted to meet you, because your Father is one of my neighbours. My land is between his and the coast."

Argent smiled genuinely, with no hint of indulgence.

"I know, Lady Constance, I grew up there. I doubt you'll remember me, a small boy who walked the lanes and drove the cows. I went to school in Falmouth, I had to walk there each day. Perhaps you can remember that; I passed your gate daily, but there is no reason why you should."

The Lady looked openly at Argent. It was plain that she was not going to make any statement that was untrue.

"No, Captain, I confess that I do not, but plainly it did you no harm. Here you are now a successful frigate Captain, dwelling in everyone's good opinion."

An image of Broke came immediately to Argent's mind, but a modest response was now required.

"If I am, Lady Constance, I have my crew to thank and my good Officers here. I am but a part of it, an important part, but merely a fraction."

Lady Constance smiled and looked directly at Argent, examining his face, but she gave no reply. If one was forthcoming it was cut short by the dinner gong, being rung at the end of the room by an immaculate Steward. Grant leaned towards Lady Willoughby, offering his arm.

"Lady Constance, allow me."

Before she took Grant's arm, she bade her farewell to Argent.

"Perhaps later, Captain, if not sometime in the future."

She looked at the three Officers, stood dutifully beside Argent.

"Gentlemen."

All bowed. They disposed of their glasses and followed Grant and Lady Willoughby out of the room and through the inevitable double doors to a glittering table, enough for perhaps 15 each side. The table centrepiece was a silver warship, in the style of the Dutch Wars, even the tablecloth shone, enough to rival the silver, and the crystal glass reflected the light from the massed ranks of candles on the table into small pools around their sculptured stands. The room was high; matching the one they had just left, with light oak panelling covering all wall surfaces. This was uninterrupted by any paintings of any description, all that did punctuate their long expanse were several polished brass candle holders, whose charges shone their light up to a magnificent ceiling where dwelt the ornamentation of the room; shipwrecked sailors coming ashore amidst a howling gale.

There was no board displaying place names and so the four grouped themselves at a far corner. Each place had several ranks of knives, forks and spoons and Sanders looked horrified, but Fentiman did the reassuring.

"Don't think it complex, Jonathan, it isn't. Start from the outside with your cutlery and work inwards."

The food arrived as a succession of small, but tasty dishes, well prepared and well presented. Each course was accompanied by a different wine and the glasses were whisked away with each course, along with the plates. The chinaware and glass departed and was replaced with the precision of Marines on manoeuvres. It was all very sumptuous and plainly very expensive. Argent remarked to Fentiman.

"Our Port Admiral must have serious sources of funds."

Fentiman raised his eyebrows and nodded. They and Sanders drank little, but Bentley imbibed mightily and asked for more, he was the furthest up the table of the four, and conversed almost solely with the person next up, he being unknown to Argent. The last course came and went, and so arrived the port and nuts. Time for the Loyal Toast, before the Ladies departed, but time went on. Broke, as host, should have taken the initiative, but after copious quantities of wine throughout the meal he had rather lost track of where they were within the accepted timetable; the wine had worked its effect upon his now befuddled thoughts. Grant, seeing the Ladies remaining, when they should have departed soon after the arrival of the port, took over.

"The Loyal Toast, Gentlemen. Who is the Junior Officer here?"

Broke heard all and immediately answered, drunkenly.

"Who else, but our ex-topman? Down there."

Broke leaned forward to look at Sanders, who, to his credit, looked straight back. Broke, detecting neither embarrassment nor awkwardness, felt the need for further jibes.

"Does he know, that we don't stand, in the Navy?"

Argent angered immediately and glared back up the table. Sanders was one of his Officers and he knew of nothing concerning Sanders that could justify such comments.

"I think it right, Sir, that we allow Lieutenant Sanders to conduct the toast and then, afterwards, judge for ourselves. Sir!"

Sanders seized his own glass and spoke up, clear and steady, whilst raising his glass for all to see. Argent and Fentiman followed his example, lending strong support.

"Ladies and Gentlemen, if you could please ensure that your glasses are charged."

Some were not and, in obedience; for the words had rolled down the table like a quarterdeck order, so they held up their glass to the Stewards for some wine, or used the port already on the table. The gravity in Sanders's words and gesture caused several to act with some urgency and eventually all had some alcoholic liquid of some kind. Sanders spoke, clear and steady.

"Ladies and Gentlemen, I give you The King."

The response was loud; after so forceful a proposal, it could be nothing else. Some tapped their hands on the table edge, in appreciation. The Loyal Toast had been well done. Argent patted Sander's sleeve, twice.

"Well done, Jonathan. Well done."

However, he could see that Sanders was angry.

"Don't let it disturb you, Jonathan, you are going to meet them. I've met them, and all you can do is your duty, in the best way you know, which you have done. Let that be your answer, and tonight we can look to what we've accomplished; and you were a part. There's a French 42 under the guns of The Tower. None can gainsay that, and there's no better answer. Have a drop of port."

Sanders looked at his Captain and smiled. His face changed upon hearing his Captain's good opinion. The Ladies left and the port circulated. The three, for sometime now minus Bentley, talked of their ship and what they hoped to improve, her good features and her bad and what this could mean for future frigate design. It was friendly, professional and convivial. When this was done, Fentiman amused them both with an anecdote of how he was once called upon to stand in for an indisposed Vicar in a masked pageant. Suddenly, came a call, a shout even, from higher up the table.

"Captain Argent!"

Argent looked along the table in the direction of the call. It was the heavily built Post Captain, now leaning forward, distinguished by his immaculate uniform. If his body length counted for anything whilst sat down, he was indeed tall; even sat, he rose above his neighbours. His complexion was pale over a flattish face, which held two large eyes that seemed to be permanently startled, above a smallish nose, but a wide broad mouth. Fair hair hung down past his ears in irregular waves. Argent and he were separated by four places and on opposite sides of the table. Argent addressed his inquisitor, expression open and cordial.

"I am he. How can I help?"

"We have been discussing what makes a good ship. Tight, as we say in the Navy. An expression you're familiar with, I'm sure. As you've had some success of late, perhaps you could add to our discussion?"

All had gone quiet. Was it because of who had just spoken, or were all interested in what Argent had to say? However, first, Argent had one question.

"I'm afraid you are not known to me, Sir. If I may know your name?"

"Cheveley. Herodotus."

The Christian name was omitted and the brevity of the reply carried a chill. This was not lost on Argent, he sensed the challenge, the note of superiority; a sense heightened by the fact that, at the table, Cheveley was the neighbour of Broke. He began his answer slowly, carefully choosing and weighing each word. There was no other sound.

"What makes a tight ship? I take it, by that you mean what makes an effective ship; able to do its duty, whatever that may come to be. Well, plainly, in my opinion a tight ship comes about when every man is well able to carry out his own duty, and knows well what that is. As a frigate Captain, you are sometimes faced with 240 men, all different, but all must be blended to become part of an effective crew. That done, you have a tight ship."

Broke hiccupped, but Cheveley continued. His tone and expression made it clear that he hoped to tighten the screw, bring about some error.

"And what brings that about?"

Argent replied immediately, doing his best to convey bonhomie.

"Why, practice and instruction, Captain Cheveley. You rehearse and practice every situation that a ship can find itself in. You practice until your men get it right. And when they know for themselves that they are getting it right, just as skilled seamen should, and they feel that there's nothing they can't face up to, nor complete, then they call themselves the best crew in the fleet. Then they'll do whatever you ask. That's your tight ship."

He smiled, hoping for agreement. But cold silence. The reply rested with Cheveley.

"So where does following orders come in? You give your orders and expect them carried out. If not, then you give them The Devil."

"Were the task simple, you would have a point. But a man o' war is the most complex machine that man has yet developed."

Nods of agreement occurred around the table.

"Running such an instrument takes years of skill and no small amount of knowledge. That's why you cannot buy promotion in the Navy as you can in the Army. The effective handling of a man o' war only comes with instruction and practice. The threat of punishment doesn't put the skill in their hands, nor the knowledge in their heads. Correctly trimming a sail or laying a gun doesn't happen simply because you say it must; it only comes through rehearsal and practice. Again, as I say, when everyone in the crew counts themselves as right "man o' war's man", then you have your tight ship."

Heads were nodding, even at Cheveley's end of the table. The argument was slipping away. However, Broke, although befuddled by drink, had rehearsed this argument over times innumerable and it all came lurching into his mind. In addition, his anger had fully surfaced, released by the alcohol. Here was a "one swab" Johnny Newcome Captain, not even one year, the son of a common farmer whom he hated, who had taken a French 42 with a smaller ship and no more damage than a few knocked out splinters. It would rank in Naval annals second only to Cochrane taking the El Gamo with a two-masted sloop in the Year One. Cochrane at least was a Lord, but on top, this damn jumped up would now be placed at least on a par, and, worst, he had now shown himself to be a soft damned liberal; in his lexicon, the worst kind of Captain!

"No-one disputes the need for practice, Argent, but I tell you one thing that I know and it's true. The threat of the lash don't half concentrate their minds and stir their stumps. Appealing to some "higher spirit" counts for nothing; it doesn't dwell there. If they know what comes across their backs from laziness or not heeding their orders, they'll learn what they need to know in half the time. Drive 'em. I tell 'ee. Drive 'em."

Several closed to him sounded "hear, hear" and rapped the table. Argent had heard the argument before, from Officers above, including Captains. However, he, too, had rehearsed the arguments before, in his own mind.

"Permit me, Sir, but I beg to disagree. I put it to you that even the most average of seamen can work out for themselves the importance of being able to fulfil their duty, and if they don't their own messmates soon apply the necessary correction. The possible disasters are obvious. I invested the time in practice and tuition, and success breeds success, I find. When my men counted themselves as "right seamen", then they conducted themselves as such. We arrived there without the lash, and it didn't take too long. Within a month I had a worked up crew. Within two, a first rate crew, who continue to improve."

Argent felt the argument true, but it sounded lame, boasting of his own achievements. Cheveley re-entered the fray.

"I stand with Sir Arthur. They have to be more damned afraid of you, than they are of the enemy. Then they fight. What?"

He looked around for support, and got it. More heads nodding and fingers beating the table edge. Argent continued, his own emotions rising. Fentiman saw the change and grew apprehensive. He leaned over to whisper.

"Careful, Sir. They've made you the bull in the ring."

However, Argent pressed on, with some disregard.

"I disagree, Captain. Take Trafalgar. When the Belleisle, the Temeraire, and the Tonnant came into action and fought alone for so long, what kept them fighting? Why didn't the men desert their posts and run down to the bilges?"

Cheveley threw back his head and guffawed."

"Self preservation, I shouldn't wonder. They'd have been hung!"

Others joined in the mirth, but Argent continued, his own temper now showing. He spoke with some passion.

"They'd have been released when their ship was taken. What kept them going was the fact that defeat was simply not possible. Unthinkable. They were Nelson's men, manning one of Nelson's ships, part of the most potent fleet that ever sailed, and invincible. Now that doesn't come with the lash!"

Broke's own drink-fuelled temper finally snapped.

"And I say your damn namby pamby ways will ruin the Navy. We get the dregs and scum of society. Fear of the lash gets 'em there quick and keeps them there. Anything loose and lax they'll take advantage of. They hate us, their Officers, and I for one, hold them in like disregard. They're dregs and scum that we have to lick into shape."

Argent rose to his feet, his face reddened. Fentiman and Sanders looked very concerned. Fentiman placed his hand on Argent's forearm. Was a challenge on its way? Argent ignored him. Bentley merely looked befuddled.

"Sir! My record speaks for me, and for my crew. I ask for nothing other! My dregs and scum and my namby pamby ways..."

"Thank you, Captain."

Grant had gained his own feet. He had noted the increasing heat in the argument with some concern, not least that the host was fuelling the fire. He did not raise his voice but his diction was clear and very precise. The fact that he was on his feet silenced the room.

"Now, gentlemen, calm yourselves. Each Captain runs his own ship in his own way and is answerable to the Admiralty if his ship fails. We all know that. How he brings his ship up to the mark is his own affair."

He paused, but remained standing.

"I may have a scheme that will lance this boil, at least to heal it somewhat. Two days hence we will receive a visit from a Spanish High Admiral. It has been suggested, by the Admiralty..."

He paused again. All knew that this was tantamount to an order from their Lordships. You ignored such at your peril.

"...that I lay on some kind of demonstration of Britannia's naval prowess. I would suggest some form of competition. One ship against another in naval skill. We show his Excellency that we achieve our expertise through honest trial, one against another. Captain Argent, may I count on you?"

Argent had re-taken his seat, but he stood again to lend weight to his words. His mood had not improved.

"Ariadne stands ready. Sir."

Grant turned to Cheveley

"And Captain Cheveley?"

Cheveley began his reply with an airy wave of his hand.

"Of course. Count me in."

Broke felt no need to quell the heat, but, instead, felt more inclined to add fuel.

"I'd back Herodotus against Ariadne any damn time. Anyway you like. I'll put 100 guineas on it."

Grant looked down at his host, but also his inferior in rank. His own patience was wearing thin.

"Thank you, Admiral. But perhaps, before we lay any money, we should decide the contest."

Broke remained silent; jaw clenched, but silent. Grant sat down, the temperature at the table had, thankfully, fallen somewhat, but it was Cheveley who made the suggestion.

"Standard sailing and gunnery. Five targets all moored close, and we sail up through a start line, then broadsides. Tack and repeat, all to time. The fastest to destroy the targets. How say you, Argent?"

Argent leaned forward so that Cheveley could see him, to then speak with some force.

"Agreed, but make it six."

Again the dismissive wave of the Cheveley hand.

Broke now pulled himself forward, needing to use the table edge, to then peer down the table at Argent. He was allowing nothing to drop.

"And a wager, Argent? 100 guineas suit you?"

Argent's shoulders fell and his face saddened.

"I'm afraid that 100 guineas is beyond my purse, at this moment."

Broke and Cheveley grinned and shared the moment, each nodding in the other's direction; "Lower deck Captain."

"50, then."

Argent looked up, he thought that could be raised, on the strength of the forthcoming prizemoney. However, Grant was not pleased, in fact, angry. Both Broke and Cheveley were rich men, using this to bait a Captain who had brought the Navy nothing but credit. He'd seen and heard for himself the crowds thronging the quayside and he spoke his own answer.

"I'll take you up, Sir Arthur. For the full 100!"

Broke looked shocked as silence fell across the table. Then Fentiman spoke up.

"And I'll take the 50!"

* * *

The gigantic landau, gleaming black, its wheels resplendent with bright yellow spokes and hubs, but scarlet rims, proceeded self-importantly down the wide road that marked the edge of the wide green called Plymouth Hoe. The black sides reflected, as would a mirror, the neat kerbstones and white garden walls that ran off before them to show their future course, but the reflection became lost across an ornate and extensive heraldic design, mostly red and gold, that showed gaudy on the side of each wide, high, door. Two high stepping and large black horses trotted over the worn cobbles, their tossing red feathers and gold tassels matching the rhythm of their hooves, which added their noise to the rumble of the well-sprung wheels over the wide stretch of pale and dusty stones. Inside, almost hidden by the high sides, was a collection of ribbons, cockades and fringes that bobbed and fretted in the strong breeze. At the rear, on their platform, rode two liveried Footmen, statue stiff, unbothered by the sedate progress. The carriage made its leisurely way to gradually close with The Tower at the end of The Hoe and then, journey done, it clattered onto a wide parade ground.

There, patient for over an hour, were paraded the Garrison Company of the Royal Marines. With the arrival of the carriage, the whole came to a noisy and emphatic "present arms" and then waited, their Captain with his own gleaming weapon, his sword, pressed thoroughly against his nose. The landau halted at right angles to the immaculate red ranks and both footmen jumped down and jogged around, one to open the door, the other to lower the footstep. This done, they resumed their statuesque pose. Nothing happened. What could be seen were the ribbons and fringes bobbing forward, until a hand reached across the door opening to seize the gleaming handle fixed on the far side. An amazing uniform was then hauled upright to stand in the doorway and extend forward a tentative foot towards the footrest. All then descended. The eye fell first on gleaming ranks of decorations, then upon sashes, lace and brocade, backed by a royal blue coat above a scarlet waist sash, all above scarlet pantaloons. The vision was furthered by an enormous sword, which touched the ground before any foot of its owner, whilst at its top existed a huge polished brass handguard holding a collection of golden tassels. Most incongruously, one could then not do other than focus on legs sheathed in high cavalry boots, each sporting a silver spur. The uniform was completed by an enormous bicorn hat, this worn athwart ships; it being also blue and scarlet, not that much of this colour could be seen through the crowded cockades and decorations all clamouring for attention. In between the hat and the coat was an ancient face that resembled a burnt walnut, in a yellow box, formed by the front edges of the impossibly high collar. The Admiral took four paces forward and stopped, the movement accompanied by an orchestral amount of jingling, which included the spurs. Two, almost equally gorgeous, Officers, the Admiral's Equerries, descended after him, then came Admiral Grant, very plain by comparison, which included the footmen.

Grant hurried forward and gestured towards the Marine Captain, who would provide a guard for the forthcoming inspection. The Captain lowered his sword and then brought it back to the salute. The introductions were made and the Admiral plodded forward, Grant at his side, the Marine Captain just behind and the Admiral's attending Officers just behind again. Each Marine bested the Admiral's height by at least a head, this accentuated by their gleaming black shakoes. Each Marine remained expressionless; who this mobile pile of cloth and bullion was, they had not a clue. The inspection done, the party, with no increase in pace, set a course for The Tower, and entered. Whilst the Marines marched away, the gaze of any onlookers was drawn to the top of the imposing stonework, where, at their ease, with their lenses blindly scanning the sky, stood a rank of telescopes, all secure on their tripods. At length, the hats and cockades appeared through the crenellations and the telescopes were quickly seized upon to examine the harbour. Soon all were focused on two frigates, stern on, one larger than the other, both under minimal sail in the South West wind, both on the starboard tack to hold themselves against the incoming tide.

Once in place at the battlements, and after a period of studying both frigates, one of the Equerries approached Grant.

"His Excellency would be grateful to know what form this competition will take place."

"Ah, yes. Permit me."

Grant walked to place himself beside the Admiral and began to explain, slow enough to allow a translation.

"Tell his Excellency to train his glass on the six rafts moored before us across the gap between the mainland and the island. Moored to give the frigates a beam on wind, or close."

This was translated but His Excellency turned around, looking pained.

"¿Emita en?"

"His Excellency asks, what is beam on?"

"Your pardon. The wind hitting the side of the ship at right angles."

Grant added further explanation by butting his own fingers directly into the palm of his left hand. The translation was made and His Excellency nodded, releasing an "ahhhh" like a hiss of steam.

"On the raft are targets, panels of wood"

This was passed on. His Excellency returned to his telescope.

"Each ship sails up, shoots at the targets, and sails back, if needed, to finish the job. The winner is the quicker, timed from their going through the start line, then sailing back across it."

The translation took place and this time His Excellency took his eye from the telescope and grinned, brown stained teeth showing between the purple lips.

"¿Cómo hace esto su Marina mejor?"

"His Excellency asks, how does this make your Navy better?"

"Honest competition between two ships, friendly rivalry, that is. We consider that it encourages both vessels to perform better. The crews have to handle both their guns and their sails. It's a good test."

Post translation, His Excellency nodded.

"Ah, si. ¿Y dónde está la línea de meta?"

"His Excellency asks where is the start and finish line?"

"Grant pointed to a small vessel moored far out in the Sound, showing a long pennant from its short mast."

"From us to that longboat."

A short burst of Spanish and His Excellency peered through the crenellation to re-direct his telescope and then peer through it. Grant continued, patiently

"Please inform His Excellency that we would like him to decide the winner. It is a balance between speed and gunnery. A ship may be quicker, but not destroy all the targets. We would like him to make a judgment as to who is the winner."

The translation was made and again came the despoiled grin. His Excellency showed approval with a nod and a wave of his hand, in which, somehow, had arrived a huge cigar, possibly from the second Equerry.

The first Equerry turned to Grant.

"His Excellency will be pleased to make his judgment."

Grant bowed to the Admiral and then turned to Captain Baker.

"Time to start proceedings. Does Cheveley know he's up first?"

"Yes Sir. Yes to both."

Baker walked to the furthest cannon, surrounded by a waiting crew, it's Gun Captain stood back, lanyard in hand. Baker nodded and the lanyard was jerked back. The gun roared and all was shrouded in smoke blown across by the wind. When it cleared, all eyes were placed against the rear of a telescope, trained on the larger frigate. The Herodotus set her jibsails and turned into the wind. The details on the side of her hull grew for the watchers as she swung around to begin her run in; she would run directly across their line of sight to the longboat. Cheveley set all plain sail and his ship gathered speed, her 21 gunports each with the black dot of its waiting gun-muzzle, run out and ready. The minutes passed, whilst many consulted their watches, then she crossed the startline. A gun along the battlements spoke again. Many spoke the time; 11.42.

Admiral Broke, who had stood aside whilst the Spanish Admiral was being spoken to by Grant, now approached Grant, he being now stood, without telescope, looking out over The Sound.

"Care to change the betting, Grant?"

"As is, Arthur, 100's rich enough for me!"

Broke grinned and rejoined his small party of Officers.

Herodotus was approaching the line of targets directly, taking the wind fine over the larboard quarter, so at some stage she would have to change course to run along the line to the furthest target. Speculative conversations grew amongst the Officers. One spoke somewhat above the level of the others.

"Ah, I see what he's doing. He'll turn right, to wear onto the starboard tack, for target two, sail down to take four and six, and then come back to take five, three, and finally one. He hasn't the sea room to take number one first, which gives him only one crack at it. What will he do for the turn back, though, that's the issue?"

The Officer had divined truly. Cheveley wore ship someway off the first target and Herodotus' did turn right to swing her stern round through the wind. The sails came round and, with the wind now perfectly from starboard, Herodotus presented her full broadside at 50 yards range. All her guns exploded at once and the target disappeared. She sailed silently past the next target whilst the guns were reloaded and dealt out the same to target four, on then to ignore five but to destroy six. She now had to sail back, to destroy targets five, three, and then one and cross the finishing line. With the wind large on his starboard quarter, Cheveley elected to tack, to turn South and get some sea room, the better to pick up the wind for the run back to the finish.

With the wind strong on his starboard beam Cheveley felt his ship had enough speed to turn down seaward and cross the wind and then come back up on a North West course. The helm was turned into the wind and all sheets were released to prevent the sails backing against the masts as she came around to point straight into the wind. Cheveley had the big stern driver hauled out hard to starboard and the wind hit it to push the stern round. The jibsails were hauled over, but the Herodotus had slowed appreciably, the only discernable movement from The Tower was her stern swinging around across the water, pushed by the driver.

All on The Tower held their breath, would she get round? However, soon the jibsails drew the South West breeze and she began to make headway. The mainsail, forsail and all topsails were hauled round, sheeted home and began to draw. Herodotus began to make headway and pick up speed, the wind perfect, just astern of directly onto her hull. It had been a risky turn, but Cheveley had pulled it off. Many on The Tower applauded, Broke with extra vigour. Her starboard gunports stood ready. Herodotus sailed down onto each target, but, for the return leg, the wind would not allow a parallel course, only a convergent one, 100 yards range onto target five, 75 onto three, then 50 onto one. But, even at long range, her full broadside turned them all into flying splinters. She raced on to cross the finishing line, to prompt another gun, achieving a time of 16 minutes 5 seconds. Broke was ecstatic.

"Damn me, if that wasn't ship handling of the first order. I'll take that 100 now, if you choose, Grant. Argent won't better that. That's as clean a piece of sail handling and gunnery as I've ever seen."

"We'll see, Arthur. We'll see."

However, Grant was indeed apprehensive for his 100 guineas, but at least pleased to see the party of Spaniards all nodding in approval.

Argent had watched all from the foretop, accompanied by Fentiman. They conversed but little, content to watch, but learning little, certainly not enough to change their chosen course. The ship idled on the incoming tide, fore and main topsails just holding her against the incoming sea. They had to wait for the gun, which showed that the targets had been rebuilt and it took three longboats, each taking two targets, almost an hour to rebuild the wooden targets. Within the interim, the party on The Tower took a little refreshment, no beer, in deference to their guests, instead some white Spanish wine and canapés. Grant did duty, through translation; politely acceding to the fact that the Spanish armies would very soon clear the French out of Spain.

Down on the Ariadne's gundeck, the crews from the Starboard Watch were deep in conversation, the guns ignored for now, everything having been checked and re-checked numerous times. Joe East, Gun Captain of No. 4, the next to Sam Morris, called over. Morris was habitually staring at his flintlock, should he check for the 10th time that it sparked?

"Sam. I heard tell that the Captain's got 200 guineas ridin' on this."

"Heard tell from who?"

"Eli Reece."

"That sprung waister! And where'd he get it from?"

"Skipper of a bumboat, what got it off a Steward."

Joe Dedman was sat on the shot garland, checking the spherical quality of the first ball they would fire.

"Eli Reece was born deaf in one ear, and lost the hearin' of the other at Copenhagen. 200 guineas! Bloody ten, more like."

Their volunteer, Jacob Pierce just polished the gun.

"Deaf's right. An' 'ee can't take in no more than five words at a time."

All within hearing gave a deep chuckle, but at that point a dull report came to them through the open gunports and the deck tilted heavily to larboard.

Ariadne was coming round sharply, her bow pushed by her full set of jibsails. As soon as she moved across the wind and took the strong breeze fine over her starboard quarter, she kept in there. All plain sail suddenly appeared on her yards and soon all lower starboard stunsails were added. Ariadne immediately picked up speed, faster and faster, but on a heading much more off to starboard than that of the Herodotus. All on The Tower watched, fascinated; none spoke, all were trying to divine Argent's intentions, but what they noted first was the speed. The loud voiced Officer was the first to speak.

"God, she's going like a racing yacht! Twelve knots, and plus, I shouldn't wonder. But he's heading out, ignoring number one."

A pause.

"He's going straight for number six!"

All watching could do no more than agree and speculation grew as all argued the merits of this different course of action. Ariadne crossed the line and, as the gun sounded, several called the time; 12.59.

On the Quarterdeck of the Ariadne, Argent was in conversation with his Gunner. Behind him Henry Ball came to the Binnacle to turn the glass and ring two bells. Argent had handed Tucker his telescope, which he was focusing on the nearest target, showing white against the dark water.

"What do you think they are, Mr. Tucker?"

"I'd say standard targets, Sir. Flats, six foot by six. Made of board, coffin wood, most likely."

"What should we use?"

"At what range, Sir?"

"100 down to 50."

"Grape on ball, Sir."

"Not chainshot, nor bar?"

"No Sir. Both them can swing about. Grape and ball both fires truer. 'An you gets much the same spread."

"I agree. Make it so, for the starboard battery."

"Aye, aye, Sir."

Tucker beetled off and Argent looked forward to the first target he would take, calculating when he would make his turn. The deck righted itself gently beneath his feet, back from larboard; the wind had slackened, just slightly, she'd slip a little less to leeward when she made the turn.

Back on The Tower, all were in agreement as to Argent's intentions, but many failed to see how it would work. The loud Officer again voiced the thoughts of many.

"He's going to wear round onto number six and sail back, taking each target in turn. But that will be evil slow. He'll have to give his guncrews time to load, he's got to take each one as he passes so he'll have to reduce sail. Too fast, they'll miss a target, they won't reload in time, but giving time for reloading he'll be too slow, and the loser. This game's done!"

On the gundeck of the Ariadne, the grapeshot was arriving from the magazine, carried by labouring Powder Monkeys. Two of the young boys dropped the white bag at the muzzle of number three, the inch balls inside knocking heavily against each other. Morris congratulated their own Powder Monkey, one of the two.

"Well done, Smallsize. And to your mate. Now go get us another."

The shout came down the gundeck, from First Mate Henry Ball.

"Load starboard battery. Grape on ball. White 6 foot target, first 100 yards off, comin' down to 50."

The guncrews sprang to. The tacklemen feeding the muzzle with the bag of gunpowder, rammed down, then a carefully prepared 18lb ball, all then fully rammed down. Morris nodded in their direction, he had felt the pricker pierce the bag down through the touchhole, all was as it should be. He then pushed the quill filled with fine powder down to meet the powder inside the first bag, then he cocked and primed the flintlock. The loaders then fed in the white bag of grape, finishing with a wad of guncotton; all rammed down. With the final exit of the rammer from the barrel, the four crewmen seized the tackles and hauled the muzzle through the gunport, the gun truck hitting the side with a thud. Morris took sight, with Dedman and another adjusting the quoin to elevate the gun for a six-foot target at 100 yards, Morris hoping to anticipate the heel of the ship with the wind on her beam. Then the deck moved beneath their feet, Ariadne was coming round.

Argent had called "up helm, larboard tack" and Ariadne had answered, swinging left, to larboard. With the wind still just astern of beam on and fair over the larboard side, she didn't drop a knot. Fraser used the unoccupied Larboard Watch for his sail handling and the big stern driver was hauled round to point straight over the taffrail and catch the wind, thus to push her stern around quickly. Likewise the square sails already set on the spars were hauled to the correct angle that would catch the wind, the starboard yardarms braced well back. The stunsails extending these remained in place, they were doing no harm, probably some good. Argent gauged the run of his ship; she was not picking up quick enough.

"Mr. Fraser. Main and mizzen staysails. Foretopmast staysail."

At his prompting Bosun Fraser had his men set the three lowest staysails. These, running down the centre of the ship, met the wind perfectly and so Ariadne sped on. Argent had the same problem as Cheveley on his run back, so he also chose not to sail fully up to his first target, not closing to 50 yards, because then they would have to turn back into the wind to sail parallel to all six. It could mean losing the wind, so he also chose a convergent course that would take them from 100 yards range down to 50 when they finally reached number one. Ariadne settled onto her course and the deck steadied. Sam Morris stared along the gunbarrel, calling for the elevation as Pierce changed the quoin for what Morris judged to be 100 yards distant.

On The Tower all eyes were glued to whatever telescope was available. Their view was fine across Ariadne's starboard bow as she bore down upon the targets, her 16 guns now visible, black muzzles mute but threatening beyond their gunports. The same conclusion came from several directions.

"She's too fast, they'll never reload in time. Impossible."

Another made his contribution.

"And that's 100 yards, too far to be certain. He's taking the same chance as Cheveley."

Ariadne was nearly up to target six. Sam Morris crouched behind his gun, peering along the greyblack length of its barrel out through the gunport. Looking forward through the gunport, he caught a glimpse of white before number one fired and came back inboard on a squealing truck. He had three seconds before the target was inline with his own weapon, but it was now obscured by smoke. He yelled at Dedman and Pierce, both stood ready to lift the casable, wooden handspikes already between the carriage and the casable.

"Up a half."

The sturdy handspikes strained under the heavy casable, as number two gun fired. Pierce pulled out the quoin one half of a mark on its upper surface. Morris pulled the lanyard and his gun roared and sprang back to be held by the heavy breeching rope. His crew sprang forward to reload.

The audience on The Tower watched Ariadne open fire, each gun as it bore. At the extreme range on a six foot target each gun did damage but much remained upright. Then, after six, the guns stopped, but it was just a pause. Guns thirteen and fourteen from the last four on the starboard battery fired in quick succession and finished the work. As the Ariadne sped on, the target was left behind as several pieces of flotsam. She reached target five and guns seven to twelve fired in succession. At closer range the target was practically destroyed, but the final two guns of the starboard battery fired anyway, knocking down the last upright.

The watchers waited, thinking that they knew what was happening, but not sure and almost unbelieving. Just before target four it was confirmed, the first six guns from the bows emerged from their gunports and fired in succession, this time wholly destroying their mark. The bow six were taking targets six, four, and two, the next six to the stern were to hit targets five, three, and one. The last four guns waited loaded and ready, insurance against anything remaining upright.

The loud Officer closed his telescope with a snap and beat it into the palm of his left hand.

"Well, ain't that the neatest. He's gambling that six guns will do the job, half a battery at a time, giving time for each half to reload before they reach their target. Trusting his gunners, and I for one applaud. Seeing's believing. Good seamanship but even better gunnery! Damn fine shooting. I've never heard of the like, never mind seen it!"

Grant watched as target three dissolved from the stern battery of six guns. He turned to look for Broke and found him, but the latter looked as if he had swallowed a wasp. From over the battlements came the last two volleys, then the finishing gun sounded, then someone called the time; 01.11 precisely. Ariadne had completed her run in 12 minutes.

Broke walked over to Grant, still looking as though he were chewing on something with a rotten tooth and that he was also in pain somewhere else, but he was pulling out his pocket book. A companion was handing him a pencil. Grant stood still and was pleased to see the Spanish navy walking his way. The English speaking Equerry spoke first.

"His Excellency says that there is little to decide. He thinks that the Captain of the second ship made the better decisions."

"Please inform His Excellency that we thank him for his .... informed judgment."

The thanks were passed on, and His Excellency waved his hand, this time containing another cigar. The Equerry continued.

"His Excellency asks that he meet both Captains."

Broke looked up from writing the note, deep apprehension plain on his face, but Grant made an immediate reply.

"At dinner this evening, if that suits? At the Admiral's Headquarters." Grant looked around at Broke.

"Is that possible, Broke? I can send over some rations, if needs be."

Broke nodded at Grant, then turned and bowed to His Excellency. The Equerry did not see the need for translation.

"At your 8 o' clock."

Grant smiled as the Spaniards headed for the stairs, a smile that broadened as Broke finished the note for 100 guineas and handed it over, with ill grace plain on his face. Grant could not resist striking home further.

"You'll need to write another. Argent's First, if you remember. He took you up for 50!"

* * *

Having crossed the finishing line, Ariadne tacked South, to gain some sea room. Argent saw no need to anchor so close to the shore. Using all jibsails, she eased her way around to gain enough wind and then, on the starboard tack, with no more than jibs, lower staysails, and driver, she slid around the now anchored Herodotus. Argent looked over. He could see the Officers of his erstwhile opponent looking across at his own ship. He turned to his Officer of the Watch.

"Lieutenant. Dip the Ensign."

"Aye, aye, Sir."

Sanders went to the halyards himself and loosened the rope that held the Ensign aloft. The huge Ensign, white, with its red cross and Union Jack, fell and billowed out to larboard in the continuing stiff breeze. No longer held aloft by a taut rope, a corner touched the water. Sanders counted to ten, then rehoisted, and soon the Ensign was taught from the end of the driver boom. All on the quarterdeck looked over for a response. They saw an Officer on Herodotus go to their halyards and begin, but he soon stopped and spun around, coming to the attention. He didn't touch the halyards again. Argent looked away and gazed along his own deck to the forecastle, wryly nodding his head, speaking dryly, but more to himself, his voice thick with irony.

"Like that, is it? I see."

He watched and heard as Fentiman oversaw the anchor being dropped and all sail was taken in and furled. All was secured. With the ship safe at anchor and the crew stood down, up from the gundeck came a volume of laughing, cheering, and shouting, to be taken up by the Larboard Watch ranged along both gangways. Many timepieces throughout the ship had confirmed the victory. He turned to Fentiman.

"I think a tour of the gundeck would not be out of place."

Fentiman grinned openly.

"I agree."

They took themselves to the head of the starboard companionway and began down, to be immediately spotted by First Mate Henry Ball, stood at the bottom.

"Man your stations!"

Silence came quickly.

"Attention!"

Argent and Fentiman looked upon a scene, somewhat confused, but wholly still. The guns were being housed, some still stood in the middle of the deck, still being sponged out, some almost fully bowsed up against their closed gunports. Shot garlands had conspicuous empty spaces, and rammers, sponges, and handspikes were lying around, some on the deck, some leaning against the guns. But each man was at his place as though for an inspection, Gun Captains to the right of each gun. Argent considered some kind of speech, but thought his normal walk along the deck would suffice. He started forward but stopped at guns 13 and 14. "Unlucky for Some" was carved neatly on the carriage of 13. He spoke, looking at both Gun Captains.

"Evans and Wood. Well done, good shooting to finish that first target."

Evans, on 13, saluted, and felt that on this occasion, saying something extra would be counted forgivable.

"Aye, Sir. Thank you, Sir. Wiped the eye of those lubbers up there! Sir."

He leaned forward to look up to the bows, clearly indicating the identity of the "lubbers" and where they stood.

Argent grinned.

"Perhaps so, Evans. Perhaps so."

They passed on, picking their way through the confusion, not in any way solemn, this time all grinning openly, behind the salutes and spoken names. They made their way to the last gun, then came quickly back astern so that all could see him, including those on the gangways above. He looked at Henry Ball and spoke, quietly.

"Stand the men easy, Mr. Ball."

Whilst the order was ringing down the deck, he turned and removed his hat. Fentiman took his cue and copied his Captain, but with an openly wider grin.

"Men. I take my hat off to you. If there's a finer crew, anywhere, I'd like to see them, and we'd best them anyway."

Shouts of agreement came back at him. The carnival atmosphere was growing. He looked up at George Fraser stood on the starboard gangway.

"Mr. Fraser. I think that this evening we can double the grog!"

Cheers echoed all round, as Argent waved his hat before replacing it and ascended the companionway to the quarterdeck. At the top he was met by Midshipman Bright.

"Sir. A signal from The Tower, Sir. All Captains, 3 bells, 2nd Dog. Admiral's residence."

* * *

"Easy all. Toss oars"

Once more, again in the yellowing light of evening, the Captain's barge glided smoothly to The Tower steps, speed perfectly judged by Coxswain Whiting. The Captain's barge of the Herodotus, had departed their ship at the same time, but, being nearer, had arrived just earlier. It had passed them on its return, empty of its Captain, and saying nothing. As they crossed, Argent had looked up onto the quayside that was but minutes away and saw a black carriage drive away. He became annoyed and thought to himself, "That's damn poor. They must have seen me, and couldn't wait. Or wouldn't". It had dawned on him, that Cheveley had beaten him to the carriage and had required it not to wait.

Abel Jones secured the boat and held the gunwale steady, as his Captain stepped out and onto the same granite steps, now dark in shadow from the Westering sun. Argent turned back to his Coxswain, he remaining at the tiller. He had decided, on the way over, that he would not keep his barge crew waiting at the steps, waiting perhaps until the small hours for all he knew, whilst their crewmates celebrated back aboard.

"Take yourselves back, Whiting. I'll spend the night ashore. Have a drink for me, won't you."

Whiting looked relieved, the same thought had passed through his mind.

"Aye aye, Sir. You can be sure of that, Sir. Thank you, Sir, and enjoy your evenin'."

Argent had grave doubts, but replied his thanks. Jones was soon back in and the oarsmen shoved off and were soon gone. The thought of what lay back on the ship lending extra energy to their long, regular, strokes. Argent ascended the steps and looked for some form of transport for hire. He looked at his watch, 7.15. It was little more then a mile to the Port Admiral's residence but he would be late for 7.30. There was no vehicle to be seen, so he began walking. He had cleared The Tower, when he heard a carriage and horses behind, then it drew level and stopped beside him. The crest on the door he recognised; The Willoughby's, then a footman descended and opened the door, quickly adding the unfolded footrest to the evident invitation. He entered to find himself facing, not only Lady Willoughby, which he expected, but also Admiral Grant and a young woman. He smiled his greetings, a smile made wider and more genuine by his relief at having been spared a walk and then being embarrassingly late.

"Good evening, Lady Willoughby, Admiral Grant. I'm very grateful for your stopping. It seems I missed the carriage which, I assumed, picked up Captain Cheveley."

Lady Willoughby spoke, whilst Grant silently beamed his unspoken pleasure at seeing Argent.

"Captain Argent. May I introduce my niece, Charlotte Willoughby?"

She was directly opposite. Argent took the proffered hand and bowed over it, with as much emphasis to the requirement as he could manage, whilst still remaining in his seat. The interior of the carriage was gloomy, but it was clear that Charlotte was a beauty; classic features, especially her hair; fair to golden and pulled back, after the fashion, but enough hanging curls to frame her striking good looks.

"Your Servant, Miss Willoughby. It's a pleasure to meet you. I trust you are well?"

"Quite well, Captain, I thank you. I have been looking forward to meeting you."

This spoken in a clear voice, with very precise diction, and containing just an edge of haughtiness. Grant at last spoke up.

"I thought some Ladies would add to the occasion, Argent, don't you think? Can't have a whole evening talking shop, something unavoidable with the High Spanish Navy at table, I shouldn't wonder."

"Yes Sir. Most wise, in my view."

Grant paused and shifted himself forward and across, as if there were others to hear what he didn't want them to.

"Exceeding fine display this afternoon, Argent. Exceeding fine. You made me 100 guineas richer."

He reached inside his Admiral's coat, the rings of rank on his arm reflecting the dying sun.

"Here's a note for 50, for your crew. From me. And here's Grant's note for another 50, for your First. Your performance cut a dash with our Don Admiralty, I can tell you."

He placed a finger on Argent's cuff as if to indicate further conspiracy.

"Which has given rise to a little luxury coming your way. You're to stay the night at The George; Plymouth's best in my opinion, at His Excellency's expense. He's staying there also, so you'll breakfast with him. He insisted, clearly you impressed him, which will more than satisfy Their Lordships, Heaven be thanked. "

He paused and leaned even further forward, very, very, conspiratorially.

"You know, I think that there may be a bit more of a seaman in this particular Don, than meets the eye."

He sat back, beaming again whilst nodding vigorously and released a downward sigh of deep contentment; a man released from a difficult job, now done, all most satisfactory. Grant then realized that he had better start the conversation, so he looked at Lady Willoughby, then to Argent, the Admiral smiling like a child that had much bounty bestowed upon him.

"Lady Willoughby and Charlotte saw the whole thing, isn't that right Constance, from a high window from their house along The Hoe?"

Lady Willoughby grinned back at Grant and nodded.

"Yes, Septimus, the whole thing, as best we may, through telescopes. My eye still feels damp, and almost depressed; but I understand, Captain Argent, that congratulations are in order."

"That's very gracious of you, Ma'am. It was a good contest, fairly played out. I count myself lucky, a good ship, well Officered, and manned by a good crew."

Charlotte now spoke.

"It seems that success trails on your heels, Captain."

"So far, Miss Willoughby, yes, I've been lucky, but luck can change. In common with all sailors, superstition dwells not too far below our surface."

"I'm surprised that a modern Captain, such as yourself, if I have the correct impression, allows such primitive ideas to guide his actions."

"Perhaps, Miss Willoughby, but I take no chances..."

He grinned at his conjunction with superstition, but pressed on.

"I don't allow superstition to affect the running of the ship. Whatever is good for the ship, then I count that as contributing to our own good luck. For example, there is the superstition of not sailing with a woman on board. But we have one, the wife of my Sailing Master, Mrs. Eara McArdle. She assists my Surgeon, and the men would have no other. All would defend her presence aboard, because she is so fine a nurse; and knowing, especially of that which is required for the care of the sick and injured. She has an unparalleled knowledge of what I'll term "home remedies"; herbs and such. My Surgeon also remains most content that she be part of his sickbay. Thus superstition comes a poor second."

Grant slapped his hand on his knee, nodded, and grinned some more, but Charlotte Willoughby looked mildly shocked.

"You have a woman, caring for men?"

"Why yes, my reading of history tells me that is not so strange. And we are a man o' war, Miss Willoughby. What works, does; if you take my meaning."

Lady Willoughby looked at her niece.

"I think you will find, Charlotte, the more you hear of Captain Argent, that he does indeed run a modern ship. If new ideas work, he keeps to them. I am correct, Captain?

Argent was not going to gainsay such as Lady Willoughby.

"Yes, Ma'am. I'm ready to try anything that strikes me as being for the good of The Service. For example, I've heard of a new shell called "shrapnel". Really it's for the Army, but I've requested some, to take a look. New ideas should be given a fair chance, I believe, I don't see how we can do anything other. It's a tough fight out there."

Lady Willoughby smiled, a fine thought coming to her mind.

"Perhaps; unless your ship is the Ariadne!"

Argent bowed.

"You are too kind Ma'am, but I see no cause to argue."

The carriage lurched to a stop, rocking on its springs. Almost in a second, the doors opened and the footrest was unfolded. Grant exited first and he then aided Lady Willoughby down to the swept gravel, leaving Argent to do the same for Charlotte. With the Ladies safely alighted, Grant acted as escort to Lady Willoughby, giving Argent no choice but to do the same for Charlotte. He held out his left arm and she placed her hand upon it, but first looking at Argent with an expression whose emotion he could not divine. However, thus arranged, they proceeded up the steps and through the opened, and to Argent, now familiar, doors.

In the Hall, all under the command of Captain Baker, stood more servants, who came to take the Ladies cloaks. This revealed the gorgeous dress worn by Charlotte Willoughby, a chemisette, made from the finest satin, with just enough edging and embroidery to convey its hand-made quality, and it accompanied by an extensive string of pearls, swooping low from her neck. She was, indeed, a very handsome woman. Baker, for once taken wholly aback and stumbling over words he had spoken a thousand times, led them forward to the ante-room that served for Argent's first banquet, that of unpleasant memory. There, looking rather lonely in the centre of the wide floor, stood the five other guests, Broke, Cheveley, His Spanish Excellency and the two Equerries. The four entered, the Ladies on the arms of the two Officers and Baker announced their presence.

All conversation ceased. Lady Willoughby and her niece glided forward and all advanced to meet them. Broke, as host, was required by convention to address himself first to Lady Willoughby, leaving Cheveley to advance further to greet Charlotte. Cheveley ignored Argent, who remained supporting Charlotte's right hand.

"Charlotte, what an unexpected pleasure to see you here. So very splendid to see you again. I thought this occasion was going to be wholly Naval. Permit me to find you a glass of sherry."

With that he turned to walk rapidly towards an ornate mahogany server that carried nothing but a chased silver tray and some small glasses of the dark wine. No words had passed between them on the way in, but Argent now spoke.

"I had no idea, Miss Willoughby, that you are acquainted with Captain Cheveley."

"Why yes, on more than one occasion he has been gracious enough to take us out for an excursion into The Channel, on a day not too taxing for myself and my Aunt. His wife accompanies us, also."

By now, Cheveley had returned and, offering the glass to Charlotte's left hand, he stood in front of Argent with his back to him and his own left arm raised, clearly expecting a transfer.

"Charlotte, let me introduce you to our Spanish guests. They are anxious to meet you, I know."

Charlotte transferred her hand from Argent's arm and allowed herself to be led over to His Excellency and his two Equerries, who stood stock-still and wide-eyed at the arrival of this English vision. Charlotte and Cheveley progressed away, Charlotte moving as though on casters, were it not for the faintest rise and fall of her hem, tailored for perfect length. The High Admiral came forward to take her hand and bend low over it.

Argent was left standing, but he raised his eyebrows and sighed. He expected little else. His only two allies this evening, he knew, were Grant and Lady Constance Willoughby, but they were both engaged in conversation with Broke. He sighed again and took himself over to the server where a single glass remained. He took this, but did not drink, but turned to see the Spanish Admiral still holding Charlotte's hand in both his, whilst gazing up into her face, this being significantly above his. An Equerry was translating, equally and utterly absorbed, whilst Cheveley and the other Equerry were all smiles.

Argent had no option but to take himself over to Grant and Lady Constance, although this meant being in the petulant company of Admiral Broke. He walked forward, Broke's face changing with every footstep that brought him nearer, but Argent knew that he would have to greet his Superior. He smiled as pleasantly as he could, although his eyes did not match the warmth he spoke.

"Good Evening, Admiral Broke. Thank you for inviting me, Sir."

Broke felt no need to be gracious.

"As our Spanish guest would have it, Argent. As he would have it, not I."

But Lady Constance, after frowning pointedly at Broke, immediately dispelled the chill.

"Tell me, Reuben, how are things with your Father?"

The weather around Broke turned thunderous, but around Argent it brightened, not just at the use of his Christian name, but also at the support provided by the open friendliness showing on Lady Constance' face as she looked up at him.

"Thank you for asking, Lady Willoughby, but the last I heard, he was in good health and the farm was holding up. Nothing that could be termed as prospering well as such, but doing well enough."

"You have a sister, as I recall, or is it two?"

Argent now grinned openly.

"Sisters yes, Lady Willoughby, two, Emily and Enid, and one is married, Enid, the elder, with a small child. I'm an uncle!"

He continued to grin and looked at Grant and Broke. Grant beamed back in fatherly fashion, whilst Broke stared back with a scowl that came straight from the Arctic, but Grant intervened.

"Now, Argent. You are here because our Spanish guest wished to meet you, both of you, Cheveley and yourself, that being. I must take you over."

Argent was still holding his glass and he knew that this would be awkward, he must lose it somewhere. He looked around but the server was too far, however Lady Willoughby realized his plight and came to his rescue.

"I'll look after that for you, Captain, whilst you do your duty."

Argent bowed and smiled his thanks.

She took the glass and Argent turned to accompany Grant, but he caught a glimpse of the withering look that she gave Broke now that they were left alone, made more so because she was slightly taller, thus it was delivered down the fine line of her nose. His Excellency had released Charlotte's hand, but was wholly monopolising the conversation with her, severely taxing the translator, thus his concentration upon her was absolute. Argent realized what he was breaking into, but Grant was doing the breaking. Grant stopped close to the Spanish Admiral and leaned forward to attract his attention, whilst Argent maintained an inferior's distance.

"Your Excellency, I'm sure that you would wish to meet the other Captain. The one that you so graciously declared to be the winner of the competition earlier today."

His Excellency looked alarmed at the interjection between himself and Charlotte, but the translation calmed his expression. He turned to observe Argent, who, upon being regarded by his Eminence, came to the attention and saluted. Argent took the wave of the glass as acknowledgment and dropped his hand. His Excellency remained regarding him, up and down, with a strong look of puzzlement on his face, but Grant did the honours, first waiting for the translating Equerry to hurry round to Grant's side to hear.

"Your Excellency, may I present Captain Reuben Argent, of His Majesty's frigate, Ariadne?"

His Excellency grinned through the puzzled expression and nodded. Grant continued.

"Captain Argent, this is His Excellency, the High Admiral Joaquim Don Alaves D'Sentillo."

Argent remained at attention and bowed. His Excellency nodded again, waved his glass and then returned to Charlotte. Argent remained at attention, until he saw Don Alaves D'Sentillo's back, then he relaxed himself. He thought "job done", and felt more than a small sense of gratitude for the presence of Miss Charlotte. However, he felt that he should "hover" as he may be required and therefore stood on the edge of the group. Doing, he felt, no harm and remaining standing there, made him at least half-way occupied, attending his superior Officers. His place, just offset from the talking group, but near enough to hear, caused him to catch the question that explained His Excellency's puzzled countenance. His Excellency, still holding firm to his position at Charlotte's elbow, spoke rapidly to the Equerry translator who posed the question to Grant.

"Why has this Captain no decorations, merely one epaulette?"

Grant's reply was to the point.

"His rank. He is a Post Captain of only one year, entitling him to wear one, just one. After three he is entitled to two epaulettes."

The answer was conveyed to His Excellency, who received the answer with merely an inclination of his head, his eyes remaining on Charlotte. Argent remained at his post, as he saw it, but was grateful when the gong sounded, rung by the same Steward as the occasion before, to call them into dinner. He allowed all others to move off, before he took a pace forward himself, but his spirits sank when he saw that, tediously, Cheveley was hanging back, evidently intent on exchanging some words. Argent was, however, determinedly polite. He nodded his greeting.

"Captain Cheveley."

Cheveley made no reply that could be counted as an acknowledgement; he merely began to unburden himself with what he had been bursting to say since Argent entered the room.

"Damned sleight of hand you demonstrated this afternoon, Argent."

Argent was expecting as such and spoke indulgently, wearily, after giving release to a deep sigh.

"Sleight of hand? How so, Captain?"

"You broke the rules, Captain. We agreed broadsides both sides, up and back. And, if I'm not mistaken, you used grapeshot."

Argent looked at Cheveley as one would at a petulant adolescent.

"I recall no hard and fast rules being spoken of, Captain, nothing so clearly defined as "full broadsides", both "up and back", nor specific type of shot. Six targets to be destroyed by gunfire. You took your decisions, I took mine."

Argent looked hard at Cheveley. His own temper was rising and he saw no need to be diplomatic.

"You were bested and that's it. Next time, things may be different, but this time the winner was my Ariadne and my crew. Look to yourself and to your own crew as to the reason. You may call it sleight of hand, but we did what was needed so that the job got done, done quick and done thorough. Something you may find pretty useful yourself when you come up against Johnny Frog. He's not bad himself with the odd trick or two."

Cheveley's face turned black with anger at so thorough a riposte. He could think of no reply other than to growl in the back of his throat.

"And I still say sleight of hand."

His own outburst had calmed Argent somewhat, so he regarded Cheveley with a blank expression, then replied.

"Well, whatever was done, it was at least done open and above board. Out in The Sound in full view! And at least we amused the Ladies and impressed His Excellency."

By the most fortunate of chances, one of the Ladies had observed and was approaching to end a confrontation that had the potential to finish with a challenge to a duel. Lady Willoughby had waited for them to come up to her, she being stood in the doorway of the dining room. One glance had told her that bad blood was running between the two.

"Captain Cheveley, please sit by me."

Cheveley's face improved to merely look as though it were made of stone; he even constructed a rictus grin to convey agreement, before managing to speak.

"As you choose, Lady Willoughby."

Thus Argent was the last in and found himself on the end of the table, furthest from the Admirals, and next to the Equerry who could speak no English. Unsurprisingly, for Argent the dinner was a dull affair; apart from the food, that he did enjoy; it being plain, from good ingredients, and well cooked. As Junior Officer, it fell to him to propose the Loyal Toast, which he did, and he settled for that as his main contribution to the evening. Unsurprisingly, his High Excellency requested that the Ladies remain, and so it continued as before, His Excellency, his Equerries, and Cheveley unable to take their eyes off Charlotte. Grant and Lady Willoughby, were both opposite Argent, but deep in their own long conversation, and whilst Broke drank himself into a stupor, or at least some level of drunkeness, Argent sat daydreaming and twirling the stem of his glass. However, this social arrangement dissolved with alarm when the English-speaking Equerry interrupted the conversation between Grant and Lady Willoughby.

"His Excellency wishes to inspect the victorious vessel. Tomorrow morning, would be his pleasure."

Broke choked on a glass of port and he spoke before Grant could reply.

"Please inform His Excellency that the first ship made a fine showing and, being larger, is more fitting for an inspection conducted by such as himself."

The translation was made, but soon His Excellency was shaking his head.

"His Excellency says no. He wishes to inspect the winning ship. Perhaps there may be something that he can learn. No?"

Grant looked over at Argent, who had, belatedly, realized that the conversation had moved to a subject that very much concerned him. Behind his confused face Argent's mind raced to make sense of the few words he had heard. Grant didn't help.

"Argent, is there any problem that you can foresee? Four bells of the forenoon?"

Argent looked blank, but Grant helped him out.

"For the inspection, I mean?"

It fell into place and Argent could foresee a hundred problems, but none that he could speak of, not least that he was tied to His Excellency all night, so how he could warn his own ship? Also, being ordered to remain ashore, he would be unable to supervise the preparations himself. He could do nothing other than look across the table at Grant, then at His Excellency.

"Si, mi Admiral."

The Admiral beamed his brown grin at the affirmative reply in Spanish, and returned his attention to Charlotte. Argent sat in silent thought for a minute, then he made his excuses and left the table, ostensibly heading for the guarderobe.

* * *

Aboard the Ariadne, jollity and celebration still proceeded unhindered. The Officers dined in the Captain's Greatcabin, with Fentiman at the head of the table, in his Captain's stead. All Officers were present, save Bentley, he being on Watch, and all were in good spirits, which included even Sailing Master McArdle, who, despite not having partaken of the wine and port, had caught the good mood of celebration and was even seen to smile. The Loyal Toast had long passed and now the conversation had passed on to whichever amusing story those gathered around the table could come up with. Currently, the Ariadne's Marine Captain Reginald Ramsey was regaling all with a tale about some washing belonging to a High Spanish Matron that went missing whilst he was on garrison duty on Gibraltar. He had just introduced the idea that the Garrison Mascot, a goat, may have had some part to play and, when this became clear at the finish and the laughter had died, even to the echo, someone began singing. At this point, the Surgeon, Harold Smallpiece, made his excuses and rose from the table. The tune was quickly taken up, therefore few noticed his leaving nor heard that he wished to check on his patients. Although there was a quicker route, he chose to go up and via the starboard gangway and then down through the forecastle to his Surgery, the Orlop Deck. The corridor led out onto the gundeck, through which existed the quickest route but the gundeck was alive with a cavorting crew, drinking their grog, dancing hornpipes, telling tales and generally making merry. On the way along his chosen dim gangway he saw three figures, not joining in with the merriment, simply talking and sharing the moment as they drank their portion of the potent mixture of rum, water, lemonjuice and sugar. Smallpiece felt the need to say something, not merely to pass by, for he had recognised them as George Fraser, Zachary Short, and Henry Ball.

"Good evening, gentlemen. Not partaking of the celebrations?"

It was George Fraser who spoke up.

"No Sir. For the moment we can't quite find the mood, Sir."

"In poor humour? Why so? Surely after our victory, a good mood is not so hard to come by?"

"Normally you would be right, Sir, but we knows the cost, Sir."

"Cost, to whom?"

Fraser jerked his thumb in the direction of the Herodotus, anchored but a cable length away.

"The lads over there, Sir, on Herodotus. There'll be some bloody backs over there this evening, I can tell you that for sure, Sir. Which fact puts a bit of a dampener on our own carousing, Sir."

Smallpiece looked beyond Fraser to where he was indicating. Herodotus sat black on the black water, identified only by her riding lights, with her masts and spars standing out from the few lights of Plymouth behind her. There was no light even from her stern cabin. Smallpiece knew well the ways of the Navy, and thought it best to make no comment, but to pass on. He nodded and went his way, disappearing down the companionway into the forecastle. All three turned to lean on the rail, each took a drink from their tankards, and each said nothing for some minutes. It was Henry Ball, who broke the silence.

"What's this comin' our way? Someone ordered up a few "town ladies"?

"Ladies of the Town" it was not. What it was, was a jolly boat, with four Marines at the oars and what looked like an Officer, unbelievably, at the tiller. Ball reacted; Marines they may appear to be, but a challenge was required, nevertheless.

"Ahoy, the boat. State your business."

The Marines ceased plying their oars and tossed them vertical. The boat glided on and the figure at the tiller stood up, now unmistakably an Officer.

"Fetch me your Officer of the Watch. Tell him that Captain Baker, Royal Marines, wishes to speak to him."

Henry Ball, surprised and confused, replied their obedience.

"Aye, aye, Sir. Directly, Sir."

Ball hurried to the quarterdeck to find Lieutenant Bentley standing his watch, none too happy at missing the fun emanating from the glazed open hatch in the quarterdeck, as he stood aft of the binnacle.

"Beg pardon, Sir, but there's a lobster, I mean, Marine, Captain, in a jolly boat just over the side, Sir. Says he wants the Officer of the Watch."

Bentley took himself to the centre of the gangway and heard what the Captain had to say. All was overheard also by the three Warrant Officers. Were it possible to see it, Bentley's face now registered deep shock and it was still there when he thanked Baker for his trouble. He then took himself down to the Great Cabin, where charades were in progress, Lieutenant Sanders in mid execution of some contorted pose. However, Fentiman noticed the look of grave concern on Bentley's face as he entered and stared, almost helplessly, at his First Officer. Fentiman realised that something was amiss and waved his hands, calling for quiet, but still speaking cheerfully.

"Gentlemen, pray silence. I do believe that Lieutenant Bentley has some news of great import."

Bentley looked even more concerned and his eyes rolled around the room, meeting the gaze of the eyes fixed on him. Finally, he returned to the inviting and concerned look of Lieutenant Fentiman.

"We've just received a message from a Captain Baker, Sir, Captain Adjutant to the Port Admiral. He says that we are to expect an inspection at four bells of the forenoon, Sir. A Spanish Admiral, and two English. Two Spanish Captains, and the Captain of the Herodotus. Oh, and two Ladies; in addition. Sir."

* * *

The longboat was full, deep laden, of both oarsmen and passengers. The two ladies sat on the longseat in the stern, their parasols out and spread against the playful wind that was picking up the droplets from the strokeside oars and carrying them over the side, but their voluminous cloaks gave further protection. The Admirals, both British and Spanish, sat together, deep in their double conversation as it passed back and forth in both English and Spanish, these translations provided by the Equerries. Cheveley looked as though he couldn't wait for the purpose of their journey to begin, him being a picture of eager anticipation, his mouth working into various angles of amusement. Argent sat almost apart, unaware of events within the boat, deep in both thought and worry. Strictly speaking, he was the host and the others his guests, therefore hospitality fell to him, but all seemed content enough and so he felt no need for any effort on his part. Baker sat beside him and, recognising his anxiety, left him to himself. Argent had thanked him fully for his efforts the previous night to forewarn his crew.

After the dinner had broken up, he had paid his respects to the Ladies and then accompanied the Spanish Officers back along The Hoe in their landau, both himself and Cheveley. He was grateful that Cheveley was only too keen to answer the Admiral's questions on the Royal Navy in general and, therefore, but little requirement came Argent's way, even though he disagreed with much of Cheveley's proclamations. As they made their slow progress to The George, for as much of the journey as he could politely manage, he had studied what could be seen of Ariadne from the distance. Also, after politely taking his leave, for much of the night, he stared some more, sitting in his room that overlooked The Sound. His only consolation was that she showed many more lights than were considered common practice for a ship riding at night at anchor; she could even be described as "lit for the King's Birthday".

Breakfast had proven to be leisurely, but for himself with a far higher level of involvement. His Excellency was curious as to the origin of the Ariadne, he saw much that was familiar in her. Argent saw no choice but to come straight out with the answer; to be honest and frank. He told them that she had been captured in 1802 and immediately taken into service, but his Excellency, surprisingly, was pleased, as were his Equerries. A Spanish design had proven to be superior, which gave rise to a discussion on the comparative design features of British, French, and Spanish warships. Argent was heavily involved, ship design and the set-up of their masts and rigging, were a particular interest of his. Cheveley contributed little, but His Excellency proved to be very knowledgeable and a good discussion ensued, albeit slow and somewhat stilted, due to the requirements of translation.

The longboat now approached Ariadne and the oars were tossed to allow it to glide to the ladder up the larboard side from the waterline to the entry port admidships. The helmsman gave the required call of "Flag", meaning that the boat held Ariadne's Admiral and, obviously a bevy of guests. As Captain, Argent was required to be the first out of the boat to enable him to greet his visitors as they came on board. He stood up in the boat and, with great apprehension concerning the events of the coming hour, he grasped the hand ropes that hung beside the ladder, this being composed of mere wooden protrusions from the side. It was at that moment that he noticed that the steps were newly varnished and the hand ropes were pale, made from brand new rope. He began his climb to find himself passed by two seamen going down ropes into the boat, a bosun's chair being lowered between them, behind him as he climbed, so he paused to quickly turn around and look. It was not just any bosun's chair, normally a plank with four ropes secured at the corners, this was a whole chair seat, including the back, but minus legs. There was ropework all over it, including a thick plait across the front to prevent the passenger slipping out and even small ring hitches around the supporting ropes to the seat, to show where they should be held by the delicate hands to come, these there to enable the passenger to feel fully secure. The Ariadnies involved were immaculate in the uniform of the Captain's bargemen; Gabriel Whiting and Abel Jones both taking charge. Argent continued up the ladder and when his eyes came level with the deck, he couldn't fail to notice that the decking at the port was covered with a neat Carrick mat. He continued up and placed his foot upon it. Two more of his bargemen, the mighties Moses King and Sam Fenwick, stood rigidly to attention either side of the port, holding the ropes that would pull the bosun's chair inboard over the deck before it was lowered down to release its passenger. Both were decked out in their "barge" uniform. The Bosun and his Mates stood close, shining bright and immaculate, ready with their gleaming silver calls to pipe the Admirals aboard.

What he then saw were the men paraded in groups mostly based on their role in action, at "Quarters". Not surprisingly the first to catch his eye were the bright scarlet uniforms of Ariadne's complement of two dozen Marines paraded on the opposite starboard gangway. His Officers paraded on the quarterdeck, lined along the starboard rail. The great majority of the men were at their guns, both larboard and starboard batteries. The forecastlemen that were not part of any guncrew, were on the gangway opposite the Marines. Finally, he noticed the topmen, paraded from gangway to gangway over the width of the forecastle, but Argent had no time to take in any more detail. He quickly turned to face the opening of the entry port and Fentiman came to stand by his side. Moments later the first of the guests began to arrive, hoisted by the bosun's chair, using the muscle of a dozen of the foc's'lmen, all pulling to a clean and steady rhythm, as called by a Bosun's Mate.

The first was Lady Willoughby, it was to be "ladies first". She was disengaged by King and Fenwick, then she came smiling out of the bosun's chair to be formally welcomed by both Argent and Fentiman.

The chair disappeared back over the side and so, she now being safely on deck, Lady Willoughby decided to take herself off to the Officers on the quarterdeck and begin a conversation, not with the Lieutenants, but first with Midshipman Bright. Next came not the second Lady, but Cheveley, up the ladder, to be piped onto the deck, him then standing to await the rapid arrival of Charlotte in the chair. He gave her his full attention to conduct the removal of herself from the hoist, Jones and Whiting having ensured that she began the journey as safely secured within as possible. Cheveley escorted her to the quarterdeck and they both stood beside the binnacle, Cheveley pointing out various features, the best or perhaps the worst of the Ariadne, no-one could. The party assembled and Argent took this as the time to begin the inspection. He looked at Broke.

"Sir. Where would you like this to begin?"

Broke was in ill temper and his impatience added venom to his tone.

"This is your affair, Argent. Take us where you will."

"I thought first, the Marines."

Broke did no more than lift his hand and extend his fingers, these carrying many rings, Argent noticed for the first time, as they flashed in the sun. He led the party forward to the starboard gangway. Strictly speaking, this was Argent's inspection and so it was he that had to lead the way to inspect for himself, but His Excellency was close by his shoulder. Ramsey immediately discerned their approach to his own command. He called his men, already at attention, to present arms. The Naval pattern "Brown Besses" came off all shoulders to 'the present" as one, followed by the left foot forward, with the same precision. The attached bayonets, all remaining erect and parallel, reflected the high sun and the brass trigger guards shone bright, as did the ramrod guides. Ramsey's sword came to the present and all was immediately statue still. Argent walked down the parade, but taking his pace only from His Excellency, who looked up into each blank face before examining the weapon, then the uniform. He was impressed, but he had seen Marines on the day of the contest. They progressed up to the forecastle, where were lined up the topmen, the elite sailors of the ship. They were in divisions by mast: foremast, main, and mizzen, Captains of the "Tops" in front, which placed Whiting in advance of his men. The four involved in the "coming aboard" had run quickly to their places with all guests now safely on deck.

The topmen were the cockscombs of the crew, both athletic and capable, and they took pains to show it; their uniform was a variety of nautical finery. Apart from the standard tarred hats, black shoes with brass buckles and white duck trousers, there were a variety of shirts, shoulder cloths, and neckties, in addition to the multiplicity of earrings and pigtail ribbons. All were spotless and with neither a crease nor a wrinkle; each man stock still, staring ahead. Behind them were the guncrews of the two forecastle carronades, not outdone in finery, at attention besides their stubby black weapons. Whilst His Excellency looked admiringly at the topmen, Admiral Broke, with Cheveley, left the party and took themselves behind the ranks of sailors, to examine the deck, the carronades, and all nooks and corners. They returned with set faces, Broke's countenance even blacker.

However, His Excellency had now noticed the guns on the forecastle, these with their unique stubby barrels, on wheeless slides, and with their large 24lb cannonballs, shiny black, in the garlands nearby. He also, followed by his Equerries, took himself behind the paraded topmen and began to examine the guns. Fentiman quickly took himself to the Admiral's side to answer the inevitable questions and meanwhile the rest of the party waited his convenience, save Broke and Cheveley, the latter escorting Charlotte. These three progressed on to the foc's'lmen, paraded on the larboard gangway, these being the oldest men amongst the crew, mostly around their fiftieth year or more and now too elderly to work aloft, so they worked the deck, wherever and whatever. 30 stood paraded, and if their time aboard ships were totaled, between them would be almost 1000 years of seagoing experience. Almost all were once topmen and had lost none of their ability to show themselves as once such, but now, at least, they counted themselves as good able seamen. They, too, stood flawless, awaiting the inspection party. Broke halted before one of them, seemingly the eldest, and Broke looked aggressively up into his face. Charlotte looked concerned, but Cheveley stood waiting, as though something was coming that he had long been anticipating. The chosen sailor stared over the Admiral's left shoulder.

"Name?"

"Eli Reece, Sir"

"Service?"

Reece looked blank, there came a silence that would soon become offensive to any Admiral, least of all Broke. However, the next to Reece saved his back by speaking from the side of his mouth.

"Your ships."

"Oh, beg pardon, Sir. I joined in '65, a ship's boy, the Merchant Marine. I was in the slave trade for nigh on twenty years, until I was pressed out and put aboard the Antigone and then the Euryalus, Sir. Then on the Glatton at Copenhagen, Sir, Captain Bligh, the one off the..."

Broke exploded.

"Don't presume to teach me Navy History, Reece!"

"No, Sir. Beg pardon, Sir. After the Glatton was sent for long refit, I found myself aboard the Ariadne, yer. Sir."

"And your opinion?"

"About what, Sir?"

Broke's voice grew even louder.

"This ship, man?"

Reece was staggered by so direct a question. Never had he been asked such by a superior Officer about a ship run by other superior Officers. He had to think hard for the correct adjectives and those that came were wholly naval.

"As I see it, Sir, this is a full worked up ship, Sir, with a good crew of true man o' war's men. Men as is contented. Sir."

Reece maintained his stare over Broke's shoulder. Broke looked hard into Reece's face.

"Contented?"

Reece was in a quandary. He thought his answer would satisfy, but now he was required to think further. His face screwed up in thought, then came inspiration.

"Men as is content with their lot. Sir."

Broke continued staring at Reece's face, as though hoping his eyes would penetrate Reece's skull. He then looked at his clothing, but he could find no offence with that, either. Meanwhile the rest of the party had almost caught up, however, His Excellency passed the elderly foc's'lmen, looking, nodding rythmically, but not stopping. Next was the gundeck and Argent led them down the nearest companionway, turning at the bottom to check on the progress of Lady and Charlotte Willoughby, but all was well; Admiral Grant attended the former, Cheveley the latter. Before examining the guns, Argent, on Divisions would normally take himself to the Galley, which was on the same level within the ship and neighbouring his own cabin. Here all meals were prepared for the crew and he thought this a useful addition to the tour.

The short corridor took them to the domain of "Bible" Mortimor, Ship's Cook and Captain's Steward. They all allowed the ladies through first, assuming this to be more to their interest and the stoves were at full production, attended by Mortimor himself and his two assistants. Both were Lascars, named throughout the ship as Johnson and Jeremiah, although no-one could tell them apart, but one, at least could, this being Mortimor himself. Being Spanish built, the Ariadne had special provision for the Officers, which meant a smaller stove built in, especially for their food. The larger was for the crew, supporting and heating three cauldrons of stew, peas, and potatoes. At the arrival of the guests all came to the attention, but Lady Willoughby, realizing that the food may spoil if left unattended, told them to continue with their work, however, she addressed her questions to Mortimor himself.

Argent grew anxious. Even beyond McArdle and his wife, Mortimor was of the deepest of religious persuasions, a strict Methodist, and most of what he said to anyone aboard the ship could also be read in the Bible. The unassailable gravity of these Christian quotes inevitably gave him a certain amount of licence, but, because of this feature, conversation with him could become quite tedious. Lady Willoughby assumed him to be in charge.

"How many men do you have to feed from here?"

Mortimor looked at her as though she were a woman who had questioned his interpretation of some deeply profound Biblical text.

"213."

The Ma'am was omitted. Argent grew even more worried and gave Mortimor a withering look, but Lady Constance continued.

"All at once?"

"No, Ma'am."

Argent breathed a sigh of relief.

"In Watches, Starboard first. Honest toil gives appetite to the righteous. Eat, that thou mayest have strength, when thou goest on thy way, First Samuel, 28, verse 22."

She smiled, then pointed to the smaller stove.

"And this is for whom?"

"The Officers, Ma'am."

"Is it different?"

"No."

"No difference at all?"

"Perhaps a bit better quality, Ma'am. The Lord maketh poor, and maketh rich: He bringeth low, and lifteth up. First Samuel, 2, verse 7."

"You seem very fond of the Book of Samuel?"

"I am fond of the full span of the Bible, Ma'am. Seek ye out of the book of the Lord, and read. Isaiah, 34, verse 16."

She looked into the cauldron.

"May I taste some?"

Mortimor's expression did not change; he handed her a stirring spoon. Lady Willoughby dipped the spoon delicately into the brow stew and brought the liquid and a small piece of meat to her lips. Finding it not too hot, she swallowed all. Her face became thoughtful and she looked at Mortimor.

"More salt, I think. Salt is good: but if the salt have lost its saltness, wherewith will ye season it? Mark, 9, verse 50."

She handed the spoon back to Mortimor and all passed through, Fentiman bringing up the rear, still chuckling mightily at Her Ladyship's bright riposte.

"Better do as the Lady says, Mortimor. After so tasty a quote as that, you can count it as a prayer. Oh, and why aren't these grates blacked down the sides?"

Mortimor's face twisted into further gloom and irritation, a look appropriate for a crime on the same deep level as if someone had dropped a Prayerbook during a sermon.

"Seems my grate blacking has disappeared, Sir. The full stock. Thou shalt not defraud thy neighbour, neither rob him. Leviticus, 19, verse 13."

"Just so, Mortimor. Just so."

They emerged onto the gundeck. The guncrews had awaited their presence for 30 minutes, each man at his station. Besides each gun stood the four man crew, plus Gun Captain, just forward and to the left, his Second was to the right, the remaining three of the crew spread evenly behind. The guns themselves were bowsed up against the ship's side, muzzles above their gunports, looking for all the world like begging dogs, gazing up at their caring Masters. The guntackle was draped tidily and uniformly along the side of each gun carriage, and the gun tools, spikes, sponges, rammers, etc., all clean and polished, were up on the deckbeams, arranged on their hooks, inch perfect. Behind each guncrew, stood their Powder Monkey, thoroughly scrubbed and polished. Being in front, the Gun Captains were made prominent by their uniform, this being unofficial, but it added to the impression of order and readiness. Their buckled shoes all stood the same plank seam along the deck. All crews stared straight ahead.

Argent walked forward, the invitation for the others to follow, but His Excellency was allowed to be second, after Argent. This time there was to be no greeting, this was inspection, to see that all was as it should be, and it was. The deck had been holystoned, and all shavings and sweepings removed. Each gun was burnished down to the dull greyblack sheen of its gunmetal, the flintlocks shone as the polished brass they were, finally any examination of the guncarriages would find them thoroughly scrubbed. All shot garlands were full, each shot as black as the main firedog and grate within any stately home.

Argent could do no more than conduct the party down the row of guns, each in a thorough state of readiness for inspection or for action. However, when he came to the mainmast, he stood in puzzlement. A look back at the Mizzen and the mast forward confirmed his impression; he turned to find the figure who should be bringing up the rear of the inspection party, Bosun Fraser, there to make note of any of his Captain's concerns.

"Mr. Fraser."

Fraser hurried forward.

"Sir?"

"What's all this on the masts?"

"Beeswax, Sir."

"Beeswax?'

"Sir."

"To what end?"

"Well, some of the lads thought it might smarten the place up a bit, Sir."

Argent looked from Fraser, to the mast, and back again. He looked again at the mast.

"Very well. But see that it doesn't interfere with their duties."

"No, Sir. Aye aye, Sir."

Broke and Cheveley had heard all and seen all, but nothing of what they wanted. All was clean and very shipshape, and they could be certain that the continued gun inspection would reveal nothing that could be remarked on in criticism. Frustration and resentment grew in both. They came to Number Three, Starboard side, Samuel Morris' gun. Morris stood to the left of the gun, his second Joseph Dedman, to the right. Behind Morris stood Jacob Pierce, their Volunteer. For Cheveley, all was as he would wish aboard his own vessel, but what he most wanted was not there. There was none of the anxiety he rejoiced to see in the faces of his own crew, instead he saw a stern, hard-jawed, confident gaze forward on the face of each man; "There's nothing here to trouble you, old cock!" He gave the gun little more than a cursory glance, but a movement on Pierce's face caught his eye. Pierce was winking, at him he felt certain. His pent up frustration erupted.

"Captain Argent!"

Argent turned. He knew that it was Cheveley and he turned to him, noting the already reddening face. Something was happening that was not good. Cheveley was rooted to the spot, but Argent could not leave His Excellency. By good fortune, Admiral Grant saw his dilemma and hurried forward to take over, then, with Lady Willoughby, the tour continued. The Spanish moved on and Argent returned to Cheveley, the latter working up further heat.

"Captain? Is something wrong?"

"That man there, Argent, winked at me. Damned unbelievable insolence! Is there no respect for a Captain's uniform on this ship? I want him flogged. Four dozen; do you hear me."

Cheveley turned to Admiral Broke, some way behind.

"Admiral Broke, did you not see? That disrespectful devil there. Winked at me, damn him and all his kind."

Broke hurried up to the gun.

"I did, yes, that I did see. Very indicative of a poorly disciplined crew!"

Both turned to Argent, who looked at Pierce, now doing his best to control his eyelids.

"Pierce. Step forward."

Pierce did as he was bid and came to attention before his Captain.

"These Officers say that you have showed them great disrespect. Winking at them. What do you have to say?"

"Beg pardon, Sir, but there has been something amiss with my left eye for some days. It pains and irritates something cruel, Sir."

Argent looked carefully at his left eye, to see that it was, indeed, red and swollen. Pierce was probably telling the truth.

"Why have you not taken yourself to the Surgeon?"

"Thought it might clear up, Sir."

Argent turned to Cheveley and Broke, both stood at their full height, in a state of high dudgeon and higher irritation.

"Admiral Broke, Captain Argent, it is my belief that this man does genuinely have a problem with his eye, it is there plain to see. Pierce, here, is a volunteer, diligent in his duties and quick to obey his superiors. A first rate member of my crew, never once a defaulter. I can only apologise on behalf of the ship, and ask that you give this man the benefit of the doubt."

Broke looked as though he was about to strike Pierce himself, but if was Cheveley who spoke, his words stark and vicious.

"Are you telling me that this man cannot control himself for the short time he is in the company of his superiors? I want him flogged!"

The last spat out, each word carefully emphasised. Argent was in a quandary. Cheveley had a point, but Pierce did not deserve a flogging. However, it was Charlotte Willoughby, who had remained, that spoke up to aid him through his dilemma.

"Captain Argent, do you not have a Surgeon?"

"Yes, Miss Willoughby, we do."

"Then should we not allow the Surgeon to clear this matter up? This man either has something seriously amiss with his eye, or he has not. I believe that the Surgeon should decide what is essentially a medical question."

Argent looked at Broke and Cheveley. It rested with them to deny the request of a Lady, so, of course, they said nothing. Argent seized upon the idea gratefully.

"I fully concur, Miss Willoughby. I thank you for your presence of mind."

He turned to Pierce.

"Pierce, take yourself off now to the Surgeon. Give him my compliments and ask him to examine your eye. We will be down directly."

Pierce hurried off, grateful at the chance of avoiding a flogging. Argent was still worried, his inspection was falling apart, because it was now split into two; the Spaniards, Grant and Lady Willoughby halfway down the larboard battery, the remainder still stuck at Number Three. He motioned Fentiman forward.

"When they are done, take the Admirals into my cabin, Jonathan, along with Grant and Lady Willoughby. Tell them what's happened and tell Mortimor to break out the best Madeira, the best, mind. I'll join you when I can."

He turned back to the remaining three, four including the Bosun.

"If you'd like to follow me. I suspect that by now our Surgeon has already begun his examination."

He led them further down into the ship, to the lower deck, the men's quarters, now deserted. All along the side of the gangways, their messtables stood vertical, lashed up against the ships side planking and between the tables were their chests, containing their few belongings. They went further down, below the waterline, under the low beams and along to the orlop deck, the sickbay. As they entered, they saw Pierce stretched out on the Surgeon's table, with Harold Smallpiece bent low over his face, holding a large magnifying glass over Pierce's left eye. In the Surgeon's right hand were a tiny pair of tweezers which he was using to gently open the recesses of the eye. Eara McArdle stood, tall, black and lugubrious above Pierce's head, her hands either side of his face, holding it still. No one spoke.

After a minute Smallpiece stood up, examining the end of the tweezers. He had long been aware that an audience had gathered, but not that it was mixed.

"There we are, Gentlemen, this, oh, forgive me, Lady, ...this is probably the answer, what was once part of the ship's side, I suspect. A tiny splinter, and, coming from a place that is none too clean, at least medically, it has set up an infection. Too small for its presence to have been noticed, even as it lodged there, doing its evil work."

He showed the miniscule piece of woodwork to Argent, who, as he peered forward with narrowed eyes, could barely discern anything between the jaws of the tweezers. Smallpiece held the instrument up for Broke and Cheveley, but neither made any movement forward, but Charlotte Willoughby did, for a thorough examination. Argent looked at Pierce.

"Where were you, Pierce, when the first shot hit us from the La Mouette?"

"Fetching a ball from the garland, Sir. I was showered in dust and other bits."

Argent turned to confront both Broke and Cheveley.

"Sir. Captain Cheveley. Once again I ask for your indulgence. Arguably, this unfortunate occurrence has been caused by a wound obtained in action. It is my strong opinion that any punishment that stems from such would be most unjust."

For some seconds the two stood still, staring at Argent, but neither could bring themselves to concede. It was Charlotte Willoughby who broke the silence, speaking quietly.

"I, too, believe that to be so."

Eventually Broke ended their silence.

"We'll let Grant decide."

With that both spun on their heels and left the sickbay, Cheveley ducking under a beam, Broke walking comfortably beneath it. Smallpiece had heard all.

"This eye irritation has caused a problem, Captain?"

"Yes, but I hope it's finished now, or as near as."

"Good, I'll mix a salve, for Pierce to rub on. That should help"

At this point the formidable Mrs McArdle spoke up, frank and to the point.

"An ointment's nay good for an eye, Doctor. A wash is best for an eye and I think I know the one. At least, we should try a wash first, in my opinion."

Smallpiece looked back at her with his eyebrows raised, then up to the deck beams in thought. He did not argue.

"You think so, Mrs McArdle? Well, can I leave that to you, please?"

"Aye, Doctor. I'll get straight about it."

She turned to a large Welsh Dresser, possessed of many shelves, all full of jars, bottle, vials, and packets, and she set about her business. Charlotte Willoughby followed her and stood quite near. Eara McArdle acknowledged her presence by merely looking up and at her, before continuing her work with mortar and pestle. Charlotte Willoughby was wholly absorbed.

"You know of these things?"

Eara McArdle saw no need for deference.

"Aye. I do."

She continued to punish the contents of the mortar.

"What are you using?"

"This is fresh garlic, but I will make it into a wash with water from this bottle."

She held it up, a small jar. Sitting inside on the base was a large silver coin."

"I'll strain some of this water through this crushed garlic. It's the silver as does it and that'll then be the wash. A few drops each day should make the difference; with the blessing of the Good Lord."

She continued her work, leaving Charlotte to watch or leave, as she chose. She watched further as the water was mixed in and then the whole strained, but Argent was anxious that he had deserted his guests.

"Miss Willoughby, we should rejoin the others. I'm afraid my cabin is where we are needed, especially myself."

She turned at his request and smiled.

"Yes, Captain. I believe you are correct, but I'm not sure that I could find my way out."

Argent smiled and motioned with his hand for her to lead on, out of the sickbay. She showed the grace to bid farewell to both Smallpiece and Mrs McArdle. Argent guided her towards the necessary companionways and soon they reached the gundeck. The crews were still at their places, but Bosun Fraser hurried over.

"Sir, beg pardon, Sir, but is the inspection over? Can we send the men to their messes to get their dinner, Sir?"

Argent smiled and nodded.

"Yes, Mr. Fraser. You may stand the men down. Well done to you and to your Mates. And the men, of course."

Fraser grinned and saluted, before hurrying off, shouting for his fellow Bosuns.

Argent looked at Charlotte Willoughby and smiled; he felt pleased, although he knew that Grant had yet to pass his judgment on Pierce. Nevertheless, he felt the need to say something, if only to release his own feelings. It came after a deep sigh of relief.

"That's the third time my crew haven't let me down."

She looked puzzled, but didn't press it further. She had a topic of her own.

"So that's your Mrs. McArdle? And your own qualified Surgeon deferred so readily?"

"Yes. Smallpiece is the best I've seen with saws and knives and whatever. However, he's a Surgeon; his knowledge of medicines is necessarily limited, whilst Mrs. McArdle has a lifetime of "home grown" remedies, as I said before in the coach, when we first met. Almost always they work, and so Smallpiece is happy to defer. With such medical concerns the crew trust her more than him. Pierce's eye will be cured and that will further confirm, and enhance, her status amongst the men."

They had reached the end of the gundeck; behind them was the commotion of the men falling out from their places, before them was the door to the corridor that ended at his greatcabin. At the door stood the Marine Sentry, who came to an immediate "present arms". He allowed Charlotte through first and they entered the wide space that was both his office and quarters. The Spanish made a beeline for Charlotte and Argent bowed as they parted, he had a concern of his own, Grant's verdict on Pierce. He gave that priority and went towards Grant, him in heated argument with Broke and Cheveley, both these with faces aflame. At the moment that Argent approached, it was Grant that held the floor.

"Dammit, Broke, let it fall. If you can't judge what's to be seen on this ship, I can. You won't see better on a Flagship. And as for the man, well, the Surgeon fetched a piece of the ship's side out of his eye. To end this with a flogging...ah."

He had noticed Argent

"Captain Argent. Your Surgeon confirms that your man has an infection and that a splinter caused it?"

"Yes Sir. Yes to both, it was a splinter, almost certainly obtained during our combat with La Mouette."

Grant nodded, then he looked impatiently at Broke and Cheveley.

"A splinter! That fact has not been relayed to me. In action, you say?"

"Yes. Sir."

Grant paused.

"No matter, it confirms my own thoughts. And this man has no past record of indiscipline?"

"None Sir, and he's a volunteer."

Grant turned to look directly at Broke and Cheveley. The first two sentences were spoken with great care.

"This is my verdict. He will not be punished. To flog a man for that, would be the same as punishing a man who had lost half his leg in action, punishing him for cutting capers as he clumped his way down the deck, stump still bandaged! Or failing to make his proper respects whilst holding himself up on crutches."

Broke and Cheveley looked as though they would argue more, but Grant held up his hand.

"No more! This is done, and what's worse, it could embarrass us before our guests. That I'll not have. It's done!"

The last was spoken with a tone of such weight that any further argument was out of the question. Also Grant was more than worried by the evil mood showing on both Broke and Cheveley's faces.

"Now, if you two wish to take your leave before the rest of us, please feel free."

He turned to Argent.

"Would that be possible?"

"Yes, Sir. I will make it so."

Argent now looked at both. If each were capable of speech, they made no use of it, therefore Argent took their silence to mean that they wished to go. He motioned for Johnson (or Jeremiah?) to come to him.

"Go to the Officer of the Watch. Tell him that two Officers wish to leave immediately. They will be at the entry port directly. Go now."

The Lascar saluted and hurried off. Argent looked at Broke and Cheveley, then he spoke, his words, clear, level, and formal.

"Gentlemen, if you would care to take yourselves to the entry port, your wishes will be fulfilled directly."

He formally saluted Broke. Both took themselves out of the cabin without a word. Grant looked at Argent and he sighed and smiled.

"A good inspection Argent. I've seen nothing wrong with this command of yours. Broke spoke earlier of the lack of shine on that which could. No surprise there, but I told him, if you don't know what you have seen here today, then you should; here is a ship ready to fight. Ready for that, nothing more, in fact, in my opinion, there is nothing more!"

Grant leaned forward and swung his glass around to place it close to Argent's chest, his protruding index finger touching the left lapel.

"In addition, His Excellency gives his compliments. He said, "Buque apretado". I think it translates into "tight ship".

Chapter Three
Affairs Ashore

The crew of the Captain's barge were all assembled on or above the foretop, all stood erect on the small platform, but holding tight to any convenient shroud or lift, for they were 40 feet above the deck and they were all giving deep consideration to the mid point of the spar that normally held their foretopsail. The spar had been lowered down on its lifts, down to rest on the small expanse of planking. All there assembled, at various times and from different angles, looked from the spars' midpoint to the other point of deep concern, another 20 feet above, where the spar usually met the foremast. There above them and clinging to the foremast shrouds were two more of their select crew. They had all been sent aloft by Boson Fraser to check on the robbands, the loops of rope that held the canvas onto the spar's stout round timber, but the job had taken a turn for the worst. All stood, making close examination, faces screwed in decision, swaying with the movement of the mast that they were all perched upon. Gabriel Whiting drew his gaze away from the point of contention, to look up to the two men above him.

"Silas. How far through?"

Silas Beddows, Foretopman and Stroke of the Captain's barge, swung around to examine the front of the foretopmast.

"Nearly through, Gab. I can just about make out the woodwork."

Whiting clenched his teeth and took a deep intake of breath. This job was turning out not good, certainly worse than he had expected and it worsened yet more, for at that moment a fierce face appeared over the edge of the foretop. His feet were on the futtock shrouds, this being the ladder of ropes beneath the foretop, his hands were on the shrouds extending up to the mast above, his chest against the platform edge, but his face and voice through a square of shroud rope told that he was none too happy.

"And what the 'ells 'appenin' up yer? You shirkers 'avin a make and mend? Jobs not done, why?"

Whiting looked down at George Fraser, Bosun, who had, thankfully, come no further. He was precariously perched, but this state of peril never entered his mind, for to himself he felt as safe as though he were in some armchair in his favourite public house.

"It's the frapping, Bosun. Worn through on both, the spar and the mast. We can't send it back up, we reckon it's got to be changed."

Surprisingly, Fraser's annoyance did not grow, instead his face became calm and concerned. He completed his journey up and took himself to the front of the foretop where the spar was lashed secure. He peered over to view the coils of thick rope that were wound around the spar to stop it chafing on the wood of its mast. The whole smelt of the galley, it often having being lubricated by fat left over from Mortimor's efforts with the pots and cauldrons. The rope was almost worn through, barely a few shreds left. He looked up to Beddows.

"Be you sayin' that 'tis nearly worn through up by you, an all?"

Beddows hung out from the shrouds to the mast and fingered the equally shrivelled coils around it. He could feel where there was very little left.

"'Sright, Bosun. Wood's showin'"

Fraser copied Whitings expression earlier, then he made his decision.

"Right, 't'as got to be changed. King, follow I down. I'll give you the new. The rest of you, get on with it."

All drew their knives, they were set for a long job. The rope could not simply be unwound, the months, years, of galley slush had hardened like tar. Each coil would have to be cut away, but at least, stood on the foretop the job was easier, far easier than the task that now faced Beddows and Abel Jones, now together attempting this job above. Their only access point was from the swaying rope ladder that was the topmast shrouds and that was too far over for such work. Two bosun's chairs had to be constructed first, these to enable them to hang down to the required level. However, all involved began; the job was defined and set on; discussion of it ended. After a period of silence the topic arose which had been the cause of discussion in their messes earlier, but not, so far, thoroughly aired. The topic was the £50, donated by Admiral Grant. Sam Fenwick spoke first and all knew what he was talking about.

"Well, I think it should be spread out, in coin. For us to decide what 'tis to be spent on. 'Tis our money, we won it."

Whilst yanking off a whole coil, Whiting gave his opinion.

"If 'twere spread, what would it be, a few pence in coin? What the Captain's decided to do makes good sense to I. A fine spread of decent beef an' greens, along with beer, apples or whatnot, and fresh soft tommy; that suits me just as well; better. You couldn't buy that with the few pence we'd get. Our Purser will get a good bargain for us with that £50, flinty sod that he is, and that's something better on top. When was the last decent pint you had? What d'you think, Mose?"

King had returned with the new rope.

"Well, I don't worry too much, but I'll say that I'm all for a good feed. What's more, it sends me a signal, bein' that during repairs we'n stayin' aboard. When I was in the afterguard of my first ship, the Sirius, we had a refit and the whole crew was marched off the ship to barracks, guarded by Marines, like we was bloody felons. They was too worried about desertions. This tells me that we'n stayin aboard, even though the repairs is but small. Better than a week in some evil barrackroom."

Whiting looked up at the two above, swinging on bosun's chairs, sawing away at the heavier mast frapping with their own knives.

"What's your verdict up there? Feed or coin?"

The answer came back, in unison.

"Feed!"

"There, Sam, you'm outvoted."

Far below and at the opposite end of the ship, Argent sat in his greatcabin, a spread of papers around him. The compass repeater in the ceiling above him told of their course, steady now for some hours, West South West, a direct course from Plymouth to Falmouth. His orders rested on the desk just above his right hand, "proceed to Falmouth for re-supply and repairs. Report to Commodore Budgen", signed Admiral Broke. The day after the inspection, Captain Baker had handed him the heavy paper, closed by thick red wax containing a huge seal. Baker had wasted little time and had caused himself to be rowed out early in the day.

"Here are your orders, Captain. It seems that our Port Admiral can't wait to see the back of you. You are to sail to Falmouth, directly."

Argent had taken the papers and then offered his hand.

"Thank you, Captain Baker. I never got the chance to thank you properly for coming out and warning my crew about the inspection. We are very much in your debt."

"No thanks required. Fair's fair, is all I can say, and on top, we can't have The Service let down before a few visiting Dons. Jobs done well, I'd say. Good luck to you, Sir."

"And good luck to you, Captain Baker."

Argent had watched the boat row off and he gave a wave, before giving his orders to weigh anchor and leave. Now they were but an hour's sailing from Falmouth. A good stiff Southerly was now meeting her just off her best point of sailing, two points large, a "beam on" wind. A Westerly out of the harbour had caused them to make one run South out of Plymouth, but the wind then changed perfectly to South to be gratefully picked up for one run across to Falmouth.

Fentiman sat opposite. He'd come down to finalise their re-supply and minor re-fit. That done, they were sharing a glass of madeira. Argent spoke first.

"Can't say I'm sorry, Henry, to be quit of the last few days. High drama don't describe the half of it. Was it not all somewhat fraught? That's how I see it, not even a peaceful meal ashore! Still, we've emerged the other side, and with some credit. I think that can be spoken."

Fentiman took the final drop from his glass.

"Yes Sir, I would agree, but we've gained a few antagonists also, if that's the correct word, but that's The Service. Not all of us are the best of shipmates."

Argent smiled.

"No indeed, and more's the pity, but, deep rivalry between ships has always been with us, and to the good, I feel, in the main."

He took a last look at the list of supplies.

"Oh, good, you've included grate blacking. A full supply, and more. Mortimor's been giving us nothing but quotes about thieves and vagabonds since our guests went over the side. He does require to be mollified in some way."

He held up the list for closer examination.

"I hope this does it, more than he lost, or should I say was relieved of?"

Both laughed and were still smiling when Midshipman Bright knocked and entered.

"Beg Pardon, Sir, but the Officer of the Watch, Lieutenant Bentley, asks that you be told, Sir, that Falmouth is up on the starboard bow."

"Thank you, Mr. Bright. Inform him that I will be there directly."

He stood and put on his coat, the one, of the two he possessed, that he called "his undress", this being faded from several soakings in salt water and patched from wear and rough contact with unforgiving projections. Up on deck, all was in order in the bright afternoon sun. Two Master's Mates were throwing the log and McArdle was studying the passing coastline. Their ship rose and fell in the easy swell as she coasted along under plain sail; driver, main sail, foresail, maintopsail and outer and flying jibs. All was easy on a ship at ease with itself.

Argent saw the mainsail go limp, then fill again. He looked first for a change in the wind's direction and saw none, still steady South East; so the wind must have dropped, but not significantly, it would seem from the streaming pennant up at mast height. He looked for a Bosun's Mate and saw Henry Ball.

"Mr Ball. Set foretopsail."

Henry Ball looked back in consternation.

"Beg pardon, Sir. But we've had to change the frapping on the foretopsail spar. 'Tain't yet finished, Sir."

"Very well, fore and main topgallants, then."

"Aye, aye, Sir."

First Bosun's Mate Ball hurried off forward. What to do? The foretopmen were still about their work, it was courting disaster to ask them to leave all unsecured whilst they set new sail above the point where they were working. He did what was very rarely done. "Mainmast topmen. Set the foretopgallant."

This allowed mainmast sailors into the preserve of the foremast. They swarmed eagerly up the foremast shrouds to set the sail as ordered and to exchange looks of pure hatred from Whiting and his cronies as they climbed up, past and above them. There was some ascerbic conversation between them and it frequently included descriptive words such as "slabsided waisters", "pikehands", and "grasscombing". There was also some comment about the "bloody state of this running rigging." However, the foretopgallant was soon set and the foretopmen then had their preserve back solely for themselves, their adversaries now ascending their own shrouds to set their own topgallant. The new frapping was soon finished and buckets of slush collected from Bible Mortimor, Moses King's arrival being accompanied by "Evil pursueth sinners. Proverbs 13, Verse 21", but King knew enough not to accept such, without some form of retort.

"What you mouthin' off at me for? I'm a topman. 'Tweren't I as stole your bloody blackin'. Buggery to you!".

Soon the lifts took the spar back up to its rightful place and all was shipshape for entering harbour. The foretopgallant was immediately took in, pronounced as "lubbers work" anyway, and replaced by the sail below, the foretopsail. Thus, on all lower sails and the maintopgallant, Ariadne glided up to the bar of Falmouth Harbour, but soon Argent ordered a shortening of sail down to just foretopsail, maincourse and driver. Argent took in the whole picture, not just the wind, the sails, and the "lie of the land", but the tide also. He had divined for himself that it was still "on the make", not far off high tide, the best of situations, but nevertheless he called again upon the time of Henry Ball.

"Mr. Ball, we'll have a leadsman, if you please."

Argent wanted the depth beneath the keel checked as they eased their way in. Henry Ball ran to find a foc's'lman who would be best for such a task and found Eli Reece.

"Eli, get on the lead, quick as you like"

Reece nodded and shambled to the locker that contained the lead and line. He pulled out the lead and checked the tallow in the cavity at the bottom. There wasn't enough and so he added some more. Soon he was by the starboard cathead and casting the line to find the depth, then his monotonous call echoed back through the ship.

"By the mark, 12, plus half. Coarse sand, some shale."

He cleaned the tallow, which had told of the condition of the seabed and re-cast.

Falmouth was one of the finest natural harbours along the South coast. An easy entrance stretched between Pendennis Castle and St. Anthony's Head, then, to the West of the entrance, the deep anchorage of Carrick Roads. Coming from the East, Argent had to do little more than sail straight in.

"Down helm. Steer West Nor'west."

The answer came, calm and obedient.

"Down helm. Steer West Nor'west, aye aye, Sir."

"Mr. Sanders, you have the deck."

Argent had passed the sail trimming to Sanders as Ariadne made the small adjustment to her course. Sanders grinned a reply and first gave orders for the driver to be let further out to starboard, then he called for the squaresails to be trimmed as Ariadne turned more into the wind, but the latter call was unnecessary, the hands were already at the sheets and braces. All done, Sanders then stood at the taffrail, looking smug and satisfied, checking the canvas for false movement.

Argent and Fentiman, standing together, saw the battlements of the Castle slide past and noted the Union Flag raised high on its tower. On past the end of the castle wall came a large, but not ostentatious, house, pale pink, with gardens that dropped down to their own seawall. Gardeners continued about their business, the common event of a ship entering harbour of no great concern. Argent pointed over.

"Lady Willoughby's townhouse. Very fine, in my opinion, and having the best position in town, I'd say."

Fentiman turned for a good look, whilst Argent returned to the business at hand.

"Mr. Sanders. Hands to stand by the larboard anchor."

Sanders passed on the order to the nearest Bosun's Mate and soon there was a gathering of the labourers of the crew, foc's'lmen, waisters and afterguard. Bosun Fraser placed himself in charge, his presence very necessary, as he saw it, to oversee the dropping of an anchor. Ariadne had to be brought to the harbour mole that jutted North from the castle point, up into the harbour. Therefore her bows had to be turned right around to face South and then she could be warped forward to lie alongside the mole using a strong towing cable. To tack around would need the whole harbour and that would risk running aground, therefore, Argent, with a gentle tide running, had elected to pivot his ship on her anchor. Drop the anchor and drift past, then allow the ship to turn on this fixed point, however, the closer to the end of the mole the better, the less then, that the ship would have to be warped up by muscle and sweat to her final berth.

"Up helm. Steer West by North."

Argent heard the helmsman repeat and then continued.

"Mr. Sanders. You have the deck."

Sanders sent the driver back to starboard, and called out to Henry Ball for the foretopsail to be set for the larboard tack, However, as previously, the order was superfluous, Ball had set all in train as soon as the bowsprit began to move left across the backdrop of green hills. Argent waited his moment and allowed his ship to settle onto her new course towards his chosen point off the mole. He took himself along the larboard gangway, to ensure that he would be heard.

"Now, Mr. Fraser."

"Let go!"

The anchor fell with a huge splash and Ariadne drifted past, then Fraser watched the anchor cable carefully as it grew taut in the water as the anchor gripped the bottom.

"Cable up and down, Sir."

"Thank you, Mr. Fraser. Furl the foretopsail."

Ariadne was turning on the anchor cable and soon the foretopsail would be backed in the Southerly wind if they took no action. However, it was "started" loose and then furled, almost in the time it took Argent to regain his quarterdeck and turn to regard events. The driver would push her around, that to the good. Ariadne ceased her swing around her anchor and soon she was still, sat motionless in the gentle current of the final incoming tide. Argent looked for a Midshipman.

"Mr. Berry. Get a line up to the dockside."

"Aye, aye, Sir."

Berry hurried off to see Bosun Fraser, as much for advice and instructions, as to give orders. However, soon the jolly boat was over the side, with four of the most competent seamen in the ship on the oars and on hand, also with a Bosun's Mate on the tiller. Fraser was not going to have the ship disgraced by any false moves at this point. The line was eventually secured on the quayside to a large bollard, watched by Berry, but quality controlled by Henry Ball.

The rest was a question of muscle. The first job was to recover the anchor, then winch in the final distance by the cable now stretching from the mole. The anchor messenger went onto the capstan then onto the anchor cable, this too thick to be wound around the capstan and so the whole crew stood by for their turn on the capstan bars, which began to turn with the efforts of sixty men. Ariadne moved forward, the slack cable to the bollard on the quay being gathered up as the anchor cable shortened and came aboard. She was coming in easily and there was a growing crowd who watched the proceedings, which, Bosun Fraser decided, were a mite too sombre and did the ship no credit, especially with a growing audience.

"Elliott. Go get your fiddle. Start with "Liverpool Judies""

He turned to glower at the assembled crew.

"An' when he gets back, I wants all you tripehounds singin'".

Ben Elliott, ship's fiddler and member of the afterguard, disappeared and returned post haste with his instrument. He was hoisted atop the capstan, stamped his feet for a rhythm and began. Soon, the entire dire choir were joining in with the familiar song, as were those on the bars and the capstan, who continued to stamp around to the rhythm. All the hands took a turn and the first task, the anchor cable, was soon recovered, then the cable onto the mole was bent onto the capstan for the final effort. The ship closed to the mole, fenders ready over the larboard bow. 30 minutes later the frigate was bowsed up and secure against the stonework, with a gangplank across, guarded at both ends by an immaculate Marine. One of the first across was the Purser, Merryman Maybank, although how he got a name like that was a ship's mystery, in dour sobriety he surpassed even McArdle and Bible Mortimor. However, he was well wished on his way with the £50, as the crew finished the job of finally securing the anchor and mooring the ship. Also in his deep pocket was the supplies requisition to be taken to the Naval Ordnance Depot.

Those nearest, for the benefit of the landsmen watching, pointed to the damaged bulwark, just in case these secure on terra firma hadn't worked it out for themselves, for it conveyed the desired and important self aggrandising message, "This is shot damage. We've been yardarm to yardarm with the Frogs."

Argent leaned on the larboard bulwark rail of his quarterdeck, accompanied by Fentiman, the deck beneath their feet as dead as though they were stood on the lifeless stone of the quayside spread beneath them. The ship was moored and secure.

"Henry, I'm going to ask you to oversee things for the next day or two. The repairs and the re-storing need no decisions that you are unable to give. I've a mind to see my family, they are very close to here. You can see the farm almost from where we are now, come, I'll show you."

They walked to the other side of the quarterdeck, Argent taking his Dolland from the binnacle drawer. He pointed to a far hillside.

"There, atop that furthest hill, but just down a mite. That's our farm, the white building."

Fentiman focused the Dolland.

"Yes, I think I've got it. Is there a large tree behind?"

"Yes, a colossal horse chestnut."

Fentiman continued with the glass.

"There's cattle moving. Looks like a female driving them."

"Yes, that'll be one of my sisters, probably Emily, my younger sister. Enid will be caring for their baby, being married, you know."

He paused.

"Now move the glass up the hill, to the next building."

Fentiman moved the glass a fraction.

"Have you got it?"

"Yes, a grey pile, large, bleak and square."

"Most graphic and most exact. That's Broke's place, called Higher Barton. Ours is called Lanbe Barton. Don't ask me how it got a name like that."

* * *

The dawn had moved into early morning as Argent cleared the last of the buildings that could claim to be attached to the good town of Falmouth. He rode a hired mare that he allowed to take the journey in her own time, he was in no hurry. This was a route familiar from his childhood and he had tipped his hat to the school gate that once held behind it at least half of his world. The horse walked on and then, for some reason, she broke into a trot, perhaps impatient to get done the business of the day. Upon his way, he had seen in the route no change from years ago that could cause him any disquiet; trees, bushes and gates were all still there, as were the buildings, some now improved, some now run down, but all in their remembered place. The hill steepened and it was at this point that he passed the gate to the main Willoughby estate, it showed not a speck of rust within the green paint, but it was closed and barred to him and the world. On the opposite side of the road, in counterpoint, rose the dark and weathered wood of the impressive lych gate of the church, a solid and authoritative symbol of the Anglican Faith. The church itself, all built by the Willoughby's, sat hidden behind a collection of yew trees, its tower just rising above the highest. Argent smiled at the memories both good and bad; he had seen his sister married there and seen her place her bouquet on the grave of her Mother. He had sat through many a service, the last the Christening of his nephew.

The hill came proper and the mare ceased her trot and resolutely set about the climb. Argent looked forward and all appeared before him in the same order as it had years before; first the chestnut tree, then the barn roof, then the thick chimney, then the thatch of the cottage roof. Last in view came the namesign, newly painted, Lanbe Barton. Soon came the yard gate and he turned the mare into the gap and dismounted. He tied up the reigns and shouted.

"Anybody here? I've caught a rustler and a poacher!"

A curious sound came from within the barn, but undoubtedly female, and his younger sister Emily came hurtling out of the barn, whisps of straw on her coat and dress. She flew straight at him and seized him around his waist with both arms.

"Reuben! You're wicked, you've given us no warning."

She stepped back and whacked him on the chest as punishment.

"And you've grown thin. Don't you order them to feed you on that ship of yours?

She pushed him again, then pulled him forward by his captured arm, held in both her hands.

"Come on, Enid's inside and Beryan, and baby Jake, too.

She linked her arm through his and, at the door, used her grip to pull him through. Inside all was as he remembered, bar the large cradle in the middle of the room, over which his elder sister Enid was administering to her baby son, Jacob. Her face lit as though it were a ship's nightlantern, but Jacob's needs were necessarily completed before she, too, flung herself at him to begin a fierce embrace. That done, she also fired off her admonishments.

"Turning up with no warning! You're very sinful!"

"I've already told him that. I said he was very wicked."

However, by now Argent was holding them both tight against his side and he kissed them both, but it was Emily who broke away first.

"And you're a hero! We've got the paper. It's days old now, but we're going to keep it, always!"

She bounced over to a huge, plain, and somewhat crude desk with a tall back section of several compartments and protruding from one was a broadsheet. Emily pulled it out and held up the front for Argent to see.

"There!"

She looked at him, then looked around at the paper, this still being held at an angle for Argent's benefit. She read the title.

"Frenchmen fall before Britannia's Naval Sons."

She turned the paper to enable her to read on.

"On 30th June, HMS Ariadne, a 32 gun frigate, engaged and captured the French frigate, La Mouette of 42 guns. The Ariadne was under the command of Captain Reuben Argent. That's you!"

Argent laughed, but Emily continued.

"Second in Command was First Lieutenant Henry Fentiman, and these two fine sons of Albion, supported by their good crew of stout British Tars, made a prize of the French ship, displaying just the same spirit and pluck as shown by our lamented hero, Admiral Lord Nelson."

She looked at Argent, glee and joy spread all over her pretty face, which not even a morning's work with the cows could disguise.

"There's more!"

But Enid broke in, but cheerfully.

"He can read it for himself, Emily."

Emily lowered the paper to gleam at Argent, whilst Enid went to the cradle and lifted out baby Jacob, or perhaps more accurate to say that what emerged were the brightest pair of blue eyes that Argent had ever seen, then he noticed the round healthy face in the white bonnet that matched the rest of the swaddling. Inevitably, she talked to the baby, rather than to Argent.

"This is your Uncle Reuben. He's a famous Navy Captain. You've not seen him for a long time."

The contented baby was passed to Argent who cradled the substantial bundle awkwardly in his left arm. Nephew Jacob looked up at him in puzzlement and Argent was immediately certain that the child was about to burst into tears, so he looked down with growing anxiety, a study that was broken by the arrival in the room of Beryan Trethewey, his brother in law. Enid took the baby and both men shook hands, or rather Beryan took the hand of Reuben in a grip of appalling ferocity. He was a hand shorter than Reuben, but built like a wrestler, which is exactly what he was; at many village fairs around, and usually successful. Argent had always warned him to stay out of Plymouth, Falmouth too; any pressgang would pursue him to the Devon border in order to add such as him to their crew. Both shook each other by the shoulders, even though Beryan was two years older, through their childhood and early teens they had been good friends. He spoke first.

"You look older!"

"You look younger. Married life must be doing you good. Would you recommend it?"

"With a good woman, Reuben. With a good woman."

And he held up his right arm for his wife to run in underneath and wrap one arm around him, while the other held the baby. He kissed her hair. Both Reuben and Emily smiled at the depth of tenderness shown by each to the other, then Argent turned to Emily.

"Where's Father?"

"He's ploughing the three strip in the North field. Are you going to go up there?"

"Yes."

Enid broke in again and detached herself from Beryan.

"Then you can take his croust."

She seized a satchel from the back of a chair, it hanging by it's strap, then she turned her attention to some portable food that was arranged on a shelf besides the cooking range. She wrapped each in separate cloths and put them in the satchel, then she cut a loaf in two, carved a cheese quarter in two, and added that. However, as she worked, Argent's memory jogged.

"I've brought something. It could become a family heirloom, over time. Give me a moment."

He hurriedly exited the door, but soon returned, carrying a long object in a piece of blanket. They all looked expectantly as Argent unwrapped a sword, still in its scabbard, all black leather and brass. Their faces showed surprise and no little wonder as it was revealed.

"This belonged to the Captain of the La Mouette. As I was entitled, so I claimed it, it coming from my first prize. I'd like it to remain here."

He gave the sword first to Enid who weighed it in her hands, as did Emily, but it was Beryan who drew the blade, almost to its full extent. The fine steel shone clean and bright. Beryan looked up and spoke, but to no one in particular.

"I think it should go on hooks above the mantle, or on one of the beams."

Enid pronounced her verdict, and then drew them back to the issue that mattered more to her.

"We'll let Father decide. Now; your croust. There's two pasties and a fuggan, with bread and cheese. There's some for Father, and some for you. I know how you like fuggan, so you and Father will have to share. That's your fault. Had you given warning, I'd have made two."

"I'm fine, I ate aboard."

"Now we know why you're thin! Missing meals, that's why. There's some in here for you, and no argument!"

She threw in four apples for good measure and then hung the satchel strap around his neck. He passed his right arm up through, so that it hung down his right side, but she still had a question.

"How long are you staying for?"

"Two nights, I must return the day after tomorrow."

"Right, I'll set another place for this evening. Now, out, I'll see you on your way."

Beryan grinned.

"You're under orders, Reuben. You've got your quarterdeck, Enid's got hers."

Argent smiled.

"And this is one I'd never try to board, not even with a company of Marines!"

They grinned together, then Enid pushed him to the door.

"Enough from you. Out. Father'll be waiting."

But outside her mood changed. She turned him to face her, her face anxious.

"You'll find Father none too happy, Reuben. Something's working at him. We don't know what it is. Please try to find out; he's so silly about these things, when we may be able to help."

Argent's face fell and matched her's for seriousness. He unhitched his horse and mounted, then looked down to further examine his sister's concerned look.

"I'll try, but you know what he's like. He takes all upon himself and keeps all of most of it to himself."

Argent loved his sisters dearly and loved each for their differences, for, to him, they were as different as chalk and cheese. In many ways he defined each in relation to his own life. Enid was a solid merchant ship that steadily sailed her set course, reacting calmly and sensibly to whatever came her way, whilst Emily was a gleeful racing yacht, at full sail when the wind, any wind, was favourable, yet subdued and worried in times of storm. Enid rarely showed any emotion, bar impatience with members of her own family, especially Argent himself, yet Emily was all emotion; joy and optimism, or sadness and anxious worry.

He pulled the mare's head around and set her to the gate, giving Enid a wave as he took the track up. It took him past the drive that led from the track to the main gate of Higher Barton and 20 yards down it stood the gate itself, between two high pillars in the recently re-built wall. The gate being high, black, ornate, and forbidding. Following his route, the high wall curved around to mark the track that led over to Long Barton. This hamlet was a small collection of cottages, though each was a substantial building and here dwelt the eight families named amongst those that farmed the three giant fields to their North, West, and South. East was the High Barton estate. The fields were strip fields, a system that had pertained from Medieval times, for there were 40 or more strips in each and every family held, in ownership, several strips in each of the three fields.

He passed above the hamlet, over the top of the group of cottages, and entered the corner of the field, huge in its expanse, no hedges, but a few trees. He passed the first stone markers that spoke the ownership of each strip and there were some of new stone and new carving, the letter B, claiming Broke's land. He knew where their family's three strip was, just over the horizon, and for some minutes more he saw nothing, then a tiny figure grew in the distance, tiny in comparison to the two huge horses that hauled the plough through the deep red soil. Even from that distance Argent recognised the Bakewell Blacks, each 20 hands high, which his Father used and bred. Whilst Beryan was a wrestling champion, Edward Argent was a ploughing champion, this given witness by the rosettes, in a variety of states of fade or pristine, that covered their stable wall.

Argent continued up the track that marked the edge of the field, past the evenly spaced out markers, until he saw the sign for his family, a square with a diagonal, bottom left corner up to right, chiselled into the stone. Three holes were in the surface beneath the square, and each carving showed its age, the once clean edges of the lines now worn into rounded grooves. Argent dismounted, took the hobble from the saddlebag and used it on the mare's front hooves. She wandered to the drinking trough and then began to crop the grass at the verge. Two bags of fodder lay nearby, clearly for the plough horses. He stood and watched and finally had to acknowledge the apprehension that was growing within him. It had been no surprise that Edward Argent had wanted his only son to follow him onto the farm. Argent becoming a Midshipman had caused a serious rift between them, such that his Father had not come to their gate to wish him farewell and good fortune on his first leaving. Disapproval had clouded each return home ever since, however, or so Argent hoped, the arrival of Beryan, and baby Jacob, secured the succession for the farm. Perhaps his Father's attitude had changed, hopefully for the better.

Luckily, his Father was on a return. On arriving, Argent had pondered what to do best, walk up the newly ploughed furrows to meet his Father, or wait for him to plough back to the track he now stood on. Chance had taken the decision for him, he had but to stand and wait, but he chose to sit, on the low stone marker. The horses grew in size, hiding his Father, but details appeared, the chains and the leathers, these not the show harness, but that for the workaday. What impressed Argent most, and always had, were the horses keeping in perfect step, how his Father trained them for such, he never knew. The sounds of the team grew, the jingling harness and the spoken instructions from his Father, the sound of his voice bringing a lump to Argent's throat.

There were but yards to go to the end of the furrow and the horses stamped onto the margin. His Father called "Come round" and the two swung left, and for the first time Argent saw his Father and, simultaneously, his Father saw him, as he stood up from the stone. His Father was but an older version of Argent, although slightly shorter, with grey streaks in the thick main of hair. It was Argent who spoke first.

"Hello, Father, how are you?"

Argent Senior gave no reply, other than a flat, "Reuben. Good to see you."

He continued to tug on the reigns, concentrating on bringing the horses parallel to the track, but Argent felt the need to break the silence.

"What's the crop?"

"You'd know you'd stayed."

Argent sighed, becoming a little angry.

"Father, that's well back now, in the past. I made my choice. I didn't stay, but I'm back now to see how you are, and Emily and Enid, and to see my nephew. He's a bonny lad."

Argent Senior seemed to soften a little at the mention of his grandson and his posture became less tense.

"Yes. He is that. And the crop's fodder beet."

He stood and looked at Argent and almost smiled.

"Well, come and make yourself useful. Lead them forward whilst I unhitch the ploughhead."

Argent walked forward and took the bridles of both horses in his hands, their heads rising high above him. His Father detached the chains that led from the ploughhead to their collars.

"These are even bigger than I remember. Are these still Bakewell Blacks?'

"Yes, but a new strain, "Fens", not so pretty but better on a long run. Take them on, now."

Argent led them onto the track, to leave the plough isolated at the end of the furrows. Argent looked back along these, all stretching away into the far distance, but each ruler straight.

"Shall I take them to drink?"

"Yes, but take the bits out first. Time for their feed."

Argent obeyed the instructions and soon each horse was wearing a nosebag, filled with good oats, then he opened the satchel Enid had given him to share out the contents.

"Enid gave me this for your croust."

The Cornish word for midday meal seemed alien to him, but he spread the contents onto the warm grass, using the wrapping cloths for protection as best he could. His Father frowned.

"There's more here than she puts up for me. She intends that we eat together?"

Argent felt the old anxiety, but pushed on.

"Yes, but you are to get first choice. That's because I arrived with no warning, so I get the leftovers."

For the first time Edward Argent genuinely smiled.

"Well, you can have one of the pasties, but the lion's share of the fuggan 's mine. You can make do with the apples. The bread and cheese is equal."

However, what had to be shared was the water bottle, a long cylinder of grey clay. Argent took the top off and offered it first to his Father, who drank from it, several times, before beginning the food. Argent took his drink, but it wasn't water, it was small beer, that tasted familiar and all the better for that. He said nothing, leaving his Father the space to speak or not, but he soon did.

"So, you've been successful. Making quite a name for yourself."

Argent nodded and drank again.

"Yes, we took their ship, right enough. It even made the broadsheet. We left the result swinging round her anchor in Plymouth Sound."

"Swinging round her anchor?"

"Yes, Father. It means idle; safe and idle."

Argent Senior nodded and almost smiled again.

"Yes. It's pleasing to see our name in the paper, there for the right reason."

"Could it have been there for the wrong reason?"

"Yes, but that's a long time past and best left there."

Argent felt relieved, and fell silent, judging it best not to pursue what was plainly an old, but unknown to him, family disgrace. They shared the rest of the food in silence, but when it was finished, Argent felt bound to speak of Enid's worry.

"Father, Enid's worried. She's worried because there is something worrying you. I'd like to know. I may well be in a position to help, taking that French frigate may just have given me enough influence to make a difference."

Argent Senior looked at his son and frowned, but he was plainly thinking. He paused some more, then moved his head to look at the ground, but a twist of his mouth showed that he had made up his mind.

"You know that Broke bought the estate, about twelve years back. That makes him a landowner in our fields, the biggest, and no surprise there. I've heard that he wants to enclose; the three fields and the common, and Cinch is backing him. He probably has lawyers drawing up the Bill as we speak. More than likely they'll get it through Parliament. I've not heard of any enclosure that's been turned down. The Government now wants enclosures, the end of the old Three Fields, they want separate farms, with each having their fields grouped close around. Farming is changing."

Argent looked with concern over at his Father.

"Cinch is your Member?"

"Yes, Sir Digby Cinch. Our Honoured Member for Cornwall and many other places."

Argent noted the irony in his Father's voice, but kept to the subject.

"Right, but is that so bad. Think of the time it takes for you to walk to all our strips. What do the others think?"

"Most is for it. They think like you, but there's one big snag. To claim a farm after all's gone through, you have to have your Deeds, to prove ownership of land."

Argent could foresee what was coming and he grew fearful.

"But you've got ours?"

"No. I can't find it. I can find Bills of Sale for the extra land that's been bought over the years, but the bulk is on the Deeds, and that I can't find."

Argent's spirits sank, the family farm was now in deep jeopardy! Troubled thoughts came quickly concerning Enid and Emily, Beryan and Jacob, however, his military mind worked subconsciously and created a solution, at least partial.

"Father, if it does come to eviction, I've got the prizemoney from La Mouette to come. It'll be a fair sum. You may not be able to stay here, but there'll be another farm to buy. I'll not see you with no-where. Don't worry, that's a way around if the worst does happen."

Argent Senior looked at his son and smiled, his son's anxiety worried him and his concern touched him. He placed a workworn hand on his son's shoulder and shook him gently.

"That's good of you, son, and a comfort. But it may not come to that, this may pass over, in the best way. Meanwhile, leave it for the future, because now, this ploughing needs finishing, that's my immediate worry. If it's not ploughed and sown, we're down on fodder for winter, nearly as big a disaster. I'll push on, I can't sit here nattering with you."

The lift of his Father's head told him that his Father was determined to work through this new trouble, in the same way that he had carried the family through the difficult times of the past. His Father stood, so did Argent.

"I'll help, with the ploughing, like I used to."

His Father nodded.

"As you choose. So, right, fetch them back."

In minutes the shires were back before the plough and Argent Senior's hands were on the plough handles, but now his son led the horses forward, leaving his Father to concentrate on making good furrows. Thus, the hero Post Captain, the toast of the Navy and probably Royalty also, now walked down the plough line, leading the horses for his ploughman Father, walking between their giant heads, a hand on each bit. He was glad that he'd chosen to wear his sea boots.

All was done with much daylight left, but the sun was Westering. The plough had to be taken down to the farm and so Argent Senior pulled the ploughshare upwards to lodge secure between the wheels and his son led the horses home, whilst his Father steered the plough. The mare tailed along, tethered to the plough. They reached the farmhouse, their route using the track above it, and Argent called back a question. For what seemed the first time and perhaps because of the possibility of losing it, he looked carefully at the house in which he had been raised. It was squat and broad, with barns built in and a low, wide, chimney. The walls were as thick as some men were tall; the lower half was large pebbles, set into the cob mixture. There were few windows. It looked almost medieval.

"How old is the farmhouse, Father?"

"Couldn't say. It's come down through generations way before me."

On arrival, all was stabled and stored and, as soon as they entered the room, Emily brought out the sword.

"Look Father, look what Reuben brought home. It's French, taken from the Captain of La Mouette. Reuben was entitled to it."

Argent Senior took the sword in both hands, one hand each end, and gauged the weight. His face showed a smile, but not an open grin. He pulled out the blade, but only six inches, and stopped.

"There's something written on it. It must be French. "Pour defence de la Patrie". What's it mean?"

Argent answered.

"It means "For the protection of our country". I have a Lieutenant who can speak French. I don't know how, he had no formal education and he's never been to France."

It was Enid who answered.

"There; the French think of their country, just in the same way that we do about ours. Which makes this war doubly stupid!"

Emily broke the heavy mood.

"We were wondering where to hang it, Father. Beryan thought above the fire, or from a beam."

Argent Senior nodded and took the sword to place it in a corner.

"Plenty of time to think about that. Now; Reuben, let's get clean."

He led the way to the back scullery. They washed together from the same tub, in silence, the only sound the splashing of water.

The evening meal was jolly and cheerful; Emily especially, joyful and in good spirits. Father maintained a smile at the top end of the table, but with the clearing of the last of the plates, Argent saw the time.

"Father, you've got to tell them. There may be something that can be done, they may be able to think of something, just as well as you."

His Father looked up at him, but he wasn't annoyed, more resigned. He took a deep breath and told the story. Emily and Enid's faces showed increasing degrees of shock, but when his Father had finished, Argent spoke first, addressing his sisters.

"But don't worry, my prizemoney will buy a farm. You'll still be somewhere, how big remains to be seen. If that's what it comes to, we've still got that money, but we must pray that it may not."

Enid had grown both serious and annoyed. She rarely admonished her Father, but this was such a time. Argent had noticed the self assumed authority, now that she was both a wife and a mother.

"Why didn't you say? You know how many boxes and chests there are around the house and barns. And you know what your eyesight is like these days; you can't read anything closer than your elbow! We're going read every piece of paper in every box and chest. We'll find it, we will. We'll be alright."

Emily joined in, equally heated.

"Yes. Yes, we will! It must be somewhere."

Argent Senior looked at both his daughters with more than a little pride, in both he saw the feisty spirit of his late wife. He smiled and nodded.

"Right. Then I'm leaving that with you, you and Enid. I thought that sending you to school would pay, and I was right. Now, I'm for a pipe and a quiet sit. Reuben, Beryan, you'll join me?"

Argent hated tobacco, but this was a development of such significance between him and his Father that he could not say no. He determined to puff at the pipe, take in the smoke and blow it out again, no matter the consequences. Beryan first went off to fetch the pair of shotguns that needed cleaning and soon he returned and disassembled the guns, and then the three were sat by the empty fireplace, empty that time of its winter fire, all fussing with pipes and guns, whilst the two women fussed equally with the plates, pots, and child. They talked of nothing of the war, nor enclosures, but instead of social changes, both near and far. The power of the landlord and landowner, the continued power of the House of Lords, the rise in the importance, if not the status, of the working man. Rebellion not being unknown throughout the history of Cornwall, both Beryan and Father had some sympathy with the French Revolution, but Argent couldn't countenance The Terror, nor the ambitions of Napoleon. The fact that none of the likes of those sat talking was allowed to vote arose, but was quickly dealt with. There was nothing to argue over.

With the last of the light, the discussion wasn't worth lighting a candle for and so they retired, to rise early the next day. After breakfast, the three took the horses and both rakes, the course rake and the chain rake, back up to strip three. With three of them they could carry the back edges of the two rakes, one atop the other, the horses supporting from the front, Argent's horse carried the bags of beet seed. The course rake levelled the field for planting, then the three walked the flattened tilth and spread the seed by hand. Perversely, Argent enjoyed the simple labour of such a task, to walk the field scattering the fine seed in rhythm to his walking feet, helped sooth his mind from the stress and tension of the past few days. Eventually, the seed was on the ground and they ran the chain rake over to cover it so that, as the sun turned down to the West, the job was done. Argent Senior pronounced the epitaph.

"A good job, with the ground most fit. All we need now is a nice drop of rain."

* * *

Argent hurried into the Port Commodore's Office to avoid further soaking. On his journey down from the farm the gathering clouds had turned his thoughts away from his emotional farewell from his family, not least the memory of his Father's warm handshake and the way his Father had gripped the muscle of his right arm. Nor the fierce embrace of both sisters. He approached the desk that supported the variety of tasks of an elderly Marine Sergeant who acted as Secretary for Commodore Sidney Budgeon, he that ran the harbour and both gave orders and passed on more weighty instructions from those placed above him. The Sergeant noticed early Argent's single epaulette and sprang to attention and saluted.

"Morning Sir."

Argent nodded and smiled.

"Thank you, Sergeant. Please sit down."

He waited until the Marine was settled.

"Please tell me your name."

The Sergeant was surprised and non-plussed. Few were this polite.

"Venables, Sir. Michael Venables."

"Well, Sergeant Venables, I was hoping for a word with the Commodore."

"Yes, Sir. That should be possible. I don't think he's busy; he's just had his mid-morning coffee and rolls taken in from the coffee house over the square. I'm sure he'll see you, Sir. But, please Sir, who are you?"

"Captain Argent, of the Ariadne."

The sergeant's face lit up.

"The Ariadne! Sir! Captain Argent. Yes, I'll ask directly, Sir."

The sergeant stood and disappeared down a corridor, leaving Argent to decide if he would sit and wait or stand and wait. The debate lasted but a moment, for the sergeant returned, all smiles and bonhomie.

"If you'll go straight in, Sir. The door that's open, Sir. Right at the end."

This accompanied with much smiles and nodding.

"Sir, just before you go in, Sir, allow me to say Sir, bloody good business with the La Mouette. First rate, Sir."

Argent nodded.

"Thank you, sergeant. I couldn't have done it without my Marines!"

"No Sir. Course not, Sir. Now, he's just down the end there, Sir."

Argent walked the corridor to soon make out the corner of a desk, seen beyond the doorframe. Argent reached the opened door, reached forward and knocked on one of the panels. Argent saw a balding head with frizzy tufts above the ears before it saw him. The figure behind the desk gained his feet, or rather his head moved more sideways than up. The rotund figure was only a little less tall sitting down as he was standing up. He took with him a very long knapkin that dangled from his collar.

"Captain Argent. This is a pleasure, I was hoping to meet you sooner."

The last contained a hint of displeasure, but he came around the desk with his hand outstretched, leaving his Commodore's jacket on the back of the chair. Argent dropped his hand from the salute and Budgen shook it vigorously. Then he waved him into a chair, before he returned to his own side of the desk and regained his seat, but Argent couldn't be certain if Budgen's feet were touching the floor. The Commodore pointed to the miner's flask of coffee and the plate of crusty rolls.

"Would you care for some coffee? Captain. And perhaps a bread roll?"

"Yes to the coffee, Sir. Thank you."

Budgen moved his head to one side, as if to shout around Argent.

"Venables, another cup. Tout suite!"

The reply came from the distance down the corridor.

"Tout suite it is, Sir. On its way."

The sergeant arrived, smiling, with the cup, it being vigorously polished with another knapkin. He saluted and left, still smiling. Budgen poured the coffee, then sat back, his fingertips meeting before him, his elbows on the arms of his chair, to regard Argent somewhat sternly. Argent followed the movement with his eyes to note that the view from the windows behind Budgen, of the harbour, included his own Ariadne, still moored securely some distance away. He noticed carpenters at the damaged bulwark.

"Now, Captain. You've come seeking orders?"

"Yes, Sir. I received none within my packet as we left Plymouth."

"No, that's because your orders now come from me, unless I hear different. You are to be based here to patrol the triangle."

He dropped his hands and sat forward.

"You know what that is, from here to The Fastnet, to 48 and 8, then back to here. You don't stay out as you have done, ranging up and down, but you do the three legs, then back. Their Lordships consider that to be a better use of you; you being within the few ships at their disposal."

Argent had been rapidly pondering "48 and 8" He felt that he could safely assume it to be a particular point in the Atlantic, 48 latitude, 8 longitude. In his mind he saw it as the same latitude as the island La Quessant, off the Brittany coast, and the same longitude as The Fastnet.

"Yes, Sir. Do I leave when ready, Sir?"

"Yes, day after tomorrow, if reports about progress aboard your ship are correct. The repairs are taking a little longer than the re-supply, but I think you can work with that."

Budgen finished a swig of coffee and reached for the flask.

"Now, you'll be anxious to get back to your ship, but first I have to ask where've you been?"

"I took the chance to visit my family, Sir. I haven't seen them for over a year. They farm just below the estate owned by Admiral Broke."

Budgen jerked his head back.

"Well good luck to them with that. As for swanning off to see them, I'll make it allowable this time, but, next time, I expect you to report first to me."

The cherubic face had taken on a very stern set as Argent made his apologies.

"Yes, Sir. Sorry Sir, it's just that I didn't know whose orders I was under. My orders from Plymouth didn't actually state a change in my Commander, Sir. So, I assumed no change."

"Perhaps, but perhaps there was also a question of courtesy, towards the Office of Port Commodore?"

"Yes, Sir. I apologise."

"Well, if, as you say, there was some confusion, then you have something on your side. But it'll be right from now on, yes?"

"Sir."

"Right, off and on your way, but report before you sail. There may be a change."

Argent left the office and then the building, but not before formally returning the immaculate salute, delivered whilst stood to perfect attention from Marine Sergeant Venables, him wearing his hat with chinstrap down. Once out, he made straight for his ship and took himself up the gangplank, both following and preceding barrels of salt pork. Once in his cabin, he saw on his desk a small pile of correspondence, each of which he dealt with in turn. They were mostly to do with the re-supply and repair of his ship, but what stood out was the letter in heavy cream vellum, with a generous spread of sealing wax and the wide seal in the centre. He recognised the crest within the seal immediately, distorted even as it was within the thick red wax. He opened it and read the simple line.

"Lady Willoughby requests the pleasure of the company of Captain Reuben Argent and two other Officers of his choosing for Dinner at 7.30 on the 16th July. Signed Lady Constance Willoughby."

His first reaction was to cover his face with his hands, "Oh, God. Not another joust with Broke and Cheveley", then it struck him. 16th July! That was today. When was it delivered? The day he left for home. He rose from his desk.

"Sentry! Send for Lieutenant Fentiman"

Fentiman duly arrived and Argent slid the paper towards him, for him to read the simple line, but it was Argent who spoke.

"Another Dinner. After the last two, I could do without. I tell you true."

"The penalty for being the hero of the hour. Everyone wants your company. To take a good look at you."

Argent ran his hands over his thick hair.

"My fault, the penalty for self indulgence. They want us there this evening. Can you get yourself up to the mark?"

"Yes, of course."

Fentiman then read it carefully.

"It asks for two. If I'm one, who's the other?"

Argent pondered.

"Not Sanders again. He went through enough at the hands of the dear Admiral and Captain. What about Middy Bright? She seemed well taken with him when she came aboard for the inspection. Can we shine him up in time? Is Mortimor still aboard?"

"Yes to both."

"Then tell him to spend his time on Bright. My dress uniform will do me well enough. I've not worn it much more than thrice, two of those in the last week."

* * *

For the next two hours, there came down the corridor various exhortations from Bible Mortimor towards Midshipman Bright. "Shine your belt", "polish that buckle," "that'll disgrace the ship," until finally, "The excellence of dignity. Genesis, 49, verse 3". Later, at 7.00 pm, an open landau, of no level of ostentation, appeared on the quayside. At the foot of the step they had given Bright a final check, but all was as it should be. Mortimor had even used some of his precious grate blacking on the curious four cords that supported the brim from the top of Bright's Midshipman's hat. The badge on his crossbelt, the handle of his dirk, the buckles on his shoes, all shone to match their owner's name..

The streets were almost empty as they rode in silence through the town to the outskirts. Conversation was difficult in any case, the road being almost all cobblestones, these setting up a fearsome rumble during the argument with the steel rims of the wheels. The footmen opened the elaborate green gates, they entered and the wheels crunched on the sea gravel, soon to take them up to the imposing portico, which they drove into and then alighted. At the open door was Lady Willoughby herself, with Admiral Grant as escort and their welcome was genuine and cheerful, unshaped by any formality. Argent grew hopeful for the evening, with a greeting so warm and unceremonious. Grant shook hands with Bright and even carried in his hat, whilst telling him a tale about his own Midshipman's hat, from many years ago. Grant passed it to a servant and then, himself, handed out the glasses of sherry to each of them.

"There, enjoy that, and you are most welcome."

Argent noted that there were a modest number of guests, about 10, mostly what Argent took to be local landowners. The four sailors were the only representatives of the military, save an Army Officer, that Argent thought was probably a Major, but he couldn't be sure from the distance, but what he did notice were the white facings on the turnbacks of his red jacket. He was stood in a small group that also, Argent very quickly noticed, included Charlotte Willoughby. However, she had seen him first and Argent saw her excuse herself to her companions, then touch the Officer's forearm and, as he bowed towards her, she left the group. Argent spoke sideways to his two companions.

"Stand by for a coming alongside. Off the larboard bow!"

Both Fentiman and Bright looked left and came to the attention as they saw who and what was approaching. Charlotte smiled warmly, clearly pleased to see Argent, then she extended her hand for him to bow over.

"Captain Argent."

"Miss Willoughby, a pleasure to see you again. May I present my second, Lieutenant Fentiman, and one of my Midshipmen, my youngest, William Bright."

Fentiman maintained enough presence of mind to bow over her hand and speak his greetings, but young Bright was absolutely sunk and could but jerk forward and remember just in time to release her hand, and then stand transfixed. Charlotte addressed herself first to him.

"I remember you from the recent inspection. I seem to recall seeing you twice, once on the Captain's deck, what's it called?"

"The quarterdeck, Mmm."

"And where else was it?"

"Larboard battery, Mmm. Bow section."

"Now explain. Larboard means?"

"Left side, looking at the bows, Mmm"

"And bow section?"

"Guns one up to eight, Mmm, coming back from the bows."

"There, I've learnt something. Learnt it from you. And you are in charge there are you?"

"Yes, Mmm, when at "Stations". But also I keep Watch, Mmm."

"And you were at "guns one up to eight", during the fight with the La Mouette?"

"Yes, Mmm."

The dinner gong sounded.

"Mr. Bright, would you be pleased to escort me into dinner? You will sit by me?"

Bright looked as though he'd been asked to work out a difficult navigational problem in his head. Argent recognised the confusion, but, luckily, Charlotte was stood sideways to him, but Bright was directly facing Argent. He pointed to his own left arm, then raised his forearm to the position for a Lady to place her hand to gain escort. He lowered it, just not in time, as Charlotte turned and smiled at him, before returning to Bright, who by this time was stood in the required form, left forearm raised. Charlotte placed her right hand upon it, and the pair, Charlotte nearly a head taller, followed the other guests into the Dining Room. Argent stood watching them until other guests closed behind them.

"Well, that's him lost to us for the next few hours or more."

However, when he looked at Fentiman, he was equally statuesque with a faraway horizon in his eyes, both very wide open.

Argent, almost out of habit, was the last into the room, immediately noticing it to be furnished in the best of taste, a high pale yellow ceiling with green highlights in the plaster discretely picked out in the corner mouldings. The walls were not panelled, rather a cream, satin wallpaper, very much in vogue and the table was a panorama of fine glass and silver. The only place vacant was beside the Army Officer. Fentiman would be opposite, and Bright, would be between Charlotte and Lady Constance, Charlotte was on the Officer's right, the only vacant place for Argent, remaining on his left. As usual, he was on a corner, so Argent sat down in the space and, whilst organising his knapkin, he took the initiative with the introductions.

"How do you do? I'm Captain Reuben Argent, HMS Ariadne."

The Officer offered his hand across his body. He looked in his early thirties, his eyes were young, but his face was haggard.

"Major Algernon Blake, 32nd Foot."

His face grew serious.

"I suppose that really I should call you, Sir."

Argent threw a mock frown, made so by a twisted grin.

"Oh no. I do think we can dispense with that!"

Blake beamed a smile and attended to his own knapkin. Soon the first course arrived, this being the soup. As the pale liquid, it was a fish soup, was ladled out, Lady Constance leaned forward from three places up.

"Algernon, you must have an extra portion."

She leaned back to address a servant.

"Biggs, see to it."

The she leaned forward to continue her instruction of Blake.

"You are convalescing. You have to build your strength back up. I expect to see you eating extra."

An extra ladle was dispensed to place his bowl in danger of brimming over. Argent looked at him and grinned.

"Orders! No argument, Court Martial otherwise."

Blake grinned and began the task of consuming the soup. Argent was curious and, in any case, felt the need to begin the conversation.

"Convalescing? A wound?"

"No, swamp fever. The Regiment's in Walcheren, now, as we speak, and the men are going down like flies with it. I was lucky, one of the first to contract it and so I got myself evacuated."

He plied his soup, then his bread roll.

"We've captured a fair proportion of the place and we've got ourselves around Flushing, but the French are entrenched and we can get no further. Thus we're stuck there, in the marshes, the most disease ridden place outside the West Indies. It's a God Awful mess! We'll have to pull out soon, or we'll have no army left."

Many at the table had been listening and, feeling the need to set a relaxed and good-humored tone to the meal, Lady Constance again leaned forward.

"Algernon has an amusing anecdote of his time in the Low Country. Haven't you, Algernon?"

Blake plainly saw his cue and the requirement placed upon him. He dropped his spoon and grinned at the recollection.

"Yes, a bit of bad form, really, but it amused the men immensely. It was in the trenches at Flushing. The French, to their credit, made a sortie out and counter attacked. I was having a shave, it was an attack at dawn, you see, so there I am, all lathered up, just about to apply the first razor stroke, when the alarm went up, "stand to". Well, plainly, I had to answer, so I shot out of the tent, shirtsleeves, no jacket and placed myself with the Grenadiers. Then I heard them laughing and realised that I'd even forgotten to drop the razor! Well, the French were some way off and so, without a mirror, I have to say, I finished the job. Didn't even cut myself, I'm proud to say."

All laughed, none more so than Argent.

"And the attack? And the razor?"

"The attack was beaten off, but the razor lost. I was distraught, it was a very fine one."

More laughter, but Lady Constance again addressed the table in general.

"Now leave him alone. He must eat his soup."

The soup plates were cleared and the main course arrived; roast mutton with roast potatoes, of both of which Argent was very fond. The plates were loaded up with the fine food, Blake's more than anyone's, at Lady Constance's insistence, so the end result was quite a construction. Blake leaned towards Argent.

"I say, Captain, you couldn't help me out with some of this, could you? Her Highness'll be in a helluva lather if I don't make a clean plate."

Argent leaned forward himself to check that Lady Constance was looking in the other direction. She wasn't, she was attending to Bright, but suddenly she turned away to address another gentlemen further up the table. Argent pushed his plate over and Blake lifted across some meat and potatoes, then each set to eating, as though nothing had happened. The food was excellent and Argent began to feel, thoroughly, that he was in good company, good people ready to like and be liked, then came the shout from down the table.

"Captain Argent!"

The thought immediately arrived, no change, not even here. It was one of the country gentlemen, so Argent turned to face up the table. He said nothing, he considered looking back at the gentleman to be sufficient, but the full and ruddy face was plainly friendly and open.

"I'm told that your family farm up at Barton? Name's Portbury, by the way, James Portbury."

"How do you do, Mr. Portbury. Yes, we farm up there."

"I farm in the next valley over. Warrenbury. I hear that enclosures are afoot at Barton. How does your Father feel about that?"

Argent felt a pang of unease, but he decided to remain noncommittal

"He's not certain. Having farmed there for two generations, he's quite content with the ways he's used to."

"Well, tell him from me to welcome it. No need for worry, he should support it."

Even though the conversation was at some distance, Argent wanted to know more.

"What are the arguments in favour, Mr. Portbury?"

"I speak from my own experience. My furthest field is now less than one mile away from the house, although I've now got double my acreage. I can grow what I like, where I like, when I like. No more compulsory rotation of wheat; barley and fodder; then fallow. I'm trying new methods and new breeds. I do just as I choose and my yields have doubled. It has to happen, there are a damn sight, oh, apologies, Ladies, many, many, more people in this country now. They need feeding, and there's money there for farmers like us to make."

Many heads were nodding around the table, but it was Argent who continued.

"Forgive me, but how did enclosures double your acreage?"

"Land came up for sale. There were various reasons, but one is that some old farmers had no proof of entitlement, so their land passed to the Crown and came up for auction. I found the finance and bought. Best thing I ever did!

Argent's face smiled, but his spirits sank. However, he politely nodded his head.

"Thank you for that, Mr. Portbury. I'll certainly pass that on. My Father will be very interested."

Argent concerned himself with finishing his food. Blake was talking to Charlotte, on his other side. Gloom and worry resurfaced, but he reassured himself with the La Mouette prizemoney, knowing what could be done with it. The meal soon finished, terminated by some kind of soufflé. Argent had been keeping his eye on Bright up the table and was growing concerned that the 15 year old hand reached frequently for the wine bottle. There would be the loyal toast and then drinking would move to the port. Argent caught Fentiman's eye, pulling him away from him regarding Charlotte across the table. He pointed up the table with his left hand and covered his own glass with his right. Fentiman divined the message and looked at Bright. After a few moments Argent saw that Fentiman had caught Bright's attention, because he repeated Argent's gesture. Fentiman nodded that the message had been received and, Argent hoped, understood and acted upon. The port arrived, time for the Loyal Toast and, of course, it fell to Bright. However, it was done well enough, after all, he had completed it often enough on board.

"Ladies and gentlemen. Please charge your glasses."

A pause.

"I give you The King!"

The toast was repeated, then there was applause and several, "Well spoken, young fellah."

Charlotte spoke.

"William has been in action against the French. He commanded a whole section of guns against La Mouette."

An elderly farmer gave reply.

"Then I raise my glass to you, young Midshipman Sir."

Then Argent grew anxious for another reason, besides the wine, how would such a teenager cope with this lavish amount of praise and attention? However, Bright did not reach again for the port bottle as the Ladies made their excuses and left, but cigars appeared and Argent saw one offered to Bright and he took it. Anxiety rose again to the surface as a cloud of smoke emerged from his vicinity.

Blake had drunk as much as anyone, but in him it had produced a mood of subdued contemplation. He turned to Argent, but his speech was clear and plainly weighed and considered.

"You know, Reuben. May I call you Reuben?"

"You certainly may, Algernon."

"I count myself as a thoughtful fellow. I think about the game we're in, a lot, perhaps too much, some may say, but I would value your opinion on something. Something that's splitting the army in two. It's this, you see, more and more of our Regiments are being given names, that is titled by the county that they have been affiliated to, often quite arbitrarily. Thus, the 32nd Foot are now also The Cornwall Foot. Would you have an opinion?"

"Concerning what? Where is the controversy?"

"It flies in the face of cherished army traditions, many say. They are adamant on retaining and using only the old Regimental Number, which designates seniority in the line. Horse Guards believe that giving Regiments a county or a town will somehow make them more effective, which I presume means to fight harder."

"I would suspect that it has more to do with gaining recruits; men volunteering for their own home regiment. We have The Press, you don't. Other than that, the only difference that occurs to me, is that you'll get a louder cheer when you march through Truro. Although there's probably something in the notion of your men not letting down the name of their County; making the people back home proud of their own regiment, as it were."

"But your men don't need a county not to let down, do they?"

"No, and I definitely can't see sailors taking as much pride in their ship if she were known merely by a number, rather than some stirring name, like Mars, Bellerophon, "Billy Ruffian" to her crew, or Agamemnon. We fight for the ship, and for self-preservation. If she's sunk, then we're in a very parlous state."

Blake grinned and nodded agreement, but he was plainly thinking further.

"I suppose that we, too, fight for what we are stood on, a piece of ground in our case. But, I have some opinion that there's much more to it than not letting down the people of a particular county back home. For example, to withdraw, when others stand their ground would be an appalling disgrace. Or to lose a Colour, for another. I mean, for such as that, is there any difference between us and the men, do you think, in terms of disgrace, that is? That kind of thing worries the likes of us terribly, Officers have blown their brains out because of it, but the men?"

"I think our men are capable of feeling dishonour, just as we are; they feel terribly any disgrace to their ship, but I am of the strong opinion that our men fight more for each other, than for any other reason. To keep each other alive, they fight the enemy. Personal honour matters little to them, certainly not as much as it does to us. And, in my opinion, they have more the right of it."

Blake sat back and thought, his face quizzical, his eyes far away.

"Honour and glory, yes, certainly a strong currency in our, so called, higher society."

He then leaned over, almost conspiratorially

"You know, in that line, this is something I found very remarkable, almost astounding. We were in the Peninsula, last year, the first to land. After we had clattered the French at Rolica and Vimeiro there was an armistice whilst that God Forsaken Convention of Cintra was set up. Thus, there were two armies, not fighting, just looking at each other. What staggered me, was that there were regular duels between Cavalry Officers. One chap, from the Life Guards, would ride out and call out the opposing French. He did it three times, and each time killed his opponent, killed him; whilst both sides looked on, but not interfering; dueling code, you see. So, there's a dead Frenchman stretched out on the ground, between the lines, and this Life Guard would pick him up, drape him over his horse, the Frenchman's that is, and lead him back to the observing French. So, there's Johnny in a total fume, but can't do a thing, it's all been conducted in the most proper form, then he comes back to the cheers of his own side, like a cricket match. Lust for honour and glory; what do you think of that? Can you imagine yourself poking your nose into some French port and calling out the local frigate?"

Argent openly laughed at the thought.

"Very unlikely, if only for the reason that we are most often sent out for a purpose, which must not be put at any hazard by having some joust with the local opposition. Sometimes, we are sent on "seek and destroy", as for my last cruise, but usually it's picket duty or relaying information. Nothing must be allowed to interfere. A Captain who risks his ship whilst under orders to the contrary could find himself in a fine pickle."

Argent paused and smiled again.

"But to send in a message conveying a challenge? Now, there's a thought, but I can't see it."

The carafe of port passed across them from right to left and Argent pushed it across the table to the gentleman next to Fentiman. However, he also moved it to his left, but it was at that point that Grant decided that the time had come to rejoin the Ladies.

"Gentlemen, shall we adjourn?"

Grant stood and was soon joined by all others. Blake stood and placed his hand briefly on Argent's upper arm.

"An interesting discussion, Reuben. I value your opinion. What you have said I have found valuable. And informative."

"Likewise, Algernon. It's a topic that I too have concerned myself with. In fact, I recently had just such a discussion with a fellow Captain, but he had a very different view. I'm sure you would be interested to hear it, but, we should leave that for another time and take ourselves back to the Ladies. Admiral's orders!"

However, Argent then went straight up to Bright and made a careful examination. The cigar was half smoked down, but Bright's complexion seemed untroubled.

"William. Are you feeling quite well?"

"Why, yes Sir. Quite well. Is there a problem, Sir?"

"No, William, but I would strongly suggest that you now leave that cigar here. You wouldn't be the first to trouble the swabbers by smoking a whole cigar, after a full meal and glasses of wine and port. You've conducted yourself very well, I'm proud of you. Let's hold what we have, yes?"

Bright dropped the cigar onto a plate.

"Yes, Sir. If you think it best, Sir."

"I do. It's happened before, and the person it happened to was me!"

Bright looked up astonished.

"Very good Sir. Thank you, Sir."

They were the last to enter the Drawing Room, which was considerably bigger than the Dining Room. Whilst the theme of the Dining Room was cream, here it was maroon, counter pointed by the careful inclusion of blue and pink. The deep and large armchairs were of light maroon, upholstered in soft silk, whilst the thick carpet was deep maroon. Whatever in the room was made of wood, it was polished mahogany, all of the same shade, as if it came from the same tree. The light from the chandeliers shone back up from the wood almost as much as down from the ceiling. There were sweetmeats arranged in glass dishes on a low table in the centre of the room and four of the Ladies were grouped around a card table, engrossed in their game. Argent and Bright joined Fentiman on a long settee, from where he could and did, Argent discerned, enjoy an uninterrupted view of Charlotte Willoughby. The three talked aimlessly about good food, good wine and making the most of this memory; they would soon be back at sea. Suddenly, Blake stood up.

"Let's have some entertainment! Who can do something? Charlotte play us a tune."

Charlotte looked up and at him, with mock annoyance.

"Algy, you are a thoroughgoing nuisance. This is the best hand I've had since sitting down."

"Never mind all that, what's a game of cards! Do that thing that you did last week, by that Mozart. A Requiem, as I recall."

"Very well, and it's called Lacrimosa. And really it's for a choir."

"All to the good, we'll take out the furniture and get an echo going!"

"Fool!"

Charlotte took herself to the grand piano, gleaming black, which occupied but a small proportion of one corner of the room. From the piano stool she found the music, she opened the lid, then sat, and played and sang. It was a very accomplished performance and, at it's finish, through the genuine applause, Argent was not surprised to hear Lady Constance mention to one of the other guests that Charlotte had had singing lessons at an Operatic Academy in London. The mood had been set, this was to be an evening that involved the guests

each doing a turn to further the entertainment, what you could do, you did. Two of the gentlemen farmers stood up, one of which was Portbury. In stark contrast to what had gone before, together they performed a comical recitation between two farmers, arguing over a blocked road. In rhyme, the argument was passed back and forth. It began,
"That's your haywain."
"No, it b'ent. That's the one what Arnold's rent"
"You should move it."
"Shut thy trap! B'en't my wain and so that's that."
"Road's all blocked."
"B'ent my fault. Go see Arnold, hay's his bought."

This continued between the two belligerents until the haywain was burnt to the ground along with half the village, the other half being wrecked by two teams of carthorses running amuck. Whilst each blamed the other for the catastrophic events, which both had done nothing to prevent, the village was reduced to ruin. No one could fail to laugh and none did, it was a performance that would stand up in any theatre. The accents were perfect, along with the gestures and facial expressions and it drew loud applause. Next Blake himself sang the "The Blue Bell of Scotland", accompanying himself on the piano. Argent and Fentiman became increasingly uncomfortable, performances were coming from everywhere, soon the finger would point at one of them. Another landowner, or farmer, stood for another recitation, this time serious; Tom Wharton's "Ode to Sleep." Another gave the first six verses of the Rhyme of the Ancient Mariner. He insisted that he knew more, but did not want to be tedious, nor "hog the limelight". Then came the inevitable, from Major Blake.

"I think something now from the Navy!"

All through Argent had been cudgeling his mind about "Horatio at the Bridge". Although there were serious gaps, he had felt obliged, until a voice came from his left.

"I can sing, Sir."
"Sing, what, young Midshipman?"
"The Sisters."

"I know it, and therefore, I will accompany you. We'll call it a combined operation; Navy and the Army."

Blake went to the piano, played the introduction and Bright sang, word and note perfect. Come the last verse, a strong affinity had built between singer and accompanier and so Blake joined in, his bass baritone perfectly complementing Bright's tenor. They finished to loud applause. It was a high point to end a splendid evening. Argent clapped his hand on Bright's shoulder.

"Well done, young William. We'll have to shove you atop the capstan next time we weigh anchor!"

Many heard and grinned, but it was time to go. However, Argent hung back. He told Fentiman and Bright to go to the carriage and wait, he needed a word with Lady Willoughby. However, she and Grant were seeing their guests off through the door, Charlotte besides them, until, finally, only Argent himself remained in the entrance hall. He walked forward, towards all three, them expecting smiles and fond farewells, but Argent was driven by his own concerns.

"Lady Willoughby, may I have a word. Excuse me, please, Charlotte, excuse me, Sir."

Grant looked concerned, his face in sudden contrast to the bonhomie that it had worn moments before.

"Local business, Argent?"

"Yes, Sir. I'm sorry Sir, but it concerns my family."

"Right, your affair. Let's leave them to it. Charlotte?"

He held up his forearm for her and led her back into the Drawing Room, however, as he waited for them to get out of earshot, Argent noticed her looking back anxiously. He turned to Lady Willoughby.

"Lady Constance, I am so sorry to finish the evening on so low a note, but I must beg your help if you can give it."

"Why, of course, Reuben, whatever can be the matter?"

"It concerns enclosures, as was raised by Mr. Portbury earlier. Do you think it will come about?"

"Yes, I think it will. Both Broke and Cinch are behind it, and Cinch has influence. On top, the Government want it. Portbury was right, more food is produced from enclosed farms to feed us during this war, and who can say for how long it will go on."

Argent sighed.

"What Mr. Portbury said has deep relevance to my Father. He cannot find his Deeds. My sisters are looking, but I fear the worst. Can you think of any avenue that could be explored? Perhaps you have documents that could furnish the proof just as well. For any help that you could provide, you would have my deepest gratitude."

Lady Willoughby looked directly up at him, placed her fingertips on his chest and smiled, almost maternally.

"You can count of my help, Reuben, of course you can. I have dealings with all the solicitors in Falmouth, and I'll instruct them to conduct a search, as a favour to me. None will want my disfavour, be assured. I'll do what I can."

Argent felt such gratitude that he surprised himself. He seized her left hand, kissed it and then shook it."

"Whatever the outcome, Lady Constance, you have my family's undying appreciation of your efforts."

Lady Constance was moved by Argent's evident fretfulness and anxiety

"Don't worry, Reuben. I'll get them to come up with something."

Argent bowed deeply.

"My thanks again. Now, I'd like to say that this has been a most enjoyable evening; my thanks for inviting myself and my Officers. Thanks, once again. Good night, Lady Constance."

"Good night to you, Reuben, and Godspeed, to you and to your ship."

Argent nodded and smiled his further acknowledgment and took his leave, to descend the steps to the landau. In it Fentiman sat waiting, Bright sat sleeping, the wine and port having finally had an impact, more in the leaving than in the taking.

* * *

The next day, Fentiman interrupted Argent's breakfast.

"We've got a runner."

"Who?'

"Wilmot. Afterguard of the Starboard Watch and one of Morris' guncrew."

"He was pressed, wasn't he?"

"Of sorts. He was tried and condemned for some minor offence against a landowner up Okehampton way. Sentenced to "Service until released by His Majesty."

"Have you informed the Provosts?"

"Not yet, but I'm about to."

Argent looked even sadder and sighed as his shoulders sagged. He seemed to bear it heavily and Fentiman noticed.

"Don't take it to heart, Sir. It's not your fault. If I may say so, Sir, you run a taught but contented ship, as far as can be achieved on any man o' war. You know as well I, how hard a seaman's life is, whatever we try to do, although others don't, I know. To a landsman, it's an appalling life, and Wilmot is such. To be honest, I'm surprised it's just one. Every ship laid up like ours, that I've ever heard of, loses several, unless they're marched off to some barracks, of course."

Argent nodded.

"Yes. No surprise, really, but a disappointment, all the same."

He rose from the table.

"Let's hope the Provosts don't take it out on his family. If they don't find him, then with his home, they'll be none too gentle. Now, repairs and re-supply, I need to check, especially the former."

He took his undress coat from the peg and went along the corridor, briefly, almost sadly, acknowledging the sentry's salute.

On the lower deck, the event was not being regarded with such equanimity.

"Bloody Wilmot! God rot the bastard."

Morris and Dedman were attending to their own personal affairs in the gloom of the lowerdeck, attending to their possessions in the light of a small candle that was lodged between them and shone its paltry light into the depths of their sea chests, these holding all the world of both.

"God will rot him if the Provosts gets hold of him. It'll cost him his neck?"

Morris sobered a little.

"Well, true, I'd not wish that on him, but now we'n one short. Who else, but some blown winded old fo'c'slman is what we'n goin' to get. All is given to somewer' from the afterguard and waisters."

"Well, look on the bright side. A fo'c'slman'll know what he's about, even if he ain't got the strength to do it."

A movement from the aft companionway caught their eye, the flash of white breeches, two pairs. That meant Officers, so both closed their chests and sprang to attention. The Captain and the First, no less, were on their way forward, accompanied by Frederick Baines, the Ship's Carpenter. The repairs to the shothole had necessarily extended between both the gundeck and the lowerdeck. They had come to inspect where the new planking now showed on the side planking of the lower deck. Morris and Dedman came to the attention and paid their respects by knuckling their foreheads. Argent looked closely at both in the gloom.

"Ah, Morris. You've lost a man over the side. Was it you that first missed him?"

"Yes, Sir. At breakfast, Sir, which we reported to Mr. Ffynes. He didn't turn up to our mess, Sir."

"How did he seem."

"Never content, Sir, and always afeard. Our set to with La Mouette had him full terrified, Sir. When her shot first hit us, I saw he could barely stand, Sir, but he was alright when we started firin' ourselves. Sir."

Argent nodded in the gloom.

"Very well, Morris, but now we've got to get you a replacement, haven't we?"

"Yes, Sir. Any idea who that might be, Sir?"

"Mr. Fentiman, here, hasn't yet decided, but you'll know soon enough."

"Aye, aye, Sir."

The three, Officers and Warrant Officer took themselves along further and, at the appropriate point, Mr. Baines held up the lantern.

"What do you think, Mr. Baines?"

"Oh, 'tis a good enough repair, Sir, along with the bulwark we've just seen. And I've checked outside, and the caulkin' is all sound. I'd say, that we're now repaired, Sir."

* * *

Many sea miles across The Channel and further, Kalil Al'Ahbim looked across at the point on the Biscay coast that he had chosen as his place of shelter. They had made a good landfall, to the island the French call L'Ille d'Yeu, although this he would not have known. Nor was he to know that it was termed thus because it was shaped like an eye, the right eye, but "right" had been omitted from the title. What pleased him was that they had arrived here in good time, unmolested by the French, but also avoiding the English cruisers. Moving close to the shoreline, he had avoided the English and posed themselves as French. A Tricolour flew above his head, any that saw him had taken him to be a French galley, her oars manned by condemned prisoners.

However, his oarsmen were pirates, like himself, but more accurately, slavers. Al'Ahbim and his men found themselves able to take advantage of the preoccupied Navies of France and Great Britain and re-new Tunisian interest in the slave trade that had taken prisoners from the coasts of France, England, and Ireland. These unfortunates were then carried back to North African ports, there to be sold as slaves. For such a long voyage North, Al'Ahbim would take only those that fetched the highest price; children and young women and the highest price amongst these were for the white skinned women and children of this region. Now, they were at their destination, well hidden under the cliff of their sheltering cove, having warped themselves in close by their banks of oars. It had been a hard voyage, so it was worth now taking the time to ready his ship and make his plans. Soon their raiding could begin, then, the sooner they filled the slave deck and the sooner they could begin their voyage back, to the markets of Tangiers.

Chapter Four

Sinaid Malley

The Irish Sea had been less than welcoming, growing in temper the more they encroached upon it, leaving the Lizard and Land's End two days past. They had departed Falmouth on a morning tide and soon gained enough sea room to tack across the strong South Westerly and make a long run up the coast to clear The Scillies. The dawn of that day had come reluctantly and in the rain-washed light, the ship lifted and dropped to a growing swell. However, Ariadne was taking the wind "two points free, beam on" close to her best point of sailing. Argent began his Watch by consulting Ship's Master McArdle."

"Any thoughts on the weather, Mr. McArdle."

"Aye Sir. I'd say a blow of some kind, but no a bad one. Expect tae remain on lower canvas, for safety, but I'm thinkin' it'll not grow intae anythin' that'll cause us tae change our chosen course."

"I'm relieved to hear it, Mr. McArdle. We can only trust in the accuracy of your valuable experience."

"Och, I've seen the like in these waters before, at this time of the seasons. I don't expect it'll come tae much."

The seas mounted and surged over the weather bow, this the larboard, and the daily practice at the guns and on the masts became impossible After the crew had gone to dinner, Fentiman had safety lines rigged as the waves rose high up the larboard side to cause churning water to boil through the scuppers and spurt in around the gunports and sneak below, into the ship. This volume also being increased by the all too frequent solid waves that rose up and spent themselves fully over the bulwark. Both Watches were ordered to double lash the guns and look for any kind of movement in any cannon that could work loose into that most feared "runaway", a loose cannon. The ship pushed on through the waves, still making nine, sometimes ten knots, and McArdle was right, no canvas could be spread higher than the main and foresails, but the wind never rose high enough to such a shriek that would cause these to be taken in or even reefed. Nevertheless, this was not comfort sailing. The Irish Sea was making its presence felt and the water ran down into the ship, through the lower deck, past the hold, down to the bilges. Come evening Frederick Baines reported to his Captain, him not having quit the deck since daybreak.

"Six inches in the well, Sir."

The well gave knowledge about the level of water in the lowest reaches of the ship, and six inches could not be ignored, if only for its weight altering the ship's trim. Thus, throughout the night the pumps clanked, with all men, from topmen to fo'c'slmen, from waisters to Marines, taking their shift to wind the handles, up and down, these that lifted the scoops up through the full height of the hull to tip the foul water out onto the deck. There was little conversation as the men laboured at the exhausting task. All would prefer to work the capstan than to take a long turn at the up and down of the winding handles that exhausted their lower backs and arms. The seas rose further in the night, but not the wind and, with the arrival of the next dawn, the pumps still clanked but they had held the well to six inches. Dinner saw the seas abate and the ship took little more water aboard, merely the spurt through an ill-fitting gunport. The pumps gained on the well and, finally, the evening meal was taken in silence, no clanking pump, but the men too tired to talk. The next dawn came with a stiff breeze, South Southwest, carrying alternate banks of rain and mist, that hurried on to soak the Welsh coast, but the heavy seas had abated. Ariadne sailed on, no change in her course, nor extra sails set. The Watches changed, the Bell was rung, and Dinner was not so far in the future, then a cry from the mizzentop broke the set routine.

"Deck there. Sail on the starboard bow."

Bentley was Officer of the Watch.

"Where away?"

"Four points. Two miles, nor more."

Bentley immediately turned to Daniel Berry, standing Watch with him.

"Fetch the Captain."

Berry saluted and hurried off. Bentley continued to interrogate the lookout.

"What size?"

"Small, Sir. Best I can say, Sir, but a mist has passed across her."

Bentley gave a sigh of relief. Small. He could leave the decision to clear for action for the Captain.

"What now?"

"Still hid, Sir. No, she's coming out."

Argent had arrived, buttoning his jacket.

"Four points, Sir, off the starboard bow. Two miles off."

"Thank you, Mr. Bentley."

Argent now called to the lookout.

"What can you see?"

"She's small, Sir, but bigger than a fisherman. She's seen us, Sir, and hauled her wind. I can see her better now, Sir, a lugger, two masted, schooner rig. She's deep seagoing, Sir."

A pause.

"Mist has got her again, Sir."

Argent was left to ponder. She might be a trader, between Ireland and the English coast, obviously legitimate. She might be a deep-sea fisherman and they could buy her catch. That would be good. On the other hand, she might be a smuggler, and therefore should be apprehended. His own ship was running West Northwest.

"Down helm! Come to Nor'nor' West."

The steersmen repeated, but Argent was talking over them, to Berry.

"Mr. Berry. Take yourself down to Mr. Mortimor, and tell him to hold up Dinner."

As Berry disappeared, Bentley smiled.

"Glad you sent him and not me, Sir."

Argent ignored him.

"Clear both batteries to fire, Mr. Bentley."

"Not "Beat to Quarters", Sir?"

"Mr. Bentley, have I not made myself clear? I want both batteries cleared ready to fire, as for a salute, and that alone. Now please to set about it."

"Aye, aye, Sir."

Bentley hurried down the companionway to the gundeck, hoping to find Bosun's Mates. Argent, meanwhile, was walking along the gangway to take his Dolland up to the foretop and once there he consulted the lookout there.

"Where did you last see her?"

Moses King pointed and Argent trained his glass in that direction.

"Look, Sir, she's coming out again. Look right, Sir."

Argent did as advised and soon saw the vessel. She carried a press of canvas, and was running North East before the wind, lug sails set either side, to gain the maximum of the wind, jibsails out in addition. He spoke to King, but in a way that could best be described as "thinking out loud".

"That's an escape. Hopes to outrun us, get lost in the mist, and hold off till night."

The lookout gave his opinion.

"I'd say she was fast, Sir. Two big masts and flying all she's got."

"Yes, King. But not as fast as Ariadne!"

"No, Sir. Nuthin's that fast, Sir!"

The two exchanged grins as Argent disappeared onto the futtock shrouds below. Back on his quarterdeck he gave his orders, Bentley had gone and so he turned to Daniel Berry.

"Mr. Berry. Get the Larboard Watch up from the lowerdeck. Set topsails, topgallants and main royals."

Berry looked horrified, the Bosun and his Mates handled such things, but they were involved with the readying the guns. Argent couldn't resist some sarcasm.

"Off you go, Mr. Berry. At the top of your voice, you tell them the sails you want set, and, you'll be amazed Mr. Berry, but the men will actually come up and do it."

"Aye, aye, Sir. Which sails again, Sir?'

"Topsails, topgallants, and main royals."
"Topsails, topgallants, and main royals. Aye, aye, Sir."
"Yes, Mr. Berry, you have the right of it. Now please to take yourself off."

Within a minute the off duty Larboard Watch, once sat waiting for their Dinner, came up onto the gangways and jumped into the ratlines. A few extra minutes and the sails were set and sheeted home. Argent was sure that he felt Ariadne accelerate as the extra canvas drew. He took his speaking trumpet and shouted up to the mizzentop.

"Fredrickson. Do you have her, is she still in view?"
"Yes, Sir, but she's heading for a mist bank, Sir. A big one."
"Any change of course?"
"No Sir, she's still crossing us, Sir. Moving over to starboard."
Argent turned to his helmsmen.
"Down wind. Steer North East."
"Down wind. Steer North East. Aye, aye, Sir."
Bentley returned.
"Batteries cleared and ready, Sir."
Argent gave Bentley a withering look.
"Yes, Mr. Bentley, a minute slower than had you gone about your business immediately!"
"Yes, Sir."
"Now, find Mr. Fraser, we're wearing ship. Before the wind."

Fentiman arrived, buttoning his jacket, disturbed from a sleep that would have recovered him from a night combating the storm. Argent noticed his arrival and his voice contained no sarcasm.

"Mr. Fentiman. I'm pleased to see you. We're wearing ship to North East. Please to give it your full attention."

Fentiman made off forward, to first find any Warrant Officer now on deck, because not much seemed to be happening. The big driver, over to starboard, bellied out above the quarterdeck, drum tight, but soon it would swing over to the other side for the starboard tack as the ship wore round. However, at the will of Fentiman, Fraser, and Ball; the crew were soon about their business and all hands trimmed the sheets and braces for the starboard tack, while Argent considered options, both his, and the rival Captain's. A lugger could not outrun a frigate, his only real hope was to tack South, hoping to skip past in the mist and leave Ariadne to plough on North East, seeking what was no longer there.

"Frederickson, what can you see?"
"We're gaining on her, Sir. You can probably see her from the deck, now, Sir. She's fine off our larboard bow."

Argent jumped into the mizzen shrouds with his Dolland and, with a naked eye, saw the white speck. He focused the telescope and saw her clearly. Once again Argent detailed her Captain's options to himself. She could run on through the mist, but Ariadne would come through and catch her. She could heave to in the mist or steer off a little and hope that Ariadne would run past, but Ariadne would follow her in at the same point, and very probably see her. Also the mist was running on the wind, it would soon clear any ship, hove to and stationary. She could run on something North of West, as she was, keeping in the mist, then turn down South West to her previous course. That would keep her on the wind and take her across Ariadne, as she now steered, but it meant holding to the course Ariadne could plainly see her steering and surely he would reason that his pursuer would be likely to follow.

Or she could tack in the mist and run West, to wholly diverge from Ariadne. He thought more carefully about this. She was a lugger, a fishing rig. They could tack on a sixpence in half a second. He looked again. Someone was at her taffrail with a telescope trained back on him, then the lugger ploughed into the mist and was swallowed. He made his decision; whoever was looking must have seen Ariadne cracking on North East, under a press of canvas.

"Mr. Fentiman. Wear ship, larboard tack. Helmsman, come to West Nor'west, soon as she draws."

Loudly, to his Captain, "Wearing ship. West Nor'west. Aye, aye, Sir."

To his mate, "Soon as she draws, like we was a pair of grasscombing lubbers!"

Argent was gambling that the lugger's Captain would tack back, away from Ariadne as he last saw her. The frigate came around to her new course hardly losing a knot. On the larboard tack, sailing West Northwest Ariadne was running along the edge of the bank of mist, too fast, Argent thought. If and when the lugger turned back South West his ship must not be astern of her.

"Furl all topsails and topgallants. Furl mainsail."

The orders were shouted along the deck and soon obeyed. Ariadne slowed to a bare three knots in a wind just astern of beam on. Nothing to do now, but wait. Argent re-assessed his gamble. He confidently thought himself right, but the minutes passed. They had come to the end of the bank of mist, soon they would know if the lugger had kept on with the wind or tacked and dodged back, as Argent had gambled.

"On deck. Sail ho. Off the starboard bow. Same lugger, Sir."

There she was and Argent pictured the consternation on her deck as she saw Ariadne square across her course, guns run out. Argent looked around his quarterdeck and saw Midshipmen Ffynes.

"Mr. Ffynes. Request Morris, on number three, to put a shot across her bows."

Ffynes gave his "Aye, aye, Sir," on the run.

"Walk, Mr. Fynes."

Ffynes hurried on, whilst still holding to something resembling a walk. The quarterdeck was all smiles as telescopes were raised.

Progressing along the gundeck to number three, Ffynes found the same mood amongst the men manning the guns he passed, only spoken.

"The Captain's got her!"

"She's a size, that's a dollop more prizemoney."

Ffynes came up to Morris.

"Morris. The Captain wants a shot across her bows. Now."

"Now, Sir? I thought he might wait awhile."

"That's enough from you, Morris. Now."

However, Morris had already laid his gun for a shot across the bows. He bent down to check the direction, required Dedman to lever the gun slightly right, then jerked the lanyard. The gun roared and the smoke spurted from the touchhole beneath the flintlock, as the gun hurried back to jerk to a stop against the breeching ropes. On the quarterdeck they saw the splash of shot, it must have passed alarmingly almost under her bowsprit. The lugger was now faced with the Ariadne's full broadside. Her Captain started his sheets and she fell idle, slumping into the swell, the sails soon in the process of being furled.

"I suspect her to be a smuggler, and I suspect her to be French. Mr. McArdle, you have an opinion?"

"I do, Sir, aye. Half lugger, half schooner looks French enough to me!"

Were it intended as a joke, from McArdle probably not, but, nevertheless, all laughed just the same. With this success and with the mood pertaining on the quarterdeck, the thinnest of jests would have been taken as the highest of humour.

"Send for Mr. Sanders, and ready the longboat."

An idle signalman was sent to instruct both the Lieutenant and the Bosun and, whilst the latter busied himself busying others, the former arrived on the quarterdeck, having hurried up from the gundeck. He approached and saluted.

"Sir?"

"Mr. Sanders, with six Marines and the same of topmen, row over and take possession. Include my bargecrew; tell Whiting what you need."

"Aye, aye, Sir."

Soon the longboat was over the side and filling with its Marines and seamen. The mast was stepped and braced, then its sails, merely two, but extensive, were set to use the good wind to carry them across. It took but five minutes from them leaving the side of the Ariadne until they were all climbing the side of the lugger to disappear onto her deck. Argent felt the need to be nearer, and saw Fraser, just along the starboard gangway.

"Mr. Fraser, back the foresail, I want some leeway down onto her."

Fraser knuckled his forehead and ran off, gathering seamen. Soon the foresail was backed to work against the driver. Ariadne could go neither forward nor back, so she drifted sideways, down onto the lugger. The time passed, during which Argent thought of his next move.

"Mr. McArdle. What's the nearest port of any size?"

The reply was instant.

"Kinsale, Sir. Close on North West of here."

"Thank you, Mr. McArdle."

Ariadne drifted down onto the lugger until a mere 50 yards of distance. Argent joined Fentiman, who was using his telescope.

"I think our boarding crew are sharing a bottle!"

Argent fetched his own glass and focused it. True enough, the Marines and seamen were passing around a bottle.

"That's either Irish or brandy. My money's on the latter. The French have no taste at all for whiskey."

"Should we have a word, Sir, on his return?"

"I think not, Henry. I think we can turn a blind eye to that, but you'll have a point if they start a second!"

Argent fetched his speaking trumpet from the locker and climbed into the mizzen rigging.

"Ahoy the lugger."

Sanders appeared in the rigging.

"Mr. Sanders. What have you discovered?"

"She's French, Sir, and full of contraband. Tobacco and Irish linen."

"Very good, Mr. Sanders. Get underway to steer North West. You can follow us to Kinsale. And Mr. Sanders?"

"Yes Sir?"

"If you find a second bottle aboard, we'd all appreciate it coming back for the Officer's table."

* * *

Ariadne, with her new consort and the longboat in its tow, turned to anticipate the bearing as calculated by McArdle, which he gravely delivered to his Captain.

"Steer North West by West. Sir."

Many, if duties allowed, came up to the starboard gangways and examined their new prize. There was much speculation.

"I'd say she'll be bought into The Service. As handy a supply ship as ever I saw."

"More like for the coastal trade. She'll soon be snapped up."

The mood was high throughout the ship, bar the inevitable "Bible" Mortimor.

"The potatoes has turned to soup, and the greens is not far behind. The land shall be utterly emptied, and utterly spoiled. Isaiah, 24, verse 3."

Nevetheless the food was issued for the much delayed meal. It was all good cheer on the lowerdeck; the quality of the fare, poor or otherwise, being ignored for the more current topic. Both vessels pushed on with the good breeze steady from the South and by sunset they had raised the Irish Coast, but darkness had set in, their landfall was impossible to accurately recognise. Nautical prudence took over, which dictated that, with a depth of ten fathoms beneath them, both vessels anchored to ride out the night and soon the sounds of singing came across from their prize, she being called the Erienne. Fentiman and Argent were at the bulwark rail of the quarterdeck, looking at the shadow of their prize and gauging her length from her riding lights. It was Fentiman who first voiced their thoughts.

"I suspect another bottle."

"So do I, or perhaps finishing the first one, but were you to enquire I know the answer you'd get."

"What?"

"We'n just havin' a singsong to keep ourselves amused and our spirits up. Sir. Keep out the chill, Sir."

Both laughed. Fentiman continued.

"Shouldn't Sanders be taking things in hand?"

"Think back to your time as a new Lieutenant. What chance would you have had of finding a bottle amongst a dozen old salts all on the deck of a strange ship? And what kind of Officer would stop the men singing, especially after taking a prize."

Fentiman nodded in the glom, then changed the subject.

"What would you say? 40 foot?"

"45. And she's handy. She's a good prize, and then there's the value of her cargo, she being a smuggler. Nothing aboard there of low value."

"But Irish linen as contraband?"

"It doesn't surprise me. A shortage of fine cloth within Johnnyland doesn't surprise me at all. They can't even get cotton yarn, not from Egypt, nor from the other side of the Atlantic, that's for certain. The Americans would sell them all they could, but there's our cruisers ranging up and down the Bay. The Channel and the Med are even more impossible. No, a bale of fine Irish linen will fetch a worthy price."

The next day saw a clear dawn, but McArdle judged them to be off the narrow bays of Kilarney; they had come too far West. However, the Southerly breeze still held allowing them to cruise the coast, heading East Northeast, and McArdle, continuously consulting the chart, grew ever more confident of their position. Meanwhile, Argent took the chance to organize his squadron and its duties, so he had the longboat return and take himself over to the prize. On her deck he found Sanders stood foursquare overlooking his command, Whiting at the helm and all the crew either cleaning the deck, checking the standing rigging, or replacing some of the running rigging. Sanders found the need to explain.

"The men felt the need to tidy her up a bit, Sir. They thought that getting her a bit more shipshape may add a few more pounds to her value, Sir."

Argent studied the scene around the deck, as both seamen and Marines brought the vessel up to Navy standards, or at least as close as possible.

"Very good, Mr. Sanders. Who could fail to approve? Now, Kinsale has a long throat to its harbour. Ariadne will anchor outside and we'll take this in and hand her over to the Port Authorities. Is she full laden?"

"Yes Sir. Full all round. There's not a space that hasn't a bale of something, Sir. Either linen or tobacco."

"And the crew?"

"Under the main hatch, Sir, with two Marines guarding."

"And there's no other way out of the hold?"

"No Sir. I had your bargecrew check, Sir. They found nothing from any other point in the ship and if there is one, it's deep under the cargo, Sir."

"How many in the crew?"

"Six. All very disgruntled, Sir. Her Captain thought he'd played a fine trick, but he complained bitterly, Sir, repeating several times, "Votre Capitaine est un Deveil"."

"I'm a Devil?"

"Yes Sir. That's what it means."

Argent chuckled.

"The luck of The Devil, perhaps. I took a gamble and it paid off. Another time, who knows?"

"Yes Sir."

Argent paused to further appraise the craft.

"She's handy, holding onto Ariadne well enough. And stable, and, from what you say, "capacious.""

"Yes, Sir."

Argent took his Dolland out from under his arm.

"Did the Captain have a spy-glass?"

"Yes, Sir, I have it here."

He pulled a medium-sized, but quality telescope, closed down, from his pocket.

"It's yours! Now, accompany me forward with it."

Argent and the grinning Sanders went to the bowsprit, then both trained their glasses forward.

"Mr. McArdle said to watch for a hilly island, on the end of a narrow causeway, and I do believe this is it. Beyond its head is the entrance to Kinsale. We're nearly there."

He turned to his Coxswain.

"Whiting, lay me closer to Ariadne."

"Ease to starboard. Aye, aye, Sir."

Whiting gently turned the newly polished spokes and Erienne eased closer to Ariadne, the longboat bobbing and snubbing at its towline. It took but 15 more minutes to clear the island and the entrance to Kinsale opened before them. Argent called across his orders and Ariadne took in sail and dropped anchor with enough sea room for an easy departure, but Erienne stood on to enter the harbour. Kinsale revealed itself to be as good a natural harbour as Falmouth, only with the quays at the furthest side of a kidney-shaped bay, rather than just inside the entrance. They gained the attention of a few local craft, all going about their business of coastal trade, or hauling up lobster pots, but there was no greeting; the red uniforms of the Marines identified them as being about the business of King George, this rarely to the good of such as themselves. The quayside grew closer and Argent was cautious with his approach, not only from an unfamiliar fore and aft rig, but the unfamiliarity of the harbour. The tide was falling, so he had Able Jones in the bows sounding the lead which they had found aboard, this being an item all sailing craft had full need of. In the same way as they had for the craft they had passed in the bay, the Marines' uniforms identified them as Royal Navy and, therefore, a reception party had assembled on the quayside, their uniforms showing Officers in both red and blue. The quayside moorings were almost fully occupied, but there was one space of enough size and Argent had the sails dropped and Erienne drifted to a stop, but yet close enough for Moses King to throw a line a staggering distance and then Erienne to be slowly hauled up to the quayside and finally secured at both bows and stern.

As this was being done a gangplank was swung out and lowered from the quayside and two Senior Officers, one from each of His Majesty's Forces marched down. Argent greeted them as they came over the side and saluted.

"Good Afternoon, Sirs. My name is Captain Argent, HMS Ariadne, she now being outside, anchored at the entrance to the bay."

The wearer being Navy, he in the blue coat spoke first. He was a short, thin man, with a face curious, yet not unkindly, but deep, almost feverish blue eyes above a sharp nose. His uniform fitted where it touched.

"Port Commodore Harper, Captain, and this is Colonel Michael O'Dowd, 2nd Cork Militia."

It was the Colonel who extended his hand, then Harper did the same, but it was Argent who began.

"How do you do Colonel? Sir, if I may report?"

Both nodded.

"This is a French smuggler that we took yesterday, about 30 miles South East. The crew are French and are prisoners below. She is full to the gunnels with tobacco and Irish linen. I was hoping to leave her here, Sir, in the hands of the Government Agent, and then continue my patrol, as are my orders, Sir."

Harper spoke first.

"Whose orders?"

"Commodore Sidney Budgen, Sir. Port Commodore of Falmouth."

"Hmm, that sounds familiar, one from my own past."

He paused, eyebrows together in thought, however he soon abandoned his trawl through the files of his memory.

"Come ashore and we'll make the arrangements and get you on your way."

At this moment Colonel O'Dowd spoke his curiosity.

"Irish linen, you say?"

"Yes Sir. I'd say there are about 200 bolts of it aboard, perhaps more, plus about 50 barrels of tobacco."

"So; French smugglers are taking Irish linen?"

"That's the conclusion, Sir."

"Bring a bolt ashore with you, Captain."

Argent gestured to Sam Fenwick.

"Fetch a bolt and follow us, please Fenwick."

Fenwick, not being prepared to pass up the chance to demonstrate "proper Navy" to these two and anyone else looking on, came to full attention and saluted.

"Aye, aye, Sir."

However, he was soon "at ease" and holding a canvas covered bolt of linen that had been immediately thrown up to him by Moses King. Argent stepped onto the quayside and was immediately struck by how busy the harbour was, this reflecting the amount of shipping crowding the quayside. There were carts and donkeys aplenty, all busily being unloaded or laden, with a full collection of people, either working, supervising, or simply idling. Tall, solid, newbuilt warehouses stretched out as a backdrop, but Harper and O'Dowd led the way off to the right towards two buildings, these separate from all others. Both were painted the same royal blue, of medium height and equally well made, and they both overlooked the harbour, the one the furthest, indeed, having a lookout window. Argent walked respectfully just behind the two superior Officers and, thus, he was in a good position to both see and hear O'Dowd call over a member of his Militia.

"Fetch Mother McDaid. Bring her to the Harbour Office."

The Militiaman saluted and made off, running. The four entered the first building which quickly revealed itself to be the administrative centre of the harbour, at least eight clerks sat at high desks, all attending to their ledgers, quill pens either writing furiously or being dipped purposefully into inkwells to facilitate yet more ledgering. The four were separated from this eager effort by a high counter. Commodore Harper addressed the nearest.

"Tell Mr. Brideswell that we're here."

The clerk disappeared out through a door in the back of the office and after a minute or two he reappeared with a tall middle-aged man, dressed entirely in pale brown, bar a high white collar. Thin, wispy hair hung down over an almost cadaverous face, itself stretched over with sallow skin, almost the same colour as his coat. The set, over both his eyes and mouth, was one of his surprise and concern. He was greeted by Harper, unceremoniously.

"Ah, Brideswell. The Captain here," indicating Argent, "has brought in a French smuggler as a prize. You have the capacity to act as Government Agent, yes?"

Brideswell nodded, still looking concerned.

"Please to draw up the papers that show your receipt of her from Captain Argent, then we can get him on his way, off and about the King's business."

Brideswell nodded again and swung like a crane around to the nearest desk, from there to gather paper, quill, and ink. He looked at Argent and placed the materials on the counter. When he spoke, Argent was taken aback to hear the sounds of the Yorkshire Dales, and Brideswell spoke with surprising confidence and authority.

"Please to give me details, Captain. Dates, places, names and the like. Details about your ship, the prize and her cargo. The more details you can give, the less confusion, you'll find."

Argent picked up the pen and began writing, whilst all stood by patiently, including Brideswell. Argent carefully listed the details, then stopped and turned to Fenwick, still cradling his bolt of linen.

"Fenwick, when did we first sight her?"

"Must have been about seven bells of the forenoon, Sir. Dinner was spoiled."

"Ah, yes, quite right."

At that point a bundle of black cloth entered the door, this held open by the Militiaman dispatched previously by Colonel O'Dowd. The bundle was a little over five feet high, which included a black bonnet. Argent took this to be Mother McDaid, although Mother or Father, it would be impossible to tell, the figure was so bound about by black cotton clothing. A hatchet nose jutted forward from under the bonnet, flanked by the triangulation points of two red cheeks and a like coloured chin, from all of which protruded a collection of thin white hairs. Above these were two watery eyes, both blue, but one startlingly more ferocious than the other. O'Dowd gave the greetings.

"Ah, Mrs. McDaid, so very good of you to come, and so very good of you to give us your services."

He indicated the bolt of linen, now placed, in accordance with his gestures, on the counter, and he began to remove the cloth wrapping.

"We'd like you to tell us its origin, where it was made."

Argent, with few details of his own left to list, looked up astonished. There were no markings anywhere, neither on the linen nor on the wrapping. Mrs. McDaid walked forward and two surprisingly muscular hands emerged from the black folds, each with a single finger top missing. With the practiced ease of a professional she picked up the bolt and spun it to immediately unravel about two yards of the cloth. Upon this, then fell the close examination of the ferocious eye, the linen being both held away in the light, then minutely examined at close range. She turned to O'Dowd.

"Oi whant to examine it in the dayloight, houtside."

O'Dowd motioned to Fenwick, who lifted the bolt, whilst Mrs. McDaid herself carried the end of unravelled cloth. O'Dowd opened the door and the two exited out into the sunlight. Argent looked at O'Dowd.

"Forgive me, Sir, but am I to understand that this lady can tell us where the linen was made?"

"That is exactly the right of it, Captain. Certainly linen from these parts and someway beyond. Mother McDaid can tell you the loom it was made on, never mind the manufactury."

Argent held his peace, but looked necessarily amazed. He finished with the details and pushed the paper across to Brideswell and both said thank you to the other in unison. A minute passed, then two and the pair returned, Mrs. McDaid dwarflike besides Fenwick, him bringing up the rear with the bolt, but all eyes were upon the black clad woman. All was returned to the countertop and a final close examination was made. She looked at O'Dowd and pronounced.

"This was made in Killannen. Malley's mill. It's amongst the finest you'll find, anywhere."

With that she held out one of her maimed hands to O'Dowd.

"Oh, yes. Of course."

He extracted a silver coin from his waistcoat and placed it into the etched palm. Mrs. McDaid said no more, but turned and took her leave through the open door, this held open for her passage by the same Militiaman. Harper looked at O'Dowd.

"We've got to pursue this, we've no choice. Linen from the Killannen mill is ending up aboard French smugglers. You'll send a company around to investigate?"

"I will, but it'll take a day, and more, to get around the mountain. If they are up to something, they'll know soon enough that we're on our way and hide everything away, and that's assuming that there is anything; anything that would give evidence, which is very unlikely. In that case, we can do no more than get around there and make our presence felt, at least show them that we know. It would be more effective, if the Captain here, took his ship around there, landed quickly and held all as found, until we got there. It's only half a day's sailing."

O'Dowd looked at Argent, his look posing the question. Argent looked from one to the other of his superior Officers.

"My orders are to run the triangle, Sir, and then report back to Falmouth for my next commission. My Port Admiral will be curious regarding any delay, Sir. Bringing in the smuggler has already cost me time from this commission."

It was Harper who replied.

"I'm changing your orders, Captain. This is now an order from me. You will take your ship and hold Killannen until Colonel O'Dowd's men arrive. Is that clear?"

"Yes Sir. As you order, but I would appreciate it in writing, Sir. And you'll question the French Captain? Sir?"

"That you can safely assume."

* * *

The Officers were all gathered in the great cabin, save those keeping Watch, these being Lieutenant Fentiman and Midshipman Berry. This was the evening meal and Argent was in his place at the head of the table, Captain Ramsey on his right in Fentiman's absence. The repeaters attached up through the ceiling to the binnacle on the quarterdeck relayed both the wind and course into the greatcabin. Just above Argent's head, both showed no change, both good for Killannen, which they should reach sometime well before dawn. The mood was good, created by gaining another prize and, somehow, a whole saddle of French mutton had appeared for their main course and it now sat demolished in the middle of the table. Good French wine had been the liquid accompaniment and, while Jeremy and Jerimiah cleared all away for the next course, which promised to be a large figgy duff, Argent saw the chance to ask a question that he had been burning to ask for sometime.

"Lieutenant Sanders. Please explain to us all why you are able to speak French so fluently."

Sanders looked up the table at him and Argent became a little disturbed, even conscience stricken, by the anxious look that Sanders gave both to him and then to Bentley and Ffynes sat opposite him. Nevertheless, Sanders recovered himself, sat up with his forearms resting on the table and his expression soon changed to cheeriness, as though he were about to impart a humorous story. He launched straight in, hiding no detail.

"When I was taken aboard the Defiance from the orphanage to be a ship's boy, I was immediately made a Powder Monkey to a guncrew, and, of course, they became my messmates. They were all French! Fishermen that once were."

Bentley and Ffynes exclaimed together, eyes wide, even horrified, although it was initially hard to tell from what cause, for there were two possibilities, until they both exclaimed the same word.

"French?"

"That's right. They were refugees from Brittany. In '90 there was a rebellion there against the Revolution and the army stormed in. In those days, anyone could accuse you of being an "aristo sympathetique" and they didn't have to prove you guilty, you had to prove that you were innocent. Over the years the fishermen had prospered, which immediately made them suspect, or the target of jealousy, so they loaded their families into their boats, three of them, and sailed for Cornwall, with all the family valuables. They hoped to be able to carry on fishing, but the locals burnt their boats; they didn't want the competition. However, the valuables were sold and they bought a warehouse just off the quay, where their families could live. But, no boats, no fishing, no money; so all the men joined The Service and sent home their pay. They were very good to me. I'm not sure of my age, I believe that I was about five then, perhaps more. They were the only family that I had, and I still go there to see them, when I can. The Defiance fought at Copenhagen and Trafalgar, as I'm sure you know, and it was Captain Durham who sponsored me as a Midshipman. By the time of Trafalgar, I was a topman."

Captain Ramsey looked kindly at Sanders, who looked anxiously around the table, not sure how the story had been received, but Ramsey was touched that Sanders, whom he regarded as a good Officer, with an impeccable record, was not able to even state his own age.

"So, you were at Trafalgar? And Copenhagen? On the Defiance?"

"Yes, Sir."

Ramsey nodded, long and steady, with a "that'll do for me", look on his face. However, the exact opposite was displayed on the tipsy faces of Bentley and Ffynes, each looking as though they'd just drank some very sour wine. It was Bentley who spoke.

"You were taken out of an orphanage?"

Sanders recognised the tone of the question and challengingly returned the look to both.

"Yes, that's what I said."

Argent saw the direction in which that question would be going and intervened, helped by the arrival of a huge figgy duff, steaming, speckled and translucent from the boiler, carried aloft by both Johnson and Jeremiah.

"Right, that gives the answer. Now we know. Messed with a French guncrew; it could only happen in the Navy."

The figgy duff suffered the same fate as the saddle of mutton and, after the port and the Loyal Toast, the gathering broke up. Argent saw his fellow Officers out of the cabin and followed the last into the corridor, this being Sanders. Argent clapped him twice on the shoulder, not speaking, but at least demonstrating his very good opinion.

Argent reached the quarterdeck, in time to see McArdle supervising the "taking of the log" in the light of a lantern. "Taking the log" stilled all conversation, the silence at last broken by the Master's Mate.

"Eight knots and a half, Sir."
McArdle answered.
"A half? You're certain? No a quarter, nor three quarters, but a half?"
Before the fearsome gaze of McArdle, seen even in the half-light, the Master's Mate's confidence dissolved like a sculpture in smoke. He looked at the point where his fingers had nipped the line and checked either way.
"Well, Sir. Perhaps just over a half, Sir."
McArdle made a noise somewhere back in his throat and turned away, taking the lantern with him and the Master's Mate made himself scarce. Using a board, that he rested on the glass and mahogany structure that formed the greatcabin windowlight, McArdle busied himself with calculations of distance involving both speed and time. This he transferred to the chart, which was the next occupant of the board. He looked several times from the chart to the coastline, a mountain silhouetted against the starry sky. After more work with ruler and dividers, he turned to Argent.
"Ye'll be well advised to anchor at five bells of the Middle Watch, Captain."
Words of advice such as this from the likes of Leviticus McArdle came to those such as Argent like words of fire on tablets of stone.
"Five bells of the "graveyard". That's my Watch. I'll make it so. Thank you Mr. McArdle.
With a growled, "Sir", McArdle departed to his cabin, there to join his wife for their final reading of The Bible, before retiring. A Bosun's Mate rang the eight bells for midnight and the Middle Watch began, and Argent now had the deck. However, all was well, nothing to command his attention, as his ship slipped easily across the sea and through the night. His thoughts dwelt solely on what he should do when he reached Killanen, what was the correct procedure that would persuade O'Dowd that he had acted correctly? What could be found to prove involvement in smuggling? A French Revolutionary cap? Should they search anyway? The Captain had revealed that the linen was transferred ship to ship in one of Kilarney's long bays, which meant nothing. He had said that the other vessel was a fishing boat, it smelt!
On a sea still inky from night, they set out. At four bells he called for George Fraser to make his preparations and at five bells the sails were taken in and the anchor let go. In the steady breeze Ariadne swung around her anchor and they all settled to see what the dawn would reveal. As the sky lightened, details grew on the shore and they could see that McArdle was almost perfect in his calculations, perhaps only 300 or 400 yards further would have been an improvement. The longboat, the Captain's barge, and even the jollyboat were soon readied to carry all Marines and as many seamen as possible to the shoreline.

Killannen grew out of the dawn and all that were able see what was exposed on the shore by the growing light, wished that the dark had lingered further. If it was a harbour then that defining word was being stretched almost to breaking point. There was no more than a grey stone, weed-covered wall at the head of the beech, halfway up it being black from weed and scum. They were coming in on a rising tide, half in, and Argent calculated that high tide would take the sea about two foot up its height. Two buildings stood prominent; one above the quay and this Argent decided must be the mill, not just for the fact of its prominence but also that a mill leat discharged its water tumbling down beside the quay's stonework. The second, more in silhouette in the half light, was set far back. However, even at the distance its size could be easily judged, appearing more like a castle, with solid walls and a dark, squat, and somehow sinister, shape emerging from the top of the outline. Most that could turn their eyes upon it from examining the abject poverty of the village, took this to be the tower of the keep, but this was not yet clear in the half-revealed dawn. However, what most depressed the spirits of those approaching was, indeed, the sight of the village itself, that being the dwellings, if that word could also be stretched to describe each as such. Each looked like a pile of earth slumped on the hillside, topped by filthy thatch reaching almost to the ground, dark, probably from moss. Small windows and a low door showed themselves apologetically beneath the unkempt, overhanging straw. The most impressive points about the village were the four solid and well maintained fishing smacks drawn up on the beach.

Few people were showing themselves and they did no more than look curiously, and briefly, at the approaching flotilla, one of the boats full of redcoats. All continued with their daybreak chores and Argent thought to himself, "Either they're playing a canny game, or they've nothing to fear, because nothing's happened to be fearful of." The boats crunched onto the shingle and the Marines poured ashore, led by Ramsey. Argent heard Ramsey shout his orders.

"Hold them all indoors. Anyone who comes out for their morning business, get them soon back in. No-one leaves their house."

The Marines ran up the single street, followed by armed seamen, Sanders, Bentley, Ffynes and Berry were their Officers. Soon there were the sounds of arguments as the occupants were forced back through their own front doors, but soon this settled to little more than the odd swearword as the street was cleared. Argent walked up the street between his men, still with questions churning over in his head. "What now? How long before O'Dowd arrives? Do I search, and for what?" The sun rose above the mountain and the strong yellow light gave some minimal cheer. Argent called Berry to him.

"Get yourself taken back to the ship. Tell Mortimor I want some food coming across to here by eight bells. Go now."

"Aye, aye, Sir."

As Berry ran off, back to the jollyboat, Argent took a good look around. The dwellings were little more than hovels, but the mill was well built and well maintained, a sound slate roof and good timberwork. The castle was as imposing in the sunlight as it was in the gloom of the dawn, its outside walls more formidable than the crenellated mansion encircled within and the gate, now revealed, was of impressive, studded timber. Suddenly, the door in the side of the mill opened and out came a female figure, full skirt finishing just below her knees and matching the maroon of her hair. The skirt finished taut around a narrow waist and from there her figure expanded upwards in a white blouse that covered shoulders just short of masculine. She stopped outside the door, arms aggressively akimbo on her hips, spotted Argent and then strode forward. At that moment Argent knew that he would soon be in a fierce engagement. Should he walk forward and be the first to speak a greeting, or should he hang back and wait? He decided on the former, to appear uncaring and aloof would not serve. He walked forward to meet the striding figure, thinking of a greeting that may mollify even this evidently angry harridan, because it would need to. He remembered what he thought to be the cheeriest Irish greeting and spoke it.

"The very top of the morning to you."

"And the very bottom of it to you! What do you mean by holding these people in their homes? They need to come and earn a day's pay, and I need them for a day's work. What's all this about?"

She had halted less than a yard before him, assuming the same stance as she had adopted at the mill door, but this time aggressively leaning forward. Argent noticed immediately her bright green eyes, which he was certain were throwing sparks, but what was equally as striking was her deep auburn hair that tumbled down beyond her shoulders. Argent felt it best to fall back onto formality.

"I am Captain Reuben Argent, of His Majesty's Ship Ariadne. We're..."

She interrupted, loudly.

"And I'm Miss Sinaid Malley, of Killannen Mill. Now answer my question!"

Argent continued.

"We're here because 200 bolts of your linen have been found aboard a French smuggler, which we captured yesterday. We're here to investigate."

If anything, her temper grew.

"And what, in the name of all the Saints, am I supposed to know about that? I've 10 looms in there; we make 20 bolts in a week. A week! Ten weeks and that's what I've made. Sure, how am I supposed to keep a knowledge on where they go after they've been sold? Anyone who buys my linen could ship it on to the North Pole, for all I know, and I don't, because it's none of my business."

Argent had been fearful of this answer, because he had none to counter it, but he made the best reply he could.

"I understand what you say, but, from our point of view, the linen was made here, and so this must be the place where we make a start."

"Start what? Let me tell you that no smugglers have landed here nor taken off, and that's what you'll hear from everyone else, and, on top, you'll not find any evidence of any kind to prove French feet in this village because they've never been here!"

The last delivered at the top of her voice with her chin jutting further forward with every word. Argent stepped back, but held onto his own self-control.

"Then tell me, please, where your linen does go?"

The constructive line of questioning seemed to calm her, somewhat.

"At least half goes to himself, up there."

She jerked her thumb over her shoulder at the castle.

"For what he buys, I don't get charged to use his damn road. He charges enough to bring in the flax. Where he sells it on to, I can't be certain. I think a lot goes to a merchant called Vanyard in Kilarney."

"Right, thank you for that, and who is he, up there?"

"Mr. James Fallows. Landlord and owner of everything you can see, bar those boats and my mill."

Argent saw that she was calmer.

"I will go and talk to him. Now, your workers. I will allow them over to your mill, if you go around these cottages and name, from those inside, those whom you wish to work today, and then allow my Marines to stand guard on your mill, both inside and out, to oversee affairs, as it were."

She looked up at him quizzically, turning her right shoulder slightly away and inclining her head slightly towards that shoulder, but a frown still furrowed the light brown skin of her forehead. Clearly, she resented needing his sayso and goodwill, but eventually she saw that he was offering a good compromise.

"Very well. How many Marines?"

"I will leave that to my Captain of Marines, Captain Ramsey there. With your permission, I'll call him over, and you can begin."

Her expression turned sullen, but she nodded. Argent turned to find Ramsey.

"Captain Ramsey, your attendance here, please."

Ramsey took his sword in his left hand and jogged over, his face widening with delight the more he could see of Sinaid Malley. He arrived, slightly breathless.

"Good morning, madam. A pleasure to meet you. Captain Arnold Ramsey, Royal Marines, at you service."

However, the reply he received was a look of stone. Argent continued the dialogue.

"This is Miss Sinaid Malley. She owns the mill, there. I've agreed that she can call out the workers she needs from the cottages, and that we will put sentries in place to watch over all that happens. Can I leave that with you?"

Ramsey saluted Argent, who then saluted Sinaid Malley, who maintained the same stoney look. Ramsey and Sinaid Malley began their walk to the nearest cottage and Argent started up the hill, gathering two Marines as he went. After a steady, but not too arduous climb, they reached the gate. As they approached, its impression of medieval solidity grew. It was clearly designed for defence and, examining its imposing timbers, Argent felt it futile to knock with his hand; instead he required one of the marines to strike it with the butt of his musket. The sound echoed back into what must be a gatehouse behind and soon the left door swung open, but only enough for an unshaven, early middle-aged, unkempt head to peer around, but under the homespun jacket his shoulders appeared broad and substantial. His mouth had a downward slant, from a curved scar, as though he had been kicked by a horse.

"Good morning. I assume that I am at the residence of Mr. James Fallows?"

The head nodded.

"Then please tell him that Captain Argent of HMS Ariadne would like a moment of his time."

"He'll not see you before breakfast!"

This spoken through a wide mouth, full of suspect teeth.

"I'm afraid that if Mr. Fallows does take that attitude, then you need to tell him, that I am here on the King's business. It won't wait, and if I need to come in, I'll come in with Marines at my back."

Suddenly an English voice was heard from behind the door.

"It's all right, Michael, go about your business. Ready a horse, I'll need one soon."

The head of Michael disappeared to be replaced by the full torso of a medium-height, slightly overweight, man; evidently a gentleman or dressing himself to be such. He was wearing a man's clothing that was more the fashion of 40 years previous, a frilled shirt, a long waistcoat, knee breeches, buckled shoes and, most old mode of all, a threequarter wig. But what was evident was the quality; silk, velvet and brocaid were much in evidence. His face was full and showed easy living. It was he that spoke first.

"I saw you marching up, Captain, from my window. I thought you would appreciate being met at the gate. Now, you have business with me."

It was spoken as a statement of fact and Argent responded.

"Yes, Mr. Fallows. A cargo of 200 bolts of linen, definitely made here, has been found aboard a French smuggler. 200 bolts. I'm told that you take the majority of the production from the mill there. Can you shed any light on how such a quantity can be assembled?"

Fallows face remained expressionless.

"No. All the linen I buy goes on to various merchants. Vanyard in Kinsale takes the most but not the majority. There are five or six other merchants that I sell to. Where it goes after them, I cannot say."

"No, Mr. Fallows, that's understood, but if you could furnish me with a list of all the merchants you sell to, that would be appreciated. If I could send one of my Officers to collect the list sometime this afternoon, would that be convenient?"

Fallows folded his arms and thought, his face registering the annoyance he felt at this prying into his concerns. However, the alternative was the unwelcome military doing their own prying. The latter came uppermost.

"I'll do that for you, Captain, with pleasure."

He stepped back to take hold of the door edge.

"Now, unless there was anything else?"

"Yes, I'm afraid there is. My orders are to search the village, which does, I'm afraid, include your residence here."

Fallows' attitude changed utterly.

"I'll have none of you in here. You away, and be damned!"

Argent set himself squarely on his feet.

"I can understand your concern, Sir, but it must be done. We will be searching everywhere to find, or not, evidence of dealings with the French. I have the force of the King's business behind me, and I'm sure you do not want me to use my Marines to achieve entry and then search. If it eases your concerns, I will allocate for your premises, only my Officers."

Fallows retained a look of thunder, his eyebrows knitting together over narrowing eyes in a reddening face. Argent stood and waited, then Fallows spoke, his jaw almost clenched.

"Only your Officers?"

"Yes, you have my word. They will arrive directly and you may give the list to one of them, if you choose."

Fallows gave a curt nod, face remaining stormy. Argent made his reply.

"Thank you and good-day."

The door thumped together without another word. Argent led the Marines back down the hill, satisfied, at least with that outcome. He went straight to Ramsey.

"Is all well, Arnold?"

"Yes, Sir, but I say, what a "looker". No wonder they speak of the 'Emerald Isle' if they all have eyes like that."

Argent smiled.

"You'll get no argument from me. Right, take yourself, please, Bentley and Ffynes, up to the mansion there. Make a search. He's expecting you, but is wholly displeased, as you can imagine, nevertheless take a look, top to bottom. You can take all day if needs be, but you're looking for anything that can prove recent dealings with the French. Whatever; anything; from a bottle of wine with no dust yet settled, to a gold Napoleon."

Argent looked around, but all was in order.

"These poor Devils have nothing to do with this, Arnold. It's all they can do to keep body and soul together, never mind assembling a 200 bolt cargo of highest quality linen. If it's anyone here, it's our Lady Malley up there, or the Lord of the Manor, further up there. Whatever, we'll hold all here and search. As soon as the Militia arrive, it's not our problem."

"Right, I'll take myself off, Sir."

Ramsey strode off up the street, gathering Bentley and Ffynes to him. Argent looked over to Ariadne. Fentiman had eased the ship in further on minimum sail and she was now no more than 100 yards off the beach. Argent looked and saw, at the same time, the four fishing boats being readied on the shoreline. He called over to Whiting.

"Whiting. Go over to those fishermen. Tell them we'll buy whatever they catch. Top price."

On the run, Whiting delivered his "Aye, aye, Sir, and knuckled his forehead. Argent looked for Sanders, saw him and called him over.

"Jonathan. Captain Ramsey has placed the men as sentries on the cottages, with his Marines occupied at the mill. Organise two men at each cottage to go in and search. Emphasise strongly, strongly mind, that nothing is to be damaged. They are looking for anything to prove recent contact with the French. But, tell them to take very great care."

"Aye, aye, Sir."

A salute, then a run to the first cottage. Whiting then returned from the fishing boats.

"I did my best, Sir, most only speak Gaelic, but one. He had some English, Sir, and I think I got through."

"Very good, Whiting. Thank you for your efforts. Now, I do believe that you will soon be employed. Re-join your party."

This time respects were formally made and Whiting walked off to the cottage that was guarded by the men of the Foretop. Sanders waited for Whiting to arrive.

"Whiting, and you, Jones. The Captain wants a search to be made, but nothing to be damaged. No damage. None. Can I leave that to you both?"

Whiting knuckled his forehead and spoke his response whilst walking to the door. Jones followed and Whiting knocked on the door. He had seen the son leave for the mill and assumed the man of the house was upon the boats just leaving. As it opened he stepped slightly inside, but the woman, plainly terrified, took herself to the back wall, her children running to her. Whiting looked at them and smiled, whilst moving his hands up and down in the best gesture of placation he could think of. It had no effect, but at least they were out of the way. Whiting looked back at Jones.

"Search! What's to bloody search?"

His point was obvious. What little there was, was all on shelves or wooden pegs hammered into the cob wall and nothing more was there beyond shawls, shifts and shirts. The shelves contained mostly emptiness, bar a stack of earthenware crocks and some crumpled and forlorn packets of such as flour. There was no table, just a bench and some stools by the grate, where a black pot hung on a chain over the peat fire, now smoking on the earthen hearth. Whiting noticed that the floor was also bare earth, and when he looked up, he saw but empty rafters and dirty thatch between them. There was one opening in the wall to the left.

"Take a look in there, Abe."

Abel Jones went over to do no more than stand in the opening after drawing back the hanging cloth, whilst he looked through into the room.

"Just sacks of straw, Gab, and a few old rags as bedclothes."

Whiting nodded.

"Look under, but make sure they goes back as found."

Jones disappeared and Whiting turned to the still cowering Mother and children. He crouched down to the level of the nearest child and smiled and nodded, but the response was an even more desperate clinging to her Mother's leg. Whiting rose up as Jones reappeared.

"I've seen enough, Abe. Check round the back, and then we're done."

He looked at the wife and children, still cowering, but perhaps less terrified. All he could do was smile, nod some more and then he allowed Jones to leave before him, before pulling the door to. As Jones took himself around the back, Whiting took his seat on the low wall, to lower his shoulders and shake his head.

Sanders, having dispensed his orders, returned to Argent.

"All done, Jonathan? And no damage?"

"Those were my orders, Sir."

"Very good. Now, more urgently, I ordered some food brought over. Any sign of it? I sent Berry, as a gesture of faith."

Sanders turned towards the ship.

"I think your faith may be justified, Sir. Something seems to be casting off now, with not too long a journey."

Argent looked over himself to confirm what Sanders had seen.

"Good. I'm going to send you around again. One man from each cottage to go to the shoreline and draw rations."

Sanders saluted and went first to Whiting's cottage. Argent saw Fenwick leave and stride off for the beach, after being spoken to by Lieutenant Sanders, so, with that in train, he took four steps up the street and stopped, none too happy. They now had to search the mill.

Whiting was sat with Jones, King, and Beddows, all sat on the wall before the cottage. He gave his firm opinion.

"Well, this must be the most miserable damn place that I been in for many a long year. They don't live in much more than a hole in the ground with a bit of straw spread over. In the winter this must be the most glum and dismal muck pot as can be imagined."

All nodded, but Jones more than most.

"So this is Ireland. I've seen more cheer in a graveyard. Childers all thin and weedy, an' all of 'em, adults too, I bet, wears all day what they wakes up in, one bit of clothing each, and that's that.

Fenwick had arrived with the food, a mess canister suspended from each hand, a bag of ship's biscuit tucked under his arm.

"'Tain't very hot, but what's worse, there's nothin' to eat it with, nor from. That's been forgot."

He set down the canisters and the five sat and looked in at the contents. It was King who spoke first.

"Well, do you think we could borrow some, from them inside, like?"

Whiting answered.

"You can try, but good bloody luck to you. The ones I spoke to spoke no English. Just heathen Gaelic."

King rose, went to the door and knocked, needing to almost bend double under the thatch. The door opened and the again terrified woman stood to greet him, half behind the door. The light showed her shapeless in a cotton shift, light blue and stained, beneath which thin legs extended down to crude leather slippers. Her face was blotched and thin, with unkempt hair, but she responded faintly to King's wide grin. When he asked if they had any plates, the reply was a blank look. There was then enacted, by him, a farcical pantomime that had his mates in stitches of laughter, which ended with the giant King sat on the ground going through the motions of eating and making round circles with his hands to show where the plate would have been. Three children had come to watch, to soon laugh as loud as anyone. Then one uttered something and disappeared back into the hovel. She reappeared with five crude earthenware platters and five spoons, of various designs and age. King's messmates had been speechless at his antics, but with his success, their thinking changed.

"You should be on the stage, Mose."

"That's right. Sweepin' it."

However, the plates were spread amongst them, along with the spoons, and the food began to be shared out. With the canisters almost emptied they looked to start, but it was then that they found they had an audience; five children had emerged from the door to stand and watch. Whiting stopped his spoon midway to his mouth as soon as he saw the look on their faces. He gave a deep sigh that emptied his lungs, then held out the spoon to the nearest child, the one he guessed to be the second eldest. She ran forward and allowed Whiting to feed her. He repeated the feeding, then he simply handed over the plate and the spoon, which action was soon copied by his fellow topmen. With all five children busy eating the beef, peas, and potatoes, he looked across at his messmates, all sat resignedly, with their elbows on their knees.

"Looks like we'n makin' do with the biscuit."

However, by this time, their mother was at the door and Whiting was the first to notice.

"Abe. What's left in they pots?"

Jones leaned forward to form an answer.

"Some, but not much."

"Tip all into one and give it to Mother there. Throw in a couple of biscuits."

Jones obeyed and offered the food to the mother. She took it with both hands and a grateful smile, but then disappeared back into the cottage. However, within seconds she was back returning the empty canister. Whiting realized immediately what she had done.

"God Damn, she's chucked it into the family pot! Savin' it for tea. God Damn, what a bloody place!"

However, he watched in fatherly manner the five chewing faces lined up before them. When the food was gone, then the plates were carefully licked, then the spoons, then their fingers. He placed his huge and distorted hands over his face and uttered something between a cry and a shout.

"Lads, this is breakin' my heart. We got new prizemoney due. What say we uses some of it to buy supplies off the ship, which we got plenty of, more'n we needs now that we'n nearly half through our stint?"

The rest looked at him puzzled, but it was Beddows who spoke.

"What, you mean buy some barrels of salt pork and suchlike off the Purser and give it to these here?"

"That's exactly what I means. We can go and talk to the other lads around and see what they says. If they agrees then we'll talk to the lads back aboard and see what it can amount to."

"You needs to see the Captain, first."

"Not yet, only after we've seen the others, here on shore. That's first, so stir your stumps."

In response to the orders of their Captain of the Foretop, they took themselves off to the men guarding the other cottages. The response was wholly positive, like themselves and for the same reason, few had eaten of the food brought ashore. Whiting went to talk to Captain Argent, while most looked on. They saw their Captain stood stockstill, saying nothing, then nodding his head, then speaking. Whiting returned to his fellow conspirators.

"The Captain says yes. He says allow for three shillings per man. I'm to take that back aboard and talk to Maybank, to see if there's any charity somewer' in there. I'm to take the jollyboat, so Sam, Moses, I needs you on the oars."

Soon both were sculling off to the ship, but Argent gave these new developments little thought, he had to deal with the mill. He took himself up to the door and entered, to be immediately saluted by the first sentry. He looked around and saw Sinaid Malley examining some linen yarn. From all round in the mill came the fierce clatter of looms working full out, backed by the rumble of the waterwheel. He eased his way around some carts full of bobbins and went and stood in front of her, because to try to speak to call her attention was useless. The frown of earlier immediately returned, but Argent pointed to the door. Outside she placed herself almost as aggressively as before and said nothing, but waited for Argent.

"Miss Malley. There are two things I have to say. Firstly, that I have to search your mill. Secondly, my men have made a collection and with it they are going to buy some food supplies from the ship, to give out to the people here. Each man is contributing three shillings, each Officer six. It'll come from our prizemoney from the French smuggler. When it comes ashore, what's the best way to distribute it, do you think?"

Sinaid Malley's stance softened slightly, but her face grew suspicious, but the idea of a search of her mill didn't seem to concern her.

"You're going to give the village some food?"

Argent spoke as if to a child that had finally understood.

"Yes, that is right, we are, well, my men are, mostly. But how should we give it out, to each family?"

Her face changed and she almost smiled.

"What form will it take? What kind of food?"

"Well, salt pork and salt beef in barrels, sacks of dried peas, potatoes, flour, biscuit, apples and such, I would guess."

Everything changed about her, like a young girl in her first dress of fashion. Her pose matched her new mood and above that, an incandescent smile, that reached up into her deep green eyes. The change hit Argent like a hammer and he had to re-gather his dismembered thoughts.

"Well, Captain, Reuben, if you land it on the shoreline, the people will collect it from there."

"Yes, er, Sinaid. But I'm thinking that some should stay in the barrels. It'll keep better then, for future use."

Her knowing half smile was disarming, coquettish and alarming, under the befuddling green eyes.

"That's a grand idea. Now, you organize your bit of it, and I'll do mine."

"And the search?"

"Ah, see Patrick. He'll open anywhere you've a mind to peer into."

With that she ran off to enter the nearest cottage. It wasn't long before Argent heard shouts and screeches coming through the glassless windows. He found a Corporal of Marines.

"Collins. Get three men, no just two, and search the mill. No damage, am I clear? No damage. Someone called Patrick will conduct you around. A thorough search, but no damage."

Collins gave a sharp salute and jogged off to the mill.

The westering of the sun saw the supplies landed from the laden longboat, so full that there was only room for half the usual oarsmen. Many hands, at least half of them Irish, carried the barrels, boxes and sacks up to the shoreline, where they were transferred into handcarts and wheelbarrows. Some barrels went to the mill, Argent assumed for storage and, by the time all was packed away, the day was dying, long shadows from the mountains extending over to claim the village for the coming night. More cooked food came across from Mortimor's galley and the men ashore this time ate the food undisturbed, for, as they were certain, a fine feast was happening indoors, under the thatch.

However, at the end of the meal, things began to happen. The villagers, in their best clothes, such as they were, began to assemble on the large paved square by the mill. Soon came the strains of a ceiledh band, going full tilt, and the accompanying sounds of reels and jigs. Argent and his men stood and watched, but from a distance, until Sinaid Malley came across to him.

"Won't you and your men come up and join us, Captain?"

No more Reuben, he thought, the joy of that moment now gone with the daylight.

"My men would like that very much, I'm sure, Miss Malley. May I bring some more of my crew ashore?"

"Why sure, of course! The more there is, the better it becomes."

With that she jigged back to the dancing, skipping in time to the music.

This claimed his gaze for some while, then Argent called over to Sanders, whilst examining his watch.

"It'll be the Starboard Watch off duty. Get them ashore, and leave an anchor watch from the Larboard, and don't forget Elliot, and there's someone who has a squeezebox, Smart, I believe. Bring him too, and as many Marines as can be spared from the Watch."

Within an hour the Starboard Watch and most of the Larboard, were ashore and occupying the high bank above the square, shouting, cheering, and clapping to encourage all the dancing below. Elliott and Smart had joined the band. An ancient was stood on a barrel conducting the dancing and, although his Gaelic was unintelligible, many sailors went down and joined in. Eight girls then held the audience with a performance of Irish line dancing and so, not to be outdone, the dancing team of the crew took their place to perform a series of jigs and hornpipes, with raucous and incessant encouragement from their own shipmates. Little could be heard of the music above the cheering and clapping. Argent was stood just off and just out, he felt that this was an affair for the men, but, suddenly a waft of perfumed soap came to him and, to his great disquiet he found himself stood besides Sinaid Malley. For him, words wouldn't come, but they did for her. She had a plan.

"Would you like to take a walk along the quayside, Captain?"

A jumble of awkward thoughts shaped his equally awkward reply.

"Er, yes, but only if you think it will be right, er, proper? Isn't "walking out" of great significance here, in Ireland. Isn't it something very formal, I mean, I don't want to do anything that will affect your reputation, here."

She looked at him shocked.

"Well now, what an English stuffshirt you turn out to be! Sure, it's just a walk! And we aren't that backward, nor held down, that two people can't take a walk together."

She waited for a reply. None came.

"It's this way."

She took his arm, not the formal placing of a hand, but she looped her arm right through his and held the wrist of her arm with her other. She guided and pulled him to the quayside until the sound of the dancing was muted around the corner and they could hear the waves of the full tide. She spoke first.

"I'm giving my full thanks for the gift of the food."

Argent was still groping for something to say.

"Well, I can't accept it. It was the idea of my men. They thought of it and they have paid for most of it."

"But you had to say yes or no. Right?"

"Well, that is true."

"There. So, you can accept my thanks and say no more."

She paused and looked out to sea.

'What's you ship called?"

"Ariadne."

"That's a nice name. Where's it come from?"

"It comes from Greek legend, you know Greek mythology."

"I'll stick with the word legend. So, what's the story?"

Argent laughed.

"Well, to cut a long one short, in the Greek legend, there was this character called Theseus who had to go on a voyage to get this golden fleece, from the King of Crete. That's an island, but the King would only give Theseus the fleece if he got out of a labyrinth, sort of maze, guarded by a Minotaur. Half man, half bull. Ariadne was the King's daughter and offered her help only after Theseus promised to marry her and take her back to Athens. She tied a thread to him so's he could find his way back. He did kill the Minotaur, by the way. But, once off Crete, Theseus deserted her."

"Typical sailor!"

"Ah, but it didn't end so bad. Some say she was spotted by a God, Dionysus, and he fell in love with her, married her, and Zeus, the chief God, made her a God, and she's up there in the stars, or at least her crown from her wedding. We call it the Corona Borealis, or the Northern Crown."

"Can you see it?"

Argent looked North

"Ahmmmm, yes. It comes up in May, yes there it is, I'll try to point."

He pointed at the group of stars, checked the alignment of his finger and then moved away, hoping his hand held still.

"Follow my finger, it's a sort of chain, making a horseshoe that's tilted left."

She came close, in front of him and he smelt her again. She stooped slightly to look along his finger.

"I can't make out anything like that. Are you sure?"

Argent put his head beside hers to look along his finger.

"Well, I am off a bit. Look right a bit, there's a red one, that's the main one. Then there's two up to the right. Then two immediately left."

Silence.

"Then two up to the left."

She held his forearm with both hands and looked along his finger again.

"I think I can, yes , I can. So, that's Ariadne, at least her crown."

"Yes. And that's her out there as well, on the water, but her lights make an upside down horseshoe."

Sinaid turned to look at the lights, defining the now vague silhouette, but her shoulder still touched his chest.

"And you won't desert her?"

"Never!"

"Do you like your ship, Captain?"

"Yes, of course. She's fast; very fast, handy on any wind, stiff, and surrenders hardly any leeway. And dry."

"I'll assume all that is good, though I barely understood half of it."

Argent laughed.

"She's Spanish built. We captured her."

"So, she's a Spanish ship, with a Greek name. Why isn't she called Maria or somesuch?"

Argent laughed again.

"Girls, gods, goddesses, heroes and flowers are the favourites of the Royal Navy. English girls names."

There was a pause and she shifted to face him.

"You've good men aboard your ship."

"Yes. I think as much of my crew as I do of my ship. I've had to rely on them totally three times now, and on none did they let me down. But don't tell them!"

It was her turn to laugh, then silence fell, but he knew she was looking up at him.

"You've been very good, Captain, you and your crew. I thought you must be different when you allowed my people out to come to work, and now your gift of food confirms it, and the way your men are joining in the dancing, and all."

Argent could only sidestep the sentimentality in her words, and voice.

"Oh, they're not backward with joining in with any fun, nor starting it, of that you can be certain."

Argent was glad of the excuse to laugh, the emotion was building up. He changed the subject.

"So, this is your mill. It and fishing support the village, I would guess?"

"Support is too strong a word. We make the best linen in the South, as I see it, but it has to be the best, only then can I sell all I make, but selling's one thing, profit's another."

"It makes little money?"

"It would, but himself up there, has his foot on my neck. He charges a toll to use his road. It's only the quality that gets the stuff sold and out. With his charge, our price for a decent profit would be way high, so I have to lower it right down to make any kind of market. There's little left as profit."

Argent, having been raised on a farm, knew something of business and understood what she was saying. He looked out over the water from the quay. He could see that beyond the wall the sea came quite close.

"But a small quay out there, would make it possible to bring in and out by sea. A small coaster could nudge in there."

"Yes, Captain. A very good idea, but where's the money coming from? You need skilled masons and good stone to build a quay. And a boat with a proper hold that would protect the cargo, sea water ruins flax."

She paused to allow Argent to answer, but none came, so she changed the subject.

"I'll say you're better than the other representatives of King George we've had around here."

"Such as?"

"O'Dowd and his Major, Kibley. God rot him."

"Well, on that subject, I'm afraid that the Militia are arriving tomorrow. I expected him today. They must now be on their way here, at least."

She took his arm again and turned him around.

"I should have guessed, with all this talk of smugglers. And it being my linen. Right, the music's stopped. All are away to bed. Will you still be here in the morning?"

She walked forward and, with her arm through his, he kept pace with her.

"Yes. My orders were to land and wait for the Militia. I have information for them which I gained from Mr. Fallows, though I doubt it'll be much use, but it shows I've tried."

"What information?"

"Who he sells your linen to. Merchants inland."

"Oh, I could have told you who they are. I sell to the same, but no matter."

They were at the door of the mill. At the square the gathering had greatly thinned. He turned to face her.

"Well, good night, Sinaid. It's been a grand evening, for me and my men. We'll still be here in the morning, and I'll come and say good bye before we go."

She said nothing but he could see her looking up at him in the light of the lanterns remaining from the ceiledh, but when she did speak, she astonished him.

"You can kiss me, if you like."

He was so astonished that he froze rigid, so she took the initiative and kissed him, looping both arms around his neck. Before he knew it, his arms were around her waist, his mind turning cartwheels, then she broke away.

"There. Now. Good night to you."

With that she turned and opened the door, giving him a little smile before she closed it behind her. Argent went down to the shoreline and had himself rowed out to his ship, following his rowdy crew, but once in his great cabin and in his bed, he didn't sleep much.

The next day saw what he had been expecting, but dreading, even against hope. For that reason he had had himself awoken early to return ashore, but as his barge left the ship's side, he saw that he was late, perhaps too late. A company of Militia were already at the top of the village and spreading out to enter the cottages. Argent's own Marines and seamen were around their fires on the shoreline, some had noticed the commotion and were standing up. Argent turned his head and spoke to Whiting, at the tiller.

"Whiting, I want to be ashore inside a minute. You can see for yourself what's afoot, up at the top."

Whiting looked up and through the village. He needed no explanation.

"Up the rate, you bastards, beg pardon, Sir. We needs the shore, sooner than now."

Argent felt the kick in his back as the four bent their oars in the water. Soon the barge crunched deep into the gravel and Jones leapt out to hold it steady. Argent immediately climbed the beach, the loose shingle frustrating his progress. Ramsey saw him coming and saluted.

"Ramsey, the Militia are here, and I don't like the look of it. Put your men in line and follow me."

Ramsey ordered a skirmish line and the Marines formed it in seconds, with the seamen following close behind. They passed the mill, it's din proclaiming full production, but Argent only had eyes for what was happening at the top of the village. From there came screams, shouts and cries of anguish and misery. The Militia were running to the cottages and entering; then, judging by the screams, what was happening inside was none too gentle. At the centre an Officer sat a black horse, waving his men to various points with his riding crop. Argent hurried upward and his jaw clenched together, as a table and chair were thrown out of a door and smashed by a musket butt. Another Militiaman was dragging a woman outside by her hair, his hand grasping a handful at the back of her head, her children screaming behind her. She was thrown to the road, stamped into the dirt, spat on, then shouted at.

"Catholic scum. Feneian whore!"

Argent judged about 40 Militia. He had 24 Marines and about twice that from his crew. However, many of the latter were unarmed, but they could see as well as anyone what was happening and they crowded up behind the Marines. Argent broke into a run, and eventually, 100 yards off, the Officer noticed a Navy Captain, other Navy Officers, Marines and seamen hurrying in his direction. He stopped from directing his men to the site of their next predation and sat his horse, staring ahead, awaiting the new arrivals. He spoke first, after a perfunctory but cheery salute, with his riding crop rather than his hand.

"Good morning. Major Kibley, 2nd Cork Militia."

However, his expression soon changed when he saw the evident rage on Argent's face, even more so when Argent began to shout.

"This stops. Now! Either you stop it, or I'll order my men to. But it stops, now."

Major Kibley's face showed both shock and surprise in equal measure. He rose in his stirrups and shouted, both left and right.

"Form up, on me. Four ranks, on the road."

Some heard and obeyed, some were simply too carried away by their eagerness, and some were in the cottages therefore did not hear. Argent turned to his Marine Captain.

"Ramsey."

Ramsey needed to further bidding.

"First section to your right. Second to your left."

No further orders were necessary; the Marines pitched straight in. The only difference between their uniforms and those of the Militia, was the black midshipman's hat and blue facings that the Marines wore, whilst the Militia had a shako with a face plate and lime green facings on their tunics. Confusion could have resulted, but the Marines ran forward and quickly got amongst the Militia. These suddenly found themselves confronted by angry strangers, wearing a red jacket, but none too gentle with their musket butts, nor in any way averse to use them, quarterstafflike, to emphasise what they wanted. One Militiaman ran out of a house, carrying a chest, prior to smashing it, to find himself tripped up and kicked back down to the ground by a glowering Marine Sergeant. The Militiaman scrambled up and soon, now thoroughly cowed, the last of the Militia formed up with their comrades, all looking puzzled and not a little intimidated.

Kibley had watched his men being roughly handled, rounded up and shoved out of the cottage gardens. He turned to Argent, his face now showing both shock and anger, but he recognised now that he was dealing with a full Navy Captain.

"But Sir. My orders were to search the village."

Argent looked up, his own anger still in full spate.

"Get down off that horse, come to me and report!"

Kibley did as obeyed and stood before Argent at attention.

"Report."

"I have been sent here to search this village, Sir. My orders come from Colonel O'Dowd."

"And did your orders include that you should commit wanton destruction on these people?"

"Well, no Sir, not specifically, but it's what we do. Any instance of lawbreaking, such as this smuggling, well, we teach them the consequences, Sir, as a form of punishment."

"Punishment?"

"Yes Sir. Punishment."

"Under the law, as I understand it, citizens of King George are punished after having been found guilty of some crime. You would agree?"

Kibley's face fell, as did the set of his shoulders. He could see where the argument was going.

"I'll have to report this, Sir. That I was stopped from carrying out my orders."

"Your orders were to make a search. Well, I can save you the trouble. We've already made one, and found nothing, nothing, including the residence of Mr. Fallows, which was searched by my Officers. What I have discovered is where the linen goes after it leaves here. Here's a list."

He pulled out the paper, with Fallows handwriting and signature and presented it to Kibley. He took it, studied it briefly, then folded it and put it into the pocket of his jacket.

"Regarding the search, Sir, I would like to point out that you do not have our experience. Of searching, Sir."

"No, Major Kibley. By God, no! Me and my men have no experience of such as we've just seen. Now, I suggest that you take your men away, the sooner, then, that you can start your report on your return."

Kibley had recovered some of his composure, which stemmed from years of unchallenged superiority over all around him.

"I'll have to put all this in my report, Sir."

Argent nodded, but at this moment Captain Ramsey stepped forward. His anger had matched Argent's and it had reduced in no measure.

"My name's Ramsey, Captain of the Royal Marines. Then you'd better put this in your report, Major, because it'll be in mine, if called upon. What I saw here was mutiny. Mutiny. Men out of control and beyond the influence of their Officers."

Shock reappeared on Kibley's face.

"Mutiny? How so?"

"The moment your men entered this village, they embarked upon pillage and destruction. And robbery. Far exceeding their orders, and yours. That's mutiny, and men are hanged for it. Hanged for robbery, too."

Kibley's men, overhearing every word, shuffled and murmured their concern, which was growing with the slow encroachment of sailors up along either side, their faces seen behind the Marines, each with intent of dire retribution written large and clear. The sobs of women and children could still be heard and were full enough to maintain the seamen's anger. Argent now saw the time to make an end.

"I would sincerely suggest that you now about turn and march away. You have my information, and I'm telling you that your mission is accomplished."

Kibley looked once more at Argent, then he turned and mounted his horse. With no word to anyone, he mounted, turned his horse, then rode back up the road. Ramsey looked at the Militia Sergeant and did no more that incline his head in the same direction as Kibley was taking. The Sergeant shouted his orders and the Militia marched off, at Light Infantry pace, although it wasn't ordered, for some reason it happened naturally. Argent watched them go, as did his men. He turned to find Bentley.

"Lieutenant Bentley. Get back to the ship, please, and request the attendance of Surgeon Smallpiece, and Mr. Baines and his mates."

He looked at the bloodied heads and the smashed furniture, before looking down to move a small, jagged piece with his foot

"I think that there is work here for them both. Ask if Mr. Baines has any spare timber. I think it can be put to good use. And, Mr. Bentley."

"Sir?"

"Request Mr. Fentiman to ready the ship for sailing at eight bells of the afternoon watch."

Argent had one more order.

"Jones and Beddows. Get atop that mountain and watch them all the way, watch that they keep going."

* * *

Argent watched Baines and his Mates climb into the longboat and noted that he was now the last remaining on shore. A gang of sailors, spread either side, pushed at the longboat until it floated and then they hauled themselves up into it. His own barge remained at the shoreline, washed by the gentle waves, so benign that Jones and King had little need to hold it steady.

"Wait here, Whiting. I'll not be long."

He began the climb up the shingle, back into the village, but when his footsteps inclined towards the mill, knowing looks were shared amongst his barge crew. Perhaps she saw him walking up, for she appeared at the door, the same door as she had appeared through in the early morning of the previous day. Argent began speaking as soon as the distance allowed it.

"I've come to say goodbye."

He continued to walk closer. She stood the same spot, using both hands to wring a fold in her dress, but saying nothing. Argent continued.

"My crew and myself can only apologise for what happened earlier. I wish there was more we could do."

She examined his face before she spoke."

"You did all you could and more. You stopped it, and put right what you could. You'll be welcome here, so you will, you and your men."

Back at the barge, the crew, all experienced men with women and the ways of the world, saw Argent nod and saw Sinaid Malley continue to wring the fold of her dress and gaze up at him. Whiting sighed with exasperation.

"Bloody kiss her, fer Christ's sake."

Then more exasperation as he saw her shake her hand.

"Our Captain. He can capture a French 42 with no more than a strained gut in the afterguard, but when it comes to women!"

Moses King finished it for him.

"All aback, topmasts over the side!"

Argent was walking back, face both sad and serious. Whiting stood up above the shingle.

"Well, I be goin' to give her a wave. Do that, at least."

Which he did, and her face was lit by a smile as she waved back. Argent saw what Whiting was doing and, finally, the same thought, in some measure, crossed his mind. He turned and formally saluted. Her arms fell to hang at her sides, but her smile was warm and genuine.

* * *

Killannen Bay had fallen below the horizon, all that remained as evidence of their past stay was the high mountain, now far astern, but still in view. Supervised by McArdle, Midshipman Ffynes had the deck, and was now setting a course, pushed on by a good West wind, for 48:8. Argent and Fentiman stood together, looking over the taffrail at the disappearing peak.
"Do you think the Militia will return, Sir?"
"I think not. Jones saw them well on their way, and they don't know if we are still there. They'll not be eager to return and find us still there."
"What about the smuggling?"
"Who, you mean."
"Well, yes."
"Either Miss Malley or Fallows. Who else could put such a cargo together? Those other poor Devils haven't got two coins to rub together. There's no profit going in their direction. If I point a finger at anyone, it's Miss Malley. She can't get her linen out without Fallows charging passage. If anyone has a motive to load linen into a smuggler and send it to France, she has."
"Smugglers don't buy at top price, Sir, they sell at a high price; they've taken the risk."
"Yes, there's that. I don't know; but it's no longer our worry and, for that reason, I'm glad to be out of it. A deep and dirty business. Anyway, one good thing, we had three volunteers from Killannen, they saw us as a way out of the place, I'm guessing, but three good recruits."
Below on the gundeck, one of the volunteers was being introduced to Samuel Morris by George Fraser.
"Right, Morris. Here's your replacement for Wilmot. We think he's called Tooley. We don't know it that's his first name or last, because he only speaks Gaelic."
Fraser looked at Morris and grinned.
"I'm sure you'll get along just fine!"
Morris did anything but grin as he looked at Fraser's disappearing back, then to Tooley, then to Dedman, then back to Tooley. Morris pointed to himself.
"Morris. Gun Captain. Gun Captain! Who are you?"
Tooley grinned and offered his hand. Morris sighed in exasperation and took it; Tooley was young and well muscled. He then pointed to each of the rest of the guncrew, giving their names. Dedman pushed him to his place and thrust the rammer in his hand. This morning's gun practice was going to be interesting.

The noon of the following day found Ariadne, sails hanging limp, riding above her own reflection, the gentlest of breezes ruffling the surface into the smallest of waves. The noon bells were rang, and the noon sight was being taken, McArdle customarily glowering at all assembled under his baleful gaze. His own board was held in his crablike hands behind his back, whilst his pupils read their instruments and Almanacs, then transferring their reading onto their boards. Finally, the last was displayed. McArdle made a growl in his throat, which could mean either pleasure or anything opposite. All the boards agreed with his own reading, or, at least close enough for accurate navigation, 47 40/ 8 10. Argent stood with arms folded, regarding the class and, smiling, remembered his own experiences with the Noon Sight. McArdle dismissed the class with one word.

"Awa!"

"Your tutelage is bearing fruit, Mr. McArdle."

"Aye, Sir, perhaps. But a more scurvy crew of festie beasties has yet to be assembled."

Argent gave a chuckle, as did all those within hearing and he looked up to the pennant at the masthead. It was showing more life than it had in the past hour and from the North West.

"Down helm. Steer East North East. Mr. Fentiman, jibs and all plain sail."

The helmsman repeated the order, as did Fentiman repeat his portion to the Bosun's Mates below. Ariadne swung her bows over to head for the furthest point West of the French coast, the island of Quessant, off the coast of Brittany. Fentiman came up to Argent, him standing on his privileged weather side.

"East North East seems a little far South, Sir?"

"It is, but I see no harm in taking a look at the French coast, then taking ourselves close hauled back to Falmouth. You never know what we may find."

The next day dawned warm and clear with bright sunshine. The wind had moved dead South West and strong, which would give easy sailing back to Falmouth. At five bells of the forenoon watch the cry came from the masthead.

"Land ho!"

Bentley had the deck.

"Where away?"

"Four points on the starboard bow."

Bentley turned to Ffynes, on Watch with him.

"Inform the Captain."

Ffynes disappeared down the companionway to the gundeck, but Bentley noticed McArdle striding forward, extending his own glass as he went. On the forecastle, McArdle climbed onto the starboard carronade and focused. He held the pose for two minutes before closing the glass and returning to the quarterdeck, his return coinciding with the arrival of his Captain. Argent looked at him, his expression posing the question.

"Yon's Quessant, Sir. Nay doot."

"Thank you, Mr. McArdle. Helmsman, steady as you go."

"Steady as we go, aye aye, Sir."

Ariadne's course would take her parallel to the North coast of Brittany. However, with Ariadne just off Quessant, the main French port of Brest was just around the corner, on the South side of the Brest Peninsula. Perhaps a potential prize would show itself, but Argent was resolved to avoid a major engagement, reinforcements were too likely in such a place busy with much French shipping, both maritime and martial.

"Mr. Bentley, double the lookouts."

As Bentley shouted down to the nearest Bosun's Mate, Argent walked to the forecastle himself and took up the same position as had McArdle, minutes earlier. Quessant was not unknown to himself, a flat, featureless island, burnt brown in the extending summer. It's main feature, he knew was a deep inlet to the South West, an excellent shape for a harbour, apart from the fact that it was on an isolated island and totally open to South West gales. He returned to his quarterdeck and awaited events, but the day wore on. He shortened sail and Ariadne idled past the French coast at four knots. The ship's bells were rung and the hands took their meals and the Watches changed. Quessant was falling away astern behind the Brittany headland when there came a cry from the mizzen masthead.

"Sail Ho."

Argent answered himself.

"Where away?"

"Three points off the starboard quarter, just off the island."

Argent gathered up his glass and climbed to the mizzen top, then continued beyond and above, to the mizzentopmast crosstrees. There he found the lookout, who pointed the direction.

"Just off the island, Sir. She's crossing the island, coming East."

Argent sat on the spar and wrapped his arms around the topmast. Thus secured he focused his glass. What grew in the lens was a craft outside his experience, a long hull with three stubby masts and no sail set, but with white water beside her hull, evidently a wake, only very white; it appeared, then went, in rhythm. He studied her for some time, but remained puzzled and finally, he handed the glass to the lookout, a seaman but a few years older than himself.

"What do you make of her, Cooper?"

Cooper took the glass and focused it for himself. He gave himself a minute with his Captain's personal telescope.

"She's a galley, Sir, flying the French flag."

He studied some more.

"Best word is a Xebec, Sir. Lateen sails on short masts, but with a bank of oars each side, 'though with this wind I can't figure why she's nothing set. But that's it, Sir, best call her a galley."

"Perhaps nothing is set because she's in the lee of the island. Happy to do it on oars alone?"

"You could be right, Sir."

Argent nodded.

"Well done, Cooper. Draw a measure of rum from Mortimor, eight bells of the forenoon."

The lookout's face lit up as he carefully returned the telescope to his Captain.

"Much obliged, Sir."

Argent took a last look. The Xebec had cleared Quessant and was on a heading direct for the coast. Back on deck Argent called on Fentiman and McArdle.

"It's a galley heading for the coast, three masts rigged for lateen and she's oars each side. Cooper called her a Xebec and she's flying the French flag. I'm for a try at her, what do you think?"

McArdle's face knitted into a deep frown.

"I'd advise strongly against it, Sir, we'd have tae tack back. She'll see us and use her oars t'get up wind, and if she gets into the bay in Quessant or anywhere that puts us on a lee shore, we're in a reek of a situation. If she's in Quessant bay, with this wind, we'll never get out if we go in t'get her. She can sit in there and laugh at us."

Argent turned to Fentiman, who shook his head.

"Mr. McArdle's right, Sir. I'm sure you know, Sir, but fighting oared galleys on their terms is the Devil. They can go where we can't, being so much more manoeuvrable. They can spin; go backwards, even, if needs be. She can put us on a lee shore that'll put the ship at grave risk, Sir."

They both saw Argent's jaw clench and his mouth stretch, but then he nodded, his face resigned.

"As you say. Perhaps not this time, but what are they, these French galleys?"

McArdle answered.

"Punishment ships, Sir. They put their convicts in them and they're handy enough for their close coastal trade; especially if you're under blockade, as they are, but they're nae use for deep ocean water, Sir. Too shallow draught."

Argent nodded.

"Right. My thanks. So, Mr. McArdle, lay a course for Falmouth, if you please."

He turned to the helmsman.

"Up helm. Steer due North."

"Up helm, Sir. Due North."

Whilst his crew made the changes and amidst his own topmen, Argent took himself back up to the Mizzen crosstrees and Cooper took himself out onto the yardarm to make room. Argent looked back at the Xebec, but soon she was lost as she finally closed with the coast. A last look at her, then he took some minutes to study all around for himself, but saw nothing. He was about to leave, when Cooper began to speak.

"Look back, Sir, where that Xebec was. There's smoke coming up from where she closed the coast."

Argent focused the glass. There was, indeed, a thick column of smoke rising from that point and moving his way on the wind. Judging by the amount and its distance, the fire beneath was extensive and about 10 minutes old.

* * *

Kalil Al'Ahbim was not pleased. He looked at the meagre group of prisoners coming back up the gangplanks either side of the bows of his galley. They were of the right type, but too few for the cost. He had come in on oars alone; sails would have been seen when they were still far out, giving warning, and then his galley, after its stealthy approach, had thrust itself into the beach of the small harbour town and his men had poured down those same gangplanks to assault the houses above. However, the small number of soldiers on guard, old, but veteran, and the fishermen on the quayside, had put up a very stout resistance and sold their lives dearly. Knowing there was no point in surrendering to slavers, they had made a fight of it to the last, which had allowed the civilians, amongst whom were those that Al'Ahbin most desired, to escape. This brave defence had cost him many slaves, he felt sure, and many of his own men now lay amongst the bodies of the defenders. Also, were many more wounded, now being helped back aboard. The casualties were not too great a concern, he had allowed for this and had set out with the galley much overmanned, but, nevertheless, it was a poor return for the cost. He saw some of his own, too badly wounded to recover, being despatched rather than be left behind alive or clutter his ship. This had added to his anger and he had ordered the town to be fired.

Chapter Five

La Pomone

On this occasion, Argent's timing caused him to follow the coffee and rolls into the Commodore's building, arriving just as the door shut close. His appearance then placed Marine Sergeant Venables in a state of quandary, his hands being full of his Commodore's comestibles, just as a Post Captain entered the door. However, this he dealt with by returning the whole collection to the delivery boy, with the instruction to take it down to the bottom office. He then sprung to the attention and saluted, although he was mortified that he was hatless, that being minus his burnished Marine shako. However, Argent returned the salute with parade ground formality, then waited as Venables regained his seat.

"Good morning, Sergeant."

"Good morning, Sir. Good voyage, Sir?"

"As far as a jaunt to Ireland can be, Sergeant. But I take it, from the delivery, that the Commodore is present? In his office?"

"Yes Sir. I'll just go down and announce you, Sir."

Argent lifted his hand, waving the old Marine back into his seat.

"No. No need. I'll go down and announce myself. If he cannot see me, no matter, I'll come back."

Argent started down the corridor. He had to acknowledge to himself that he did have a more than significant soft-spot for the old, fiercely partisan, Marine. He looked back over his shoulder.

"Good to see you looking well, Sergeant."

"Thank you, Sir. You too, Sir."

Argent wrapped on the door, to receive an instant response.

"Come in, Argent. I thought it was you, recognised your voice, you see. Take a seat."

Argent sat down, to look at Budgen, who took time to busy himself with his coffee and rolls, organising the various pots, plates and cups, finally a large napkin appeared in the same place as Argent's last visit, lodged under the Commodore's well-upholstered chin. Again, came the same offer.

"Coffee, Argent? And a roll?"

The reply was the same as previously and the result the same, Venables came "tout suite" with another cup. Having now fully organised his mid morning second breakfast, Budgen spoke.

"Rumour has it, Argent, that you've taken another prize. A rich smuggler, by all accounts."

"A smuggler, yes, rich, well, that remains to be seen, Sir. I don't know the price of linen and tobacco, but I'd hazard that it's worth far more over the water than it is here, but it's all in my log Sir; which I sent to you immediately we dropped anchor."

Budgen reached out a pudgy hand to his right, at the same time somehow dropping some adhering crumbs onto the desktop. He brought the log nearer, but did not open it.

"Yes, Captain. I read it with interest."

Budgen dropping his name and substituting Captain, put Argent on his guard.

"Seems you got yourself caught up with affairs on land, which extended your mission; considerably. In two directions, time and events."

"Yes Sir, but I'd like to point out that I acted under orders. The written order is in the log, Sir, from Commodore Harper, Commodore of the Port of Kinsale. He made it a formal order; I had no choice but to co-operate. But, er, excuse me, Sir, but Commodore Harper seemed to find your name familiar."

"He's right. We were Lieutenants together, briefly, on the Egmont. I didn't like him, but what's that? No matter."

He sat back in his chair, elbows on the armrests, fingertips posed together.

"But what does matter is you getting involved with their local Militia."

Argent waited for more, but none came.

"I felt it my duty, Sir. The Militia were destroying every home. I saw no justification, and, as superior officer at the scene, I stopped it."

Budgen's eyes became hard and stern and seemed to withdraw into his face.

"In future, Captain, keep out of it. Ireland's a God awful tangle at the best of times. Get off and away at the earliest, and that's more than advice, that's an order!"

"Sir."

"Now, new orders. This is from Grant. You are to get your ship to Plymouth, at the earliest."

Argent could see his ship, out in Carrick Roads, idling around her anchor, with some topmen working on the spars.

"You'll sail on the afternoon ebb. Any supplies you don't have by then, you get at Plymouth. Here are your orders, and your logbook."

Budgen pushed the book across, with the various communications, including the orders, protruding. Argent gathered the book under his left arm and saluted with his right. Budgen waved a finger in acknowledgement, but not pausing on its way to procure another roll. However, on his taking of his leave, the exchange between Argent and Venables was much more "proper Navy". Argent had a "soft spot" for that, as well.

Argent found his barge where he had left it, his crew in deep and frivolous conversation with a pair of local girls, who, for some reason, had stopped on their way back from the fish market. The bargecrew sprang to attention and the two girls turned all agog, as the seamen fiercely saluted and Argent replied. Both girls remained transfixed to watch as Argent took himself directly down the steps to the barge, Jones having preceded him to hold the barge steady and Argent placed himself inside and took his seat. In minutes the barge was skimming across the harbour, Beddows grinning at the diminishing figures of the girls, and soon their vessel was weaving its way between the small harbour traffic, which included some supply boats moving to and from Ariadne. Argent had dismissed from his mind the mild rebuke from Budgen, such was nothing new in his Navy experience, but what did preoccupy him was the instruction to return to Plymouth. The whole thing sounded urgent, but it was useless to speculate.

He climbed the side ladder to be piped aboard by Fraser and Ball, whilst various sacks and barrels were being swung aboard above him. He made to return straight to his cabin, but the worried countenance of Master Gunner Tucker made him stop. Joshua Tucker was standing besides a stack of six boxes on the starboard gangway, looking anxiously at these, then at his Captain. Argent stopped beside him.

"Mr. Tucker, you seem to be in something of a quandary?"

"Aye, Sir. It's these what's just come aboard. I've ordered no ordnance, but these have arrived, and b'ain't even Navy, Sir. It says "shrapnel shell' on the box, which I en't never heard of. I think this is army, Sir."

Argent looked at the boxes himself and confirmed Tucker's conclusion. Also, over the side, he could see that Ariadne had swung on her anchor to the beginning of the ebbing tide.

"Yes, Mr. Tucker, they are Army, but I ordered them, some time ago, for us to have a look at something new. But our priority now, is to leave harbour. I assume they're dangerous, so get them below into your magazines. If we can't make any use of them, we can always drop them over the side."

"Aye, aye, Sir."

Argent continued to his cabin to find Fentiman stood at the desk, studying papers that concerned the on-going re-supply. Argent dropped the log onto its surface.

"Ready the ship to catch this ebb tide, Henry. Rumour has it that we are needed urgently in Plymouth. Budgen has ordered us to sail directly."

"Aye, aye, Sir, but I've spotted something strange in the supply manifest. Something called "shrapnel". I'll attend to our sailing, Sir, and leave that with you."

Argent took the paper, studied it, and found the word, "Shrapnel, six boxes, 72." Argent nodded, dropped the paper onto his desk and followed Fentiman out on deck.

* * *

A good Southwesterly was coming over the starboard quarter, which promised a fast passage to Plymouth. Argent was relieved that such a breeze had sprung up with the dawn, their exit on the ebb tide to shape a course for Plymouth had been hampered by a wayward wind, never West of North, and sometimes full East. Now, more content, he was timing the gun practice and his men were consistently achieving better than three shots in five minutes, which involved two reloads. He had timed the third broadside at 4 minutes, 40 seconds; he flexed his hands behind his back in pleasure, that was exceedingly good, but now, practice finished, the guncrews were being stood down and the ship returned to peaceful sailing. At Number Three, Morris and his men were stowing their gun, Morris watching Tooley very carefully. He was proving to be strong and agile and had even begun to understand the English names for his part in the process of loading. The commands "sponge" and "ram" were both now understood, signifying clearly to him the operation needed, and he rotated easily between both. As part of housing the gun, Tooley was carefully placing the sponge onto its hooks on the deck beam, the crew had no complaints at gundrill, but what did amaze his messmates was the amount he ate. Anything consumable, he consumed. No biscuits remained from breakfast for a mid-Watch snack, but they did notice that rum had a rapid and profound effect on him, such that, at grog time, he had to be carefully watched in case he committed some tipsy blunder.

To Argent's satisfaction, a good use had been found for Tucker's shrapnel shell. If fired from a carronade, by adjusting a fuse, which Tucker quickly fathomed, it could be made to explode about 200 yards from the ship. The smoke made a perfect target, and all Ariadne's Officers had been pleased to see the balls fired during the practice grouped closely behind as they fell into the sea. With his ship making 10 knots under a full set of canvas, Argent took himself up to the forecastle, curious to see his Master Gunner still there and he found Tucker in conversation with the Starboard carronade's Guncaptain, one Bill Marshall. Both were examining a shrapnel shell, a curious combination of a cannonball, but with a fuseport and it bolted to a wooden disc. Both came to the attention and saluted, and Argent asked his question.

"So, how do these work, Mr. Tucker."

"Well, Sir. This fuse, here Sir, is fired by the explosion within the gun. In flight the fuse burns to explode the shell over a target, Sir."

Argent examined the fuse.

"It must burn extremely quickly."

"Yes Sir. The powder's the King's Red Grain, the best, Sir. It burns fierce, but even. But, Bill Marshall, here, Sir, has spent some time with mortars ashore. High angle stuff. We was thinking how we could, perhaps, use these like that, Sir, sort of dropped out of the sky. If we ever had to go up against something on shore, Sir. Or such. Then they could be useful. "

Argent looked at Tucker, then Marshall.

"But the fuse would have to last a very long time."

"Yes Sir. That's what we was talking about. How to make the fuse last longer."

Argent nodded.

"Good. I'll not argue with that. Dropping these into their laps, were we to engage shore batteries, for example, would help our cause no end, I'm sure. But can you get enough elevation on the carronade?"

Marshall spoke.

"Yes Sir. We've solved that, Sir."

This was spoken so confidently that Argent didn't enquire further.

"Good, but have you any ideas with the fuse?"

This time Tucker answered.

"One or two, Sir. Can we have your permission to try a few over the next hour or so, Sir?"

"You have, and I wish you well."

Both saluted as Argent returned to his quarterdeck to stand besides Fentiman.

"Technical discussions, Sir?"

"Yes, that shrapnel. Devilish inventions, and such. But, expect a few experiments fired over the side over the next hour or so."

Thus it went on, from both carronades on the forecastle. Gunner Tucker was up and down from the deck to his magazine, each time with one of his Mates carrying a modified shell. The first efforts exploded a good number of seconds after being fired, but still much too soon, but eventually one exploded 400 yards from the ship, just above the surface, this being greeted by much cheering and backslapping on the forecastle. Argent grinned at the capers being cut at the bows and spoke to Fentiman.

"Good. Now for a bit of peace."

Fentiman replied, with a chuckle.

"Yes Sir. And not a moment too soon. That's Plymouth opening on the larboard bow."

* * *

Broke's Office held no surprises for Argent and he entered through the door opened for him by Captain Baker, who also announced him. They had met again as friends and exchanged a warm handshake. Grant, Broke and Cheveley were leaning over a chart, spread over the copious square yardage of the desk, a Marine Colonel standing with them. Grant looked up and grinned, Broke and Cheveley raised their heads and scowled. Grant spoke his greeting, but Broke immediately demonstrated that nothing had changed.

"You're late, Argent."

"Sorry, Sir. Headwind off the ship."

Broke looked both angry and puzzled at the same time, the wind was off the sea, but the opportunity to take this further was cut short by Grant.

"Captain Argent, may I introduce Colonel Benjamin Shortman, Royal Marines?"

Shortman extended his hand and he took Argent's with a grip of iron.

"Your servant, Sir."

"Your's, Sir."

Argent flexed some life back into his hand as Grant continued.

"Captain, we have a problem on the far side of The Channel. The French have got a 44-gun frigate, La Pomone, into St. Malo. Their Lordships consider her a menace, so we've been given the job to cut her out, burn her, sink her, or do her some harm. Preferably the first."

He pointed to the map spread on the desk.

"This is a chart of the harbour."

He stood up and indicated a harbour plan as Argent took a place opposite Broke and Cheveley. Argent saw that it was fully detailed and he didn't like what the details revealed. He looked over at his superiors, expecting some plan or ideas, but nothing came, both had their eyes boring into the thick paper. So, Argent began some questions of his own.

"Do we know where she's anchored, Sir? Or berthed?"

Grant placed his finger on a point inside the harbour.

"Reports say here."

Argent saw that the map showed four arms protruding into the anchorage, two from each side of the harbour and they were not opposite, but alternated back into the depths of the anchorage. Grant's finger was opposite the third arm, where the harbour was at its widest. Argent had noted that there was a bastion on each of the first three arms. A ship entering would meet the first bastion from the left, then the second from the right, then the third from the left, by where La Pomone was reportedly anchored, but the first bastion was on an island, fairly isolated. Again Argent waited, but nothing came.

"Do we have a plan, Sir?"

All three looked at him, Broke and Cheveley in annoyance, Shortman impassive, Grant in hope. Argent studied the chart further.

"Do we have any Marines, Sir?"

Grant answered.

"Yes, that's why Colonel Shortman is here. Four Companies, about 320 men, including yours and those off Herodotus."

Argent placed his finger on the first bastion.

"That's our first problem, Sir, but it's isolated. I would suggest that we first capture that, to ease our way in, and also ease our way out."

All three, bar Shortman, looked at him, expecting more. Shortman looked at the chart and began nodding his head. Argent continued.

"Well, with the first fort secured by the Marines, if Ariadne goes in first, carrying the second Marines, we could board La Pomone and cut her anchor. On an ebb tide she'll float out. Herodotus comes in after and engages the first bastion on the right, the biggest, judging from this, whilst Ariadne engages the second bastion on the left. In the smoke and confusion it should work, Sir. Especially if we come out of the dawn, taking them by surprise, with the tide on ebb."

This spoken to Grant, but then Argent looked at Cheveley and spoke straight at him.

"Herodotus will be against the main bastion."

It was spoken as a fact, but plainly posed the unspoken question, "So, how do you feel about that?"

Cheveley's face registered no emotion. Broke was working his gaze up and down the chart and made his first contribution.

"How will you turn to sail out?"

"Anchor turn, Sir. Drop an anchor off the stern, then let the tide swing us around it, to point back out to sea. We'll have to cut the cable, but that's worth the sacrifice if it gives us a rapid exit."

Grant looked at Shortman.

"How do you feel about this, Colonel?"

"Well, Sir. I like it because so far it's simple. Once inside, things will get much more complicated. Best to start simple."

Grant looked at the two opposite Argent.

"Broke, do you agree?"

Broke looked confused, but said nothing. Instead he nodded his head.

"Cheveley?"

Cheveley looked annoyed. Argent had made all the running, so he felt as though he was following Argent's orders.

"What about the Marines? We'll have 300 plus. 100 will be going in with Argent here. The other 200, and more, will be landing independently on the island. How will that be done?"

He looked at Grant, to then answer his own question.

"We'll need two coasters. One for the landing at the first fort, a large one, and one to go in with Argent."

He then looked at Argent.

"The Marines in their own vessel means that you can board her from both sides."

Argent smiled and nodded vigorously.

"Yes, good idea, but I'd suggest two small for the landing. They can get off two vessels quicker than one, and get a good force quickly up to the wall. Colonel?"

"True enough."

Grant nodded and Argent continued.

"So, let's hope our agents are right, and she is anchored out in their Roads. And she's not out cruising. Nor berthed, especially." Grant responded.

"If she's berthed, you must assume she's secured against a quay, probably here."

His finger touched the chart where a quayside was indicated, on the right of the harbour, looking from the entrance.

"If so, I leave it to the boarding party to decide if she can be cut free and the tide carry her out, but be prepared to abandon cutting out. Just do what damage you can. The Marines with you, Argent, will have demolition charges."

Broke voiced another worry, directed at Argent.

"What about you and the prize getting out?"

Argent looked directly back at him to answer.

"Ariadne and La Pomone will come out with the tide, which should be running strong by then."

"But you'll be passing before the largest bastion, right under their guns."

"Yes, but hopefully, by then Herodotus will have pulled some of their teeth."

Then Argent looked directly at Cheveley, right into his eyes.

"We must leave together, to divide their fire, and answer with both our broadsides, us together. Herodotus doesn't cut her stern anchor until my bowsprit is over her taffrail."

Cheveley stared directly back, saying nothing, but his temper was growing. Another order from Argent, but it was Grant who forced the issue.

"Captain?"

Cheveley's jaw clenched together and his eyes narrowed, but it was his Admiral speaking. He answered whilst meeting no-one's gaze.

"Agreed."

But then Broke finished the discussion, looking directly at Argent.

"Cheveley is Commodore. Understood?"

* * *

The night was ending off to the East, the day but a suggestion on the far horizon. Having kept well together, with Ariadne leading, Argent saw the other four vessels emerging into sight as light replaced the gloom. Herodotus was the last, with the three luggers between and behind Ariadne; one off her starboard stern quarter, the remaining two off the larboard. They had left in the late afternoon and sailed through the night, keeping together with their masked lights showing only astern, both frigates with only minimal sail, allowing the slower luggers to keep up and hold their station. Argent looked at McArdle, who had been glued to the binnacle all night, studying the compass. The log had been cast every 15 minutes and it was McArdle who had called for increasing or shortening sail to use the steady wind, just South of West.

"Mr. McArdle, what is your opinion concerning our position?"

Argent could see his face fairly clearly in the light from the binnacle and he appeared as satisfied as ever he had been.

"We've held our course, Sir. With this beam wind, there'll be some leeway, but that I allowed for. I agreed our course with the Master of the Herodotus and I think we have cause for confidence."

During the previous four days, whilst they waited for the correct tide, McArdle had visited the Herodotus. He had returned looking even more grim and disatisfied than usual and had gone straight down to his cabin.

Their position at dawn was vital, they had to sail straight out of the dark to take the island fortress by surprise. The first lugger had a Master's Mate from the Herodotus and both she and the second would go ahead of Ariadne, to take the island and allow Ariadne to enter unhindered by the fort's guns. McArdle spoke again.

"I calculate that we are one mile and a half awa', Sir. The first luggers should move ahead."

The luggers had sailed with all possible canvas set, almost on maximum speed, so, for the pair to pull ahead meant Ariadne slowing. Argent gave his orders to shorten sail and the first lugger drew up and slipped past and ahead, followed by the second. Eight bells had finished the "Graveyard" Watch and as the Starboard Watch re-ordered the deck from the sail change, Argent and McArdle walked to the forecastle with their telescopes extended. As the light grew they searched the half dark and, much relieved, Argent could clearly make out a dip between the outlines of two hills, about one mile distant, fine on the larboard bow. He spoke to McArdle.

"Is that St. Malo? Do you think?"

McArdle closed his telescope and turned away.

"Aye Sir. That's that place. We're there, sure enough."

Argent felt the urge to slap McArdle on the shoulder, but, this being McArdle, the urge was necessarily resisted. He returned to his quarterdeck.

"Clear for action, Mr. Fentiman."

The tide would be high, they would arrive just at the beginning of its ebb, not strong enough to stop them sailing in, but in full spate later to bring them out. Argent followed McArdle back to the quarterdeck, acknowledging the respects of his topmen, most saying Captain as they raised their knuckle to their forehead, they were tense and those not veteran plainly afraid. When Argent regained his quarterdeck he could see the two luggers far ahead, under all sail, making maximum speed through the growing light. Down on the gundeck his men were stood to their guns. All was prepared, nothing to do now but await their own arrival. The dark of dawn was lingering, but Argent could now see the first island, it would be even clearer to the luggers, now two cables, four hundred yards, ahead. He extended his telescope and focused on the fort, it began with a low wall, but the gun embrasures were on a wall above and inside that. The Marines would have to carry both walls to silence the guns.

Coaster rig was common throughout the Channel and the Atlantic, so two luggers coming out of the gloom wouldn't necessarily be identified immediately as foe. Argent hoped that this would get them a measure closer before the alarm was raised and he trained his telescope on the two vessels; no redcoat could be seen, they must be lying on deck. He looked beyond them to the island itself to see a small quay on the entry channel side. The luggers steered straight for it, dropped their sails and immediately several gangplanks fell onto the stonework, to be soon covered by running Marines, many carrying ladders and grapnels. Suddenly, a rocket shot skyward. The alarm had been raised, but the Marines were ashore. Argent responded.

"Set all topsails and topgallants."

The topmen had been waiting, most already in the rigging and, within a minute, the sails had dropped and seconds after that sheeted home. Ariadne surged forward and past the fort, coinciding with the Marines being already over the first wall and scaling the second to take the guns. Blue-coated figures could be seen through the embrasures above them, running to their stations. The sounds of musketry immediately followed.

Argent hurried to the forecastle. Ariadne was now in the harbour, with her own lugger, chosen because she was fastest, full of Marines and doing its best to keep up. The daylight was now full and his gaze swept the harbour to find La Pomone. Where Grant had indicated, she wasn't, merely a collection of small merchantmen, anchored safely in the Roads. Argent looked to the wharves on the right; nothing. Over to the left, and there she was, berthed against a quayside, bows in, stern out. She was moored out of the tide. Cutting her out was impossible, she would need to be freed from her moorings and then towed out into the current, which would need at least three longboats, fully manned. All that could be done was to damage her. Argent ran back to his quarterdeck and seized the loudhailer. He jumped into the larboard mizzen shrouds and shouted across to the lugger alongside.

"She's off to larboard. Get across her stern and board. I'll be near to tow you off. You've got five minutes, then away. Use your charges."

The lugger was commanded by Lieutenant Sanders and contained Ariadne's own Marines. Argent saw Sanders wave his hat, and he could swear that he was grinning. It seemed that Sanders had already seen La Pomone and had decided that course for himself, for with all canvas drawing, the lugger was already steering directly for La Pomone's stern and all the Marines lined along the bulwark, their muskets trained over the side. He could see Ramsey in the bows, sword raised, shouting to his men. So brave a sight commanded a moment of his time, but then he attended to his own urgent concerns, as he heard McArdle confirm the Log entry with Fentiman.

"Ah'm enterin "Entered St. Malo at 5.10", Sir."

Argent heard Fentiman's "Make it so", then he issued his own orders.

"Mr. Ball. Get King into the starboard bow with a throwing line."

Ball knuckled his forehead in acknowledgement and then shouted the order to King up in the foretop. Ariadne would be passing La Pomone at 80 yards range, give or take. The Frenchman's stern would be unprotected long enough for one larboard broadside before the lugger came across to mask it. Argent called down to Bentley, overseeing the guns.

"On her stern, fire as you bear."

The order was shouted up to the bows and the firing began to roll back to the stern as each Gun Captain waited for his gun to bear on the moored ship. La Pomone's stern began to disintegrate and Argent thought to himself, "At least we've done her that bit of no good." Then he attended to his own concerns, the anchor turn. An easy task, if he took all the room available, but they had to turn and then come to a stop just off the lugger, close enough to get a line across during the process. The anchor was lashed to the larboard side of the quarterdeck, with Fraser and two of his mates standing by with axes to cut the lashings. If they were going to get a line across to the lugger, Ariadne would have to swing left, to larboard, so that her bowsprit, as it swung round, would almost touch the lugger's rigging. The last gun fired and at that point the French guns opened fire. The fort across the bay was over half a mile away, but 32 lb cannon could easily reach beyond that and would soon find the range, however, for now, the shot was falling some way off and sending up huge gouts of water. They could be 42's! However, Argent's biggest worry was the bastion on their side, two cables ahead, with three side embrasures looking straight at them, each framing a black, threatening gun muzzle. Then they fired. A 32lb ball sailed through the rigging, with a fearsome humm, parting some shrouds. Then two more, but thankfully taking the same course. The topmen swung through the rigging to make repairs.

Argent looked back to his left. Dwarfed by La Pomone's masts, the lugger had crashed into the damaged stern and the Marines were swarming over and onto the Frenchman's quarterdeck. Argent saw Ramsey jump down sword in hand, but he now had to fully concentrate on judging his vital turn. The time was right. He bellowed sufficient for them to hear in the foretop.

"Start all sheets!"

The sails went slack and Ariadne slowed rapidly in the ebbing tide.

"Let go."

Three blows with the axes and the anchor was gone.

"Down helm."

"Down helm. Aye aye, Sir."

The Quartermaster Zachary Short answered as if they were tacking the ship safe in the roads of The Channel, but Ariadne had enough momentum to swing away from the wind, just enough for the tide to catch her on her starboard bow and push her left. She moved sternwards with the tide until the anchor caught her and she began to traverse, swinging round like the arm of a crane. Ariadne's bowsprit passed within yards of the side of the lugger, now empty of Marines. King, poised at the starboard bow as Ariadne turned with the tide, flung his line cleanly onto her deck, to see it seized by one of her crew, he then passed it down the outside of Ariadne to bring it to Fraser, still on the quarterdeck. It was attached to a towing cable coiled there, which the lugger's crew began to draw in. Ariadne stopped with a lurch, her bows now pointing seawards, the anchor had held, but now their own stern was exposed to the bastion just further up the harbour; about one and a half cables behind them, an easy distance for trained gunners.

The first ball hit the taffrail and took off the head of one of the crew of the starboard carronade, sending splinters, large and small, flying across the quarterdeck. One hit Argent in the thigh, another, larger, pierced the chest of a Bosun's Mate. Argent fell to the deck, not sure if his leg was broken or not. The second ball passed through the mizzen topmast spar for it to hang drunkenly down to starboard. The third passed right through the rigging to hit the forecastle bulwark where King had been standing. Argent raised himself on one elbow to turn to Gunner Tucker, stood close on the quarterdeck.

"Mr. Tucker, if you can do anything with your shrapnel, to those guns behind us, do it now!"

Tucker and his gunners had already partly anticipated the need and the quarterdeck carronades were already swung around to now be quickly elevated and, with that, they began the process of loading. This started with adjusting the fuses to make, what they hoped, was the correct length. Eli Reece and another Forecastleman had run to their Captain and raised him up, so that he could, at least, lean on the quarterdeck rail. They remained at his side and Argent looked over to Bentley stood down on the gundeck.

"Mr. Bentley. Open fire with the larboard broadside. Rapid fire at the bastion on the far side of the harbour. Rapid fire, cover us in smoke."

Tucker's carronades fired together. Each had been loaded with three shrapnel shells, and they exploded low and short, but the smoke from the explosions hid Ariadne from the three embrasures, at least temporarily. Tucker and his mates worked on the next fuses, whilst the carronades received their gunpowder charges, this time a little extra. Argent noted that some guns of his starboard battery were firing, one, two, and three, three being Morris', they had found targets beyond the lugger, and, at the far end, Evans and Wood, Gun Captains of 15 and 16, could see right down the quayside. They had agreed between them to load grapeshot to give the Marines some support.

This noted, that his ship was fighting in all directions, Argent looped his arm around Reece's shoulders, whilst his mate took Argent's waist.

"Thank you Reece. Help me to the larboard side, if you would be so good."

"Aye, aye, Captain", came from both, and they practically carried him to the rail. Argent looked across the full width of the harbour at the bastion opposite, through the gaps in the smoke. He called for his telescope and studied the affect of their own gunnery from the larboard battery. Some shot were hitting the stonework, but too few to make any difference, but by now Herodotus should be in action. He changed direction to look down the harbour through the thinning smoke and saw her in the middle of the harbour roads, stationary in the centre of the tide, but too far down. There had been some misjudgement somewhere, but nevertheless, trained back, her broadside would hit the bastion. Just as Argent thought this, she opened fire, as single guns in a rolling broadside, making huge clouds of smoke. He looked at the bastion, merely a few balls had hit, but at least some. More importantly, at least, as he saw it, Herodotus would draw some fire and in answer to this thought, some waterspouts erupted off her stern.

His own quarterdeck carronades fired again. This time the shells must have been over the bastion behind them, because he saw no explosions, but perhaps they were drowned in the smoke from the French guns at the embrasures. He looked at Tucker, who answered.

"That's the longest fuse, Sir. I reckon it don't matter if they lands to bounce around their feet!"

"Just so, Mr. Tucker. My compliments to you."

Argent thought how ridiculous was the phrase he had just used to Tucker, then another ball from the bastion astern ploughed up planking from the starboard gangway, then ricocheted up and over the bows, parting some standing rigging, bringing his mind back to his own predicament. His leg hurt and his ship was taking damage.

Then a signalman called out to him.

"Sir, signal from Herodotus, Sir. "Withdraw."

In shock, Argent took himself to the larboard side, ignoring his limp, but still supported by Reece. What he saw, by looking down harbour, he looked on with horror. Herodotus was going, definitely moving seaward and out, already some way down the Roads, she'd cut her anchor, if ever it had held her. The fire from the main bastion still looked on her as a target, but soon all would be on him, but he could not abandon the Marines, now all aboard La Pomone and doing their best to wreck her.

"Acknowledge."

"Aye aye, Sir."

Then, under his breath.

"For all the damn good that will do."

Reece and his mate carried Argent to the other side to look at La Pomone and what he saw gave some hope. The Marines were coming back over the taffrail and jumping down onto the lugger. One minute more and they could pull her away. Explosions were occurring on La Pomone and there were some fires. They had, without question, done some damage, probably significant.

His own starboard guns, those five that could, were still roaring away at any target they could see. At Number Three on the starboard side, Morris had already sunk a small coaster with three aimed shots on her waterline, now there was a Signal Station that he was systematically knocking to pieces, his crew loading and running out with smooth precision. Morris had no complaints about Tooley. Evans and Wood had loaded solid to batter some buildings that contained French soldiers, who were firing at the Marines from the windows. Fynes was running up to the forecastle and then back down, trying to find targets for his three guns, including Morris', Berry coming up to the quarterdeck for the benefit of his two. Bright and Bentley were encouraging their men to fire at maximum speed, Bright taking the place of a tackleman felled by a splinter.

Argent studied the lugger, surely these were the last of the Marines, then he knew they were when Ramsey came over La Pomone's taffrail to jump down into his vessel. Argent turned to Fraser.

"Stand by, Mr. Fraser."

No more Marines appeared.

"Now, Mr. Fraser."

The sharpened axe chopped twice, the anchor hawser disappeared and Ariadne immediately began to drift downstream in the strong current. The towrope to the lugger snapped taught and Ariadne lurched, but the lugger began to leave La Pomone's stern, her bow swinging round to follow. Tucker fired for a third time and this time explosions could be seen all over the bastion. His work had made some difference, but only to slow the rate of fire, men felled by the shrapnel could quickly be replaced.

Argent limped to the centre of the taffrail to look over the stern, Reece never leaving his side. Argent had to con his ship down the harbour, but now running the gauntlet of the opposite main bastion. Fraser, without orders, had prepared all plain sail, bar the Royals, dropped but not sheeted home, so, at present they hung limp. Argent couldn't move himself forward, he couldn't even stand on the leg, certainly not walk, and so he gave his orders so that Fentiman would hear.

"Sheet home."

Whilst Fentiman relayed his orders along the deck, Argent spoke to the helmsman.

"Up helm. Take us out, Mr. Short."

"Up helm and course out. Aye aye, Sir."

Zachary Short moved the wheel four spokes, then held it steady.

Ariadne's starboard broadside roared out. With the lugger away and coming around astern, La Pomone was cleared and the guns that had been forced to hold their fire gave her a double shotted farewell. Decking, planking and railings flew up into the air and within the ship fires continued. However, Argent had observed none of this. They were now within the fire arc of the front battery of the bastion they had just dropped shrapnel onto, it looked directly out over the harbour and, in addition, they were also heading directly into the fire of the main bastion across the harbour. This no longer had Herodotos as an opponent, she was going through the harbour entrance and was now well out of range. He turned to Tucker, to ask for some more shrapnel, but the roar of the carronades gave him an answer. The shells exploded above the embrasures that threatened them anew from astern. Argent yelled above the din.

"Mr. Tucker. Keep firing. Cover us with smoke."

Both Ariadne's batteries were roaring away and, in the noise, Tucker could do no more than knuckle his forehead. The bastion behind them fired, but it was wayward, this being their first volley, apart from one shot that hit the mizzen topmast, for it to descend to fold down and point at the quarterdeck, held by the rigging. A shower of blocks and splinters descended to be caught by the splinter net strung above the deck. For that bastion the range was now lengthening, but to the main bastion, across the harbour, the range was shortening, soon it would be down to three cables, with Ariadne presenting her full length as a target. She was picking up speed, with her canvas perfectly set, but only slowly. Whilst, in that wind and alone, she could easily manage 12 knots, the lugger would do well to achieve nine. Sanders had set all sail and, without the tow, Ariadne would be faster, but the lugger slower. Argent would not leave the Marines to face the full fury of the bastion's fire and, as that thought passed through his mind, the main bastion fired; Argent had estimated about 12 guns. Most were wayward, but all felt the shock through the hull of those that hit, and one crossed the deck to hit the starboard bulwark below the mainmast shrouds. The shrouds jerked outwards as their anchoring davits flew out over the sea, the water then being covered by the shower of splinters.

Argent knew his ship couldn't take too much more, 32lb balls, never mind 42lb could knock a frigate to pieces, but so far Carpenter Baines had not come to talk of the height of the well. He took stock, his mind working rapidly, under three cables was just within Tucker's range. The smoke would shroud them, but the topmasts would show above, fixing him as a target, but one was already gone, courtesy of a French gunner.

"Mr. Tucker. Give them some of your shrapnel."

"Already in hand, Sir."

"Mr. Fraser. Lower fore and main topmasts."

It was a complex affair, to lower the top part of a mast, but a good crew could do it in less than three minutes. Fraser was already sending them aloft and when the task was done they would be better hid by their own gun smoke. All four of Tucker's carronades roared out, but the affect was hidden to Argent on the quarterdeck, however, one of Tucker's Mates was in the rigging.

"All short, but just."

Argent looked at Tucker.

"Maximum range?"

"Just about, Sir."

"Keep firing anyway. It'll give 'em a headache if nothing else."

Tucker grinned, as did Short on the wheel. McArdle stood his place, as if made of granite.

Ariadne was making about 9 knots waterspeed, but, with the tide, about 15 landspeed. Only minutes more and they would be at the point of maximum danger, well within accurate gunnery range from the bastion. It occurred to Argent that the Battery Commander was holding his fire for just that moment. He looked aloft, the foretopmast was down, the larger, maintopmast on its way. His larboard guns were firing at battle speed and above, hitting back, but the bastion had a lower tier, men and guns safe inside a gallery. Argent heard the deeper roar of the bastion's heavier cannon and he felt the hull jerk as the shot crashed into her. Argent saw the forecastle bulwark explode inwards, the splinters killing all the guncrew on the carronade there, which crashed backwards across the deck, crushing another man's leg. The other hits were to the gundeck or below.

"Mr. Fentiman. Go below and find out what damage. I have the deck."

Fentiman ran down the companionway to reach the gundeck. What he saw made him clench his jaw. Three guns were back inboard, the cannon of each off its carriage. Another was slewed back in; it had lost its breeching on one side, but the crew were working frantically to get it back into action. At least two dozen, probably more, dead and wounded were stretched on the deck, some ominously still, some writhing in agony, some trying to raise themselves, some examining minor wounds. Blood was running across the deck to mingle with the sand, then he saw two blue coats amongst the fallen. Meanwhile, the rest of the guncrews grimly served their guns, battering the stonework of their tormentor. They might get one through an embrasure.

Fentiman descended further into the ship, to the lower deck. There he found Frederick Baines and his Mates. Four shot had hit there, two above the waterline, two just below. The latter were spurting jets of water right across the deck as Baines and a Mate hammered home large shot plugs. The jets stopped, it continued leaking, but that was minor. The two higher was admitting water at odd times with the odd wave, but shot plugs cured that. Fentiman returned to the quarterdeck.

"Three guns wholly out of action, Sir. Four shot on the waterline that we've found, and plugged. Mr. Baines is checking for more, and he's certain there are."

"Casualties."

"I'd say two dozen from that, Sir. About five dozen so far."

Argent felt surprised to feel relieved at such a level of damage and injury. The two minutes, and more, that it would take for a French battery to reload, should see them out of effective range, they would only then remain within range of a lucky shot. Then a Signalman touched his sleeve to gain his attention.

"Sir. Look at the lugger, Sir."

Argent and Fentiman turned to look. The lugger was well down at the stern, she was badly holed. A 32lb ball, hitting a small merchantman such as this, would pass from one side to exit at the other, they were built light, to better their speed. Argent guessed that this is what had happened, that she now had two gaping holes below the waterline, she wouldn't float much longer, and she had nearly 100 Marines aboard, plus her crew. As she took in water she was growing ever more sluggish, dragging Ariadne back and both were still under the guns of the bastion. Argent decided immediately.

"Start sheets."

At this order, then from Fraser's prompts, the topmen loosened all the sheets to the sails, that soon hung curling in the wind.

"Down helm."

Ariadne swung slightly to starboard, then stopped in the water, the lugger dragging her back, but this vessel still had some seaway with all her sails set. Her bowsprit came thrusting over Ariadne's taffrail.

"Lash this secure."

The Afterguard hurried forward to do his bidding. Argent used his good leg to climb further up the taffrail to look at the lugger, but Sanders had divined for himself what to do. The bowsprit was their way off and all aboard were hurrying forward, carrying the wounded, but the water was already onto the planking of her quarterdeck. The Marines got the wounded off first and then began their own evacuation. Marines and seaman were swarming along the ropes and woodwork to come aboard, some coming up netting thrown over to them and then secured. Then the guns on the bastion fired again.

Argent's slight change of course, down wind had placed her stern on to the bastion. Dangerous at short range, but thankfully creating a smaller target at long range. In addition, the carronades were firing just to make smoke, adding any ordnance was now pure waste. If any shot hit a hull, it would be the lugger's, now half sunk with her bows only held up by her bowsprit lashed over Ariadne's stern, also her sinking stern had raised her bows right up, providing further shield. Two shot hit the lugger, one ploughed into the sternward sloping deck, sending up a shower of splinters that killed two Marines and injured two more. Their mates ran back to get them. The second killed Captain Ramsey, stood with Lieutenant Sanders, both ensuring that all were off, before they, themselves, followed. The ball took off his right arm and most of his shoulder, before passing on and over. Sanders knelt down to him, but saw that he was beyond help. He left his body for the waves and helped one of the wounded along the bowsprit, securing a line around the injured man's waist himself, to prevent him being lost, down into the water below.

With all off Fraser took his axe to the lashings of the bowsprit simultaneous to Fentiman ordering the sails to be re-sheeted home. With both coinciding, Ariadne jumped forward and the bowsprit slid back with a groan, as if acknowledging the coming fate of its ship. The island fort was now coming up to starboard, it still being held by the Marines under their Colonel and Argent trusted them to hold their position until Ariadne could get safely past before the French re-occupied the fort. They were holding off a cloud of skirmishers attacking across the narrow causeway that joined the island to the mainland. Fentiman saw them first and called down to Midshipman Berry, now in command of the gundeck. Bentley was dead.

"Starboard battery, load grape."

Argent spun on his good leg and balanced himself on Reece's shoulder to focus his telescope on La Pomone. Through the glass, he could see the extensive damage to her hull from their shot, but her fires seemed to be out, she now being shrouded in thick blue smoke. She was far from a wreck, but she was out of action and it seemed a poor return for the carnage aboard his own command. Then there was an explosion and her mizzenmast lurched, he heard his own crew cheer and Argent felt better, then his leg began to really hurt.

The French skirmishers saw Ariadne emerging with her guns run out and ready. The veterans amongst them knew what was coming and ducked down behind the rocks, calling their comrades to follow. Soon, all musketry ceased and the Marines began to evacuate, jumping down from the walls onto the higher rocks, or using the ladders. There were no wounded, these were already back aboard their own luggers and soon, but a few Marines were still running to their vessels, both of which were shoving off from the quayside to ease their bows out into the running tide. Some French skirmishers, braver than most, emerged to obtain a sight of the luggers, so Fentiman called down to the gundeck.

"Fire, if you see a target."

Two together, then a third, gun, fired to send grapeshot sweeping across the rocks and the causeway. Two skirmishers were caught and flung backwards like discarded ragdolls, but no more showed themselves. The two luggers got their bows out into the current and soon swung around to point themselves for home, and to follow Ariadne, now raising her topmasts and setting what sail she could. McArdle was the last to speak within the harbour, confirming with Fentiman.

"Ah'm enterin, "Left St. Malo at 5.41", Sir."

"Make it so."

Herodotus was a white shape, almost on the horizon.

* * *

Argent was at his place at the quarterdeck rail, not standing, but sat on a chair brought up from his cabin. His injured leg was resting on a bucket. He watched his crew busy everywhere, knotting, splicing and replacing rigging. The whole mizzen topmast, a jumble of wreckage, was being cleared and sent over the side, piece by piece. Masts and spars could be replaced, but Ariadne had suffered severe damage to her hull. He could see her bulwarks, smashed in at several places, then there was the gap in the stern taffrail behind him, then there was the shattered planking. Fraser was supervising some kind of repair to the davits of the starboard mainmast shrouds. There was a long row of canvas covered shapes along the larboard gangway, many showing large patches of red. Fentiman came to stand beside him.

"You should go below, Sir, to Mr. Smallpiece. Let him take a look at you."

"I'll not. Not just yet. It's not broken, look, it would bend in the middle if it were."

He indicated with his hand that his leg, horizontal on its support, remained straight. But Fentiman was not giving in.

"Perhaps, Sir, but it may be fractured. All is in hand up here, Sir. You do no extra good here, but you may be doing yourself harm."

Argent looked up into his concerned First Lieutenant's face and frowned, he knew that Fentiman was right. He waved forward the ever attendant Eli Reece and his mate, whom Argent now knew was called Ben Raisey.

"I should see the Surgeon, so I am told."

Fentiman smiled, as Reece supported Argent on the side of his injured leg, his left. With Raisey hovering below, he was lowered, step-by-step down the companionway to the gundeck, to be helped along its length through the scene of the guns being housed, and what could be repaired, being repaired, and what secured, secured. The last included three dismounted guns that were being lashed to any fixed point, the mainmast and nearby breeching rings. Splinters were being swept up and blood swabbed away, some were chopping at the jagged shot holes, at least making the edges cleaner. Many saw their Captain being helped along the deck, limping badly, and these took the time to examine him carefully, genuine concern on their faces, but reassured at seeing no sign of blood, at least. Argent rested at the mainmast, leaning his hand against it, then looking at it, now pockmarked by splinters.

"This beeswax needs touching up!"

His men laughed, relieved, despite the tired voice, and their concern fell away.

"We'll get that done, Sir. Never fear."

He held out his left arm for Reece who immediately placed his shoulder under it, giving support. His men watched as he continued to the end of the deck, to reach the companionway that led further down and, as he passed, all stopped work and nodded to their Captain, carefully paying their respects. On the lower deck they found Frederick Baines, hurrying in the opposite direction. They could hear the pumps clanking, worked by their Marine passengers.

"How much in the well, Mr. Baines."

"Nine inches, but holding, Sir. I'm sure there's another hole somewhere. We're going to the aft magazine."

"Very good, Mr. Baines. In you I have the fullest confidence."

Argent shook his head. Where did he get these phrases from? But Baines was gone. They continued down further to reach the orlop deck and here they found a scene from Hell. Blood seemed to be everywhere, spread by men writhing on the bare planking. In the gloom of the battle lanterns Surgeon's Mates ran hither and thither with water and wadding, and lengths of lanyard for tourniquets to circle shattered limbs. In addition to what he could see, was what he could hear. It was impossible to distinguish the scream of one man from another; even the screams of the man on Smallpiece's table, losing his right leg, below the knee. Through it all moved Mrs. McArdle, moving like a Saint in Perfect Light. Wherever she was, came calm, even if she were merely wiping a face from sweat and grime. Her hands touched others to achieve peace and ease their worry, the wounded knew that they were being cared for, that succour had arrived. Argent leaned against the bulkhead and turned to Reece and Raisey.

"My thanks to you both. Now leave me here and return to your duties."

Without thinking he patted both on the arm, which simple gesture brought surprise to both faces, such was unknown to them from any superior Officer. Both came to the attention and saluted, then left. Suddenly, Argent felt very weary and close to fainting, his head slumped down and his arms went limp. Eara McArdle, who seemed to notice everything, saw him and hurried to his side, to take his left arm over her own shoulders, but Argent recovered himself.

"I'm alright, Mrs. McArdle. I can just stay here, whilst you attend to those in real need of your help. I can wait."

Eara McArdle looked at the Captain of her ship and her husbands superior Officer.

"You'll not, is what I'm telling you. Get yourself over to this bench and sit."

Argent obeyed immediately and sat on the bench.

"Now, Captain. I can see no wound."

Stated as a fact, but an obvious question, Argent gave his answer.

"I was hit by a splinter, the back of my left leg, my thigh. Some think it may be fractured."

"Then stand and let's see!"

Argent look at her in astonishment, then obeyed, whilst she gave physical support.

"Now, full weight on it."

Argent gingerly transferred his weight and the pain intensified, terribly.

"Now, Captain. Where does it hurt? If it's the bone, ye'll feel it, right in the centre. If just bruising, the pain's on the outside. So, where?"

She looked challengingly at him, "Make your mind up".

Argent looked querulously back, then searched for an answer, then felt relief. The pain, although appalling, was, indeed, at the back of the muscle.

"At the back, Mrs. McArdle. It feels on fire, but below the surface and not too far in."

"That's good. Ye've bad bruising and nae more. It hit the meat of your leg and that took the shock. Ye're lucky."

"Yes, Mrs. McArdle."

"Now, drop your breeches and sit ye back down. I'll put a bandage around for support and make ye a potion and a rub when I've more time."

Argent began to undo his breeches buttons, wondering about the state of his linen underneath. Eara McArdle had disappeared but soon returned with a thick bandage.

"Turn round and lean over the bench, Captain. I need to see the bruising."

Argent stood, with his breeches around his ankles, then draped himself over the bench, his stomach taking his weight. Mrs. McArdle sounded satisfied.

"Ah, I can see the bruise coming out now. This'll no take long, and it'll help."

Argent felt the bandage being expertly applied, neither too tight nor too loose, but from his position, Argent could see Smallpiece's operating table, and on it Midshipman Ffynes was losing his right arm.

* * *

Ariadne entered Plymouth with the next dawn. Progress had been slow for all three craft despite the favourable wind, the luggers were naturally slow, but Ariadne could set little sail, her rigging had suffered more damage than Fraser had thought and so, as she crept over the sea, she left a trail of jettisoned wreckage. This had brought her to Plymouth in the dead of night and so she anchored to await the new day. She was creeping up to Drake's Island, mostly on fore and aft sails, so few of her common sails could be set, such was the damage to the required spars and running rigging. Argent was in his cabin, writing the Ship's Log. On the desk, in front of him was a crutch, crudely fashioned, but sturdy, the forcastlemen had made it and it had been delivered whilst he slept. Argent had given himself the luxury of a good sleep, allowing the same to Sanders, knowing that they would both be summoned on their return. Argent was halfway through describing the events of the previous day and, on top, he needed to make some entry concerning what damage had been done to La Pomone. He called in the sentry.

"My compliments to Mr. Sanders. Could he please come to my cabin?"

The Marine delivered a sharp salute and disappeared. Argent noted that the Marine's white leggings and coat were very dirty and torn, he had been on La Pomone. Sanders arrived with his own bandage, on his left hand.

"Morning, Jonathan. How's the hand?"

Sanders looked at the bandage, as if that would give the answer.

"Not too bad, Sir. Top of a finger missing, the little one. How's your leg?"

"Better. Perhaps I should thank this."

He indicated a jar of pale brown ointment and small bottle that seemed to contain liquid mud.

"A paste and a potion from Mrs. McArdle. One smells foul, the other tastes disgusting. "It'll ease ye're bruisin', Captain.""

Sanders laughed at Argent's mimicry.

"Well, Sir, as my "French Mother" used to say, "the worst the taste, the more it does you good"."

"I'm sure she was right. Perhaps we could send it to her. Now, aboard La Pomone. What did you do? I have to ask you, you're all I have, you know why."

Sanders face fell, but then brightened a small measure.

"Yes Sir. Well, we took her upper deck and gundeck, but could get no further than the mainmast along her lower deck. We cleared her gundeck by throwing our charges at them, but could not fight our way to a magazine. It needed more than half of us to hold the French on the quayside. So, with time running out, we dropped our last charges down her hold and took our leave, Sir.

Sanders face grew serious again.

"I'd like it put on record, Sir, that Captain Ramsey was the last off her. He commanded the rearguard, and finally saw even those away, before himself."

Argent looked at Sanders, whose eyes were level, looking straight back at him. Argent nodded.

"So noted. What about her damage? How long would you say she will be out of commission?"

"Well, her gundeck was a wreck. You raking her did that. Her mizzen was wounded, as was her main, and I hear that an explosion moved her mizzen some more. And we started some fires that burned for some time. And then there's the broadside you gave her on leaving. I'd say one month minimum, and for that, they'll have to work on her night and day."

Argent began writing immediately.

"Thank you, Jonathan."

They both heard six bells of the Morning Watch.

"Up hammocks. And this is your Watch, is it not?"

"Yes Sir. But none of the crew slept too much last night."

At that moment Midshipman Bright knocked and entered. His eyes were red-rimmed from lack of sleep in a face still black with gunpowder.

"Sir. Excuse me, Sir, but we are just clearing Drake's Island."

"Thank you, Mr. Bright. I'm on my way."

Argent rose on his good leg and lifted his crutch, to place it under his left shoulder, then stump out of his cabin. He passed across the rear of the gundeck, now clean, but still much in disarray. The companionway to the quarterdeck was a problem for him, but soon he stood his place, on the weatherside. Some fishermen and coastal craft were nearby and their crews stopped working, to watch her enter, alerted by the clanking of the pumps. Some silently watched, but others cheered, as Ariadne slid in, looking as though she'd received the malignant attentions of a French two decker. They remembered what she'd looked like when she brought in La Mouette; they saw her as a fighting ship, this now confirmed by very different evidence.

Off to starboard was Herodotus, so Argent took himself to the starboard bulwark to take a look, they were near enough not to require a telescope. Many Ariadnies were on the starboard gangway, such as was left of it. Fentiman was at Argent's side.

"How much damage can you see, Henry? We're looking at the side that was in action."

"Three, perhaps four, holes, Sir, that I can see, but we don't know what's below the waterline."

"No. But I agree about four at the most."

At that moment they saw Cheveley come to the corner of his quarterdeck to watch Ariadne crawl up to anchor. Argent turned to the ever attendant Reece.

"Reece, my glass, please."

The glass was obtained and he focused it quickly on Cheveley. The face that he saw was impassive, but then he saw it quickly change to fury. Argent was nonplussed; he could see no reason for the change. However, what he did not know was that, from his own ship, two bare backsides were being displayed from two gunports and another through the largest shothole.

A Signalman came to stand beside him.

"Signal from The Tower, Sir. Our number and Herodotus'. Captains to Flag."

* * *

They had landed their Captain safely, helped him up the steps and into a waiting carriage, accompanied by Lieutenant Sanders, so now the barge crew watched the carriage disappear past The Tower. They had noticed a similar barge moored empty at the same steps and drew their own conclusions. Now they were looking around for the crew and they found them along the quayside, sat on some bollards and piles of cable. Whiting looked down at Able Jones, checking the moorings of their barge, it with two large patches, both of which leaked.

"Abe. Up here."

Jones gave the knot a final tug and ascended the stone steps, to assemble with King, Fenwick, and Beddows. Whiting pointed to the other bargecrew and they walked over. The sailors looked up and saw the Ariadnies approaching, their faces soon showing that they could expect trouble. Whiting noticed first that they were all Bosun's Mates and then he saw the Bosun himself, his hat having the plate on which was the face of an old Greek Sage above the word "Herodotus". Whiting walked to the Warrant Officer, his superior, but saw no reason to change his intentions.

"Mornin' lads. That's a fine ship you serves on. A fine sight, she makes, 'specially when you'n lookin' at her stern as she sails off, out of harbour."

Between sailors, normally, this was fighting talk, but they just looked up, grim and subdued. None made any move. Whiting continued.

"So what happened? Was it time to polish your bell or summat, or was it gettin' a mite too hot, with what the Frogs was sendin' your way?"

The Bosun looked directly back at Whiting. He was meeting the challenge.

"'An what makes you think that it's we as gives the orders?"

"She's your ship."

The Bosun stood up and looked directly at Whiting.

"You know how many was flogged on the way back? Twenty one. Where's that number come from? Every Gun Captain of the larboard battery. An' you know how many he flogged after you bested us against them targets? Every tenth man from the whole bloody crew! Every tenth man in the ship got a dozen. The lads smashed those targets sweet as you like, but 'twere Cheveley's ship handlin' as lost us the trial, 'im bein' out thought by your Captain, yet 'twere us as took the brunt across our backs. You wants us to stand up for our ship? This is what I thinks of my ship."

He took off his Bosun's Hat and threw it on the floor.

"Don't ask me, nor my mates here, to stand up for Cheveley's Circus. You'm knockin' on the wrong door. Her and 'im can sail into Hell for all we care."

He shifted his stance, and continued, returning to the subject of St. Malo.

" A bare five shot we took? Five, and one through some shrouds and that alone were enough for 'im to cut the anchor and take off. We 'ad time for three broadsides, no more, an' you can believe me or not, I don't care, but the lads was servin' their guns as best I've ever seen. They wanted to fight that frog fort, give 'em a batterin'; that's a fact I know."

The Bosun paused to let that sink in, then continued. He wouldn't defend the ship, but he'd defend the crew.

"An' I'll tell you summat else, an' all. We've got gunners as've served on fightin' ships. The best! We'd sorted out spotters to watch the shot hit, us an' the Gunner's Mates. Cheveley's Officers wouldn't know their arse from their elbow. We opened as a rolling broadside an' we was getting' the range. The last thing I heard before he ordered cut the cable, was a spotter shoutin' for number 12 to lower a half."

Whiting looked at the Bosun. In his face he saw what he had rarely seen in any seaman. Sorrow and shame for his crew and his ship, such that was bringing him near to tears. Whiting bent down, picked up the hat and dusted it off. His expression became resigned, his sadness matching theirs. There could be no argument here, these were true man o' war's men, berthed on a bad ship and no fault of theirs.

"We was figurin' to buy a bottle from The Benbow down there. Perhaps you'd like to share a drop or two."

He handed back the hat, and the Bosun took it.

* * *

Simultaneously, Argent and Sanders were ascending the steps to Broke's residence, now all very familiar, a familiarity which included Captain Baker, who immediately came forward to help Argent over the steps, but Argent waved him back.

"I'm fine, Captain Baker, I can manage, but I thank you."

Baker remained concerned, which grew when he saw Sanders bandaged hand.

"Not too serious, I hope?"

"No, just a tiny bit gone, and I drink my tea with my other hand, so it's that little finger that I need to stick out!"

Both Argent and Baker laughed and were still laughing when they reached the door of Broke's office. Baker opened the door, still smiling, and Argent and Sanders entered, Baker following. The four already present were sat on chairs before the fireplace, with one chair vacant. Grant stood up and immediately noticed the crutch, the misshapen leg and then Sanders own obvious wound. He began speaking as Argent stumped forward whilst Baker went to sit at the desk and assemble a stack of plain paper.

"Captain, please take this chair. I hope your wound is none too painful, but we did not know that you were bringing Lieutenant, er, Sanders, is it?"

Sanders and Argent both nodded, but Argent spoke.

"I thought it would be useful to include him, Sir. Lieutenant Sanders actually got onto La Pomone and he is the only Officer off her to survive. Captain Ramsey was killed."

Whilst saying this, Argent looked directly at Broke, who looked both annoyed and confused. Cheveley looked at the fireplace, but Marine Colonel Shortman rose and came forward to shake both their hands and then fetch another chair. It was he that took Argent's log and put it on the desk, alongside that of the Herodotus. Soon all were sat and waiting for Grant to start. He sat up, stern faced, and spoke.

"I've called you here because I want a simple report of what happened, and what you think you achieved. I'd like to start with you, Lieutenant."

Sanders sat up nervously, but when he began his voice was firm and his speech clear.

"We got aboard her, Sir, over her stern, after Ariadne had raked her. Captain Ramsey led, but she was full of sailors and workmen, and a squad French Marines, but there were many dead, after Ariadne's broadside. Captain Ramsey put half of us along her starboard gangway to hold off any reinforcements from the quay, but French soldiers were coming from everywhere. The Marines held them off, especially when Ariadne fired grape along the quay in support. Captain Ramsey led the rest down to her gundeck, and we cleared that, too, but we had to use some charges. They tried to get down to a magazine, but were held on her lower deck. I knew that we had five minutes and it was running out. Captain Ramsey sent back a runner to inform me of the position and what did I advise? I said throw the remaining charges down into the hold. This they did and we got back onto the lugger and Ariadne towed us out, until we were badly holed. It was then that Captain Ramsey was killed, just before we transferred to Ariadne. Sir."

"Five minutes?"

"That came from Captain Argent, Sir. He shouted it across."

"Across when?"

"When we got into the harbour and saw where she was, Sir, and we both made a course for her stern."

Grant nodded, then continued.

"And her damage?"

"Her masts are damaged, Sir, and dislodged, and she took a dreadful beating from Ariadne's guns. Also some fires burned in her. I think she's out for a month, at least."

He paused, but was not interrupted.

"I would like, at this point, to commend Captain Ramsey and the Marines, Sir, if I may."

Grant nodded, as did Shortman.

"You may. Thank you."

Grant turned to Argent.

"Your report, please, Captain Argent?"

Argent knew what he could set in motion, regarding Cheveley and the Herodotus. But he decided, for now, to confine himself to the bare facts concerning only his own vessel and let the rest emerge, as it may.

"We entered the harbour, Sir, and she wasn't in the Roads, she was moored to a quayside on the left. I remembered your orders, Sir, to take, or burn, or damage. To cut her out was impossible, so I decided that all that we could do, was to do damage her in whatever way we could. I'm confident that Lieutenant Sanders here, independently reached the same conclusion regarding our aim, for he began steering straight for her, just as we were. We raked her, then we were engaged by two bastions. I received a signal to withdraw, but we held our position for a short while longer until the Marines came off; we gave her a last broadside, then withdrew. We towed the lugger clear and made our escape, engaging the main bastion as we passed. Sir. It's all in my Log, Sir, there on your desk."

"Your estimate of her damage?"

"We got two broadsides into her, Sir, and every shot told. An explosion dislodged her mizzen. I've no reason to disagree with Lieutenant Sanders, here."

"Your own casualties?"

"23 dead, Sir, and 12 amputees. 18 wounded, 10 badly, 6 like to recover. I lost two Officers, Marine Captain Sanders and Lieutenant Bentley, and a Midshipman, Rufus Ffynes is an amputee. 56 in total. Sir."

Broke shot forward, his face showing genuine concern.

"56! And Bentley, dead?"

"Yes, Sir. On the way out, when we came under the guns of the main bastion, opposite La Pomone."

Broke sat back, to look away, he was genuinely worried. Grant continued.

"What damage to your ship?"

"Extensive damage to deck and planking, Sir. We have about six shot twixt wind and water, 32lbs, I believe, but my Carpenter thinks there are more. We lost our Mizzen topmast and damage to both standing and running rigging is extensive. Three guns overturned and a carronade."

Grant nodded, plainly saddened.

"Not far short of what you gave La Pomone."

"No Sir, but at least we weren't raked."

Grant looked at Shortman.

"Have you anything to add, Colonel?"

"Not a great deal, Sir, other than to say that we took the island and came off when Ariadne came out. I'm grateful that Ariadne covered our withdrawal with their guns. It saved us casualties, I'm certain."

Argent now spoke. Time to raise the issue.

"And I'd like it placed on record that I am grateful for Colonel Shortman for holding the island until Ariadne had sailed past. If the French had regained the fort, they could have done us further damage, such that could have finished us off."

Shortman spoke.

"No fear of that, Argent, we'd spiked the guns!"

Argent laughed.

"Thank you, Colonel. I guessed that you might have."

Grant continued his questioning.

"You haven't mentioned Herodotus? Where were you in relation to her, on the way out?"

"Some way behind, Sir. We came out alone, Herodotus had already left."

Cheveley looked angrily at Argent, but Grant sat forward and up, plainly this was taking a serious turn.

"You were not in consort with Herodotus?"

"No, Sir. That's correct, Sir, but Captain Cheveley can answer for his own ship."

Showing increasing shock and concern, Grant looked at Cheveley. This was new and, potentially, very grave.

"Captain Cheveley?"

Cheveley looked at Broke, shifted himself on his chair, and then he looked at Grant. Cheveley was plainly affronted. He both chose and spoke his words with great care. Grant stared straight back, eyes hard and stern.

"Captain Argent is quite correct. When we entered, I also saw La Pomone securely moored. I turned in the harbour and tried to anchor. However, in the Roads the tide was stronger that anticipated and we slipped too far down. I could not engage the main bastion directly, but we came under their fire. With La Pomone moored I considered the mission impossible to carry out to any significant effect, which seems to be borne out by what Lieutenant Sanders has said, regarding the actual amount of damage inflicted. I ordered withdrawal, sent by signal. I took my own ship out to save her further damage. I saw no point in sustaining damage and casualties when we could inflict so little on the enemy. I expected Ariadne to follow."

Grant looked at Cheveley, his face blank.

"And your damage and casualties?"

"Five shot into the hull, one dead, five wounded."

Grant's expression remained unchanged. He had a hundred questions, but he was uncertain if this was the time, almost certainly this would go further. He looked at Broke.

"Admiral?"

"I have nothing to add, Sir. I'm of the opinion that each Captain acted correctly according to their own circumstances, although Captain Argent does appear laggard in obeying the order to withdraw."

Grant looked at Broke, his face cold, but he had more serious issues to concern him. There was no change when he turned his baleful gaze to Cheveley.

"Captain Cheveley, I have to tell you that I am not satisfied with your answers, therefore I will stop this conversation amongst us now. The agreed plan was that La Pomone be cut out, sunk or damaged and that you support Ariadne as she withdrew with the boarding party after, after, I say again, they had inflicted what damage they could. It was clearly agreed that you would give support, if only by dividing the enemy's fire. There is now grave doubt that you complied, thus leaving Ariadne to make her exit unsupported. I must make it clear that I will mention this in my report to the Admiralty. If they wish to pursue the matter further, I'm sure you will hear from them, as I'm sure that I will."

Cheveley sat forward, not even slightly chastened, his natural anger building at any slight against himself. He clearly did not want an end to the discussion at this point but Grant had raised his hand, palm out, and then he stood up.

"Our meeting is finished, gentlemen."

Cheveley looked as though he were bursting to say more, but Grant had turned to Broke.

"Is the dry dock free?"

"At the moment, yes, but I have a Revenuer that needs attention."

"Ariadne goes in first. She gets priority. Am I clear?"

Broke nodded, as they all rose from their seats. Cheveley was the last to rise and, being in a state of mounting anger, would have re-opened the argument, but Broke went to him and pushed him gently towards the door; then they both left together. Grant placed his hand on Argent's arm, saying nothing, but, plainly, he wanted him to stay. Sanders looked back, alerted by his Captain's absence.

"If you could give us a moment, Lieutenant."

Sanders saluted and left, then Grant looked at Argent.

"Just between us, Argent. What's the truth?"

Argent's face went blank.

"We got across her stern and began to damage her in any way we could. I saw Herodotus anchored in the Roads, she was far down, but not so far as to be unable to engage the bastion. I saw her fire a broadside and I saw her achieve some hits. She was taking fire, true enough, and I saw the fall of shot around her, but she was answering fire. My signalman told me of his signal to withdraw, but she must have sent it after cutting her cable, when I looked she was already on her way out, whilst I was still waiting for the Marines to get back aboard their lugger."

"You were stationary when Herodotus cut her anchor?"

"Stationary? Yes Sir, absolutely, we were still fighting at La Pomone."

"So, Herodotus leaving whilst you were still across La Pomone's stern made it impossible for you to leave together, giving mutual support."

"Impossible Sir, yes, that's correct."

Grant nodded and Argent was saddened himself to see the Admiral's normally genial face so cast down.

"My thanks, Argent."

"Sir. I'll get back to my ship."

"Yes. Get her around to drydock, immediately."

Grant fetched Argent's crutch himself, from off the floor.

* * *

The carriage containing Argent and Sanders followed Cheveley's at a distance, but they inevitably caught up at the quayside. At the sight of the carriages, both barge crews came to the attention, both in line. Cheveley remained at his carriage, because Broke was still inside and they were having further words through the open door, therefore Argent's and Sanders' coach drew up behind before Cheveley departed the quayside. As they arrived and Argent and Sanders alighted, Cheveley had reached the steps down to his barge, but, seeing both arrive from behind, he stopped, to leave his own barge crew waiting below. Cheveley turned to both Argent and Sanders with a face of thunder, his hands clenched, but his eyes directly on Argent, who stood impassive, expression blank. Cheveley dearly wanted further words and so the temptation for him was irresistible. He strode forward, across the front of the lined up Ariadne barge crew, to stand before Argent. His face was livid, eyes burning, mouth twisted. He overtopped Argent by some inches and it clearly appeared that a physical assault was about to fall on their wounded Captain. Whiting nudged King to be alert, but Cheveley only leaned forward, each word spat out.

"You disobeyed a direct order. I ordered withdrawal, and you failed to comply. I hold you responsible."

Argent looked at him impassively, but contempt grew on his face. By his code, he was dealing with a coward and a bully.

"Responsible for what? That we didn't leave together? I was still engaging the enemy when you cut your cable. I withdrew, yes, obeying your order when I could, when I would be taking the Marines with me, and that being merely minutes after seeing your signal. My bowsprit over your taffrail, that was the agreement, before you would cut your anchor to leave, together with me. Why that did not occur, only you can answer, for only you know!"

Cheveley leaned further forward and Whiting nudged King again. Their Captain remained calmly leaning on his crutch, but Sanders had moved to his shoulder, even partly covering Argent in front, face and chest jutting forward at Cheveley, eyes fixed on him, obviously prepared to defend his Captain, a fact not unnoticed by Whiting. However, it was Argent who spoke further.

"You can ask for an enquiry yourself, Captain, if you feel your name has been sullied in some way. I suspect that one will come about in any event, and that will give you every opportunity to put your case and justify your conduct. That's for the future, but now, if you have no objection, I have a sinking ship to attend to."

Cheveley straightened up. He gave Argent a last withering look, then turned on his heel to descend the steps. Soon, his barge was moving off across the harbour, no one within either looking up or looking back. Argent and Sanders stood at the top of the steps to allow the crew to descend first and Whiting motioned his men to follow him, but as he passed Sanders, the Captain's Cox'n looked at him directly and nodded his head. Sanders, once before-the-mast himself, knew the meaning and smiled knowingly in reply.

Once back alongside their ship, the noise of the pumps having grown louder in their ears as they drew nearer, all was hoisted up to be made safe, Argent with a whip around his armpits as a precaution, as he ascended the ladder one step at a time. He reached his quarterdeck and gave his orders.

"Longboat over the side. Signal to harbourmaster, "Request a tow".

Meanwhile Whiting and his mates had reached the lower deck and begun to relate the lurid tale of the confrontation with that "floggin' bastard" Cheveley. The "floggin' bastard" had raised his fists to the Captain, but the Captain had given him "one muzzleload into his ear", and Sanders had stood before their wounded Captain and put in a hand to block Cheveley, simultaneously telling him to "shove off and sink". Sanders' personal star was well in the ascendant.

Come the evening Ariadne was in the dry-dock, having been towed there by two longboats and warped in. The removal of the water had revealed two more hits, low down. The water had taken much of the impact, but the balls had penetrated nevertheless and these were the sources of the continued ingress of water, a yard below the waterline. As a nearby church clock chimed six of the evening, Argent ordered the whole crew stood down and to a late supper. An hour before their own meal with his Officers in the greatcabin, Argent sat with Fentiman and Frederick Baines, to establish priorities. The hull came first, which would require the hold to be emptied, also the forward magazine and, once watertight, Ariadne would be moored to the quayside to complete her repairs. There was no need for the masthoy, her own crew could raise a mizzen topmast, so, tomorrow, at seven bells, which began the forenoon watch, the larboard watch would begin emptying the required spaces and the starboard would continue with the spars and rigging. Baines, his business finished, took his leave.

Management complete, both took a glass of madeira, Fentiman doing the pouring. Argent's leg was painful and tired so he gratefully took his ease. However, with both seated and provided for, Fentiman took Argent by surprise, such a change of subject that Argent could only attribute to Fentiman feeling light headed with fatigue.

"Do you think I have any chance with Charlotte Willoughby?"

Argent could not prevent a look of shock, which he quickly removed.

"I don't see why not. You're from a good family, landed, and with a good income. Salt, isn't it, your family are in? And aren't you some kind of Honourable?"

"Yes, and Father's had a canal dug, linking us with the Trent. Funds won't be a problem. But; what do you honestly think?"

"What can I say? I'm no expert on the ways of women, nor their society; of which she's a major part, at least in this area. Have you had any communication, at all?"

"Yes, I've written and received a reply that I would describe as most kind and gracious. It's given me some hope, as you can imagine."

Argent pictured Charlotte Willoughby, a stunning beauty, who would not be out of place at The Palace; she would grace even the Royal Court. He remembered how Cheveley was always pushing his attentions forward in her direction and the Spanish couldn't take their eyes off her. Fentiman was a fine, brave, Officer, with good prospects within the Navy, but a suitor for Charlotte Willoughby? He had his doubts, but it was not impossible.

"I wish you good luck, Henry."

* * *

The yacht had been easy prey. Almost becalmed, she had been overtaken by the eager oarsmen on the galley and now her passengers, disbelieving and traumatised to the point that their minds had almost ceased to function, were being brought aboard the galley. All were crying uncontrollably and in deep shock, they couldn't believe what was happening to them and worst, couldn't believe what had happened to their menfolk and the crew. They were all dead, butchered by the slavers the instant they took the ship. Kaled Al'Ahbim felt some satisfaction, some gain at no cost; two women, three girls, two boys, all would fetch a good price. Weeping and barely able to stand, they were pushed below decks, surrounded by men of a strange race, each with a cruel and malevolent grin spread large over an alien face. They disappeared down into the stench and gloom as fires sprang up aboard their yacht. A pleasure cruise just off the coast by two families of wealthy merchants from La Rochelle had ended with their lives in ruin.

Chapter Six

New Shipmates

Ariadne's hull seemed to be full of hammers, all busy and all competing; the large and the small, the tuneful and the discordant. It had been decided to bring forward Ariadne's refit and so, besides the carpenters pulling at her decks and planking, she would receive new copper on her hull and a thorough check of her masts, spars and rigging. The existing copper was old, green, and Spanish; thin, and the victim of corruption. It was also peeling off the hull in all directions, revealing her timbers and, more importantly for her Captain, slowing her speed, but the noise from it's removal and replacement during the working day was incessant. Argent's leg was better, he could stand on it, but not walk normally and the crutch was still required, also, in addition to the noise of the hammering, Mrs. McArdle's potion made him sleepy and absent minded. To his consternation, she had sent a second bottle and he dared not fail to do as he was bid; yet wicked thoughts were circulating in his fuzzy head about dispensing doses out of the cabin window.

The new coppering had progressed to the larboard quarter, adjacent to his cabin and the hammering was echoing around his cabin and twice as much inside his head. There was no reason to remain there and no administration to occupy him; there remained only the signing off of the repairs and that was in the future. He took himself out to the gundeck. All the guns were housed and bowsed up, two with conspicuously new carriages and conspicuously new carving, "Bad Language", and "Mad Joseph." He continued to the quarterdeck companionway and threw up his crutch, then he followed it, one step at a time, but at least independently. A September wind was blowing off the sea, chill, but refreshing to his cotton-wool head, a cold precursor to the Autumn now arriving with the ineluctable rotation of the planets. He looked forward and felt in some way further disorientated, the reason being, he could only conclude, was because beyond the ship's side there should be water, either moving or still, instead, there was the damp grey and green brickwork of the dry dock, with uncountable wooden spars leading from the dockside to Ariadne's tumblebhome, thus holding her upright and steady, although Argent would swear to a lean towards starboard.

The lack of affairs concerning his ship had turned his thoughts to the affairs of his family. Had there been any developments, had Lady Willoughby found anything, had his sisters? He felt that he could justifiably take himself away for a day, or perhaps two, albeit that his ship was now in Plymouth and that much further away. However, it was easier for him to get on and off the ship, also to get letters off the ship, and so he resolved to return to his cabin and write to both his sisters and Lady Willoughby to warn them that he would be with them the day after tomorrow. However, for the moment, he would take a few more lungfuls of fresh air and a few more minutes of respite from the incessant din. He hammered his own fist against the new and extra backstays that now ran up to the join of the maintopmast and the mast above it, the maintopgallant mast, backstays ordered by Fraser and to be anchored from the unusual point of the mizzenmast shrouds. He hammered to no effect, both were as solid as the bulwark rail under his elbow, so then he leaned against the starboard bulwark to ease his leg and watch his crew sending up a new mainsail spar, with all attachments, including the huge sail. The old spar had been found to be sprung, which gave much ammunition to the men of the fore and mizzen tops about the "half blind lubbers" of the main top. The huge assembly was going up powered by almost all the crew on the capstan, all accompanied by the harsh admonishments of Bosun Fraser, shouting warnings to all involved about what could happen if they were to fail in their proper attentions. If that were all that had the potential to cause him disquiet, that being what he saw from his quarterdeck, Argent would be a contented man, but the worries of his family nagged at him. He was just about to lever himself off the bulwark and lean upon his crutch, when Fentimen brought over a piece of paper he had been studying. He handed it to Argent.

"Replacements, Sir."

It was a long list. At the top it said Lieutenant Benjamin Wentworth, a recently passed out Midshipman; second on the list, a new Midshipman, the Honourable Thomas Trenchard; and third a Captain of Marines, Reginald Breakspeare. Beneath that was a list of 59 names, to replace the casualties amongst the men. Argent noted that the description "pressed" or "convict" came up with depressing regularity as an addition to many of the names, but, at least, there were nine volunteers. Seven said merely "Marine". Argent handed the paper back.

"The usual mixture, in the usual proportions. We must spend time with their instruction. They are replacing good men. Are any of the Officers known to you?"

"Not personally, but I've heard of Trenchard's family. A political one, I believe. But there is no replacement for Bentley. I assume Sanders remains "acting"?

"Yes, until we hear otherwise. Until then, I'm well content. That's not a boat that I intend to rock."

Fentiman smiled and nodded.

"Nor I. He's liked by the men and respected. A rare combination. From somewhere, somehow, they know his background, which gives him a head start above most."

Argent nodded, but he wanted to change the subject.

"Henry. How are you fixed, work wise, over the next two or three days?"

"Nothing formal, Sir, bar the odd day-to-day. Fraser and his mates are taking care of most things. I was just studying this list for something to do"

"Good, then I'm going to take my leave for two days, day after tomorrow. There's a Mailpacket, leaves early each day for Falmouth and beyond. I intend to take passage on her and visit my family, and the Willoughby's.

"Oh, the Willoughby's. Would you do me a great favour and deliver a letter to Charlotte?"

* * *

Argent leaned on the weather bulwark, out of habit, but not that of the quarterdeck. Not just for the change in place, he was dressed as a civilian, but also because, uniformed as Royal Navy, he would not be left to himself by the Officers of the Mailpacket and he relished the time of freedom from his normal level of high responsibility. To that end, he told himself to resist the temptation to assess the sails that were set, if more or less canvas, or sheeted more here or less there, but he had failed. Captain's instinct frequently took his gaze aloft, but he could find no complaint. The cutter, sporting two masts with a fore and aft rig, was moving beautifully in a wind just before the beam, a wind steady, just East of South. All around and above showed the crew all to be "right seamen", well practiced and long accustomed to their ship. She being "official", a Mailpacket about the King's business, she was therefore exempt from the Press, no man could be taken from her. They had made good speed since their Noon departure and now Pendennis Castle was growing in detail off the starboard bow.

Argent was quiet inside, still subdued from his morning attendance of the funeral for his men. For common seamen there had been no last bugles, no fired salute, simply a brief, standard sermon over the mass grave dug fresh amongst other, older, mass graves, and the sermon read routinely before the earth could be shovelled over the long row of 31 simple coffins. As the Cleric walked away and the gravediggers began their work, he had bade them halt and had himself taken the time to cast a handful of earth on each, followed by McArdle, Short, Fraser and two of his Mates.

He took himself back to the break of the quarterdeck, mostly to get himself out of the way, for soon the Captain would be ordering the same change of course as he had made himself, some weeks previously. The order came, the wheel spun and the sails came over for the starboard tack. The Mailpacket, needing to sail on at the earliest, found a longboat out waiting for her in Carrick Roads and the two were made fast together. Then, Argent, two mailbags, and a corpulent Merchant were transferred and soon Argent was at the door of the same stable where he had hired a horse before. The owner had remembered not only his name, but also his fame, and offered a better horse. However, Argent was content to again use the same mount as before, which he termed "that good mare, which now knows her way." Thus he came to the gates of the Willoughby Estate and they were open, which somehow gave Argent hope that they had received his letter.

He thethered the mare, ascended the steps and approached the door, the familiarity of both making him feel welcome, this stemming from recent happy memories. He knocked and a liveried servant opened and bade him enter, then to take his cloak.

"Lady Willoughby is occupied elsewhere, Captain, for the moment. But she is expecting you, and I'm told to take you into the Drawing Room and offer you tea. I will tell her that you have arrived, and I am sure that she will be with you shortly."

Argent stumped to the door of the Drawing Room, giving the servant ample time to swoop round and open it for him. Once inside, rather than sit, Argent felt the need to stand by the French windows and look out over the green and immaculate lawns. Bright flowers, shrubs and bickering birds presented a soporific scene of tranquil calm in which he submersed himself, and also came thoughts of the jolly evening the last time he was there. Hardly had he observed all the detail before some tea arrived and the maid presented him with a cup that he drank whilst remaining standing in order to continue to look over the garden. She moved a stand close to his right hand to support the cup and saucer and waited until he had finished, then poured him another. Half way through it, Lady Willoughby arrived. She began with the usual greetings but then noticed the crutch under his left shoulder and the odd shape of his left thigh.

"But you're wounded!"

"It's nothing, Lady Willoughby. It's getting better every day, look, I can now stand on it. Even hop!"

He removed the crutch and waved it aloft, endangering the curtain pelmet, whilst his left leg stood steady and he jigged up on it, once. The maid giggled, but was immediately shooed out by Lady Willoughby.

"But you must sit. Please do, by me."

Argent joined her on the long settee, but her anxious look had not been banished by his antics with the crutch.

"How? Is it painful?"

"What we call a splinter, Lady Willoughby, a large lump of wood hit me from behind. It was painful, but it's a great deal better now. I wonder if you can remember me mentioning the wife of our Sailing Master, Mrs. McArdle?"

She nodded.

"Well she has been doctoring me vigorously with various unctions and ointments, and, I must say, I am now well on the mend."

She smiled, evidently relieved.

"I am very pleased to hear you say so, Reuben. Septimus told me something about the affair. He has some concerns over it."

"Yes, Lady Willoughby, so I understand, but I'm a mere frigate Captain. For me such things are on another galaxy, beyond the thoughts of mere mortals such as I."

Argent looked steadily at her.

"I mentioned in my letter the main reason for my visit. I was hoping that you might have some news."

Her face fell, at which expression, Argent's did also.

"No Reuben, I'm afraid I have no good news. I have tasked each Solicitor in Falmouth but the best that they can come up with is a mention of your family's land as only that, land to the North of here, but no inclusion of any name. I'm sorry, and from two, it's worse. They are of the opinion that the mere mention of your family name is not proof of ownership. You may live there, but do you have the right to live there? Broke and Cinch's lawyers could drive straight through that. I'm so sorry. Wheeler and Simpson, the solicitors who hold my own deeds, have also drawn a blank. I wish there were more I could do."

Argent smiled encouragingly.

"You have done all you could, Lady Willoughby, and all that I asked. I sincerely thank you for doing what you have done."

He rose from the seat, making full use of the crutch to hoist himself up.

"May I excuse myself now? I wish to visit my family and I have to be back on my ship the day after tomorrow."

She rose also and walked to the bell pull, but did not pull it.

"I have some news also, Reuben, which I hope may cheer you. Septimus and myself are to be married. This month, the 18th. The morning spent in Church, the afternoon on the lawn of our harbour house. Only a small affair, we are both well past any sort of fuss, but I do hope that you will come, if you are able."

Argent's face showed genuine pleasure, which in turn cheered Lady Willoughby.

"My fullest and heartiest congratulations, My Lady. I will make every effort to come. If I cannot get away, I'll bring my ship! I wish you every happiness, and a long life together."

The last seemed a bit clumsy, but Argent was relieved when Lady Willoughby laughed.

"Thank you Captain"

She pulled the bell.

"Now, you must go to your family."

Within seconds the door was opened to emit the same servant, who positioned himself to hold open the door. Argent arranged his crutch to comfortable then reached inside his coat with his right hand to extract Fentiman's letter.

"My First, Lieutenant Fentiman, asked that I deliver this, from him to Charlotte. May I leave it with you?"

She took the letter, her face blank, but when she looked at him she smiled again.

"Good day, Reuben. Good luck to your ship, and good luck with your quest. If anything does come my way, I will let you know immediately."

She extended her hand, which Argent took and then bowed over it.

* * *

Perhaps the good mare did remember the way, for, once out of the gate, Argent had barely to touch the reins and she trotted contentedly down the road, her hooves making a cheery "clip clop" against the hard, stony, earth. When she met the hill she set about it with a will and the order of sights for his journey to the farm passed rapidly. It was as if his sisters were waiting for him, for both stood in the road at the gate, their joy at seeing him was genuine and both instinctively moved forward to hasten the time they would meet, but their joy turned to consternation when they saw him drop the crutch prior to him dismounting. Once descended, he picked it up and placed it under his left shoulder. This brought shrieks of concern from both and each rushed to support him as though he were imminently about to expire and it was only his laughing at their distress that reassured them that he was to remain alive, at least yet awhile. It was Enid who spoke first, in admonishment.

"Why didn't you tell us you were wounded, and give us some warning? That you were still in one piece, at least?"

Argent's answer was to take both in his arms and kiss both, Enid first.

"I didn't because it's nothing. Just a bruise. Of no mind."

Emily broke away.

"It's not, you're hurt."

She gave him her customary push as a punishment, luckily from the right, so that he was still supported by the crutch, then she realised what she had done. Her hands went to her mouth, then she grabbed him, unnecessarily, just in case he did fall over. Argent grinned.

"Let's go in. A morsel to eat would not come amiss."

He took himself to the door, both sisters anxiously examining his progress. Inside there was a fire, on that day the wind was chill atop the hill and Argent took a seat where he would feel the heat. Enid came over to place the kettle on the fire.

"How long can you stay for?"

"One night. Then I must get back, to Plymouth. Ariadne's in dry dock there."

Emily was carving some ham to add to some cheese and bread on a huge plate.

"Then she's damaged. How? We heard nothing."

Argent smiled at her.

"I'm not surprised. It wasn't any kind of notable success, such as would interest the newssheets. Although I saw enough courage to fill the pages of a dozen such."

Seeing Argent's serious face, changed her own as she brought over the plate of food and Argent could see that her face was near terrified.

"So it was very dangerous?"

Argent looked at her calmly, his mouth half smiling.

"We had a fight with the French, Emily. They're our enemies, it's always going to be dangerous, more or less."

He considered adding, "I've come back", but stopped himself. He took a mouthful of food and looked at her, then at Enid. No one spoke until he swallowed, then he did.

"So, how's Jacob, and Beryan, and Father?"

It was Enid who replied, but she seemed as anxious as her younger sister.

"Jacob's fine, asleep next door. Beryan's in the South field, and Father's in the North. Both well."

She paused and looked at his bandaged leg and the crutch beside it.

"You can use that horse of yours to take around their croust, that'll save us both a journey."

Argent smiled and nodded.

"Pleased to, but that's not why I came. The Deeds, what did you find?"

Emily sat and clasped her hands together in her lap, but remained silent, looking sideways, then downwards. It was Enid that replied; though busy wrapping food in a cloth.

"Nothing, we found nothing. Some Bills of Sale for some odd strips, but for the main and the house itself, we found nothing."

Argent kept silent about learning the same with Lady Willoughby, why pile on more misery? However, he did have some good news.

"Well, I've increased my prize money. Not by much, but some. We captured a smuggler, which will add to the amount. So, as I said last time, we may not be able to stay on this farm, but, we can always buy another one. And now, perhaps a little bit bigger than before."

Enid did her best to respond to his attempt to cheer them and Emily managed a smile.

"So, all is not lost."

"No, indeed, oh sisters mine! A roof will be maintained, if not this one."

Their faces fell, he wished he'd not added the last, but he was determined to be cheerful. Enid had finished the food parcels, so he stood and limped over, deliberately forgetting the crutch.

"Now, which is which? Which for whom?"

"Father's in the red check and Beryan's the green."

She looked up into his face, laughing.

"Can you remember that? Yours is back here, when you return. You can finish what's still on that plate."

If there was a reason why Argent loved his sister it was for her courage, her rocklike fortitude, against whatever came their way, good or bad. He leant over her outstretched hands that held the food and kissed her. She, in response, smiled and pushed the food against his chest.

"The sooner they get theirs, the sooner you can come back and finish yours."

He limped and hopped to the door, but paused at the spot. Above the door was fixed the sword of the Captain of La Mouette, supported by two brass hooks. He noted that all three were carefully polished and wholly free of any dust. He turned around to look at Enid.

"I see there's been an improvement in the ornaments that you have around here now."

She gave a smile, but not quite a laugh.

"That's enough from you. You've got your orders. Now go."

She placed her hands on his shoulders, but remembered not to deliver the usual push.

Argent decided to visit Beryan first, the South field was nearest and he wished to spend more time with his Father. He soon found Beryan, moving hurdles to pen in their cattle, the South field this year was set for grazing. They greeted each other not just as good friends, as they always had been, but as family, each now sharing the fortunes of the other. Argent dismounted but remained holding the reins as he took the green check bundle from the saddlebag. He looked at Beryan.

"No good news, then?"

Beryan instantly knew the subject in question.

"No. They searched high and low, in every chest and bag. Bills of Sale, but no Deeds."

Argent nodded. Some re-assuring words came to mind, but Beryan was not a child. He knew the threat they were under and well understood the possible outcome, but Beryan did smile when he noticed the ridges of the bandage around Argent's thigh, and pointed.

"So what's that? Is that where Navy boys wear their money belt?"

Argent laughed.

"No, just a bit of frapping to give me comfort in this saddle. Now, give me a lift up"

Argent placed his left foot in the stirrup and pulled himself off the ground with his hands on the pommel. Beryan gave him a shove up for the remaining distance. Argent looked down at him.

"See you at supper."

Beryan nodded and Argent pulled the mare's head for the track. He set her for a trot along the short cut to the North field and there he found Argent Senior, on the same strip that they had ploughed weeks earlier, but this time hoeing, creating rows from the robust seedlings. He had his back to Argent, so Argent hobbled the horse and walked the row up to his Father. Father must have heard or sensed something, for he turned before Argent could speak and saw his son within the rows and, Argent was pleased to see, surprise and happiness came to his face.

"Hello, son. Delivering again?"

"Hello, Father. Yes, this one's yours, I've just taken Beryan's over."

Argent Senior dropped the hoe and sat on the ground, opening the parcel. Argent sat with him, but his Father noticed him wince as he placed weight on his left leg.

"What's the matter? Some injury?"

"Yes, Father, just a whack, but it's on the mend."

He looked at his Father, now chewing vigorously.

"No good news on the Deeds."

Argent Senior swallowed.

"No, but I've heard that the County Court in Truro may keep some kind of records, copies even. I'm going to take a visit there, soon, sooner the better."

Argent brightened.

"Who told you that?"

"Oh, a few friends. You know."

Argent stopped there. He knew that nothing more would be forthcoming.

"And the Enclosure Act?"

"Going through. It's with Parliament as we speak."

Argent looked at his Father, trying to detect some emotion, but there was none. His Father continued to bite into his food.

"Your visit to Truro, delay it until I can come with you. After our next patrol, I'll get some leave and we'll go together. I'll wear my full dress uniform, which'll stir some stumps. County officials are always chary of the military, and a bit of apprehension in their minds won't come amiss."

His Father chewed and looked at him. He then took another bite and chewed some more. Argent spoke further.

"I've increased my prize money as well, so don't forget that."

No reaction.

"This beet's come up well. Must be something to do with the ploughing. And the sowing."

For the first time for some minutes, his Father nodded.

Evening supper was surprisingly cheerful, made more so by Jacob joining them, now that he was big enough to sit on his Mother's knee and be fed. The way he happily devoured whatever came his way on the spoon raised the spirits of them all. With the meal finished and the table being cleared, Argent, his Father and Beryan sat by the fire and talked, mostly prices, both for buying and selling. This being a faraway topic for him, but important to his companions, Argent was content to keep out, go through the motions of puffing the pipe and study the fire. The cloud of worry that was over them all was not mentioned and remained in the background, out of their conversation, if not out of their thoughts.

In the morning Argent rose late and found both his Father and Beryan gone. His taking of his leave was both fraught and emotional, why his sisters should be so, he didn't ask, nor did he raise any issue. It could be that his leg reminded his sisters of the dangers he could be exposed to, or the worry of the farm, or the two together. He handed the crutch down to them from the saddle.

"Put that in a corner for me. I'll need it come old age."

They both smiled into a day that had no sunshine, but it made Argent feel warm despite the grey clouds.

* * *

With the setting of the sun, he was ascending the gangplank of his own ship, welcomed by the calls of Bosun Fraser and his mates, as he crossed the deep void below him, for Ariadne remained still in dry dock. The next morning saw the new arrivals, each arriving in very different fashion to each other. The seven Marines marched up, with no NCO, having organised themselves into three two's and a one. They waited for the Sergeant to come down to the quayside, one handed over their papers and then they filed aboard. Their place was taken by a very different spectacle. The new crewmen were marched down under close guard from the local Militia, all in a group, volunteers, pressedmen, and convicts, all gathered together. Although all were in a tight group, it was not difficult to discern the three types. The volunteers stood looking eagerly at the ship and the high masts, they were dressed better and most had some kind of satchel or sack slung across their shoulders. The pressed men could be identified if only by the angry look on their faces. They looked resentfully at the ship and angrily at each other, sharing their resentment to curse their ill fortune. Their hands were bound before them. Likewise the convicts, only for them there was extra, a tether from the back of their neck to the hands of the man behind and thick ankle chains. All these were scruffy, dirty, and unshaven. Most couldn't bring themselves to look at the ship they had been condemned to. The majority of the Militia guard were grouped around these latter.

Fentiman took the book of the Ship's Muster down to a crude table that was set up on the quayside, at the beginning of the gangplank. First, the volunteers. These gave their name and their previous occupation, then they signed their name, or made their mark. They were then given their volunteer's bounty, 3s and 3d. Then came the pressedmen, but less willingly and with blank anger. When they had given their name, their bindings were removed to enable them to sign their name or make their mark. No bounty for them. Finally the convicts. First their chains were removed, then they were asked their name. The question regarding occupation was omitted, each was entered as "convict". Then their neck bindings were removed, but those around their wrists only taken off if they could write. It was assumed that they could make a mark with hands tethered. Then, with all bonds removed they were allowed up the gangplank. One, in utter desperation, for there was no water to jump into, tried to run along the quayside, to be halted by the butt of a musket into his face. Semi conscious and bloody, he was carried up the gangplank, to be dumped on the deck, at the end of the assembled gathering of new "recruits".

Argent waited for Bosun Fraser and his Mates to shove them all into two lines along the starboard gangway. The volunteers were to Argent's right, waiting eagerly to hear what he had to say. In the centre, the pressedmen looked at him with pure hatred, the convicts on the left, looking anywhere but at him. Most of the latter were thinking, "Will this be worse than gaol?" Many, amongst all types, looked anxiously at the battle damage not yet repaired. With all assembled Argent nodded at Fraser.

"Attention."

The volunteers all came to a stiff upright, the pressedmen made no move, but most of the convicts achieved a better posture. Argent began. He had to search for words, this was his first time to address such a gathering.

"At ease."

At each end of the line, but not the middle, shoulders were lowered.

"Welcome to HMS Ariadne. We are a 32 gun frigate, a 6th rate, and such as we are spend most of their time at sea, but returning to port quite often. You will be allocated into what we call Watches, Starboard or Larboard, then into what we call the afterguard or the waisters. It is there that you will learn the skills that you will need to help us work the ship. There we can assess you. Perhaps you have it in you to become a topman, which will raise you up, both actually, you climb the masts, and also in status, it gains you higher pay."

What humour registered showed only on the faces of the volunteers. Argent paused.

"Perhaps you've heard of Ariadne. We've had our triumphs and always try to do our duty. This ship has a good name, which is something that many of you cannot claim for yourselves. This is your chance to change your lives, but I deduce you probably think it has been changed anyway. This is a ship that fights, she fights to keep the French from our shores. It matters not what you were before, what matters now is what you become, from now, from this moment. I urge you all to make yourselves into a seaman and become a valued and respected member of this crew."

Argent nodded at Fraser, then walked towards his quarterdeck to descend the companionway to his cabin. Fraser stood before the parade, with his Mates at his back. His Captain was leaving.

"Attention!"

The sight of Fraser caused all to become more upright. Fraser gave them time to look at him.

"My name is Boatswain Fraser. These behind me are my Mates. Boatswain's Mates. My job is to look after the ship. She's my mother, my wife, and my sickly sister, which makes her a damn sight more important to me than any of you. You don't want to know me. You think of the nastiest, most ill-tempered, double foul bastard you've ever known, then double it and treble it, then you'll get somewhere close to me. You fail this ship and you fail me. You fail this ship and your lubber's work could send us all to the bottom. Your shipmates acts like right seamen because it keeps them alive and you too. So listen to what you're told, get it right and look lively. Then you'll not feel a touch of this."

Fraser held up his "starter", a short, thick, length of rope, with a knot on the end and he smacked it three or four times into his palm. He replaced it behind his back, then paused further and looked towards the quarterdeck. The sole Officer was Midshipman Bright.

"You won't be thinkin' this. You'll be thinkin' your world's come to an end, but I'll tell you this. You could be a damn sight worse off elsewhere, on some other barky than this one, what's called Ariadne. There's plenty as would transfer onto this deck, given the choice."

He paused to allow that to sink in.

"Now, we'n goin' to take you down to the gundeck, and decide wher' you'n best placed, like Captain Argent said."

He paused.

"Stand easy."

They all relaxed for Marines to then lead the way and some Marines to follow behind, shepherding the men forward with their muskets. Down on the gundeck each was assessed. Most would be waisters, the most unskilled, but some, most likely those pressed out of merchantmen, would be made immediately into the higher status afterguard.

In his cabin, Argent busied himself with the letters and lists that had built up in his absence and from them he learned that his ship was to leave the dry dock tomorrow. He had just finished, when Ramsey's replacement arrived at Noon, Marine Captain Alloysius Breakspeare. Argent had studied his papers and marked him as one of the older Marine Captains, but very experienced with a string of ships and a list of land actions. Breakspeare knocked before being called in and stood to attention with his shako under his right arm, his left hand on his sword hilt. Argent stood to greet him and came around the desk to shake his hand. The shako was smartly transferred.

"Captain Brakespeare, welcome to the ship. My name is Reuben Argent."

"Alloysius Brakespeare, Sir. Thank you, I'm most happy to be joining the company."

Brakespeare was slightly shorter than Argent, but broader. There was a scar across his left eye, and part of his left ear was missing. Argent immediately assessed him as a solid, capable, and experienced Officer. Nothing more need be said.

"We're happy to have you. Did you know Captain Ramsey?"

"Yes Sir. His sister is married to my brother."

"Well, part of the family then, or was."

"Yes Sir. He was a good man, Sir."

Argent nodded.

"Right, I'll let you get on, to settle in. The Marine sentry will show you to your cabin."

Argent shook his hand again. Brakespeare, took one pace back, saluted and turned. Argent thought to himself, "a bit stiff, but he'll fit in". He felt confident, then with Brakespeare's departure, Argent returned to his papers, to soon be disturbed by another knock on the door. The sentry entered to announce another new arrival.

"Lieutenant Wentworth, Sir."

Argent stood again.

"Show him in."

What came in was an odd and narrow apparition, made stranger by the fact that he was so tall that he had to hold his head at an angle to avoid the deckbeams above. Seeing this, Argent was anxious that Wentworth quickly take a seat. Again, he came around the desk.

"Welcome to the ship, Lieutenant. Please take a seat."

Wentworth sat down and arranged his four long limbs into various angles of comfort. Argent repeated his greeting.

"Welcome to the ship."

"Th-th thank you, S-S-S-Sir."

Argent smiled and nodded, hoping that the stutter was the product of nerves caused by his boarding his first ship. Argent returned to his place.

"You've just passed out?"

Wentworth nodded, which Argent found unacceptable.

"Just passed out?"

"S-Sir."

"And with high marks, and commendations, so I have read. Well, with your arrival, I now have three Lieutenants, My First, Henry Fentiman, My Second, Jonathan Sanders, and you. My Sailing Master is Mr. Leviticus McArdle, a very religious man, you need to know. All three are very experienced and have faced the French. Talk to them, they'll help you to settle in."

Argent suddenly felt anxious at what he had said, as though he had hit upon a problem.

"You will find all to be a fund of knowledge and experience, from which you will benefit, if you take the trouble. Now, have you met Lieutenant Fentiman?"

"No, Sir."

Argent felt better.

"Sentry!"

The sentry arrived.

"Take Lieutenant Wentworth to the First."

The Marine held the door open and Wentworth unwound himself from the chair. Argent stood and leaned across the desk, extending his hand.

"Do your best, Benjamin. We're pleased to have you."

"Tha-th-thank you, S-Sir."

Argent felt worse. How the Hell did he get through his Board? Desperation on the part of the Admiralty, must be.

The hammering continued throughout the day, but Argent's days away had seen the end of the fixing of the new copper. Frederick Baines and his mates had spent the day making a careful check, adding extra copper nails as they thought fit and that also was now finished. Tomorrow the dock would be flooded and Ariadne returned to her natural element, then she would be towed out to a quayside, to complete her state of readiness. With the sun glowing orange, then red, through his stern windows, he took himself onto the quarterdeck. His crew were still busy, but most were now cleaning, ridding the ship of the evidence of longshore contamination. Ariadne was looking more like her old self, albeit with several patches of new decking and planking. Soon he would be going to Broke for orders, or receiving them by courier, more likely.

The next day, in the forenoon, saw the last of the new arrivals and it was a memorable entrance. A huge, closed, gleaming coach progressed down the dockside, with two liveried coachmen at the rear and another beside the driver. Argent was at the dockside bulwark and leaned on the rail to observe. The coach halted at the gangplank, before the sentry, and one of the coachmen ran forward to open the door. The door opened and out came a young man of mid teens, clad in an immaculately tailored Midshipman's uniform. He stood at the door of the coach for some time, until finally a highly elaborated female kissed him and an equally immaculate man descended from the coach. The adult immediately gave orders and the standing coachman went to the rear and produced two large chests, each being picked up by himself and the other coachman. The young man shook hands with his Father, who motioned the coachmen towards the gangplank. They both began to ascend to the deck, followed by the youngster.

Argent didn't like what he was seeing, on two counts. He walked along the gangway and stood at the top of the gangplank.

"Halt. Go back."

The coachmen looked astonished and surprised. They halted, but did not retreat; instead they looked back at their Master. Argent advanced down the gangplank.

"Go back. Go back, I say."

Seeing a uniform coming down at them, this time they did return to the stone of the quayside. They stood aside to allow their Master to walk forward to meet the oncoming Argent, who did not extend his hand, for the "Master" was stood hands behind his back, beginning to look angry.

"Good morning. My name is Captain Argent".

Argent placed himself at the end of the gangplank.

"Two things. Firstly, two chests is one too many. The Midshipman's Berth would seem to you, if you saw it, to be no more than a large cupboard, and it already contains two incumbents. Secondly, only my crew come aboard my ship, they are, after all, the crew. Others only with my permission. Therefore, the midshipman here, carries aboard his own dunnage, that being one chest."

He paused to await some reaction from the Master. None came, perhaps from surprise that someone had prevented him and his minions from carrying out his fixed intentions. Argent continued.

"I must ask, therefore, that you reduce the Midshipman's belongings to a single chest, in whichever way you choose, before he comes aboard."

A female expression of great impatience appeared at the window of the coach door. The Father, a block of a man and as finely tailored as his son, only with more embellishments, placed himself squarely before Argent, setting himself for the imminent confrontation.

"Do you know who I am?"

Argent returned a blank stare.

"I assume you to be Mr. Trenchard, Father to Midshipman Trenchard here, but what is more important is that you know what I know. As the Captain of this ship, I have to decide what happens and in what way. No one takes up more room than he is entitled to. No one, including me. Your son is entitled to only so much space in his berth and we find that to be adequately described by one sea chest. If you find that to be unacceptable, then, well, I already have two Midshipmen, I can get by with that number. If you understand me? So, well, the choice is yours."

Argent paused to find himself viewing a look of blank astonishment, but nothing spoken.

"So, I'll leave you to your deliberations. Good day."

Argent turned, then stopped to face them again.

"Your pardon. One thing I should have said. If you so choose that he does join our crew, I would strongly advise that you include any instruments that you may have provided for him, especially his sextant. And writing and drawing materials."

Argent then turned again and ascended the gangplank. At the entry port he instructed the sentry.

"Only the Midshipman is to come aboard, carrying his own chest, just one."

The sentry grinned and flexed his hand around his musket, it with bayonet fixed.

"Yes Sir. Well understood, Sir."

"And if he does come aboard, he leaves his chest here, within your care, and you ask a seaman to conduct him to my cabin."

The sentry shouldered his musket, came to the attention and saluted.

"Sir."

Argent walked back along the gangway and gave himself the luxury of a look down over to the coach. One chest was still on the quayside; the other was being pushed into the coach by a coachman. Of Father, Mother, or Midshipman, there was nothing to be seen. He continued back to the taffrail and took a satisfied look over, at the mighty gates that held back the waters of The Sound, soon to be opened, but both gates were of such thorough and precise construction that but a trickle of water edged down between the two and a little also at each side. He returned to his cabin and idled away the time, sat at his desk toying with a letter opener and soon came seven bells of the forenoon watch, half an hour before dinner. The minutes idled away and he was considering returning to the deck when there came a knock on the door. It opened to admit a seaman and behind him stood the youngster.

"Midshipman Trenchard, Sir."

The seaman held open the door for Trenchard to enter. This he did and he took himself straight to a chair and sat, without removing his hat. He seemed to have not a care in the world. Argent nodded to the seaman, who left, closing the door.

"Midshipman. We are going to try that again. Stand up, and take yourself back to the door. There, you come to the attention, salute, wait for me to return it, and then remove your hat. Do that now."

Argent saw the same astonishment as he had seen on the quayside, but Trenchard stood up and did as he was bid. His salute was a wide circle that came down from above the top of his head. He then removed his hat.

Argent began his instruction.

"Replace your hat."

Trenchard did so.

"When we salute in the Navy your hand does not come any higher than your forehead, just above your right eye. Straight up and straight down. The decks are too low for army circles. Like this."

Argent demonstrated and Trenchard made a passable imitation.

"Now, come and sit down."

Trenchard did so, his expression now showing some concern.

"That's how you make an entrance into the company of a superior Officer. Every time. That way."

Argent paused to let that sink in.

"Now. You are Midshipman Thomas Trenchard."

"Yes."

Argent looked up at him, glowering under his eyebrows.

"Incorrect. Try again."

"Yes Sir."

Argent continued to study the papers, allowing the silence to build. He spoke as though giving facts, not asking questions.

"This is your first ship."

"Yes Sir."

"You are sixteen years old."

"Yes Sir."

"Right, then you have a vast amount to learn before you are of any use to me at all, never mind in the future your going before the Board and passing out as an Officer. Two things. Keep your Journal as though an Admiral were due to look at it tomorrow, and, secondly, never be satisfied with your navigation. What you are unsure of, study and become sure of. You will be taught navigation by our Sailing Master, Mr. McArdle, and perhaps the other Officers in addition, but Mr. McArdle is the finest navigator I have ever sailed with. That makes you privileged. You will be given Watch duties, and a place at Quarters, by the First Lieutenant, Mr. Fentiman."

Trenchard looked puzzled.

"Quarters? Sir."

"Yes, Mr. Trenchard. Where you perform your duties when we come to fight the French."

Argent saw a slight anxiety come over Trenchard's face, but he continued.

"You have two other companions in your berth, Mr. Berry and Mr. Bright. Both are progressing well, so you can learn from both. An important point is that you will find the food aboard very different to what you have been used to, of that I'm sure, but there will be plenty of it, at least under normal circumstances. Don't complain. Berry and Bright have been surviving on it now for over a year."

Argent then sat back and regarded Trenchard sternly.

"One final thing to remember. Everyone on this ship knows more than you. Everyone, right down to the youngest Powder Monkey. If you treat everyone with respect, they will give you the time that will improve you as a sailor, time more than you ask for. "Top it the nob" as the seamen put it, and no one will grant you more than they have to, and your education as a Naval Officer will be that much slower, and poorer. You follow my meaning?"

"Yes Sir."

"Now, after leaving me, you recover your chest and ask the sentry to find a seaman to take you to the Midshipmen's Berth. You ask him. Ask him!"

"Yes Sir."

"That was an order. The correct reply is aye, aye, Sir."

"Aye aye, Sir."

"Now go to the door and repeat what you did when you first came in, but salute last."

Trenchard rose and placed himself at the door. His salute was passable. Argent returned it and watched the door close.

Down on the gundeck other introductions were being made. Henry Ball was escorting a new recruit to the site of number three gun. Ball was even more terse than Fraser.

"Tooley. Out of it. We'n making you a topman. Morris, this is the replacement, calls hisself Landy Main. Good luck to 'ee with 'im. "E just tried to do a runner along the quayside."

Morris looked at Ball with no small annoyance.

"Well, thankee, Bosun's Mate Ball. We'd just sorted out Tooley an' now you'n whiskin' on 'im away to be a mast monkey!"

"'S right, an' 'ere's the man to fill the hole."

He pulled Tooley out and thrust Landy forward.

"These is your messmates. Fine gen'lemen all!"

With that he walked off taking Tooley with him. Morris looked at Landy, then at Dedman.

"I knew that bugger Wilmot takin' off wouldn't end in satisfaction."

He looked back at Landy Main. He wasn't impressed. A ratlike face, bloodied, on a fleshless head above thin shoulders and a sunken chest. Thin, lank hair hung dark around his face. What muscle he had was on his arms and legs, but neither was too conspicuous.

"So, you tried a runner along the quayside?"

Landy's eyes swivelled up, then shifted down.

"Just how bright was that?"

No answer.

"'An for it they spread your nose over your face."

Neither reply, nor movement.

"You hungry?"

Landy nodded.

"Well, dinner's soon and there is one benefit, at least we'n shot of that scrapsbox Tooley."

He pulled a piece of rag from a box beside the gunport.

"Here, wipe your face. There's a bucket of water over there."
Landy took the rag and walked to the bucket. So far he had spoken not one word to anyone.

* * *

The dock sluices opened and the water began to reclaim the space with a roar, spurting yards into the dock from the huge pressure beyond the gates. In what seemed no time the water was covering the copper and the crew felt the deck lift. Although there was no movement, something under their feet told them that they were again on a living ship. The spars to the dockside wall fell away to be recovered by their handling rope and Ariadne was towed out towards the dying sun and then warped up to the quayside for her final supplies and the finishing touches to her repairs. Not least the touching up of the figurehead, to which they could now give some attention; something had taken her nose off. The workmen left at the daydone hour and Ariadne returned to seagoing routine.

With the dusk Captain Baker rode onto the wharf and came aboard. Argent had been told of his arrival and took himself to the quarterdeck to meet him and they met as good friends, this shared by Henry Fentiman, who brought himself back down the ship to greet the Marine Captain at the entry port. Baker handed over the sealed package of heavy paper. Argent looked at him and grinned.

"Thank you, Captain. You'll take a glass with us before you go?"

"Well, just the one, Sir. There's a young lady in great need of my attention, although she doesn't know it yet."

Argent and Fentiman laughed, and Fentiman spoke.

"Oh yes, and in just what manner, exactly, do you expect to correct that?"

"A local choir, very cultured and very profound."

"And you sing, where?"

"In the bass section. Bass baritone."

"And she sings, where?"

"Soprano section. The higher orders."

"And, confronted with this, how do you expect to meet and make her acquaintance."

"Ah, well, I've been working on that, and I think I've found just the duet!"

The laughter was genuine. Argent eased him towards the companionway.

"Then we'd better give you a glass, vital lubrication of your vocal chords."

In the cabin, Fentiman poured, whilst Argent slid off the wax seal. For all the bulk, the orders were simple, to sail the triangle and return to Falmouth, where he would again be under the orders of

Commodore Budgen. It was signed by Broke. Argent dropped the papers and picked up his glass.

"Here's to your singing, Captain, and your duet. When the time comes may you never sing a bad note. And always maintain the required impression."

All raised their glasses and sat back, but it was Baker who broke the silence.

"I feel the need to warn you, both of you, that the St. Malo affair may well be taken further. Both Bentley and Ffynes, were, are, well connected, and so there are strong rumours that pressure is being placed upon the Admiralty, not only by Parliament, but also from Court, no less. I'll not be in the least surprised if there's a Board of Enquiry."

Argent raised his eyebrows and extended his mouth into a thin line, then looked at Fentiman, before returning speak to Baker.

"Any resistance to this? I have no idea of the connections of Broke and Cheveley, but I would assume that if they have any, they would use them to put a block on the whole idea."

Baker leaned forward.

"What I've heard, and there's been a lot of talk about St. Malo, is that Cheveley would actually welcome it. What he's been saying is that your plan was poorly conceived and not feasible. It did not take account of the strength of the tide in the middle of the roads, nor the strength of the bastions, nor the holding ground for the anchor, which was why he ended up half a cable down. Also, that you failed to respond to his signal, which he flew the instant he saw where La Pomone was. Had you responded, you would have left together. Utter stuff, in my opinion, but that's the drift and that's the rumour."

Argent clenched his jaw and slowly nodded, whilst pursing his lips. He looked at Fentiman and saw an expression that matched his own thoughts, namely that Cheveley was going to lay as much of the blame onto Ariadne, over as many aspects of the affair, as he could, using as many falsehoods as necessary. Argent sighed deeply, anger growing at Cheveley's dishonourable calumny and downright distortion. He looked at Baker.

"We're grateful, Captain. Truly."

All glasses were now empty.

"Another?"

"Thank you, no, or I'll miss the opening bars."

"Well, at least you'll make a grand entrance."

"More like a flogging. The choirmaster's a retired Admiral."

With Baker's leaving, Argent and Fentiman were left to ponder. Argent poured each another madeira, then, as he handed over the glass, asked the question that each was wishing to ask of the other.

"So, what do you think?"

Fentiman gave no immediate answer. Plainly he was still thinking. Eventually he found that he could do no more than state the obvious.

"We can do no more than hold to what we've already said, that being what's in the Logbook. It's all detailed there and so there can be no point in deviating from it, that would not look good, to Log one thing and give evidence of another. We can do no more than hold to the facts, that being that we did carry out the agreed plan and we did do our best to obey orders and damage La Pomone. It's Cheveley who's under pressure from what actually came about, not us. The enquiry will be looking most at his conduct, not ours."

Fentiman took a drink and looked at Argent, who nodded and replied.

"Yes and no. At the back of it is why Bentley was killed and Ffynes lost his arm. They were both on our ship, not Cheveley's, but, you're right on one count; it is him that's under pressure. If an Enquiry is raised than we must both re-read the Log. If we both hold to what's in there, then we should both get through. But Enquiries; brrrh, the idea makes me shiver. They can go in all kinds of directions."

He finished his glass and showed cheerful.

"That's for the future. Tomorrow we sign off our repairs and sail, with new, clean, copper under our hull. Let's see if that produces an extra knot or a half."

* * *

Argent watched his men order the deck as Ariadne settled on the larboard tack in a wind just East of South. The spirits of the crew rose with the lift in their ship as she once more sought the open sea. He saw many that smiled and there was much joking and horseplay, but this was soon ended by Bosun Fraser and his Mates, but even these sea hardened Warrant Officers seemed to have some measure of good humour behind the scowl. It had taken much of the morning for them to tow themselves out into a Southerly wind and gain enough open water to set enough sail to take them East across Drake's Island and then tack around to pick up their heading for The Lizard. They had passed the moored Herodotus but nothing had been exchanged between them, neither formal nor informal. Their course now took them along the coast and to their starboard were spread the green fields, farms and villages of South Cornwall, in plain view in the bright September sunshine.

Argent stood on the weather side of his quarterdeck and almost subconsciously looked up at the towering sails and flexed his leg, both at the same time. His leg still hurt some mornings, but with the passing of the day, it eased. It was his Watch and he spent the morning deep in thought, content to leave the deck to Sanders, who stood as the proudest of Commanders at the quarterdeck rail. Argent's thoughts oscillated from Enquiries to Deeds, then to the lift and send of his own ship. He was pulled out of his reverie by the Noon Sight and the casting of the log, this beginning with McArdle invading his side of the quarterdeck, for on this side shone the sun.

"Beg your pardon, Captain, but it's now approaching eight bells."

"Of course, Mr. McArdle. The weatherside's all yours."

McArdle made no reply, but awaited the gathering of his class; at the same time watching two of his Mates cast the log. Soon the class arrived, the three Midshipmen, a Master's Mate and Lieutenant Benjamin Wentworth. All five carried their sextants in their right hand, Trenchard's conspicuously new. It was the new Midshipman who looked the most nervous, even though both Bright and Berry had given him hours of tuition whilst they were still in harbour. The bell was rung and each lifted their sextant, for the sun to be brought down on the stroke of the eighth bell. McArdle consulted his instrument, consulted the Almanac, chalked the latitude and waited. Lieutenant Wentworth had arrived at his answer before even McArdle, but the other four took their time and examined their instruments very carefully before moving on to use the chalk. Trenchard tried to compare his instrument with Bright's but McArdle's sharp eye above the aquiline nose spotted the illegal collusion.

"Nay talking! None! Your own answer, Mr. Trenchard, if ye please."

Finally, all chalked their answer to then display their board. All said 50 degrees and a quarter, as did McArdle's, save Berry's. His said 48 and a half. Trenchard was overjoyed, but Berry utterly despondent. McArdle fixed upon him with a look that nailed him to the deck, his anger adding to the depth of his Scottish accent.

"Mr. Berry, tak' ye'r ignorant self forward and practice, till ye obtain what's right."

Berry was about to take himself to where he was bid, when Wentworth intervened.

"L-let me t-try with your s-sextant, M-Mr Berry."

The sextant was handed over and Wentworth quickly and assuredly brought the sun down to the horizon. He then read the instrument and spoke the reading to McArdle.

"It r-reads, 48 and a half, S-Sailing Master. The r-reading was c-correct by this instrument, wh-which we c-c-can only s-say is inac-c-curate."

McArdle fixed an even more penetrating look onto Berry.

"Mr. Berry. Have ye damaged ye'r instrument in any way? Such as dropped it, now?"

His gaze remained as fierce as ever upon Berry who looked as though he were about to faint.

"I, er, did drop it a while back, but it seemed to be unharmed, Sailing Master."

"Dropped it. Dropped it, ye say! The one thing that can keep ye from running onto a reef! Dropped it. What use are ye now tae me, or this ship? What use?"

From his extra height Wentworth looked down at the dissolving Berry.

"We'll go forward and see what can be done."

No stutter, then he looked at Argent.

"Wi-with your p-p-permission, Sir."

Argent nodded.

"Carry on, Mr. Wentworth. I hope your efforts prove effective. Take the other two with you."

All three Midshipmen followed Wentworth along the larboard gangway, himself examining the instrument closely, Berry looking hopeful and Trenchard looked as though he wished to perform cartwheels. Argent and McArdle shared a knowing look before Argent gave the deck to Fentiman for the Afternoon Watch, but Argent had been pleased with what he had seen. He left the quarterdeck and turned at the bottom of the companionway to then step aside as the messcooks returned to their messes carrying the Noon meal for their messmates. All quickly disappeared down the companionways to the lower deck. At two bells came the turn of the Starboard Watch to eat and it was Jacob Pierce who performed the errand for Number Three gun and returned to the table carrying the cooked rations. The six guncrew sat a bench three each side, including their "ship's boy" Smallsize, as known by all. The table had been lowered from the deck beams and hung suspended between the two benches. Morris sat as the head of the table on the end, on the right, and the food was placed before him and the six square wooden plates. The food was quickly divided, including the beer, and all immediately set to. During previous days, the guncrew had occupied their meal times with topics of their own, but now their attention turned to their new messmate, him sat between Morris and the young Smallsize. It was Morris who opened the questioning.

"So how'd you get a name like Landy?"

Landy Main had spoken not above 50 words since coming aboard but two days before. He made no pause to his devouring of the food, but shrugged his shoulders between rapid spoonfuls. Dedman looked up at Morris.

"What was you sayin' about losin' that grazer Tooley. No one puts food away like this 'un, not such as I've seen."

Morris nodded and paused over his own food. He looked at Main.

"So where're you from? You must know that."

Landy Main swallowed his mouthful.

"Plymouth."

"Plymouth? No other place, you've always lived there?"

Landy Main nodded and spooned up the last portion on his plate, way before the others. His plate was clear so he stood up and looked into the skillets, which he also found to be empty, but the hunted look on his face showed that he evidently wanted more. He fixed upon the plate of the ship's boy beside him and seized it away from the astonished youngster to tip the food onto his own plate. He again began to make use of his spoon when a pointed knife came plunging down into the middle of his plate, held in the huge fist of Sam Morris. Main looked at the fist and the knife and then into the livid face of the owner.

"Main! We 'as none of that yer. Not in this mess. What's shared is your portion and that's all, now tip that back for Smallsize, or you'll find yourself on the end of a few shipboard punishments such as you've not 'eard of yet."

Despite the anger all around him, Main's face showed no fear, it remained matter of fact, resigned even. He'd been stopped, well, no matter, and he gave it no thought, it was instinct that had told him to obtain more food. He did as he was bid by Morris and sat still. Around him there was no more conversation, simply a succession of angry looks in his direction, which seemed to concern him not at all. Morris tossed him a ship's biscuit.

Above and at the stern the off-watch Officers were taking their midday meal, in the Captain's cabin. Argent looked at Sanders and his new Captain of Marines.

"Today's the 17th, if I'm not mistaken."

It was Brakespeare who answered.

"The 17th, Sir. Yes Sir. All day."

He smiled at his own joke, as did Sanders, but Argent showed thoughtful. He looked at the compass and wind repeater above him in the cabin ceiling. The wind remained steady, South by West giving them little choice but to hug the coastline on a course West South West. That was the most Southing they could achieve, for, even to manage that, Ariadne was showing more fore and aft staysails than common square canvas on her spars.

"Jonathan, please hand me that book of tide tables."

Sanders reached back and got his hand onto the thick, well-used, book. He passed it to Argent who quickly thumbed through to the place he required, then to find what he needed and look up.

"So tomorrows the 18th, and…"

He again regarded the tide table.

"Yes, I think it can be done."

He looked at Brakespeare.

"Alloysius. I want your men ready for an Admiral's inspection at noon tomorrow. That's possible?"

Brakespeare looked up surprised.

"Why, yes Sir. Eight bells this evening if you choose."

"No. Consider it to be a parade. Ready yourselves for that, at Noon tomorrow."

He turned to Sanders.

"Jonathan. Your Watch all turned out in full fig, at the same time?"

Sanders looked equally incredulous.

"Yes Sir. Of course, Sir."

"Right, I'm off to see Fentiman."

* * *

The fine September weather held for the next day and at 3 bells of the Afternoon Watch Ariadne was idling towards the entrance of Falmouth Harbour, on no more than two jibsails, the main and mizzen staysails, and driver. The wind had moved to South Southwest, just at breeze strength; the tide was full and just on the turn to run out. Reece was at the bows taking soundings and his flat, monotonous call, the regulation cadence for the delivering of such, toned back along the ship. Argent and his full complement of Officers, including Midshipmen, were on the quarterdeck, all in full dress uniform, but their attention was, for the moment, wholly fixed on the conning of their ship. Argent had the deck and he called down to Bosun Fraser, him equally decked out in his full finery, the nameplate on his hat gleaming fiercely.

"Loose all topsails. Larboard tack. Fine on the quarter."

Whilst Fraser ran shouting along the deck, Argent turned to his Quartermaster, Zachary Short, one of four helmsmen on the two wheels, but Short was at the rear, on the weatherside.

"Steer due North."

It was Short who replied.

"Steer due North. Aye aye, Sir."

As the topsails fell and were sheeted home, Ariadne came around perfectly to enter in the main channel. The details of Pendennis Castle, with its Union Flag flying confidently from the highest battlement, revealed themselves on the larboard side. Argent took himself over and looked along the shoreline. Ariadne was coasting in on the breeze, but the ebbing tide was proving too strong, so he made his response.

"Mr. Fraser. Foresail and topgallants."

Again Fraser bid the topmen up into the rigging and Ariadne quickly gained speed to push strongly against the tide and so, soon, Argent could see the house he was looking for, Lady Grant's, ex-Willoughby, town house. He lifted his Dolland glass and, sure enough, the lawn was covered in guests enjoying a post-wedding gathering. He studied further and picked out Admiral and Lady Grant. There was Charlotte and Major Blake and Broke and Cheveley, which surprised him, but he permitted himself a small grin of satisfaction and contemplated a small departure from strict Naval etiquette. He decided yes, and signalled for Bosun's Mate Ball.

"Mr. Ball, I can see no harm by informing the crew that Admirals Grant and Broke are on that lawn and also the Captain of the Herodotus, Captain Cheveley."

Ball perfectly understood Argent's motives in making such facts known and he grinned.

"Nor I Sir, no harm at all. Aye, aye Sir."

Argent raised his Dolland again and waited for what he was sure would happen and soon it did. The guests saw Ariadne entering the harbour and they all took themselves to the seawall to watch her entrance. Argent saw the moment.

"Parade by Divisions. Topmen aloft."

The three Midshipmen were stood close alongside the three Lieutenants and Trenchard looked forward at the sights and events and looked baffled. He turned to Bright.

"What's all this about?"

Fentiman heard and turned on him.

"Silence there, hold your parade. And for your information we're turning up to a wedding. The Captain made a promise."

Fentiman paused, but felt the need to say more.

"The Royal Navy puts itself out for ladies!"

With the ship settled on her course and Quartermaster Short at the wheel the whole ship's company paraded on the gangways and forecastle, lined up from the quarterdeck up to the bows came first the Marines, then waisters, afterguard and foc'c'slmen. The topmen arranged themselves along the spars of their respective masts. All were in their best finery, even the new recruits had been given clean slops and a black hat. The ship was under perfect control, sailing in against the tide and Quartermaster Short eased his ship as far to the seawall as he dared and within 100 yards, and opposite their audience, Argent lifted his hat. This was the signal for all Officers to do the same and for Bosun Fraser to call for three cheers. The Marines presented arms as the three huzzas rang out across the water accompanied by the lifting of the sailor's black hats. Not needing his glass, Argent could see Lady Grant stood beside her Admiral, who had come to the salute, as had most other Officers, but Broke and Cheveley conspicuously not. All the girls and even some of the older women were clapping with delight. With her huge White Ensign billowing off to starboard and her sides clean and freshly painted, Ariadne looked the very epitome of Naval pride and elegance. At perfect parade speed she pushed on through, forcing on against the strengthening ebb tide.

What their audience could not see, was a cluster of stone filled barrels lashed to the starboard side. Ariadne stood on for 300 yards more, then Argent ordered the foresail and topgallants to be furled. With the loss of their leverage, Ariadne slowed and Short swung over the wheel to turn to larboard and at the same time the barrels were cut loose to act as an anchor, lashed to the starboard quarter. The tide pushed her back, but the improvised anchor held and she swung around for a perfect anchor turn to reveal her starboard battery, with 13 guns run out; an Admiral's salute. The sails were trimmed for the starboard tack, the "anchor" cable cut, and, with just enough steerageway, she began her exit. The crew repositioned themselves to parade on the starboard gangway and once more she passed the happy couple and their guests. This time there was no cheering, but Smallsize was on the gundeck below with orders to fire the guns between a careful four pace interval. He was to pull each lanyard, take four deliberate paces to the next, then fire it. Each gun had a salute charge and he was given a lighted match in case a flintlock failed and, with each gun fired from the stern, so that the smoke would not mask the ship, the salute rang out. With her crew stood stiff to attention she once more passed the wedding gathering, almost all of whom, this time, were applauding. As her stern passed and, as the last gun barked its addition, a signal broke out from her halliards; "Congratulations."

As Argent sailed his ship out into the open sea, he climbed into the starboard mizzen shrouds and lifted his hat to those whom they had entertained. After climbing down, he thought it would be bad form to look back any more, especially with his Dolland glass, but his imagination had the picture clear in his mind anyway, especially the expressions on the faces of Grant and his Lady and the very different expressions on those of Broke and Cheveley.

* * *

"Mr. Fraser. I want 14 knots. Let's see if we can't make the Fastnet in record time."

Fraser wasn't sure how to answer, having been asked for something that may not be in his power to give.

"14 knots, Sir? Depends how we lie on the wind. And how she performs in it. Sir."

"Right, and, as we speak, it's coming large over our larboard quarter. Her best point of sailing."

"What're we on now, Sir? Our speed."

"Twelve."

Fraser looked up at the masthead, the highest point of the ship, the top of the mainmast. The pennant was almost ruler straight in the stiff breeze, firm between Southwest and South. He took a look at the sea conditions on the weatherside and saw a choppy sea, but no steep waves to fall into and then climb out of, which would markedly slow any ship down. He then looked at the vacant spars, all those above the topsails.

"All plain sail then, Sir."

"All plain sail, Mr. Fraser."

Fraser ran off gathering his Mates, then the topmen.

"Captain wants 14 knots out her. So, set topgallants and royals. See what that does."

The topmen swarmed up each mast and soon every spar was possessed of its sail. Argent allowed the deck to settle, then called for the throwing of the log. Minutes later a Master's Mate came to him with a number chalked on the board. He said nothing, assuming his Captain would read it and it said 13 and a half. Argent considered; staysails or stunsails? He gauged the wind direction and decided, staysails would not draw with so much common sail taking their wind. He looked for and found Fraser on the starboard gangway.

"Mr. Fraser. Larboard stunsails. Main, top, t'gallants and royals. Starboard mizzen stunsails."

Again the topmen climbed aloft to send out the extensions to the larboard yardarms and haul up the square stunsails that would go into place alongside the common sails already set. It was a long job to secure the extensions, especially for the mizzen topmen who had to extend on both sides, then attach the sails, then sheet home. It took fifteen minutes, then all was done, with Whiting and his crew of the foretop looking smugly across at those of the maintop, the foretop having finished their work first. With the deck settled again, Argent asked for the log. Minutes later, his grin matched that of the Master's Mate and also that of the population of the quarterdeck. The board read 14 and a half knots. Argent looked at McArdle.

"Any comment, Mr. McArdle?"

The Sailing Master looked once at Argent, then looked away. To him praise was an alien, irreligious, language that he rarely bestowed on anyone, or anything, but perhaps this time was one of those exceptions.

"Ay, she's fast Captain. Over 14 is something outside ma experience, but nae ma hearing, I need tae add. But ye've got tae credit the new copper, as well as the ship."

Argent stood at the quarterdeck rail and indulged himself for a while, luxuriating in his ship racing over the choppy sea, scattering spray downwind. It added to his mood to see the crewmen on watch looking over the side at the ocean racing past and he concluded that their conversation circled around the guessing of their speed, but the actual figure was passing between them anyway. Fraser came back, having checked that all was well and secure. He stood waiting until Argent turned towards him, feeling bold enough to ask his Captain the question.

"Did you get 14, Sir?"

"14 and a half, Mr. Fraser."

Fraser grinned from ear to ear. Such heights of happiness seen upon his normally hypercritical visage were beyond the memory of all aboard.

"14 and a half! My, but she's fast. Sir."

"I can only agree, Mr. Fraser, but I'll wager good sail trimming must take some of the credit."

Fraser resumed his grinning in response to the shared delight between himself and his Captain.

"No argument from me, there, Sir."

"Right, Mr. Fraser, but now I feel the wind strengthening. We are in the Irish Sea after all, so, royals, and stunsails off. It's time for the guns, let's see if we cannot set a new record there."

There was no new record, in fact slightly slower for three broadsides and two reloads, four minutes and 50 seconds, but Argent was not unhappy. There could be no surprise, with so many new men and so many of these not even close to the physical condition needed to haul out the guns at the maximum speed for repeated broadsides. In fact he was pleased that the veterans of his crew had integrated the new men sufficiently to only drop five seconds.

Argent may have been pleased, but this was not the case at Number Three, and the object of Morris' displeasure was Tooley's replacement.

"We might as well give that rammer to Smallsize for all the lively that you be showing with it."

He confronted Landy Main full on, with arms akimbo.

"Now you listen, 'cos I'm now tellin' you how 'tis. You can ask any man down this battery, that what matters, when you'm yardarm to yardarm with Johnny Frog, is beatin 'im to that second broadside. You've got to take his first, like 'ee takes yourn, but it's the crew as gets off the second as wins. An yer's another truth, winnin' means a lot less of us gets killed, includin' you, but right now I'd be 'appy enough to sew you into yer 'ammock and 'eave you over the side for the fishes."

He paused.

"An' they'd probably chuck you back!"

However, when Morris looked at Main he became even more depressed by the look he received back; dead eyed and uncaring. What he liked even less was that Sanders, their new Officer of the Gundeck, was speaking to their new Midshipman. As Sanders walked back astern, their new Section Commander came to them, this being Trenchard, who stood to look up at Morris. There couldn't be a wider gulf between them in terms of shipboard experience, but one was "Officer", the other "before the mast".

"Your gun was last for both reloads. You must improve."

Morris made his respects, as did the rest of the crew, completed by Main being kicked by Dedman to add his salute.

"Right Sir. We've a new man, Sir, but we'll get there."

It didn't enter Trenchard's mind to retort that almost every other crew had a new man and so, rebuke delivered, or so he thought, he returned back to his position at Quarters. Morris made up his mind, Main would load the charge. It was the simplest of all the operations, to take a charge from the powderman's saltbox, load it into the muzzle and push it down far enough to make room for the wad before the rammer. He looked at the tackleman that he had most faith in, that being Bearman.

"Tom. You'n on the sponge an' rammer. Main, I'll show you now what you do."

Three more broadsides were called for. The time was still four minutes 50, and Number Three was still the last, but not by so wide a margin. The guns were stowed and the Starboard Watch went to Supper, which was also being taken in the Midshipman's Berth, the food having been obtained by Trenchard and shared out by Bright.

Trenchard had fitted in well. Both Bright and Berry had taken to his cheerful and ingenuous character, not only because he seemed willing to reveal, if only for the sake of conversation, all kinds of details about himself and his family home. He was willing to learn, confessed any ignorance and never disparaged conscientious effort in others. Just as important, he shared what he had, which included three pounds of sweetmeats that he had brought on board in his pockets. As the third son, not even the "spare to the heir" he had been pulled out of Public School and packed off to the Navy at the earliest age when Mother could contemplate being parted from her youngest. It was to their betterment, for both Bright and Berry would have agreed that the loss of the sarcastic Ffynes had rendered their berth a more cheerful place. As the rations were portioned out, Berry was giving his sextant a final polish. Wentworth had made the necessary adjustments and Berry was now regularly obtaining Noon Sights that enabled him to avoid the worst of McArdle's displeasure. However, it was Trenchard, as usual, who opened the conversation.

"What's it like, being in action?"

Berry looked at Bright, who had taken his first spoonful of food. Berry said nothing, but Bright swallowed to answer.

"Ship to ship, when we took La Mouette, it was not so different from gun practice. The Captain wholly outmanoeuvred that French Captain and all we had to do was fire quickly and accurately. We took a few shot into the hull, and had some men hurt, but worst was at St. Malo. We came through that just by sheer luck and the Captain."

He paused and looked at his equally experienced companion.

"What do you think, Daniel?"

Berry stopped eating and subconsciously rubbed his forearm. He'd been hit by a splinter that gashed his arm and both his coat and his arm had been sewn up in identical manner, so that both now showed similar evidence of the injury. Truth be told he had never been so terrified in his life, from the endless bellow of the guns, the sickening noise of the balls smashing through the sides and on across the gundeck. On top were the screams and the sight of the appalling wounds. He knew, that had they received another series of hits from the shore, he would probably have run off to the bilges if he didn't faint first. He was in a quandary as to what to say, either to put a brave face on it or tell the truth. In the end he did neither, he spoke from halfway.

"It was awful, but we got out of it."

Bright recognised Berry's discomfiture and, although he knew that Berry was limited in the technical arts, he liked his friend and spoke up in his aid.

"The ship did her duty, that's all you can say. Despite taking a pounding."

Berry brightened up.

"Yes, that's it. We stuck it, that's all you can say. If you weren't badly wounded, you were lucky. If you were on your feet, you stuck it."

Trenchard became far less than comfortable at this last, but it was Bright who continued.

"One thing about the Navy is, that you do your duty. That's your orders. Do that, and you're safe, fail and you get punished."

'What kind of punished?"

"Could be anything, from a rocket off the Captain to being chucked off the ship and into gaol. Even hung, I suppose."

"I've met the Captain. He seems a bit of a stickler."

"He is, if you foul up. Avoid that, and, as I say, you'll be fine. By and large we've all got a lot of time for him, if only that he puts prizemoney in our pockets."

Berry now joined in, but he was still on the previous topic.

"I've seen the likes of us stretched across a gun, breeches down and whacked with a cane."

Bright nodded and Trenchard looked up.

"Not much different from school, then?"

"No, not so different, except that it's laid on by a bloody great sailor rather then some spindly schoolmaster!"

Berry laughed as loud as anyone at his joke and the three then fell silent and resumed serious eating, until a thought came to Bright.

"This is your third day at sea. Are you feeling quite well? I mean, by now, after three days, I couldn't eat a thing."

Trenchard took another huge mouthful. He allowed that to be his answer.

* * *

As soon as they were sailing across routes from Ireland to France, Argent ordered the doubling of the lookouts, but nothing was seen and Ariadne stood on to the Fastnet Rock, the reaching of which coincided with a Noon Sight and so most knew what their Latitude answer should be. Argent decided to turn around the Rock to make their second leg of the triangle and then set course for "48 and 8". Most came up to take a look at the incongruous, conical lump of rock, a barren, bleak and cheerless spectacle. In the Autumn light it showed more grey than black from the habitation of countless seabirds that claimed it as their home, but it had claimed the life of many a sailor as it proved to be the graveyard of their ship. Known as the teardrop of Ireland, not just because of it's position of "dropping" off the mainland, but also for the tears it had caused to be shed by those seeing the last of Ireland and also the relations of those sailors lost on it's unforgiving shoals.

The wind had veered and was now stiff from just South of West and the waves provided a spectacle as they rolled up to pound and surge over the low cliffs of the island. As the desolate and noisy sight passed along the larboard side, Argent ordered a course South Southwest to complete their middle passage and in the strong wind Ariadne was confined to topsails alone. Nevertheless, stiff and short of canvas as she was, she now began to "corkscrew", a motion disliked by any crew. As she obliquely crossed the run of the waves, her bows dipped up and down with the peaks and troughs and her deck tilted right then left as she climbed to the crest tilting to larboard then descended the other side leaning to starboard. Within an hour the new crewmen were on deck hanging over the bulwark and not a few of the old, either. This included Bright, elbows leaning on the quarterdeck bulwark rail, looking oddly green and wishing he would faint or die. It was not his Watch but he felt an obvious and undeniable need to be at the rail. Trenchard was in attendance, it was also his Watch, but he was occupying the time taking alternate bites from an apple and a ship's biscuit, he found the "lift and send" of this most splendid ship eminently enjoyable.

For days the motion was unrelenting and gradually the stronger or more experienced stomachs were able to indulge in larger portions from rations, this being because many of their messmates were still prostrate on deck. In some cases dehydration became severe and Surgeon Smallpiece found the need to intervene, not by asking the Captain to change course, but by the tried and tested method of having the worst cases hoisted into a hammock and then held steady until the sickness abated and they could stomach a little water. The only consolation from the wind was that it provided a perfect driving force for their destination and three days later, the Noon Sight gave their position as 49 degrees 10, 8 degrees 20. Argent gave orders to again head for Quessant and, with the sea now following from astern, the motion eased considerably and almost all seasick cases recovered. With a fast passage on the first two legs, Argent was content to idle his ship along to draw out the time spent in close proximity to the French coast. The weather turned wet and misty and visibility came down to little more than a mile, but McArdle brought them to within sight of Quessant, flat and brown and now more than familiar, at five bells of the forenoon. Argent held a course just North of East to enable them to track along the line of the French coast, which they held off at just under a mile. Immediately after both Watches had finished their dinner came a cry from the masthead.

"Sail ho!"

It was Sanders who had the deck.

"Where away?"

"Three points off the larboard bow"

She was outside of them, further into The Channel. Sanders sent Berry to tell the Captain and then he climbed to the mizzentop with his own glass to join the lookout, who was draped in the crosstrees 20 feet above him. The lookout pointed and Sanders trained his glass. What came into focus was a strange craft, small, with three masts that carried three square sails, one jibsail and a small driver. The mizzen carried the driver, the main carried two sails, and the foremast supported one square sail and the jib. She was moving South West, on the starboard tack, a course to cross theirs, but, as he watched, she must have seen Ariadne, for she came about and headed almost North. She was trying to run, she must have concluded Ariadne to be British. Sanders slid down a backstay to the quarterdeck and ordered the change of course, due North, hauling their wind to bring it beam on. He shouted to Fraser to make the sail change for the larboard tack, just as Argent and Fentiman arrived, the former disturbed from his sleep. Both went straight to Sanders who spoke to both, as the ship was settling on her new course.

"Now off the starboard bow, Sir. An odd looking thing. Small, some kind of coaster, I should say. I don't think she's a warship, Sir."

Argent climbed into the starboard mizzen shrouds and focused his own glass, but only to confirm his quarry's heading. They were both on practically parallel courses, with the wind abeam, directly over the larboard side. Ariadne would inevitably catch her sooner or later, but Argent preferred sooner. He turned to Fentiman.

"Double the lookouts. We don't want some heavy two decker sneaking up whilst we're about our business."

Whilst Fentiman gave his orders, Argent shouted at Henry Ball. Ariadne carried no more than all topsails and driver.

"Mr. Ball. All lower staysails. All topmast staysails. Inner and outer jibs."

The fore and aft staysails and jibs flashed out and were sheeted home. Ariadne jumped forward to the added leverage of sails that were perfectly positioned to make full use of the beam on wind, but Argent wasn't satisfied.

"Mr. Ball. Main and foresails."

The two sails fell and were secured, then the yards were braced around for the larboard tack and the big sails drew. Ariadne claimed another knot. Argent took himself along the starboard gangway to the forecastle to take a look unencumbered by his own rigging. There he found Bosun Fraser making his own examination and he focused the glass then passed it across.

"What do you make of her, Mr. Fraser?"

Fraser gave himself a long look before he answered.

"Well, unless I'm mistaken Sir, that's a French rig. I think they call them "bah toe cannon ee air" if I'm sayin' it right, but probably not. They'm shallow draught and designed for coastal work. Definitely not weather boats, Sir."

"Shallow draught, you say?"

"Yes Sir. Which means she won't be holdin' too much. They haven't got much of what you'd call a hold, for cargo. An' they gives up to lee somethin' shockin'. Sir."

Argent took another look for himself. In the short time of adding more sail Ariadne had cut the distance by more than a quarter; she was catching the Frenchman rapidly, eating up the distance between them. Within minutes Argent could focus on her taffrail and see the Captain focusing on him, either him or his ship. He then saw the Captain turn away and almost immediately a white flag was hoisted and the sails were started and furled. The Frenchman was giving up his escape.

Argent retained his own canvas until they were within a cable, then he took in all common sail to ease up to the Frenchman on the staysails alone. All the crew came up to view their latest capture, the Officers too, standing on the quarterdeck, Quartermaster Short had the wheel.

"Take us upwind of him, Mr. Short. Close as she'll lie."

"Upwind, aye aye, Sir. Close as she'll lie."

"Mr. Ball. Start all sheets. Furl driver."

Ariadne lost all her canvas and, on momentum alone, eased up to the Frenchman, her starboard side against their larboard. They all noticed that she was pierced for two cannon, so she must be a warship of some kind. Short took Ariade to within feet of the Frenchman's hull and the beam wind pushed them closer, to the extent that she could be boarded simply by swinging over on a rope and, as they closed, the full run of the Frenchman's deck was covered by the intimidating muskets of Ariadne's Marines. Argent turned to Sanders.

"Lieutenant Sanders. Make ready, if you please. Swing yourself over and obtain her surrender."

A rope was attached to the very end of the main yardarm and Sanders swung over the nine or ten feet, across to the deck that was some six feet below theirs. All on Ariadne looked down to see that she was indeed a warship and her cannon were 24 pounders, no less. The ships were so close that Fraser ordered fenders over the side to protect both hulls, and then grapnels were thrown over to hold both vessels together. They all watched Sanders approach the Captain, when formal salutes were exchanged, begun by Sanders, and finally the Captain handed over his sword. They then had a short conversation, but it was too long for a mere formal surrender. Soon Sanders was standing the Frenchman's deck below them, but opposite the quarterdeck. All were listening intently; there was not a sound to be heard beyond the slap of the imprisoned waves complaining between the hulls. Sanders started speaking.

"Sir. This is Captain Dagonnel."

At the sound of his name, the said Captain lifted his hat and bowed. Argent touched the peak of his own.

"He says that this part of the coast and around Brest has been raided several times by a slaver, an oared galley. They are raiding small villages, capturing young women and children and sometimes firing the villages. There has been another raid and they are trying to find the slaver. An oared galley. Sir."

Fentiman was stood near and spoke as soon as Sanders had finished.

"Sir, do you remember what we saw, much about in this place, back in early August, after we left Ireland? An oared galley and a big fire on shore. I'd say he's not trying to pull the wool over our eyes, Sir. We saw what we saw."

Argent looked at him, then looked at Sanders, his face becoming grim and angry. The signs had been there, obvious, and with a modicum of thought they could have worked it out, but they did nothing and now this slaver, probably up from the North African coast, is still at large, practicing its Devil's work.

"Mr. Sanders. What does he know?"

Sanders spoke to the Captain, then turned back to Argent.

"He says that they raided a village close to Roscoff three days ago. They suspect that they have headed back down Channel."

"Why is this type ship doing the chasing?"

Soon Sanders was translating the reply.

"Because they are shallow draught, Sir, and can go where a galley can. And their 24's could reach them if they are beyond her draught. She's what they call a "bateau cannoniere."

Argent looked along the gangway at his crew. Most had heard and were talking amongst themselves in serious tones with serious faces. He turned to Fentiman; he had made his decision.

"I'm letting her go. She's on a humanitarian mission. I'm letting her go."

He leaned forward over the bulwark.

"Mr. Sanders!"

"Sir."

"I'm releasing him. Give him back his sword. Tell him to try the South West bay of Quessant. We saw him back that way in early August. He was around there then, and he's still here now, so he must have a base, and that's as good a place as any to try. Tell him that, and tell him good luck."

Sanders turned to the Captain and spoke, as he handed back the sword to the astonished Captain and soon he was nodding furiously both in the direction of Sanders and Argent on the quarterdeck above him. He insisted on shaking Sanders' hand and raising his hat to Argent, then to the whole of Ariadne's watching crew. The response was a whole forest of raised arms and fists, then clapping and waving and many encouraging words, but shouted in English. The crew of the cannoniere responded in kind, a strong common affinity had been thoroughly established, then they tossed back the grappling hooks holding the ships together, as gently as possible, as throwing such a thing could be achieved. Soon Ariadne had hoisted her staysails and drew ahead of the cannoniere, which wore right around to become close hauled and resume her course down Channel.

Argent, Fentiman and Sanders watched her go until she was but a speck in the distance. Argent knew what he had done, released a French warship, which was a serious decision. He spoke to both.

"I want to make it plain that this was my own decision. We all need to agree what goes into the logbook, but when it's there, it's me that will sign."

Fentiman looked at Argent, then at Sanders, who looked back at him.

"I don't agree Sir."

Sanders spoke.

"Nor I Sir. It was humanitarian. I'll put my signature to that. We saw corroborating evidence back in August. We had no reason to disbelieve him. I'll sign to it."

Argent looked at Fentiman who nodded in response.

"And I. Yes. Absolutely!"

Argent was moved.

"I thank you both, sincerely."

He paused, then looked at both.

"So, we'd better be about it, using up the pen and ink, that is."

* * *

Their return to Falmouth was nothing like as spectacular as their last visit. For one it was in the gloom of evening and for another, the Willoughby house was dark, closed up and deserted. Ariadne came in on a heavy, flooding tide, and dropped anchor. They transferred to a mooring buoy, recovered their anchor and closed down for the night, with no more than an anchor watch. Argent invited all his Officers, including the Midshipmen to his cabin for Dinner, but the atmosphere was subdued. The sole high point of their voyage had been achieving fourteen and a half knots; the rest had been routine and mundane. On top, it had provided evidence that they should have done more when they first saw the galley back in early August by Quessant Island. The talk was of the history of slave raids from North Africa, a practice that had gone on for centuries but had died away over the past century, some surmised because of stronger navies operating from Spain, France and Britain. Now that they were back and operating again and some reasoned because all three were now preoccupied with war. An oared galley could voyage up, unseen over the horizon and run for shelter at the coast if a storm hit and that was plainly what was taking place. However, what was unspoken was that they had had their chance to make an end, even if it meant a serious operation to get into her lair and sink or capture her. Most concluded in their thoughts that a carronade could have been mounted on a longboat and sent in. The meal continued gloomily, momentarily cheered up by them teaching Trenchard how to make the Loyal Toast. No one stayed for port and nuts and Argent was left with his own company. He re-read the log and closed it, noting, once again, with some emotion, the two added signatures. Tomorrow he would have to present it to Budgen. He hoped, perhaps, also for time to visit his family, but he doubted it.

On the lower deck there was also a portion of spreading gloom. With the ship stood down in harbour, many took the opportunity to see to their own affairs, making, mending, organising and trading from their personal sea chests, this regulation box encompassing their whole world of possessions. Few had any kind of padlock, most were held shut by a simple spike through the hasp. Gabriel Whiting was not happy.

"Silas. Did I lend you that clasp knife what I won off that lobster back awhile. B'ain't yer. Did you borrow it?"

Silas looked at his Captain of the Foretop.

"No, an' I was about to ask you if you 'ad them silver earrings of mine. Did you borrow them for goin' ashore with the Captain?

"No, Silas. I didn't."

Both looked at each other, but it was Whiting who spoke further.

"I'd say we got a thief."

The next day Argent timed his departure from the ship to enable him to arrive at 10.00 o'clock at Budgen's office and so, to give himself half an hour, he left at three bells of the forenoon. As his bargecrew propelled him towards the shore, he couldn't help but notice that all were sour faced and out of sorts. This was confirmed when he overheard the first line of their conversation as he departed for the Commodore, King asking of Jones.

"So what have you lost? Anything?"

Argent entered the outer office and was cheered up by indulging in the parade ground formality of greeting Marine Sergeant Venables, both coming to the attention when salutes were most properly exchanged. However, within Budgen's office the atmosphere was nothing like as convivial. There was nothing on his desk for him to eat nor drink, perhaps because all was delayed for some reason, but Budgen's greeting was formal and perfunctory, his mood was plainly not of the best. He wasted no time in finding the pages of the log for the past voyage and quickly skipped over the sections that spoke only of course and speed, but his head did lower itself to enable a better look at the page that spoke of a speed of 14 and a half knots. It lowered itself even further, when he came to the incident with the cannoniere. Budgen read it twice, then looked up. His face showed his discontent, for, as Commodore he was entitled to a share of any prizemoney.

"This..."

He looked again.

"...cannon ee air, you let her go?'

"Yes Sir."

"She was a warship?"

Argent made no reply.

"And you let her go."

Another pause whilst his face changed to show both puzzlement and annoyance.

"Why?"

"As it says in the log, Sir, amongst other details, I and my Senior Officers concluded that she was on a humanitarian mission. It would seem that slave raiders are back, at least on the French side of The Channel."

"I suspect they were spinning you a yarn, Captain."

"Possibly Sir, we did consider that, but, if you refer to the entry for August 3rd, Sir, you will see that we almost certainly saw that slaver. The description of the type of vessel that the cannoniere gave, agrees, and we also saw smoke from what must have been large fires on shore, this being mentioned by the cannoniere's Captain."

Argent waited for Budgen to speak, but, nothing forthcoming, he continued.

"I, and my Officers are in no doubt that there is a slaver operating over there, and I classed her attempted apprehension of said slaver as humanitarian. On top, two things. I concluded that a cannoniere is of no use to the Navy, they have no keel and can capsize in even a moderate sea."

Budgen sat up, incensed, and interrupted, almost shouting.

"That's not for you to decide, Captain."

"Perhaps not, Sir, but I was the Senior Office in place, I had to decide and there were other considerations. As I was saying, secondly, if a slaver has come this far, he'll think nothing of going farther, to raid our shores. A cannoniere has a good chance of taking him, if he finds him. They're better designed for the job, Sir. I thought it best to give them that chance, to secure our own safety, using a vessel that we could make no use of. Sir."

Budgen looked how he felt, bad tempered and minus some prizemoney, but Argent had a case. However, he wasn't going to concede that quickly.

"I'm still not satisfied. Because of your decision, a French warship remains French. I'm copying your log and sending it to my superior, Admiral Grant."

Argent's face became, if that were possible, even calmer.

"I stand ready to answer for my decisions, Sir."

Budgen scowled. He knew that Argent stood well in Grant's favour and little would come of it, but "face" had been saved. The log was closed and pushed to one side; that subject now closed. Argent turned to his own affairs, he knew it was hopeless, but he felt the need to ask anyway.

"Sir, I was hoping for half a day away from my ship, to visit my family up Barton way."

Budgen looked at Argent down a gaze as unequivocal as a run out battery, his sentences delivered as would be a rolling broadside

"No. Out of the question. Besides, I've your latest orders. Yourself, your Officers who were there, and your Senior Warrant Officers, Master, Bosun, and Quartermaster, are to take yourselves immediately to Plymouth. An Enquiry has been convened to look into the St. Malo affair, chaired by Vice Admiral Lord Holdsworth. You leave at first light tomorrow. You go overland, by coach; your ship remains here. And there's another thing. Get your ship up to the quayside, bows out, I'm hearing that a frigate may be needed for a voyage. Get her supplied and up to the mark. Is your First up to the job?"

"Completely, Sir. You may have every confidence, as I have."

Budgen's head jerked back, but if he thought that to be the end of the interview, then he was wrong.

"If I'm to appear before an Enquiry, Sir, I think my Logbook may prove useful."

Budgen placed a pudgy hand on the logbook and slid it across.

"Give it to Venables with orders to copy those two entries. Call back for it later today."

He spoke no more as Argent left.

* * *

Kalil Al'Ahbim was anticipating a large profit. He gazed avariciously at his "stock", all required to parade past him, all naked and shivering in the chill wind of late September, and all pushed forward by the menacing scimitars of his crew. He examined each white-skinned figure with some satisfaction and money-flavoured thoughts came into his mind; they had made a quality haul and each would fetch a good price at the slave markets of Tangiers. The last passed him by and, with sobs and cries, they all descended to their prison in the depths of the galley. They had made five raids which included both sides of the Brest peninsula and the capture of the yacht had been a fine and easy bonus. They had room for the proceeds of two more, say a dozen from each, but he knew that, by now, word of his predations would have spread and the French navy was not so worn down as to fail to make a search and perhaps find him. Two dozen more would turn a good profit into a very handsome one. Two more raids, but not here, with the increasing risk of being caught. They were this far North, why not venture a little further, out of the range of the hunting French navy? He was proud of his ship, she was more seaworthy that most Xebecs; being wide-beamed she was more stable in a rough sea. Ireland was possible and also England. He turned it over in his mind. So, which first, Ireland or England?

Chapter Seven

Witness or Defendant

There are some buildings that add gravity and weight to the events that they host, there are some that gain it from the events played out within them. The Port Admiral's Official Residence, hosting the Board of Enquiry, was one such of the latter; imposingly built as it may be, it was, nevertheless, merely a place of domicile. Argent was the first out of the coach, property of the Royal Mail, but especially hired to convey, post haste, the three summoned Officers and the four Warrant Officers. Argent looked at the familiar façade and portico, but its familiarity did nothing to ease the tension growing within him. Stood as he was now, before this particular building, the weight of the occasion caused the neat architecture to bear down upon him even more, rather than to give any salve to his anxious thoughts. His intimate knowledge of the interior, coupled with the memory of past fraught occasions inside its walls, could do nothing to ease his troubled mind, only to add to his building sense of apprehension. The thought was never far beneath the surface; this could easily end with any resulting opprobrium poured upon his own head.

Fentiman and Sanders emerged after him, then McArdle, Short, Fraser, and Ball, all more concerned to stretch their cramped limbs than to examine their grand surroundings. All seven had been carried from Falmouth in less than five hours, leaving before dawn to arrive in good time for the post noon gathering. They had travelled in silence; it was not so much the social gulf between the travellers that inhibited any conversation that may be termed "pleasant and convivial", but more because each knew what awaited them and each was more consumed with their own thoughts on what they would say when their turn came to give their own observations and opinions.

Ball, Short, and Fraser gave the building little more than a glance, for them its imposing frontage was merely part of the ordeal. In contrast, McArdle, perhaps more appreciative of fine structure and mathematical proportion, stood awhile and nodded his head. Argent was carrying the logbook and he had stood for no more than a minute, before a Naval Captain that he did not recognise, came forward to relieve him of it.

"Captain Argent?"

Argent nodded.

"I am Captain Nathan Dunstaple, acting as Clerk to the Court. May I take that, the Members wish to compare the two logbooks before the Court assembles?"

Argent knew the answer, but he wished for complete clarity.

"Compare?"

"Why yes. Your version, and Captain Cheveley's. Before the Court sits."

Argent nodded, handed the weighty volume to him and Dunstaple turned and disappeared up the steps immediately. Argent, now joined by Sanders and Fentiman, then saw, at least, one friendly face, Marine Captain Baker, who descended the steps whilst grinning in open friendship, then warmly shaking the hands of all three.

"I'll bid you welcome, if that's the correct word, and wish you well for a good outcome."

All three grinned and nodded in reply, but it was Fentiman who spoke first, the question that they had all been wondering.

"Who's on The Board?"

"Vice Admiral Grenville Holdsworth is Chairman, along with our own Grant and Broke."

Argent continued.

"Holdsworth we don't know. What's he like?'

"Unknown to me. He was at Copenhagen, but not under Nelson. He was Hyde-Parker's Flag Captain when Nelson decided he "couldn't see the signal", so you can read into that whatever you like."

Argent nodded.

"Right. An unknown quantity."

Argent knew that Broke would support Cheveley, and could only hope that Grant would be fair to him. He changed the subject.

"Is Cheveley here?"

"Yes, and inside."

"What's the word?"

"Well, the talk at table in these parts is much as I told you last time and he's holding to it. He's saying that he judged for reasons of prudence... damn weasel word that is... that an immediate withdrawal was necessary to save the ships in an impossible mission. He sent his signal and you should have obeyed quicker."

By now the four Warrant Officers were close and overhearing all. The mouths of each face set hard into a thin line, but only McArdle emitted a kind of growl, he feeling that the Ninth Commandment was now in some deep jeopardy. Argent looked at Fentiman, the unspoken fact showing clearly on his face, "This could go very wrong."

Baker broke in.

"I should tell you, that Bentley's people are here, and so is Ffynes, with his. I took them to their places myself. Also Charlotte Willoughby and Lady Grant."

Argent sensed Fentiman shifting beside him, but continued on the subject of Bentley and Ffynes.

"Are they inside? Ffynes and Bentley's people, that is. I must go to them, before things begin. Could you point them out?"

He began to mount the steps and Baker turned to ascend beside him.

"Yes I can, assuming they've not moved."

Argent's companions followed and they entered the main reception room where they had entertained the Spanish Admiral, but now all was set for a Board of Enquiry; one table covered in green baize, nothing on top bar a block and gavel, four chairs behind and many ranks before, bar one, a chair very alone three yards before the table. The heavy paintings, of battle and disaster seemed to shrink back into obscurity in the face of the profound magnitude of what was about to occur. Baker looked around.

"There they are, where I placed them, seated towards the back right. You can see Ffynes, then the two couples to his right. His parents, then Bentley's."

Argent followed the directions and was successful, then he turned to Baker.

"Where are we sitting?"

"Witnesses in the front two rows. I'll take your party down there now. Shall I save you a seat? Are you going back to them now?"

"Yes to both. Save me a seat. I think it right that I pay my respects immediately."

Saying no more, Baker motioned for Argent's companions to follow, leaving Argent to stand where he was. Being stationary made him noticeable and so Ffynes saw him and his face showed that he had. Argent made his way back to them and he saw Ffynes lean sideways to talk to his parents. It soon became evident that he had told them that his Captain was on his way back to them because both Mother and Father turned their eyes upon him, but not before Father had passed the word down the row to Bentley's parents. Soon all five pairs of eyes were on his approach, but only those of Ffynes showed any light of welcome. Argent concentrated on Ffynes, still wearing his Midshipman's uniform, but with his right sleeve pinned across his chest. Ffynes stood as Argent neared him and, poignantly, stood to attention. He seemed thinner and paler in complexion. Argent extended his right hand, but palm down, and Ffynes left hand lifted to meet it, making a satisfactory handshake.

"Rufus. I'm so very pleased to see you again."

Argent stopped himself just in time from asking after his health. It seemed crass and pointless.

"How do you do, Sir? Permit me to introduce my Mother and Father"

Argent blessed his good memory for names, from the time when Midshipman Ffynes was first delivered to the ship.

"Sir Harold and Lady Ffynes. I am pleased to meet you again, although I would have wanted for better circumstances."

Sir Harold, heavy set, pomaded black hair, dressed all in navy blue and white, and leaning forward onto a silver cane, did not rise to shake hands. His wife's mouth moved to form but the slightest smile, before her head turned so that the edge of her bonnet cut out the line of sight between herself and Argent. Sir Harold felt no need to say anything, he simply continued to regard Argent coldly, clearly he felt no need to be polite, but Argent did have something to say.

"I do hope that you received my letter."

Father answered in the affirmative and Ffynes continued with the introductions.

"And Lieutenant Bentley's parents. Sir Matthew and Lady Cynthia."

Sir Matthew, him in black and white, matching the clothing of his wife, stared back stonily, from a full face that spoke of opulent living, but his eyes were angry. Those of his wife, in contrast were close to weeping, but it was she who spoke.

"We, also, received your letter, Captain Argent, and we're grateful for the kind things you said. I found your letter a great comfort."

Her husband's angry gaze turned on her, but she continued.

"I know that he'd never have amounted to much of a leader of men, but I do feel, that since he joined your ship, he was growing in character, and for that I thank you. In your service, I grew very proud of him."

"Thank you, Lady Cynthia, and I meant what I said, because it was true. He met his end alongside his men, encouraging them all to stand by their guns. He led by example, which is all that any of us can do. That's our memory of him and it will always remain so."

At this Lady Bentley did begin weeping and she managed to gasp a "Thank you" before she brought an already damp handkerchief to her dampening eyes. However, her husband was having none of it. He looked up at Argent, the anger that was in him growing further.

"We're here to find out what happened, Captain. Why our son died in so hopeless an escapade, and where the blame lies. Have you any thoughts, now, at this moment?"

"I do, Sir Matthew, but I must hold them for the Board that is about to assemble. I am pleased that you are all here, and I hope that it will give you some comfort, when it's done."

Both Sirs gave a curt and formal nod, but with Argent, they were plainly less than satisfied, in their eyes blame already lay thickly upon him. Argent concluded that it was time to go; his continued presence could do no good. He smiled to both sets of parents, but received nothing like back in reply.

"I should take my place. I'm sure this will soon begin and I should be where I am needed. Should you wish to talk to me afterwards, then I am at your disposal. So, I bid you good afternoon."

He bowed, then turned, but paused to pat Ffynes, who was still standing, on the muscle of his left arm. Amazingly Argent perceived him as being more cheerful than when he was serving on ship.

"Good bye, Sir. I'll write. I'm getting quite good with my left hand." Argent smiled and nodded.

"Please do that, Rufus. We're always pleased to hear from an old shipmate."

The word struck home and warmth came into the face of both, but Argent had to go. Servants were entering from the side door, its room evidently contained the Members of the Board. Argent gained his place in the front row, as the four entered, Grant first, then Holdsworth, then Broke, him being the shortest, between Holdsworth and Dunstaple. Each of the first three wore their full uniform of rank, gold epaulettes on each, but only on the epaulette of Lord Grenville Holdsworth could a second star be seen, designating his superiority as a Vice Admiral, as did the extra ring on his cuff. He carried in the books, both under one arm and, on reaching the table, these were then set within easy reach before he took his place. Broke and Grant stood waiting for him to be sat in his own chair before they took their own, then Captain Dunstaple entered with a sheaf of paper and took the fourth seat.

Whilst each member was placing himself Argent leaned towards Fentiman.

"I've just been speaking to the people of Ffynes and Bentley. Not good."

"Where are they?"

"Towards the back right. Ffynes is alongside."

Fentiman rose slightly, looked for Ffynes and saw them, but proceedings were beginning. With each settled besides him, Holdsworth looked up and sat with both elbows on the green baize, his fingers interlocked to form a rest for his chin. His face was impassive, thin, weather-beaten and stern, but his eyes glared out; impatient, annoyed, a gaze that could pierce fog. With these he regarded the assembly, left to right, up and down, as though gathering their attention. Silence he already had and he began with no welcoming formality.

"This Board of Enquiry has been set up to examine the events of August 10th 1809, namely the raid on St. Malo against the French frigate La Pomone, as carried out by HMS Herodotus, Captain Cheveley, and HMS Ariadne, Captain Argent, in the company of 320 Marines under Marine Colonel Shortman. This is not a Court Martial, but part of our brief is to discover if there should be one, as may lead on from our deliberations here."

He paused.

"I would remind any Officer here, about to give evidence, that they are automatically on oath, on their honour as Commissioned Officers of The King, to tell the truth."

Argent's stomach had churned at the mention of his own name out of the thin lipless mouth, but Holdsworth had now paused to look at both his companions, a look of enquiry in case they wished to add anything. Both shook their heads and so Holdsworth began.

"Marine Captain Baker."

No request, no please, just the bare name. Baker came forward with a file and sat in the single chair. Holdsworth immediately corrected him.

"Captain Baker. Please stand and read to the assembly the notes you took of the meeting of 7th August to agree a plan for the raid."

Baker did so, laying particular emphasis on the "cut out, burn, or do what damage that can be done". He also stated slowly and clearly, "Herodotus to begin her withdrawal in close consort with Ariadne, to both bombard together the enemy bastion as they leave and force it to divide its fire." Baker remained standing, while Holdsworth looked left at Grant.

"Admiral Grant. You were Senior Officer at that meeting. Do you agree with that account?

"I do."

"And you signed off those Minutes?"

"I did."

"That's all Baker."

Baker saluted, which wasn't returned, and walked to his seat. Holdsworth consulted his own notes.

"Lieutenant Henry Fentiman. HMS Ariadne."

Fentiman sat bolt upright at being called so soon and looked over to Argent, who nodded encouragingly. Fentiman rose and strode, somewhat disjointedly, to the single chair. Holdsworth adopted his earlier pose to support his chin, but his mouth still worked well enough and his eyes were cold and level.

"Lieutenant Fentiman. You have heard the plan of the raid read out."

Fentiman nodded, but Holdsworth continued straight on.

"How would you describe your relationship with Herodotus during the raid?"

Fentiman looked puzzled and he frowned.

"I can't."

"Can't?"

The word exploded out of Holdsworth's face.

"No Sir, I can't because we were never in any kind of relationship during the whole action. Herodotus came in well astern of us and went out well ahead. The only relationship that we were in, if it can be termed thus, is that we received her signal. And, I suppose, it can be said that we, that is Ariadne, bombarded the main bastion at long range, whilst she engaged it at effective range. Other than that, the relationship can only be described as independent action. Sir."

Holdsworth glared at him, he wasn't pleased at such frank opinion.

"So, how would you describe independent action?"

"We each fought the French in our own way, Sir, according to our own circumstances. I cannot relate to you any level of co-operation at all. Sir."

"But you say you engaged the main bastion across the harbour together with Herodotus?'

"Yes Sir, but our fire, Ariadne's, was almost completely ineffective, the range was too far. We opened fire more to cover ourselves with smoke. Sir."

"That's all Fentiman. Captain Argent, come forward, please, and take his place."

Argent rose and took himself to the chair, around one way, whilst Fentiman departed around the other. Holdsworth fixed Argent with the same stony look.

"Captain Argent. Please describe the action as it applies to Ariadne."

Argent took a deep breath and began. He outlined the events as he remembered them described in the Logbook, which was just as well because Holdsworth had opened the Log and was following Argent's description, word for word. Argent finished with a description of their battle damage and casualties, he then sat and let the silence hang. The drama of what he had said had reduced the hall to total stillness, the utter silence conveying fully the impact upon the audience of the intensity of the action. Holdsworth looked up from the Logbook.

'Let me get this clear. You entered and saw La Pomone berthed in neither of the places intelligence told she was likely to be?"

"That's correct, Sir. She was berthed bows in, stern out, under the guns of the third bastion. Sir."

"A dangerous place, Argent."

Holdsworth let the point hang.

"Yes Sir. But our orders were to burn if we couldn't cut out, and damage if we couldn't burn. Her stern was vulnerable, Sir, and so we attacked. To do her what damage we could. Sir."

Holdsworth showed no reaction, he merely lifted himself up and looked either side at his companions. He then turned back to Argent.

"And when you learned of the signal to withdraw, what was your immediate reaction?"

"To look at the situation with the Marines, Sir, who by this time were aboard La Pomone and had been for some minutes. They were still aboard her at that point but the first were coming back off. I had the tow in place to bring their lugger away and so I waited until all were off. The last was Captain Ramsey and when he came I knew that there could be no more Marines remaining. At that moment I began my withdrawal and cut the anchor cable for the tide to carry us out."

"So, if I understand your Log here correctly, you set off, out, with the lugger in tow?"

"That's correct. Sir."

"Once you were out in the Roads, where was Herodotus?"

"Almost left the harbour, Sir, certainly by the time we got ourselves into the Roads proper. At that point she was passing the island bastion, Sir, either opposite or past it, I didn't study her too closely, I had concerns of my own."

A hubbub came forward to him from the audience; all had listened avidly, but many were now commenting on the conduct of Herodotus. Holdsworth's voice cut through the murmur.

"So, how did that sit with your agreed plan?"

"Not at all, Sir. My understanding from our meeting to plan the raid, was that Herodotus would not cut her anchor until my bowsprit was over her taffrail. We used those exact words, and written orders confirmed that."

Again, the deep growling set up behind Argent. "What was he about?" was heard clearly and more than once. Holdsworth sat back, plainly he considered that he had heard something significant. He studied what was evidently a copy of the orders, then looked at Grant, then at Broke, who took his cue.

"You engaged the main bastion together on your exit, Captain?"

Argent looked squarely at Broke, directly into eyes that he saw were worried, more than a little, but were, nevertheless, equally hostile.

"No Sir. Certainly not in the way that was planned. When my guns came within effective range, Herodotus was gone; she was no longer within any kind of range, even extreme. We passed the bastion alone, Sir, and we engaged it on our own. It was then that I sustained my worst damage and the majority of my casualties. We took all their fire and..."

Broke interrupted.

"I understand Captain. I hear your answer."

Argent looked at Holdsworth.

"If I may finish, Sir?"

Holdsworth nodded, Broke screwed up his face.

"We took all their fire and it was then that the lugger was sunk, but we got the crew and Marines off her. Sir. Then we took ourselves out, to pass the last fort, that was still held by the Marines."

Holdsworth looked blankly at Argent but perhaps his eyes were no longer the previous mere slits of malevolence.

"We may call you again, Captain. Is your Quartermaster here?"

"Yes Sir. Zachary Short."

Holdsworth spoke no more, it was plain what he now wanted. Argent rose and walked around the chair. Zachary Short was shuffling along his row, treading unconsciously on feet, anxious to reach the required place. He did so and sat, but Holdsworth had other ideas.

"Stand up, Short."

Zachary Short did so and saluted, instinctively. Holdsworth turned to Dunstaple.

"Give him the Oath."

Dunstaple picked up The Bible and the Oath was repeated, nervously and some parts twice. Holdsworth resumed his "chin on hands" pose.

"Now, Short. You were at the wheel of the Ariadne throughout the whole?"

Short came to the attention and stared just above Holdsworth's head.

"Aye Sir. Yes Sir."

"When you got under way to come out, what order did you receive?"

"I remembers it clear, Sir. Up helm and take us out."

"So you steered for the harbour entrance?"

"Yes Sir."

"What did you see of Herodotus?"

"When, Sir?"

"When you got into the Roads!"

"Yes Sir. Well, the wind was abeam, Sir, so I eased her over, and, like you ask, got into the Roads to gain the full tide."

Holdsworth's mouth set in a tight line of impatience.

"And Herodotus?"

"Well Sir, when we got in the Roads I lay for the entrance Sir. 'Twere then that I was looking down harbour. All I could see of her as I lay for the entrance, was her stern, Sir. Driver out to starboard and about where Cap'n Argent said, Sir. 'Twere too far to be more accurate 'bout exactly where she was, certainly how far ahead of us."

"Short. I'm asking for her exact position."

Short was growing in confidence.

"I couldn't give it, Sir, I couldn't say to no more accurate than a cable or more. She was too far."

"How far ahead of you?"

"Well, when I got us square in the Roads, Sir, you've got to be lookin' at somethin' not far short of a mile ahead!"

Holdsworth looked down and sat back.

"Dismiss, Short."

Amidst the recurring growl of muted discussion, Zachary Short came to the attention and saluted. He then returned to his place, smiling, this time avoiding feet, but not the congratulatory slaps on the arm from his mates. Holdsworth was speaking again.

"Marine Colonel Shortman."

From some way down the row from Argent, Shortman rose and marched to the chair, sword hilt in his left hand, shako tucked under his right. He came beside the chair, came to the attention and saluted, but did not sit.

"Please to sit, Colonel."

Shortman did and arranged himself whilst Holdsworth waited.

"Colonel. You were present at the meeting to conceive a plan for this raid?"

"I was."

"And what is your recollection of how the three vessels would leave on completion of attacking La Pomone, that being both frigates, plus the lugger?"

"In close consort, Sir, with Ariadne towing the lugger. Captain Argent has the words correct. Herodotus would not cut her cable until Ariadne's bowsprit was over her taffrail."

"And was this the case?"

"No Sir. Herodotus came down alone, and Ariadne much later."

"How much later?"

"A good five minutes, Sir. Approaching ten."

Holdsworth again sat back, stretching his forearms forward on the table, this now his signal that the questioning was done.

"You may go, Colonel."

"Thank you, Sir, but I'd like to say one further thing, Sir. I watched Ariadne put up a fight in that harbour such as I've never heard of. If the Frogs ever thought we've gone soft since Trafalgar, they don't now!"

Applause broke out around the hall and Holdsworth seized his gavel to pound it on the table.

"Silence! Silence!"

When he could be heard without shouting, he spoke further, dismissively.

"That's all, Colonel."

Whilst Shortman marched back to his place to about turn and sit, Holdsworth was in discussion with his Board. Silence fell as they deliberated, then Holdsworth looked up.

"Lieutenant Sanders."

Sanders rose and quickly reached the chair to immediately sit.

"Lieutenant. You commanded the lugger that attacked La Pomone?"

Sanders nodded and spoke.

"Sir."

"What did you see on entry to the harbour?"

"I saw La Pomone berthed over to our larboard, Sir. Stern showing."

"And what did you do?"

"Made straight for her, Sir."

"You did not look for orders from your superior?"

"Well, no Sir. "Cut out, burn, or damage, Sir, were our standing orders. So we set off to set about the damaging. Sir."

Sanders actually smiled, good naturedly, as he delivered his answer, as though the answer were already plain and obvious and behind him laughter actually broke out. Holdsworth used his gavel again and having stared the assembly into silence, he continued.

"Your zeal for your duty does you credit, Lieutenant. You speak as though you acted independently."

"Why, no Sir, that doesn't quite apply. We sailed in alongside Ariadne, just off her larboard quarter. Captain Argent hailed across that we should get across her stern, to use our charges, and that we had five minutes on her. Sir."

Holdsworth did not assume his "finish" posture, but nevertheless, Sanders was waved away.

"Sailing Master McArdle."

McArdle rose from beside Zachary Short and eased his way along the row, taking his time, looking up, along and over, to the four at the table. Once beside the chair he stood, at his full height and awaited the arrival of Dunstaple, whose approach down the tunnel of McArdle's gaze gave Dunstaple the strong impression that this Warrant Officer regarded him as some kind of ignorant imbecile to outrageously presume that he, McArdle, needed to take an Oath to tell the truth. Nevertheless, McArdle took The Bible, held it aloft for all to see and spoke the words, spoken as though at the end of a Hellfire sermon, delivered to commend the congregation to even deeper righteousness. This done he turned his baleful gaze upon Holdsworth and waited. Holdsworth seemed more than slightly intimidated.

"McArdle. You are the Sailing Master of HMS Ariadne?"

"That is correct. Sir."

"When Ariadne entered the harbour and you saw La Pomone, how did you assess the task ahead?"

Perhaps from irritation or for some other reason, McArdle's Scottish accent became even thicker.

"Nay too difficult, Sir, with guid seamanship and ship handlin'. Timin' was all important, but we achieved it. Sir."

"Achieved? Elaborate."

"I tak' it ye're asking aboot the trickier parts, Sir, but they were completed well enough. We sailed up past La Pomone, close enough to rake her, completed our turn, at the same time gettin' a cable to the lugger, then held our place on the anchor, the exact place, I wish to make clear. When the time came, we cut our cable and towed her out, Sir, that bein' the lugger full of Marines."

"And your escape?"

McArdle looked at Holdsworth as though he were one of his pupils taking a Noon sight, one that had placed them somewhere in the Sahara.

"We got out, Sir, because I'm here tae tell ye aboot it, but I'm of a mind to say that I'm of the opinion that they was firin' 42's, Sir, nae

32 pound. Sailin' past that bastion alone, Sir, I don't mind tellin' ye, I said a very long prayer, us being wholly alone and full in the hands of the Good Lord."

More laughter and more gavelling. Holdsworth rose and stood, as did his companions and he waited for silence.

"We will now adjourn for a short time. Assume resumption in 30 minutes."

With that, leaving McArdle at attention, all four took themselves away to the door from which they had entered, again in line astern, with Dunstaple bringing up the rear. The door closed behind them, at which point Argent looked at Fentiman and gave a deep and prolonged exhalation of breath. The look they exchanged carried the same message, "So far, so good." Argent turned and looked at Short, also McArdle, now back in his place, he having dismissed himself.

"Well spoken. Well spoken to you both."

He looked directly at Short, for his next words could not apply to McArdle.

"It couldn't have been easy. You shaped up well."

Both spoke their thanks in unison and the three Officers stood, if for no other reason than to stretch their legs. Many others in the hall were doing the same and Argent looked around. He saw Charlotte and Lady Grant, both remaining seated, and both gave him a cheery wave, which he returned, but their regarding him was interrupted by Cheveley, who placed himself in a vacant chair before them, to turn and engage them in some conversation. He appeared neither worried, nor under any strain, but Argent didn't care what happened to Cheveley; as long as Ariadne emerged with her reputation unsullied, that was the only result that mattered to him. Sanders was talking to Fraser, Short and McArdle, but Fentiman came to stand at Argent's side.

"I've heard that the defendant's case is taken last, in a Court of Law, so at least we can take some comfort in that. They don't seem to regard us as being amongst the accused."

Argent turned to his Lieutenant, with a smile that matched the hope in both.

"A turn around the deck, I think."

"Good idea, Sir."

For some minutes they perambulated around the hall, keeping to the outside, sometimes stopping to examine a naval painting, usually commenting on the impossibility of what the artist was showing, given the deduced direction of the wind, tide and other factors, but they both indulgently forgave all in the name of artistic licence. They came up to Captain Baker, but there was little to say, other than to voice the obvious, "So far, so good." The door opened and Dunstaple reappeared to stand and wait, which fixed posture conveyed the message to all assembled that they should quickly resume their seats. With that achieved, Dunstaple looked through the door and the three entered. Once sat, Holdsworth lost no time.

"Captain Argent. Return if you please."

Argent noted the polite addition, but he did not allow his face to show any emotion. He quickly came to the chair and Holdsworth began.

"Captain Argent, it seems to me that, with La Pomone berthed so securely and under the guns of two powerful forts, that to proceed further was reckless in the extreme, and would put at risk two valuable frigates and a good number of men."

Holdsworth let the statement hang. With nothing more forthcoming Argent concluded that he must respond, but not too soon. He allowed a quizzical look to pass across his face.

"That is a point of view, Sir, but I don't share it. La Pomone was, is still, a major threat. Our orders were to "cut out, burn, or damage", and we were there, in the harbour and could see her vulnerable at the stern. I concluded that the chance to damage her was clear and achievable. I followed orders."

"Whose orders?"

Argent was taken aback.

"Why, Sir, the written orders of Admiral Grant, which became the standing orders for the raid"

Broke placed his hand on Holdsworth's sleeve, he wished to intervene and he looked at Argent, pure hatred present in each part of his face.

"Captain Argent, you were the Senior Officer in the position to make the judgement. You proceeded, and you proceeded recklessly."

Argent was incensed, not only by Broke's openly aggressive tone but also by the words forming his questioning.

"Yes Sir, I did proceed, but those were my orders. I followed my orders. I was not made Commodore; you gave that post to Captain Cheveley. It was not for me to decide to set those orders aside, Sir, and break off the action, or any other deviation."

Broke glared back with a look of triumph.

"But you received an order from your Commodore, did you not, Argent? An order to withdraw."

Argent could see where this was going.

"I cannot speak for when the order was given, Sir, I can only speak for when my signalman brought it to my attention and I could act upon it. That time, Sir, was when the action was well under way. Well under way! The Marines were committed and on La Pomone. We had raked her, turned, and anchored across her stern. Only then, after those things had taken place, did I get the signal"

"The time of the signal is not in your Logbook."

"No Sir. Under the circumstances no one thought to look at their timepiece."

"Then we can only look to the efficiency of your ship, Captain, that being the relaying of orders from your Commodore, in this case Captain Cheveley."

"I have no reason to doubt the efficiency of my signalman, Sir. His task was to watch Herodotus for signals. As to when the signal was first flown, you will have to ask Captain Cheveley. All I can say in addition, Sir, is that there was a lot of smoke, and, when the signal was made known to me, I obeyed as soon as I could, but I was not going to abandon the Marines, Sir."

Comments came from behind Argent, within hearing distance of the table, "damn right", "hear him", "impossible". Holdsworth looked at Broke, with a frown, but giving him the opportunity for more. However, Broke was finished and it was Holdsworth who spoke.

"Thank you, Captain Argent."

But Argent's temper was roused.

"I'd like to say more, Sir, in that we did damage La Pomone, after all, she is out of commission. We did manage to fight our way out, but my damage and casualties would have been a lot less if we weren't alone, and also the fort that did us the damage would perhaps have been less potent, had Herodotus engaged her for some while longer. She, after all, Sir, was the 42 gun frigate!"

Argent rose, amidst the buzz of open conversation, but feeling no better for his outburst. He marched back to his chair and sat. Holdsworth looked blank, showing no reaction, instead, he lowered his head and consulted his notes.

"First Lieutenant Lord Harrison Charles Langley."

A slim figure of medium height rose over on Argent's left and made his way to the front of the audience. In line with the chair, he strolled towards it, at the same time feeling for the correct arrangement of his shirt cuffs that protruded from his sleeves, which Argent noticed were made of lace. His whole couture was immaculate, the additional decoration to his uniform just the wrong side of acceptable, but, plainly, Langley expected to get away with it. There were black bows and brass buckles at each strategic point and gold braid gleamed. On reaching the chair, he stood before it and shot his coat tails backwards before seating himself; he would take no risk of creasing the drape of so splendid a piece of naval tailoring. Thus arranged, he looked at Holdsworth who assumed his questioning posture of fingers counterpoised, chin upon the arch, elbows on the table.

"Lieutenant."

Langley seemed pained at being addressed by his lowliest title.

"Your Log shows that you entered St. Malo at 5.15, five minutes after Ariadne."

Langley nodded and Holdsworth continued.

"Once in position, for how long would you say you exchanged fire with the main bastion?"

Langley pursed his lips and rotated his thumbs together. Holdsworth looked annoyed.

"I'd say somewhere in the region of ten minutes, give or take."

"Give or take what?"

"A broadside or two."

Giggles came from where Langley had been sitting and he smiled at his own "bon mot". Holdsworth continued, no longer feeling, nor looking, indulgent.

"And then, after the lapse of that time, your Captain, Captain Cheveley, ordered the cable to be cut and you made your exit?"

"That's the right of it."

A pause.

"Sir."

"So, in your estimation, you engaged the main bastion for ten minutes, made your signal, then began to leave. Yes?"

"No. That's not quite right. We made our signal after about five minutes, continued the action for a further five, then cut."

"Where was Ariadne when you cut?"

"Still hanging about with La Pomone. We'd waited five minutes, we couldn't wait any more. I wish she could have been sharper about her business."

More giggles, more frowns from Holdsworth, then he fixed Langley with a look like a poised hatchet.

"Explain "hanging about". Was Ariadne engaged with La Pomone?'

"Well, it would be duced poor if she wasn't! There was certainly a lot of noise and smoke."

"Noise?"

"Gunfire."

"So, let me get this clear. You saw Ariadne up against La Pomone. You engaged the bastion for ten minutes, sent the signal after five, and then waited for Ariadne for another five? All the while under fire from the bastion?"

Langley was now grinning openly.

"That's precisely the correctness of it. Sir."

Holdsworth looked at Broke who shook his head, but Grant had already begun.

"Lieutenant, could you develop further, "couldn't wait any more", if you please?"

Langley looked puzzled and in no little way apprehensive.

"We were coming under heavy fire. Sir."

"Heavy fire! Hmmm. Now, Lieutenant, how many hits had your ship sustained when you sent the signal?"

Langley's face changed to deadpan; expressionless. He took some time to think.

"Three, perhaps, four."

"So, in the first five minutes, you took four hits. That's less than one a minute."

Grant waited for a response. None came, apart from a condescending look, so Grant continued.

"Less than one hit a minute was sufficient for you to cut and run?"

Langley's face changed to red anger.

"I cannot comment. That was my Captain's decision."

Grant remained staring at Langley for some seconds, then he turned to Holdsworth and nodded. Holdsworth took his cue, but his tone spoke of his displeasure at Langley's foppish attitude.

"Thank you, Lieutenant. That is all."

Langley rose and looked at Grant as though he wished to call him out, but he spun on his heel and stalked off. Holdsworth followed him with his eyes, his next witness was next to Langley's vacant chair.

"Captain Cheveley. Please come forward."

Next to Argent, Fentiman was incensed.

"Ten minutes, I wouldn't allow them to say five. It was a pack of damn lies, and so will this be."

Argent had re-gathered himself and was able to speak slowly.

"I agree Henry, I feel the same, but keep calm. It was only to be expected."

Cheveley sat down, large, confident and immaculate. Holdsworth began.

"Captain Cheveley. What did you see when you entered St. Malo?"

"I saw our quarry securely berthed under the guns of two forts. One just upstream of her, that being on her side of the harbour, and one directly opposite. I ordered withdrawal."

"What happened next?"

"To whom?"

"Let's start with Ariadne."

"She sailed on, against my orders, and attacked La Pomone."

"And you."

"We sailed in, turned, and came out. I expected Ariadne to follow. She didn't. I hold Captain Argent responsible."

"When did you send the signal?"

"As soon as I saw the impossibility of the mission."

"As it states in your Log?"

"Yes. "Entered St. Malo at 5.15. Signal sent at 5.25." It took ten minutes to finally appraise the situation."

Holdsworth sat back, this time it did mean that he was done. He looked at Broke, who looked very cheerful. He turned to Grant, who sat forward, his face dark and very disturbed. His mouth set into a purposeful line, chin jutting forward. Grant began.

"Captain Cheveley, there is something I am very much in need to clear up."

He already had both Logbooks open in front of him.

"Your Log states that you entered St. Malo at 5.15?"

"Yes."

"Your Log also states: 5.25. Sent signal to Ariadne, she not yet engaged."

"Yes."

"Ariadne entered before you, say five minutes before you. So by your own Log, she was in at 5.10 approximately, as Ariadne's own agrees, yet 15 minutes later, a quarter of an hour, 5.25, by your Log she had still not engaged the French, and all she had to do was sail up a couple of cables. Any comment?"

"I stand by the entries I have made."

"But your own First Lieutenant has just stated that when you sent the signal, Ariadne was still "hanging about with La Pomone" presumably within very effective cannon range?"

"I stand by the entries I have made."

"Ariadne's Log states that she left at 5.41. She came in at 5.10 and you're saying that she had not yet engaged, even at 5.25. Therefore, everything she did in that harbour until she sailed past the last fort, every piece of every action, start to finish, including the 5 minutes of the Marines aboard La Pomone, all happened inside a mere further 15 minutes?"

"I stand by the entries I have made."

Grant stared at him for several moments, his expression cold, yet questioning.

"Captain Cheveley. You are an experienced officer?"

"I count myself as such."

"How many actions have you been in? Whilst in overall command, I mean?"

Cheveley shifted uncomfortably. He looked down, then up, then back at Grant.

"None."

"None?"

"No. St. Malo was my first, as a Commodore, I mean."

"Right. So there you are, taking your ship up to engage the enemy, the last in, but following the plan as agreed, in all fairness."

He took a deep breath to control the emotion in his next sentence.

"Before you are your men, those you command, in their vessels engaging the enemy, piling into the enemy for all they're worth. They are obeying orders, doing their best to carry them out, which was to damage the French."

"I cannot argue with those facts, but I judged the risk of further action to be too great."

"You did, Captain Cheveley. Yes, you did. But they didn't!"

The last three words hit like a thunderclap. Grant paused and looked calmly and levelly at Cheveley, whose face reddened. Courage and cowardice were now in question, particularly his. Once again he shifted himself on the chair.

"I made my judgment. I was Commodore."

It sounded lame and growls from behind, of disapproval, confirmed it as so. Grant continued, his face coldly humorous from the poor answers.

"So, despite your order to withdraw not being carried out, and any experienced Officer here will tell you that instant communication in battle is a myth, it was plainly laid out before you that your men were following the plan and doing whatever damage to the French as was in their power to do!"

Cheveley nodded. Grant pressed on.

"Now, let's consider your signal. You ordered a withdrawal and it was acknowledged? It says so in your Log."

"I did order withdraw and it was acknowledged."

"And you concluded from the acknowledgment, what?"

Cheveley was recovering.

"That Argent was going to comply."

"So, you concluded that Argent would soon be on his way out. Surely it crossed your mind that he'd need some time, and so, you stayed, of course, knowing that the plan required you to engage the bastion until Ariadne arrived, to reduce its effectiveness and to draw some fire. As a good Commander, despite the hopeless cause, as you saw it, you stayed to help your men fight their way out?"

Cheveley's hands twitched and his head jerked upwards. His face reddened further, it then spread behind to the back of his neck. Subconsciously, the audience sat forward, the better to hear the answer. It was mumbled.

"No, but...I waited five minutes more after sending the signal to withdraw. I thought..."

Grant interrupted.

"You're saying no. You didn't stay to support your men, bar the five whole minutes you quote. This five minutes is "dancing on a pinhead", is it not? A mere nothing. It can only lead to the inevitable conclusion that when you began taking hits, you took your ship out as soon as you could turn and then lay a course out for the open sea. Out! You did not stand your ground until your men came up to you. The facts are that you spent 10 minutes in that harbour, from passing the first fort, before you decided you'd had enough, which included a mere five minutes under fire. Then a mere five minutes later, you cut to break off the action entirely. Ariadne's log says her stay in there was close on 30. Twice as long as yours. What say you?"

Cheveley suddenly looked smaller.

"I took my ship out or I'd risk losing her. I expected Argent to do the same."

Grant was turning the knife. He listed the facts.

"So, you came under sustained fire. You couldn't remain a moment longer. You sent a signal to withdraw, that was acknowledged?"

Cheveley seized on the notion like a lifeline.

"Yes. Remaining was impossible."

"Your ship was under sustained fire, it was causing you severe battle damage, damage so great that it was impossible to hold the place that the men under your command were expecting of you. Your ship was being knocked to pieces."

Grant paused to allow Cheveley to nod his head. He then nodded himself.

"And your casualties and damage from this sustained fire was?

Grant leaned forward.

"Remember, I have your Logbook."

Cheveley twisted in his seat, his hands grasping the sides.

"Five great shot hit my hull, causing one killed and five wounded."

Almost the whole audience sat back, shocked. Naval Officers exchanged looks of horror, or contempt or sadness, the question either thought or spoken, "What now for The Service?". However, Grant had not finished.

"Five hits, and six casualties, Captain, therefore, gave you cause to abandon your men to their fate; the men who had sailed in, sailed up, and attacked the French with all the vigour they were capable of. Their brave conduct carried no weight with you?"

He paused to give emphasis to his following words. Cheveley remained slumped yet fidgeting.

"The men of the Ariadne and the Marines must now have very good cause to curse the French gunners in their aim; that they hit your hull and not your sails, which perhaps would have forced you to remain at your post a little longer."

Grant folded his arms and sat back, rubbing his forehead with his fingertips, looking down at the green baize, saddened and forlorn. He had taken no pleasure from exposing the conduct of a Royal Navy frigate is such manner. He gave no look to Holdsworth; he could now take whichever course he chose. Holdsworth chose to make an end.

"This Board will now retire to reach its conclusion."

All four stood, all with grim faces, although for different reasons. Both stony faced and hard eyed, Grant, and then Holdsworth exited through their door, but Broke's face showed no small depth of anxiety. Almost the whole audience rose, amongst the last being Cheveley. He was still in some shock from his treatment from Grant, but when he did rise, he took himself straight outside, meeting the gaze of no one, to sit and suffer in his own carriage, alone.

The Ariadnies remained in their places, as did most of the assembly. The high drama that had just played out before them filled their thoughts such as to give no admission to the idea of moving or even standing. Sanders looked across Fentiman to ask of Argent.

"What do you think, Sir?"

Argent was as much moved by what had just taken place as anyone. He took a while to collect his thoughts and find the correct words.

"I think it now rests with the whim of the Board, which, in my experience means it can go either way. Whatever, Ariadne and yourself have emerged with some credit. There can be no criticism of you. If any bad decisions were made, they were mine. My responsibility. If the Board wish to draw attention to that, well, that is their choice."

He paused and looked down, his face serious, then he looked back at Sanders.

"I'm for some fresh air."

He stood, as did his two Officers. Argent looked back at the four Warrant Officers sat behind. Being addressed by their Captain, they stood also.

"There is no need for you to remain in here. The decision will take some time, I'd say over an hour."

He pulled out his half hunter.

"3.15. If you return here not long after four, it will be plenty time enough."

All four came to the attention and saluted.

"Aye aye, Sir."

The three Officers acknowledged their salute. It was a small, but profound gesture, each to the other. It did not go unnoticed by those around.

The chairs were emptying, few now contained their occupants, almost all had come to the same conclusion as Argent and so the spaces to the side and behind the chairs were crowded with members of the assembly, many of which were military. Bosun George Fraser looked at the throng and didn't like the idea of his Captain having to fight his way through such a press. His three Officers were now gathering their hats and gloves. He turned to his companions.

"Henry, Zack, you too, Mr. McArdle if you've a mind. We'll see the Captain through this lot."

He set his Bosun's hat squarely on his head, having given the Ariadne badge a brief dusting. When Argent, Fentiman and Sanders entered the crowd, they found their way being gently, but firmly, created by the four Warrant Officers, Ball, Short and Fraser using hands and voices, whilst McArdle needed neither, merely the look, from his great height, of the condemnation of Judgment Day. Many Naval Lieutenants saluted, Captains tipped their hats, women smiled. Outside a crowd had gathered, they had heard that something was afoot with the upper classes and it involved Ariadne, she that dwelt high in their regard and probably their affection. The sight of Fraser's hat coming down the steps, set off clapping and cheering. The details of her fight in St. Malo had emerged and they had themselves seen her damage when she came home to harbour. The four Warrant Officers set off through the crowd, each with their own idea for the next hour, but this did not spare them the backslapping and good wishes, which brought a smile, of sorts, to even the lugubrious face of the Sailing Master. Ball, Fraser and Short made straight for The Benbow. Once sat and with their drinks, the conversation opened, begun by Ball.

"That lyin', floggin', bastard Cheveley."

Replied to by Short.

"An' Broke. Crawlin' bilge rat!"

Sailing Master McArdle was elsewhere, on his knees in the nearby Pentecostal Church, praying that The Good Lord would guide to righteousness the thoughts of the now deliberating Board.

The three Officers had taken themselves around to the garden and, being amongst the first out, had found a seat, sheltered from the chill sea breeze of late September. However, this was soon surrendered when they saw the approach of Lady Grant and Charlotte Willoughby. Argent immediately walked forward to greet them, followed by Fentiman. He bowed over the hand of Lady Grant and then did the same for Charlotte. Argent's mind and emotions were still in turmoil after the trauma of the past two hours and his greeting was crass and clumsy.

"Lady Grant, Miss Willoughby, you have come to distract us as we wait in our hour of deep anxiety."

To Lady Grant such over-blown language was of no consequence, her reply was as gracious as ever.

"Captain Argent, gentlemen, if we can provide some comfort or distraction, then it is our pleasure to do so."

With that Argent led both to the now vacant seat. Sanders gave his own greeting.

"Lady Grant, Miss Willoughby. I am Lieutenant Sanders. I hope your remember me from the dinner at Admiral Grant's, sometime back?"

It was Lady Grant who spoke.

"Yes, Lieutenant, I do remember you, and you are too modest. The occasion was marked as that immediately after your taking of La Mouette and it was you that gave the toast. I remember it well."

Sanders smiled and bowed as both ladies occupied the seat. Fentiman had put himself forward, offering his hand to Charlotte.

"Miss Willoughby. I was wondering if you would care for a short walk around this garden. There are still many blooms to be seen and it is quite sheltered."

Charlotte looked at Fentiman, then at Lady Grant, then back at Fentiman.

"Why, yes, Lieutenant, that would be most acceptable. Some mild exercise after being sat in the hall would be most welcome."

Fentiman leaned forward, offering his arm, the gracious smile on his face not even rivalling the delight in his eyes. Charlotte placed her hand delicately on his left forearm and rose from the seat, then both promenaded slowly across the lawn to the shrubbery. This left Lady Grant alone on the seat, with Argent and Sanders now standing.

"Won't you both please sit down?"

Argent and Sanders obeyed, with Argent in the middle and Lady Grant on his right. He began the conversation.

"If I don't get the opportunity, will you please pass on our gratitude for what Admiral Grant said in there. It was most supportive and a great comfort that some words were spoken for our side."

Lady Grant looked at him and smiled.

"Between ourselves, Captain, and Lieutenant Sanders, Septimus needed no bidding, but he took no pleasure, I can assure you. He said to me, 'I must do my duty'. He has been brooding on this for some weeks now. He has no concerns regarding the role and conduct of Ariadne, but he has some concerns, beyond St. Malo even, regarding Captain Cheveley. You need give no thanks, he gave himself the order."

Argent exhaled a laugh and looked at Sanders, who was grinning likewise.

"Well, I must say something to you for what he said and that must be my thanks."

He paused. He was still in a state of emotion.

"There is little we can do now but wait. However, I have no fear for the reputation of Ariadne. Whatever The Board says now, I feel that she has come out of it well."

Lady Grant placed her hand on his forearm and smiled.

"That was never in question, Captain. It has not escaped my attention that you and your men, and your ship, gain applause from the crowd wherever you go."

Argent sighed. He was feeling calmer, more in control.

"That's very kind. To us, being her crew, the ship is everything. That's how it is."

Sanders joined in.

"Yes Sir. Yes. That's right. Whichever part of her sinks, hull or reputation, we sink with it!"

All laughed and allowed silence to settle. Soon came the return of Fentiman and Charlotte, and both seated Officers stood to give her the full space of the garden seat. Argent spoke to the other two.

"I think a turn around somewhere outside will not come amiss for any of us."

Fentiman hovered, wanting to stay, but Argent wanted him away. He felt that Fentiman's continued attentions of Charlotte were bordering on the overbearing. He knew that he may be wrong in that, but he did need to say something to both his Officers.

"I wish to speak to you both."

He turned and bowed to Lady Grant and Charlotte.

"If you'll both excuse us. We need a "quarterdeck conversation".

A smile from both ladies was the reply and so the three walked off, from the garden to the residence gate and soon they were looking out across The Sound. Fentiman and Sanders had been waiting silent all along and now Argent spoke.

"I want you both to know, that if this does go badly for the ship, I will write to the Admiralty to have it placed in your records that you both acted under my orders and followed them to the letter, despite the personal danger."

It was Sanders who spoke.

"There's no need for that, Sir."

Both their anxiety and regard for their ship was still high within each. Sanders continued.

"Ariadne has come out well, and everyone knows....."

He paused.

"Perhaps it's not my place to say this, Sir, but everyone knows that this Board is some kind of effort to make repair to Captain Cheveley's reputation, Sir. Sorry to speak of a superior Officer, in that way, Sir, but that's how many see it."

Argent replied.

"Don't make a habit of it, and I fear that you are wrong. The push for this Board has come just as much, if not more, from the parents of Bentley and Ffynes, who, by the way, I want you both to make a point of seeing. Both parents have influence, either at Court or in Parliament, and they want someone to blame, these being Captain Cheveley and myself, either or both. We were in command; if both, then most on him or most on me, it matters to them not one jot. They want someone to pay, and this is the method they've chosen to use. Cheveley's conveniently using it to shift any stain that he feels has alighted on him. That's why my own reputation is unlikely to come out of this unsullied. That's why I'll write, to clear you both."

Neither argued further. They stood in silence breathing in the clean air. Then Argent looked at his pocketwatch, it was time to return.

* * *

The four Warrant Officers returned in good time, the three from the Inn returning just after the one from the Church. McArdle looked disapproving, but when did he not? However, he had spent too long amongst sailors and, more pointedly, man-o'-war's men, to allow the daily occurrence of drinking, to cloud his opinion too much concerning the men he served with. He'd never say it, but all three stood in his high regard. It was they who greeted him.

"Mr. McArdle."

All three smiled and nodded. McArdle lifted his head to them, but looked blank. Short posed the question.

"How do you think this will come out, Mr. McArdle?"

McArdle folded his arms and looked, face still blank, at the vacant table.

"If ye're seekin' my opinion, I'm thinkin' that this whole thing reeks of shiftin' blame. It went wrong in that harbour, as well ye know, as well as I, and I'm thinkin' that, depending on the way the wind blows between those three, one Captain will get the lion's share, but they'll both get somethin'. That includes Captain Argent."

The three stared back at him, hoping for more. None came, so Short asked further.

"Which one? The most, I mean?"

"That's nae for me. We can only hope that The Good Lord takes them down the correct path."

All three looked away. The introduction of The Good Lord made further fishing for the thoughts of McArdle impossible. Also, this coincided with the arrival of their Captain and his companions and so all four stood to the attention and saluted. They regained their seats only when their three Officers were in theirs. All sat in silence, which lasted but minutes before the door opened and in came Dunstaple to signal to all still stood around the room that they should immediately return to their seats. When he was satisfied, he looked back through the door and in came the three. This time, Argent noticed, Dunstaple was carrying the Logbooks. The three took their places and all in the audience looked hard at those faces to try to glean some hint regarding the nature of the verdict, but all three faces were as blank and inscrutable as any stone statue. Neither Broke nor Grant showed any emotion, Holdsworth probably couldn't.

Holdsworth sat up and hoisted his hands to form the apex of a triangle with his elbows on the desk and then he began, his words coming as they came to him. He used no written statement.

"The Board has reached its conclusion. What I say now will be appended to a report that will be sent to their Lordships at the Admiralty. We have made no recommendations regarding further action, that being a possible Court Martial. Their Lordships will look at the evidence that we have gathered and draw their own conclusions. However, we do feel justified in providing some pointers for their thoughts."

He paused and lowered his hands to drape them over the table edge against his chest.

"We start with the Commodore, Captain Cheveley. Both his actions and decisions were highly questionable. That his ship would be at great risk if she remained under the guns of the bastion is not in question, but what is in question is his early withdrawal to quit that position, abandoning his men to make their own way out, alone and unsupported by his ship. She being the strongest adds to his questionable decision. He must have known that his early withdrawal did not follow the agreed plan that his under Officers were expecting him to comply with. His decision was precipitate and showed little regard for the men he commanded."

He paused and raised his hands again.

"Regarding Captain Argent, he stood his ship on into the harbour in a manner that can only be described as reckless, brave certainly, but over the borderline of naval prudence. To tackle La Pomone where she was, placed his ship and the Marines at great risk. There was time for a signal back to his Commodore to gain orders, but he did not make one. However, Admiral Grant here..."

He turned to look at Grant, then turn back.

"...has insisted that this valid point be stated now, and included in our written report. It is, that, had both vessels immediately turned and exited the harbour, inevitably sustaining battle damage, but having done no harm to La Pomone, then we would now be conducting an enquiry into why an attack on her was not pressed home to the best level possible."

He looked both sides at each companion. Grant smiled, Broke looked glum.

"Our final conclusion is that both Captains closed with the enemy, but each took decisions that could have been better judged. This Board is now closed."

Holdsworth picked up his gavel and smote the block. All three Admirals rose, but only Holdsworth took his exit through their door of entrance. Broke took the nearest course for the main door and out, Grant the quickest way to his Lady. Argent remained sitting, wholly still, then he rubbed his face with his hands and sighed. He looked at his two companions blankly, a wan smile, eyebrows raised. Fentiman spoke first.

"I'd say that was good enough, Sir, if all they could say was we should've sent a signal. How much time have you got during a raid like that? And signal what? "Shall I proceed?" They had to load something on you, us, and that was it. "Small beer", I say."

Sanders grinned and nodded.

"I agree Sir. All that about a signal sounds more like an offence against naval etiquette. What matters, Sir, high blown as it sounds, is that no one questioned our courage in the affair. That question went elsewhere."

Argent smiled and nodded, he did not disagree and felt at ease. He turned to the four behind and they too looked well content, then he spoke to all six.

"Back to the ship."

This time Argent led the way through the thinning crowd. This time no salutes, nor slaps on backs nor arms for any of them, just looks of approval. Argent suddenly found himself confronted by Baker.

"I hope you are content with their findings, Sir? I have my opinion and it does not differ too much with what Holdsworth said; after you take out that total stuff about a signal, that is."

Argent laughed, as did Fentiman and Sanders stood just behind. Baker smiled, he was pleased.

"By the way, have you seen Captain Cheveley, Sir?"

Argent looked puzzled.

"No, was he not here?"

"No Sir. It seems he did not reappear to hear the verdict."

"Well, his choice. Now. We take our leave. We'll be seeing you again, no doubt. Our thanks for your support."

"Yes Sir, but don't forget your Logbook, down there."

Argent looked at the table, it being now deserted and somewhat forlorn, but supporting both Logbooks, one atop the other. Dunstaple had expected both Captains to come forward, but Cheveley was absent and it had slipped Argent's mind. He turned to Fentiman and Sanders.

"I'll get them. You seek out Ffynes and Bentley's parents to pay your respects. I'll see you outside."

He turned to his Warrant Officers.

"Wait here for me."

Salutes and "Aye aye, Sir" came from all four. Argent took himself down to the table and saw that the Log of Herodotus was on top and there was a marker protruding. Conflicting emotions arose within him; it could be construed as dishonourable to look; yet Cheveley had acted very less than honourably himself. After the lies he had just heard, he convinced himself by saying that it was right that he should know what was being written about his own ship, and he was, after all, second in command in St. Malo. Therefore he opened the Log at the marker. It was the entry for the raid and he scanned down the description and grew angry at the entry he saw, that as stated by Grant, "Signal sent at 5.25", after that there was another; "Ariadne not yet engaged". It was an utter untruth. His own Log, initialled by McArdle, stated their entrance to be at 5.10. By 5.25, he knew, he was considering ending the action. Clearly, Cheveley had made false entries into his Log to support his case. Argent was angry, but what did it matter now? Also, to a Board, contradictions such as that proved nothing; in any naval action Logs rarely agreed. He closed the heavy volume and moved it sideways to expose his own. Suddenly a voice.

"I'll take that."

Argent looked up. He was looking at a First Lieutenant. Argent was still incensed, and angered still further at the omission of the required formal introduction, even though he was well aware of the identity of he who stood before him.

"And you are whom?"

"Lieutenant Lord Charles Langley. First of Herodotus."

"Well, Lieutenant Langley, I would remind you that you are speaking to a Post Captain, and I require you to come to the attention and address me as "Sir".

He let the words strike home, but Langley didn't move.

"Attention!"

Langley shuffled himself together.

"And you want, what?"

"Our Logbook."

A pause.

"Sir."

Argent pointed down at the table.

"It's there! For all it's worth!"

He scooped up his own and left. Langley may or may not have seen him opening their Log; that he couldn't care about, he just wanted away. He arrived at the back of the Hall, by the exit, and his four Warrant Officers fell in behind and they left. However, on the steps down he had to halt again, the parents of Ffynes and Bentley were calling him and were approaching. Argent told the four following Warrant Officers whose parents they were, handed the logbook to McArdle and then turned to the two couples, at the same time coming to the attention and saluting. His Warrant Officers did the same and it seemed that the two sets of parents appreciated the gesture, certainly the two mothers. It was Sir Matthew Bentley who spoke.

"Captain, we would not wish to go without imparting our thoughts to you."

Sir Matthew turned to Sir Harold, who nodded. Fraser, Short and Ball had drawn their own conclusions from the stern look on both men and Fraser closed up to Argent, better for these toffs to see his hat badge and that their Captain had him right at his shoulder.

"Captain. We would wish you to know that we are satisfied. What blame there is attaches but lightly to you."

He paused, and Sir Harold took over.

"We have heard what has been said, and are of one mind that the responsibility for what happened to our sons lies elsewhere, at least the great majority. I would wish to add, that Rufus himself attaches no blame to you for his injury. Despite his wound, he is resigned to say that he was luckier that some, unluckier than most. He says often that his ship went straight at the French, of that he is very proud, and that everyone took their chance. In addition his character has changed, and we think for the better. We now think it right that this matter is settled and confined to the past."

Sir Harold looked at Sir Matthew, then at the two mothers.

"We will take our leave now. We wish you good day."

Argent came to the attention once more, and again saluted. Both mothers smiled and nodded, then he was looking at their backs. Fentiman came up and saw who Argent had been talking to.

"Is all well?"

Argent looked at him.

"Yes, all's well. Now."

"I've just left young Ffynes. He's leaving the Navy to run the family estate. He's got himself engaged, on top. A lovely girl, she was in the crowd and we were introduced. Just deserts for a naval hero!"

* * *

They arrived back in the middle of the night, rattling down onto the quayside to identify Ariadne by her silhouette against the stars and the faint moonlight of the night sky. She was moored as Budgen ordered, bows out. Earlier, in Plymouth, they had found their mail coach, but it was wholly stood down in need of some minor, but vital, repair. Informed thus, the seven took themselves off to The Benbow for food, refreshment and some conversation that might ebb away the anxiety of the day. The three Officers kept their own company, because Ball, Short, and Fraser, minus McArdle, who wished to make his own arrangements that took him elsewhere, had found old shipmates and immediately cleaved unto them. Three hours later, in the gloom of a wet September evening the Mail coach turned onto the turnpike for Falmouth. All, bar McArdle, had been drinking, all had felt the stress of the day fall away, all were sailors who knew the value of sleep and soon all were slumped down on the bench seats, unconsciously supporting each other as the coach swayed and rocked.

With no formality, save the 'present arms' of the Marine sentry, all ascended the gangplank and took themselves to their own quarters, there to indulge in two or more extra hours sleep. By some unknown telegraph the crew took their breakfast all knowing of the events of the previous day and the stories circulated of how Ariadne, according to the judgement, had "gone in like a game plucked 'un," and that Cheveley and his Herodotus "must have all fell over dizzy when she spun around so fast." However, whilst the mood aboard should have been overall good, it was not. Many were far from content, especially in the mess of the foretop, namely Gabriel Whiting the Captain of the Foretop and his four messmates of the Captain's barge crew. It was Whiting who was speaking.

"What else can it be, but a thief? I've lost two particulars now and so have you, and so have others, one at least. T'ave only come about since we took on all them quay sweepings a while back, so it has to be a thief!"

Able Jones answered.

"So, we does what?"

Whiting was angry, but that always concentrated his mind.

"We does some askin'. Ask each Guncaptain what's gone from their mess. Leave the topmen; none of the convicts went into any mast, they'n all in guncrews. Let's see what comes back and what sort of picture it draws."

Thus were some days spent. Whilst minor repairs were attended to and stores came aboard, the Captain's Barge crew conducted their enquiries. Come an evening meal three days later, each reported back. All but three guncrews had suffered theft; Eight and Ten, of the Larboard Battery, Number Three, Starboard Battery, Sam Morris' gun. Gabriel Whiting looked puzzled.

"So, this thievin' is all over the ship, just about. All bar Sam Morris' crew an' two others."

Moses King added what he knew.

"Only Sam Morris' has a new recruit. T'other two is all Ariadne of long standin', from one place or another."

"Who's Sam got in his guncrew? Anyone know?"

His fellow topmen spoke of what they knew. They named most, including Smallsize, but it was Beddow's recollection that was the most telling.

"His recruit's a convict, as replaced Tooley, now gone for a mizzen topman. A shifty lookin' bugger as I recall."

Gabriel Whiting paused to think.

"I'd trust Sam Morris, straight as a gun barrel. And his crew, least those I knows."

It was Silas Beddows who spoke next.

"That don't prove too much, Sam. Could be just that our thief ain't got round to them three yet."

"Could be. On the other hand, perhaps our thief has some kind of feelin' for his messmates, but that I doubt, more like he's worried that they'll see in his chest any particulars that he's half inched from them, when he opens it, alongside theirs, where they're stored all together. When he's inside his own chest, could be that one of his mess comes up to see, as is very possible. Strikes me as 'tis a convict that'll 'ave that kind of cunnin', an' 'tis Number Three as've got a new man, a convict."

Sage-like nods circulated the table. Whiting slapped his hands on the table.

"Right. That's a start if nothin' else. I'm off to see Sam."

Gabriel Whiting took himself along the lower deck and found Sam Morris sat on his chest in the company of his guncrew, they being sat on theirs. Whiting spoke immediately.

"Sam. A trip to the heads."

Morris knew exactly what Whiting was asking. The heads, the furthermost part of the ship was the crew's latrine, when at sea. Officers went there but very infrequently, so there they could talk privately. They ascended the companionway and crossed to the starboard carronade. Whiting began in response to Morris' concerned face.

"Sam, all guncrews has suffered some thievin', great or small, save three, your'n bein' one. No one's accusin' you or your lads, not right off, but it's a place to start, on account that yours is the only one with a convict new recruit."

Morris made no argument, but nodded.

"That's a fair call, Gab, and that's the one I wouldn't trust, him new joined. One Landy Main. He's a convict and one very odd sod. If you have to start somewhere, startin' there makes as much sense as anywhere."

"Right. Come mornin' I'll see my Watch Officer, Sanders. He knows how this works. Meanwhile, keep an eye out and keep one on this Main."

Morris nodded and clapped his hand against Whiting's upper arm. The conversation was finished; agreement reached.

* * *

The next day Whiting approached Lieutenant Sanders.

"Sir, may I beg a moment of your time?"

Sanders remembered Whiting from their confrontation with Cheveley, post St. Malo. He did no more than was needed, to nod and smile, but the smile soon faded.

"We got a thief on board, Sir. All messes has suffered some kind of loss, one or two men, each one or two items, 'cept three. Eight and ten, larboard, number three starboard. But number three is the only one with a convict new come aboard. Eight and ten has long standin' shipmates, Sir."

"That's no proof, Whiting."

"No Sir, but perhaps it's where we should start. Losses are all over the ship, Sir, 'tis no good thing."

Sanders needed no convincing. A community such as a ship, with all on board trusting and depending on each other and all living cheek by jowl, was highly vulnerable to theft and the trust that could take years to build up, would be quickly destroyed. He looked at Whiting, a man he knew. With different circumstances, their positions could be reversed.

"I can start a search, but we don't start with number three, we start with number one. If nothing is found at Morris' gun, starting there nevertheless piles all suspicion onto them. But we will search."

Sanders shifted his feet to consider further, remembering how such was dealt with when he was a topman.

"You find a dozen men, who've all had items stolen. Meet me by the mainmast at four bells. This you can do?"

"Yes, Sir. Me, an' Silas Beddows is two, for a start."

"Good, but not all from your mess. It looks better if from amongst the whole crew; and quietly and discreetly. We don't want to give any advanced warning."

"Aye, aye. Sir."

Both parted company, Whiting for his search, Sanders to find Fentiman, he being off watch but not asleep, as was Argent. He found him on the quarterdeck.

"Sir, Gabriel Whiting, Captain of the Foretop, has come to inform me that there has been a severe outbreak of thieving in the ship. I'd like to make a search of the men's sea chests."

Fentiman looked grave.

"Theft?"

"Yes Sir. All over the ship. The men are both disturbed and incensed. I think we have to do something, to show that we know and take it seriously, at least."

"I agree. Can I leave it with you?"

"Yes, Sir. You can. I've already made a start. I now need Fraser and his mates to send all the crew to the lower deck to stand by their chests, at the appropriate time."

"Agreed. Make it so."

Sanders hurried off to find Fraser and tell him what was required. At four bells the Bosun's whistles blew and the order was shouted around the ship, to stand by their chests, but not yet to open them. Sanders collected four Marines and then Whiting's collection of victims. Fraser came also. They began with number one gun, starboard side. Each in turn was required to open their chest and reveal the contents for Whiting's men to examine. Nothing was found. The search at number two gun produced the same result. They came to number three. Morris' sea chest first, then Dedman's, then Bearman's, and Pierce's. Next Landy Main, but he opened his chest and spilled the contents onto the deck. There was nothing but odd items of clothing, a tarred hat, and a few rags. All stared hard at the miserable contents, but Whiting had thought of something.

"What about the ship's boys, Sir? Each gun's powder monkey?"

The ship's boys stored their belongings down in the hold, in smaller chests. Sanders turned to look at Whiting and nodded, then he turned to Fraser.

"Mr. Fraser. Each ship's boy to bring his chest up to the lower deck."

With these words spoken, Smallsize legs collapsed and he scampered back to the bulwark to sit with his arms over his head, face in utter distress and wailing uncontrollably. Sanders looked at Fraser.

"Fetch him forward."

Fraser walked to the cowering Smallsize and lifted him up by his left arm, almost off the deck. He dragged him forward and stood him before Sanders and when his arm was released he collapsed again and so Fraser had to haul him upright again. Sanders noticed that Main, stood at the back was beginning to look nervous and agitated, but, for now, he looked down at the agonized face of Smallsize.

"Now then, you know..."

But before Sanders could finish the sentence, Smallsize began to speak, or more like wail at the top of his voice, pointing back at Landy Main.

"It were 'im, Sir. 'im. He made I do it, he said he'd 'ave the eyes out of my 'ead, Sir, if I didn't."

The Marines were moving forward to cut off any escape. Sanders allowed Smallsize to take a few deep breaths, sucked in between heavy sobs.

"Didn't do what?"

"Store what he stole, Sir. In my chest."

Sanders looked at Morris.

"Take him down and bring back his chest."

"Aye aye, Sir."

Morris took Smallsize away, holding him upright to the extent that his feet barely touched the deck. Sanders allowed silence to arrive all round, with all looking at Landy Main. Sanders' time as a common sailor shaped the contempt he now felt. He stared straight at Main.

"Anything to say, Main?"

The answer was no more than a blank stare in return. Silence reigned with Landy Main pinned to the spot by the malignant looks from the men surrounding, many of whom having left their place to come to the origin of the commotion. Within minutes Fraser returned with Smallsize's chest, the steel shim still in through the hasp. Smallsize began again to blubber as Fraser removed the shim and tipped out the contents. The chest was almost full and the scattered contents were all saleable items; earings, scarf rings, knives of all kinds and three small purses of coin, each with holes remaining from stitching that had previously shown initials. Main must have cut away the embroidered letters. Sanders turned to Whiting and the others.

"Is any of this yours?"

As many of the dozen as could see strained forward and each pointed. Each called an item that they identified as their own, but there were many left over. Sanders now turned to Fraser, but pointed at Main.

"Put him in irons."

Fraser, in turn, motioned to the Marines, who eagerly sprang forward to seize hold of Main's spindly frame and one accidentally dropped his heavy musket onto Main's foot. He howled in pain, to then be dragged, limping, off to the forward end of the lower deck where he was quickly thrust down to the deck and his ankles locked into manacles whose chain passed through iron rings set into the planking. Nothing was actually thrown in his direction by anyone, but the looks of contempt were withering. Main sat still, unconcerned.

With the disappearance of Landy Main, Sanders looked down at Smallsize, still in a state of tearful terror. He then looked at Sam Morris.

"What's his name."

"We all calls 'im Smallsize, Sir. No one knows his given name."

Sanders nodded, then looked back at Smallsize, slightly calmer, but this changed when Sanders gave Morris an order.

"Bring him with me."

Smallsize set off wailing again as Morris propelled him, more carried than walking, along the deck after Sanders. They came to the Marine guarding the entrance to the Captain's cabin.

"Is the Captain awake?"

"He is, Sir. Bible, I mean his Steward, has just taken in his breakfast."

Sanders turned to Morris, still supporting the distraught youngster.

"Wait here."

Sanders entered the corridor, approached the Captain's door and knocked. "Come in" sounded immediately and he entered. Argent had finished his breakfast, merely coffee and rolls, he rarely ate more at this time. Sanders saluted and began.

"Sir, we've caught thieves, Sir. Two of them, one a convict recruit in the afterguard, the other, his accomplice, a ship's boy."

"Where are they now."

"The afterguard, that being one Landy Main, is in irons, the other, the boy whom the men call Smallsize, is outside."

Argent looked at Sanders, who could see that his Captain was saddened.

"I'll see the boy now. The other can wait, until we're at sea."

Sanders left, but once in the corridor, he saw Morris giving the terrified Smallsize some strict advice, the latter gazing back and up in awe and horror. He paused to allow it to finish.

"Now, when you gets in there, before the Captain, you comes to the attention, pays your respects, then goes back to full attention. An' you answers full and respectful. Be that understood?"

Smallsize nodded furiously, shaking some long standing tears onto Morris' duck trousers. Sanders called out.

"Morris, send him down."

Morris pushed the trembling boy forward, not roughly, but enough to move him, when he clearly would rather not. Smallsize entered and carried out Morris' instructions to the letter while Sanders followed and closed the door. Argent had the Ship's Muster open before him, at the page for Ship's Boys. Smallsize stood, remaining at attention, but looking at the deck beams.

"What's your name?"

"They all calls me Smallsize, Sir."

Still looking at the deck beams.

"There is no name like that here. What were you signed on as?"

At last the boy lowered his eyes to regard his Captain. He saw a face almost friendly, not at all what he had been expecting.

"I was signed on as Wheeler, Sir. That's the name I had at the Foundling Home."

Argent ran a finger down the list and found Wheeler, but no Christian name.

"You have no Christian Name?"

"No Sir. None that I can remember."

"And how old are you?"

"Sorry Sir, but I can't say, Sir. Don't know. Sir."

Argent fixed his age at around ten or twelve, but under nourishment could have wholly thrown that awry.

"Right. We're going to call you Wheeler. Now, to this thieving. You could be flogged, Wheeler, even hung!"

More terror passed over Wheeler's face, but his expression improved to mere deep anxiety when he saw that Argent was neither stern nor frowning himself. The boy made a few noises, gasp like, then stopped. Argent spoke encouragingly.

"Take your time, say what you think, but first take a deep breath."

Wheeler did the latter, and then began.

"It were soon after he came into our mess, Sir. He grabbed me when I was alone down in the hold. Grabbed me, Sir, and said he'd have the eyes out of me, Sir."

Argent held up his hand, palm out. The description stopped.

"That's all he did? He did not interfere with you in any other way? At any other time, in any unnatural fashion?"

The implication was lost on Wheeler, but not on Sanders. The next answer, if matched what Argent was suspecting, would mean death for Main, possibly also for the boy, but Wheeler's face grew puzzled.

"Stickin' a knife under my eye were enough for me, Sir."

Argent nodded.

"Continue. How did this work, between you and Main?"

"He'd do the thievin' Sir, and give me what he took to take down to my chest, Sir. He never came down to the hold again, Sir, just reminded me, like, by pointin' at his eye, each time he gave me summat, Sir. He'd say that he had a list of all he'd given me, and, when the time came, it'd better all be there, Sir."

Argent nodded and looked at Sanders.

"Any other problems with this boy?"

"No, Sir."

Argent returned his gaze to Wheeler. He looked at him for some while, his face serious and concerned.

"You've been in action alongside us, haven't you Wheeler?"

"Yes Sir. Against La Pomone and in St. Malo."

"That makes you a veteran, and a shipmate of everyone in this crew. Doesn't it? You served your gun as well as anyone."

"Yes Sir."

"Do you have any family?"

"No Sir. I'm a foundling."

"So, who acts as your family now, I mean, who are those that look after you? See to your needs, that is. Keep you safe?"

Wheeler needed to think.

"Why, my messmates, Sir. Sam Morris and such."

"And others in the crew, I don't doubt."

"Yes Sir. Eli Reece and others teaches me much about bein' a sailor."

"And now you've been party to stealing from them."

Wheeler's face fell and his shoulders slumped down.

"Yes Sir."

Argent sat forward, his arms across his desk.

"I'm going to be lenient with you, Wheeler, this time."

Wheeler looked puzzled. He didn't know what lenient meant.

"I'm giving you back to your mess and they'll decide what is to be done with you. You'll receive seaman's justice. That's what you are, are you not? You're a seaman?"

Wheeler brightened up. He wasn't going to be flogged on a grating, nor hung for thievery.

"Yes Sir. I am"

"But also now a thief."

No answer, bar a full slump down of face and shoulders.

"But until now you've been a good shipmate of ours; and you'll never steal again, nor be part of it. Will you?"

Wheeler straightened up.

"No Sir. Never Sir."

Argent lowered his face and looked at Wheeler very gravely, from under his eyebrows.

"And that's your word, to us, here, now, us, as your shipmates?"

Wheeler nodded vigorously.

"Yes Sir, never again Sir."

Argent nodded slowly, whilst fixing a serious look on him.

"Now, about your name. We must correct that. Have you any name that you prefer?"

Wheeler looked amazed and thought for a second.

"I've always liked the name Christopher, Sir."

Argent smiled, so did Sanders.

"Christopher it is. You'll be entered as Christopher Wheeler. Now, as we speak, you are but a ship's boy."

Wheeler nodded.

"Well, I'm sure he won't mind me saying, but Lieutenant Sanders here, he came aboard one of His Majesty's ships as a ship's boy, and now he's an Officer. It can be done, you'd agree, Lieutenant?"

Wheeler turned to look at Sanders, no small wonder showing on his face. Sanders smiled and nodded.

"That's right, it can be done."

Argent looked up at Sanders.

"Do we educate the ship's boys in any way, do we? To read, write, and cipher?"

Sanders shook his head.

"No Sir. We do not."

"I want that changed. Any boy we have above the age of ten is to be taught. Give the job to Wentworth, with Berry, Bright and Trenchard to assist. One hour every day."

Argent sat back and toyed with his letter opener.

"Now, take ship's boy Christopher Wheeler here, back to his mess and tell Morris that they are to decide his fate. There's a cane in the corner, over there."

Wheeler's face fell to his shoes and there was no improvement as Sanders shuffled him out the door, now carrying the cane. They proceeded along the gun deck to the companionway and down to the lower deck, where Morris and his crew were still at ease, being off watch. All rose at the approach of Sanders and made their respects. Sanders pushed Wheeler forward.

"I am returning ship's boy Christopher Wheeler, commonly known as Smallsize, to you. He has told all to the Captain, confessing that he is a thief's accomplice. The Captain has now decided that his fate is in your hands, as his messmates. You decide what happens next."

Wheeler was looking down at the deck, up at the beams, anywhere but at the stern faces above and around him. Members of other messes had also gathered and Sanders placed the cane on the nearest sea chest.

"He's all yours!"

Morris spoke first.

"Look at me."

Wheeler did his best, but couldn't hold it for long.

"Look at me."

Ship's Boy Wheeler managed to return the gaze of as angry a look as he'd ever seen. Morris' reaction was to clip him neatly but firmly alongside his head, then push him over to Dedman, who did the same, until he had gone all around the mess, to be cuffed by something, a hand or a cloth hat. He returned, chastened, but not tearful, to Morris, who placed Wheeler before him, whilst he sat on a chest.

"Now you listen to me."

This time Wheeler did immediately look up and meet his eyes. The return look was stern, but not unkind.

"If anyone ever threatens you like that again then you comes straight to me. You got that?"

Wheeler nodded, but Morris wasn't content.

"Yes. Gun Captain."
"Yes Gun Captain."
Morris nodded.
"Now, you take a look around yer, now, and see who you've got on your side. Any trouble, you've got them at your shoulder and they'll see it right. You got that now?"
"Yes Gun Captain."
"Right. An' I don't know where all this Wheeler stuff came from. Round yer you'm still Smallsize, till I says different."

* * *

Argent read, for the tenth time, the simple note from Budgen.
"Ready your ship for a mission to Portugal. Likely departure post 10th October."
Argent was confused. "Hold the ship ready." What extra could there be about sailing to Portugal? 10th October was four days hence and he was even more confused in the light of the fact that his ship had sat there for three days already since their return from the Enquiry. He resolved to see Commodore Budgen, so he stood up, quitting his cluttered desk to then take his hat as he made for the door. Within five minutes he was exchanging the now traditional salutes with Marine Sergeant Venables and then he was sat before Budgen, who looked somewhat affronted at this sudden arrival.
"What brings you here, Argent?"
"Your note, Sir. I'm confused, what extra readiness would I need for a voyage to Portugal? I must say that I'm surprised we're not out already, Sir, on patrol."
Budgen sat forward, as far as his stomach would allow, still in unquiet mood.
"You go when we tell you, Argent!"
He paused to alter his face into an even more sour picture.
"State of readiness means that your ship is so far up to the mark as to ensure that she will definitely get there with no mishap, Argent. Everything shipshape, checked, and re-checked."
"Have you any idea of the nature of the mission, Sir?'
"None. I only know that you are to remain in a state of high readiness. Ready to go on the earliest tide after the tenth, when we know your mission, of course."
"I feel confident that Ariadne sits in that state now, Sir. As we speak."
"That may be so, Argent, but it's for you to be certain that it is."
Argent stood up. Ideas for the next three days at least were forming in his own head. He saluted, very formally.
"Very good, Sir. I'll be away and be about it. Sir."

Budgen waved a finger and Argent left, but what Argent exchanged with Sergeant Venables would not have disgraced Horse Guards parade. Back on board, he sought out Fentiman and brought him down to his cabin.

"We have been ordered to hold ourselves in a high state of readiness to sail on or after the 10th, that being four days from now. How would you put our "state of readiness"?"

"As high as you can get it. All stores on board, well stored and checked. Every rope, sheet, and hawser doubly examined."

"And the men?"

"I've run out of ideas. They've run the guns in and out so often we've had to change axles on some. They've been up and down the masts so often the population look upon it as a regular entertainment. I've got them now on knots and splicing, much to the disgust of our "old salts". I'm now short of ideas."

"Paint! Paint and grease. And longboat races. We've got one, borrow another."

Fentiman looked shocked and quizzical, but Argent ploughed on.

"I'm taking myself away for a day or so. If Budgen calls for me tell him I've gone to Truro. Tell him anything, tell him I've gone to see a swordsmith there."

Argent's face showed a moment of revelation.

"In actual fact, that won't be so far from the truth. That old spike of mine could do with a clean up, the removal of a few notches. Yes. Tell him that."

Thus energised Argent rose from his chair and started throwing shirts, hose and linen into a canvas bag. In contrast he pulled down a large leather portmanteau and carefully folded in his best uniform and best shoes. Within minutes he was ready.

"I'll be back day after tomorrow."

Fentiman looked at his Captain with no little humour.

"Yes Sir, but if you're going ashore to get your sword seen to, then perhaps you'd better take it with you."

He shifted his gaze to the almost ancient scabbard up in its cradle on a deck beam, terminating with the dull gunmetal bell guard at one end. Argent reached up to seize it.

"Yes, yes, you're right, of course."

Two hours later, just on Noon, he was walking into the door of Lanbe Barton to receive the screeched admonishments of his sisters for again arriving without warning. Emily practically pushed him back out the door, but not quite, mostly because of his protests.

"Fine way to treat a wounded sailor! Not so long ago I was gravely wounded, remember? For all you know I've come back to get my crutch. I may have decided that I have some permanent need of it."

Emily suddenly looked genuinely concerned, but Enid would have none of it and threw a towel at his head. However, with all that done Argent embraced both and kissed both, twice.

"Are you all well?"
Both smiled and nodded.
"Where's Father?"
Enid answered.
"Outside, over the back. He's clearing a drain."
He looked from one to the other, each still within the crook of his arm
"Nothing found? No news?"
Both shook their heads and detached themselves, pushing their hands against his chest. Both seemed more depressed than last time.
"I've come for that idea if mine, to go to Truro to the Records Office at the County Court. They keep copies of Deeds and such. It's worth a try. If Father can't come I'll go alone, but this is our chance. I have to sail on the 10th, but not before. There's time."
They both looked at him and hope grew in their eyes, but only a glimmer. They had been disappointed too often. Argent looked at both.
"I'll go and find Father. If we leave now, we'll be there come mid afternoon."
Both nodded and he went through the room to reach the rear of the house. There he found his Father, stood in a ditch in stout leather boots, clearing out the soil and rubbish to ease the passage of the winter rains. Argent Senior saw his son and ceased work, which for Argent, was a good sign.
"Son. Nice to see you, but why've you come? What've you in mind?"
"That trip to the County Court at Truro I talked about last time. I've three days off and I've got my best uniform. If we leave now, we'll be there before they close."
There was no change in his Father's expression. It seemed that hope within him was all but gone and Argent recognised it.
"If you'd prefer Father, I'll go alone. If you're busy and have something urgent."
His Father levered himself out of the ditch, using the spade as a hoist.
"No son. I'll come. I can't deny myself the chance. Besides, I have a better idea what to look for. I'll come."
He placed a dry but grimy hand on Argent's arm.
"Give me a chance to get clean and changed. We'll take the dog cart."
Argent brightened up.
"Yes, Father. Right. I'll get changed, too."
Within an hour, the dogcart, with Argent Senior's riding horse between the shafts, was rattling along the Truro turnpike. Little was said. Argent began most conversations between them, rotating around all sorts of topics, from new types of plough to how far Jacob could now walk, but all were soon exhausted. Argent asked himself if his Father really was now so fully despondent, but he consoled himself

with the fact that Father never had been the most garrulous of men and "slow and stern" were the best descriptors for his character. It had occurred fully to him, as his anxiety forced his mind around the topic, that they could expect no help from Broke, their nearest neighbour, more probable full scorn on any document they found that could help the Argent cause. Broke would be first in line for a cheap purchase of Argent land.

When the more accurate clocks of the town were striking three, they pulled up outside the County Court. The horse was tethered at the trough and, side-by-side, both ascended the steps and entered. At the sight of Argent's dress uniform the Hallclerk lowered his pen and stood upright to await their approach. Dressed in black, with a white cravat so voluminous that Argent wondered if the clerk could see anything beyond it, Argent found demeanour enough to look at him as he would a defaulter.

"We have business at the Records Office. Can we be conducted there, please?"

"Yes Sir. And your names, please, Sirs?"

"Argent. Both Argent, Junior and Senior."

The Hallclerk made a note, looked at the clock, then placed his hand over a small bell, raised it in his fingers and shook it. Almost immediately a heavy, rough-clothed porter arrived in the archway that led off from the entrance hall. In his turn, the Hallclerk looked disapprovingly at him.

"Take these two gentlemen down to the Records Office."

The porter took a pace back to clear the arch of his burly frame. Both Argent's recognised the invitation and walked forward to follow him down the long, dark corridor. Argent came up to his shoulder.

"What is your name?"

The porter turned, surprised. Few made such an enquiry.

"Parsons, Sir."

"Well, Parsons, this for your trouble."

Argent held out a coin, which Parsons turned to accept, but said nothing.

"Anyone else been here, over the past few weeks, of any note?"

Parsons turned to look at him.

"Few come here, Sir, but we did have Sir Digby Cinch here a while back. He stands out in my memory."

Argent nodded and then looked knowingly at his Father. He returned to Parsons.

"He came to the Records Office?"

"Yes Sir."

They had arrived at the required door. Parsons opened it for them and closed it after their entry. Both were now in a room that reminded Argent of the harbour office of Kinsale, many clerks behind a high counter which kept them separate from the visiting public. Immediately upon their entrance one of the Clerks stood and came to them at the counter. Argent spoke first.

"Do you have an office where we can speak?"

Argent wasn't going to have their business overheard and it had the desired result. The clerk pointed to his right.

"The next door down, Sirs."

They exited the office and entered the next door to find the clerk waiting for them, sat behind a scruffy desk. The only other furniture in the room was a bench and so this they used. Argent began.

"We wish to see any records you have, any record, concerning a farm called Lanbe Barton, Falmouth District.

Argent was looking at the clerk and asked himself if he detected a slight shifting of his eyes, a change in the set of his mouth and also the lines of his forehead, but the clerk now spoke.

"Which Parish?"

"All Saint's."

The clerk made the note. Argent continued.

"How long will the search take?"

"If you return at Noon tomorrow, Sir, we will have found all that we have."

Both Argents rose, but Argent Junior continued.

"Noon tomorrow, then. In here."

"Yes, Sir. In here."

"May we know your name?"

"Fellsham, Sir. Michael Fellsham."

Argent walked to the desk and placed a guinea on it. Fellsham looked up, this time with fully elevated eyebrows.

"You'll make a full search. Yes? Everywhere you can think of. Show us any document you can find with Lanbe Barton written on it."

A thin hand extended from a frayed cuff and closed over the guinea. Argent looked full at him.

"Another if you find what we need."

Argent allowed that to sink in.

"So. Until Noon tomorrow."

Both left the office and made straight for the street. Argent looked at his Father as they approached the dogcart.

"Cinch!"

Argent Senior didn't look up as his released the reins.

"It could be nothing. He is the MP and a landowner himself. He could well have his own business here."

By now both were in the dogcart. Argent took up the reins.

"Let's hope. His own business, not ours."

Argent then looked at his Father.

"What do you want to do, Father? There's an Inn just along there, we could stay the night, or return home. Which one would you prefer?"

Argent Senior answered instantly.

"Home. I can't waste a day, waiting, then travelling. That's if you can ride back, to get what they've found, or not found."

Argent nodded.

"As you choose, Father, and yes, I'll come back, hopefully for something that favours our cause."

The journey back was even more silent and faster, the horse sensing his stable at the end of the journey. Once back, their entrance through the door coincided with the preparations for the evening meal. Emily and Enid looked both confused and annoyed. Enid voiced their feelings.

"We didn't expect you back. I doubt there's enough."

Argent Senior appeased her.

"No matter. Bread cheese and cider, will do for us both. Don't worry yourself."

He sat in his chair and eased off his boots, then sat for a while to regard the fire. Argent came to sit with him and both Enid and Emily drew near. Enid spoke.

"It's a good thing to try, Father. There could be something, in all their dusty records. They've got papers there that go back centuries."

Both Argent and Emily nodded and their Father smiled.

"As may. Could be. So let's hope so."

With their Father more cheerful, the meal was also. Of course there was enough stew, potatoes and greens, and none at the table had need of the large loaf of bread to fill an empty corner. As before, the three men sat around the fire, but Argent, for a reason he could not fathom, whilst sitting comfortably before a good fire, could not stay awake and so he dozed whilst the other two talked farming talk. Come morning, Argent allowed himself a long stay in bed beyond dawn, but once up, he lost no time and set out for Truro on his "good mare", wearing again his best uniform. Behind the saddle, his sword swung on its slings.

He reached Truro close on 11 am. He rode to the swordsmith's that he knew and left the sword in their expert hands, but if the look of distaste on their face carried a clear message; it would not get their most careful attention.

"When shall I return? I must rejoin my ship tomorrow."

"At 2.00 o' clock, Sir. We'll have it ready. Should we attend to the scabbard, Sir?"

"To do what?"

"Polish the fittings, Sir."

Argent shook his head.

"No need for that. I've come up through the Navy, I know how to polish brass, but thank you, all the same."

He left the workshop and led the mare down to the County Court. He tied her up at the same horse trough and sat in the unseasonal sunshine. Enid had packed some food and he debated how much to eat, none, some, or all. He chose some and ate, as much to occupy himself as to ease any hunger. At 11.55 he entered. The same Clerk rose to ring the same bell, but someone other than Parsons took him down. Very much other than; thinner, shorter, and older. Argent took himself into the main office to announce his arrival to Fellsham, then he left to go further down to the side office. Within minutes Fellsham arrived, bearing a heavy velum folder. Argent's hopes rose, but were dashed when the folder was opened. It contained but three pieces of paper, none particularly old, two pieces of quarto, one of foolscap. Argent allowed Fellsham to speak.

"I have three documents here, Sir. Two are summaries of two Court cases between Edward Albert Argent and Admiral Sir Arthur Broke. One concerning drainage, the other concerning access. The third is a requirement on William Reuben Argent to provide a statement of the members of his family, dwelling in Lanbe Barton, as at 1st January 1768. It gives a list."

Argent's face turned grim. Not at all what he wanted, but not without some use, for it proved their residence there almost half a century ago, but he knew that it would satisfy no court, were someone of the ilk of Broke or Cinch to make a challenge. He looked at Fellsham.

"This is all?"

Fellsham nodded.

"And, if needs be, these can be quickly recovered?"

"Yes, Sir. They can be held in this file for six months, as an ongoing matter."

Argent stood up, whilst Fellsham shuffled the papers.

"My thanks to you. I would be grateful if you would hold them as so."

Argent recovered his hat and left the office. It was then that Fellsham sat and smiled. This had been most lucrative, Cinch had paid him five guineas if he destroyed any Deed to Lanbe Barton he found. He had found nothing where something should have been, but he had taken the five guineas anyway, telling Cinch that he had found a Deed and destroyed it. Now another guinea had arrived on top. A most satisfactory affair.

* * *

Kalil Al'Ahbim was now a more than contented man. Ireland had provided a good haul, but this was now a bonus upon that, another fishing village, this time on the English coast. Both had provided a young and white-skinned cargo, so he was now full, more than so. His craft was leaving the shingle, backing off using her oars, his men straining to take her out to sea, the oars in rapid beat. The arrival of the soldiers had been an inconvenience, so they were now pulling off with merely the odd musket ball hitting the hull as a less than fond, but very useless, farewell. Leaving the village early had cost nothing, merely hastening their exit, for he did not wish to confront regulars. Some of his men, killed and wounded by the men of the village as they defended their hearths and homes, lay on the beach, some still moving, one struggling in vain to reach the ship, but they could be abandoned and sacrificed. He saw the soldiers, some still buttoning their tunics, running to the quayside to board the fishing boats to make a chase, but he was confident he could escape, rowing into the wind, where they could not follow. He watched, with great glee, the last of the prisoners being driven below, but then shouted in anger. Some of his men were too active with the points of their swords, he wanted neither marks nor scars that would lower any value on the auction block. His haul now totalled 128, all young women and children.

Chapter Eight

A Question of Duty

Argent had barely slept at all. The despondency and unease that he had seen at Lanbe Barton, had not been left behind and the regular tolling of the ship's bell through the night, usually ignored, had broken into his sleep at almost every ring. Now he was fully awake with the three bells of the Morning Watch sounding on the quarterdeck above; this being 5 o' clock early morning to those safe in their beds in their homes ashore, provided they were awake enough for it to register. He could still see Emily chewing her lower lip, Enid stern and shockproof, his Father staring at the fire. A whole day had now intervened, but his anxiety had not lessened. He turned over in his cot and stared at the grain of the planking slowly revealing itself in the growing October dawn. He knew that his deep worry for his family would soon become a luxury; he had a ship to run and to ready, for some important mission as yet unrevealed. Today was the 10th.

Three bells having sounded, in came Mortimor with the customary rolls and coffee, but this time augmented with a sausage and two rashers of bacon, but Argent paid the food not one moment of attention after Mortimor had finished his one piece of news.

"Slavers have raided Ruanporth, Sir, and got away with something like two dozen women and children. 'Tis all over the town. There's killed, too, both them and the fishermen. Sons of Belial hath beat upon our house, Judges, Chapter 19, verse..."

Argent broke straight in.

"Ruanporth, Mortimor, you say Ruanporth?"

"Aye, Sir. That's the place, right enough."

Argent sat up, horrified. Beryan had family there; it's where he came from. Argent looked at Mortimor.

"Fetch Lieutenant Fentiman. Immediately."

Argent began to dress himself urgently, missing buttons and making a shambles of his cravat. Fentiman soon arrived and quickly concluded that his Captain was far from his usual state of calm and collected.

"Sir, you sent for me?"

"I did. Have you heard? That slaver has raided Ruanporth. Nothing like has happened for almost a century!"

Argent stood, his face in shock. Fentiman looked puzzled, he fully understood the implications of the news, but had he been urgently summoned for a history lesson? He didn't recognise his Captain at all.

"Yes Sir?"

"My family has relations there. They often go there to stay, my sister, her husband and their child. With my brother in law's parents. They may have gone there yesterday. I need to find out."

Argent looked anxiously at Fentiman.

"I hope you understand?"

Fentiman immediately realised why he had been summoned.

"Yes Sir. You must go, of course. There's no need for you to remain on board, but every need for you to be certain of your family."

By now Argent was wearing his coat. He nodded, but his face showed his gratitude.

"Thank you, Henry. This I'll not forget. I'll be back sometime in the afternoon."

Carrying nothing, Argent hurried on deck and off the ship to the quayside and his hurry along it did not go unnoticed. Fraser and Ball, on Watch, studied the figure dodging and scurrying his way through the early morning dockyard activities. Fraser put into words what they had both concluded.

"That slaver hittin' Ruanporth, must be the one that Frencher was on about. Cap'n's got family 'round there. He'll be worried and be off to discover. No blame from me for that."

Ball nodded.

"So, 'ere's hopin'. Bastard slavers, I thought they was now back in times long gone. The memory sent a shiver through my grand folks."

Almost running, Argent soon reached his usual horse stable and had to knock up the ostler. He came straight down on seeing him and had no need of explanation as to why he so urgently needed a horse. He saddled and bridled the usual mare, noticing that Argent, both hopping and fidgeting, could barely contain his impatience. Once in the saddle Argent began at the gallop, but soon allowed the mare to drop back to a canter, then a trot. The familiar sights passed on each side, seen by sight, but unseen by his troubled mind. Soon the last hill and then the gate, but no one could be seen. He partly tethered the mare, then ran to the door to push it open, barely breaking stride. His relief was palpable as he saw Enid feeding Jacob, with his Father and Emily still at breakfast. They were as shocked to see him, as he was relieved to see them, all safe and well. Argent now realized that he was out of breath and gasped his explanation.

"I've just heard that slavers have raided Ruanporth. What's the news? Where's Beryan? What of his family?"

Emily saw his state of anxiety, which only added to her own, but she was the first to rise to bring him to the table and then his Father pushed his own cup of tea before him. The small domestic gestures went a huge way to calm him and as he drank Enid spoke the answers.

"Beryan's safe, but wounded. But they got Jane Worleggen, his sister, and her two children."

The cup left Argent's lips, the terrible question clear on his face. Enid continued.

"He's not wounded badly. Not badly. He was down there when they came and he joined the fight against them, so's they didn't get too far into the village, then the Militia turned out. Thank God there was a company of them in the Church. He's still down there, with Michael, his brother in law. So there, be calmed, that tells you he's not badly hurt."

Argent had not drunk again from the cup and, at his sister's words, he gave vent to a long sigh and his shoulders and chest fell with the ending of his anxiety. He looked back at Enid.

"Who did they get? Anyone we know? I've been told two dozen."

"Yes, about that, but closest to us is Beryan's sister and the two children."

Argent's jaw clamped back together. He had met Beryan's sister at Enid's wedding and at other times since. She was pretty, slender, and blond, and her children likewise. He made up his mind and rose from the table.

"I'm going back into Falmouth. I'm going to ask that Ariadne be sent after him. She's fast and can cover a lot of ocean, tracking back and forth. Tell Beryan that if I'm let out onto that ocean, I'll get them back."

He rose and traversed the table to kiss his sisters and Jacob. His Father rose to shake his hand and there was a light in his Father's eyes that he had not seen before, as his Father looked at him and gripped his right elbow. Argent smiled and nodded, then he gathered his hat and left.

The horse, poorly tethered, had wandered, but only to a hayrick. Soon Argent was trotting back down the hill and then further, almost to the outskirts of Falmouth. However, when he passed the gate of the Willoughby estate there were a group of servants clustered just inside. Argent stopped and noticed that in the centre of the group was the serving maid who had given him tea the last time he called, she was plainly distraught, crying with huge sobs into her apron. Argent dismounted and led his horse to them. They soon noticed his uniform and all turned towards him, some with grim faces. Argent looked back at them.

"The raid?"

The largest man and the angriest, replied.

"Yes. They got her sister. Barely a slip of a girl."

He squared around to Argent to say what he really wanted.

"You're the Navy. 'Tis you as is supposed to keep the likes of these filthy Heathens away. Protection! That's what we expects from you."

Argent couldn't argue. The image came to his mind of Herodotus and her feeble, far between, Fastnet patrol, barely leaving harbour. He only had one reply.

"I'm sorry. We've all lost family, including me. It's the war, we can't fight the French all over the ocean and cover every cove and harbour back here. I'm sorry."

At the fact that Argent had also lost family, the man softened, but said no more, so Argent continued.

"I'm hoping to put to sea soon and give chase. I'm the Captain of the Ariadne. If those are my orders, that's what I'll do, be assured."

One of the women comforting the maid turned to him.

"If you're the one sent after them, Sir, then Godspeed to you."

Argent smiled and nodded, but she continued.

"Her Ladyship's, too, got a wounded man indoors. One of those as fought them off. A Ruanporth man, one of her servants, but badly wounded, that she's carin' for. 'T'ave hit the most of us."

The thought struck Argent immediately, that from this man he may learn something. Argent remounted, intending to ride up the drive, but he noticed again the serving maid. He couldn't leave without saying something, but the girl had now collapsed onto the bank, her face still covered by her apron. Argent looked at the woman.

"Please tell her that the Navy won't give up. If it's possible to get her sister back, we will."

With that he rode up to the front door, dismounted, tethered the horse securely to the hitching post and knocked. He was greeted by the same footman as before.

"I am Captain Argent. Please tell Lady Grant that I would like to see her wounded servant, if that's possible."

The footman stood back from the door to allow Argent an entrance.

"Yes Sir. I'll do that immediately. She is with the wounded man now."

He walked to the door of the same room that Argent had waited in before.

"If you'd like to wait in here, Sir, I will fetch her Ladyship."

Argent entered and sat, impatient and thinking intently; the man may know something, something that could make the difference. However, his patience was not tried too far because soon Lady Grant entered the room. Argent stood immediately.

"Reuben. You wish to see James? He's received a stab wound in his chest, but is conscious, at least when I left him. You'll not stay too long?"

"No, Lady Grant, just a few questions."

She left the room expecting him to follow and both went down the corridor that led to the rear of the house. She entered a room at the end, off to the left and, on entering, Argent saw James, a man of early middle age, with his chest bare and a wound below his right collarbone oozing blood. A serving woman was dabbing at the wound, ineffectually, presumably hoping it would stop if she continued wiping. James was lying back with closed eyes. There was also a livid bruise with a cut, showing on his forehead. Lady Grant went to him.

"James. Captain Argent is here. Can you answer a few questions for him?"

James opened his eyes and cast his gaze around to find Argent. He nodded and Argent went to his bedside.

"James. First, well done, to put up such a fight, well done. That was brave."

James nodded, but clearly he was very weary and not well.

"What did the slaver look like? Anything you can tell me about him will help."

James closed his eyes and lay back.

"Black hull, Sir, lots of oars."

He swallowed and the woman gave him some water.

"And her sails, they was furled but they was red, a dark red."

"Anything else?"

"She was broad on the beam. Wide as a frigate and nearly as long"

"Any guns?"

"Not as could be seen, Sir. I recall two banks of oars and bare planking above 'em, up to her rail."

"What kind of men?"

"Arabs, Sir. Dark skinned Devils, all wearin' loose clothes, their heads wrapped in cloth.

Argent patted his arm.

"That's helpful James and very important. Well done and thank you. You rest now, you're in safe hands."

Argent looked at the wound on James' chest. It was clean and probably deep into the muscle. He looked at Lady Argent.

"What's worse for him is the blow on his forehead. That stab is less serious, it will heal. My advice is to sew it up, just sew it up, with clean cotton. That'll stop the bleeding. Then he must rest, but get a Doctor to him as soon as possible."

The serving woman looked up at him, then at Lady Grant, who nodded. The servant left and Argent spoke again.

"Does Admiral Grant know?"

"Yes, he does and he's despatched Herodotus to give chase. She's probably on her way now, as we speak."

Argent's spirits sank and it showed on his face. How could he place any faith in Cheveley and the likes of his First, that fop Langley? Lady Grant saw his face cloud with worry and said what she should not.

"Reuben. Septimus told me that you are to sail soon, with strict orders. Otherwise he would have sent you."

She placed a hand on his arm and looked into his face almost with desperation.

"Reuben. Ruanporth is part of my estate, they are my tenants and they are devastated. I look upon them as I would my own. I know you will be under orders, but find them, Reuben, please find them. Do all you can."

Argent looked back at her, his face equally serious. She was asking him to disobey clear orders, but he made a reply that reflected what was already growing inside him.

"This mission I'm being sent on. If it sends me down through the Bay of Biscay, I'll find them. They're Arabs, up from the Barbary Coast. They've been raiding France for some time, that I know. I'd hazard that they are now on their way back, probably back to where they came from, with enough of what they came for, damn them. But if I'm sent down there, I'll find them."

He looked down at her concerned face.

"There are two kinds of duty and I understand both, very well, be assured. But, now I must go."

He left, he felt it best. Lady Grant was near to tears.

* * *

He strode quickly along the dock beside his ship, but did not board her. He had but one foot on the gangplank when he saw Sanders at the top in the entry port.

"Sir, we had a message, but minutes ago. You are to report to the Commodore's Office."

Argent about turned and walked quickly around the dock to enter at the familiar door. Venables rose at the sight of him, but he, too, showed the same level of shattering depression that he had seen at Lady Grant's. They exchanged salutes.

"It's hit you, too, Sergeant."

"Yes, Sir. I've no relations there, but it's the thought of it, Sir. Young women and children, prisoners aboard a slaver and bound for who knows what kind of Hell. It don't bear thinkin' about."

Argent nodded, his own face giving equal expression to the thought which the Sergeant had just given voice to.

"Well Sergeant, we're not letting him go, just like that. Herodotus has been sent after him."

Venables' face did not change. Argent nodded again and walked down the corridor to Budgen's office. He knocked and entered, Budgen had made no reply, but was sat at his desk with a large, cream, vellum package before him on his desk, the package held closed by a huge red seal. Besides that was a single piece of paper, covered in a handwriting he did not recognise, and this he pushed first in Argent's direction.

"Your orders, Argent, drawn up by Admiral Broke, Grant wasn't available. You sail on the next ebb. You are to make fast passage for Figuiera da Foz; North Portuguese coast, and deliver that to General Wellesley. If he is not there, then you place it in safe hands, safe hands, mind, to ensure its sure arrival with Wellesley."

"That" was the second thing pushed across. Budgen continued. "This has come down from the highest, Argent, from Castlereagh himself, never mind the Admiralty. It is essential that Wellesley receives it, at the earliest. They've even given you this, to carry it in."

He brought up a shiny black, thick leather satchel, which he dropped onto the desk.

Argent studied first the thick bundle, with some awe, then the glorious satchel, which had the Royal Crest embossed on the flap in red, blue and gold. Then, back again to the velum package, it probably having been sealed by the Secretary of State for War's own hand itself.

"May I know what it is, Sir?"

"You may know this much. It's a communication to Wellesley, telling him that the Austrians are out of the war. They will sign a Treaty with Napoleon at Schonbrun. It will release French soldiers to come against him. It may affect any plans that he has about invading Spain from where he is, that being Portugal. He may think the French army to be one size, but this Treaty could enable the Johnnies to double the force against him. He has to know this, at the soonest."

Argent looked up at Budgen.

"And this slaver? Sir. If I see him? I'll be taking the same course, if he's returning to the North of Africa."

Budgen stared back at him hard and slammed his hand onto the desk.

"You are to do nothing that jeopardises the rapid delivery of that package! Nothing, Argent, nothing. That must be totally clear. That package is the affairs of nations, whilst the work of that damned slaver; well, no more than a bad shipwreck. We get over it. Am I clear?"

Argent stood and saluted.

"Yes Sir. Perfectly clear."

He picked up both the package and his orders and placed them in the satchel, which he slung over his shoulder, his left thumb hitched comfortably where the strap joined the cover. On passing Venables, the old Sergeant stood at his passing.

"Good luck, Sir."

Argent looked back, as reassuringly as he could.

Back on board, he issued orders right and left. The ebb was but an hour away, he wanted to be on it, out and away. First he ordered the longboat over the side to be ready to tow Ariadne's bows clear of the harbour wall, then he gave orders to remove all the gangplanks and mooring ropes that connected her to the wall via the stout bollards. Next a look at the pennant told him that the wind could ease her out into Carrick roads to pick up the ebb tide, after she had been worked clear of the mole. Fraser was informed to make ready the foresail and foretopsail, but, for the moment, Argent thrust both of his problems to the back of his mind. He took himself to his cabin and dropped the satchel into his own sea chest and then took himself back to the quarterdeck.

By now the longboat was over the side and was being made ready to receive a towline that was being fashioned up on the forecastle. He turned to the Midshipman on Watch, the new Thomas Trenchard.

"Mr. Trenchard. My compliments to Mr. Fentiman. I would appreciate his presence on the quarterdeck."

"He's only just gone off Watch, Sir."

The withering look that Trenchard received both defined and finished the argument.

"Aye aye, Sir."

As he waited, leaning on the rail, his dilemma reasserted itself. It was in his power, if he found the slaver, to put it right, for family, for friends, and for all the poor souls now overcome with grief. He thrust the thought back as Fentiman arrived, he had hurried, evidenced by the fact that he was still buttoning his coat. Quarterdeck etiquette would be strictly observed.

"You sent for me, Sir."

"Yes, Mr. Fentiman. We are to put to sea immediately and I want to catch this ebb."

"Aye aye, Sir. Is this the mission we've been held for, may I ask?"

Argent turned to him, his face stern. He had too many worries to be concerned with the niceties of politeness.

"We will discuss that when we are at sea, Mr. Fentiman. Meanwhile, let us get the ship out and onto it."

"Aye aye, Sir. Your orders?"

"I've given orders to tow her head away from the quayside, then please to ease us upstream on foresails. Mr Fraser has that in hand."

"Aye aye, Sir."

Fentiman took himself over to the starboard side to check that all was now gone. It was. The gangplank was square against the quayside edge and all mooring ropes coiled, bar one at the stern. He took himself to the forecastle and found it prepared under the supervision of Bosun Fraser, there was no more reason for delay. The stern mooring was cast off and the bows towed away from the quayside, next the sails were dropped and sheeted home and Ariadne began to ease upwards from the quayside and into the open water. The longshoremen on the quayside gave their shouts of encouragement and farewell; their assumption of Ariadne's mission was clear. The replies from the crew showed that they, too, shared that same assumption.

The breeze on the foresails made the task of the towing crew very much easier, until, with clear water all around, Fentiman ordered the longboat recovered. Now, Ariadne, under foresails alone, was no more than drifting up against the ebb. A crowd had gathered to watch her departure and all gathered there also assumed that she was being despatched to intercept the slaver. There were many calls and shouts to confirm their belief, which added to Argent's despondency and torment, but once in enough open water he re-ordered his thoughts and turned to Zachary Short, at the wheel.

"Take us into the Roads, Mr. Short."

"Course for the Roads. Aye aye, Sir."

The next orders to increase sail he gave himself.

"Mr. Ball."

Henry Ball, on the starboard gangway, immediately turned round and came to the attention at the sound of his Captain's voice.

"Main and mizzen topsails and driver. Main topgallant."

Ariadne would be carrying a lot of sail for manoeuvring in harbour, but Argent saw no cause for prudence at the top of the tide, he wanted his ship out and on her voyage. The tide was now on full ebb and, as Ariadne's bows eased into the fast flowing water, she began to swing downstream to point to the harbour entrance. Argent waited his moment to turn to gain it, for the wind West Southwest meant a close run to the Eastern arm of the harbour entrance.

"Up helm."

The repeat came, then Argent called out to Henry Ball.

"Close hauled, starboard tack."

Next to Short.

"Course out, Mr. Short."

The repeat came and Argent detected the eagerness in Short's voice. His Quartermaster was pleased to be at sea and, in the seaman's mind that was Short's, the reason was well formed.

Full in the tide and with all sails drawing Ariadne sped from the harbour and as she passed Pendennis Castle, her crew could hear cheering to speed her on her way. Argent could not help but wonder; in what manner had they sent Herodotus out onto the ocean? A large crowd was waving and cheering; in their minds, if there was any ship that could find and take the slaver, it was Ariadne.

"Mr. McArdle. A course for Quessant. Mr. Ball. All plain sail."

* * *

Quessant was due South of Falmouth, and with the wind steady on North West to North, close to her best point of sailing, Ariadne leapt and sped over an unquiet sea. Those of her crew on Watch, having decided on her mission, looked to their duties as though every care must be taken with sail trim and they made themselves ready for any change required, indeed even pointing out to the Bosun's Mates anything less than perfect. Argent sat at his desk in his cabin, his head resting in one hand, deep in thought, his mind oblivious as his ship rose and sank in the fretful rollers. If his mind wasn't mired in thinking of the family farm in peril, he was thinking of the slaver and his strict orders. No amount of thought eased the situation of either. He was grateful when Fentiman knocked and entered.

"Sir. We have the question of the thief, Seaman Main. He is still in irons."

Argent sat back. This also was no subject that could give him any comfort.

"Let's have him in."

Argent sat waiting until Main was brought in, hands and ankles still in irons, himself puny between two burly Marines, with Fentiman stood to the side. Argent looked at him, his own problems adding to his anger with this thief.

"Main. Step forward."

The convict recruit shuffled forward and stopped, hands manacled before him.

"Main. Do you dispute your guilt regarding these thefts?"

Landy Main returned a blank stare and Argent's temper broke.

"That requires an answer, Main, or I'll have you flogged for insubordination, then come back once more to these thefts and start again."

Main shuffled in his sets of irons.

"Yes. It were I."

Argent sat back, his voice suddenly weary.

"I don't know if you recall, Main, but my words to you, when first you came aboard this ship, were, that it matters not what you were before, what matters now is what you become, from now, from this moment. Become a seaman and become a valued member of this crew."

He paused to gauge Main's understanding. He failed against the blank look.

"Did you understand those words?"

Again, the blank look.

"Insubordination, Main."

"Yes."

Argent fixed him with a fierce look and Main recognised the requirement.

"Sir."

"But they had no impact upon you. You decided not to change. You decided that you were a thief and a thief you would stay and, at the earliest opportunity you would begin thieving. And you did."

Argent waited for a reaction, but none came, and so he continued.

"As far as I can tell, all of those that came aboard with you; convicts, pressed men, and volunteers, have settled in well. Bar you."

Argent paused to give gravity to his next words.

"I waited until we were at sea to hear your case, Main. In harbour you were under English Law, and, as a convicted felon, offending again, you would have been hung."

Another pause.

"Hung"

Main's eyes shifted slightly, but no other reaction.

"Out here, you are subject to Navy Law, and that states that I determine your sentence."

He paused.

"Two dozen lashes."

Main showed no reaction at all, this sentence was nothing new, he'd been whipped before, in town squares. Argent turned to Fentiman; he wanted this finished and dealt with.

"What bell?"

"Five, Sir."

"Punishment to be carried out at six bells. Inform the Carpenter to rig the gratings and the Master at Arms. And Bosun's Mate Ball, of course."

Fentiman left immediately to inform all, including the Officers, because a flogging was a very formal affair. Main was shuffled away, whilst the Marines marched, taking him back to his open gaol at the forward end of the lower deck. His punishment was rapidly transmitted to those whom the Marines passed; "Two Dozen."

When the glass had but an inch to go the Bosun's calls sounded, "All hands to witness punishment". The whole crew came on deck and assembled along the gangways and forward of the mizzenmast. All with deadly serious faces; most had witnessed a flogging before but it was unknown on the Ariadne. All Officers were to oversee from their regulation place on the starboard gangway just along from its meeting with the quarterdeck. The punishment was to be carried out on the gun deck, immediately below the quarterdeck rail. Only the Marines would not see all, they were paraded at the stern end of the quarterdeck, taking their line forwards from the taffrail. At six bells Main was led up from the lower deck, on his right side was the Master at Arms with drawn sword, this being one fierce Yorkshireman, Joseph Ackroyd, the Sergeant of Marines. Fraser and Ball came on Main's left, Ball carrying a red bag. Landy Main's irons had been removed and he walked freely up to face the grating, his course being guided by those beside him. Fentiman came up besides the Master at Arms and saluted.

"All ready. Sir."

Argent stepped forward to the quarterdeck rail.

"Article of War 29. All robbery committed by any person in the fleet, shall be punished with death, or otherwise, as a court martial, upon consideration of the circumstances, shall find meet."

He paused.

"Ordinary Seaman Main. You have admitted to a great number of thefts aboard this ship. Your sentence is two dozen lashes. Strip him!"

Two Bosun's Mates stepped forward and removed Main's shirt, then they pulled him onto the two gratings, one grating lying on the deck to which his feet were lashed, one vertical to which his wrists were lashed, as far above his head as possible. Landy Main was spread out, helpless. The last act of one of the Bosun's Mates was to place a wooden gag in Main's mouth, between his teeth, and tie its cords around the back of his head, so that it would not fall out when his mouth opened, as they knew it would. He was given good advice.

"Bite on it, now."

Meanwhile, Ball had taken the cat of nine tails out of the bag and was combing out the strands. He knew that such would soon be needed and had therefore fashioned one from a piece of thick hawser, incorporating the knots at the end of each of the nine strands, which were required for thieving. Ball took his place with the lash curled loose and malevolent on the deck beneath his right hand. Argent spoke.

"Bosun's Mate. Do your duty."

All Officers removed their hats and Ball threw back the tails of the cat behind him. The first stroke sounded like a wet sheet being smacked against a wall. It slammed all of Main's breath out of his body and his mouth flew open, but the wood stopped him biting his tongue. Ackroyd shouted.

"One."

Then he turned the quarter minute glass. Ball waited for the nod, Main for the next stroke. He was fighting for breath; he had never been hit so hard. Ball got the nod and the next stroke broke across his back, slamming him into the grating. At five strokes the blood began to flow, at eight quite copiously. The Midshipmen; Bright, Berry and Trenchard looked on with different degrees of nausea. Berry and Bright had seen such before, but not Trenchard and Bright could sense Trenchard swaying besides him. He turned his head as far as he dared and then spoke from the side of his mouth.

"Close your eyes."

Trenchard did and had only to put up with the sound of the cat, different now as it slapped against the flowing blood. Main was pulling himself up the grating as far as his tethered ankles would allow, the muscles of his scrawny arms standing out like taught ropes. At one dozen, Surgeon Smallpiece walked forward to examine him. Smallpiece looked first at his back, but it showed nothing unusual for a flogging, but a look at Main's face from the side showed him gasping for breath and his eyes bulging from their sockets. He wasn't sure, but he was certainly concerned. He turned to Ball, who had taken the time to comb out the bloody lengths, and nodded. Four more were placed on the riven back, but then Smallpiece held up his hand and walked forward again; early, it should be on the half dozen count. Main had sagged down entirely and was held upright solely by his tethered wrists. He looked at Main's face, he had fainted; his jaw was slack and hanging open, the wooden bit slack. Smallpiece knew that Main could be faking, he had experience of such, so he nodded to Ball and one more was laid on, but Main's face showed no change. He was utterly unconscious and, to someone of so sparse a frame, any further could be fatal. What decided Smallpiece was that Main didn't seem to be breathing, so he walked out to look up at the Captain and he shook his head. Smallpiece was saying that the prisoner could take no more; any more could be a death sentence. Argent nodded.

"Cut him down."

Bright told Trenchard to keep his eyes closed as a bucket of water was thrown over Main's back and then he was cut down to collapse in a jumbled pile of limbs, bleeding back and lolling head, all coloured by scarlet water. Four seamen carried him, by his wrists and ankles, along the gun deck to be taken down to the orlop deck, Smallpiece's sickbay. The gratings were removed and the last act, as all trooped away, was for two swabbers of the Watch to swill away the blood from the deck. All knew that the affair was finally terminated when Argent issued an order.

"Set main staysail."

Those on Watch looked to the sail, those not, continued down to the lower deck, many commenting on the fact that he couldn't even take his "two dozen"; this being unheard of. Also, all knew and some said, that most Captains would have carried on.

The three Midshipmen returned, grateful, to their tiny berth. Berry and Bright unburdened themselves of the accessories of their dress uniform, these being the hat and belt with their dirk. Both were pale, but Trenchard was green. Bright took down the bottle containing their small stock of brandy and poured a measure for him. He had no qualms over using their precious supply in such a way, for Trenchard was close to keeling over and, anyway, the brandy had been brought aboard by him. The spirit revived him and he perked up, but only to look thoroughly shocked and shaken. He looked up at Bright, then at Berry.

"You know, if any of us ever make Captain, it'll be us that will have to order such as that, to our own men."

Berry and Bright nodded, and Bright poured him a drop more.

* * *

In the Captain's cabin, Argent and Fentiman had confined the affair to the past; Argent had more pressing and insoluble concerns, much beyond the simple decision to halt a flogging. Both were sat on the bench beneath the stern windows that extended between the two stern chaser guns, both bowsed and secure, but, nevertheless their casables protruded incongruously out into the room from under their canvas covers. Argent placed his right foot on the rear wheel of one of the guns.

"Our orders, Henry, are to deliver a package to General Wellesley, down in Portugal, putting in at Figuiera da Foz. It's a package from Castlereagh himself, telling Wellesley that the Austrians are out of the war, meaning that his is the only army fighting the French, to any degree. That could affect his plans, I don't need to tell you."

Argent paused to let that sink in.

"We are charged to deliver the package at the earliest, which is probably why Ariadne was chosen."

Fentiman saw the change come over his Captain, anguish, or close, came over his face. He continued listening anxiously as Argent spoke further.

"But the slaver? What do we do? I'll not countenance doing nothing, if anything is in our power. He's off home, of that I'm now certain. He's been around here for months, as we learned from the cannoniere. He's got what he came for and will want to be across the Bay of Biscay before the weather turns foul. He's in front of us. What do we do? What are your thoughts?"

"Hasn't Herodotus been sent after her?"

"Yes, but you know what Cheveley will do. Set a course for Cape Finnistere and sit there. He'll reason that the slaver has to round the Cape to run down the coast of Portugal. Cheveley will sit there and wait for a day or so and then, feeling uncomfortable or bored or short of fancy food, he'll give up and come home. He hasn't been that far down in years."

It was Argent's next words that convinced Fentiman of the torment inside his Captain.

"What the Hell does Cheveley care about the likes of a few peasants captured off some beach?"

Fentiman assembled his own thoughts and they lighted first on their orders.

"Orders are orders, Sir. We get the dispatch to Wellesley. You set a course to expedite that. If..."

He paused.

"...if we meet the slaver, then we've got to take her. There'd be a shocking row if we did not, despite our orders."

He paused.

"But the point is, Sir, do we go looking for her? If we do we are acting against our orders. Whatever we do, we must be able to justify as being part of making as fast a passage as possible to Figuiera, and the Log must make that clear; clear and accurate."

Argent looked at him. He knew Fentiman was making sense and it was Fentiman that continued.

"If we go roaming around Biscay, searching, or looking into every cove and backwater on the coast, instead of cracking on to Finnistere, then, well, it's a Court Martial, Sir. And we won't have much of an argument. The Log will show it."

Argent nodded.

"Very well. But if we encounter the slaver, we take her. No one would argue against that. If I understand you rightly, we set the best course possible for Figuiera hoping that that will bring us up on him. Hoping he's made the same choice as us."

It was Fentiman's turn to nod.

"That's about it, Sir."

"We agree then. Whatever we do has to be justified as part of executing our orders."

"Yes Sir."

"Right, but we must do something about the impression existing amongst the men. They think we're out after the slaver, nothing else."

Argent sat silent, as did Fentiman, waiting for his Captain's decision. They heard seven bells ring above them.

"At eight bells I'll address the crew."

Eight bells came and, as this was a Watch change, both Watches were on deck. McArdle took the Noon Sight alone, as the Bosun's calls sounded for assembly and all the crew made their way back aft and found a place where they could both see and hear their Captain. Argent stood in the centre of the quarterdeck rail waiting for all to arrive and fall silent.

Fraser took charge.

"Attention."

All obeyed and Argent began.

"Men. I feel I must put right what may be in your minds regarding why we are at sea. I have to tell you now that we have not been sent after the slaver."

No one spoke but many exchanged looks and shifted their position.

"We have been ordered to take a vital dispatch down to Portugal to give to the Commander of our army there. It is vital that it arrives at the earliest and that is our charge. Lives could be spared because of our speedy arrival."

He paused.

"However, we are in the same waters and heading in the same direction as that slaver, and if we see him, we will take him."

Faces changed and fists were clenched amongst the crew, albeit by their sides at attention.

"So. If he's on our piece of ocean, we must make sure we see him. We'll double the lookouts and change halfway through each lookout duty. If you're up there keep your eyes skinned, we don't want Ariadne speeding past him for want of an open pair of riding lights!"

Some smiles as he turned to Fentiman.

"Dismiss the men."

As Argent descended the companionway to go to his own cabin, Fentiman dismissed the crew and Argent heard them speak about still "Gettin' that Hellsent Devil". As Argent entered his cabin, he began a reasoning of his own. The slaver was not built for the open ocean and possible Atlantic storms. He was broad beamed, as Argent knew, with too little freeboard between the oar ports and the waterline. He had managed to cross The Channel, but he would need to run down the coast, on this he had no choice; he had to steer just over the horizon from the land, yet keeping close enough to get shelter if a storm hit. However, Argent had to justify Ariadne following the coast that would give the best chance of taking him, but he knew that the fastest passage to Finnistere and on to Figuiera meant a straight line, full across the Bay of Biscay.

All around the ship there was but one topic of conversation. In the Foretop mess and that of Number Three starboard, confidence grew that "the Captain will find him" and many vowed to volunteer for extra lookout, but in the Midshipman's berth they shared Argent's own thoughts. It was Berry who spoke first.

"We have to go straight across with the dispatch, but the slaver could carry on raiding down the coast."

Bright replied, for Trenchard knew too little to contribute, as yet.

"Don't forget the wind. I've never gone straight across the Bay yet. Nine days out of ten, there's a South West wind right in your teeth. It hits you the moment you leave The Channel. You either tack out or tack in."

Trenchard needed more information for his contribution.

"This slaver's a galley. Right?"

Both nodded.

"With oars?"

More nods.

"Then how do we take him? We won't be able to get close enough to board him, the oars'll keep us away, and we can't sink him because of the prisoners. What do we do?"

Neither had an answer and looked at each other puzzled, but Bright sidestepped the subject.

"Well, first we've got to find him. Then, that's a puzzle we'll be happy to have."

By dead reckoning, within the dark of night, McArdle placed them just off Quessant and, sure enough, with the light of dawn came the cry from the masthead that land was sighted. The wind had veered to West Northwest and so Argent took Ariadne to the West of the island, but close, unnecessarily close, so as to cause more than a few eyebrows knitting together in puzzlement on the quarterdeck. However, McArdle, Wentworth, Sanders, and Fentiman could read Argent's mind; he wanted to look into Quessant Bay. Fentiman approached Argent, stood alone on the weather side, then he spoke softly, more than a little concerned.

"Sir. Can this be justified?"

Argent turned to look at him.

"I believe so. To take a look will lose us nothing, yet he may be there. We are merely sailing past on our legitimate course"

"And if he is there, Sir?"

"Then we have to take him, as we agreed."

They sailed so close to the Western tip of the island that sheep and startled shepherds could be seen on the featureless, dull green pasture. The sheep keepers stood thoroughly surprised at the sight of this British man-o-war with the minimum of sail, drifting past wraithlike, with no sound of her own but accompanied eerily by the mournful mewing of hundreds of gulls. Wentworth raised his own telescope to examine the life they could see on the flat pasture beyond the surf and low cliffs. He was not well regarded amongst the men, referred to as "Old Splutter Pump." They respected his seaman's skills well enough, but how could you respect an Officer who could barely utter five words together? The men of his battery had grave doubts, whilst Trenchard, him knowing practically nothing, was well liked. Wentworth reported to his Captain.

"S-Sir. Th-those are shepherds, Sir. And sh-sheep. A large flock. Sh-surely the slaver, were he there, would have slaughtered m-many and killed the men? Sir."

Argent lowered his own glass.

"You may be right, Mr. Wentworth, but it's worth a look, nevertheless."

Argent turned to Quartermaster Short.

"Down helm. Come to South East."

The order was repeated and Ariadne answered and, with the wind almost dead astern, Fraser supervised the adjustment of the sails. The western arm of the bay eased past and the large expanse opened. At least a dozen telescopes were levelled over the larboard quarter, but Argent took himself far aloft to sit on the mizzen topgallant spar, accompanied by four lookouts. He examined the far end of the bay until his eye ached. He could see right down to the furthest beach and also clearly along the sides of the bay, but there was nothing. Merely what he thought were a few barrels and boxes; perhaps evidence that the bay was, indeed, once the slaver's base, but more likely just washed up flotsam, trapped in the inlet. He descended, his disappointment plain to see, but there was worse. The decision was now upon him; in front of them was the Bay, which course to set? It should be direct for Finisterre and the Northern wind was set fair for such a passage straight across. The Officers of the Watch on the quarterdeck stood waiting and Argent took himself to the weather side. He looked and felt very much alone.

On his side, working on the mizzenmast shrouds, were his only companions, foc's'lmen Eli Reece and his constant companion Ben Raisey. Reece was voicing his great concern.

"Look 'ee at that sky, Ben. That herringbone. 'Tonly means one thing in the Bay, and that's a bad blow. There's a bad one comin' up from mid Ocean, you mark my words."

Raisey answered without ceasing his splicing of a broken shroud.

"You ain't wrong there, Eli, I noticed it too, an' not for the first time. I seen that sky afore, tellin' I Summer's well gone. 'Tis get yer wet gear out yer chest, right enough."

Argent, wishing not to think, had instead listened to all being said.

"Reece."

On hearing their Captain's voice addressing one of them, both came to the attention and made their respects.

"Reece. What's this you're saying about a herringbone sky?"

Reece spoke all he knew.

"Why, yes Sir. I've heard it many a time and gone through it. If you sees the clouds comin' across in that pattern, herringbone some calls it, in these waters, then you can be sure there's a blow comin'. There's many as says that, Sir."

Argent turned to McArdle.

"Sailing Master. Is this something you have experience of?"

McArdle drew himself up to his full height and clasped his hands behind his back, one wrist in one hand. His chin rose as though he were about to pronounce a subdued and intimidated couple to now be man and wife.

"Aye Sir. Aye. That's somethin' ah've heard. In these waters, it shows a storm could be comin'. An' it'll be a bad one, right enough."

McArdle knew what his Captain was seeking; he also knew the choices facing an oared galley.

"Out in the Bay could well be no too good a place to be, over the next couple or so days. Not for any kind of ship."

"And the wind after?"

"Generally East. Sir."

Argent looked at Reece, who nodded agreement, then Argent looked at Fentiman. The look that passed between them conveyed all, they now had reason enough to follow the coast. Argent had decided.

"Mr. Short. Come to South South East."

Then to Fentiman.

"All plain sail. Break out the larboard studding sails."

Then, finally to McArdle.

"Mr. McArdle. A course for 20 miles off La Rochelle, if you please."

He descended to his cabin, opened the Log and entered the date, 10th October 1809. Then he logged his course and the reason for doing so.

* * *

Ariadne had sailed through days of murk. In the evening of her clearing Quessant Island, the wind had backed to South West, feeble strength, carrying grey clouds and curtains of fine rain. The full spread of sail had flapped and twisted fitfully. For the lookouts the weather drove them to despair, the fine rain draped and hung on the meager wind, clearing out to show miles of good visibility, then closing to mere yards. A wind now coming from the South West, as Ariadne gradually turned South, soon left her common sails useless and so she progressed to her point off La Rochelle on staysails alone, but slowly. The weather was clearer on the coastal side so there, at least, they could seek out their quarry, but there also was nothing to be seen of note, bar the odd fishing vessels. They had seen a barrel and failed to bring it aboard, but it gave hope, yet that was now two days past. The lookouts were changed regularly and often, all as eager as ever to be the first one to see the galley, but Argent and his Officers grew less hopeful. They were as likely to have sailed past the slaver in the fog and rain as to have see him.

The bells rang, the Watches changed, the ship's routine ran on with the same inevitability as her progress through the grey and sullen sea, but nothing was seen, not even French shipping. Perhaps the herringbone sky presaging a storm was known as thoroughly to the French on shore as on their own ship and Ariadne continued to ease her way down the coast entirely alone. On the fourth day, the Noon Sight pronounced their position as 46;32 North, 2;32 West, half a days sailing from their point off La Rochelle. Argent knew that they could follow the coast no further than that, for at that point they would have to tack out into the Bay to make an offing for Cape Finisterre. He spent as much time up on the highest crosstrees of the mainmast as he did on the quarterdeck, up there he felt that he was at least doing something, because there, at least, or so he told himself, he could better use his good telescope. McArdle had calculated that, at their present speed, they would be off La Rochelle at sunset, which depressed him further and, with the sinking of the sun, so sank their hopes. With the evening all changed, the skies cleared and the wind backed fully to South East, and strong; now a perfect wind for Finisterre. He had no choice. They had kept a detailed Log of wind and weather to justify keeping to the coast, but this new wind now forced them to leave the land and track across the emptiness of the Bay to round the Spanish coast. His order sounded like a death sentence.

"Down helm. Come to West Sou'west."

Short's acknowledgement came back swift and cheerful, but Argent's own spirits had sunk. He had no choice now but to make a fast passage, so he turned to the Officer of the Watch, Lieutenant Wentworth.

"In all staysails, Mr. Wentworth. Set all plain sail, and larboard stunsails."

Wentworth's stutter disappeared when he shouted and so after the "Aye aye aye, S-sir," he bawled the order clearly to Bosun Fraser. The Second Dog Watch was the Starboard's and so the men ran to the shrouds to set the massive increase in sail. The crew remained eager, they had grown nothing like as despondent as their Captain, they thought the change to increase her speed was done to bring them up sooner on the slaver, but at dinner in the Captain's cabin that evening the conversation dwelt on their pursuit but briefly. All Officers there were sure, as much as they could be, that hope was all but gone and the topic was covered in but a few sentences. Breakspeare asked the question.

"What are our chances now?"

An answer did not come, so Sanders looked at Argent who was morosely arranging his cutlery. He decided to answer himself, as optimistically as he felt made sense.

"He may still be ahead of us. We came down very slowly and he may have cut the corner and be further out. He may still be out there."

Argent looked at Sanders and smiled, but added nothing. Mortimor, with Jeremiah, had brought in the fish soup. All fell to eating, trying to think of another topic, bar Argent. He knew it was likely that he had failed, he had tried, but that was little consolation. They may yet see the slaver and Herodotus may catch him, but the chances of both were slim.

* * *

Dawn found Ariadne held tight in the wind and bursting through the waves that she overtook rolling swiftly on towards the deep Atlantic, her course still West South West. The sky had cleared to the far horizon and all lookouts were in their place. Noon came and with it the ceremony of the sight and the throwing of the log, and now the afternoon was wearing on. Argent was on Watch; over the past days he had rarely left the quarterdeck, but he was on the weatherside, his hand on the backstay, gauging whether to take off sail. There was no more space on any of the masts, even lower staysails and bowsprit sails were set, in addition to the larboard stunsails, for Argent was determined to now make a fast passage. The last log had shown close on twelve and a half knots and he was thinking that the Royals may be driving her head too deep into the water, preventing the thirteen he wanted, when a cry came down from the foremast topgallant yard. It was Able Jones.

"Ship. Off the larboard bow."

The cry hit Argent like a gunshot and, seizing his telescope and breaking his own rule, he ran to the foremast shrouds and climbed, rapidly, like the most athletic of topmen. He reached Jones much out of breath, but not enough to be unable to ask Jones to point. He followed the direction of Jones' arm and scanned left and right and then he saw, four miles ahead, the shape they had seen back in late July. The slaver, if it was he, was crossing their course very obliquely, right to left, almost parallel. On their present course Ariadne would go through his wake about one mile astern of him. Argent looked again for the colours he sought. The galley had its three big lateens fully set, they were definitely dark red and the hull seemed black. He handed the telescope to Jones.

"What colour is their hull?"

Jones took the telescope and adjusted the length to focus for his own perfect eyesight. It didn't take long.

"Black Sir. Black as the ace of spades."

He handed back the telescope and Argent snapped it shut.

"We've found him! Caught them. Damn their eyes!"

Argent clapped Jones on the shoulder and each looked at the other, grinning like schoolboys.

"Keep an eye on him, Jones, report what he does."

Argent took another look. The slaver had made no change, not even to her course, nor the set of her sails. Argent descended only to stand on the foretop and then called down to the deck.

"Ask Mr. Fentiman to accompany me, up here."

Argent was anchoring himself on the shrouds as Fentiman reached him. He handed him the glass and, whilst he took a look, Argent spoke.

"That's the slaver. Just as she was described to me. Would you say she was broad; broad as us and nearly as long?"

Fentiman did not take long to answer.

"I would. So that's him. He looks nasty, alien even."

Argent took the telescope and studied their quarry, speaking as he looked.

"We've got to board him. Our guns could kill the prisoners, he won't be built to withstand shot and they could be held anywhere in his hull. I intend to come against his larboard bow, forward of that bank of oars. That way we block off his wind and the only way he can get clear of us is backing his oars and that will be slow. By then we will have him secured with grapnels. What do you think?"

"I agree that's the only way onto him, but I'm betting he'll have a large crew. He'll have embarked a lot of men to do his raiding, and we'll be going over only at one narrow point. It'll cost us lives and we may even be pushed back and fail."

Argent returned to his telescope, then spoke again.

"You're right. So...?"

The last word was long drawn out. Argent studied and thought and was about to answer his own question, but then changed the subject. At their present speed, within half a glass they would lose the weather gauge. He leaned over the foretop and shouted down, grateful to see Bosun Fraser.

"Mr. Fraser. Up helm and heave to. Furl all sail."

He saw Fraser hurry back to the quarterdeck, at the same time issuing orders to both men and mates. Soon he reached Zachary Short on the wheel and the spokes were swung across for Ariadne to come up into the wind and rapidly slow to a halt. Argent and Fentiman were on their foretop and so, as they climbed upwards to pass, his bargecrew foretopmen asked their question.

"Is that the slaver, Sir?"

Both Fentiman and Argent nodded and, grinning, the topmen passed on up to take in the press of sail, including the extending stunsails. Argent returned to the topic.

"We close him to our starboard, so, we move at least one of our larboard carronades across to support the starboard and fire through the entry port, to sweep his deck. Musket on grape should do it and through the entryport a carronade will take his defenders from behind. The other carronade, we'll have to think about, perhaps it can fire across from the foremast if we can improvise some mountings, but we'll have the Marines on the fo'c'sle, to add their muskets. After we board, then the Marines follow us over."

Argent re-used his telescope.

"Do you think we are higher than him?"

Fentiman took the glass and made a study

"Yes, just, but not by much and mostly at our fo'c'sle."

Argent nodded, growing excited at their plan, but another part of him grew calmer as they dealt with each point and, coping with each, released the tension within him.

"Any other ideas?"

"Yes. Lobbing some of Mr. Tucker's shrapnel things from here, onto his deck, on a short fuse. A job for our Midshipmen."

"Agreed."

Fentiman paused for another think.

"Sir. Do you think our topmen could swing across, over his oars, to give us another boarding party?"

"I do, but only after we've boarded at the bows. Men dropping off a rope into the middle of them wouldn't last long."

"And Officers, Sir?"

"We'll lead the boarders. You and me. Wentworth and Sanders can lead the topmen from the gangway. Tucker and his men direct the guns, McArdle has the ship, with Fraser and his Mates."

Argent looked at Fentiman, who was now silent.

"Right. That's our plan."

Argent released his hold on the shrouds.

"You see Wentworth and Sanders. I'll see Tucker. Meantime clear for action."

As soon as they reached the deck the order to "clear" was given and the men responded. Whilst Ariadne idled in the choppy sea,

Master Gunner Tucker had the most onerous task, to bring forward the larboard quarterdeck carronade and secure the awkward carriage to some anchor points at the entry port, but anyone idle tailed on and the heavy gun was soon dragged over. Gunner Tucker pronounced that the larboard forecastle carronade could be brought into action, although with a limited arc of fire completely aft. A section of railing had to be removed and a complex web of hawser rigged to restrain the recoil, but its crew set about their work more than content that their gun, "The Preacher", would play its part.

Argent and Fentiman walked the gundeck and selected 30 men each. They included Morris, Bearman and Pierce from number three starboard. Sanders and Wentworth selected most of the topmen, the remainder would be needed for sailhandling back aboard and boarding ropes were rigged from the ends of the yards.

Back on his quarterdeck, Argent studied their opponent and saw no change. He looked for the Officer of the Watch and saw Wentworth.

"Mr. Wentworth. Set topsails and jibsails and put us in his wake."

Whilst Wentworth mangled the order relaying it to Fraser, Argent studied the galley again and he could not even see a lookout. Ariadne's jibsails caught the wind and pushed her around, and soon after Argent heard Short call out the new course.

"Steady on Sou'west, Sir."

Ariadne was now following the galley, one point fully free on the larboard tack and holding the distance between them, the wind almost astern, but the galley had shown no reaction, as though her Captain was undisturbed at this new and threatening arrival. His three big lateens continued to draw and the banks of oars dipped regularly into the waves. No change. However, Argent was unperturbed, there were hours of daylight left and so he occupied himself with ensuring that all was ready. With Gunner Tucker he inspected the carronades himself and oversaw the hoisting of the shrapnel shells up to the foretop, then Tucker, a rare occurrence, climbed to the foretop himself and admonished the three Midshipmen, each with a match and flint.

"Now just you make sure, you three shavers, that these lands on his deck and not ours. They goes far out. Are you sure you can throw 'em that far?"

Each Midshipman hefted a shell and nodded, Berry, the strongest, lifted one two- handed above his head. Tucker wasn't thoroughly content, but he was satisfied enough.

"Well, even you mites should be able to clear our deck, even if it ends up in the oggin."

Tucker descended as the drummers beat to quarters, but many were not in their usual position, especially those of the boarding parties, for the guns would not be used. Argent saw no reason to delay. He looked around his quarterdeck and saw Smallsize, now reassigned as a powder monkey on the carronade. Argent was almost lightheaded.

"Ship's Boy Wheeler. Would you care to run up The Colours? Show these scurvy knaves who they're dealing with?"

Smallsize looked confused, but a Signalman pointed to the locker. "In there, lad."

Smallsize extracted The Colours and bent them onto the halliard himself, then hauled up the Ensign, his own weight barely adequate for the job, his feet often leaving the deck. Nevertheless, with the task complete, Smallsize stood back, delighted, to admire his work; the huge White Ensign billowing out to starboard, snapping in the strong breeze. That done, Argent turned to Fentiman.

"Courses and Driver."

Whilst Fentiman shouted the order to Fraser, Argent lifted his telescope to further study the galley. After a moment he made his decision.

"Take us past and lay us across his larboard bow, Mr. Short."

All topmen worked the new sails and soon Ariadne was increasing her speed, up to double that of the galley. The distance shortened very quickly and Argent climbed onto the quarterdeck gunwale, where he braced himself against the starboard shrouds and waited for Ariadne to make her turn which would bring the galley into his view. When his view arrived, Argent focused his glass onto the details of the galley that could now be seen. His upperdeck had no gunwale, merely a rail with many uprights, but not so many as to hide the fact that the upperdeck was crowded with men, Fentiman had been right, the slaver was heavily manned. He continued to look and he could see no weapons in any hand, but he lowered the telescope, curious but not concerned. Ariadne was little more than one cable away, closing to overtake and then Short would swing to starboard to place Ariadne's hull square across the slavers larboard bow, only minutes remained. He returned to the telescope but it was barely needed, only for the finer details and his own crew were in the shrouds monitoring their approach. Argent put the glass to his eye and concentrated on the quarterdeck. What looked like the Commander, better dressed perhaps, certainly more colourful, was making hand signals to his crew, waving some to come back to the stern.

Short minutes passed and Ariadne was down to one cable away, when Argent, through his telescope saw what was developing. A number of tiny figures, wrapped in white, were being pushed onto the quarterdeck. In seconds all had been lifted to stand on the rail, five in all, with a sailor holding them from behind and, through his glass, Argent could see the terror on the face of each, a child. They were not just wrapped, they were bound and Argent's stomach turned over as one was pushed from the rail. The helpless figure slid perfectly through and under the waves, making no splash and leaving no sign, as though the ocean itself felt the need to instantly hide the evidence of so heinous a crime.

"Up helm. Heave to."

A howling came to Argent's ears, this from his own crew who had just witnessed for themselves the cold-blooded murder of a prisoner, plainly a mere child. Short had swung the wheel over and soon all Ariadne's sails were flapping in the wind, no longer drawing. Fraser was yelling to all around to get aloft and secure the canvas. His crew obeyed, but not before yelling a foul insult across the water and shaking a fist. Argent focused the glass; there were still four. Ariadne breaking off had saved the lives of those remaining, but the crew of the slaver were all in their rigging gesturing and shouting at this warship that had halted her attack merely to save the lives of a few slaves. For such squeamish men they had only contempt, they who obeyed the absurdity of being bound by a humanity of which they had no understanding.

Argent dropped down to the quarterdeck, his face white with anger, his mouth grim, his eyes narrow slits. He looked at Short and McArdle.

"This isn't the end. Not by a long shot, by all The Saints, no."

He walked to the beginning of the gangway.

"Mr. Fraser. Stand the men down. Tell Mortimor to get them some food."

Then he saw Henry Ball.

"Mr. Ball. Request Messrs Fentiman, Sanders, and Wentworth to come to my cabin."

He almost jumped down the companionway to the gundeck and turned to enter his cabin, but it wasn't there, the ship was cleared for action. He ordered the nearby guncrews to get up his cabin screens and furniture from the hold and he paced and fumed whilst it was done. The men saw their Captain's mood and all was done quickly and silently. Once inside he sat at his desk with his hands over his eyes, but the image was too painful, of the tiny white figure entering the water, a bound, white, helpless shape. He slammed his hands on the desk and waited, then he noticed that he was wearing his sword. He unhooked it and threw it onto the floor behind. With its clatter came a knock on the door and the three entered. He looked at each and in each face he saw the abhorrence that he felt himself.

"Take a seat."

Each arranged themselves around the desk and looked at him, but, before he could begin, there came a knock on the door. From the shout of enter, McArdle came in.

"Begging your pardon, Sir. But what are your orders?"

McArdle was right. He had been so beside himself that he had neglected his ship.

"Sail downwind. Take us out into the Bay, then come back to follow, from far out, keeping him just in sight, us showing nothing above topsails. Double the lookouts and you, Mr. McArdle, plot his course. He's a galley, heading for Finnisterre."

A feint trace of shock came across McArdle's stony face at the last, most obvious of statements, but he paid his respects and left. Argent returned to his audience and voiced his own thoughts.

"If we renew any attack, he'll throw his prisoners overboard. He knows that if he's captured, all his crew are dead men, so the prisoners can die as well. He saw us coming and made his preparations, namely children, bound and stood up on his rail. We have to come up, when he thinks he's safe and has made no preparation for his Devil's work."

It was Wentworth who spoke. His own anger easing his speech.

"That means a n-night attack, Sir."

"Agreed. So how do we make that work? We have to come against him at the place we planned today, his larboard bow. So we regain the weather gauge, which is easy, but what then."

Wentworth continued.

"If we are t-to come up on him unseen, we must d-darken the ship, Sir. P-paint out the gunports and d-d-darken the sails we are c-carrying."

Argent was calming down.

"A good suggestion, Mr. Wentworth. That can be done and it improves our chances. But boarding him? We cannot slant in from far out, to get onto his bows in the dark, if the likelihood is that we will not be able to see him."

Sanders spoke up.

"Galleys make a lot of noise, Sir. The oars for one thing, and that gang aboard, they'll be cock-a-hoop at having seen us off so easily. And for another thing, the disturbance of the oars and his wide hull, leaves a long, wide wake."

Argent grew hopeful, but it was not yet any kind of workable scheme. He summarized.

"We get into his wake, then close from behind with a darkened ship. How do we board?"

The three looked at him, but he had his own ideas.

"We come up at full speed. If this wind holds, that'll give us nine, perhaps, ten knots, with that we can get past quickly and bore in. But this wind must hold."

"What if he changes course, Sir? In the night."

This was Sanders.

"He won't, not yet."

But the words died in Argent's throat. He was being far too hopeful and he knew immediately that he could not be that certain. His breath left his body in a deep resigned sigh.

"Yes, he may, but we have to hope. I'm reasoning that he'll expect us to expect a change, and, so, most likely, he'll not change, but keep downwind to make Finisterre."

"He could just turn in the night and row upwind."

"He could, yes."

Argent had no other answer. He had countered his own argument.

"So, do you want to attack tonight, Sir?"

Argent paused and thought. Rationality was returning.

"I'd like to, but we can't. We can't risk being seen far out from him. White sails and yellow gunports will stand out, especially if this clear sky holds, even at night. We must prepare the ship for this to work, as Lieutenant Wentworth describes. That will take longer than the few hours of daylight left. Also, they must feel secure; get through a night and a day without seeing us. We'll hang onto him through this night, and tomorrow we'll make our preparations and hold off, just over the horizon, coming over just enough to check on him. We'll plan for the following night. If he does see us, he must think it's not us, so, for now we disguise the ship. Tonight we must hold onto him, which means dropping in behind to follow, as Mr. Sanders has put it, all the noise and rowing racket."

The three left, but Argent felt no better. It was a half-baked plan, more likely to fail than succeed. He thought further; Sanders was right, he could change course and go where the Hell he liked and as for following a wake at almost half a mile distance, as was needed, that was almost fatuous, but he steeled himself. He was doing all that could be done. He reached for the Log and began writing.

At four bells in the Second Dog Watch the light was fading. They had no sails above topsails which would give the slaver anything to see of them, as they kept watch upon him from far out on the horizon, with one lookout on each bare topmast, each with an Officer's telescope. They kept watch until the darkness grew which ensured that the slaver could no longer see them, but at that time he, also, was lost to them. McArdle had plotted his course as West South West and so, in the deepening evening, Ariadne came upwind on staysails and made to match the slaver's course behind him. There was a half moon veiled in medium cloud to give some light and extra lookouts were placed in the foremast to discover the slaver's wake from the passage of her broad hull. They came onto station to find the sea choppy and, in the restless waves, nothing telltale could be seen. Argent ordered an increase in sail to perhaps close up and Ariadne tracked back and forth, left and right, hoping for signs in the dark ocean, but nothing. They strained their ears forwards to perhaps hear the beat of the oars but all they heard were the sounds of their own ship. Argent and Wentworth joined the lookouts and their eyes became sore and their minds deranged from staring at the water. Still nothing. Argent swallowed hard, having had no choice but to, earlier, stay far out on the slaver's horizon, they had left it too late to try to catch up in the growing darkness.

Then, for some reason, Wentworth looked fully off to starboard, at right angles to their hull.

"Sir. Wh-what's that, almost off our b-beam? It's a li-light, Sir, a tiny light."

Argent looked and pulled around his telescope, hung by a cord down his back, but he looked first at the light through a naked eye. A ship about her proper business, far out on the ocean, showing any lights at all, would be carrying more than that, for night safety, and brighter. He fixed on the light and raised his telescope, then he found the light and studied. Just barely visible and only because he was looking for them, against a sky slightly less dark than the black sea, were three masts with three lateen spars raised between them.

"That's him. He's come around in the night and doubling back. Not downwind, just doubling back, using both oars and sails."

He looked again.

"But that light. How the Hell?"

Argent snapped the glass shut.

"No matter. We can follow him, and come dusk tomorrow we must not look like Ariadne, at least as he remembers us. He's made a mistake, not using his oars to take him where we can't go, just changing course in the dark."

Argent raised his voice just enough for the lookouts in the bows.

"Stand down. He's out there, off to starboard. See that light? He's doubling back."

Argent quickly returned to his quarterdeck, the only part of the ship illuminated, this by their own binnacle light, but was it safe from eyes outside? It may be seen from a ship looking back from ahead. Argent was taking no chances. Bright was on Watch.

"Mr. Bright. Blank out that light, to the smallest beam. Just enough for the compass. Mr. Fentiman, wear ship, come to North East."

Bright drew out a kerchief and began his task, whilst the crew responded to Argent's orders to "wear ship". She was on a course West South West, but the slaver was on almost the opposite, steering North East. Ariadne turned easily downwind and came around to her new course and the Watch reset the deck. Wearing ship may have taken them too close to the slaver, so they steered further upwind to gain what they hoped was his starboard quarter but now on the opposite heading. Argent ran to the larboard bow hoping to see the light, but it was gone. Had they fallen too far back?"

"Set all topgallants."

The Watch quickly set the extra sails and they picked up speed. Argent waited, barely breathing, then gave vent to a deep sigh as the light re-appeared, evidently it was back in some recess and could only be seen when beam on to the slaver. Argent took himself back quickly to the quarterdeck.

"Mr. Short. Off to larboard can you see that light?"

Short looked over and craned his neck.

"No Sir. Nothin' there for me, Sir."

"So, Mr. Bright, up into the Mizzentop. Any change in the position of that light and you inform Mr. Wentworth. Especially, especially, if you think it is getting closer or further away from us. Also, of course, if it's falling behind or pulling ahead."

"Aye aye, Sir."

Bright immediately swung himself up into the mizzen shrouds and was gone. Argent walked to the larboard gunwale where he could see the light with a naked eye, bright, but tiny, perhaps a mile, perhaps less, off their beam. He remained there for some time, watching, then Bright called down to say what Argent had seen for himself.

"It's falling astern, Mr. Wentworth."

Wentworth reacted and called down to the Bosun's Mate below, Henry Ball. He did not shout, the light over the water caused all to talk in hushed tones.

"T-take in fore and m-mizzen toh-topgallants."

Argent heard Ball reply his obedience and was pleased himself, the order was exactly his own choice. He went below, found Fentiman and Sanders sat where their cabins normally were and invited them into his. His manner was forthright and urgent.

"We track him through the night, as we are. With the approach of dawn we get over the horizon as we did yesterday and watch him from there, no upper sails, and the same number of lookouts. We'll get West of him, then he will have the dawn behind him, us still in the dark and on bare topmasts we can see him whilst he can't see us. With the dawn he'll want to see clear ocean, and we'll give that to him. Then we'll work East and through the day we track him and make our preparations for an attack just before dawn the next night; we darken our sails and paint out the gunports. Any thoughts?"

Sanders spoke.

"Sir. We'll be trying to do tomorrow night, what we failed to do tonight."

"Yes, Mr. Sanders. But tomorrow, we can move up to him that much earlier. He'll be in the sunset. Any further thoughts?

Both shook their heads. Argent wrestled in his head with the idea of attacking with the arrival of the night and removing the risk of losing them in the dark, but he reluctantly rejected the thought. As common with Arab tribes, or so he reasoned, they would be entertaining themselves well into the night and be fully awake, wide awake at sunset. To take no chances it would have to be just before dawn.

"We attack tomorrow night. I want to come out of the dark, and with a darkened ship. Like that we can sit in his wake, follow and wait. The attack is just before the very break of dawn, when it's still dark, and I'm betting the whole murdering gang of them will still be snoring. So, preparations. Have we paint for the gunports?"

Fentiman answered.

"Yes Sir."
"Where do we find something to dye our sails black?"
"I think I know just the place, Sir."

* * *

They held the light off their larboard beam until their pocket-watches told them that dawn was but one hour away. The wind still held from the South East and so Ariadne reduced sail, wore around astern of the galley and headed North West for the horizon to diverge from her quarry. As they slipped silently behind the slaver, ringing no bells, the light moved across their bows, but remained bright, then disappeared; too far back in its recess Argent decided. After an hour's slow sailing North West, came the first streaks of dawn and, so McArdle calculated, they were just on the slaver's horizon. They heaved to, used the driver to turn full West and waited, stern on to the galley. With the growing light, the lookouts, again with their telescopes and perched on the bare topmasts and royal spars, found that they could see the slaver far out in the growing dawn light on the horizon. The mizzen lookout reported.

"He's heaved to, and turning."

Sanders climbed to the mizzentop.

"What course?"

"Can't see yet, Sir. What's our head, Sir?"

"West."

The lookout took a careful look.

"He's moving, Sir. I'd say back on Sou'west, Sir. Or near."

"Well done, Digby. Now keep a careful watch. We need to know where he is and what he does."

"Aye aye, Sir. We'll get him now Sir?"

"Well, I'd put more money on us than I would on him."

"Good enough for me, Sir."

The day began. Using her driver to turn further, Ariadne gained a perfect larboard quarter wind and, with no sail above topsails, half the mast remaining bare, she tracked the galley, now definitely moving Southwest, from just over the horizon, far off his starboard quarter. Paint arrived from the hold and the task began of painting out the yellow gunports. Dying the sails was much more of a problem, but Fentiman applied his good idea. An hour later, Bible Mortimor went to his grateblacking store and, instead of finding tins of blacking for his domestic requirements, he found a note. "Sequestered, by orders of the Captain."

He pointed to the empty locker for the benefit of Johnson and Jeremiah.

"Thou knowest the people, that they are set on mischief. Exodus 32, verse 22."

It was a long job to darken the sails. The largest barrel they had was raised from the hold and filled with water, this stained black, then each sail was unbent and lowered. The first came out too black, they could afford to thin it down and conserve their tins of blacking, many for Mortimor, but too few to colour almost a full set of sails, and so it went on. The biggest problems were the huge driver and the main topsail, but they would be needed if Ariadne was to overtake at maximum speed and cut off the slaver. Whilst Fraser and his mates looked anxiously at the diminishing pile of tins of grate blacking, Argent looked anxiously at the pennant that spoke of the wind. It was strong but seemed to be veering South. Too far and the course to overtake the slaver would be too far beyond any point of sailing, but, as it was, all was still possible.

The sun was westering, Noon was now three hours gone. He felt exhausted and knew he needed rest, it would be a long night with a fight at the end of it, so he decided to get some of the sleep he craved, but first to the foretop to check on their quarry. He climbed on up to the highest crosstrees where this time he found Silas Beddows, cradling Argent's own telescope. Beddows paid his respects as Argent joined him.

"No change Sir. You can see his sails, but not his hull."

Beddows handed over the telescope and pointed. He had been given a compass and he took a reading. Argent opened the telescope.

"Where away?"

"He's due South, Sir, near as. Four points off our larboard bow. Standing out plain."

Argent ran the lens along the horizon and easily made out the three dark red lateen sails against the pale blue of the horizon. His ship had been conned perfectly, steered left or right to keep the slaver way out, where he could be seen, but Ariadne could not, with her bare topmasts, invisible to any lookouts the slaver had in place.

"Has he altered course much?"

"Not a point, Sir. He's hellbent for his home port."

"Hell perhaps, Beddows, but not his home port."

Beddows grinned.

"I'll pass that onto the lads, Sir."

"Do that Beddows, with my compliments."

Back on deck, where he thought he was now finished with the ship, the ship was not finished with him. Fraser stood in his path and made his respects.

"Beg pardon Sir, but this dyeing. We've done everything below topgallants, Sir, but there's three sets left and only enough black for two. That's' topgallants, or royals, or main and fore staysails, Sir."

Argent thought. They would almost certainly need fore and aft sails. Royals were the smallest.

"Topgallants and staysails, then, Mr. Fraser. That should do it."

Argent looked up at the sails already coloured, with the mizzentopsail now being bent back onto its spar, albeit damp, but in its place it would dry. Grey water had dripped all over Fraser's precious deck.

"A fine job, Mr. Fraser. Once out of The Service I feel that there is a ready trade waiting for you."

"Right Sir. If you thinks so, but this b'ain't summat I feels I wants to get overly used to."

He held up his arms. Black to the elbows and then white to his shoulders. Argent grinned.

"No, Mr. Fraser. I can see that would turn you into something of a high street curiosity."

Fraser mumbled something of his own and took himself back to his barrel, shouting his orders for the last sets of sails. Argent made a last visit to the quarterdeck and found Fentiman.

"Time to get East of him."

"Aye aye, Sir."

Argent went straight to his cabin, giving the sentry strict orders that he was to be woken at four bells of the Second Dog Watch, at which time the sun would be touching the horizon to end the day.

* * *

He was woken by Mortimor, carrying a pot of coffee and Johnson with a plate of rolls. On this occasion Mortimor viewed his Captain from a face distinctly kindly and Argent could himself see the change, which almost bordered on sympathy and kinship. He swung his legs off his cot, still wearing his breeches.

"Where's the slaver?"

"Still there, Sir. We've held him close. This night we are in the service of The Lord, his instrument upon this earth."

"That's not a quote. Mortimor."

"No, Sir. One of may own."

"Well, Amen to it, Mortimor, all the same. Let's hope so."

"Aye aye, Sir. Shall not the Judge of all the earth do right? Genesis 18, verse 15."

Argent sipped the scalding coffee and bit into a roll, but he could not contain himself there in his cabin. He donned his coat, took the pot, the cup and a pocketful of rolls up to the quarterdeck and as he passed the guncrews he ordered his cabin to the taken to the hold. On the quarterdeck he found all his Officers, now refreshed as he himself. Most of those not required on Watch had also gained some rest, but with their cabins in the hold, they had slept amongst the men on the Lower Deck. Argent approached Fentiman.

"Where is he?"

Fentiman smiled.

"Off our starboard bow, Sir. From us bearing West Sou' west."

Argent nodded, satisfied. Fentiman had carried out his duties perfectly. Throughout the remainder of the afternoon and into the evening, Ariadne had eased around, Eastwards, moving behind the slaver, to now place him out on the Western horizon. However, despite their perfect position, still Argent could not eat, not yet. He placed his "breakfast" beside the binnacle and took himself forward to climb to the foremast crosstrees, where he found his Cox'n, Gabriel Whiting, who knew exactly why his Captain was there.

"He's out there Sir. Easy to see him now, Sir."

Argent took the proferred telescope and tracked the horizon. Whiting was right. Far out, on the horizon, the slaver was silhouetted perfectly in the yellow sky of the setting sun. Whiting felt able to ask of his Captain a question that many of Argent's rank would have found impudent.

"What do we do now, Sir?"

Argent didn't lower the glass.

"We track across in the dark and get into his wake. We follow until almost the end of night, by then they'll be closed down."

Argent closed the glass with a snap and Whiting could see the ferocity in the face that looked directly at him.

"Then he's ours!"

Argent returned to the quarterdeck in a more settled state of mind and finished his rolls and coffee. Seeing his Captain in more hospitable mode, Trenchard felt able to approach. He was worried about their role of throwing live shrapnel off the foretop in the pitched dark, which he had learnt from his First was still their role in the coming conflict.

"Sir, begging your pardon, Sir."

Argent looked down on him, chewing the while.

"Sir. When the attack starts, Sir. Would it be possible for us to have a lantern up in the foretop, to give us some light, Sir, when we have to touch the match to the fuses?"

Argent looked at Fentiman, who nodded, then back at Trenchard.

"Yes. But only when we are right up alongside him and your light makes no difference. Am I clear?'

However, as Trenchard saluted, Wentworth stepped up.

"S-sir. He may have a g-good p-point, Sir. S-suh-some lanterns from our starboard yar-yardarms, hanging over him would hel-help a lot, Sir."

Wentworth gulped more breath to continue.

"Th-the lanterns could be waiting on our g-gangway, unlit, then, at the ri-right time, lit and hoisted up to gi-give us s-suh-some light for the g-g-gunners and our b-boarding, Sir."

All had listened to the tortured suggestion and all smiled at the effort. Argent clapped Wentworth on the shoulder.

"Your thinking, Mr. Wentworth, is your best feature. I put you in charge."

Wentworth managed the next part perfectly.

"Aye aye, Sir."

Sanders spoke next; he had a suggestion of his own.

"Sir. We don't notice it day to day, but a sailing ship makes a powerful amount of noise. If we are to follow him close and sail up undetected, doing something to reduce that must be a good thing. To apply more frapping, slush and wadding in the right places would at least reduce some of the sounds our rigging can make."

Argent nodded and grinned openly.

"It does me good to know that, this evening, my Officers are at the very top of their profession. See Mr. Fraser and tell him of your suggestion."

Sanders descended to the gundeck and found Fraser, who sent for the Captains of the three Tops and soon members of each were on their way with their buckets to Mortimor, demanding a portion of his precious "slush". This placed him in not the best of moods. Normally this request came once a week, one request, now there were six, each with a bucket and making it clear that they would soon be returning for more.

"All I've got, is what I has, in there."

He pointed to the barrel. Moses King lifted the lid and dipped in his bucket. Mortimor's face grew even more dismal.

"Exact no more than that which is appointed you. Luke 3, verse 13."

"Shuddup, you miserable old bugger. When 'tis gone, then there's no more, an' that's the end of it."

Mortimor fixed him with a Gorgonlike stare, but, despite his deepest disapproval, each took themselves away with a full bucket. The topmen knew their task and within an hour the natural noise of the ship was much reduced, but still loud to those who listened, but all was being achieved that could be. Meanwhile Argent was in the foretop, calling down to ease his ship over to starboard in the direction of the slaver that could still be seen, he was always cautious, but content, that the slaver, when swallowed by the final dark, was always West of them. Soon it was just a question of judgment and a compass bearing and he ordered the forecourse to be reefed when he felt that Ariadne was, perhaps, too close. Now it was a question of picking up his wake, or the sound of him, and that came first. It sounded like an argument and the sound of whips, then the rumble of oars in their ports. It seemed almost abeam to starboard and Argent ordered "Up helm" to swing them to larboard and gain more room, then he ordered the maintopsail to be furled for them to drop back.

The wind had veered slightly towards the South but, with staysails, Ariadne was drawing well on the larboard tack and had more to give.

Argent ordered "Down helm", and she swung gently over to starboard to resume the search for the wake. A crowd of lookouts on the bowsprit and on the heads strained their eyes through the dark to pick up signs of the passing of a hull propelled by oars and soon they saw the phosphorescence of a ship's wake and, besides that, a ribbon of foam each side from the passage of oars. Argent remained on the foretop. He could now see the wake himself and, by its intensity, he judged them to be half a cable, probably just over, but not the full 200 yards. Content that his ship sat squarely within the disturbance left either side by the oars, Argent looked ahead. It was a clear night, the moon low in the West, merely a few clouds hid the stars and there was no mist. He wasn't sure, but he thought he could see something. He turned to Whiting, there leaning on the nets full of shrapnel shells, although he could barely see him.

"Whiting. Look dead ahead. Can you make out five square shapes, something like his stern windows, perhaps?"

Whiting raised himself and leaned forward using the mast as support. He stared for some seconds, then spoke.

"I'd say so, Sir. Yes. There's something there, an' 'tis dead ahead, an' in line with his wake. I'd say his window curtains b'ain't as thick as they should be. Or he's got a bonfire in his cabin."

Both smiled in the dark and both looked for some time, but the shapes did not move, nor grow any more, nor any less distinct. They were holding their position and, more important, holding their distance.

"Right. That's our guide. Expect Lieutenant Fentiman. If there's any change between now and when he arrives, tell him. I want that held, fixed right on our head."

"Aye aye, Sir."

Subconciously, in the dark, Whiting paid his respects and soon Fentiman arrived and Whiting reported no change. Ariadne was set and locked on, biding her time.

* * *

From his place on the quarterdeck Argent spoke to Sanders and Wentworth.

"Go forward. Quietly pass the word, "To quarters" and then you both remain at your posts."

Each moved off and soon Argent saw the result, topmen mustering on the starboard gangways and the carronade crews manning their guns. He looked East, was the sky less dark, now grey and growing lighter? Was that a faint line showing the first light on the Eastern horizon? He could not see the pennant to gauge the wind, he could but move to the weather side and feel it on his face. Still a good breeze and still on the beam, a little more astern would be her best point of sailing, but this was well good enough. His pocket watch showed near sunrise, it must soon be time, delaying any longer would gain them nothing, perhaps they would be waking up. He walked forward and climbed to the foretop, there he found Fentiman and Whiting, still in position.

"Any change."

Fentiman answered, in a whisper.

"No, Sir. There's his cabin lights, still up ahead, Sir."

Argent leaned out on the shrouds and saw for himself the five dull rectangles just showing through the gloom. He descended to the forecastle for his final check and found Henry Ball.

"Are we still in her wake?"

"Yes Sir. It's going right under our forefoot."

"Where's Bosun Fraser?"

A voice came from the dark behind him.

"Here Sir."

"Right. Get your topmen onto the yards and your waisters ready. They understand the signal?"

"Yes Sir, they do."

Meanwhile Sanders and Wentworth were discussing their coming role. It was Sanders who had broached the subject.

"Have you ever boarded a ship on the end of a rope before?"

"N-no. C-can't say as I h-have."

"I was a topman, once. I know all about swinging around on ropes, but to board a ship? What's the best way, do you think?"

"Well, I've only seen il-lil-lustrations, but as I recall, the b-b-best way is t-to h-hang on with your le-left arm and have a pistol in your ri-right. Then you c-can sh-shoot the first to come at you, and throw the p-pistol at the next. Then you land."

"That's why you brought up a rack of pistols."

"Y-yes."

"The Captain was quite right about your thinking. But would it not be a good idea to have another in your waist band?"

"It wou-would, but I'm of the v-v-view that they shou-should be shared out, and we all take our ch-chances."

In the dark Sanders nodded.

"Well, I've got a brace. I took them off a prize, they're French. I'd be proud to offer you one."

"Thank you. Th-that's very k-kind."

Wentworth took the handle, checked that the hammer was down and stuck it into his waistband. Their men had stood silent, listening to all that had been said. Then the pistols were shared out and each checked theirs, after that each checked that their cutlass came easily out of the sling around their waist. Each stood still and silent, each with their own thoughts. Then came the order, not shouted, merely spoken.

"Let fall."

They heard the canvas fall on the foremast, then its writhing and snapping until the waisters ran past them to sheet home. This was the signal for all other canvas back from the foremast to the mizzen to be dropped and secured. Inside two minutes Ariadne was under a full press of canvas from topgallants down, lower staysails included. The waisters and forecastlemen worked furiously to trim the yards to fully catch the wind. Ariadne heeled and accelerated under their feet, immediately about her business.

Yusef Bin Yusef was dozing on the quarterdeck, leaning over the side, facing larboard, across the black sea, but seeing little, his head lolling as he drifted in and out of a shallow sleep. A shout from the oar deck brought him back to wakefulness and he looked down at the barely discernable straining arms and chests of the oarsmen at their turn, but there he saw nothing untoward. Now awake, he looked out over the sea; he was, after all, on Watch, but all on board felt confident that they had lost the warship of two days ago, sacrificing that child had been worth the loss. He began chewing some khat leaves and his thoughts drifted, but then he looked again. There was an odd shaped wave off their larboard quarter, gaining on them, and standing out white in the starlight. It wasn't part of their wake and it had come up past that point anyway, but then, the unmistakable shape of a bowsprit rose into the grey of the horizon and then a ship's bows came clear and then a tower of canvas above that. He paused before shouting a warning, it didn't look like the warship, the hull was all black and all sails dark. He paused to look again. She was moving at twice their speed, rapidly up their larboard side, her bows already almost level with their stern, what he had first seen was her bowave. His eyes widened in terror and his mouth dropped open, the khat leaves falling to the dark ocean, for even in the dark he could see the unmistakable shape of a muzzle protruding through her entryport. He began to run forward, taking a breath to shout, but the words died in his throat as a grapeshot from "The Preacher" on the quarterdeck took off the top of his head.

All four carronades had fired, as ordered, as soon as a target presented itself. At the horrifying sound the galley oarsmen dropped their oars and rose with their weapons in their hands and scrambled up the ladders to the upper deck. The alarm passed on through the galley and, soon after, the sleeping watch was emerging from their quarters below, these too fully armed. The galley's crew had responded quickly to the need to defend their ship, now slowing with the oars now unmanned, but time had been lost and more time still would be needed to organize a solid defence.

Argent and Fentiman stood on the forecastle, their men behind them, waiting for Short to judge his turn and send the ship against the bows of the slaver, the smoke from the carronades running away downwind into the gloom. Astern from them at the mid-point of the gangway, Sanders and Wentworth stood with their men, holding the ropes that they would soon use to pull themselves up onto the rail of the gunwale before swinging over. Wentworth looked at the shining black of the slaver's hull, defined more by the foam passing her side, that any other form of light. A tangle of emotions competed within him; fear, anxiety about his own ability and a righteous sense of duty for what they needed to do. These emotions emerged from him as a sentence as clear as that of any Commander in history's pre-battle speech to his men. He turned to his own, gathered behind him.

"Men. Aboard that slaver are Christian women and children being shipped off to who knows what kind of Hell. I, am going to get them out of there, or die choking on her deck!"

Silence, for a long pause, a silence somehow heavy with astonishment, but then replies emerged from the dark.

"Right with you, Sir."

"Same from me, Sir."

"At your shoulder, Sir."

In the dark Wentworth nodded and took a better grip on the rope, as did Sanders and those with him.

On the forecastle Bill Marshall, Gun Captain, starboard carronade, was sighting along the short barrel, because for the second shot it had been trained right round to point aft, as much as possible, along the anticipated line of the slaver's deck. Easau Grimes was doing the same just over to his right, as his piece was heaved forward to fire again. Either side of him were Ariadne's Marines, their muskets already trained over the side. Marshall felt the deck heel to larboard as Zachary Short turned the wheel hard over, but they had both allowed for that. To their right, back along the ship, pairs of lanterns were being hoisted to shed their helpful, but paltry, light onto the deck of their enemy and, sighting along their gunbarrels, they found that they required only small, quick adjustments to make the elevation perfect. From above a spluttering shrapnel shell arced down onto the slaver's deck, Berry, the strongest, had thrown far and true to begin their assault. Ariadne's hull hit the larboard bow of the slaver with a huge crash, to be replaced by the sound of the two ships grinding together and that of splintering wood as the foremost oars were crushed between the two hulls and then came the explosion of the shrapnel shell, this to be replaced by the sound of screaming. Grapnel hooks sailed over into the slaver's rigging and the two hulls were joined.

Marshall could see down onto the slaver's deck, he knew he had to wait, but he was not required to do so for long, for the carronade at the entryport, traversed fully towards the bows, as was the carronade further back on the quarterdeck, fired a second time. Marshall saw the discharge of musket balls and grapeshot cut a swathe through the slaver's now crowded deck, bodies being flung down like discarded dolls. He checked the alignment of his own weapon, called for one final adjustment then jerked the lanyard. The smoke from the discharge hid the effect and then Easau Grimes fired his second and Ariadne's last, into the slaver. Burning shrapnel shells were now raining down from the foretop above, almost all reaching the deck of the slaver, but one hissing into the sea below.

Argent and Fentiman seized the gunwale for balance as the impact nearly threw them off their feet. Both Officers climbed onto the gunwale and looked down and across, the jump was five feet over, but a drop of three. They heard Breakspeare shout "Fire" and then the volley from the Marines crashed out. The slaver's deck was shrouded in smoke, but the gap was still visible, Argent measured it out, and gripped his sword.

"Onto him, boys. Ariadne's the shout!"

He jumped and landed with a jar to both legs, then he slipped on what can only have been blood. His men followed, yelling their ship's name, and he saw that Fentiman had landed better and remained upright. The smoke was clearing and, as he regained his feet Argent could see only the smashed bodies of dead and wounded men, writhing in agony or moving slowly as death claimed them. The carronades had cleared a space, but figures were moving further across the slaver. He felt, rather than saw, his men arriving behind and to his side.

"At them, boys. Straight at them!"

He sprang forward to be confronted by an Arab with a short boarding pike. He dodged the stab forward and smashed the metal guard into the man's face. The man fell back, but then Argent was overtaken by a tide of his own men, now supported by the Marines. Argent's own opponent was quickly bayoneted and, after a brief but brutal fight they had control of their portion of the deck, no more opponents could be seen beyond the gloom and smoke. Argent looked around and saw immediately in front a companionway leading down to a lower deck. Fentiman was at his side with Breakspeare just behind.

"Captain Breakspeare. Take your Marines to the right and fight your way aft. Support Sanders and Wentworth, but when you can, get down below, find the prisoners."

As the Marines made off , Argent spoke to his fellow sailors.

"Follow me, lads. Down here. Find the prisoners."

For their attack, Wentworth and Sanders had climbed onto the gunwale, stretched their arm up the rope as far as they could and launched themselves out. Their time in the air was fixed in their minds as a long and desperate moment and beneath they had a brief glimpse of the foam of the waves writhing between the two hulls and the tangled oars trapped at all angles. Wentworth made it to the side of the slaver and used the side rail as extra leverage to finally land squarely on the deck, after discharging his pistol at the nearest Arab and then landing in the space created by his victim falling back into the oar deck. He threw his pistol at the nearest turbaned head but failed to draw his cutlass in time to ward off the next assault, however, the maddened, raging face acquired another hole as one of the topmen following Wentworth shot the slaver in the head. Wentworth got out his cutlass just in time to block a savage swipe as they all found themselves fighting for their lives with their backs to the remains of the side rail, now with much missing from the grape shot. A slaver besides Wentworth stabbed over the rail to send an Ariadne down into the water before he arrived at the deck, but more topmen were coming and Wentworth cut the slaver across the back of his neck, almost severing the head. He saw Sanders, head now bloodied, defend himself from the assault of two, but their own numbers had grown and they were holding their gains. Suddenly, their opponents to their left melted away to be replaced by the redcoats of Ariadne's Marines, led by Breakspeare, his sword dark even in the poor light. Sanders gave the order.

"Clear this deck of the bastards. Leave none alive."

They moved rapidly aft, a vengeful tide of sailors and redcoated Marines. Soon they had the gangway cleared on both sides and they looked down into the oar deck to see near pitched dark, but there came up to them the sounds of fighting in the bows. Sanders decided to take the chance.

"Marines! Reload."

The Marines reloaded their muskets in seconds and Breakspeare took over after Sanders had explained what he wanted. Breakspeare issued his orders calmly.

"Form at the rail."

The Marines lined up along the gangway rail to look down into the darkness of the oar deck below.

"Make ready"

A pause.

"Present. Into her waist, aft of her foremast."

The Marines adjusted their aim.

"Fire."

The volley went off with a deafening crash and the space was filled with smoke. As screams emerged from below, Sanders looked around and saw two companionways either side of him. He pointed left.

"On my left, get down there, with Mr. Wentworth. On my right, with me."

Blood was running into his eyes but he led his men down. Going right, they would arrive near the bows, at whatever fighting was going on. At the bottom of the companionway lay the results of the Marines volley and any wounded were trampled down as Sanders and his men leapt from the stairs of the companionway. The fighting that ensued was of the worst kind. In the dark and the smoke they fought their way forward, the Marines forming a line of bristling bayonets to fight their way up to the bows, battling their way across the benches and discarded oars, whilst the seamen fought off assailants from behind. Wentworth had gone left and found his task easier, there was less smoke, but it was Hellish enough, fighting in the dark over the oars and benches there. However, they were drawing off enemies from the backs of Sanders men, but assailed on all sides themselves.

The slaver crew were making their do or die stand amongst the tangle of the oar deck. Argent and Fentiman had led their men down their companionway, but got no further than the last steps. In the almost negligible light of the lanterns above, what they saw was a sea of desperate faces and raised scimitars, but they nevertheless began the fight by slashing down and kicking forward. Some of his men jumped sideways off the companionway to land deliberately onto the chests and faces of their opponents and, inevitably, some of these Ariadnies perished in such close quarter fighting, but others followed to continue the appalling conflict. It was the experience of a nightmare, a matter of chance, with nothing to stand on but the dead, dying, and the wounded, all lying over benches, or the deck underneath, with a treacherous oar handle waiting to trip those trying to fight between them.

Gradually they fought their way off the steps and away, to secure some space on the walkway between the oarsmen's benches. In the smoke and gloom, as desperate as the slaver crew, Argent and his men battered their way aft. A turbaned figure emerged before him, swinging his scimitar at Argent's left arm, but Jacob Pierce was at his side and he blocked the swing with his own cutlass. Argent punched forward with the bellguard and the man fell back to roll unconscious under a bench. Argent raised his sword for the next blow that may come from the gloom and smoke before him, but he stopped. What did come next was a bayonet on the end of a musket, followed by a Marine. Argent pushed the bayonet to one side, just in case, but, fantastically, the Marine saw that he was faced by his Captain and presented arms! Argent saluted him back.

The sounds of the fighting were dying down, but the oardeck was thick with bodies. It was impossible to walk on planking and, in the dark, all stood on whatever seemed firm. The walkway was theirs, but screams and shouts still came out of the darkness, because off to the sides of the wide hull, the last of the crew were being either captured or their lives ended. Finding himself in the middle of the vessel, Argent thought of their next move from where he was stood.

"Sanders! Wentworth!"

Replies came through the gloom.

"Take your men aft. Search this level, then get deeper down and search there. Find the prisoners."

"Aye aye, Sir", came back through the dark.

"Mr. Fentiman. The same, take some men and go forward."

Then, mercifully lanterns were lowered down to them. The topmen, remaining on Ariadne, had seen the need and lowered them to the slaver's deck and now they were being passed further on down to the oardeck. In the yellow light a Marine shouted to Argent.

"There's a way down here, Sir."

The Marine held his lantern up to show a low set of railings, surrounding a companionway down.

"Let me through."

Argent made a way to the railings, as best he could, and he led the way down, his sword first, the seaman's hand holding up the lantern second. They descended to what was clearly the hold, barrels and crates were to either side. Argent looked forward to see lanterns bobbing through the gloom at the bows, which he took to be Fentiman. He looked aft and saw nothing, when he should be seeing the lights of Sanders and Wentworth if there was a clear run back to the stern. He directed the seaman to follow him as he edged astern and soon they heard a terrified, unintelligible gibbering from just ahead. Taking the lantern forward revealed a cowering Arab, on his knees, supplicating with both hands raised towards the advancing foreigners. He was kneeling on a walkway, before a solid bulkhead of timber, the walkway leading to a door in the same. The jibbering increased in volume and rose to a wail as the point of Argent's sword approached his chest. Argent seized the cloth of his tunic and shouted.

"English?"

The result was more wailing, more supplication, and the shaking of his head. Argent pulled him out of the way and examined the bulkhead to each side, then the door. The bulkhead stretched across the full width of the hold and the door had a large keyhole above a large handle.

"I'd say this was it. But even if it isn't, we go in here anyway. Bring him up."

The Arab was pushed forward, more calm, now that it was clear to him that he was not going to be immediately and summarily done to death. Argent placed his hand at the keyhole and began to turn an imaginary key, whilst looking at the Arab. The result was an exhibition of deep distress at his only being able to disappoint his captors, so he was pulled back again and kicked to one side. Argent looked again at the door, it was very solid, too solid for musket butts.

"Find something to smash in this door. There must be something."

The result was all lanterns being raised to examine the contents of the hold. Argent was relieved to hear what came soon.

"There's some kind of spar here, Sir. It's long but if we all get on it and it's rigged, too, with plenty of rope."

"Perfect, get it up here."

Weapons and muskets were laid aside as the lateen spar, long and unwieldy, was lined up with the door, but, once in place, many hands were able to take hold of the attached rigging and every muscle was then applied to drive it forward. The door splintered at the lock after the third blow and swung back. A foul stench emerged, but what came next amazed them all.

"Who's that, who's there?"

This from a female voice with a profound Southern Irish accent, but Argent answered.

"We are the crew of His Majesty's Ship Ariadne, ma'am, and I am Captain Argent. We have captured this ship and intend to take you off."

There was no clear response, but, nevertheless, sounds of some kind were heard, seemingly gasps and sobs. Also some French reached him, "Nous sommes secourus par la Marine Anglaise." Even Argent didn't need that translated, but then came the very Irish reply.

"I'm sure we're wholly grateful, Captain Argent, but if any one of youse comes in here, you're surely going to get a fist in the mouth. There's not one of us with a stitch on!"

Argent looked back at his men, all now grinning.

"Get some clothes down here. Strip the dead, but include none too bloody. And search down here as well, the clothes they were captured in must be somewhere aboard."

Somehow Midshipman Bright had appeared.

"Bright, I'm leaving you in charge. You examine whatever is passed in and it must be at least vaguely wholesome."

Argent returned to the gap of the open door.

"We hear you, ma'am, and we are going to find you some clothes, which we will pass in as soon as we find them, but they may be the clothing of dead sailors. I'm sorry."

He reached back and took a lantern, then continued, speaking at the door edge.

"We're passing in a lantern or two. Please be patient, we will do our best. You are safe now, under the protection of the Royal Navy."

He slid the lantern around the door and the smell hit his nostrils as the lantern was seized by a female hand and taken away. He turned to those behind him.

"Two more."

Carrying these he returned to the door edge and pushed them through. Then came the next thought.

"Ma'am, would you like some buckets of water? Perhaps you'd care to wash before you come out?"

A pause, then the same Irish voice, equally aggressive.

"I'll take that as a concerned and helpful suggestion, Captain, rather than some sort of unkind and pointed comment. We would like a wash, yes, and I'll say thank you."

Argent nodded and looked again at Bright.

"See to it, and be patient. This will take some time, and, in any case, I do not want them to come out until we have cleared the decks above of bodies and parts of. So, await orders. Clear?"

"Aye aye, Sir."

Argent raised his voice to the men waiting.

"Above. We've work to do."

However, the female Irish voice had not finished.

"So, that's you, Captain Argent."

Argent returned to the door edge.

"Yes, ma'am."

"Captain Reuben Argent, of the frigate Ariadne, that's fast and stiff and surrenders hardly any leeway. Named after a few stars!"

"Yes to both, ma'am."

"Well, this is Sinaid Malley in here, and I'm pleased to renew your acquaintance, and we're all surely grateful that you've arrived."

The adrenalin of battle, still flowing within him, helped Argent recover from the shock.

"I'm very pleased to encounter you again, Miss Malley, but that light, shining from this hull, last night. Did you have anything to do with it?"

"Yes. It was me."

"Why am I not surprised?"

* * *

Argent picked his way back to the top deck which the growing light was revealing as a charnel house, worse than that of the oar deck below. The grapeshot had ripped bodies to pieces and unidentifiable body parts were strewn around, but he need give no orders. His men knew what came next and all were being unceremoniously tipped over the side, save the bodies of their own shipmates, which were carefully laid out. Soon the bodies from below were brought up and followed over into the reddening sea. Argent took stock of what they had, she was wide, but lightly built with three stubby masts carrying the big lateen sails whose spars jutted far above the mast tops. Some Officer, probably Fraser, had rigged a gangplank between the two hulls, both now being well secured together and his own wounded were being helped back on board. He observed the care that the sailors afforded their own shipmates, watching for a while, then he began to walk around the slaver's deck and at that point he felt a wound of his own, a cut on his arm, through his coat and he saw that blood had run out through the wrist. However, his mind was returning to calm after the heat of the battle, so the wound now hurt and it suddenly re-occurred to him that he was under orders not to have done this, but to get a despatch to Wellesley as soon as possible.

His absent minded tour of the slaver brought him to the quarterdeck where were grouped a mass of prisoners, 80 or more, many wounded, but all guarded by a strong line of Marines, with a pile of weapons heaped behind them. Argent thought that the slaver's crew must have been almost the equal of their own and was grateful for the work of the carronades, even though the result was too stomach churning to look upon for too long. Many of the prisoners were wounded and no one was doing much for them, but Argent felt little disturbance to his own conscience. His own wounded came first and he knew that he was now stood at the very rail where the child had been murdered, pushed off to perish in the wide, cold sea. Nevertheless, someone, perhaps more Christian than he, was bringing buckets of water for the prisoners at least to wash their wounds and then make some repair. He came up to a Marine Sergeant, and found him to be Ackroyd.

"Do we know which is the Captain?"

The Sergeant saluted.

"No Sir. We've no idea, Sir. He may not even be alive."

Argent nodded, but Ackroyd continued.

"There's one problem, Sir. We found eight chained to their oars, Sir. Two of them claim to be English, taken off a merchantman. Another says he's a Yankee!"

Argent nodded again.

"Which?"

The Sergeant pointed and Argent was able to quickly identify the eight, still with manacles around their wrists. Two noticed Argent and stood.

"Sir, sir, your honour, Sir, we're English, Sir. Captured by these Heathen Devils off the William Johns, Sir, an Indiaman. We'll sign on, Sir. We're English."

Argent fixed them with a look of scorn.

"Sit down and wait. We'll discover soon enough your role aboard this ship. Now hold your peace."

The two sat down on the deck, glum and miserable, then Argent continued around the deck, pleased that his men had set to cleaning and swabbing away the worst of the blood. He took himself down below again, back to where Bright still stood at the shattered door, now joined by Trenchard. Piles of arab seaman's clothes were arriving and being passed in by Trenchard, who had given himself the duty. Everything that was being offered was being taken back behind the door. He walked up to it and knocked.

"Miss Malley. Anyone."

A voice answered that was not Irish, but Cornish.

"Yes."

"This is Captain Argent. How long do you think you will be? We must be quickly on our way."

"Not long, Captain. We're all washed and soon all will be dressed."

A pause.

"Captain."

"Yes, ma'am."

"I'm from Ruanporth. I'm Jane Worleggen. My two children were taken with me. Are you an Argent from Lanbe Barton?"

"Yes, ma'am."

"My brother married one of your sisters. He's called Beryan Trethewey. If you are Reuben, I can remember you both playing together."

Emotion welled up inside Argent almost to the point where he could not speak. He choked out the words as best he could.

"I left Beryan very well and, ... he was worried for you. But you should worry no longer, we are going to get you home."

"Thank you, Captain, and we'll all be out soon."

Argent was grateful for the dark as he wiped away a tear and swallowed hard. He turned to the dim shapes of Bright and Trenchard.

"When they come out, bring them straight up."

"Aye, aye, Sir."

"And well done, well done to all three of you. I'm proud of you. Pass that on, will you, to Berry?"

Trenchard answered.

"We will, Sir, and thank you, Sir."

They both saluted in the dark.

Argent regained the top deck, now washed to a faint pink. He looked over the side. The wind was moving both ships across the sea together and a trail of reddened water stretched out behind them. Some kind of sea creatures were active there, disturbing the surface.

Ideas were forming in his head, not least the wish to be on his way again well before Noon. He looked for an Officer and found two, Fentiman and Wentworth, talking together.

"Where's Sanders?"

Fentiman answered.

"Back aboard, Sir. He was wounded; a cut to his head and another to his arm. Neither is severe, but they need stitching."

Argent nodded, then began on his own business.

"Get every spare man from Ariadne over and onto this; I want his sails off him and back with us. Then search everywhere, anything of any value take back on board, including the weapons back there. We'll let the prisoners take their pick of it all, which is small recompense for what they've been through, but something better than nothing. I want to be shot of this and away."

Fentiman was surprised.

"You'll not send this back as a prize, Sir?"

"No. She's no kind of ship that's of any use back home, Navy or Merchant, and we cannot spare a prize crew. A fast passage to where we should be now, gets priority. What's our butcher's bill, by the way?"

"As a know of at this moment, eight dead and ten wounded, two seriously."

Argent nodded and looked at the shrouded shapes, eight, as Fentiman had said, waiting to be carried back to their ship. But Fentiman could not contain his own concern and he pointed aft.

"But what of those, Sir? We have over eighty prisoners."

Argent began walking away, but replied over his shoulder.

"Did I not say, "shot of and away".

Wentworth and Fentiman exchanged horrified looks, but took themselves back to their ship to find seamen to carry out their Captain's orders.

The women and children did not arrive up on deck as promised and so, in the interim, the Ariadnies searched the galley from top to bottom, taking back to their ship any item that could possibly have any value, where it was then stored between the masts on the gundeck. By Fentiman's orders, Gabriel Whiting and his fellow topmen found themselves over on board the slaver when the women and children did finally emerge up onto the oar deck. All eyes turned to them, all wearing outsize Arab seaman's clothing, but Whiting's blood turned cold when he looked at the children, one especially that was running towards him. He fell to his knees and caught the child, she was the girl that he had fed back at Kilannan and he wept himself as she clung to his neck. Through the tears he could see other children that he recognised and his voice quivered with emotion.

"Oh lads, what's to do?"

As he stroked the girl's head, he saw Sinaid Malley. He looked at her.

"Ma'am. The child they murdered?"

"Her brother."

"What about her Mother, ma'am?"

"They didn't take her. I think she's still alive, back in the village."

He muttered a curse under his breath then raised himself up with the child still in his arms. Other crewmen were stood near and he gave an order.

"Get these off, off this. Too soon'll not be soon enough."

Each small child was picked up by a seaman and carried to the top deck and then to the gangway. All was well until the girl that Able Jones was carrying was brought up into the sunlight, when at that moment she started screaming. Jones could do nothing to comfort her and she struggled even when Sinaid Malley took her from him and whispered soothingly in words of Gaelic. Her struggles were so violent they had no choice but to tie her arms to her side and also her legs before she could be carried over the perilous gangplank. Jones, now with no child and Whiting still carrying his, looked at Sinaid, their lack of understanding clear on their faces. Then she spoke.

"She was one of those they took and bound. They took away five and brought back four and she hasn't said a word since they brought her back. She's been wholly silent until now, I'd guess it was when she saw the sea again."

Jones had no jacket, but Sam Morris took off his and wrapped it around the girl's head so that she would not know where she was going. This calmed her and perhaps, also, did their soothing words. Wentworth had seen all and he was as moved by it as anyone.

"Take her st-straight t-t-to the si-sickbay. To Mr. Smallpiece."

Able Jones again raised up the child and stepped onto the gangplank, all the while talking soothingly, but he was thinking, "not Smallpiece, Mrs. McArdle."

Silas Beddows had no burden, but his anger was in full spate. He looked at the prisoners still squatting at the stern and raised his fist and screamed obscenities at them. He made to run back to them, violence in his eyes, but the giants King and Fenwick stopped him and their own pats on his shoulders and soothing words calmed him. However, this did nothing for the tension now growing amongst the slaver prisoners, who had seen everything, which had added hugely to their own fears.

Argent was examining the Captain's cabin, when he heard the commotion above, but he relaxed as the noise subsided. From the cabin everything moveable had been cleared, but all the papers were in Arabic script and so they remained, scattered about. He decided that all aboard the slaver was done, bar one thing; the Captain and the eight chained oarsmen. He took himself onto the top deck and saw, for the first time, Sinaid Malley. She was pale, her face still dirt-streaked and her lustrous hair hung in rats' tails, but this did nothing to diminish her self-assurance. On seeing Argent, she stood straight and tall, with her arms on her hips and her bare feet comfortably apart, the voluminous Arabian clothes seemed to suit her. Her knowing smile had not changed, nor the coquettish angle of her head.

"Captain Argent."

Argent came to the attention and bowed. As usual he fell back onto the comfort of formality.

"Miss Malley. I did not expect that we would meet again, certainly not in such circumstances."

"No indeed, Captain, but it pleases me, all the same, for all kinds of reasons. As you can imagine."

Her eyes flashed straight into his. Argent cleared his throat.

"Can you identify the Captain for us? Is he one of the prisoners? If not, then, obviously, he must be dead."

"I can't, but there's one who can. She and her child were taken to spend many hours with him and they came back sobbing, every time."

Argent gave no reaction and held his silence at the implication. He knew exactly what she was conveying.

"Is she still here, or on board Ariadne, do you know?"

Sinaid looked around at the line of captives filing up and onto the gangplank and by good chance, a pale, dishevelled, woman, with light brown hair, came up the companionway and Sinaid pointed.

"This one. Her name's Bridie Mather. She's Irish and speaks no English."

Argent took a deep breath.

"Please ask Mrs. Mather if she can come with us to identify the Captain, back there."

He inclined his head to the group of prisoners. Sinaid gently placed her hand on the woman's shoulder and her and her two children stopped. Sinaid spoke the Gaelic and the woman nodded, but her face grew fearful. Argent saw this and he looked at King and Fenwick.

"Come with me. Keep close to Mrs. Mather, as if a guard."

He turned back to Sinaid.

"Miss Malley. If you would care for the children a while."

Sinaid bent down and put an arm around both, as the four left her and walked back along the galley's topdeck to the prisoners. Argent looked at Mrs. Mather and smiled encouragingly as did the two huge seamen beside her. She seemed comforted and walked back to the first line of prisoners, stopping there to examine all in front and then those beyond. Many dropped their heads as she looked across them all, then her face changed to one of rage and fury and, before anyone could stop her, she had leapt amidst the prisoners to tear at the head and face of one sat close to the back and near the siderail. She had been too quick for King and Fenwick, but they recovered and pulled her off. They released her, and then seized the man she had attacked, but she, now free, renewed her assault. Fenwick hauled the man to his feet, whilst King restrained the berserk Mrs. Mather. Argent had seen enough.

"Bring him. Take him back aboard and put him in irons."

Fenwick hauled the man out of the group and both were just passing Argent, when Argent held up his hand. Fenwick knew exactly what his Captain wanted and he held Kalil Al'Ahbim in front of him. Argent looked into the face before him with all the hatred and contempt he could muster and he recognised the man on the slaver's quarterdeck who had ordered the children to be brought back to the rail. The Tunisian slaver looked straight back and upwards, with all of the same depth of hatred, staring back from a face lean and cruel, somehow all the more so for the carefully trimmed beard and moustache, and the fierce black eyes. Argent inclined his head and Fenwick dragged the Arab off. Mrs. Mather was now in tears and being comforted by the muscular arm of Moses King, but she freed herself, quickly returned to her children and each comforted the other. Argent looked over the prisoners and thought, "Was it one of you that pushed that child off this very deck?", but the thought was interrupted by the two manacled "Englishmen".

"Your Honour. What about us, and these other six? We was galley slaves. Chained to an oar. What about us?"

The fact that they showed concern for their fellows, also in chains, moved Argent just enough. He turned to the Marine Sergeant Ackroyd.

"Get those eight out and back aboard and remove their chains. There's just enough about them to justify at least hearing their story."

As the eight were extracted, Argent heard the same wailing that he had heard at the door of the prison and he looked to see the same man squatting on the decking, but he did nothing and turned away. However, Sinaid Malley was waiting and stopped him.

"That man, the one making all the fuss. He's called Kaled, and he's the only one that showed us any sort of kindness. Doing his best to keep us fed and clean. He doesn't deserve to be killed or sunk or executed, or whatever you have in mind."

Argent looked at her and her expression fell when she saw the anger in his face.

"He's still a slaver. He still signed on. He'd take his share of the profit from this Devil's venture."

Her face softened.

"I don't think you're right. We're pretty much sure that he's the Captain's slave. He often came in with a bleeding face, all the crew knocked him about. What's more he did take some pity on us, so please show some pity for him."

"He took pity on you to keep you spruce for the auction block!"

She took a deep breath.

"Perhaps, but, please, show some mercy, for my sake. It's what I want, so would the others."

"He'll most likely hang, back in England!"

"Yes, perhaps, but it was him as told us you were close, when they took the children. It was then that I saw the need for the light. So, for now, please."

Argent turned away, but not before nodding to the nearest Marine. Kaled was motioned forward and shoved towards the gangplank, which he needed no further bidding to quickly scamper cross.

Argent returned aboard Ariadne and found Bosun Fraser.

"Get our boats out, and then make ready to tow him off. Then find me one of the so-called Englishmen that was just brought aboard."

"One of those in chains, Sir?"

"The same."

Fraser made his reply and hurried off. Fentiman and Wentworth came up and Fentiman spoke.

"May we ask your intentions, Sir? With their vessel, I mean."

Argent looked at both, still angry, but his position as Captain took over.

"As I said, he's no use as a prize and we cannot spare a prize crew. However, I am not prepared to indulge in mass murder, however much they deserve it, but these are not getting back home to the Med, of that I'm determined, that's why I took their sails. Next, he's all wood, with no ballast. I'm going to sink him, but he'll still float and drift. He'll end up ashore somewhere, France or Spain, and they can take their chances there."

Fentiman and Wentworth looked at each other, both faces alternating between puzzlement and horror. Fentiman spoke first.

"They could drift out to sea and that would be a lingering death. Sir."

Wentworth added his thoughts.

"W-we could leave them one s-s-ail, Sir, the foresail, th-then they can set it to b-b-blow themselves to the shore whe-when the wind is fa-favourable, Sir."

Argent gave no reaction, but turned to McArdle.

"Mr. McArdle. What would you estimate as our distance from the French coast?"

"Something over 40 miles, Sir, but nae much more. I'll know for certain come the Noon Sight."

Argent nodded. Meanwhile Fraser had arrived back with one of the English galley slaves and Argent looked at him, but none too kindly.

"Do you speak their language?"

A pointing arm indicated whom Argent was referring to.

"Yes Sir. I do."

"You are to tell them to bring some food stores up from their hold to the upper deck. Tell them that they have but little time."

As the man nodded, Argent now spoke to Fraser.

"Take him over. When he has spoken, then bring him back aboard and all the Marines on guard. Then our gangplank. Oh, and give them back their foresail."

Wentworth spoke.

"Their oars, Sir. W-with those under the wa-water, dragging, it will make the s-sail useless."

Argent nodded.

"Tell them to bring their oars inboard, also."

As Fraser and the man hurried off, Argent turned to Fentiman.

"Starboard battery cleared for action, with crews at stations. Load single roundshot, supply for six rounds."

Fentiman still looked concerned as did Wentworth, but the former hurried off. Argent watched Fraser and the man, by now over on the slaver's quarterdeck. He saw him speak to the slave crew, then he hurried back, followed by the Marines. All came over the gangplank and then Fraser ordered Ariadne to detach herself. The gangplank quickly came aboard and the mooring ropes between the two were cast off. It took some 15 minutes for the boats to tow the slaver 40 odd yards downwind of Ariadne, then they also were recovered aboard.

The prisoners on the slaver's quarterdeck sat bemused as they were released and then abandoned. One stood up, then others. Soon all were running to their companionways and all disappeared, then the oars were pulled in and boxes and barrels appeared on the top gangways, to be followed by many others. Then all activity ceased as they looked to Ariadne. Her gunports were being raised and the black muzzles appeared to the rumble and screech of their guncarriage wheels, each gun making its own naked threat. Many on the slaver fell to their knees and began their prayers, others ran to the opposite ends of the ship. From all over came cries of anguish and distress.

Around number three, starboard battery, Sam Morris' guncrew hauled their weapon up to the gunport, completing the job one man short, Morris himself on a gun tackle.

"Where's that piece of shite, Main? I know for a fact he wasn't part of any gang of boarders."

It was Tom Bearman who answered.

"Time will tell, Sam. Meanwhile, there's this."

Fentiman was walking the whole length of the gundeck, speaking the same words.

"Twixt wind and water, men. Sink her, but no casualties."

Sam Morris heard it for the fifth time and called for the quoin to be eased in a fraction to lower his aim. He was perfectly on target and raised his arm. Fentiman looked along the line of guns, to see all arms raised.

"Fire!"

Sixteen lanyards were jerked and the guns roared out practically simultaneously, to then speed back inboard and slam against their breeching ropes.

"Reload. Await the next order to fire."

Argent had watched as the perfectly aimed roundshot hammered into the slaver's hull just below the oar ports, and just on the water line. As the smoke cleared the shot holes could clearly be seen, already allowing water into the hull. Argent looked along the gangway, where his topmen and the ex-prisoners were watching, none making a sound. With the smoke cleared and the guns re-laid Fentiman gave the second order to fire. The result was the same and, with the clearing of the smoke, they could see that the planking at the waterline was badly shattered and the galley had taken on a list to larboard. Those aboard the slaver had run to the far side and off to the bows and stern.

Gabriel Whiting had not watched the second discharge; instead he had descended to the gundeck and stood behind number three. He tapped Sam Morris on the shoulder as the gun was run out. Sam Morris needed only to see Whiting's face to know what he wanted and he handed him the lanyard, but he did say one thing.

"Captain's orders, Gab. Only at his waterline."

Whiting nodded and squinted along the barrel. He ordered one change to the quoin and raised his hand, then Fentiman called "Fire." His teeth were clenched as he pulled the lanyard and the gun roared and flew back in towards him.

The impact of shot for this third volley did much to restore some calm and quiet within Argent. It was the same as the previous two broadsides and the galley's deck was tilting markedly, many of the slavers were crying and waving to the Heavens; many were on their knees praying. Argent ordered cease fire after a fourth discharge; the water was above the oar ports and these were now allowing huge quantities of water into the hull. The slaver slowly settled into the water. Argent ordered the guns to be housed, then looked at the pennant above him. The wind had veered further to the South. Ariadne could come onto the larboard tack to take this as a good beam on wind and sail just South of West, it was a more Northerly course than he would have liked to make Cape Finnisterre, but the wind felt strong and his ship would not be slow. As the galley settled to show just a foot of freeboard above the water, he gave his orders for setting sail. Soon Ariadne was speeding away from the stricken galley and Argent watched the single lateen being raised to catch the wind, then he looked no more.

* * *

One and a half days later they were turning onto a Southerly course, for they had emerged from the Bay of Biscay. Ariadne rode the waves rock steady, using the stiff breeze coming over her starboard quarter, as if the ship knew the serious requirement of a firm and steady deck for what was about to unfold. Nine dead were all sewn neatly into their hammocks with three eighteen-pound balls evident as shapes at their feet; nine, for one had succumbed to his wounds. All were gathered around, not on vantage points but to form a solid and united congregation, the sailors all Divisions dressed and presented and their passengers smart enough. Their clothes had been found, bound in chests, ready for sale in Tunis.

Argent read the ceremony, slowly, sadly, and sonorously, beginning with the 23rd Psalm, followed by the whole crew singing the burial hymn. Those that they had just rescued added their voices, all accompanied incongruously but poignantly, with the ship's fiddles and squeezebox. The many French amongst those rescued stood in silent respect. After the careful telling of each name, as though this made their final mark upon this earth, each was lifted onto the bier to be covered by the Union Jack and the Marines fired a volley for each as they were slipped over the side, the boards being tilted by their tight faced messmates. Argent read the traditional Protestant Prayer for each one, the repetition adding potency rather than reducing it from over familiarity. The passage of Ariadne through the waves hid the sound of each entering the sea.

Afterwards, down in his cabin, Argent sat with his head in his hands and his thoughts in turmoil. One part of him told him unequivocally that what they had just accomplished was utterly right; on the other hand another part told him that his career was probably at an end. However, he wrote up the Log and signed it, just as Fentiman entered. He came to the desk and placed a list on Argent's desk.

"Final losses, Sir."

"What of the wounded?"

"All like to recover, given time, and Mrs. McArdle's attention."

Argent ran his eyes down the list. Alongside the top nine names was the "dd" that would be entered alongside their names in the muster: "discharged dead." However, the last name had an "r", standing for "run". It was alongside the name of Landy Main. Argent looked up at Fentiman.

"What's this "r" concerning Main?"

"We can't find him, Sir. We've searched from the bilges to the tops and he's nowhere aboard."

Argent looked up at him to hear the reply.

"He must had got himself aboard the slaver and stayed there."

Chapter Nine

Delivery

Many would say that October gave the Peninsula its best weather, but Argent cared little for the clean, swept blue, that stretched from horizon to horizon, broken but sparsely by pure white clouds that scurried on, anxious to remove their presence that they should not spoil so perfect a day. The sea also gave a benign addition to the picture; playful waves chased and fell upon each other, but none so steep as to give Ariadne any pause in her headlong passage Southwards. Argent spent hour after hour, staring at the sea, the pennant, the heel of his ship and the set of his sails. Ariadne, on the starboard tack, sped on under a vast spread of canvas, regularly logging twelve knots in the good breeze coming just aft of amidships, its steady pressure causing each sail to draw cleanly and push Ariadne quickly on, obeying her Captain's bidding. For once Argent was stood merely gazing, no more possible sail adjustments were suggesting themselves as being of any benefit and the full spars, including stunsails, even on the mizzen lee side, gave no cause for impatience over canvas not spread but, perhaps, possibly could be. Fentiman came to stand by his side. He had something to impart to his Captain, otherwise he would not have dared to join him in the sanctuary of the weather side for mere social reasons.

"Mr. McArdle estimates we will make Figueira the day after tomorrow, Sir. That'll give us a ten day passage from Falmouth. No one can complain of that."

Argent responded in kind, he knew that Fentiman was trying to cheer him, but he remained in a slough of despond. However, he did manage a small smile at the kind efforts of his First Officer.

"Ten days is a good passage, no doubt, Henry, but without the slaver it would have been eight. There's no escaping that."

He looked fully at his First Lieutenant, grateful for his understanding, but changed the subject.

"How are our passengers?"

"Oh, well enough, Sir, very much so. Indeed, as one would expect, all now in better spirits to some degree or other, but some know they've lost their men folk, and that, well, obviously..."

Fentiman let the sentence tail off as Argent nodded.

"And what of the little girl?"

"She's the worry, Sir. We cannot bring her on deck without her falling into hysteria, and she has spoken not one word. She remains permanently in the sickbay. With her, there seems to be no recovery, I fear that her mind has gone."

To add emphasis came screams of laughter from other children playing pat-a-cake games on the starboard gangway with Kaled. Argent looked at them and smiled, then at Fentiman.

"I think I'll go down and take a look."

Fentiman saluted and Argent turned for the companionway. Once down in the sickbay he found Surgeon Smallpiece and Eara McArdle tending the aftermath of the combat aboard the slaver. These included Lieutenant Sanders, because the wound on his head was not healing as well as it should, but his nursing was provided by a French girl, one of the rescued, she of much the same age as himself, perhaps a little younger. Argent passed amongst his men first, carefully asking after their wellbeing, trying to make some gesture himself, usually to give a drink of water or adjust a dressing. He found Eara McArdle preparing a potion and felt the need to cough to announce his presence. She turned and immediately fixed him with a frowning look.

"Captain! Are ye ill, in any way?"

"No, Mrs. McArdle. I have come to enquire over the little girl. I hear that there is no improvement."

Her frown deepened, she understood immediately to whom he referred.

"Nay. Nay improvement. She's over this way."

She took a candle and led the way to a small cot in the corner. The child lay there, attended by Sinead Malley, she wetting the child's lips and speaking soothing words, talking as though her Mother, smoothing the child's lank hair. She looked up at the approach of the two, but resumed speaking to the child.

"Look who's come to visit. It's the Captain."

There was no response, the catatonic stare remained, her eyes boring upwards but seeing nothing, her body rigid on the narrow bed. Sinead looked up again and shook her head. Argent knelt beside the bed and took the child's hand, kneeling close to Sinead. He saw for himself the expression of terror and the fear in the child's eyes, then he stood again to look at Eara McArdle.

"What's to be done? If you want my opinion, she's still feels herself stood on that rail, bound and helpless. What's to be done? Does she sleep?"

"Nay Captain, neither sleep nor eat, at least not much, hardly enough tae keep her alive! The Surgeon's in a dilemma, so am I."

Argent looked down at the child, showing deep concern.

"I'm no medical man, but we have to get her out of the place where she's put herself. Can you put her to sleep? For a long time. My Father always calls sleep a great healer. Is it worth a try?"

Eara McArdle looked back at him, responsive to his evident concern, but sceptical of his opinions on such a matter.

"I can, aye, for all the good it'll do, but for little more than three days, I'd say. Beyond that spells danger, if you want my opinion. She eats and drinks so little, y'see. I doubt the use, but ye're right, Captain, we have to try something."

"And whilst she's asleep, is there anything we can do that may help? When asleep she can still hear. Can we speak to her, some words of comfort or familiarity. Will that do any good?"

Sinead Malley looked at Argent in the candlelight, moved herself at this stiff Captain's deep and genuine anxiety for the welfare of a mere peasant child. She had a suggestion of her own.

"We could sing her cradle songs, lullabyes, and at the same time, tell her she's safe and going home, her Mother is waiting, things like that."

Both Argent and Eara McArdle nodded and Sinead continued.

"Other women here would help, singing and talking, taking over when one gets tired."

Argent spoke again.

"And we've some good voices amongst the crew. They'll stand a Watch, of that I'm certain."

Sinead spoke again.

"She much enjoyed the Ceilidh, the dancin', the fiddle and all."

"We can manage that too."

Both Argent and Sinead looked at Eara McArdle and her response was positive.

"I'll mix the potion."

* * *

The eight filed in, all highly bedraggled and ragged, but at least now clean and their chains removed. Fentiman had arranged them into some form of order and he followed them in, to begin the introductions, from left to right.

"The first is Edward Cable, Sir, the second is William Beech. Both say they were taken when their Indiaman was captured and then both were sold to the galley."

This was accompanied by vigorous nodding from both Cable and Beech.

"The next five are of various nationalities, Sir, and speak no English, but Cable and Beech have been able to inform us of their names and where they come from. We have...."

He stepped forward to point.

"Two Frenchmen, Dubois and Valenciennes. Then two Neapolitans, Descatti and Frioli, last a Greek, Lamma. Last, here, is an American, James Walcott, taken off an American Merchantman and sold, like Cable and Beech."

At this point the American stood forward, pointing his finger at Argent.

"I, Sir, am an American citizen, and I wish to request that..."

But Fentiman had placed himself between the American and his Captain's desk and pushed him back into line.

"Wait!"

Both the word and the push silenced the American and he held his place, but remained stern faced and plainly angry. Argent looked at Cable and Beech.

"Which of you feels best able to translate into Arabic?"

Beech and Cable looked at each other, but it was Cable who raised his hand. It was he who had gone back aboard the slaver with Fraser to relay Argent's last instructions.

"Me Sir."

Argent's attitude to any man found aboard the slaver had significantly mollified with time and he spoke merely to enquire.

"Do these others understand Arabic?"

"Oh, yes Sir. Enough to get by."

"Right. Tell these other five, and this applies to yourselves and to Mr. Walcott, that the chains we found you all in have earned you the benefit of the doubt. We regard you all as being rescued slaves and are pleased to have freed you."

Cable spoke in syllables utterly indistinguishable from each other, but all, bar Walcott, eventually grinned and nodded. Argent paused to allow that to sink in, then he resumed imparting his decision.

"Tell the Frenchmen that they will be taken back to England. They will be well cared for, but they will be interned as enemy aliens."

As Cable translated, both Frenchman looked at Argent, but their faces registered little. They probably expected as much, they were after all, aboard an enemy warship. When Cable had finished, Argent spoke further.

"Tell the Neapolitans and the Greek, that we require them to work their passage back to England where they will become free men."

The translation brought huge smiles to the three faces. Argent then spoke again directly to Beech and Cable.

"The same applies to you two. Once back in England, I'm sure you would wish to be reunited with your families, to make them aware that you are both alive."

Cable looked at Beech, and then spoke.

"Bill, here, has family, Sir. But I've none, so I'm happy to sign on, Sir. So's Bill, but he wants to get word to his family. Your lads've told us about Ariadne and neither of us fancies another Indiaman."

Argent sat back and smiled at both.

"That's excellent. In that case you will receive the volunteer's bounty. For the moment you'll be in the Afterguard, but I'm sure that will change."

Both nodded even more vigorously.

"Aye aye, Sir. Thankee Sir."

Argent turned to the American.

"Mr. Walcott. What I said to the Neapolitans and the Greek applies to you. I feel it right that I ask you to help us sail the ship back to England, then you can go your own way. Trade is building between our two countries and I'm sure you will soon find a ship to get you home."

Walcott drew himself up to his full height, his eyes still angry, his face gathered into a deep frown.

"I have made it clear to you that I am an American citizen and, as such, I'll do nothing aboard a British warship!"

Argent looked at him, his face showing at least mild exasperation.

"We sailed short handed. We just buried nine men and I have as many again unable to perform their duties because of their wounds. The ship's company is short by two dozen. I'm asking you to help us sail her back, but you maintain that your nationality entitles you to do nothing whilst you are aboard. If I accept that, it makes you no more than a passenger, so what do you suggest?"

"That I be taken to the nearest neutral port."

Argent's exasperation grew.

"You fully appreciate, I take it, that the whole of Europe is at war. The nearest neutral ports are at the far end of the Mediterranean or the other side of the Baltic, apart from those on the North African coast, of course, but I assume you would not wish to disembark there! I do intend to return our French women and children to France, in some way. You can join them if you wish?"

Walcott's own anger now fully revealed itself.

"Then I'll never get home! There's no trade between the States and France. Your damn cruisers make sure of that."

"Or, of course you could leave us when we get to Portugal."

"And there'll be little enough trade out of there! All the Portuguese Navy is trading with you."

Argent lifted his head and looked directly at him. Walcott needed a very clear explanation that would spell out his situation, at least for now.

"It is up to you to make the choice from the following three that I can see remaining. I can land you in France or you sail with us as a member of the crew, or you remain aboard ship as a passenger. I don't see a fourth choice. If to England, and you do nothing to help us get you there, then you are a passenger and we expect a fee. If you cannot pay it, the Royal Navy may look upon you as a debtor and you may end up in a debtor's prison. Of that, I cannot be sure, but it is certainly possible."

Walcott made no reply, he was thinking of his options, but Argent was done. He looked at Fentiman.

"See that these others are signed on. Give Mr. Walcott one day to decide on his own status and what his future is to be."

Fentiman saluted and then stood to one side, an obvious signal that all were to leave. As they did so, Argent sighed. Another problem, possibly causing an international incident, but Walcott had annoyed him. He had shown not even the merest gratitude and it rankled greatly to give any of them, including him, an idle passage back to England. The ship had already paid one price, it was not going to pay another, that of an able bodied man lounging idle whilst the rest of them worked to make up for the absence of others no longer capable, and nine now no more, dead in his cause.

* * *

Ariadne was regularly logging 12 knots, sometimes approaching 13 and the coast of Portugal was now a permanent fixture on her larboard side. With the coast of Spain astern Argent could, at last, put some East into her course and, with the West wind just aft of beam on, Ariadne took it on her best point of sailing. The Noon Sight of 18th October gave a position a mere 22 miles from Figueira da Foz and so, reluctantly but submitting to prudence, Argent ordered the shortening of sail, for they needed to arrive at the top of the tide. Ariadne idled through the afternoon, evening, and night and then dawn came to reveal the lumpy headland to the North of Figuiera da Foz. Ariadne idled further forward on topsails and driver to show them the narrow mouth of the harbour itself. Argent was on the quarterdeck with Zachary Short at the wheel. Argent judged his moment with the still strong West wind.
"Down helm. Course for the harbour, Mr. Short."
The wheel was already spinning, Short's anticipation had been perfect.
"Down helm. Course for the harbour. Aye, aye Sir."
Ariadne edged Eastwards. Figueira da Foz had a very narrow entrance and they entered at the beginning of the ebb, as Argent had timed. Once inside, the area of water where they could anchor widened but little, the harbour having two, somewhat narrow, branches. The main anchorage continued East, directly inland, and a smaller anchorage turned down to the South behind the headland on that side. The hills behind showed burnt brown after the rainless summer and the town itself had two sections, the largest to the North, alongside the main anchorage and the second a mere collection of buildings, much smaller and of less import, sitting precariously on the Southern headland. Ferry boats beetled between, but most noticeable was the wide island of pasture between the two anchorages and on its flat surface roamed wayward cattle, fenced only by the tide and tended desultorily by local peasants. Under their wide brimmed hats they were far more colourful than their drab charges, each curious figure lazily herding the cattle around the grassy surface, to little

purpose it would seem, there being neither feature nor building across the whole, wide expanse. What could be seen from any ship's deck of the main port to the North was but a white line of bleached buildings, a few, presumably those with a civil function, pushing frontages and bell towers above those smaller, lining the quayside. What extra building, if any, added to the overall area of the town could not been seen, remaining hidden behind the frontage, perhaps reaching on inland across the flat interior.

Figueira was a major supply harbour for the British army of Portugal and consequently both anchorages were crowded. Vessels were against the quays three deep and the South anchorage was crowded with small coasters with rigs of every mechanical contrivance, but the main roads contained large Merchantmen and two Royal Navy warships, the frigate Minerve, and the 50 gun Grampus, both new and both very smart. Ariadne steered for an anchorage that would keep her clear of all, even when she swung at anchor, but this meant steering past both Royal Navy vessels. When she came up to the Minerve, the crew of this gleaming ship lined the rail and began hoots of derision. Ariadne's Navy colours had been restored, the yellow strake across her gunports bright and new, but she still had some sails white and some dark grey. It looked incongruous to say the least and there was no ship in the Royal Navy that would not take advantage of the discomfiture of another. Shouts such as "game of checkers, anyone?" and "make me a King", came across quite frequently in various contexts and the crew of the Ariadne stared back with implacable hatred, which they maintained in response to a similar reception from the Grampus.

McArdle's reading of the chart indicated a safe anchorage and the anchor was let go, for Ariadne to come to a halt, riding secure in the now fierce tide. Stony faced from their reception, Whiting and the bargecrew awaited their Captain below the entry port on the starboard side and soon he appeared. The despatch satchel was conspicuous and he was accompanied by Purser Merryman Maybank, who had charged himself with the task of procuring some needed supplies; including, but he would never have admitted it, some sweetmeats for the children, if some were obtainable. He descended the ladder, to take his place besides his Captain, a pained and frantic expression on his face, as though the future held something awful. Able Jones released the painter, coiled it neatly at the bows and took his place as bow oar and Whiting took over. The tide had already taken them someway downstream from Ariadne and Whiting looked around and chose a course between the two other warships.

"Give way all."

They were in their best barge uniform and the rowing was immaculate. Something needed to be done to rescue the honour of the ship and the handling of both the tiller and the oars did much towards that, at least in their own eyes, as they rowed on up to the harbour steps. Argent and Maybank exchanged few words other than which of them expected to be back first. They couldn't agree and so agreed to return at 11.00, then, with the bargecrew faultlessly holding the barge steady, both Officers disembarked. Whiting and Jones gave Argent their smartest salutes and their Captain ascended the steps followed by Maybank. Argent chose to steer a course for the building that had most British uniforms entering, leaving, and guarding and this proved to be a wise move, because, at its door, Argent learnt of the whereabouts of Army Headquarters and Maybank learned of the Royal Navy Chandlers that may be able to help. At that point they parted company.

Argent obtained a guide at this office, which seemed, surprisingly, more military than naval and his guide, a Corporal of the 27th Foot, led the way to Army Headquarters proper, a tall greystone building, sporting green shutters besides its windows. It looked as though it was once a Counting House, but was now given over to concerns more martial than financial. The Corporal came to the attention at the side of the steps up and peeled off an immaculate salute, which Argent returned, Army style. Inside he found a Captain of Dragoons behind a desk, which Argent approached.

"Good morning. My name is Captain Argent of HMS Ariadne. We have just anchored. I have here..."

Argent placed the impressive satchel on the desk.

"...an urgent despatch for General Wellesley."

The Captain looked up, hoping to be helpful and to get the Captain on his way. He closed his fingers around the strap, but noticed that Argent did not relinquish his own hold.

"Good morning Sir. Very good. You can leave it with me and I'll see that it's included in the day's documents for transfer. The General is some way away, on the border, Badajoz we believe."

Argent retained his grip.

"I thank you for your help, but this comes from Castlereagh himself. With respect to yourself, I am required to obtain the signature of the highest ranking Officer available."

The Captain's face fell at the rejection of his offer, but, nevertheless, he created a smile, nodded and rose from his chair.

"Well Sir. General Hill is at present with us. I don't think he is so busy that he cannot see you, so, if you care to wait?"

Argent bowed.

"Thank you."

The Captain disappeared behind a heavy door and Argent was left to occupy himself, the satchel over his shoulder. There was no chair and so he waited by the wall of what he now saw was a wide, sparse hallway, no cheer from a fireplace even, as would be present in any English building of such a size. The ceiling was high and of ornate plaster and any look back to the door was guided by wide, redpine floorboards. Light oak panelling showed where some kind of counter once was, but the area above was now fully boarded over. The doorway could not be examined, the sun struck the white walls on one side, giving an unbearable glare, such that nothing could be seen in the street beyond, but Argent's mind was seeing nothing beyond his own thoughts, that of what awaited him back in England. The opening of the door behind him broke in upon his dark musings.

"General Hill will see you now, Sir. If you'd like to follow me?"

Argent turned away from the glare of the frontdoor and followed the Captain down a corridor that was positively gloomy by comparison with the hall, but the impression was dispelled when he was shown into the company of a white-haired, avuncular gentlemen, plainly dressed, who seemed genuinely pleased to see him, such was the beaming smile in the bucolic face.

"Captain Argent! Such a pleasure! Please take a seat."

This meant sitting in one of two chairs, both quite close together and separate from the desk that stood, seemingly unused, at the far side of the room. Hill had enough presence of mind to wait until the door had closed before he spoke.

"Now then, Captain," he beamed anew, "What do you have?"

Argent swung the satchel onto his lap and opened it to remove the package which he held loosely in his hands.

"This is a communication from Lord Castlereagh..."

Argent paused as Hill sat back, appearing astonished, probably genuinely, his hands falling onto his sizeable knees.

"...I am charged to place it in the hands of the highest ranking Officer available, if not into the hands of General Wellesley himself. Lord Castlereagh thought it of such vital import, that I was ordered to make the fastest possible passage here."

Hill leaned forward, conspiratorially.

"Oh, highly important is it? Do you know what it is?"

Hill had not yet taken the package and Argent had not offered it.

"Yes Sir. It says that the Austrians are out of the war and will soon sign a Treaty with Buonaparte. That means he will now have more unoccupied troops at his disposal. I was required to make as fast a passage as possible in case this new knowledge could change General Wellesley's plans."

Hill guffawed.

"Plans! Not much chance of that. The army hasn't fired a shot since Talavera in July and Wellesley, he's now Lord Wellington, by the way, since Talavera; is thoroughly entrammelled with Spanish pride and Spanish politics. Currently there are no plans at all, until something workable is established with the Spanish. Being allied to them during the Talavera campaign was an awful business, you must appreciate, awful."

He leaned further forward for yet more conspiracy.

"They say one thing, then do another. Quite another! Yes! Most unreliable. But keep that to yourself, politics you know."

He slapped his hands onto his thighs.

"Now, your problem. The highest ranking Officer. Well, I'm Wellesley's Second in Command, will I do?"

Argent had genuinely warmed to the old General. Second only to Lord Wellington, nevertheless he was genial and charming company, with not a hint of hauteur nor self-importance.

"You most certainly will "do", Sir. If you could sign this receipt and date it. 18th today, I believe."

Argent had taken a paper out of the satchel and Hill took it over to the desk, carrying it face up with both hands. He obtained a quill pen, flipped open the inkwell, dipped in the nib, shook it into a box of sand on the floor to remove the surplus, then wrote the necessary. As this was taking place Argent stood, concluding that his business was done. He placed the satchel on the General's desk, while General Hill was shaking sand over his signature and blowing it off with loud puffs. He stepped twice to Argent, carrying the letter in the same spiritual manner.

"And how was your voyage, Captain, fast enough? I know how you Naval types revere a fast passage."

"It was good enough, General, thank you. Ten days."

"Ten days, my word, that's good. It took twenty before I placed a foot on any dry land!"

He looked away, thoughtful.

"But that was on a bit of an old tub, though, not in a fully worked up frigate, such as yours, what?"

Hill beamed again and Argent had to laugh.

"Yes, Sir. She's a fine ship, Ariadne. We're very proud of her."

Hill remained thoughtful.

"Ariadne? Ariadne? Now didn't I see that name in the papers a while back? Something about taking a French frigate with not a single casualty."

"Yes Sir. That was us. We took the La Mouette, a 42."

Hill seized Argent's hand and pumped it up and down.

"Then to you my fullest and heartiest congratulations. To you and your crew. They must be fine seamen, good, fighting seamen, and of the very best."

"Thank you General, you are very kind."

The General tilted back his head in a mock laugh.

"Not at all, not at all."

Then he leaned forward, even more conspiratorially.

"Now then, you cannot sail until tomorrow morning. The next high tide is in the middle of the night and if you sail today you'll never get over the bar."

His eyes took on a special glint.

"You see, enough of a seaman to know that! Now. Right. We like to entertain ourselves of an evening, nothing formal you understand, nothing like a ball nor a dinner, just a few instruments and a bit of dancing, with a bit of food laid on at the side. A local affair mostly, and if anything they make up at least three quarters of the band and the audience more than that, but we join in, us soldiers and sailors, in the square in front the Town Hall, back of here."

This described, he placed a large hand on Argent's shoulder.

"I'd like you to bring over some of your men. Your Officers at least, this evening."

Argent was in a quandary. It would inevitably be revealed that he had women and children aboard, rescued from a slaver. This gave him some concern; his diversion from his orders would be laid bare and the opprobrium, perhaps, arrive early, possibly even causing angry communications back to the Admiralty. He would have to reveal the facts now, or refuse the offer. He couldn't swear them all to secrecy and what amount of "hole in corner" conduct would that show? Did he want that to happen in such a way, which would make it appear as a secret he wished to keep? However, he could not refuse this most kindly of General Officers?

"Well Sir. Yes, my Officers would be greatly honoured, but you see, we have over one hundred women and children aboard, mostly French, some English and Irish."

As a puzzled look spread across Hill's face, Argent ploughed on.

"An Arab slaver has been raiding around The Channel. The last place he raided was Cornwall. We caught up with him off the French coast in the Bay of Biscay and took him. Now we have the rescued aboard."

In for a penny, in for a pound.

"It delayed us two days."

Hill's face changed to a thoughtful frown. Something was working behind his clear blue eyes, pieces were coming together. When he spoke, the subject had changed.

"Now let me understand this. You were charged with delivering a despatch of international importance from Castlereagh, post haste, and you break off from that fast passage to attack a foreign ship? Contrary to your orders?"

Argent sensed a change and expected an accusation.

"And you had no doubt that this ship held those taken to become slaves?"

"None Sir. We had seen him before and I had an accurate description."

Hill's face lost the frown but remained serious.

"This could mean trouble for you, Captain. Serious trouble."

"Yes Sir. I appreciate that, but I couldn't find it in myself to just sail on by, Sir. And I felt unable to ignore the feelings of my crew and Officers, Sir. Getting those women and children off him struck me as being absolutely the correct thing to do, Sir. I viewed it as a matter of duty."

Argent had come to the attention and was staring over Hill's left shoulder, as a respectful subordinate. The response was a huge hand that descended down onto Argent's empty left shoulder, to rock him back and forth, then slap down again.

"And that way of looking at it, Captain, has the right of it, absolutely the right of it, in my opinion."

The beaming smile returned, Argent felt relieved and showed it, but there was more from Hill.

"Duty, yes, duty, I feel strongly, is the word I'd use. Duty to civilians is a concept we understand well enough in this army, so, I'll tell you what I am going to do. I'm going to write a letter that could possibly give you some support."

Argent's face registered shock. Hill responded.

"Yes. I'm going to say the facts, that your arrival being delayed two days made not a jot of difference. We can lose that in this country from negotiating with the local Mayor to use his horse trough! I don't know what difference it will make, not much if I know the Admiralty, but it won't do any harm and it may do some good. I do hope you think so too?"

He nodded at Argent, who spluttered his thanks.

"Why, yes Sir. That's very gracious and I can only thank you for your support."

Hill threw back his shaking head and closed his eyes in a dismissive gesture.

"No thanks are needed, Captain Argent, none at all. It will be but the very least of all gestures. To whom should I address it?"

Argent thought for a moment before looking into the re-opened blue eyes.

"Admiral Septimus Grant. Plymouth Command. Sir."

"Septimus Grant! I know him. We met sometime back. Can't remember the place, nor the tedious occasion it must have been, but I remember him. We amused each other for hours with various stories. How is he?"

"He's fine Sir. He's just got married."

"Married! The dog! Married. Ha!"

He leaned forward again for more conspiracy and smiled with a glint in his eye.

"So, this letter. You can take it with you, after this evening. And you must bring your rescuees!"

* * *

When word of the invitation passed around the "rescuees" there were shrieks in French, Gaelic and English, all being variations on "I've nothing to wear!" The early result was the festooning of the rigging with all kinds of washing and many of the women resorting to their Arab garb, itself now clean and mended and significantly more colourful. The colourful and conspicuous additions to the braces and shrouds were the cause of many comments and catcalls coming across the water from both warships and the merchantmen. The Ariadnies made themselves scarce on deck.

Transport could have been a problem from ship to shore, but General Hill used his influence and, as the sun edged to the horizon, five longboats arrived at Ariadne's starboard side. Argent thought that he should be amongst the first onto the quayside to make the necessary introductions; formality required it, so he believed. However, whilst he was making his final arrangements with Mr. McArdle, who would command the ship during his absence, Sinead Malley led the charge over the side into the waiting longboats and three of them set off immediately, filled to capacity. All the women were as best apparelled as could be managed in six hours, many touches of colour and changes of line coming from items begged and borrowed from the crew, topmen especially. Argent looked over the side to see his carefully laid plans in utter disarray, with Sinead Malley somehow at the tiller of the leading longboat. He didn't need to watch and see what would come next, evidently it would be her and her crew piling first up the steps and around to Army Headquarters. Argent turned to Mr. McArdle.

"I expect to return at eight bells, Mr. McArdle. We must ready the ship for the morning tide."

"Aye Sir."

Ariadne's own longboat was being filled with the crew's musicians and some of those lucky enough to have been selected by the drawing of lots. The Officers, both Commissioned and Warrant, and two Midshipmen, would use the launch and the Captain's barge, meaning that Gabriel Whiting and his crew would be ashore and available for much anticipated recreation. The three ship's boats and the last two of Hill's longboats, with most of the lucky lot drawers, set off as convenient. Propelled by such expertise, it was no surprise that Argent arrived first, to ascend the steps with Fentiman and Wentworth. Sanders was not with them; for some reason, he was in one of Hill's longboats. The three Officers, led by Argent, who knew the way, went immediately to the Headquarters building to find, leaving its front, a noisy cavalcade of gambolling children, chattering women and all ranks of soldiery, all very attentive to the newcome females. Argent stood and sighed, this had gone out of his control. Fentiman noticed his Captain's anxiety and immediately spoke up.

"Don't worry about how it's all working out, Sir. No one cares much, just go with the flow! Everyone simply wants to enjoy themselves, formality's out the window!"

Argent conceded and nodded agreement.

"Nevertheless, I must pay my respects to General Hill. Please wait here."

Argent entered the building to find the desk now occupied by a Sergeant, who stood to salute.

"Is General Hill present, here?"

"No Sir, 'fraid not Sir. He's away round for the evenin's singin' an' dancin', Sir."

Argent nodded his thanks and exited the building to find the contents of the three longboats and his own crew forming their own cavalcade to follow Sinead's, Ariadne's musicians and songsters providing the unnecessary marching impetus. Argent, Fentiman and Wentworth tailed on at the end.

The square was a kaleidoscope of costumes and cultures. All around and across were British uniforms of all ranks both Navy and Army but most of those in the square were civilian. The Portuguese men were in close fitting pantaloons, black, much-buttoned and finishing below the knee. Waistcoats and hats, also black, contrasted with white shirts and hose, as did scarlet scarves and sashes. However, they were wholly outdone by the women, these highly colourful in waist shawls over black skirts, white blouses and hose, and scarlet waistcoats, but all very much augmented with multicoloured headscarves, bracelets, bangles, necklaces and circlets around their foreheads. The Irish, and Cornish rescuees looked well enough in flouncy skirts and blouses with added shawls and sashes, as did those from the French fishing villages, but the French ladies, some from the yacht, stood out, being dressed in something much closer to high fashion.

All was gathering momentum. Rumours had circulated of something extra and all who had no very pressing business were there, including, Argent noticed, several Naval Officers, presumably from Minerve and Grampus. Argent looked around for General Hill and found him, wandering around greeting all and sundry with Sinead Malley on his arm. Fentiman took charge.

"Come on, Sir. Let's see what they've laid on to eat."

As they took themselves around the edge of the square to find any tables carrying food, they could see that the entertainments were in full swing. A band, composed of instruments of great variety, and the musicians' nationalities not far behind, were straining to co-operate in Portuguese folk songs, whilst the centre of the square was occupied by tumblers of very high talent, which included several from the warships and no small number from Ariadne. Whilst the crowd yelled their appreciation and encouragement of the acrobatics, the three found a table with an array of large porcelain dishes containing a variety of types of stews, mostly fish, and others spread with preserved meats. However, there were no plates, the practice being to obtain a wide, thick slice of bread, pile on one's fancy and then eat from there, with your fingers. If you were still hungry, you ate the plate! The next table supported barrels of wine.Argent, Fentiman, and Wentworth lost no time in dipping into the offerings and stood silently eating. Fentiman, unlike the other two, who were concentrating on the food, which was very good, saw Sanders, with the French girl. Sanders, still much wrapped in bandages, was being helped with his eating by the girl, amidst much giggling and amusement. Sanders saw them and motioned for his lady companion to follow him and both came over.

"Sir, may I introduce Mademoiselle Angelie Picard?"

Mme. Picard lowered her eyes, lowered her face and curtsied. The three, despite holding their food, bowed in return, and Argent handed his "plate" to Fentiman, to free himself to take her hand and kiss it.

"Enchante', Mademoiselle, Je suis très heureux de vous rencontrer."

At that point Argent's command of French ended, but he was struck with the picture of a very pretty girl, 19 or 20, fair hair, striking blue eyes, slender, with pale skin. She was wearing a plain dress, but well cut and of good material.

"Merci, M'sieur."

Sanders looked affectionately at his companion, very affectionately.

"Angelie has not had the chance to thank you for her rescue."

He looked at her and she took her cue.

"Je souhaite à merci pour l'économie nous, surtout avec la plupart d'entre nous l'être français, vos ennemis."

Argent was lost and looked at Sanders for a translation.

"She says that she is grateful for the rescue, especially as so many of those rescued are French, our country's enemies."

Argent looked at Angelie, who did not drop her eyes, but feelings rose powerfully within him at the thought of what they had rescued this girl from.

"Please tell Mademoiselle Picard that the Royal Navy is at her service."

Sanders did so, and Angelie curtsied again. A huge grin spread across Sanders' face.

"We were both saying that this looks like a lot of fun, Sir. We intend to join in the dancing and anything else."

Now it was Argent's turn to laugh.

"You'll be the turn of the show, I'm sure, with only one yardarm and a fender of swaddling over one eye."

Sanders displayed mock affront.

"Nevertheless, I, we, intend to give it a go!"

All laughed and it seemed that Angelie also understood. With a final curtsey, she took Sanders arm and both wandered off. Argent looked wistfully at the pair but, mercifully, with enough worries of his own, he didn't let his thoughts dwell too long on the fact that the war would soon pull them apart.

A juggler had just finished and the band now felt sufficiently rehearsed to begin their repertoire of dancing tunes. An ancient stood up, shouted something in Portuguese, and within seconds there were two long lines of partners. The band struck up and immediately there followed a whirl of arms, white legs and coloured skirts, the community section of the evening had begun in earnest. Argent suggested some wine and, at the wine table, each was given an earthenware mug, which they could then fill for themselves, as full as they chose. The three then stood and watched proceedings, before wandering around the edge of the square. Argent was the only Naval Captain there, but his right hand was very busy returning salutes from both Officers and men, many from the other two ships. They passed the Boatswains of the three warships, drinking and sharing stories, their ship emblems clear on their hats, their other Mates nearby. Argent was surprised and relieved; from the reception they had received on their entrance to the harbour, their meeting on shore had a much more likely outcome, a fistfight. He saw Sinead Malley whirling past, partnered by an Army Officer, both a blur of red, white, green, navy blue and mauve, then Bright and Trenchard cavorted past, both having a wonderful time partnering two local girls. Wentworth, for the first time, had wound himself up to say something.

"Th-this is a g-good event, Sir. C-coming ashore l-l-like this, is doing us all, s-s-some good."

Argent waited patiently and indulgently.

"You have absolutely the right of it, Mr. Wentworth. If nothing else, it gives us some idea of what we're fighting for, and our rescuees are like lambs on a Spring day."

He turned to look at the dancing. It seemed that all that they had rescued were joining in the Portuguese reels and dances, getting the moves wrong, inevitably, but enjoying themselves immensely. The laughter and gaiety in such good company were plainly helping to heal the memory of what they had so recently endured and confine it back to the past.

The dance ended and so had the wine in Argent's mug. He was thinking about a re-fill when he was confronted by Sinaid Malley, stood foursquare in front of him. She was indistinguishable from a Portuguese peasant, apart from the tumbling auburn hair. She too had jacket, a' la mode Portuguese, but it looked suspiciously like that of a Gun Captain, and gold earrings such as would be typical in the ears of the most self regarding topman. All was set off by a red kerchief and a gaudy patterned waist shawl. Her green eyes looked directly into his, then she produced a letter from inside the jacket.

"General Hill says I am to give you this."

She held it up in line with his face from hers, so that he had no choice but to look at her if he looked at it. Her eyes carried the same knowing look. He reached up a hand to take it from her, but she held it just for a second so that he looked straight at her to see that insolent half smile that showed she knew everything that he was thinking. Argent cleared his throat.

"I thank you, Miss Malley. Please convey my thanks to the General."

Her head went to one side. The knowing look still in place.

"Oh no, that's for you to do. Later. What you've got to do now, is to come and dance. With me."

She saw the look of consternation, almost dismay, come over his face.

"And if you say no, then I'll get the General to order you to!"

Argent's eyebrows rose and his mouth twisted sideways. It seemed he had no choice. Fentiman confirmed it.

"Strikes me you're caught on a lee shore, Sir."

Sinead pressed home her advantage.

"Yes, so y'are, caught on one of those; whatever they may be."

Argent secured the letter inside his coat and looked at the dancing. She had timed it perfectly, one dance had finished and partners were assembling for the next. Resignedly he held out his arm and Sinead looped both hers through it to guide him to the correct place. The ancient was yelling something, then he clapped his hands to a beat; all joined in the clapping, eventually including Argent, and off they went. Sinead seemed to know instinctively what to do and what came next, whilst Argent in marked contrast was pulled, pushed, guided and shunted around the lines, groups, and circles that the dancers formed. However, after a few dire mishaps, he did begin to learn the moves, which were not that complicated and he actually began to enjoy himself, even adopting, to the appreciative glee of his watching crew, the strutting pose that was required at certain times by certain of the men. The dance finished, but Sinead would not let him leave the dance space but, surprising himself, he was not unhappy to remain out on the square. He blundered his way through the next in similar fashion, but he felt that he had finished in fine style, just as he had for the first. His men clapped and cheered him off the dance square, something that did not go unnoticed by Sinead, but this was the last of the country reels. She insisted on something to drink and so he escorted her to the wine barrels and obtained for them both a pot of white wine that proved to be very refreshing.

The next event was traditional dancing by local troupes. They stood in silence, watching the intricate display, but in between he asked what he wanted to know.

"How's the little girl?"

She looked up at him, nothing coquettish in her face now.

"No change, but she's still asleep. Your men have joined in, the singing to her, I mean, and your fiddler took several turns. It's happening now, as we speak, some of your men are singing to her, and some Mothers."

Argent nodded.

"I hope it works. Sleep and time, what else can we use?"

Sinead said nothing, but looped her arm back through his. Argent continued to face the dancing, but seemed not to notice what was happening on the square.

The entertainment had changed. The professional entertainers had finished, if such was their status, and the locals were occupying centre square, amidst much encouragement. Argent felt her arm remove from his and he looked down at her, to see that her face was bright with some idea. She looked up at him.

"I've got to go. I'll see you later. Don't move."

Then she was gone, the colours of her clothing soon lost in the welter of colour that was splashed in all quarters throughout the crowd. Now alone, Argent stood with his wine, generally examining all around. His men were on the far side, with most of the men from the Minerve and the Grampus, and many groups of soldiers were spaced throughout the crowd. The local "team" was performing what he could only describe as an intricate march, keeping to the beat of the inexhaustible band. Fentiman joined him with his own beaker of wine and both watched in silence and then they saw the result of Sinead's idea. With the end of the Portuguese performance, she marched out, with several other Mothers and older girls and both Ariadne's fiddlers and a drummer. Their emergence onto the dance square set all the Ariadnies cheering which set off everyone else who was English. The dancers all lined up, the drum beat, the fiddles played and all the women performed an excellent display of Irish step dancing. The Portuguese were stunned by the dancing, so different from their own, but were soon as impressed as anyone and joined in the clapping and cheering that came both during and after. Such was the reception that they danced another. At the finish Sinead came back to Argent, somewhat out of breath, but aglow with their triumph.

"There, honour is satisfied. I'll have another drink now."

Argent and Fentiman looked at each other, both with knowing smiles, but it was Argent who obtained the necessary. Sinead resumed her possession of his arm and all watched, or more like listened, to what came next, a singer, then a choir, of Portuguese folk songs. This was far more passive than what had gone before, but the evening was drawing to a close and this was a fitting finale and all listened attentively. A lone female sang and finished and then came the interval before the next. Argent and Sinead were talking and so Fentiman had to interrupt.

"Sir. Look it's Angelie. Sanders' Angelie."

Sander's Angelie was stood on the stage and began singing, accompanied by the accordions. It was a lovely, lilting song, and

Angelie's voice was perfect and true, but it didn't take long for either Fentiman nor Argent to detect the change in the atmosphere across the square, confirmed by the sour looks exchanged by the Portuguese around them.

"Sir, she's singing in French!"

"I know."

What stopped them from throwing things or rushing the stage, Argent never knew. Perhaps it was simply because she was a lovely, harmless, slip of a girl, singing a simple song, one from her own home.

"Get around to our men, tell them to cheer their heads off when she finishes. Sinead, could you do the same for your women and children?"

Both nodded and went off in different directions. Argent found some soldiers, the Bosun from Grampus and some topmen and ordered them to follow him to the stage. If any protection were needed, they would give it. Angelie sang on, faultlessly, and meanwhile Fentiman had reached the sailors from Ariadne. He found the Captain of the Maintop.

"She singing in French and you know what that could mean, here in a Portuguese village. When she's finished I want us all cheering like madmen, which I'm hoping will set off the rest of us English and keep the locals quiet. It should, if they see us giving her a good reception."

"You can count on that from us, Sir. We'll give a cheer right enough for Sander's girl. Them women and children is of our own, that's how we sees it."

Fentiman nodded, somewhat moved.

"Right, pass it around."

Angelie finished perfectly and Argent felt his men at his shoulder. There was silence for but a second, but it seemed like eternity, then the Ariadnies exploded into cheering and clapping added to by Sinead's women and children. This set off the other sailors from Minerve and Grampus, who by now knew perfectly who she was, then the soldiers. The Portuguese, who had just listened silently to the hated language, clapped politely. Angelie descended the stage to be greeted by Sanders and a group from Ariadne assembled by Wentworth in case they were needed. Argent thanked his guard and the moment had passed, soon to be forgotten as the band struck up a rousing tune that everyone joined in with and the crowd surged forward to be nearer the band. The song was evidently some patriotic anthem for all ended up singing, waving and swaying for its duration to finally dissolve into deafening cheering at the end.

Argent sought out General Hill as the crowds dispersed and he caught up with him on the road to Army Headquarters. Argent placed himself in his way and saluted.

"Sir. Miss Malley has given me your letter. I have it here and I cannot leave without thanking you for your support. We will be leaving on the morning tide."

Hill did no more than offer his hand.

"I wish you Godspeed and a safe passage home, Captain. Good luck to yourself and to that good crew of yours."

* * *

Ariadne was laboriously edging up to her anchor, the whole crew either at the capstan bars or awaiting their turn. A few more minutes of effort brought the cable to an angle so steep that the anchor was just holding the harbour bottom enough to hold the frigate's bows against the ebbing tide, this newly turned and not yet strong. Fraser ran up to Argent.

"Cable up and down, Sir."

Argent looked over the larboard side. A cable was running almost alongside the ship, from Ariadne's stern, the larboard quarter, then off to a fixed point further up the harbour. This would turn her in the tide, to allow her bows to swing around to face the harbour entrance then the cable would be released at the required time. Argent saw no hindrance to prevent them making their exit; it was time to start.

"Weigh anchor."

"Aye, aye, Sir."

The anchor was pulled from its ground and the cable now took the strain as Ariadne slid back sternwards, but soon she swung around in the tide until her bowsprit pointed to the harbour entrance and the cable running back to shore drew taut. Argent nodded and an axe fell, to allow Ariadne, now released, to follow the tide out to sea. The wind was the common South Westerly and jib sails, main staysail and driver gave her some steerageway in the ebbing tide. All had been perfectly executed and, as she passed, her farewell from the Minerve and the Grampus was very different from the reception of her arrival. There was no cheering and little waving, the Officers raised their hats and the crews lifted but a cursory hand to wave but they now knew the story of Ariadne's outward passage and what they now carried, hopefully home to family and safety. Waving women and children set the seal.

Zachary Short safely conned the ship through the narrow entrance and the tide and the good wind on the staysails did the rest, to take her out to the open sea, beyond the islands and deceitful shoals waiting off the coast. Argent ordered down helm and, with all plain sail set, Ariadne began her journey Northward. He felt no need to push his ship for the return journey in the manner that he had for the outward and so contented himself with studying the set of the sails and examining the clouds coming their way from the weather side. He saw nothing to give him any concern and so he fell to musing about their course and, after that, his other more personal concerns. He was interrupted by Fentiman.

"Sir, I've been speaking to Walcott. He says that he is prepared to help in the sickbay. He accepts that the wounded became wounded to help him and so he thinks it right that he helps them."

This rankled with Argent and he spoke with sarcasm.

"That's highly magnanimous of him!"

Then he let out a long sigh.

"Agree to it. That is the problem solved, albeit less than satisfactorily."

He turned to Fentiman, a glint in his eye.

"Sign him on but rate him the lowest. He has no skill for care that he has revealed to us, so put him on the lowest rate of pay."

He was satisfied. Walcott would be doing something; true, as dictated by him, but he'd get little or nothing for it when deductions were made for food and clothing. The point concerning his refusal to do what he was skilled to do, would be made, on behalf of the ship. He turned away to re-examine the weather.

Elsewhere on the ship other conversations were taking place, longer and with conclusions less well defined. One such was in the Midshipman's Berth. Trenchard, Bright and Berry were busy with their Journals. Bright had sketched the entrance to Figueira da Foz, Berry was writing about how they turned and got out and Trenchard was drawing a plan of how the anchor was raised. He had labelled all, including the personnel, but he was stuck on the title of the small boys who fastened the thick anchor cable to the thinner cable that was able to be wound around the capstan.

"What are they called, the boys that tie the cables together?"

Bright did not look up from his careful use of a brush and watercolour.

"Nippers. They're called nippers. That's the job of the ship's boys when we weigh anchor."

Berry was painfully penning the process of turning the ship in the harbour, thinking hard about the sequence of orders. Trenchard added the final word to his plan and looked up.

"Talking of ship's boys. One hour from now we have their lesson, or at least I have. Which of you two is on Watch?"

Berry raised a hand.

"What about Wentworth?"

Bright replied.

"No idea. It could just be me and thee."

Trenchard continued.

"How are you finding it? My feelings are that it's deuced awkward. They cannot even recognise their letters. We're barely off the alphabet. And most can't tell a word from a number!"

Berry spoke, at last.

"True, but it's Captain's orders. And I'll hand them all this, that they do want to learn. So, that's what we do, and I, for one, don't find it too bad."

Trenchard looked at Berry.

"Where did you finish, last time?"

It was Bright who answered.

"Simple sentences; subject, object, verb. That sort of thing."

"And how went it."

"There's progress."

Trenchard closed his Journal.

"Talking of progress. We took the slaver, but there's rumour that our Captain could be in no small amount of trouble for doing so. That our mission was not the slaver but the delivery of something to Figueira, back there. I mean, that must be right, why else would we go there in the first place, arrive, and then depart, the very next day?"

Bright gave answer.

"I was on Watch and saw him immediately go ashore with a huge and imposing satchel. One can only conclude that was our mission, as ordered."

Berry halted his pen.

"I've heard the same, about him being in hot water, but how can you be in trouble for rescuing Christian women and children from a life of slavery?"

Bright looked at him, indulgently.

"Orders! Simple as that. If you disobey them, or do not fully carry them out, it can fetch you up before a Court Martial. That's our life, we all know that, the same for our Captain, so, if he did disobey or some such, well, only time will tell."

Bright went back to his painting, Trenchard to thinking up simple sentences, Berry to his next task, listing the sails that were set to take them North. He left the berth to take a look.

Above their heads, at number three, starboard battery, other words were being exchanged, in a much less convivial atmosphere. Bosun's Mate Henry Ball had just turned away, leaving a grinning Edward Cable, him displaying a wide and anxious smile and hoping for a warm welcome, but it was not forthcoming, at least not yet. Sam Morris, Guncaptain, looked at his new recruit. He looked "right seaman" enough and well muscled, probably from his time at an oar on the slaver, but that was the problem, he'd served, although as a slave, aboard that reviled galley. Morris didn't trouble himself with introductions; he simply asked what they all wanted to know.

"So, how long was you aboard that Arab barky?"

Cable's anxiety over his reception released a torrent of information, the facts tumbling over each other.

"Six years, just over, early in '03. Pirates took our ship, the William Johns, an Indiaman, when we was becalmed off Morocco. She was an Indiaman, was the William Johns, an' they took us all off, an' we all was sold, four of us bought by that black hearted bastard you got chained up below. Two died in his galley, leaving me an' Bill Beech. One of 'em was chucked overboard still alive, ill, but couldn't row no more. So over 'e went. Nice fellah, off the William Johns too, but that were that, t'other..."

Sam Morris held up his hand to halt the torrent. His suspicion matched the others of the guncrew.

"So you says you was off an Indiaman. How long was you a sailor? An' where's your home port?"

"I bin a sailor since I was 12. Master's Mate I was, on the William Johns, till them heathen bastards took us. An' I hails from Bristol."

Morris looked at Jacob Pierce.

"This is Jacob Pierce. He's Bristol born, like you says you are."

Morris examined Cable's face and eyes minutely for any sign of anxiety or concern. But Cable turned to Pierce like a long lost brother.

"Which part. I'm out of The Marsh, St. Phillips."

Pierce folded his arms. He knew what Morris wanted.

"I'm from The Dings, next door, up the hill."

Cable looked puzzled.

"What hill? The Dings is lower, in the bend of the river. Couldn't get much lower."

"Well, we was close to Lawrence Hill."

Cable became even more puzzled, but Pierce continued.

"Where'd you go drinkin' when you got back? The Hatchet on Welsh Back?"

"The Hatchet b'ain't on Welsh Back. That pub is t'other side of the harbour. The Llandogger's on Welsh Back. Are you sure you hails from Bristol? You ain't 'ad no knock on the 'ead since?"

Pierce looked at Morris and nodded. Morris looked at Cable.

"You served a gun afore? I've got you placed on the sponge.

He thrust the worn implement into Cable's hands and he hefted it as though it were a passport to Salvation.

Elsewhere, however, as Ariadne settled to her Northward passage, her hull holding firm in the steady breeze and the even sea, greater drama was unfolding. The little girl was waking up from her long sleep. Eara McArdle had been expecting it for some time and Sinead Malley was close by, as were two Mothers and their children. By some telepathy, so was Gabriel Whiting and Able Jones.

The girl opened her eyes, blinked and sat up. She looked around and then swung her legs off the bed, to rub her eyes and scratch her neck. Then she noticed the smiling face of Sinead Malley, who gave the child her warmest smile, kissed her and spoke a welcome.

"Dia duit, Mary. Bhí tú i do chodladh."

The child looked blankly at Sinead, but rose off the bed, to stand and then walk around. Sinead looked at the others, these all watching the girl fearfully.

"I told her she's been asleep."

The girl traversed the sickbay and, after much trial and error, she found the way out of the sickbay and then climbed the first companionway she found up to the lower deck. There she stood, debating which way to go. Ducking under the hammocks, she went to the stern and found her way to the entrance to the galley, followed by the four anxious adults, Eara McArdle, Sinead Malley, Whiting and Jones. She placed both hands on the sides of the entrance and stood regarding the scene within, first seen being Johnson, busy peeling endless potatoes. He immediately noticed her and, by inclining his head, he brought her presence to the attention of Bible Mortimor, who was adjudicating on the quality of the day's beef stew but then he also stood regarding the wide-eyed child, himself, for once, lost for words. The child assessed all within, then entered. She climbed onto the wooden counter besides the stew pot and sat, regarding Mortimor quizzically, a fixed stare, but not unblinking. Mortimor looked at the thin figure and decided that some food was in order. He reached for a wooden bowl and filled it with the stew, which he handed to the child, followed by a spoon. The child dipped in the spoon, tested the heat against her lower lip, entered the spoon to her mouth and began chewing. Then she swallowed and pronounced her judgement.

"Níl go leor salann ann."

"It needs more salt."

Sinead had translated and all laughed, loud and long, as much from relief as humour. Bible Mortimor looked daggers at the child, but found the pinch of extra salt requested and spread it over the top of the stew in the bowl. The child ate up with relish, not giving Mortimor or anyone, another glance. She finished the bowl and again sat regarding Mortimor.

"A mhaith liom níos mó é, le do thoil, a dhuine uasail."

Sinead translated, barely able to contain her laughing.

"She wants some more, please, Sir."

Mortimor resumed his look of outrage at such cheek. Nevertheless something akin to emotion had stirred inside him and he refilled the bowl, this time with a combination of peas and stew, plus salt. He then landed a piece of the officer's bread on top. He saw the approving looks on the faces of Sinead Malley, Eara McArdle and the two topmen, but would not allow their obvious approval to change his outward scowl, whilst inwardly he was quite moved.

"Let her glean even among the sheaves, and reproach her not. Ruth 2, verse 15."

It was Eara McArdle who answered.

"Amen to that, Brother Mortimor. Amen."

She then returned to the sickbay, but the other three remained. The questions stood unspoken amongst them: what would she do now, where would she go, would she go to the weather deck where she would see the ocean, now growing more turbulent from a building wind? The orders to take in sail came down to break in on their concerns, so the two topmen left.

The girl finished her second helping, put the bowl to one side and sat for a further while, examining all around, not anxiously but as though appraising what she saw there. Her mouth changed to a ghost of a smile and she jumped down to stand besides Mortimor. To his great alarm she took his hand, or more accurately, closed her fingers around two of his and pulled him out of the galley. Mortimor followed, as if bidden by the God he feared. She took him up the nearest companionway onto the gundeck and there, those on Watch stopped all that they were doing and even the Bosun's Mates did nothing to force a resumption of their work. They all knew about the traumatised girl and all looked upon the incongruous sight, the miserable Bible Mortimor being led by the hand by a child, fully along the whole row of guns. The comments arrived, not complimentary for the less than popular Mortimor.

"What be this then, Bible, you grown so weak in the 'ead you needs a child to find yer way about?"

"Be she towin' you off to the Captain, Bible? You bin stealin' sugar again?"

Mortimor returned the comments with a look that would melt rock, but he would not disengage his hand. Sinead followed anxiously, then the bizarre pair came to the companionway that led to the forecastle and the child ascended, still towing the mortally embarrassed cook. Close to the top, spray from a heavier wave descended on them both, but she still ascended and on the forecastle she climbed onto a carronade, using Mortimor's shoulder for balance. She looked at the sea for a long minute, silently but calmly. Suddenly, she kissed Mortimor, jumped down and ran off to join a group of children on the larboard gangway who were making mare's nests out of string, these being taught by Kaled, who had taken on the role of "Keeper of the Children. A hint of a smile twisted Mortimor's face before embarrassment took over, then he left the forecastle, not to retrace his steps through the gauntlet of the men on the gundeck, but along the empty weather gangway. Although it made him wet, it at least preserved what was left of his dismantled dignity.

* * *

Argent heard the clear and respectful knock on his cabin door. He was standing at the cabin windows, gazing over his ship's wake, looking, but not seeing.

"Enter."

The door opened and in came Sanders.

"You sent for me, Sir?"

Argent sat at his desk and motioned Sanders to a chair. His wounds were still wrapped in bandages and he carefully arranged his damaged arm.

"We have 128 rescuees aboard, Jonathan. 92 are French. I want to return them to their own coast. Women and children are no threat to us, and should not be condemned to years of internment. Also, we could find ourselves in action, with over 100 civilians on board. Not good. You would agree?"

Sanders face lit up at the notion of his opinion being consulted.

"Yes Sir. Quite so, Sir."

"I want you to find out where they come from and decide on one port where they could all be disembarked, as one group. I want you to work that out. You know what I mean, somewhere in the middle of the cluster of coastal villages from where they were all captured, if that's possible."

Sanders stood, but his wound prevented a salute.

"Yes Sir. I'll get onto it right away. Will Mr. McArdle have a chart, Sir?"

"I'll be amazed if not, so please ask him."

"Yes Sir. Give me a couple of hours, Sir."

"No rush, we haven't cleared Finnisterre yet."

As Sanders left, Argent reached across the desk to the Logbook, a permanent feature in that corner of the desk, but he did no writing; the day's entry was done. Instead he read and re-read, for the countless of times, his entries prior to taking the slaver, imagining how a Court Martial would view the entries, perhaps as justification, or otherwise, for his choice of action. That done, he stared out of the cabin window, listening to the creak of the tiller ropes behind the cabin screen.

Sanders was as good as his word and returned within two hours, a chart under his wounded arm, which he spread on the desk before Argent.

"There is no clear choice, Sir. To place them in the centre of their village cluster, best would be Camaret, here, but there are problems."

He placed a finger below the word Camaret on the map, on the North coast of a peculiarly shaped headland below the entrance to Brest harbour.

"You can see, Sir, it's right in Brest Roads. We could, probably would, find ourselves intercepted."

"How many come from there?"

"28, Sir. The most number."

"That slaver lifted 28 French citizens from a village right on Brest Roads? Under the very noses of the French Navy?"

"That's it, Sir. There's no other way of looking at it."

Argent shook his head, but carried on.

"Where else?
Sanders ran his finger South down the chart.
"Loctudy, Sir. Much more away from Brest, and almost the most Southerly raid."
"How many from there?"
Sanders consulted a piece of paper.
"Nearly as many. 25. Sir."
Argent looked at both choices and studied. Camaret would be best for the rescuees to disperse to their homes, but it would risk the ship in the entrance to one of France's busiest naval bases. However, it would give an easy run North to Quessant, assuming the usual South West wind. Loctudy was safe from Brest traffic, but on a peculiar East facing coast, part of a Southerly headland that could mean tacking South for some miles before resuming their voyage to Quessant.

"I don't much like either. Is there no other?"
Sanders pointed to a coastal village between the two.
"Douamanez, Sir. But I discounted that one, because it's inside a deep bay and not so very far from Brest."
Argent nodded.
"You are right. How many from there?"
Again the piece of paper.
"12, Sir."
Argent adopted one of his thinking poses. Right arm across his waist to support his left elbow, his left index finger touching his chin. He used the pose for two minutes.
"Loctudy. We can come in from the South East and hove to off this headland, to the South of the harbour. That places her head well enough to sail out Westwards. The coast runs South Sou'West from there. Any decent amount of West in the wind will give us a passage out and back to our course home. Your thoughts?"
"Idling off this headland waiting for our boats to return, won't the wind push us Northeast or East, Sir, into that bay?"
Sanders finger on the map indicated his concern.
"That'll be the trick, Jonathan, to hold her where we want her, ready for a quick farewell."
Argent smiled and nodded.
"Please would you inform Mr. McArdle that I would like a course for Loctudy?"
Sanders rolled up the chart and left, Argent following him out. He felt the need for a breath of air.
Evening was upon them. Argent climbed the companionway to the quarterdeck as two bells of the second dogwatch sounded, to find the ship a soothing picture, both her decks and sails bathed in rose light by the dying sun. Argent took in the uplifting sight of his good ship, sailing on through the quiet of evening, whilst leaning on the

quarterdeck rail, not taking his place on the weatherside, which had been respectfully vacated by both his Watch Officers, Wentworth and Trenchard. Ariadne moved in leisurely mode, her hull rising and falling lazily to the long Atlantic rollers that she overtook on her passage Northwards. He turned to Wentworth.

"Heading and speed, please, Mr. Wentworth."

"N-North by West. Sir. Nine knots."

Argent nodded and thanked him. That was the least fractured sentence he had heard from Wentworth since he came aboard. Wentworth had grown in stature, both within himself and with the men, since he had led the boarding party onto the slaver. The men now, almost religiously, paid him their respects, not in any way mockingly, but with genuine warmth, and usually a spoken greeting. His seamanship had never been in question and what he had said to encourage his men prior to going over to board had been circulated and had become common knowledge, it much in his favour.

He looked along the starboard gangway to see Sinead Malley talking to the little girl he had been so worried about prior to entering Figuiera da Foz. He was amazed and delighted to see her on deck, calm, smiling and talking, now a normal little girl. Before he knew it, he was taking himself along the gangway towards them and Sinead saw him and seeing her recognition, he touched his hat. Her smile was warm, she was clearly pleased to see him, gone, at least for now, was the knowing mock impudence. Argent spoke first.

"This is the little girl, isn't it? The one we were so worried about. She seems recovered, wouldn't you say?"

"Yes Captain, I would. Your idea worked. I put it down to you."

She said something in Gaelic to the girl, who turned and curtsied, and then spoke a long sentence in Gaelic. Her big brown to green eyes held Argent in their steady gaze as she spoke, then Sinead translated immediately.

"She says that her name is Mary and she's feeling much better now. She wishes you a good evening and thanks you for her rescue. She also says that she likes your cook, Mr. Mortimor. He cooks a nice stew."

Argent broke up on the spot and could barely choke out a reply, his eyes filling with tears. He took a deep breath and clenched his teeth together to steady his jaw before speaking.

"Tell her that the Royal Navy will always, always, place itself between her and any harm, and that the whole ship is pleased that she is now well and back amongst us."

Sinead did so, whilst taking glances at Argent. The girl spoke something in Gaelic and Sinead nodded, then the girl ran off.

"She's off to the galley. She has attached herself to your Cook. She spends a lot of time there."

Argent laughed gently whilst wiping his eyes. The idea of Bible Mortimor as a nursemaid could only be viewed with great amusement on top of greater astonishment. Now it was Sinead who looked steadily at him.

"Where are we going?"

"Almost due North into the Bay of Biscay. I'm going to sail directly across and land the French at a place called Loctudy. Then we'll sail for Killannan, to land your people. Loctudy's on the South of the Brest peninsula, if that means anything to you?"

Sinead immediately bristled.

"Yes it does, I thank you, Captain. I'm not so ignorant as not to know the geography of what's immediately over the sea from my own country!"

Argent withdrew back slightly.

"I'm sorry, I meant no offence. I was simply trying to find out, to get it clear, sort of thing. If you did not know, I would have shown you. Drawn some kind of map on this rail here."

He moved his finger over the polished wood, returned her look and smiled wryly. She modified her stern examination of him to simply look at him silently with her head inclined, her body turned sideways. He broke the moment.

"Well. I'm pleased for the little girl. I'd best get back to the quarterdeck, I'm on Watch soon."

He turned to leave, but Sinead spoke up immediately, halting his turn.

"We all think, the Mothers that is, that you're looking really down. We hear that there could be some trouble for you when you get back. That you should not have come after us, not have stopped, even!"

Argent turned to face her fully. At first he simply nodded, then he spoke.

"That could be true. I don't know. It depends on how their Lordships at the Admiralty view the decisions I took to cross, more like go around, The Bay, when coming out to here. I didn't sail directly across, as we are now. I convinced myself that there was real concern for the weather and it was that decision which brought us up on him. I'm not even sure if I didn't take that excuse too readily. Even then, it's arguable that I should have sailed right past you, light or no light."

A ghost of a smile crossed his face, but anger crossed hers.

"Weather worries and sailing right past! Now what kind of a stink would that raise if a ship of His Majesty's Navy sailed right past a slave ship carrying Georgie's own citizens? He'd Court Martial you himself if you didn't, never mind the grief the Navy would get from the newssheets, and then there's the questions in The House. The whole country would curse your name if you didn't, and damn anyone who damns you for what you did do. If you don't think so, nor your Admiralty, it's the truth, to the rest of Europe you're a Christian hero. So y'are! What kind of gombeen eejit could Court Martial you for such a thing?"

Her face was alight with indignation, her feet planted firm on the deck, knuckles on her hips, just as when he had first seen her outside her mill in Killannan. He couldn't make up his mind as to what to say. There could only be a short agreement or a long counter explanation, but it was she who continued.

"Right, so that's that problem sorted out. Now, was there anything else on your mind to keep you so far down in the dumps?'

Argent grinned openly, but inwardly he was in a quandary, should he open himself up to this fearsome female? The ship's bell solved it for him, ringing four bells to finish the Second Dog Watch. Argent should now take over, so he touched his hat.

"There's four bells. I am needed on the quarterdeck to relieve my Officers. On my ship I do my share of Watchkeeping, so I'm afraid the ship pulls me away."

She looked up at him angrily, but Argent's head was swimming. The rose light did nothing to change the green of her eyes but it turned her hair into an amazing colour. He managed to turn himself away, but she wasn't finished.

"This hasn't ended, Captain. We're going to sort you out, so we are!"

Argent was not sure that something did not hit his back with this parting shot, but on reaching the quarterdeck he concentrated on returning salutes and consulting the compass. However, as he examined the sails in the last of the light, somehow he felt better.

* * *

"Up helm. Heave to!"

Zachary Short repeated the order and swung the spokes leftwards. Ariadne turned cleanly into the South West wind and lost way as it left her sails, which were soon writhing in the cross wind, but the topmen of all masts were rapidly furling them away from harm. Now that he was at his destination and could see what he was faced with, Argent became anxious for his ship. The wind could drift them past Loctudy and onto a lee shore, difficult to sail away from into a headwind. They had to hold their station and, to do that, sail right on the edge of the wind. He walked to the quarterdeck rail to see Bosun Fraser.

"Mr. Fraser. Larboard tack. Set outer and flying jib. Main and topmast staysails. Driver half to starboard."

Fraser hurried off to add to the topmen's already onerous duties and, satisfied with his ship for the moment, Argent took another look at the French coast. He had toyed with the idea of running up The Colours to let the French know who was returning their citizens, but he dismissed the idea as foolish vainglory. The longer those on shore thought that Ariadne could be French, the less time they had to send a signal across land to Brest, for worryingly, a large semaphore signal stood prominent and potent on the headland. A few white houses inching their way up the cliff marked the extremity of Loctudy, about two miles away, which distance gave him all the searoom he needed, but he expected to wear ship away from the coast, then tack back to pick up his boats.

These two were now being readied. Even the longboat could not hold 92, plus a crew. The longboat had its mast and sails aboard to make the journey and this would provide adequate power to still tow the second, the launch, which also had its own mast and a sail to give some help. Both had been fitted with a canvas shelter from the bows back to the mast, for there was a working cross sea and anyone inside either boat would soon be soaked from the waves hitting the bows of the small vessels as they faced the oncoming waves. The longboat was already over the side and the launch was being attached to the davits that had returned up from the bobbing longboat.

The French rescuees were emerging up from the gundeck, using the forecastle companionway. They had made their tearful farewells below of their Irish and Cornish friends of shared and dreadful experience and now they were passing through the assembled crew, all of whom were in their Divisions finery and, as the women and children passed through, hats were removed. Argent and his Officers were stood just along the starboard gangway from the quarterdeck, all present and all hatless. The women and children began to leave through the entry port, each carefully shepherded down the sideladder by the men of the Foretop. Perhaps unsurprisingly, none were taking any of the booty lifted out of the slaver. Gabriel Whiting and the Captain's bargecrew would be making the journey, Lieutenant Sanders in command. He, after all, Argent reasoned, spoke French, and his bandaged appearance made the point to the French that there had been a cost to the British ship of re-capturing their own French citizens. That was one small item of vainglory that Argent could not resist. He turned to Sanders.

"Remember Jonathan. In and out, at your best speed. That's the enemy's coast. I don't need to tell you how much I want it down over our horizon."

Sanders nodded, twice. It was the only response he politely could make.

"Aye aye, Sir. As fast as possible, Sir. Fully understood."

He walked forward to the entry port, but he crossed with a little girl who had just left her Mother at the entryport. She went up to Argent and held something up for him to take. He took what she offered from her tiny hand, it was a flower, made from coloured cloth, but she waved him lower. He lowered his face and she kissed him. Once again, from the simple actions of a child, Argent couldn't speak. Nor could any of the crew.

* * *

Anton Gronard was now Militia, but a veteran nevertheless. Now too old to march with the Grande Armee', he now consoled himself with his memories of marching with Napoleon in Northern Italy, the battle of Marengo, the bridge at Lodi. Now he was a sentry at his home village, paid to be such and content with his pension and the fact that he had left nothing of himself behind on any battlefield, but he had gained a small piece of iron, from something he knew not what, but this remained lodged in his left leg. However, a cut from a scimitar during the fight with the slavers still itched and irritated on his left arm. From time to time the picture invaded his thoughts and polluted his dreams, of himself and others being forced back through the village by overwhelming numbers, whilst women and children, many that he knew, were dragged screaming in terror, down to the waters edge.

Now he dozed on his musket at the end of the jetty, lulled by the lapping waves. There had been some noise about a frigate off the coast, but that was no concern of his, as long as nothing came off the ocean onto his jetty. However, his sojourn was abruptly terminated. A shout from the cliff drew his attention upwards and he saw a fisherman gesturing out to sea, to a point beyond the cliff, but it was behind the rocks and out of his view. He studied what remained for a moment as empty water, but then he saw the bows of a longboat, curious with its canvas cover, dwarfed by billowing sails, and behind was coming a smaller boat, linked by a tow rope and helped forward by its own sails. Immediately he noted the flag of truce at the stern of each; these were enemy, this confirmed by his long sighted eyes fixing on the Royal Navy uniform worn by the Officer at the longboat's stern; the single row of buttons distinguishing it from the double row of the Republican.

Despite the flag of truce, his musket came forward from his shoulder and he checked the priming in the pan but did not cock the flintlock. With his musket still facing the approaching English, he turned his head to look back along the jetty to the quay. There were some fishermen arranging nets and tackle and he yelled at them to inform the Mayor and the Constable. As they ran off, he returned to his own watch on the approaching boats, but what he saw nearly caused him to drop his musket, however, what did drop was his jaw and his old heart missed a beat. A child's head had appeared around the canvas screen, laughing and waving, then a woman's face over the top of the screen. Both he recognised and he needed no more time to realise what was happening. Still gripping his musket he ran back along the jetty yelling as loud as his ancient lungs, labouring enough from the run, would allow.

"C'est les enfants! C'est les enfants! Et leurs Meres!"

His running reduced the volume each time, but it was loud enough for two equally aged matrons to notice him and abandon their task to give him a shocked look. Gronard stopped and reached for the jetty wall for support, but the wall proved insufficient, his musket was also required, but he had enough wind to reply to the deep puzzlement on both their faces.

"Oui. Ce'st les enfants et leurs Meres. Capturé par les Arabes. Retourne' par l'Anglais. Leurs bateaux sont à la jetée."

He stopped, his breath now robbed from him, but now it was the turn of both matrons to scream and bundle themselves back into the village, yelling a repeat of Anton's message. He took three deep breaths but then lost them again when he turned to look along the jetty to see it now full of running children, their Mothers doing their best to keep up. The good Gronard did this time drop his musket and fall to his knees to embrace one child and then another. The screams of the children did not quite drown out those from back in the village as the news spread and all abandoned their houses to run to the quayside. The noise redoubled as children, Mothers, Fathers, relations and Grandparents were reunited on the quayside before the houses that they had been dragged from weeks before, only this time there was shouts of laughter, faces lit with limitless happiness, and running feet to both dance and close with loved ones in a fierce embrace.

As the final running Mother passed him, shouting a greeting, Gronard looked back to the end of the jetty to see an English Officer at the top of the steps, with two sailors silently holding the mooring ropes. The veteran recovered his musket, stood, came to the attention and presented arms. He was pleased to see his saluted answered, albeit oddly, by a bandaged arm, and the Officer turned to descend the steps and depart. Gronard hurried forward, he knew that thanks of some kind were required, but then he heard shouting from behind, which he recognised to be from the Mayor.

"Les arrêter. Les garder là."

Gronard raised his arms.

"Arrete! Arrete la, s'il vous plait."

Sanders stopped and waited. He looked beyond the sentry and saw the Mayor lumbering forward, his sash being arranged at the run. He was stocky, a fisherman's build, windblown hair and weatherbeaten face, reddening further from the running. The Mayor nodded to Gronard and passed him, the Mayor being followed by a thinner, middle-aged man in a dark blue uniform, with a striking number of buttons down to his knee. Whilst the Mayor was arranging his sash, this, the Constable, was holding onto his tri-corne hat, it in some danger of being shook off and falling to the waste covered water below.

The Mayor had reached Sanders and wished dearly to shake his hand, but it was too thick with bandage. All he could do was look into the one uncovered eye with both his own, now wet with tears, and embrace Sanders with all his strength, then kiss him on both cheeks. Much merriment sounded up from the boats below. The Constable did the same, then the Mayor took Sanders lapel between two fingers and pulled him, via it, towards the town, at the same time motioning with the other hand to accompany him along the quay. He spoke in French for Argent to follow him, but did not expect to be understood. However, Sanders replied.

"Monsieur, je parle Francais. Et oui, je vous serai fourni avec, mais nous devons partir bientôt."

The Mayor nodded his understanding at the need for a quick departure, then stopped in thought.

"Deux, non, trois, de votre hommes, nous être fourni avec, s'il vous plait."

Sanders turned to his men.

"Jones, King, Fenwick. He wants you to come as well. Follow us, and stay close."

He looked down into the longboat for Gabriel Whiting.

"Whiting, I leave you in charge. I don't expect to be more than five minutes."

The six walked quickly along the jetty, past the rigid Gronard, the Mayor clearly anxious to take these sailors back to his people still gathered on the quayside, his people themselves seemingly also anxious to view the "visiting" Anglais. The faces of the women changed from joy to sympathy as they saw Sanders, but this did not stop much backslapping and pats on any part of him that came within reach. The three topmen received the same treatment. For some minutes all that each said were several "merci"s, for the Mayor had disappeared, but now Angelie Picard came to stand before Sanders. She was crying and all he could do was smile. As they looked at each other, he spoke.

"Je reviendrai."

She smiled through the tears at his promise to return, but he thought of a better idea, at least more likely to happen in the near future that he could see before them.

"J'écrirai! Les lettres traversent toujours La Chaîne."

The idea of letters did cheer her, but only slightly. She placed her hand on the sleeve of his wounded arm and leaned her forehead on his chest, then she resumed gazing back up at him. The poignancy of the clear affection between the two had done much to quell the noise from the crowd, but it was Fenwick who spoke, responding to what was evidently a scene of deep sadness amidst such complete joy.

"Don't despair, Sir. Who knows what's possible?"

Jones added his thoughts.

"That's right, Sir. No-one knows what's 'round the corner, now. Do they?"

Sanders turned and smiled at them, then kissed her hand and shared a private, fond look with Angelie, for what became the last time, at least on that day and for the immediate future. The Mayor had returned with three worthies carrying substantial barrels, labelled "cognac". Holding hard to Sanders sleeve, the Mayor began a speech.

Meanwhile, Whiting and Gronard were alone at the end of the jetty, Gronard holding his musket in the crook of his arm, Whiting with his foot on a bollard. Each regarded the other for a good while, until Whiting nodded, then reached into his pocket for his pipe and tobacco pouch. He pulled open the strings and offered it to Gronard, who took it, peered inside, took a sniff and grinned. Good tobacco was scarce in France beyond price. Still grinning, Gronard produced his own pipe and filled it, before passing the pouch back to Whiting. Whilst Whiting filled his, Gronard found his tinderbox and made a few glowing embers in the tray. He waited until Whiting had finished charging his own pipe, then he tipped an ember onto Whiting's tobacco, before doing the same for his. Soon both were producing clouds of smoke and both leaning back against the warm stonework. The musket lay unattended, propped against the same stones. Both men folded their left arms across their waists, their right hands making final adjustments to the smouldering tobacco. Neither spoke a word; any would have been wholly unintelligible to the other, but there was nothing to stop two such as they, sharing a quiet smoke. They exchanged a look of supreme conspiratorial contentment, then Gronard passed across his flask of brandy. The moment was complete.

The length of the smoke given by the fill of tobacco matched perfectly the time it took for the Mayor to finish his speech and then for Sanders, with the laden Jones, King and Fenwick, to return to their boats, still accompanied by the Mayor, the Constable, and the population, these crowding up in the rear. Angelie was allowed between the two Officials. The crews of both boats perked up considerably when they saw what was coming down the steps, not so much the return of their dear Officer, but the three large kegs. At the top Sanders touched Angelie's hand once more, smiled and descended to the longboat. The crew ignored him, each blithely assuming his safe embarkation, all showing far more care and concern over the three barrels which were passed down as though vulnerable children. The painter ropes were thrown down by experienced French hands, oars were shipped to push off and the crew rowed themselves out to gain the wind. Whiting noticed Sanders, at the tiller, looking back much more than he was looking forward.

"I'll take the tiller, Sir. If you've a mind?"

Sanders slid over on the now vacant bench to make room for Whiting and he spent the next minutes looking back to the jetty, now crowded to its maximum, but he only had eyes for the slim figure in the white dress, until the rocks of the headland hid her from view just before he gave a last wave. He took a very deep breath, turned and regarded his command. His face remained downcast, but; first things first, for now he was thinking as the ex-topman he was. He looked over the side to the other vessel, the launch, with Able Jones at the tiller. Neither vessel had yet set any sails.

"Jones. Bring yours alongside."

Jones brought his launch close to, until hands from each could reach across to hold both boats together. Sanders issued his orders.

"Fenwick. Break out the beakers in the store."

Fenwick opened the emergency store that would be used if ever the longboat had to be used as a lifeboat and found several beakers. Sanders himself prised open the bung in one of the barrels and, now thoroughly in guise, spoke in the language of the lower deck, this time forcing some kind of smile.

"Well, lads, I think a drop of this good stuff is in order before we gets ourselves back to the barky."

He didn't have to reach very far to tip some of the fine spirit into each beaker.

* * *

Argent was pacing the quarterdeck. This was taking longer than he had bargained for, but he reasoned to himself that his hoped for, "get 'em onshore and immediately get away", was more than he could reasonably expect. Ariadne was idling perfectly towards the shore, her bows pointing at the headland, on which was the semaphore that was the subject of regular study from Argent, but the arms remained slack and idle. He turned again to the taffrail, to march back to give himself room to march forward again, when a shout came from the foremasthead.

"Longboat and launch, Sir."

Argent didn't reach the taffrail but sprang immediately into the mizzen shrouds and climbed to the mizzentop. His glass provided a reassuring picture of the longboat coming on in fine style, its press of canvas hiding that of its consort the launch, whose hull could just be seen astern of the longboat. Argent considered increasing sail to reach them sooner, but time would be lost after their retrieval. They would be much closer to the land and, with the steady breeze South Southwest, even on staysails alone, Ariadne could not sail directly into such a wind to take her leave. They would have to tack back, away from the cliff if they approached the land much further. As she lay, Ariadne was sufficiently out of the wind's eye so that she could sail directly out, albeit close hauled. Therefore, they would have to wait for the longboat and launch to reach them, both fully using the favourable wind for their course, so Argent kept his ship idling in the tide, gaining steerage way, turning into the wind, gaining some ground, then allowing the wind to push them back. The Watch was kept busy with the sail trimming and Zachary Short busy at the wheel. Three, four, then five bells sounded of the forenoon Watch before the longboat and launch bumped alongside and were secured. Argent yelled his orders.

"Mr. Fraser. All topsails and topgallants. Close hauled, larboard tack."

The topmen sprang into the rigging before Fraser said a word, as anxious as Argent to lose the French coast so clear on their starboard bow. With the large spread of canvas Ariadne sprang forward and Argent waited. The boats were being recovered, but he was gauging the wind, from both the pennant above and what he could feel on his face. He wasn't satisfied.

"Mr. Fraser. Mizzen, main and foretopsail staysails."

As these sails were spread and sheeted home, Argent noticed the three kegs being handed down from the longboat, now in its cradle.

"Mr. Sanders!"

Sanders noted the tone in his Captain's voice and the stern expression on his face. He hurried back to the quarterdeck.

"Are those the cause of your delay?"

Argent pointed to the barrels.

"Er, no Sir. The Mayor insisted on making a speech. I should have pleaded ignorance as to my French, Sir, and he would probably have allowed us to go, however, both were but minutes, Sir, and the brandy came immediately. It seemed churlish not to allow them to give some thanks, Sir. The place was overjoyed, ecstatic. Unsurprisingly."

Argent's mood from the impatient wait had barely abated.

"Let's hope your minutes don't put us on a lee shore with our French foes nicely holding the weather gauge. Unsurprisingly."

The chastened Sanders lowered his head, shifted his feet and then looked up.

"Where shall I send the brandy, Sir?"

"Send it to Mr. Maybank. If we get away from here, we can all have a tot."

By way of lightening the mood, Sanders gave reply.

"It's good brandy, Sir."

Argent's face told that he had immediately worked out how Sanders knew that it was "good brandy", and at that instant Sanders also divined what the look told him, that Argent had worked it out. He saluted with his bandaged hand, turned, and rapidly made off, his hand throbbing.

Ariadne cleared the headland and turned to starboard and came to her best point of sailing and steer almost due West, to progress, under all common sail below topgallants, along the East-West coastline, a course that would keep her clear of Brest Roads. The Noon Sight confirmed where they knew they were anyway and all obtained a reading that even the hyper-critical McArdle could not cavil over. This included Berry, progressing well under Wentworth's tutelage and a new addition, one Christopher Wheeler, also known as "Smallsize". He had proved to be an adept pupil at his letters and ciphering and was being started on the training to at least become a Master's Mate.

Argent, being content with the heading of his ship, spent much time studying the cliff, constantly off his starboard side. From time to time he studied a group of horsemen, three, perhaps four, moving their way along the cliff, keeping pace with them and, through his glass he saw that often one or two waved their hats. He put their presence down to no more than a wish to convey thanks and make a long goodbye and hoped that they were from Loctudy. He studied them once more, discerned no change, then fell to brooding over his two personal concerns. Sinead Malley had given him some comfort, because sure enough; there was a lot of truth in what she said. Public opinion would be wholly for him, but their Naval Lordships rarely took even scant notice of such as that, certainly not enough to influence their decisions. Unless something came from the King! Now that was a thought, but the thought was shattered by a shout from the masthead.

"Sail ho! Two. Off the starboard bow, comin' off the headland."

Argent hurried down the starboard gangway and climbed rapidly to the foretopmast crosstrees. Ariadne had made good speed along the coast from Loctudy to the open sea and the headland marked the end of the run of the East-West coast. From there it was a simple Northwest run to Quessant, but what he saw emerging from beyond the headland made that run anything but simple. Mere seconds through his glass showed that these new arrivals were both powerful French frigates and seconds more showed that they had spotted him and they were matching his course, turning seawards as he was and forming line abreast to block any escape, both taking in sail to reduce their speed. This would give them the option of the one engaging Ariadne, whilst the furthest sailed around to his unengaged side when Ariadne caught up with them, as was inevitable, she had no choice if she was to reach the open sea. In that event, they would come onto her from both sides.

He yelled down from his position to clear for action then himself followed the words to the deck. Once there he found the ship already alive with running figures as the ship was readied for combat, which seemed imminent. On his quarterdeck he looked again at the pennant, still showing a wind South Southwest. This gave him the weather gauge, just, but with odds of two to one, what did that matter and they were across his route home? His mind considered the options. To sail between the pair and the coast? On their present course, the gap between the shore was slowly growing. He looked through his telescope to examine the sea room he had, now a clearer picture as they finally passed the headland, but one of the Captains had thought of that. Both had shortened sail further to the point of being almost hove to, there to wait for this move, if chosen, and cut him off and have him against the coastline. If he made for the open sea, they would resume line abreast and both descend upon him, but he had to decide quickly. He decided to cut inside. They'd meet him one at a time, but perhaps Ariadne's speed would see them through and her shallower draught could perhaps give them the option of sailing inshore where they couldn't.

McArdle had anticipated the need for a chart and appeared onto the quarterdeck with the exact one. It was spread on the cabinlight and Argent saw what he didn't want to see. The chart showed no shallows, merely a deep descent from the cliff. The heavier French frigates could come almost as close to the shoreline as he, all that could get them away from the French guns was speed. He strode to the rail and found Bosun's Mate Henry Ball waiting.

"Topgallants and Royals. Mizzen, main and foretopsail staysails. All jibsails."

Ball ran to the bows gathering men for the huge task, but Argent noted the immediate reaction of the mizzentopmen, they were already in the shrouds, just ahead of all others.

On the gundeck, the crew of number three starboard listened to the orders and the running feet. Morris looked at Cable, him with his fingers nervously gripping and relaxing on the shaft of the sponge.

"Can you write?"

Cable looked quizzically at Morris, why now such a question?

"Yes, I can."

"You made a Will?"

"No."

"Then get some paper. You got time an' the Purser 'll 'ave some. This be a very bad fix we'n in, an' I suspects we'll get pummelled into surrender. Two to one, an' pushed to the shore, I don't see us gettin' out. They'll disable our sails and that'll be that."

Cable looked terrified, but Morris said no more. His crew checked their gun, Dedman the charges in the saltbox, whilst Pierce and Wilmott chipped flakes of rust from the roundshot in the garlands. Smallsize stood close to Morris as he tried the flintlock again for a spark. It did.

The two frigates had increased sail to bring them closer to Ariadne's speed so that she could not sprint past. They knew Ariadne's options and acted to cover both. They split, one to sail Northward along the coast, the other to cover the possibility of her heading for the open sea. Whichever way Ariadne went, one would engage and hold her, probably laying across her bows, until the other sailed up, perhaps across her stern to rake her. Argent had to grudgingly admit that both Captains thoroughly knew their business. The Captain of the frigate out to sea had taken his ship just to the point where Ariadne could escape by sailing close-hauled to windward, the maximum into the wind. Any course further South would be too far against the wind, even for Ariadne; she would stall, "in irons". There would be no losing these as they had out sailed La Mouette.

However, Argent had changed his mind and now looked on this direction, straight out, at least close to it, as their best chance, now that the route North along the coast was closed. He would have too little manoeuvring room against the coast, but out to sea, at least that was possible, he was confident that no ship could match Ariadne manoeuvring at speed. Argent had decided.

"Mr. Short. Steady as she goes. West North West."

"Aye, aye, Sir. As she goes."

Argent turned to the Midshipman on Watch, a ghostly looking Thomas Trenchard.

"All Officers to me, if you please Mr. Trenchard. Also Mr. Fraser."

Trenchard answered "Aye, aye, Sir", in a voice less than steady and moved to the companionway, but Argent didn't like the hunch of his shoulders.

"Straighten up, please, Mr. Trenchard. We're going into action. Your own bearing can have an effect on the men. I think you'll find that the way that they are carrying themselves will give you the confidence that you should be giving them."

Trenchard straightened up and descended the ladder. Within minutes Fentiman, Sanders and Wentworth were in Argent's presence. Fraser arrived seconds later.

"I'm going upwind as we did with La Mouette, but we won't get past that seaward frigate without taking some of his fire. So, I intend to draw him upwind to larboard and then dodge downwind to his starboard. He may expose enough of his stern if he turns upwind too far. This wind may even lock him "in irons", if he turns too far into it. So, Mr. Fraser."

Fraser came to the attention. Strife and danger seemed to make him more formal.

"Ready all staysails not yet set. All. And we must lose our common sails very quickly so's to enable our fore and aft to draw quickly and move us upwind, and hopefully draw him across that way. But, when we dodge downwind, immediately to common sail, all plain sail and set at your fastest. We will need the speed almost in an instant. Are you clear?"

Fraser had remained at attention and saluted.

"Aye aye, Sir."

"Thank you, Mr. Fraser."

As Fraser hurried off, Argent turned to his Officers.

"Load chain, larboard battery. It would be better for us to damage his sails than attempt to rake at long range at a bad angle. Round shot for the starboard. I expect an exchange with him over there at some point, so, counter battery in his case. Two quick broadsides into him to reduce his potency will serve us the best, I feel."

Argent examined their faces. Each was calm, but stern, and, in response, Argent did his best to look calm, professional, and cheerful.

"So, to your stations, Gentlemen, and good luck to us all. We are Ariadne, a "bone to be chewed". Mr. Fentiman "Beat to Quarters."

As the Marine Drummers sounded their urgent rattle, Sanders remained behind.

"Sir. Sir, I feel responsible. My delay. Five, ten, minutes could have gotten us to the open sea."

Argent looked at him and smiled.

"Dismiss the thought, Jonathan. If any blame lies anywhere, it lies with me. I should have cracked on sail as soon as we picked you up. I didn't. Your five, ten, minutes made little difference, little or none."

Argent let the pause hang, the drumming filling the space.

"Now, one thing you must do. Get our passengers down into the hold, but, if it seems that we may well sink, I leave it with you to bring them up. Pass that on to our Midshipmen. We can't have only you or I with that knowledge. Just in case!"

Argent smiled and Sanders saluted and left with no further acknowledgment. Argent raised his telescope to examine their opponents. For the first time it struck him that their hulls were more a deep purple that the usual French washed out maroon. At that moment the challenge was issued; both frigates showed their Colours, an intimidating swathe of red, white, and blue, as big as a mainsail. As if for emphasis, both raised their gunport lids and the blank stare of the gun muzzles soon appeared all along their sides. Argent turned to Trenchard.

"The Colours, Mr. Trenchard, if you please."

Trenchard strode to the locker with all the solemnity he could muster and, with due solemnity, Ariadne's Colours were, also, spread to the wind. However, despite the display of Naval ardour, the manoeuvring had continued. The frigate on the coast had divined Ariadne's broad intention, to run seaward, and her Captain was using his big stern driver to swing his stern around to point his bows to the open sea, the quicker to support his compatriot, who would now, almost certainly be in action first. Argent watched the movement of the two frigates against his own. He was content with their positions, as content as he could be in such a situation, the frigate to the left was idling in the wind, waiting for Ariadne's move, left or right. He needed to move her left, before swinging right himself, but the other frigate on the coast side was now powering up close hauled to close that door. Whatever, the die was now cast.

"Mr. Fraser. Staysails. Furl all other."

The sail change came in minutes and Argent gave his order.

"Up helm. Come to West South West."

The calm repeat came and Ariadne swerved to her new course, but two minutes later their immediate opponent had also added sail and moved leftwards, to larboard, to cut off the narrow wind channel that Ariadne had. Any further left, upwind, and Ariadne herself would be in irons, too far into the wind, and then the contest would be all over.

Suddenly came a cannon shot and Argent looked around. There was no gunsmoke either from his ship, nor his opponents. He was perplexed until Trenchard called out.

"Sir. From the headland, Sir. They've fired a gun."

As if for confirmation, another fired, the smoke swirling Northward. Argent pulled out his telescope, but it could be seen with a naked eye. The headland had it's own signal station and, there were some signal flags already up the mast and the semaphore arms were moving frantically. Argent turned away, he had his own concerns. His moment had come, desperate as it may be.

"Down helm. Come to North West."

Short acknowledged and swung the spokes, whilst Argent went to the rail to see Bosun Fraser screaming like a madman, but the topmen were already in the shrouds. The sails changed and Ariadne picked up speed as her bowsprit swung across the intimidating picture of her opponent framed within the rigging of Ariadne's bows. Then Argent saw what he couldn't believe, first one, then the other, of his opponents lowered their Colours. For whatever reason, they were not going to fight. They were not surrendering, ridiculous thought, their guns were still run out, but they were not going to fight. To confirm this, both were shortening sail, the frigate to the right actually turning into the wind to heave to. He leaned over the rail to shout at his loudest.

"All guncrews stand down. Close all flintlocks."

He was still uncertain, even perplexed, but Ariadne stood on for the open sea, on a course between the two.

"Steady as she goes, Mr. Short."

"Aye, aye, Sir. Steady as she goes."

Ariadne sailed so close to the stern of the left frigate that they could read her name. "Renard". He knew that to mean "Fox" but what drew his strongest attention were the Officers of Renard along her taffrail, all with raised hats. Argent climbed onto the larboard carronade and pulled himself up next to the larboard mizzen shrouds to stand on the rail, where he raised his own hat, very high. From behind him Captain of Marines Breakspeare drew his own conclusion.

"Seems that our call at Loctudy has spread about, Sir, and they're letting us home."

* * *

Quessant was long past and The Channel felt of late October, the long rollers parading up from the Western Approaches to assault the coasts of Cornwall and Southern Ireland alike, or push on into the space between, there to wreck the tranquillity of the Irish Sea. Ariadne, heading for Ireland, found herself traversing across their ordered ranks, causing a slow "corkscrew" for the inhabitants of her now less crowded hull, but all within were now experienced sailors enough to feel no queasiness from the up and down and the side to side. If they now had any problem it was coping with the chill in the air, such a contrast to that of the milder Spanish and French waters. The crew were now rarely seen without a warm jacket or some kind or canvas overshirt and their remaining passengers were wrapped in whatever was to hand, mostly loose Arab garments over the clothes they had been taken prisoner in. However, if the climate had grown chill their thoughts were warmed as Ariadne, under all common sail, harnessed the stiff breeze to wing them closer home.

Argent was off Watch but still on deck, where there was a whole choice of distractions compared to his cabin, where, sat alone, he would soon sink into pessimistic meditation. Feeling the need to move, he levered himself from the rail of the quarterdeck, the weather side, he checked the set of the sails and then noted some topmen working aloft. He finally set off for a turn around the deck, crossing the quarterdeck to start with the starboard gangway. He manoeuvred himself around a bunch of children being entertained by Kaled juggling with some kind of spinning top that he tossed up with a length of twine held between two handles and noted that some sailors nearby also chuckled at the sight. The laughing of the children, their evident glee, did some work on Argent and he smiled himself, albeit briefly. As he progressed forward he found himself answering the challenging stare of Sinead Malley, she having ascended the forecastle companionway as soon as she saw him leave the sanctum of his quarterdeck. Argent stopped and touched his hat.

"Good afternoon, Miss Malley."

She did no more than nod. With him she remained in ill mood, mostly because she couldn't understand, nor do anything to alleviate, the depression that she saw upon him during each occasion that he came within her closely focused gaze.

"It would seem that children playing are one of the few things that can cheer you up."

She had long dispensed with formality towards his rank, but Argent gave a half smile and nodded.

"That's about right. My sister has a child, he brings a smile to all our faces..."

But the sentence died. Sinead took it up.

"Have you any of your own?"

"No, Miss Malley. I'm not married."

She paused to look at him, the scowl disappearing for the briefest moment.

"And you're still walking around with a face like a week of wet Mondays!"

Argent managed another half smile.

"I'm a Naval Captain, Miss Malley. Most of the time I feel the weight of my command. At sea I may be the master of all around, but the responsibility that comes with it, can crowd your thoughts. It often leaves little room for humour."

She made no reply but turned to lean on the rail and watch the waves racing astern. Argent could have taken that as a termination of their talk, but, for some reason he decided not to and he joined her at the rail. She looked sideways and up at him. Had she been facing inwards someone may have seen the warmth in her look, but almost looking out over the empty ocean it was for her alone to know of it.

"When will we reach Killannan?"

Argent smiled again and pointed to a seagull scudding across the waves.

"You see that gull. He, she, sleeps on the Scillies. If this wind holds, sometime late tomorrow you'll see home again. If we hold to ten knots or close, which is nothing special for Ariadne, we can make 240 miles from Noon to Noon, you know. I'd say Killannon was about 200, so tomorrow should see it."

Now it was her turn to smile.

"Boasting about your ship again."

This time he grinned openly and slapped his palm on the polished rail and rubbed the wood as though passing on congratulations.

"Yes, and I make no excuses for that."

"About Kaled. I, we'd, like him to come off with us. He'd like to an' all, but it's your decision."

Argent paused for thought.

"You say he was a slave himself?"

"We're convinced of it."

"And he told you of our arrival?"

"That he did."

Argent turned his head and smiled at her.

"Then we'll count him amongst the rescued. He can go where he will."

She smiled back.

"I knew you'd see reason. Eventually!"

Her smile was genuine and accompanied by a complementary jerk of her head. They both fell silent and studied the ocean, with Ariadne's silhouette thrown across the azure blue by the Westering sun. Then Sinead said something strange.

"Himself'll not be pleased."

"You mean Fallows."

"The same."

"About what?"

"My return."

"Why should that concern him overly? I can appreciate that there is no love lost between the two of you, but how can that affect his affairs?"

"First, is, that shadow of a man lifted not one finger when them Heathens showed up and did as they liked. That's unfinished business between me and him and that he'll not enjoy. Second, I have no heirs. With me gone, or so he thinks, my estate would go to The Crown, and, with the contacts he has, he'll be thinkin' he'll achieve what he tried some few years back; to get me out and take the mill for himself. He'll be deeply disappointed."

She drew herself up and took a deep breath.

"When he first came he knew that he had bought the village and its surrounds, including the road. He knew well enough that it didn't include my mill, but it was surrounded by what he owned. So, he wondered just why it was that he didn't own that, as well. So, he comes along with his Lawyer man to demand my proof of ownership. It was one of the most glorious moments of my life when I told him to get his gombeen self off to Cork museum and there he'd see my Title of Deed spread out in a glass case. My mill has been there for centuries and was given to my family by Henry II, when he took over Ireland. It was one of my ancestors, I'm ashamed to say, that helped him out with that evil deed, and the mill was his reward, well, as a part of all the land he was given. My Title is a historical document, so the museum has it. But it's the first issue that I'm looking forward to dealing with!"

But Argent wasn't listening. Her story had set his mind churning like a tidal race. Historical document! Lanbe Barton was centuries old and had been in their family for centuries. How they came by it, is now lost in time, but it could be...There was a family legend about an ancestor supporting King Charles, during the Civil War.

His faraway look was not lost on Sinead. She leaned over to get in front of him as far as she could, laughing her amusement.

"Now just where are you, now, right now?"

Argent shook his head as if to clear his thoughts and smiled himself. For the first time since she had seen him again she saw a change come over his face, almost happiness, and a light had come into his eyes.

"Something's brightened you up!"

He nodded and, to her evident pleasure, he placed his hands on her arms, just below her shoulders and patted her once.

"You are right. Your story may help with my own. My family is under threat of eviction because we don't have our Deeds. They just may be historical like your own. That's new hope, and for that I thank you."

She rose herself to his sudden happy mood.

"Then you'd better kiss me. That's the right way to say such a thank you."

Surprise and shock came over his face but he replaced his hands and lightly kissed her right cheek. Her face changed to show disgust at such a paltry effort, but Argent was done. He touched his hat and moved on to reach the forecastle more by instinct than deliberate thought. His mind was working on the possibilities just revealed, but his spirits were already subsiding, for he realised he only had more of hope than substance, but the sailors working closeby, grinned and lowered their faces to their work.

* * *

As predicted, Ariadne arrived off Killannan the following day, but late. The evening was closing, the shadows of the mountain were taking the sprawling collection of cottages into the embrace of night, when Ariadne dropped anchor in the last of the daylight, less than half a cable from shore. However, from then on Argent had no choice but to land his passengers, even if it meant doing it in the gloom of growing night. As soon as they saw their village, the captives from Killannan climbed the rigging and stood precariously on the rail, waving and halooing at the few fishermen at the shore. Within minutes, came a repeat of Loctudy, the whole village was at the shoreline, many wading waist deep to be that little bit nearer to their returning loved ones; those that they had counted as lost forever.

Argent looked at the pennant, flopping lazily in the dying breeze of evening and, judging the tide as still rising, he decided there was no danger in landing the eager inhabitants, even if it meant recovering the longboat by lamplight. He'd seen the tiny bay at low tide and knew it contained no hazards. By the foresight of experience, Bosun Fraser was close at hand and Argent turned to him.

"Ready the longboat, Mr. Fraser. Let's get these people ashore. If we don't they'll end up swimming and I wouldn't want their drowning on our conscience."

"No Sir. Aye aye, Sir."

The Starboard Watch were ready at the lifts and within minutes the longboat was over the side and the now desperate villagers were at the entry port, such a rush that Argent ordered the Marines to nudge and cajole them into some kind of queue. As with the French, there were no mementoes of the slaver, but they did include Kaled amongst their number, as happy as anyone, carrying a child on his shoulders. He was exchanging farewells, by gesture, and shaking hands with some of the crew stood nearby. No one felt able to view him with any animosity; he obviously loved children and the women held nothing against him, welcoming him always into their company. Mortimor was also there, on his knees to say goodbye to the little girl, her arms around his neck. When he arose his face swivelled around to show a ferocious challenge to anyone wishing to ridicule so uncharacteristic a gesture. None did.

The topmen of the Watch saw all safely down the ladder and into the longboat where the waving and shouting to those now a little closer on shore continued even more energetically. The last to go was Sinead Malley and this time she had no compunction about approaching Argent on his quarterdeck. Her formality placed Argent at his ease as she walked up to him extending her hand. He removed his hat, the signal that all there should do the same, and he shook her hand, twice.

"I've come to say a last thank you, Captain, to you on board your ship, that is."

Argent bowed as she turned to the other Officers present.

"And to you Gentlemen also. You and your crew will always be welcome in our village."

Various replies were made in the vein of "too kind", or "it's been a pleasure", then Sinead turned finally to Argent.

"Will you not be coming ashore, Captain?"

Argent nodded.

"I will, yes, to see that all is well and if there is any simple assistance that we may give, but in the morning. For now we'll leave you to your welcome home."

Shouts were coming up from the longboat, mainly telling Sinead to hurry up. This she heard, as did the others on the quarterdeck and, although it was unintelligible, the inclusion of her name made its purpose obvious and all grinned as she turned and left. As she left through the entry port she treated Argent to a long, careful look and he cleared his throat and replaced his hat, for some reason taking extra care. He seemed relieved when he heard the "give way all".

Even in the dying light the cavorting and capers in the gentle surf and up on the strand could be seen from the ship but what struck them mostly was the redoubling of the noise. Their anticipation too great to resist, many at the water's edge waded out to the longboat, so far that the sailors were prevented from using their oars, but it made little difference. Those in the water seized the oars and used them as capstan bars to propel the boat up to the crowded beach; others took the children on their shoulders and triumphantly bore them ashore.

Within minutes it seemed there was a bonfire up by the mill and the joyful sounds of the ceilidh band. The Larboard Watch took their places for the First Watch and listened to the joyful music for most of the night, its happy sound warming them also, for they well appreciated their own role in making it happen.

Dawn broke murky and threatening fine rain. After their sleep, Argent took many of the Larboard Watch ashore with him, plus some supplies, the value of which equalled what Maybank thought the booty from the slaver would fetch at an auction. Argent had spoken to his Officers and Senior Warrant Officers and all had agreed that the crew would forego this prizemoney to supply the village with some good food, especially with an Irish winter fast approaching. As before, Argent concluded that Sinead Malley would be best to supervise the distribution and soon there was a small convoy of barrels, sacks, and boxes being relayed up to the mill. Argent went first to the mill, with Wentworth, expecting to knock on the door but she had seen him, or been warned, and she emerged from the open door when he was some way off. However, for the moment she ignored the supply chain that was leading up to her mill, through a corridor of villagers welcoming the men who had returned those they had thought forever gone. Applause and backslapping seemed to be the method of conveyance, Gaelic being beyond the crew. However, Sinead was evidently not in the best of tempers.

"Ah, Captain, you're just in time to stop me from murdering James Fallows."

Argent had no difficulty remembering.

"The day of the raid"

"That's it, that gombeen tripehound. Piece of shite! Time's now to settle his bloody hash!."

She set off on her way, accompanied by two Mothers, both ex-captive and their children in tow. Argent, staggered by the bad language, saw his bargecrew nearby, most of them quite close.

"Whiting. Find the bargecrew and follow me up to the castle. Be quick, I have a strong suspicion you may be needed."

Whiting saluted from a distance and shouted over to the only one close by, Silas Beddows, but soon the whole bargecrew were following their Captain and Wentworth, both straining to catch up with the determined striding of Sinead Malley and her companions. Still some distance behind, Argent began his questioning.

"Miss Malley. What do you intend?"

She looked briefly back at him, then spoke her reply to the locked gate, now much closer.

"I'm going to give him a very big piece of my mind, and when I've finished these ladies have something to unburden themselves of, on top of that! And if I get a chance to swing one at his lizard face, he'll get that as well."

Argent felt the need to take charge.

"Stop. Stop! Stop, I say!"

They did stop and turn, but only to dismiss his wish to intervene.

"There's no need for you to trouble yourself over this, Captain. This is for us villagers, us and him."

Argent returned her stern look.

"If it involves riot amongst the King's subjects, then it is my business. The King's business!"

Both his words and his uncompromising expression did give her pause and she progressed no further. By this time, Argent had his bargecrew behind him and he walked slowly forward. He spoke directly to Sinead.

"What exactly is the issue? I need details. What did he do?"

The last was accompanied with a pointing finger in the direction of the castle wall. Sinead adopted her argumentative pose, feet planted foursquare and elbows out, hands on hips.

"More like not do. You remember what I said about that tripehound? Well, the time of the raid, during the day, we saw them coming into the bay, that's the slaveship. We didn't need a written message to know what they were about, that they were here with bad intent, so we all ran up to his walls, here, expecting to be let in."

Her chin jutted further forward. She was utterly livid.

"The gobshite wouldn't open the gate!"

She paused to allow that to sink in.

"All the people could do was scatter and many were hunted down by those Heathen Devils. Captured up on the mountain slopes were those that they wanted most, young Mothers with little children who couldn't run as far as was needed. The Arabs took all the time they wanted. He set his men on the walls, but they didn't fire even one shot. When they'd captured all possible, they upped and left, nice and gentle like. That I know, because they had me amongst them!"

She turned to glower at the walls, as though her fierce look would turn her into a Joshua and crumble the very stonework, then she turned back to Argent, but said no more. Argent returned her look, but his was thoughtful, which calmed her.

"Tell me, please, does Fallows have an official role, here. I mean does he represent The Crown, in any way?"

Her posture didn't change, but her voice was calmer.

"Yes, he's a Magistrate. And something in The Militia. Some kind of Officer."

Argent smiled which changed her look to puzzlement.

"Then he is at fault. Massively at fault. As a Representative of The Crown, and an Officer, he has a duty of care to His Majesty's citizens, especially when they are in danger, and especially when he possesses a place of refuge, such as that."

He pointed again at the castle.

"In fact I would not be surprised if every citizen has such a duty if it is in their power to put it into effect."

He paused to allow his words to sink in.

"I can deal with this, and I will. You can come and watch and listen, but please don't say anything."

He motioned to his men and they closed up as Argent approached the imposing gate. The women and children gathered up behind them, eager to hear every word. Argent turned to Moses King.

"King. Give that door a wrap or two, let them know we're here."

King walked forward, closed his mighty fist and hammered on the door; four, then five times. The woodwork resounded like a drum inside the low arch, to be quickly opened by the same Michael, his face, scar and broken teeth appearing around the edge. He said nothing, but appeared merely quizzical and so Argent spoke.

"Good morning. I am Captain Argent of His Majesty's Ship Ariadne. Perhaps you remember?"

The misshapen head nodded once.

"Please inform Mr. Fallows that I am here and wish to see him urgently."

More of Michael was revealed and his expression grew sour.

"He'll not see you. Not before he's had his ride and his breakfast."

Upon hearing this, Argent's expression met the challenge.

"Then my answer's the same. He comes out or I send my men over your walls. There is an issue here, which throws into grave doubt the discharge of his duties both as a Magistrate and as an Officer. As a King's Officer myself, I am required to speak to him on this matter. Tell him so, and tell him I am waiting."

Michael looked more than a little intimidated and withdrew his head, at the same time closing the door, at least attempting to, but big as Michael was, the treelimb arm of Moses King came across the door and it moved no further. Argent turned to Sinead and her companions, all of whom bore the expression of washerwomen who were winning the argument. After a minute or two, Fallows appeared, to stand before the door. He was dressed in the same long-gone fashion of the mid-Eighteenth Century as he was before, an odd full length brocaded gown, but this time his grey wig hidden by an equally embellished box hat. Argent wasted no time but spoke the moment he appeared.

"Mr. Fallows. There seems to be some important questions over your conduct during the recent raid on this village by the Arab slavers."

Fallows looked shocked and puzzled but said nothing, so Argent continued.

"You remember the raid?"

This time Fallows managed a nod, but no more.

"The issue of greatest concern is that you failed to give shelter to the villagers here, all His Majesty's subjects, in your substantial home. This."

He waved his hand expansively.

"I won't say castle for the moment, but that's what it is, and you, as I understand it, being both a Magistrate and a Militia Officer, have a duty to give protection to any citizens as may need it and resist invasion to the best of your power. On top, you had a force of men here and did nothing to prevent the invaders from capturing the village and carrying off some of its inhabitants, even though you were armed and manning these walls."

Fallows face now showed both shock and anger, but Argent continued.

"I have to inform you now, that I will take witness statements and, with a covering letter from me, all will be sent to the County Sheriff in Cork, copy to the Secretary of State for Ireland in Westminster, London."

Argent paused again, only slightly and Fallows shifted his feet. Argent was growing angry himself as he laid out the story in his own mind.

"Were you a Commissioned Officer, Mr. Fallows, your arguably cowardly and inadequate conduct would merit a full Court Martial and, if what I hear is correct and I've no reason to doubt it, a guilty verdict would be fully justified. The charge would be just that, cowardice, in the face of the enemy!"

Argent's voice rose in volume as he spoke the last words. Again came a pause, but no reply.

"I trust you understand the details of the actions I am about to take?"

Fallows face turned puce with anger, his unpleasant face jutting forward.

"Do your damndest and go to Hell! You think I'd risk my home and my family to help this diseased tribe of unwashed savages?"

He reached back to seize the edge of the door, to slam it, but the substantial muscles of King's right arm again prevented its closure. After unburdening himself with his own tirade, Argent was calmer.

"Yes Mr. Fallows. Yes, indeed I do! I do expect you to take risks to protect those, whom you took an Oath to protect!"

He nodded to King who allowed the door to close. Argent turned to see the women stood stern but triumphant, with highly satisfied looks on their faces, however, he spoke to Wentworth, who had been a silent witness all along.

"Come, Lieutenant. We have some interviewing and recording to do."

The sailors and themselves began their journey back down the hill, leaving the women, standing their ground and now almost laughing. However, Argent had not gone but a few yards before he heard something shouted in Gaelic, shouted loud enough to carry over the walls to the unseen Fallows. It didn't sound at all complimentary and Argent had a very good idea concerning its origin.

Within minutes Argent had two tables placed in full view of Fallows' residence down in the village, level with the mill. Sanders and Bright sat at one table, Wentworth and Trenchard the other. Sanders and

Bright were accompanied by Patrick, Sinead's foreman at the mill, who had an adequate command of English, whilst Sinead herself sat with Wentworth and Trenchard. The Officers were there to ask questions, the Midshipmen to record, Sinead and Patrick to translate.

For the rest of the morning there came a continuous procession of villagers to tell their story and soon each Midshipman had a sheaf of witness statements. Argent prowled up and down the village. He had deliberately placed the tables in full view of the castle and gained satisfaction to see Fallows himself at a window that overlooked the scene. With all interviewed that could be described as a witness, Merrymen Maybank, ever anxious over some imminent calamity, placed all statements in his leather satchel and had himself rowed back out to the ship, there to order them into priority and identify some for copying; some for copying twice.

With little daylight left, Argent ordered evacuation. Whiting and the others of Argent's bargecrew were the last to leave the village and then assemble at the Captain's barge. Surreptitiously, they had managed to carry extra into the cottage of the family they had helped during the first visit. The Mother had survived, but the raiders had taken three of her children, the three eldest. Throughout the day her thin frame had been wracked by a tangle of emotions; she thought she had lost three children, but now had regained only two, the son was gone. Whiting and the others had done their best to give comfort, but the fisherman Father was more stoical; disease and disaster would take their inevitable toll and both were well within his experience. The extra food helped and the Father shook the hands of each, saying thanks and good wishes, albeit in Gaelic, but each sailor could now manage a rough reply in the same language. However, now the men of the foretop stood waiting at the barge.

Argent was again the very last to leave the village. He stood looking around, acknowledging the waving hands and goodbyes of the villagers stood in their doorways under their low thatch, including Kaled, who had already been taken in and now stood before a cottage, his white smile bright in his dark face. Argent, then took a deep breath and did what he finally realised he wanted to do, to see Sinead one last time and to make a serious good-bye; at least that was how he described it in his own mind. One last check that nothing had been left behind, this as much to delay the anxious oncoming moment with Sinead but, nevertheless, he finally walked purposefully to the mill. This time he didn't even reach halfway, she came out of the mill and hurried to meet him. Whiting and his mates were watching all, as before, and Whiting pronounced judgement, looking at those stood around to add emphasis.

"If he doesn't bloody kiss her this time, I swear to God I'll dump the bugger in the oggin next time he's reaching down with his foot, an' tryin' to get hisself aboard!"

Able Jones looked away from events at the mill to re-assure his Foretop Captain.

"Then I reckon he'll be stayin' dry for the next time an' the time after. Just take a look up there."

Whiting did as he was bid and his face split in a wide grin. He could not see two separate figures, merely one shape, that of two figures clinging together, Argent's hat discarded at his feet, Sinead's white arms crossing on the back of his uniform.

Chapter Ten

Praise and Recrimination

At first it was just a smudge, a suggestion, hidden by the unkind mid-October weather of the Western Approaches. All the Ruanporth women and children had been standing watch, all taking turns on a random rota, since they had cleared The Scillies off to starboard. They had been replacing each other on unofficial lookout as and when required, but now the cry of "Land ho" from the masthead sent them all to the larboard side of the forecastle. There they won the argument with the men of the larboard caronnade as to who had the greatest claim on that particular place, the seamen disputing the women's need against their own to house their gun after the finish of the daily gun drill. However, the seal had been set on the argument by the women saying it was their turn in "the heads" and so all men were banished from the forecastle rail and the lookout in the foretop was also told to turn his ugly mug around.

Land's End itself had been passed in the dark of a thick pre-dawn and full daylight found them back in the open sea, therefore their first sight of their homeland had to wait until the next landfall, achingly delayed. However, it had arrived and gradually the dark line grew and extended, then, after some study whilst stood on the carronade slide, one of the women turned to Easau Grimes, now merely marginally less put out, now that his gun was safely housed, but now having to suffer his gun being stood on and turned into little more than a viewing platform.

"Which part of Cornwall is that?"

Grimes didn't need to look up from his tasks. He'd made the same landfall more times than he could remember or even count.

"The Lizard. That's The Lizard, the furthest point South of our Great British Isles."

"How much longer till we gets to Falmouth?"

The grumpy Grimes looked up at the sails, the pennant and the waves passing by. He consulted his subconscious that had registered the bells of the Forenoon Watch, heard it say "four", then made his own calculations.

"I'd say two bells of the Afternoon Watch 'll see us there. That's about three hours, if this wind holds, but that I wouldn't count on."

The woman smiled, folded her arms, then reached down with one hand to stroke the hair of her daughter, but Grimes had more to impart.

"I'd say, with this wind as 'tis, 'bout then, he'll come up to North or such, to take us in. You may even get a sight of Ruanporth, if it clears a bit."

He consulted the sky.

"Hmmm, yes, could be. You just might!"

Grimes had doubts that became justified; the breeze was indeed dying, which gave Argent his frequent Captain's problem regarding the quantity of spread canvas. The breeze, perfectly South West but now fading to a breath, was currently coming over the starboard quarter and Ariadne was slowing to little more than four knots, yet she was already displaying all common sail that would draw. He walked to the rail to give the order himself.

"Mr. Fraser, set all starboard stunsails. Mr. Ball, warn all lookouts to keep a weather eye to windward."

As both ran off to do their Captain's bidding, Argent looked around his quarterdeck, it now crowded with Officers, both off and on duty. There were happy and contented faces all around, many engaged in cheerful conversation and Argent had to admit to himself that he was also feeling far more buoyant. The memory of Sinead Malley held in his arms was fresh each time he closed his eyes and that potent thought did much to subdue the melancholy of his other concerns. He felt Ariadne heel over slightly as the stunsails were set and sheeted home. He studied how well they drew and was not satisfied. He spoke without looking, loud enough for the helmsman.

"Down helm, one point."

"Down helm one point. Aye aye, Sir. Now on East by North."

Argent saw the stunsails tighten, then looked down to see Midshipman Trenchard on deck with his Journal and decided to take a direct involvement with his nautical education.

"Mr. Trenchard!"

"Sir?"

"Did you hear my last order? That being the one I gave to Bosun's Mate Ball?"

"I did Sir."

"And why do you think I gave it."

Trenchard thought it wise to pause in order to fully form his answer.

"In case we are hit by a squall with a large amount of canvas spread, Sir. We need maximum advance warning."

"Very good. And what is happening in your Journal?"

"I'm writing up that which we just talked about, Sir."

Argent smiled and nodded, but his mind soon moved on. The Lizard Point was becoming clear and he took his glass and walked forward to the join of the quarterdeck and the larboard gangway, here to obtain a clearer view. At first the arms of the signal station remained hanging limp, but, even as he watched, they jerked into motion. Argent knew what they were conveying, or more accurately, asking, but he waited to hear what he hoped for, that being something from Midshipmen Berry, the Officer of Signals on this Watch. He waited, then was less than pleased to hear the report of a gun coming across the waters. The signal station had grown impatient at the delay and had drawn Ariadne's attention to their request. Argent re-focused his glass on the signal arms to see them repeating their movements and his impatience matched that of the men working the signal levers ashore.

"Mr. Berry! I think you'll find that the signal station, now on our larboard bow, is asking us to make our number."

Berry himself was following the movements of some topmen on the mainmast, so it was with a sudden start, then a jumble of his own hands and arms, that he focused his own spyglass to see the end of the signal. For him, things grew worse when he saw that the signalman had anticipated everything well before Argent's order and had bent on the required flags to the signal halliards without any order from him. Berry gave a superfluous nod but the Ariadne signalman had lost further patience and the three squares of coloured bunting were already flying up to the beam end of the mizzen topsail yard, larboard side. He was not going to allow his ship to appear in any way laggard before the gaze of any lever pulling longshoremen!

Having allowed a moment to pass, Argent turned to the miscreant Berry, his voice carrying more than a hint of sarcasm.

"Now, Mr. Berry, try this. Make the signal, "Ruanporth rescuees on board.""

Berry thumbed rapidly through his signal book and gave a reply that caused some reassurance in Argent concerning the capabilities of this particular Midshipman.

"Can I substitute "captives" for "rescuees", Sir? I'll have to spell out "rescuees" and I'm already having to spell out Ruanporth. It'll mean two parts to the signal, Sir."

Argent was inwardly pleased, but did not allow it to show. He grasped his hands behind his back and turned to look along the line of his ship.

"Very good, Mr. Berry. Make it so."

The signalman had already lowered their number and was assembling the necessary combinations of signal bunting. Again without waiting for an order from Berry he hauled at the halliards and there was just enough breeze to hold the flags full out. Berry waited a minute then focused his glass on the station. Argent stood waiting.

"Signal station replying, Sir."

A pause.

"God...be...thanked."

"Thank you, Mr. Berry. Make "Amen"."

Berry did so, but remained with his telescope on the signal station; watching the "arms" rotate to face away from them, then move at a frantic pace.

"They're passing our message on down the coast, Sir, I believe. The message is not meant for us, they've turned the arms away, to point to the next station along the coast.

Argent smiled and looked for himself. The signal arms were indeed now "end on" to them and were being worked very energetically.

A throwing of the log showed that Ariadne had picked up her speed to five and a half knots. With The Lizard now passed and off their larboard quarter, Argent decided to continue to stand on Eastwards. To turn North East direct for Falmouth would put the wind full astern, not a good point of sailing, the mizzen sails would shield the main and foresails from the wind. He would hold his course, wear ship to North West, taking the wind over the larboard quarter, then wear again North East to Falmouth, with the wind over the starboard quarter. He was aware that this sequence would mean wearing ship for the final turn at a point immediately off Ruanporth, but he convinced himself that this was strictly for reasons of naval expediency; to lessen the time of his passage, nothing to do with sentiment. After the passing of two more bells came the Noon Sight and Argent surrendered the quarterdeck to McArdle and his class. Argent was pleased to see small Christopher Wheeler confidently taking a sight, using one of McArdle's old, but perfectly serviceable, sextants. McArdle studied his performance down the right hand side of his nose, the studied look of disapproval, actually conveying satisfied approval.

With the ritual complete Argent ordered his change of course and Ariadne settled onto North West, with stunsails now set on the larboard side. The wind picked up and Ariadne increased her speed by a knot and they soon closed the coast, to under half a mile. Now the forecastle was fully thronged with the Ruanporth women and children and the noise from them rose as they picked out the familiar sets of hills and, as the distance lessened even further, the noise then increased further, as did the excited jumping and skipping. Fentiman was stood by Argent at the quarterdeck rail and listened through a pause in the noise coming from forward.

"Can you hear that, Sir?"

"Hear what?"

"Bells, Sir. I think I hear church bells."

Argent could hear nothing, so he turned to Midshipmen Bright, now on Watch.

"Mr. Bright. Can you hear church bells?"

Bright stood stock still, as if to aid his hearing.

"Yes Sir. I believe so, Sir, but I couldn't tell from where, Sir."

"Just so, Mr. Bright, just so."

Argent was judging his turn, the moment to wear ship for the last time. He moved to the larboard side to better his view and saw the close gathered collection of white houses, now clear against the dark green of the rain restored hillside.

"Mr. Bright."

"Sir."

"My compliments to Mr. Tucker, but I think it will be expeditious to ready a gun, the larboard carronade. If I'm not mistaken, that's Ruanporth over there, fine on our larboard bow, and I can see no harm in us drawing attention to ourselves."

"Aye aye Sir."

Bright hurried off and soon the forecastle, at least the larboard side of it, became a wholly male preserve again. Easau Grimes loaded a signal charge provided by Gunner Tucker into the wide mouth of his carronade and waited for the order, holding the lanyard and looking back to Argent. Bright had returned and Argent turned to him again.

"Mr. Bright, I think you would do well to ask our passengers to assemble along the larboard gangway, but please ensure that none climb onto the railing. I wouldn't want any lost overboard within sight of their home village."

Whilst Bright made off forward once again, Argent had judged his moment as arrived and shouted down to Bosun Fraser.

"Mr. Fraser! Wear ship, starboard tack."

Argent turned to the helmsman.

"Up helm. Come to North East by East."

Ariadne answered her helm and her bows swung to starboard to bring her larboard side opposite the coast. As the Afterguard bustled around the deck and the topmen described acrobatics in the rigging, Argent looked along the deck to Easau Grimes, waiting patiently. Argent lifted his hat; Grimes took the signal and jerked the lanyard. The gun gave a deep bark, but, with no ball, it made no movement along its slide and the smoke curled away in the breeze. The women and children, now with a clear view of their home, redoubled their jumping, shouting, waving and hallooing. Argent pulled out his glass and focused it on the shore of the village. Some people were there and were looking out to sea, their attention gained by the gun, but as yet none waved back. Fentiman and Bright were either side of him.

"I'd say only those with a glass could see what we have aboard from this far out, but if nothing else, at least it's added to the homecoming of our passengers."

Ariadne sailed on, but Bright kept his glass on the village. After about five minutes he spoke.

"I'd say there were a few more at the shoreline now, Sir. Perhaps they've twigged somehow. Perhaps from the Signal Station."

"Yes, Mr. Bright. Let's hope so. I wouldn't want one of Mr. Tucker's signal charges shot off in vain."

Bright saw the irony and smiled.

"No Sir. Waste of powder, Sir."

Argent smiled and resumed his viewing of the deck, hands clasped behind.

"Just so, Mr. Bright, just so."

* * *

Abel Jones was serving his Watch as Foremast lookout, high in the foretopgallant crosstrees. His mate, Silas Beddows was busy below, working on the foretop. Jones shielded his eyes to aid his vision, although there was no sun and he peered ahead. The hills that marked the entrance to Falmouth harbour were clear and the gap between them growing with the reducing distance.

"Silas. Come up yer, a minute."

Beddows climbed powerfully up to his mate and joined him, hanging his muscled arms over the spar.

"What?"

"Can you see what I see, in the harbour entrance?"

Beddows shielded his eyes in similar fashion.

"And what can you see? I can see a ship, looks like a frigate, by the size of her stern, but with a lot of buggery where her top hamper ought to be. Looks like she's got but one whole mast still standing."

Jones' voice was heavy with sarcasm.

"That's what I see. Now I can inform the Captain."

He lowered himself down to the foretop and addressed the deck.

"Sail ho! Fine on the larboard bow. Enterin' the harbour. Looks like she's damaged."

Wentworth had the quarterdeck, Argent was now off-watch and was taking the time to assemble the ship's books prior to going ashore. Wentworth had only Midshipman Trenchard as a Watch Officer, but McArdle was also close at hand.

"M-Mr McArdle. Wh-what do you make of that? E-e-ntering the har-harbour."

McArdle fixed Wentworth with a frown, even though he was his superior Officer, and took himself to the larboard mizzenshrouds to gain a clear view forward and to use his own telescope. He studied for less than a minute.

"I'd say, Sir, that's a frigate, like us, with nae small amount of damage. From what, it's too far to say."

McArdle looked blankly at Wentworth and then spoke again.

"Ye'd best inform the Captain, Sir."

Wentworth nodded.

"Mr. Trenchard. T-take yourself to the C-Captain and inform him tha-that a d-d-damaged frigate is blocking the har-harbour."

Wentworth raised his own glass, at the same time imparting his thoughts to the still present McArdle.

"I'd say she was str-struggling, Sailing M-Master. The t-tide's away, is it n-not?"

"Awa's the word, Sir. This hour gone."

McArdle raised his own glass.

"She's little to spread and nae driver. That gives nae balance to her hull, ye see, makin' her a beastie tae steer. There she goes, yawing aboot, an' we'll be up on her afore she's clear, at this speed."

The hint was heavy and clear, Ariadne was carrying a heavy press of canvas to get to harbour. Wentworth looked along the weather gangway to see Bosun Fraser.

"G-get the canvas off her, Bosun. Leave only f-fore and main courses, and d-d-driver."

Fraser looked shocked at the massive reduction in sail, but he had received an order. Such was the magnitude of the task he yelled for "all hands on deck." As the Starboard Watch sprang into the rigging, and the off duty Larboard Watch climbed the companionways, Argent arrived, with Midshipman Trenchard.

"Mr. Wentworth. What's the problem?"

"S-Sir, there's a cr-crippled ship in the h-harbour entrance, Sir. I've ordered a r-r-reduction in s-sail. Sir."

Argent looked at the spars and rigging now crowded with men, all busy furling the sails. Ariadne's speed was dropping off substantially and Argent needed convincing regarding so extreme a change in their spread of canvas but he raised his own glass and was immediately re-assured. He brought the frigate into his glass and immediately saw her bows swing badly to larboard as she ineffectually battled the outgoing tide. Full starboard rudder swung over her stern to compensate, but she was now out of line for a clean entrance. She swung back to starboard, losing way in the tide. Argent lowered his glass.

"A good decision, Mr. Wentworth. I think we'll let her get fully in and clear, whoever she is, before we make our attempt. Or perhaps she gives up on her own."

Wentworth beamed at his Captain's praise, but meanwhile, in the foretopgallant crosstrees, Jones and Beddows were moving the conversation on, Jones particularly.

"Get Gabe up yer with his telescope."

To many such a descent for such an errand would be tedious in the extreme but Beddows was on deck in seconds having slid down the fore preventer stay onto the bowsprit. In little more than two minutes beyond that, both himself and Gabriel Whiting had climbed over the futtock shrouds to gain the foretop. Jones did no more than point.

"That barky yawing about in the harbour. 'Er stern looks familiar, and I think I've got her placed, but what do you think?"

Whiting looked at Jones quizzically, extended his glass, then braced himself against the foremast. He focused the instrument, studied for a minute, then pronounced.

"There's only one frigate I know with all that gash gilt all over her stern. It's only that floggin' sod as would spend such money on all that extra."

He paused to focus the glass again then spoke, his first word drawn out.

"Yes, I'd say I can just about make out Herodotus on her backside. She's lost over half her masts and riggin', I'd say. There'll 'ave been some bloody backs over that!"

Beddows looked from Jones to Whiting.

"Should we tell the Captain?"

Whiting thought, then answered.

"Nah! Officers' business, which ship comes, which ship goes, an' to where. Their business. We've told him, that's us done."

Then his face split into a wide grin.

"But I think I'll stay up yer, just to get a good look at 'er."

On the quarterdeck the situation was demanding a greater depth of attention. Argent was convinced that Ariadne, with much reduced sail, was slipping back against the tide. He used Bright again.

"Mr. Bright. Find two points in conjunction on the shore. Tell me if we're losing way relative to the land."

Bright found a hut and a tree close but not in line and within a minute they had merged, showing that the tide was pushing Ariadne back.

"Yes Sir, we are. Significantly, I'd say."

"You'd say, Mr. Bright, and your solution would be?"

"All topsails, Sir."

"A good solution, Mr. Bright. I leave it to you."

Bright's face split from ear to ear as he hurried off to find Bosun Fraser. Argent stood by the wheel, noting Quartermaster Short working the spokes of the wheel to keep their heading as the tide worked on Ariadne more than the breeze. However, soon the topsails began to draw and the coast slipped past in the right direction. Two bells came, and then three. Argent was grateful that the frigate in the entrance had, with great difficulty, succeeded in battling her way in and Ariadne was able to enter the harbour, whilst the excitement mounted to new heights on the larboard gangway. The women and children had placed themselves there for almost two hours and Fentiman saw fit to send some seamen to clear them away, but with the gentle excuse that they should get their possessions, little as they were, prior to being ferried ashore. However, their obedience was not exactly in the Naval tradition, many lingering to drink in the sight of home, until they were good-naturedly shunted away.

Sanders was studying the ship that had delayed their entrance and, almost on their entry, he walked excitedly over the Argent.

"Sir, that's the Herodotus. Wasn't she sent down into The Bay, to chase the slaver?"

Argent looked over, but he too, had recognised the heavy decoration embellishing her stern. Her name now being visible confirmed his judgment.

"Yes, Mr. Sanders, it is and she was. We can only assume that she was caught in the storm that we suspected and we set a course to avoid. And by the looks of it, she suffered, explaining her exceedingly slow voyage home."

Sanders looked again, this time examining the damage more carefully. Herodotus had lost her mizzenmast entirely, her maintopmast and her foretopgallant mast. Thus, she showed but a strange triangle of masts and rigging, descending from the foretopmast to the shattered stump at her quarterdeck. As they spoke she was coming to anchor, the first available in Carrick Roads, meaning Ariadne would have to sail quite close to her in order to reach their own, further up.

"Should we do something or say something, Sir? They've had a nightmare time of it."

Argent looked at him.

"I'd say etiquette requires that we raise our hats. Beyond that, I see no point. Take your cue from me."

Ariadne passed at hailing distance. Those on her quarterdeck lifted their hats on passing, but from the Officers on Herodotus there was no response. Some of the Ruanporth's waved and shouted, but received the merest of desultory responses, the briefest lifting of a hand from the men on deck, the crew were too exhausted. What was also missing was the usual bandinage between crews, almost obligatory, when one had lost any amount of her rigging, plainly such as Herodotus. However, this vessel and the life of those aboard her, were only too well known to the men of Ariadne and their sympathy was too strong for men whose fate, but for fortune, could easily have been their own.

* * *

The Ruanporth women and children were running along the navy mole to the main quayside to disappear into the waiting crowd, by the time Argent came to land himself. The noise of shouts and cheering was incessant. Their longboat had vacated the mole steps for Argent's barge to tie up and, with Jones again locking the painter fast through a ringbolt, Argent stepped ashore, but the din from the throng at the end of the mole gave Whiting some concern and he climbed the steps immediately after his Captain.

"I'd say you'll 'ave some need of us, Sir, to find your way through that bunged up collection yonder."

Being Navy stonework, the landward end was guarded by Royal Marines, but beyond that was civilian territory and it seemed that half of Falmouth was gathered there to greet both the rescued and the rescuer. Argent gave the matter some brief thought.

"You may be right. Leave Jones here, you other four come with me, although there does seem to be enough Marines up there to accomplish what you speak of."

"Ah yes, but beyond that, Sir. To the Commodore's Office, like."

Argent grinned, but continued to look along to the quayside. He had more than a sneaking suspicion that Whiting had another motive besides his Captain's safety and dignity, that of being close to the point where some girls may be going about their daily business or taking of their leisure.

"Very well. I'll leave it to you."

The four immediately placed themselves before Argent, the massive King and Fenwick leading at the centre. As they progressed along the medieval stonework, Argent noted that each man of his bargecrew ensured that the "Ariadne" on their hats was exactly centre, clean and most conspicuous. The Marines made a way and, using their muskets, held back the crowd. Argent walked through unscathed, apart from the clamour in his ears from the deep and excited crowd. Once through, the Sergeant in charge ordered half his command to continue as escort and so, guarded by both Marines and his bargecrew Argent arrived untouched at the door of Commodore Budgen's Office. He removed his hat and entered, leaving his guardians at the door. Inside he found Marine Sergeant Venables, already at attention, shako in place. At three yards distance he fizzed a salute up to the peak of the same gleaming headgear. Argent acknowledged and ordered Venables to stand easy.

"Good afternoon, Sergeant. I trust I find you well?"

"The very best of good afternoon's to you Sir, if I may make so bold, and I'd like to add that I've not seen this town so happy since they heard of Trafalgar. Nor I 'aven't. Sir."

Argent grinned, in some contrast to his humour prior to his entry, for, on approaching the door of Budgen's domain Argent's own spirits had become more subdued, but he did his best to appear cheerful for the old Marine.

"Well, it seems we had a slice of luck and took advantage of it. Our people are back where they belong and that's what matters."

"That's the right of it, Sir, and that Devil's sunk. Yes? Sir?"

At that moment Budgen's voice could be heard loud and clear from his office down the corridor.

"Venables! If that's Captain Argent, send him down, this instant, do you hear?"

Venables shouted back in the affirmative, then whispered conspiratorially.

"When can I get the details, Sir?"

Argent replied in an equal whisper.

"I don't doubt it'll all be in the news-sheets."

The jubilant Marine nodded and Argent left him to enter the corridor to Budgen's own office, but the thought had lifted his mood; the Press would be on his side. Feeling more cheerful, Argent entered the office to find Budgen sat bolt upright in his chair, to the fullest height that his stature could manage, but with a face as black as thunder. Argent thought it best to stand to attention and he did.

"You've no need to describe to me, Captain, just what has occurred, accomplished by you. That circus out there is witness enough!"

"Yes Sir."

The silence hung between them, but it was Budgen who took the initiative.

"You have your Logbook? It tells the full story?"

Argent took both Log and Ship's Ledger from under his arm and placed them on the desk.

"Yes Sir. The full story and in detail."

"And where is the slaver?"

"Sunk, Sir, and I have her Captain on board, a prisoner."

Budgen was taken aback. Argent's triumph was building; captives returned and the slaver himself available to be paraded in chains, but Argent had disobeyed orders, those of both himself and Broke. He felt slighted, and not for the first time, by this too self-assured "one swab" Captain. The matter must run its course.

"And the communication?"

Budgen pronounced the word as though he were spelling it, each syllable carefully spoken.

"Delivered to General Hill, Sir, whom I'm sure you know is General Wellington's Second in Command."

"Wellington?"

"Yes Sir. General Wellesley is now Lord Wellington, since the battle of Talavera, last July."

Now Argent paused.

"Delivered after ten days, Sir."

Budgen was brought even more erect, but made no comment. He contented himself with opening the Log to the relevant pages and then scanning down the entries, giving him the reason he needed to leave Argent standing there. He closed the Log with a thump for extra emphasis.

"I'm sending this to Admiral Grant, Argent. It's my opinion, and there's strong evidence in support, that you went hunting for that slaver having been ordered expressly not to do so. I'm recommending a Court Martial and I'd be surprised if Grant did not accede to one. I'd say he had little choice."

Argent was surprised at his own lack of reaction to the weighty and threatening words. Perhaps because he had been expecting it, perhaps because he had been buoyed up by their reception and the idea of the newssheets being on his side. He met the challenge, speaking calmly.

"I stand ready to answer for my actions. Sir."

Budgen's face showed his anger at the lack of impact his words had placed on Argent, but this time it was Argent who spoke further, his voice remaining calm and level.

"If there is nothing else, Sir, I wish to get back to my ship. She has to be re-supplied and I must arrange for the transfer of the prisoner."

Budgen nodded, his face and posture remaining churlish and angry. Argent saluted and left the Office, but paused, as was now customary, to exchange blistering salutes with the still elated Marine Sergeant Venables. Outside, a collection of girls had gathered around his bargecrew, but the welcoming crowd had largely disappeared. His bargecrew sprang to attention and saluted, mostly to impress the girls that they were thorough man o' war's men who knew what's what. Argent replaced his hat, returned their salutes and walked on. His crew caressed, whispered, and kissed their goodbyes and fell in around him, soon being required to hold off those closing in who wished to shake Argent's hand or do whatever they felt would best convey their sincerest congratulations. At the guardhouse at the beginning of the mole, Argent asked the sentry to fetch the Officer of the Guard and a young Captain emerged, rapidly buttoning his tunic, then coming to the attention before saluting.

"Captain Nathan Finch, Sir. At your service."

Argent nodded.

"Captain Finch. I am about to land a prisoner, him being the Captain of the slaver, which I'm sure, you've heard about. I will need a strong escort or we'll never get him to the town gaol. Can I rely on you to obtain reinforcements?"

Finch, who looked no more than sixteen, saluted again.

"Yes Sir. Aye aye, Sir. When will you be bringing him ashore, Sir?'

"Directly. Say half an hour."

"Yes Sir. We'll be ready. Sir."

Argent walked along the mole, acknowledging the greetings of those working there and he descended the steps to the already waiting barge. During the short journey his mind dwelled on the vehemence of Budgen's ill feeling, but soon they were against Ariadne's tumblehome and as he climbed through the entryport he gave further orders, his first being to order his barge to stand ready.

"Mr. Fraser. Find the Sergeant at Arms. He is to release the prisoner, but chain him hands and feet before bringing him on deck. Then find Mr. Sanders and send him to my cabin."

Argent went immediately to his cabin, threw his hat onto his cot and then sat on his chair behind his desk, leaning back, thoughtful. Now he had confronted at least one of his demons he found it more uplifting than depressing, but his thoughts were interrupted by a knock on the door. A shout of "Enter" brought in Sanders who closed the door behind him as he spoke.

"You sent for me Sir?"

"Yes Jonathan. I've given orders that our Master at Arms, Sergeant Ackroyd, bring our prisoner, Al Ahbim, up on deck. He will be in chains, I need not add, but I want you to get him off our hands and into the town gaol. There will be a strong Marine escort waiting for you at the end of the mole and my barge is waiting at the ladder. At the gaol, I suspect, you will be required to give some details regarding evidence that will lead to a charge; English captives aboard his vessel is all that we ourselves can allude to. The rest will arrive from elsewhere, I shouldn't wonder. Can I leave that with you?"

"Will your barge be big enough, Sir? Perhaps the launch instead. I can take some of our own Marines."

Argent thought. Exchanging launch for barge meant a lot of work, and for what? Ackroyd could sit besides Sanders and the prisoner sit down on the boards between them and Silas Beddows sat at stroke.

"I'd judge not. There'll be seven men, including yourself."

Sanders saluted from where he stood.

"Aye, aye Sir. Will you be coming up, to oversee his leaving, as it were?"

Argent's face twisted into a grimace. He hadn't looked at Al Ahbim since he'd been chained to the deck; the memories he engendered were too painful.

"No. I leave it to you."

Sanders left the cabin and climbed to the entryport where Ackroyd had the prisoner waiting. He still looked of high Arab status, his clothes clean and well fitting, although voluminous in the Arab style. His beard and hair were trimmed and clean, but his eyes glowered with ill will to all around him. There were heavy manacles around his ankles and also around his wrists. A long length of chain ran from the centre of his wrist manacles to the gnarled hands of Sergeant Ackroyd, then to a manacle on Ackroyd's own wrist. Al Ahbim looked up as Sanders approached and fixed him with a look of such malevolence that Sanders own expression showed his own anger and then the "before the mast" topman in him took over.

"You can look at me with all the bad mood you like, old cock, but it's the inside of the chokey for you and after that the gallows dance!"

Ackroyd and the supervising Fraser grinned, but Al Ahbim's expression didn't change, not even when a rope was wound around his chest and under his arms. He was manoeuvred to the entrance port and then pushed forward, to become suspended from the yardarm above, then lowered down to the waiting barge. When he arrived the look of pure hatred that he received from Whiting and Beddows matched his own and he squatted down on the bottom boards, to look furtively at the harbour around him, all of which was wholly alien to a North African port. Whiting released the rope, none too gently, including a few cuffs around the head, then Ackroyd came down, still holding the chain, then finally Sanders. With all settled, Sanders gave a nod to Whiting at the tiller.

"Come forward. Give way, all."

The oars were pulled, then bit into the water again. The jerk from the powerful stroke sent Ackroyd and Sanders back into the seat and Al Ahbim toppled forward slightly before regaining his posture. In no time they had cleared Ariadne's hull and Whiting set a direct course for the same steps the barge had used earlier. Sanders looked at Al Ahbim. His head was working from side to side and his fingers were clenching and unclenching, but what was most noticeable were his eyes darting from side to side. Sanders knew not what to make of it and, anyway, he found the sight of this Arab utterly distasteful. He looked away to their destination, the steps, where a squad of Marines was drawn up waiting. Suddenly, Al Ahbim was on his feet, at his full height.

"Allah akbar!"

Al Ahbim was over the side with only his own efforts to rely on. The air in his clothes working against the weight of the chain and manacles but the iron won and soon he was out of sight beneath the dark water. The chain ran out and pulled Ackroyd's wrist down into the water, but he held to the side of the barge and kept his place, aided greatly by Sanders and then Whiting, these both keeping him in the boat, he would be over the side, left to his own efforts. Sanders shouted in alarm.

"Beddows, tail on. King, back here!"

Beddows seized the chain and King tumbled back to the stern, but Beddows and Ackroyd quickly won back enough of a length for King also to gain a hold. With both topmen braced across the hull, their feet locked against the gunwhale, the chain was won back, foot by foot, but minutes had passed. It was Ackroyd who was looking down into the water and soon he shouted out what he could see.

"I can see him. He's comin up."

Beddows and King redoubled their efforts and soon what appeared over the top of the gunwhale was Al Ahbim's head, but Ackroyd shouted, almost in panic, and they saw him reach over the side.

"Stop pullin'. Stop pullin'."

Sanders leaned over the side using Ackroyd as a support and saw why the Marine had called for them to stop. With one hand Ackroyd had gained a hold on the sodden cloth at Al Ahbim's shoulder and was unwinding the chain from his neck with the other. Whiting was the first to ask.

"Is he dead?"

"We've got to get him in, give me a hand, you two."

Beddows and King reached over to take a handful of clothing and both helped to haul the limp and sodden figure back into the boat. The last loop of chain came away from the throat, but it was clear that Al Ahbim was dead, his eyes staring out lifeless but still piercing, his mouth in a rictus grin, somehow triumphant. He had wound the chain around his neck as he sank through the water, knowing it would help to end his life as they hauled his body back up, it heavy with the chains and the waterlogged, voluminous clothing. The time this took had killed him, for, even as he came to the surface, his lungs could not gain breath, the chain being tight around his throat. Sanders felt for a pulse but there was none.

"He's dead."

He drew in a deep breath and sighed. For him this could be a disaster.

"Back to your places. Let's get this ashore."

They all regained their places in the barge and Whiting took over. They reached the steps and Jones was first out to hold the barge steady. The Marines had seen all and were ready on hand to haul the lifeless figure out by the arms and onto the stone, then four of them, two on each arm, dragged him up the steps, his face bumping over the rough granite edges. Sanders followed and, at the top, found Captain Finch. He looked at Sanders with shock, but Sanders' expression was one of anger and frustration and it was he who spoke first.

"Could you detail six men, to lay this across their muskets and take it to the gaol? I'll follow, they'll need some details."

Finch nodded and named six men. Three muskets were arranged parallel on the ground and the lifeless body rolled onto them. The six each took the end of a musket and the body was lifted to be carried chest upwards along the mole to the quayside, the lifeless eyes staring ahead at all in their path from a head hanging backwards, limp and awkward, but swaying with the rhythmic marching legs of the six Marines. Many onlookers, knowing full well the identity of the body, spat on it as they passed.

It was Fentiman who brought Argent the news and told the story, having watched all from the quarterdeck and it was Fentiman who registered the greatest surprise, caused by Argent's lack of reaction.

"Saves a tedious appearance in Court."

A pause.

"When Sanders returns, send him to me."

Over an hour later, it was a very worried and chastened Sanders who once again knocked on the cabin door, but he was rapidly reassured by an unmoved Argent.

"Don't blame yourself, Jonathan. The man was determined to end his life. You would have had to chain him down on the bottom boards to remove all of such a risk. Perhaps we should have thought of it, but then he could equally have done the job by jumping off the quayside escorted by the Marines. He was determined and that's that. Don't distress yourself."

Sanders gave a worried nod, but Argent had moved on and to this end he held up a letter.

"I've just received this, it being a letter from the Clerk to the Town Council saying that they want to lay on some kind of celebration to mark our successful return, for both ourselves and the crew. They must have written it the moment they heard. I'm mulling over in my mind if we should warp ourselves alongside the mole, as we did back in July. I'm inclined, as we speak, to say not, but I'll hold my judgment until I hear from you. If I'm not here, Mr. Fentiman can decide. I want you to take charge, to liaise with the Town Council and whatever. Can I leave this one with you?"

Sanders was astonished that the interview had ended on such a note, so he nodded vigorously and saluted.

"Yes Sir, you can."

"Good, now please give Mr. Fentiman my compliments and ask him to join me."

Sanders took a rapid exit.

* * *

Argent set the good mare at the hill that rose out of Falmouth, but this time on the road for Truro, its museum and the source of his latest hopes. He couldn't decide what to think, either high hope or guarded optimism and so he thought of neither, regarding his mission as being merely one avenue of possibility, but he deliberately passed no judgement on the likelihood of success. He'd left Fentiman in charge, explaining the issue about closing to the mole and that he would prefer Ariadne to remain out in Carrick Roads, but he would have no great objection if Fentiman differed, for the sake of the occasion.

Now he felt his legs responding to the movement of the horse, rather than the deck of his ship and, knowing that Truro was but a dozen miles, he let the mare move at her own speed, a leisurely trot, which sometimes reduced to a fast walk. Sometimes Argent dismounted to walk himself, the pleasure coming from being allowed to walk so far in one direction, rather than the 40 odd yards of his frigate. The last hill saw the roofs of Truro come into sight; the height of the church towers and spires somehow aggressive against the domestic and unambitious reach of the surrounding houses and buildings. A distant chime of 9 o' clock welcomed his arrival. Argent knew Truro well enough and was able to guide the good mare to a well-appointed stable where he gave instructions for her food, rest and water. The rest of the journey he undertook on foot, which took him to the centre of the pleasant market town with its open spaces and streets that served as an administrative centre for this part of Cornwall. Also as a place of very mixed culture, this including a playhouse, a prize-fight ring, a racetrack, a cockpit, two first-class restaurants and his destination, a museum. His quest was down a side street and Argent entered the impressive Norman arch, one of the few pieces of stonework remaining from what had been erected during the time of that conquering race. He had to acknowledge that his pulse rate had increased and not just from a walk made with lungs used to a far shorter stride than he had just made from the stable.

The museum entrance hall was gloomy with myriad motes of dust hanging in the weak light that came from the clerestory windows high in the ceiling. He tucked his hat under his arm, brushed off his uniform and looked for someone to approach. There was no one. He walked on into the museum proper with its very eclectic mix of stuffed animals, flags, pots, both broken and whole, scrolls and tomes, suits of armour and vicious weapons. Along the back wall was an arrangement of glass cases and he made straight for these, to stand disappointed. They contained a collection of coins and other small metal objects; ornaments, badges, pins and buckles. He looked around to ask himself, what remained, if any, of the exhibits within the museum that he had not examined? Nothing in this gallery, obviously, so he took himself back to the entrance hall, there to see something that he had missed on his entrance because it had been behind him, against the wall containing the door he had entered by. It was a high desk, complete with a curator of some kind and Argent approached, pulse still racing.

"Excuse me."

The Curator looked up, or more accurately over, over some steel rimmed spectacles that were perched precariously on the end of his nose and held only in place by side arms that extended back to disappear into curious tufts of white hair, all that remained of hair on a head of about 35 years of age. The white stood in contrast to the pink of his complexion, it being wholly pallid, unchanged by any significant length of period in open sunshine. The risk of mishap was removed when the Curator took the spectacles off and actually stood to greet Argent. The welcoming smile completely changed the initial impression created by the bespectacled figure previously sat crouched behind the desk. He was tallish, well proportioned and neatly, but soberly, dressed.

"How may I help?"

Argent took a deep breath. He wasn't sure how to start and he hadn't yet got anything clear in his head, so he simply started talking.

"I'm here to enquire if you have any documents relating to a farm called Lanbe Barton. Pronounced "Land bee", but spelt with only one "e" on the end. I refer particularly to Deeds of Title. I'm under the impression that this Deed may be a historic document, which is why I'm here, talking to you."

The Curator's brows knitted together, more in puzzlement than annoyance.

"Such things are normally held in the Records Office of the County Court."

Argent nodded.

"I know, but I have already been there and they had nothing, neither Deed nor any reference to it."

Argent paused and took a deep breath.

"May I tell you why I am anxious to find this document?"

The Curator nodded, his face now growing concerned.

"I don't know if you are aware, but the enclosures movement is spreading all over Cornwall."

The Curator nodded as Argent continued.

"Those who cannot show proof of ownership lose their land. My family have lived on that farm for generations, centuries, even, and it will be lost if we cannot produce some Deeds of Title. Because of the time we have lived there, I was hoping that it may have some historic significance, causing it to be lodged with you."

The Curator's face showed genuine unease. He held out his hand.

"My name is Jeremiah Townmead."

Argent took the hand offered.

"Argent. Captain Reuben Argent."

Townmead moved his head from side to side, looking around, as if seeking instruction.

"Right. Where to start? If we have it, be sure we'll find it. I've just finished cataloguing and cross referencing all the museum's possessions, so all we have is recorded, somewhere."

The last word tailed off and Argent's confidence, which had grown from Townmead's words, diminished somewhat, but he had grown to like this gentle academic, who was plainly eager to help. Suddenly, Townmead became decisive."

"Right, let's start with "Land and Property". Come this way please, Captain."

He led Argent to a door in the sidewall, which he opened to reveal a room almost wholly full of chests, cabinets, and partitioned racks of loose scrolls and papers, no gangway could be walked down without turning sideways. The place was surprisingly well lit from the same type of clerestory windows as the exhibition hall and the whole interior smelt of wood, ancient paper, ancient leather and dust. Townmead closed the door to reveal behind it a bookcase above a desk, then he looked along a rank of ledgers, speaking absentmindedly.

"My favourite place, this, where I organise the catalogues."

A ledger arrived on the desk, with a hand written label, "Land and Property."

"Now, you say the farm is called Lanbe Barton?"

Argent leaned forward, hoping to see the pages for himself.

"Yes. Lanbe Barton."

Townmead set the ledger on its spine. Someone, probably him, had cut small indentations into the ends of the pages. He thrust a very clean thumb into the indentation for "L" and allowed the ledger to fall open. The turning of one page brought him to the "La"s. An equally clean forefinger ran down the list, then the finger stopped but his face showed no success.

"There is no Lanbe Barton mentioned, I'm afraid."

However, he leaned forward just to check his use of the alphabet, scanning above and below. His head dropped lower showing he had found something.

"But there is this. "Land by Barton – a document of gift."

He looked at Argent, whose eyebrows were nearly at his hairline, a wide, apprehensive, yet hopeful, smile almost joining them.

"Can you produce it?"

Townmead looked again and ran his finger across the line to the last column.

"This is a cross-reference to another ledger. CWR. Civil War and Restoration."

He closed the ledger, carefully replaced it and pulled down another, with that title showing. By now Argent was in a state of high agitation, but Townmead was as calm as though he were dusting a glass cabinet. He also stood this new ledger on its spine, entered his thumb in the "L" index and allowed the pages to fall open. Turning one page the clean finger found the words Townmead sought and Argent grew even more impatient as he saw more detail beside them. Townmead leaned forward and began to read out loud.

"Land by Barton. Fifty acres of land, given as a gift to William Bennet by Charles II in May 1661 in recognition of his loyal service to King Charles during the Civil War at the siege of Dunster Castle. In addition, his fortitude as a Royal Subject during the Interregnum during which he suffered persecution by the Puritan Government of Oliver Cromwell."

Townmead looked at Argent, almost in triumph.

"That's my writing, I wrote that. You see, May 1661 was Charles II's first anniversary on the throne. What do you think?"

Argent looked at the words, then at Townmead.

"Could be. The farmhouse is certainly old. One hundred and fifty years would be about it, and there's a family story about a Royalist soldier."

Townmead looked again at the ledger.

"Case 8. Drawer C."

Townmead turned to disappear into the narrow gap between two cabinets. Argent, whilst reading the description again, heard drawers being opened, then the rustle of paper, then a drawer being closed. Townmead quickly reappeared bearing a folder of heavy cartridge paper, which he placed on the desk and opened. Inside was a document 12 inches by 24, made of crude, thick paper, but the most impressive items were the huge coloured crest, evidently Royal, at the top and, almost as large, the stamp in the sealing wax at the bottom, containing what looked very much like the crest of some Kingly family. Townmead reached beside the desk to find a magnifying glass, then he began to examine the writing. Argent tried to peer through the glass himself, but, to his great distress, the distortion from the angle was too great. However, Townmead soon began speaking.

"Yesssss. This is in what I call Puritan English. You see, Charles' civil servants at that time were those that he inherited from Cromwell and so the Puritan language still pertained. Those educated at that time were educated by Puritans and so this is what we still have, even though Cromwell's long gone, scattered in bits around Tyburn, except his head, of course; that's spiked in Westminster Hall.

Throughout this history lesson, Argent was almost beside himself, but he cudgelled himself into patience. Townmead looked again.

"But that's what it says all right, and here it is: "unto our good servant William Bennet of Falmouth District..."

He looked up.

"Cromwell had the whole country sliced up into Districts ruled by his Major Generals, you see, strict Puritans all."

He returned to his reading. Argent ground his teeth.

"...Falmouth District, is given, on this 29th Day of May, Year of Our Lord 1661, one hundred acres of good farmland hard by the estate property known as Barton, this now in the possession of Sir Marmaduke Symonds. Know all men by these presents that this document shall count as Deed of Title to this gift and the said gift shall be known as Land by Barton and shall remain so for all purposes both commercial and hereditary. This land shall remain within the family of William Bennet as long as the Good Lord and the King shall see fit."

He set down the magnifying glass and looked at Argent.

"There. I'd say this was your land."

Argent was both grinning and nodding, before seizing Townmead's right hand to shake it.

"Yes, that's it. It is. My undying thanks to you. The current owner, Admiral Broke, purchased Barton from the Symonds family, not so far back. What else could it be? That's it."

Townmead had more. He placed a now dusty finger on the signature at the bottom.

"And that, my dear Sir, is the signature of our restored Charles II himself, and that his seal."

The finger had moved to the huge disc of wax, its volume being at least a whole stick of sealing wax. Argent looked over the document trying to read for himself, but the formation of the letters was almost unintelligible, too many "s" looking like an "f". However, Townmead was moving the affair on.

"What you have to do now is to prove that this William Bennet is one of your ancestors. Your Parish Records should accomplish that for you. That done, no Court in the land would dare dispute a Royal command such as this, attested by that Royal himself, Charles the tooth! That is why it's here, with us. I only have four more with any Royal signature, from any age. It was donated to us by one..."

He again ran his finger fully across the ledger and onto the opposite page.

"...Septimus Argent in 1754. That's a link immediately."

Argent's own mind began working.

"Can I ask you something, rather to do something? Can you produce a letter that summarises what the document says and also that this document is lodged with you as the motive for your letter? Can you do that, in order that I will have something to take away with me, back to my family?"

Townmead lifted his head and smiled in the affirmative.

"I most certainly can. And I will sign it and I'll do more. I'll get my good friend Thomas Fenby from next door to sign as a witness. He's an Attorney at Law, you see. We were at Cambridge together. He read Law. Myself, Ancient History."

Argent laughed openly.

"Well bless all the Saints for that! And bless you both for the most laudable and intellectual studies that you both completed there."

Townmead laughed as well and closed the folder of cartridge paper.

"This document strictly belongs to you. You could take it with you, but I hope you will not."

Argent placed his right hand over his left breast. He was almost light headed.

"I will indeed not. I thus bequeath this document unto the safe keeping of Truro Museum. And, if you wish to display it in a case, I'll have no objection to that, either."

Townmead laughed again.

"That I may well do, but for now, I assume that you would wish to return home, as soon as possible. So, I will complete the letter immediately, take it next door to Fenby and get him to come here. He'll want to see this, pernickity cove that he is, then he'll witness what he's seen and sign it. Come back in an hour and we'll have you on your way. And it'll be in the King's English of George III, nothing Puritan in there contained! "

Argent grinned like a child, took Townmead's right hand once again in both his and shook it vigorously. Argent left the storeroom first, followed by Townmead, him with the folder under his arm. Townmead went straight to his Curator's desk, which curiously was now in the charge of a prim, but pleasant looking woman who seemed to require the same style of spectacles as Townmead. Argent bowed in her direction, replaced his hat, wished them both a very good day and left.

He absentmindedly turned one way, his mind elsewhere, then realised this was the way out of town and so he retraced his steps, on further to a coffee shop in the town square. He had no realisation, but his uniform stood out amongst the drab civilians and so Argent was served by the owner, who approached Argent's table whilst lacing up a clean apron. Argent drank one cup, which was very good coffee, then ordered another. Half an hour passed and the euphoria that had possessed him was beginning to subside. He realised that nothing was finalised, not by some way, they still had to prove that they were descended from this Royalist hero, William Bennet. It being donated by Septimus Argent proved nothing, he could have bought it in an atiquarian shop, but Enid and Emily would undertake the search; both would fall on the Parish Registers like ravening wolves, but what if there were gaps in the Registers, caused by fire and theft? He thought his Father had a family tree, but what did that prove? Nothing at all, anyone could draw up some fictional construction. What was needed was the "tree" to be referenced back to pages in Registers, over nearly 150 years. He ordered another cup of coffee, now much more subdued, but he picked himself up when he itemised what he had achieved. A Deed to their land existed, he had found it and there was additional proof of its existence being compiled as he sat there, as further insurance. He finished his coffee, paid the owner and left. He walked the town for some minutes then returned to the Museum, in his right hand a bottle of the finest, ready to be placed, in thanks, on the Museum counter.

* * *

The good mare never fell below a fast trot all the way back, often urging herself into a canter. Argent had merely to hold himself comfortable in the saddle and her pace didn't drop even when he turned her off the direct road to Falmouth, to take the landward road to the farm. Argent felt the letter in his pocket from time to time and did so again for one last time as they reached the farm gate.

"Here you are, girl. I'd say you look on our stable as your second home from home. And we'll see you looked after."

The horse worked her head up and down as if in agreement as Argent dismounted and walked the horse into the barn. He took the time to remove the saddle and bridle and then lead her into a vacant stable and gave her some feed and water. However, his arrival on horse had been detected and in came Emily, looking apprehensive, but this soon disappeared when Argent produced a beaming smile and took her in his arms, to pick her up and whirl her once around the stable. She began to beat her fists upon his shoulders and shout in protest. He lowered her gently and smiled again, bending his knees to bring his face level with hers, his eyes wide, his voice coming from deep within his chest.

"I've found our Deed! In Truro Museum. I've seen it, and I've proof."

Her face exploded into a huge smile.

"A Deed. Then we're alright, the farm is saved!"

Argent immediately felt guilty that he had created in her mind so potent a thought that all was now solved, but he remained very upbeat.

"Bar just one thing. The name on it isn't our surname, but all we have to do is show that the name it shows, a William Bennet, is one of our ancestors. It was given to him and this proves it!"

He flourished out a cover and Emily pulled out the letter and read, then re-read.

"And this document in the Museum definitely applies to us?"

"Yes. I've seen it and what is written there, is copied directly from it. Now it's down to what's in the Parish Registers. We're one step away!"

She looked up at him and smiled, although not so ecstatic as before. She took his hand and led him out of the stable to enter the kitchen and inside were all the family, just rising from their midday meal. Emily commanded their immediate attention by waving the letter.

"It's Reuben. He's got something very important."

She held the letter vertically towards them.

"This is proof of our Deed. Reuben found it in Truro Museum."

Enid was the first to move forward. One hand went to the letter, the other onto Reuben's arm in greeting. She read quickly then turned to her Father, who was distracted enough to cease from pulling on his boots, Beryan also.

"Father. William Bennet? Was he one of our forebears? Our farm was given to him, way back in 1660 odd, by Charles II"

Argent Senior shook his head.

"It's beyond me, daughter. All I can say is what I've said before, there's some family legend about a King's man from the Civil War, but, let's see, feed Reuben and I'll find the family tree, but I doubt it goes back that far."

He disappeared through the door that led to the upper rooms, leaving Enid to swing the stew pot back over the fire, burning bright against the recent Autumn chill that came first to their high pasture. Argent came to sit in his Father's vacated chair and to warm his hands. Beryan was sat opposite and Beryan looked at his old friend and slapped him twice on his knee.

"We've heard! We've heard that you brought our people back; my sister and her children. Well done doesn't come close, joy beyond measure more like!"

Beryan clenched his jaw and smiled, both with his eyes and his mouth, then thumped Argent again on the knee. Argent nodded in acknowledgement. What silently passed between them carried more than mere words ever could.

Argent Senior returned, carrying a scroll from which he had already removed the tie ribbon. Emily had already cleared much of the table and the old man spread the parchment, which crackled with age. The Family Tree was outlined from top to bottom, the additions in many different hands and types of ink. Argent Senior spoke what he already knew, but couldn't be certain of.

"It begins with the first Argent to own our farm here, Jedediah Argent, born 1671. There's no mention of his ancestors."

Enid closed up to her Father and ran her own finger down the list, counting. She had already assessed her task.

"That's six from him to you, Father. We have to look these up in the Registers to prove they existed, then trace back from Jedediah. There can't be more than one back to 1661 and this William Bennet."

She looked at her sister.

"We'll start tomorrow."

Emily looked back at her.

"Why not this afternoon? We'll go to the Verger's house, old Pargeter, down the hill, and get him to show us the registers and then start. They'll be in the church, I suppose. He's always liked us, and the Vicar does too, Reverend Guilder. I'm sure they'll be happy to help."

Enid looked blank at her sister, then nodded. She then turned to her Father and placed her hand on the scroll, it now having re-curled itself on the table.

"Can we take this with us, Father? It'll serve as an excuse. We can say we're trying to extend it, which is just about the truth, really."

Argent Senior nodded, but his experience of the hard ways of the world had surfaced within him.

"You can, but tell no one, not the Verger, nor the Vicar, of your purpose. Money can deflect the good ways of even such as they."

Both his daughters showed shock at his serious expression and sombre words, but it was the old man who broke the silence.

"Now, feed Reuben, he's had a long ride and worked to good purpose."

Then Argent Senior looked affectionately at his son, a light in his face for him that Argent had not seen for many years.

* * *

In Argent's absence Fentiman had decided to warp Ariadne up to the mole and so it was an easy embarkation for Argent as he regained the almost white, newly holystoned decking of his ship. He acknowledged both Marine sentries at the "present" and stood waiting for the pipes of Fraser and Ball to finish, then he saluted them. All the while he had been searching for Fentiman, but his eyes couldn't fail to take in the activity to clean, polish and generally make magnificent, every part of the ship, as though a Royal inspection were imminent. He finally saw Fentiman overseeing the coiling of all the foresheets, the spare rope being arranged into wide, perfectly formed discs on the gangway, just under the bulwark. Fentiman was nodding contentedly at all within his immediate view and was about to follow the workgang onto the forecastle when Argent caught up with him. They exchanged salutes.

"Morning Sir. Welcome back. I trust you found your family all well?"

"Quite well, thank you."

Argent looked around.

"I see that the ship is being beautified!"

"Yes Sir. The celebration, if I can call it that, is set for the day after tomorrow. It will be on the quayside immediate to us, and so I thought it would do little harm to allow parties of civilians aboard to look around the ship, well, not all the ship; gangways, galley and gundecks, I thought."

Argent smiled and nodded his agreement.

"A good idea, but conducted by whom?"

"I've given that some thought, but to no conclusion. Initially, I thought our Midshipmen, as I understand it, their people will be present."

"Also a good idea. Now, any news or orders in my absence?"

"Just one, a supreme order. Ourselves, that being all Officers, including Middies; are required to attend an "evening of entertainment and dinner", given by Lady Grant. Tomorrow evening, 7.30 for 8.00."

Argent's immediate thoughts were on who would be there. As a general rule he did not like formal dinners, but this was an invitation not to be refused and, remembering the last one, he found himself almost looking forward to it, but Fentiman had more to say.

"It includes "a delegation from the crew". No number specified."

"An "evening of entertainment", including some seamen? Have our youngsters been informed? And Sanders and Wentworth? Brakespeare? Smallpiece?"

"Yes, they are below decks now getting spruced up."

"So early?"

"Yes. In response to another visitation, that being this afternoon; the Mayor and his good Lady, and the whole Corporation. Some sort of pre-visit for their celebration, one can only guess.

Argent groaned inwardly and silently condemned Fentiman for warping the ship up to the mole to ease the passage aboard of such notaries. He felt sure a trip over the choppy water on a damp November day to a distant anchorage would have tilted the noble Mayor's decision and his equally noble Council the other way, especially if the Mayoress were involved and she then exercised her undoubted influence over his Munificence. Nevertheless, duty was duty.

"What time?"

"Three bells of the afternoon."

"Right. But I want no interference in the work of the ship. We've just completed a sea voyage. I want her readied for the next one, when it comes."

Fentiman nodded.

"Aye aye, Sir, but we could lay on a demonstration of how to serve a gun, Sir. That would show willing."

Argent nodded his reply.

"Agreed. Tell off Wood, 14 starboard, to be ready."

"And this delegation for Lady Grant?"

"Let me give that some thought. I'm thinking ten. The Warrant Officers, that's five, plus five, from somewhere else. First thoughts, my bargecrew."

He changed the subject.

"They're sending a carriage?"

"Yes Sir. That was on the invitation."

"And for the men?"

"A charabanc."

"A charabanc! Lord. Enough for twenty!"

He paused and chewed his lip in thought, but returned to the immediate issue, the Mayor and Corporation.

"Right. With all other Officers invited and all now getting shipshape, that just leaves us to come up to scratch. Has Mortimor been warned to give the once over to my dress uniform?"

Fentiman's eyes fell.

"No, I'm afraid not. I'm sorry, that one got past me."

Argent screwed up his face and shook his head in dismissal of Fentiman's contrition.

"No matter. I'll do that now. As far as tasks go, that's a short one; it's been so infrequently worn. So, three bells. Prepare for boarders!"

"Correct, Sir. I expect a large party. We're very popular."

Argent nodded.

"Popular don't serve! Corporation today, dinner tomorrow, bun fight the day after. Right. Let's go and bother the good Mortimor."

The search found the good Mortimor not in his galley, but in Argent's cabin, with the dress uniform out and spread on the table, it being carefully examined for stains, frays, and anything not satisfactorily battened down. Mortimor's expression on Argent's entry was as though Argent had made an interruption in church, his brows closing together, but he nodded a greeting anyway. Argent, in good mood, allowed the desultory acknowledgement to go by.

"Good afternoon, Mortimor. I see I have to thank you for your anticipation in readying that uniform for me."

Mortimor emitted a sound somewhere between a grunt and a guffaw.

"And how much workin' out did it take, with the squeakers runnin' back an' forth for hot water to spruce up their togs."

He looked up to renew his usual scowl.

"Judge not according to the appearance, but judge righteous judgment. John 7, verse 24."

"Amen to that, Ship's Cook Mortimor. I like to feel I do my best."

To Argent's amazement, Mortimor's head moved in a tremor of agreement, then he addressed himself to his task.

"This 'ere swab looks a bit tarnished. I'll take it out for a bit of a polish."

He was looking in condemnatory fashion at Argent's one epaulette, examining it at close range with a look such as he normally reserved for the sinners amongst the crew.

It was not until three bells that the conglomeration of local officialdom finally appeared at the end of the mole and they filed aboard by way of the gangplank, many, even most, looking anxiously down at the water below, some even clinging, two-handed in their concern, to the single handrope on the right. The tedious tour, led by a dutiful Argent and an irritated Fraser, perambulated around the gangways, the forecastle, and the lowerdeck. Soon, it blurred into a memory of well fed faces whose self importance had returned, unsurprisingly, with them gaining the security of the enclosed deck beyond the gangplank.

The first questions were mildly irritating, but tolerable and not unexpected, concerning orders, obedience, and punishments. However, when the tour began, the Councilors expressions slowly changed as they saw all that conveyed life and danger aboard a sixth rate man-of-war, especially when they looked up to see the topmen at work in the rigging, some walking along the spars as though they were on the pavement of a familiar high street. The realisation was reinforced by the answer given when one of the Council made supercilious observation on the cleanliness of one section of timber compared to its surroundings. He was informed that the "clean" was new timber, the repair to a shothole, that being combat damage! The gloomy and cramped spectacle of the lower deck carried its own message.

The demonstration at the gun was observed in awed silence, the malevolent shape of the gun and its variety of ammunition suppressing any thoughts of any comment, either complimentary or critical. As the gun was run out, thoroughly displaying the evident effort required, several gasps were heard and not only from the Mayoress, when they heard from Argent that to beat the French they needed to fire three shots inside every five minutes, however long the action lasted and that Ariadne could consistently do it in four and a half. Thus, in quelled silence, they filed off to the galley. The Lady Mayoress asked to taste the left over stew from the Midday meal, but her distorted expression at the mouthful dissuaded any others curious enough to sample and none made enquiries. Mortimor's only reaction was a scowl as they left and make a simple observation to Johnson and Jeremiah.

"What do they know about what it takes to work a ship, Watch on Watch?"

It was the sole time they heard him speak without adding a Bible quote, but it was merely a pause for thought.

"If the blind leadeth the blind, both shall fall into the ditch. Matthew 15, verse 14."

All done, madeira was served on the quarterdeck by a disapproving Mortimor, aided by Johnson and Jeremiah. All Officers were present to add to the hospitality and conviviality, the Mayoress making a maternal beeline for the Midshipmen. The sounding of five bells caused much amusement and at least provided a topic of conversation to explain that it was the equivalent of 2.30pm "land time". They departed, some aided by Marines along the gangplank, for these had requested to sample the rum, in addition to the Madeira. Argent shook hands with the Mayor and felt his mood somewhat ameliorated by the genuine pleasure and gratitude shown by the portly, but personable figure. However, the Mayor was not the last to leave the quarterdeck. This was a thickset man in his early forties, short iron-grey hair, with curious dark scars on both his face and hands. He was evidently prosperous, dressed immaculately, but soberly, in a dark grey suit with the newly fashionable trousers extending down to his polished shoes. However, there was nothing in any way of ostentation, his snow-white linen showed at both his cuffs and above the plain waistcoat. Argent had noticed him often stand to merely observe the men about their duties, both aloft and on deck, his face showing contentment, even admiration, for what he saw. After the demonstration at the gun he had taken the trouble to shake Wood's hand and that of the gun's No. 2, and nod his thanks to the others. He had then pressed a silver shilling into the hand of the diminutive but delighted powder monkey. As he shook Argent's hand he had made a curious comment.

"I've not seen better, Captain. Men knowing why they work. The reason why! That's the secret."

Argent politely observed the disembarkation of all, then took himself to his cabin. He finished some paperwork and the ship's Log, then suddenly felt very tired. He took himself to bed and slept; better than he had for several weeks.

* * *

The two bells of the Second Dog Watch chimed in with the seven of the church clock on the quayside as the eight Officers of HMS Ariadne, plus their Surgeon, assembled at the embarkation port. Respectfully and back towards the bows stood the crew delegation, this being the bargecrew, Marine Sergeant Ackroyd, and all Warrant Officers, twelve in all, two extra above the ten. Ship's Carpenter Frederick Baines had been added and Senior Bosun's Mate Ball had sidled up at the back.

Arriving perfectly to time, the carriage, a large, open landau with the Willoughby crest, began using the space on the Navy mole to swing around to face the way that it had come, followed by the huge charabanc. The four chestnut horses on each could smell the salt of the sea and their heads nodded and swung throughout the manoeuvre, but the coachmen had them under perfect control. In the light of the two lanterns either side of the entryport, Argent gave his three Midshipmen a final check, but he had no concerns over the appearance of the seamen. Mortimor had got the three up to standard, in that regard they were identical, but apprehension showed on the face of Daniel Berry. It matched that in the countenance of Benjamin Wentworth, but there was little that Argent felt he could do other than to clap each on the arm.

"Cheer up, the pair of you. At least the food will be a damn sight better than what you've been used to!"

Both smiled, but then looked down and away. Each had their own Devils to contend with when mixing with high society, but both Trenchard and Bright were plainly in the highest of spirits and full of eager anticipation. Fentiman also showed something different in his eyes, but Sanders appearance reflected what he was, a competent and solid Officer, engaged, this time, on some social duty. If he remembered his last treatment at the hands of Broke and Cheveley, he didn't show it.

Each Officer wore his sword and the Midshipmen their dirks. Argent had given the matter no thought, to wear it or not, until he saw his own sword laid out by Mortimor on top of his newly laundered dress coat. Mortimor had acted on his own opinion of what a King's Officer, particularly one from his ship, should look like, then, somehow, the same message had been relayed to all others. Thus, it was as very chivalric bearers of the King's Commission that they were piped formally, and unexpectedly, through the port by the attendant Fraser and his mates, then down the gangplank. With four swords erect beside the cramped left knees of their owners, the carriage door was closed, completed with a click more akin to that from an expensive mantelclock.

The ride through the streets was dark, but no drizzle, and the conversation came from the Midshipmen who answered questions on their homes and families. What noise there was, besides the eight sets of hooves clattering the cobbles, came from the charabanc behind, twelve seamen, all in good spirits, not at all depressed by the heavy presence of Sailing Master McArdle, this thoroughly countered by the addition of Senior Bosun's Mate Ball, who was undoubtedly good company for the likes of Captain's Bargemen, Carpenters, Bosuns, Gunners, Quartermasters and Marine Sergeants.

In what seemed like no time they reached the high and imposing gates. Two groundsmen opened the gates, but they did not drive through. The coachman had positioned the coach door to face the open gates, the dark drive extending beyond them to the lights of the house, that could just be made out through the trees, all now almost bereft of leaves. All retained their seats in the carriage, with growing puzzlement, until the lead coachman turned and solved their mystery, at least partially.

"I've orders to drop you, 'ere, Sirs. Lady Grant's orders."

It was Fentiman who spoke to answer.

"But it's two hundred yards, and more, up to the house!"

"I agree, Sir, but that's how her Ladyship would have it."

Argent intervened.

"Come on. No point arguing, it's a mild night and not a damp one."

The noise from the charabanc had ceased with their arrival, the occupants overhearing the discussion with the lead coachman, but they, too, alighted at the same time as their Officers. The two carriages took themselves quickly on up the road leaving the guests to begin their walk, which they did, until interrupted by McArdle.

"Sir! This'll nay serve, Sir. To wander up yon drive like a bunch of hobbledehoys off on a jaunt. There's nigh on twenty of us, we should form up and march, Sir. That's a cable length, more, here tae there!"

Argent looked at Fentiman, through the gloom each could see little of the other and neither spoke an opinion, but perhaps McArdle was right and it would do no harm. He turned to his marching expert, Marine Sergeant Ackroyd.

"Sergeant Ackroyd, could you form us up, in some sort of order for a parade? Through you, of course, Captain Brakespeare."

Brakespeare's gravelly voice emerged from the darkness.

"As you choose, Captain. I'll gladly accede to Ackroyd over such a matter."

Once told, "We are in your hands, Sergeant", Ackroyd collected his parade and pushed, pulled, and persuaded all into some sort of order. Basically, Argent was in the lead, then his Officers, then the Midshipmen, in a line of three. The twelve seamen gave no problem, these being put into three lines of four, with himself as right marker.

"All's ready, Sir."

"From you, Ackroyd."

"By the left, forward march. Left. Left. Left right. Left. Left. Left right."

With each carefully listening to the crunch of feet on the gravel and watching as best they could the man in front, a good rhythm was achieved and they progressed with a good swing of the arms. They had marched not a minute when from both sides came a host of lanterns which must have been lit, but masked. The lights progressed from the trees marking the back edge of the lawns, to move down to the path and, in the growing light from a hundred lanterns, could be seen hundreds of people, who immediately began cheering and applauding as their small parade continued between the growing crowds on either side. Argent heard Ackroyd respond behind him, responding he hoped, for discipline's sake, to the men alone, but it was audible nevertheless, although at least two there outranked him and could have him arrested.

"Up straight, you bastards! Chests out, arms up."

Argent recognised no one but he heard the word "Ruanporth" several times and could only conclude that at least the whole population of that village were there, arranged secretly up in the trees, waiting to show their appreciation and gratitude for the return of those taken. Argent heard Fentiman, plainly moved, speak from just behind his right shoulder.

"Any doubts now, Sir, on whether we did the right thing?"

Argent shook his head in the dark, more to answer himself than to answer Fentiman. They marched on through the throng until they reached the front portico, where Ackroyd resumed command.

"Parade. Halt!"

They came to a clean halt, but they were facing along the front of the house, not turned to face it. Ackroyd continued.

"Parade. Left face!"

All swiveled on their left foot and no-one fell over. By this time Admiral and Lady Grant had arrived on the steps, all fairly well lit by several lanterns and candelabra's held by servants. Ackroyd wasn't finished.

"Parade. Off hats."

With all head-dress removed from his special guests, Grant came forward extending his hand to Argent, his face beaming, his smile showing even in the poor light falling on the drive. His Lady was just behind him, equally aglow, but it was Grant who spoke their greetings.

"Welcome, Captain. And to your good Officers and men."

He had turned to beam a huge grin further at the assembled ranks, whilst his wife placed her hands on Argents elbows and smiled up at him. Argent was sure that she was crying, but Grant had returned his attention to him.

"We hope you didn't mind the walk, but my wife's people wanted to make a show of some kind, to convey their thanks, you see, and we thought this the best way to do it."

Before Argent could reply someone shouted "Three huzzas for Ariadne!" and when that was done, the cheering and clapping was renewed. The din prevented Grant from being heard and so he waved them all inside and there he explained the arrangements.

"I've laid on something further down the hall for your good lads, in the Great Hall. We are in the Dining Room."

Argent took his cue and turned to the indispensable Ackroyd.

"Sergeant, take the men on down to the Great Hall. It's the last door on the right, just follow that fellow there."

Argent had no need to make any indication. A footman had arrived to solve the division between Officers and men and Ackroyd, the Warrant Officers, and seamen took themselves further on, to disappear off to the right. Grant stood waiting.

"Now, Captain, we are in here."

Grant himself opened the door and allowed Argent to lead his Officers through. Inside was brightly illuminated by hundreds of candles and, as the clapping started, Argent could see that all the fellow guests were on the far side of the table, all standing to applaud their entrance, as they made their way to the empty chairs on their side and take their seats. As the ovation and bravoes died away, Grant took his place at the head of the table, but he continued to stand.

"I'm remaining standing the better to make formal welcome to Captain Argent and the good Officers of His Majesty's Frigate Ariadne!"

The applause broke out again, but Grant raised his hand.

"Who, by the quality of their seamanship and courage, have returned the loved one's of our community to live once more amongst us."

More applause, accompanied by "Here him", and polite rapping on the table.

"Gentlemen, we bid you the heartiest of welcomes!"

Argent felt the need to stand again and make some kind of reply.

"Admiral and Lady Grant. Ladies and gentlemen, thank you for your generous welcome. We are overwhelmed by your kindness, but would wish to point out that what we did was merely to re-affirm the reason why the Royal Navy exists, and duty is duty, whether to the King or merely to his honest citizens. But we do thank you for this good table that you have honoured us with."

Argent sat down to more applause, but the food was arriving, prompted by a nod from her Ladyship and so Argent set about organising his napkin. It was then he noticed an amazing ice sculpture in the middle of the table, of a female figure, clad in Grecian robes and holding a crown of stars, which immediately made it impossible for her to be anyone other that the Goddess Ariadne. Looking beyond, he was able to view his fellow guests opposite and most noticeable was Charlotte, looking achingly lovely, also the two farmers from the last occasion he was there, and their wives. He recognised both Pargeter and Guilder from the church and what he guessed were two Ruanporthans, perhaps Councillors, and their wives. The one blot in the line was Admiral Broke, but at least his face was merely deadpan and not scowling.

It was the quality of the food that settled the table down from the high theatre of the sailors' entrance. All fell to eating and the meal progressed at a leisurely but well marshalled pace; soup, fish, meat, pudding, cheese and coffee. Surprisingly, little conversation came across the table and Argent was pleased to see his men attending to their plates with gusto, particularly the Midshipmen, all three taking more when it was offered. What did pass across was a question from him to Charlotte regarding the whereabouts of Captain Blake and the reply was that he was out with Wellington in the Peninsula. Some toasts were proposed, the most heartfelt coming from one of the Ruanporth men, who included the fact that his own daughter had been amongst those returned home. His wife felt the need to bury her face in her napkin, but it re-emerged to find all smiling in her direction and Sanders proposing a toast to their village, its good inhabitants and its peace and prosperity.

The Royal Toast was conducted in a most convincing manner by Trenchard and then the ladies took their leave, whilst the port and cigars arrived. This was the cue for the story of the rescue and all were questioned on the part they played, particular attention being paid to the Midshipmen, who were required to describe in detail, their role with their shells from the foretop, which gave rise to great amusement. Broke's face grew more sour as the personal tales unfolded, all modestly understating the difficulties and danger, but none mentioned the murder of the child. With the taking of the slaver being the sole topic of conversation, and it being wholly in praise of Ariadne's exploits, Broke, with no ally to provide support, could only hold his peace and suffer the many compliments crossing the table.

It was not long before they rose to join the ladies, but, as the others left, Grant gave a signal that he wished for words with Argent. They were in marked contrast to the mood of the previous events of the evening.

"I'll not beat about the bush, Argent, simply to say that Budgen has sent me your Log and is enquiring over a Court Martial. I greatly doubt that the Admiralty will even convene one and I'm sure nothing will come of it, even if it does take place, but I have little choice, my hands are tied, so I have to send it on. My own sentiments are expressed by the events this evening. I hope you understand?"

Argent smiled at the kindly but concerned face.

"I do, Sir. You have no choice. There is an issue and it must be resolved. And I appreciate that you have set yourself out on a limb, giving support this evening to events which could lead to a Court Martial."

Argent paused and took a deep breath.

"But I welcome it, Sir, I have no regrets. I welcome its being examined in Court."

Grant nodded, but his face remained serious.

"I'm pleased you see it that way, Argent, but I have another issue. Lady Grant has made known to me the problem you are having with the Deeds to your farm. Enclosures here are imminent and the County Court will be acknowledging claims next week. Now..."

He set himself, as if for some serious speech, finger raised.

"Just yesterday afternoon, whilst out on her ride, she herself saw Broke and Cinch coming out of Lanbe Barton, each with a face like a thunderhead in a force ten. It's no secret that they are both set to pounce on anyone who cannot provide proof of ownership. She also told me that Pargeter said this evening, simply in passing, that your sisters came to call and how pleased he was that they have taken the parish registers up to your house to "undertake some family research. So pleased to help in such a thing," he said. This doesn't take much deduction. Broke and Cinch left without what they wanted and those registers will demolish their hopes. I'd say they supported your claim and those two will likely also think that."

Grant looked at Argent, but the expression received in return was puzzled and waiting for more.

"I'm probably talking out of turn here, hoisting a false storm signal, but I'm speaking my mind and, putting it bluntly, Broke and Cinch are not men to easily give best, especially Cinch. If those registers stand between them and their designs on your farm, I'd be fearful. I'd be fearful for Pargeter's precious registers and for whoever possessed them. Tonight's the second night after their rebuff. They've both money enough to pay for men willing to undertake such work, so I'd advise you to be on your guard and get word to your family, if you can."

Fear for his family showed in Argent's face but subconsciously he had reached for Grant's hand.

"I must go up there myself. I must make my apologies to her Ladyship and take my leave."

Grant nodded.

"And take a few of your good lads. If my fears prove well founded, they'll be useful."

Argent was already on his way, but he took the time to turn and nod his agreement. In the drawing room he found Lady Grant holding court with his three Midshipmen. Fentiman was sat, earnest, smitten and besotted, besides Charlotte, while his other Officers were making good conversation with the other guests. He approached Lady Grant and his three Midshipmen sprang to attention, but Argent spoke, ignoring their presence.

"Lady Constance, I have received news concerning my family and I beg to be excused to attend on them now. I hope to return, but may not. If I do not, please accept my deepest thanks for what you have done for us this evening. I'm certain my men will not forget it, nor will I".

At this point Trenchard chimed in.

"No Sir. We won't, indeed not! Sir."

Argent and Lady Constance laughed but she immediately gave him the permission he sought. Argent hurried to the door that took him into the entrance hall, but he immediately turned for the Great Hall. On entering he found a fine and ancient performance in progress. With their meal finished, Jones, Ball, Beddows, King, Fenwick and Tucker were all essaying a hornpipe to the tune of a fiddle that had been produced from somewhere and also to the rhythm of clapping provided by what could well be the entire staff of the house; cooks, maids, butlers, footmen, ostlers and all. Argent went immediately to his coxswain.

"Whiting."

Gabriel Whiting immediately turned to see the troubled face of his Captain.

"Sir?"

"I need the men. My family live just up the hill from here, and I fear that there may be some trouble there tonight, even this evening. An attack, even, perhaps, of some sort."

Whiting immediately strode forward, leaving Argent standing. He stopped the fiddler and halted the dancing.

"Belay! Belay all that. The Captain's here and has need of us, all of us. There could be trouble at his house, up the hill from here."

He turned back to Argent, even coming to attention.

"As you order, Sir."

Argent nodded and saw that all were looking at him.

"Thank you, Whiting. Yes, I am fearful for my family, there may even be violence, so I'm asking for your help in ensuring their safety."

With that, needing no other word, his men immediately went to collect their hats and jackets and made for the door, Whiting kissing a servant girl that he had been courting all evening. Argent joined the group hastening through the entrance hall and then out, but from there on he took the lead, down the path through the now silent and deserted grounds to the gate. It was an anxious Argent that led all hurrying up the hill and it was only when he saw the light from the windows settling on the road outside the house that his fears began to subside. They all entered the yard and Argent noted the securely closed door, so he turned to find Sergeant Ackroyd, as the one best qualified to decide what should be done next.

"Sergeant, I leave it to you to post sentries and stand a guard. We may be here all night, so divide the men into two Watches. I'm going inside."

He opened the door and found the family all readying themselves to retire for the night, but it was Emily who saw him first.

"Reuben! Why so late?"

However, she could not hold back her news of their achievement and it came out in a torrent.

"But we've done it, traced us back to William Bennet, a Parishioner living at Land by Barton. His son Joseph died childless, he was killed in an accident, but William had a sister, Lucy, and so he willed the farm to Lucy's son, his nephew, Jedediah Argent. It's all in the Registers there. Lucy Bennet was William's sister and she married a Zachary Argent, and they had a son; Jedediah Argent, who starts our family tree. And we've found everyone in it!"

She clasped her hands under her chin and gave a little jump, then continued with more details, as they came to mind.

"Joseph died childless in 1708, and so William willed the farm to his sister's boy, Jedediah. It's all in the Registers. They show Lucy Bennet marrying Zachary Argent and the Christening of their son, Jedediah, in 1671, but what's most important is the Register showing Jedediah Argent joining the Parish to live at Land by Barton, here. It's all written down in those."

She moved to the table, pointing at the Registers, but Argent smiled, nodded, and held up his hand, halting his sister.

"Have Broke and Cinch been here?"

Emily looked at her Father stood holding his night candle. The old man answered.

"Yes. Late afternoon. They came demanding to know what we had to prove ownership of our farm. We told them the story and told them to go. We were a bit sharp with them and told them get out of our house and off our land. Why do you ask?"

"I fear that they'll not give best and will return with evil intent. Those Registers are all we have to link us back. Their destruction will give Broke and Cinch what they need, us with no proof of Title. I fear some kind of attack, here, tonight, or perhaps some other night to destroy these Registers."

Emily gasped and her hands went up to her mouth.

"But don't worry. I've several of my men, outside, now, mounting guard. Tomorrow, we'll take the Registers down to Lady Grant, there they'll be safe. We'll worry about further nights with that done."

Argent Senior walked to the door.

"Where are your men now? Enid bring the fire back up. If they spend the night here, they spend it under my roof."

He looked at his son for an answer.

"They're in the barn. I suspect half on watch, the others sheltering."

"Well, fetch those in."

He turned to his eldest daughter.

"Enid, get some blankets. Emily, get these chairs around the fire, and get the kettle going."

Whilst Emily and Beryan moved furniture, Argent left for the barn. There he found six of his men either sat on the cart or on hay bales, these being Ball, McArdle, Short, Beddows, Whiting and King. They all stood at his entry, but that to the good, as he then motioned them to follow him out.

"You're to stay in the parlour. It's warm and there's hot tea! And more, I suspect."

They all followed him to the house and entered, McArdle halting just inside the door to be bumped into by Carpenter Baines as McArdle spoke in slow and deep sepulchral tones.

"May God bless all who dwell herein!"

Amens came from various quarters, but Argent was pleased to see the relief and satisfaction on both his sisters' faces at seeing six imposing man o' war's men enter the room, all still wearing their seaman's finery and all of whom were greater, or close, in stature to their own sizeable brother. Argent Senior came forward and shook the hand of each in warm welcome.

"Now, there's a chair for each by the fire and hot tea, and we'll find more. You are welcome in my house, and we can only hope that none of us will be needed for its protection."

All nodded and smiled and took themselves to the chairs by the now rekindled fire and Enid gave each a blanket. Meanwhile Beryan had returned with two shotguns, which he placed carefully in the corner, he and Argent exchanging knowing looks. Seeing each of his men settled, Argent took himself to the door and went outside, into the dark, to find Ackroyd stood by the yard entrance. He sprang to the attention and saluted.

"I've got two down the road, Sir, two at the back and one up the road. I'm holding here. Sir."

"I'd say two up the road and one down, Sergeant. If I'm reading this right, they'll come from further up, not down. We're now on 10 o' clock, or near. Three hours on Watch and three off will take us to 4 o' clock and I doubt they'll come after that. Who's up the road?"

"That'll be King, Sir. I'll fetch Jones from down the road to join him, leaving Fraser there."

"Very good. Well done, Sergeant."

"Yes Sir. Thank you, Sir."

"King will be behind our wall, will he not?"

"A bit further up, Sir. Sat in the hedge."

"I'll join him and expect Jones shortly."

Ackroyd saluted in the dark as Argent walked off, he had an almost exact idea where King was and he called softly as he neared the spot.

"King?"

"Here, Sir."

Argent saw his shape in the gloom.

"Room for one more?"

"Yes Sir, I'll just shift over."

"Jones will be coming shortly."

"That'll be a blessing, Sir."

Argent could not be sure just how much irony there was in that, but he settled himself in. Jones arrived almost immediately and found his own place. Argent felt the need to say something, but he spoke barely above a whisper.

"So, how was the Admiral's hospitality?"

It was Jones who answered.

"Oh, the best, Sir. The very best, a fine spread."

"And you've both had a drink or two?"

It was King who chuckled an answer.

"More like three, Sir, four and five!"

Argent laughed himself.

"Right. You two get some sleep, or at least rest easy. I'll stand watch, and give you a nudge if I feel worried."

The soft sounds of the two settling back into the branches came as his answer and Argent made himself as comfortable as he could, suddenly feeling the chill and wishing he were wrapped in a blanket. He had sat little more than five minutes before his wish was answered, Beryan arriving with three. Argent wrapped one around himself and then threw one to Jones, then King, both of whom merely mumbled their thanks. Both were, as long serving sailors, almost asleep, able to slumber under almost any circumstances, dry, wet, warm, or cold. Beryan had remained.

"I'm staying. I'll not sleep whilst you stand guard out here. I'll keep you company."

Argent smiled in the dark.

"You're welcome, but none of your chatterboxing!"

But it was Argent who continued talking.

"When did Broke and Cinch leave yesterday?"

"Around midday."

"Enough time to collect some hirelings. And they looked angry?"

"Livid, I'd say, especially after your Father had finished with them."

Argent chuckled but continued.

"Would they have seen the registers?"

"Couldn't fail. They were on the table and Father was leaning on them whilst delivering his dismissal. He told them that proof existed therein."

Argent said no more and they walked slightly higher up, to a field gate set back in the deep hedge and they wrapped their blankets tight around their shoulders. Both leaned on the gate and watched the lights of Falmouth extinguish, one by one. Then Argent turned to the road to stare at nothing but darkness, what little light there was came from a moon mostly lodged behind high, but solid, cloud. They said nothing but each could feel the shoulder of the other and Argent's memory returned to the times they had sat watching over the crops to drive off the roe deer, or watch for marauding badgers who could ruin a row of young shoots in a single night. The minds of both wandered to be brought back to reality by the distant clock bells from Falmouth marking the passing of each quarter hour. A clock struck twelve forty-five and Argent was thinking that his watch was almost done when, suddenly, he was brought back from his musings by another noise, footfalls on the track and then several dark shapes passing down, their number indeterminable in the poor light. Beryan had seen them too and immediately started forward, but Argent held him back by placing an arm across his chest. Argent realized that they could be merely innocent travellers and, if so, would continue past the farm. He dropped his arm and both left the gate to gain the road, Beryan shaking King and Jones, but both had woken. Argent spoke in a hushed whisper.

"It may be nothing and they'll go on to Falmouth. But follow me, quietly."

They followed the dim figures down to the farm entrance, but there they could sense, as much as see, them halt. Whispered words came back to them, then the shape of the group moved sideways and into the yard. Immediately Argent heard Ackroyd's voice, parade ground sharp.

"Halt! Halt there. No further."

The shape rushed forward, but, as men of evil intent they were, they could not have timed their arrival any worse. The second watch was just coming out of the door to relieve the first, with a lantern held high by Fenwick, so high that it looked like a star shining above the roof apex. This appearance stopped some from closing in on Ackroyd, who had one by the throat whilst delivering punches, before he went down from a blow from a cudgel. At that point Argent and his three, and the six from the house, closed around them. The melee was brief, violent and, in the dark, confused, with many ending on the floor, including Argent, and more than one receiving a blow from their own side. The affair ended with one trying to make his escape from the yard, pursued by King, but he ran into Fraser and was soon rendered senseless on the dirt by a mighty blow from King on the top of his head.

The lantern was re-kindled and the scene revealed. Seven shapes were motionless on the floor, but the Marine uniform showed one to be Ackroyd. He was gently lifted by McArdle and Short and carried inside the house. Argent, breathless and smarting from several blows, gave his orders.

"Tie them up. Hands and feet. There's rope in the barn."

Two were regaining consciousness, this indicated by their groaning and these were bound up first by Gabriel Whiting, him making his feelings very clear, whilst he savagely tightened the rope and the knots.

"Now, just what do you think your game is, eh? Attackin' peaceable people in their homes. Women and babbies, too!"

The answer was another groan and Whiting moved onto the next and soon, aided by Ball, none remained to receive their less than gentle attentions, all had been quickly bound, hands and feet. By this time Argent Senior had arrived, stuffing his nightshirt into the top of his trouser band, but a shotgun in the crook of his right arm. He was followed by his daughters, but these were immediately ordered back inside after they had given him a candle. Argent Senior walked forward and used it to examine the face of each, lifting the head of each one.

"None I recognise. Hired ruffians."

He turned to his son.

"If they've come from Broke or Cinch, if we can prove it, we've a case in Court, surely?"

"I doubt they know who they came on behalf of. Broke or Cinch would have hired someone to hire them, keeping themselves out of it. They'd deny it anyway, saying that many had a grudge against you, and it was none of their affair."

One of the six was attempting to sit, struggling against his bindings and Argent went over to him, his anger growing. He seized the man's hair and jerked back his head, to lift the face upward.

"Who sent you? What were your orders?"

The man gave no reply, nor did the eyes show any fear, so Argent jerked the head back further.

"Speak, or you'll feel a rope around your neck and yesterday's dawn was the last you've seen."

In support Gabriel Whiting stood within view of the man and began to knot a hangman's noose. Fear arrived in the man's face.

"We was hired in Harcourt. Carried in a cart to yer. None of us knew the man, but it was £2 to start and £2 when the job was done."

"And what was "the job"?"

"To get some Registers and, if we couldn't find 'em, or get someone to give 'em, to burn this place down."

Argent drew back his right fist, but his Father stopped him.

"No, son. That's not the way."

Argent released the man, then stood. He gave an order whilst still looking at the man.

"Get them into the barn."

Each of the six was being led, or hauled, into the barn, as Argent walked to enter the house. Inside he found both his sisters attending to Ackroyd, him sat by the fire, head down with a pad of wet cloth being applied to the back.

"How goes it, Sergeant?"

Ackroyd straightened up and Argent could see that the Marine's left eye was closing.

"Not too bad, Sir. I've had worse."

Argent smiled.

"One day you'll have to tell me about it. But that was very brave, standing in their path like that. Well done."

Ackroyd's head slumped forward again and Enid applied the newly whetted cloth.

"Thank you, Sir. But if you don't mind, Sir, I'll just sit here awhile."

"Take all the time you need, Sergeant. We're in no hurry now."

He patted him on the shoulder and turned again for the door. In the barn he found his whole party glowering malevolently at the six trussed-up shapes. He walked to stand besides Fraser, a thought growing inside his head.

"How many short are we in the Afterguard, Bosun?"

"Five, Sir."

"And Fo'c'slmen?"

"Same number, Sir."

"Well, this plugs one of those holes and bit of the other!"

He looked around at his now grinning party of seamen.

"Whose been out with the Press? Anyone?"

"I have, Sir."

It was Fraser who answered.

"So what happens? Do you have to say anything? Legal or official, I mean."

Fraser screwed up his face, whilst the six, still groggy but now conscious enough to hear the conversation, howled in protest, to be heavily cuffed by the nearest seaman. Fraser gave some thought.

"Well, I went out with an Officer once, who tried to do things official and legal, like."

"What did he say?"

"Well, I'll say it now, as I remember it."

He cleared his throat, stared at his now distraught audience and drew himself up to his full height.

"Under the Recruiting Act 1703, you are hereby recruited into the Royal Navy to serve his Majesty King George III throughout the duration of the current hostilities. God save the King."

His fellow seamen cheered and applauded the solemn words, but irony was plainly uppermost. Fraser was mightily affronted, but Argent laughed himself.

"Well done, Bosun. An actor on the London stage could not have spoken with greater gravity nor dignity."

Fraser wasn't sure if Argent was serious or not and so he held his peace, but his Captain was moving on.

"Get these into our cart, gagged, and get them back to the ship. I see no reason why any noise from them should wake the good citizens of Falmouth. Mr. McArdle and Mr. Baines, stay here with me. You that are going, I want the cart back here before daybreak, and Fraser, ask Surgeon Smallpiece to come back with you, to take a look at Ackroyd."

It was Fraser who answered.

"We've got the celebration, Sir, tomorrow; today! Landsfolk will be coming onto the ship. Where to stow these pikers?"

"In the hold. And put them to work, with a Marine guard. Six, with loaded muskets. And gag them again if they decide to shout."

All stood around looking at the six and grinned, whilst they stared back, wide-eyed in horror.

"Right, you have your orders."

Argent left whilst the six were bodily lifted and tossed into the cart and, with their hands and feet tightly bound, they landed very awkwardly, either on the bare boards or on one of their companions. As they were heaved in, Whiting spoke over the top of the cart, perhaps to ease their feelings.

"Now don't take it so 'ard, boys. We could've hauled you off to the Magistrate and got you done for attempted murder! That'd mean the long haul up. Least you'm still alive and likely to stay alive, as much as the rest of us, that is."

Argent heard him and the others laugh at his legal nicety, but he paused at the door long enough to see the cart being manually hauled out of the barn followed by a ploughhorse, quickly harnessed between the shafts by Beryan. All, save those being carted, now in very merry mood and they set off, those in the cart still the butt of cruel and pitiless humour.

Once inside, Argent saw the whole family still in the parlour, waiting news, but Enid was still bathing Ackroyd's wounds and he was, himself, holding a wet pad to his eye. Argent spoke generally, to all stood around.

"They told us nothing more."

Then he grinned.

"However. I've recruited them into the Royal Navy! They'll sail with us on our next voyage. They'll not be around to be hired into anyone's skullduggery for some time, least not Broke's nor Cinch's."

He saw the pleasure and relief in the faces of all, but then thought of Ackroyd.

"Father. Can Ackroyd have my bed? I've sent for our Surgeon, who should be here in not much more than an hour."

"He can, and I'll help him there myself. Beryan, you'll help?"

The two eased Ackroyd from the chair and, still attended by Enid, Ackroyd was helped to the door that opened onto the stairs. However, Argent was pleased that Ackroyd took most of his weight on his own legs. His smashed in shako, on the table, gave evidence as to how his life had been preserved. Argent picked it up and tried to push it back into shape, but it came apart in his hands. He threw it back onto the table. McArdle and Baines had taken their seats by the fire and both were almost asleep. Argent bolted the door, used the last candle to see his way over to them, was soon at their place and was very soon in their state.

* * *

The following morning, Lady Grant herself came up to their farm, in a carriage with four coachmen. The cart had been returned and now only Argent and Smallpiece remained, so it was Argent who heard the carriage enter their yard and he came out to greet her. She spoke as soon as the door was opened.

"Did anything happen?"

"Yes, Lady Constance, some unpleasant characters did arrive, at dead of night, but my men saw them off, or morelike on. I pressganged them, all of them."

Lady Grant grinned as she alighted from the coach.

"Most excellent, a capital idea!"

She walked further, to the door, but did not enter, she remained on the threshold and knocked on the open door. Argent Senior was visible in the parlour.

"Edward. May I come in?"

Argent Senior pulled a chair from under the table as answer and Lady Grant entered to sit on it.

"I hear you've been bothered, Edward. Is there anyway I can help?"

Argent Senior looked from her to his eldest daughter.

"Enid here knows the full story, her and Emily."

Unbidden both came to the table, sat and told the story. Lady Grant listened intently, but, with the story finished, Emily went further.

"I've been talking to Mr. McArdle, one of Rueben's Officers. He's a very intelligent man and he says that we've as good as made our case, but one thing remains, to make the whole thing "copperbottomed", as he put it. To find the Will that William Bennet made to give the farm to Jedediah Argent. Do you think you could help with that?"

Lady Constance leaned forward.

"And when did William Bennet die?"

"1681, ma'am."

Lady Constance pursed her lips.

"It will be with a Solicitor who was practicing back then, obviously. I have dealings with all three in Falmouth and I'll ask them to search around that year. I suspect that Branch, Branch and Jenkins have been here the longest, and so my greatest hopes rest with them. But if any have it, we'll find it, be certain."

Emily clapped her hands and grinned, but Argent now spoke.

"Lady Constance. The men came to steal or destroy these Parish Registers."

He indicated the five volumes on the writing desk.

"May we ask that you take them into your home and keep them safe, until they are no longer needed, no longer part of the issue?"

"Of course. Be very assured of their safety with me and they will not leave my possession until all this enclosure business is thoroughly settled. Pargeter and Guilder will have no objection I feel sure, especially when I tell them the tale of what happened here this night gone and that their precious registers were and perhaps still are, under serious threat of destruction."

Argent Senior had sat beside her at the table.

"That's very generous, Lady Grant."

He paused and looked at her, querulously.

"Would you like a cup of tea?"

"I would. And some of Enid's fuggan would not come amiss, if I may be so ill mannered as to ask."

An hour later Lady Grant's carriage halted at the portico of her house. She got out and made her farewells, attended by two Register laden footmen, but then the carriage swung around to descend the drive and continue on its required journey, that being to continue on and convey Argent, Smallpiece and the invalid Ackroyd back to their ship. A short time later, the carriage was running along the length of the Navy mole, but only so far, because half the mole's length was taken with long trestle tables and the carriage was forced to halt at a collection of delivery vans from bakers, Inns, brewers and costermongers. The tables were being laid and the first, early, civilian guests of the Mayor were already arriving, these walking out onto the mole, enjoying the weak, unseasonable sunshine, but wrapped up nevertheless.

The carriage's occupants opened the door themselves and Argent strode immediately up the gangplank to call the Marine sentries down to help carry Ackroyd back on board and to the sickbay. He then waited at the foot of the gangplank to watch his Marine Sergeant as he was helped along the mole. Ackroyd's eye was very black, but it was half open, at least, and his head was swathed in bandages; however he merely needed the two Marines to steady him on his course and he took himself up the gangplank, but again closely supervised. Every Ariadne present noted his passage from the carriage to the sickbay and all, even though Ackroyd was the ship's omnipresent Master at Arms, looked and spoke sympathetically. The story had circulated.

Argent took himself immediately to his cabin and there he noted the state of his best dress uniform. He had worn it in the brawl and it looked so. There was dirt and dust all over, which showed especially on the white breeches, which also had a hole in one of the knees. Bible Mortimor had heard him walk past the galley and followed him in, and Mortimor's horrified look gave Argent clear indication that his uniform was wholly a sin against all Godliness, never mind a visit by the Mayor and his Corporate assemblage.

"Don't fret too much, Mortimor. Give the coat a dusting down and I'll borrow some breeches from Fentiman."

"An' your shoes an' hose?"

Argent re-examined each.

"I have spare hose and I'll clean the shoes myself. Now, there's the coat, do your best. I'll set about the rest directly."

"Johnson can take care of the shoes. You've a shirt to worry about, an' all."

His brows knitted in deep disapproval.

"Gettin' into fights! Do that which is right and good in the sight of the Lord. Deuteronomy. Six, verse 18."

"On your way, Mortimor."

Grumbling at everything including the jacket, Mortimor left, to be soon replaced by Johnson who left with the shoes. Argent began rummaging about in his sea chest for the necessary. One bell later Jeremiah arrived to say that the Mayor and his ensemble had arrived and were about to take their places, but Argent was brushing himself down and remarking to himself that, for a running repair, he didn't look half bad. He then made a hurried exit to oversee the formalities, but he was halted on the larboard gangway by Midshipman Berry, who looked somewhat apprehensive over what he was about to say.

"Beg pardon, Sir, but at the bottom of the gangway there's a gentleman who says he is a journalist. I'm not sure what that is, Sir, but he says he wants to talk to you about our taking of the slaver, and he would like to talk to, well, several more else in the crew, Sir, that is, with your permission."

Argent resumed walking.

"Thank you, Mr. Berry. I'll take care of it."

On reaching the entryport, Argent saw the grinning young man stood waiting, eager to come aboard, but held there by a Marine sentry.

"It's alright, Matthews, allow him to pass."

The musket was pulled back and the young man bounded up the gangplank.

"Captain Argent. I'm overwhelmed to meet you. My name's Bishop, William Bishop. I'm from the Cornwall broadsheet, The Crier. You may have heard of it. My word, but you and your ship are news, Captain. Heroes of the whole County. And beyond!"

Argent nodded and smiled in greeting. The gushing introduction had not appealed, but he knew he had little choice, "Needs must when the Devil drives!". He had to give them of his time and also allow them access to the crew, but he had no qualms about that, for they, like true sailors, would be only too willing to boast of their exploits.

"Good day to you, Mr. Bishop. I have an event to attend, as you can see, but I do have a little time and myself and my men will be of service to you in any way that we can."

* * *

The crew of number three starboard and the men of the foretop were on opposite sides of the same table. Some landsmen and their wives were next, further up towards the top table and they saw, rather than heard, the Mayor stand to make a speech, which went on too long, then the same, but much shorter, from their Captain. Broke sat smouldering, contenting himself with a mood of foul temper, but Budgen was in his element and, throughout both, continued to attack his glass with gusto. The Ariadnies listened in obedient silence, but were grateful that some beer had already been served, if not the food, and so, as the odd word came down to them over the cries of the many gulls attracted by the display, they could, at least, take a drink. Then the fare arrived, served by girls from the local inns and hostelries, which cheered them all up no end. The food was such as they rarely dined on, a variety of pies, with plenty of greens, swede, potatoes and gravy. With refilled tankards, all tucked in and there was little talk. What there was, centred on Morris' and Whiting's story, as they had relayed it to the "newspaper cove", who was still hovering around, looking for extra titbits of detail.

However, the main course was almost devoured when Tom Bearman, Number Two of Number Three, changed the subject, after he'd delivered Smallsize another helping of chicken pie and some more swede.

"So, Gab, what's this we've heard about some scrapers attackin' the Captain's family home, up over yonder? Seein' Ackroyd come aboard just now, I'd say it all got a mite close to the wind."

Whiting swallowed his mouthful.

"That's not wrong, it could have been wholly nasty, had we not been there. It was all to do with a claim on the Argent land, all around, and, if we hears true, our dear Admiral Broke has some part in it."

Morris had been listening from some places down.

"I was on Morning Watch and saw six scruffy sorts brought aboard in your company. Was they the result of all that?"

"They were, and right now they'm down in the hold under Marine guard 'till we next sails. Our Captain was like to string 'em up, there and then, 'till that thought came into his head, about puttin' the Press on 'em. Six hefty lumps like them'll not come amiss."

Whiting returned to his food, but Morris had grown curious.

"Broke behind it! How much truth could there be in that?"

It was Abel Jones, the topman, who answered.

"They was talkin' a lot about Broke and someone called Cinch, before and after the set-to. Ain't that right Mose?"

"'Sright! The Captain and his brother in law, I believe, was talkin' together and they was usin' just those names."

Morris again spoke up.

"So, 'tis Broke! Tryin' to latch onto more land, I shouldn't wonder. I've heard that some folks've been turfed off theirs from this enclosures thing that's happenin' all over. Sounds like Broke's tryin' to do much the same to the Captain's people. I've always held that Broke and Cheveley is one close moored pair of buzzards, and now we've this Cinch added. I don't like the way such as them is getting' away with the likes of what's goin' on."

He pointed his knife down the table for added emphasis.

"Common folk bein' thrown out of their homes and sent to go the Lord knows where, just so's some high society landowner can up his acreage by the odd couple've fields or such! 'Tis all wrong!"

Whiting looked down the table.

"Well, don't take it so very hard, Sam. This one we stopped, so there's one family, at least, as still has their roof over their heads."

"I hear you, Gab, an' that's fair, but there's another side to this, affectin' us. It leaves Broke with another down on us. He lost a packet after we wiped the eye of Flogger Cheveley, and now he's been scuppered again, once more by a crew off of Ariadne."

King looked up, curious.

"So Broke's got a down on Ariadne. What difference could that make?"

"Our prizemoney! That scrub Broke could put a shackle on it somehow. I don't know how, but somehow."

"You mean take it away?"

"No, I mean delay it."

The table fell silent, until Abel Jones spoke further, in hope of giving consolation.

"Well, we've got this, and such as this I've never heard of. Not even after Trafalgar. I'd say this stands up for collarin that slaver, at least, instead of prizemoney, even delayed."

Jacob Pierce of Number Three answered.

"I says it don't. 'Tis better than nothin', I'll grant, but I'd go for prizemoney for takin' that slaver, no matter how small"

Sam Morris answered, forcibly.

"And what prizemoney could come from that spatchcock, Arab built, eyesore? They'd never have took him into the service nor anyone buy him, neither. What use would such as that be in a storm down Channel?

Pierce leaned forward aggressively.

"That may be true about that slaver. The Captain did right to sink him to the gunnels with all them heathens washin' about all over him, an' then sail off, but I'm talking about prizemoney in general. Speakin' of which, Sam's right, b'ain't it about time our share from La Mouette arrived. An' that smuggler."

Sam Morris guffawed from the far side of the table.

"I've known prizemoney not arrive for a year nor more. I do swear that they delays it so's a few of the crew is dead, injured, or lost, so's to lessen the number as is entitled to it. Which saves 'em a few pound, and likely makes a bit extra for the likes of Broke."

Gabriel Whiting added his thoughts.

"What difference would a few less of us make? 'Tis fewer Officers as makes the difference, or less Admirals. They gets their share and all, a good share."

Abel Jones came in to query.

"And which Admirals would that be, in our case? Takin' a share."

"Two. Grant an' Broke."

Jones nodded resignedly.

"For not firin' one shot, nor even hearin' the wind of one."

Gabriel Whiting decided that the whole conversation had grown too morbid.

"Now belay this talkin' of no prizemoney. There's some comin' our way, in time, and, like this spread, however much, 'tis better than nothin'. And things could be a damn sight worse. We could be crewin' that busted hulk out in The Roads, yonder."

He pointed over his shoulder towards the ship which no one could see, but knew of well enough. Herodotus was awaiting the arrival of new masts from Portsmouth, at which time the mast hoy would come alongside and replace her mizzen, the shattered stump of which still gave evidence of her mauling in the Bay of Biscay.

"And here comes dessert, as the uppercrust calls it."

He leaned back on his bench to invite the serving maid to place a huge pudding on the table by him. He looked up appreciatively.

"Why, thankee, fair maid. Now tell us. Yon pudding, just what is contained therein?"

The fair maid looked once at the tanned, grinning, confident face and lowered her eyes in embarrassment, but she did answer.

"Apple. 'Tis apple."

"Which make you the apple of my eye! But do tell, which Inn do you hail from?"

"The Pale Horse, at the back of town."

"Do you welcome sailors there?"

She had recovered some of her composure.

"We might. If they had some money and behaved themselves."

Whiting sat back, his face showing mock astonishment his hands spread and open, wide open, as were his eyes.

"Well, now lads. Don't that just sound like our kind of place? Where peaceable people behaves themselves and takes a quiet drink."

He gazed up smiling at the pretty face.

"We was just sayin', we got prizemoney owin'. And your Pale Horse sounds just the pothouse to come and spend some of it. And, when we comes, who do we say recommended the place to us?"

She looked down at him, now smiling herself, quite taken with this cheerful and not bad looking sailor, but she showed mock umbrage.

"It b'ain't no common pothouse!"

She paused and looked full at him.

"And my name's Molly."

"Molly."

He nodded.

"Molly. Right lads."

He took off his hat and threw it onto the table.

"A collection for Molly, what's served us so well at this table, and told us of a good Inn to spend our future money in."

Wry and exasperated grins all round, but nevertheless, each threw some coins in and it was more than a few shillings that Molly tucked into her apron before clearing the remains of the main course, but, as she did, her and Whiting exchanged meaningful glances, more than once. Molly loaded her small serving cart with the dirty plates and placed clean dishes in front of Whiting.

"You can give these out for me!"

The others laughed at Gabriel Whiting, the Captain of the Foretop, receiving his orders from a serving maid, but it was a grinning Whiting who did spread the dishes and then himself spooned out large portions of the pudding. Molly disappeared, but not before sending a sidelong glance at Whiting. However, Sam Morris, used to such an occurrences when in the company of Gabriel Whiting, couldn't resist making some observation.

"Now, we'll just see how long that one'll last, the promise to go over and see Molly whilst spendin' some money at the Pale Horse."

Whiting looked down the quayside at the disappearing Molly.

"Well, I don't know. Perhaps that one may have hit home."

"Hit home! 'Bout as much a one passin' clean through the riggin'."

All laughed, but then commotion from further up the mole drew their attention. Fraser was hurrying down one side and Ball down the other and, as they passed, seamen from Ariadne rose and made their way back to the gangplanks, chewing a last mouthful or taking a last drink. Morris was first to speak.

"What's goin' on?"

However, Fraser had reached them and gave Morris the answer, but more than a simple order; such established shipmates were entitled to more.

"Get back aboard and ready 'er for sail, lively. La Pomone's out! A Revenuer out of Plymouth, was chasin' a smuggler, nigh on Guernsey, and found herself chased off by a frigate, but she saw a hulk with just a foremast, bein' towed by another frigate. The one as chased 'er off was the escort. They'm takin' 'er down Channel."

Chapter Eleven

A Settling of Accounts

Ariadne surged on, through a world of darkness, black sea and black sky, at no quarter beyond her living hull was there any point showing life or light, even the spray cascading over her bows from her urgent passage, sprayed across the deck as inky black. The only source that threw any light within the darkness that girded the world of those on board was that from her own binnacle; the compass within it regularly studied by Quartermaster Short as he held Ariadne on her chosen course, just East of South. Other lights did burn, but only deep within her hull and one of those burning brightly and steadily could be found in the cabin of Sailing Master McArdle as he assembled the combination of wind, tide, speed, and sea conditions into a plan for Ariadne to intercept La Pomone. His Captain had set him the task; calculate a course and speed that would bring them onto the French ships just as they reached Quessant. Not too late, for obvious reasons, nor too early, because, if they had to sit and wait at that island, the wind, just South of due East could give the French the weather gauge. Argent wanted their interception timed to when the French were almost past, giving him what wind advantage there would be. Thus, McArdle sat, calculating the likely speed of the French, with one frigate towing another, that being towed having some sail, in a steady wind in a choppy sea and a tide still building up Channel, but soon to peak and ebb. He checked his calculations for a second time, then, satisfied, he took himself out of his cabin, but not before kissing his sleeping wife and saying a short prayer with his hand on their Bible.

On deck he identified his Captain, not by his features, but by him being the only figure stood on the weather side of the dark quarterdeck.

"Sir, I've made the calculations, Sir. If we can hold eleven knots; then on this course, we should meet them as ye wish, Sir."

"Mr. Bright. Throw the log, if you please."

The log was taken and shown to be 10 knots, plus a half. McArdle spoke first.

"By my reckonin', Sir, they'll be past us and through the Quessant channel."

Argent looked aloft, but could see nothing, however, he held in his mind the picture of the sail pattern above them and now he knew he needed an extra half-knot, in a wind just forward of beam on. He shouted over the rail into the gloom.

"Mr. Fraser."

A shape moved away from the mizzenmast and Fraser's voice answered.

"Sir?"

"Set all lower and topmast staysails."

"Aye, aye, Sir."

Shouts and orders came back through the darkness, then the sound of running feet. Argent heard, more than saw, the newly set canvas whip taught and then felt the deck tilt slightly. Ariadne was responding.

"Mr. Bright. The log once more, if you please."

The minutes passed and Bosun's Mate Ball came back to ring two bells of the Middle Watch, the "Graveyard".

"Short one eighth of eleven knots, Sir. Bar one eighth. Sir."

Argent walked forward again.

"Mr. Fraser. Middle staysail. Outer and flying jib."

In the stuffy gloom of the Lower Deck, the Starboard Watch were either sleeping or working on small tasks by the light of tallow candles. Sam Morris felt the ship heel for a second time and spoke to the volunteer of his guncrew, Jacob Pierce.

"He's crackin' on."

He bit through the thread of some stitching, then continued his theme.

"How many Captains do you know as would risk springin' a mast to get into a fight with three Frogs, even though one be crippled?"

Pierce chuckled, but nervously.

"Orders! He gets 'em, same as we. Herodotus is out of it, which just left us with any chance of doin' somethin' against 'em."

"Herodotus, aye, and I'll tell thee one thing, I'd not object to seein' that over scrubbed piece of fancy work out on our lee right now, able at least to take on one of 'em. Flogger Cheveley or not, at least he could pull one away and give 'im a fight."

He pulled on a stitch.

"What we'm sailin' into I don't like."

Pierce answered, his tone seeking reassurance, more than advancing an opinion.

"He'll not play out his chances too far, our Captain."

"Oh ah? He'll have some plan, don't thee worry, an' it'll involve us goin' straight through the middle of 'em."

He examined his work by holding it close to the candle.

"Thur! Done. I'm for some sleep. An' you, Jake?"

Pierce nodded.

"The same. This day could be busy."

Ariadne held her speed and held her course. A grumbling Mortimor prepared a main meal, which was eaten before the predicted time of the dawn and, as a feint streak appeared in the South Eastern sky, the ship was cleared for action. Well within ten minutes all was ready and prepared, each man checking what they may come to use at their gun; a rammer, a tackle-block, a flintlock or simply the breech mounting. Morris was checking the cleanliness of the touch-hole when he saw someone arriving with Henry Ball and this good Bosun's Mate stopped at Number Four, but when he spoke it was to both Morris and Number Four's Guncaptain, Joe East.

"You two. "Ere's an extra man. Use 'im as you choose."

With that he bustled away, leaving the newcomer stood there, looking bemused and looking all around, but finding no answers.

"What do you reckon, Joe. A pusher?"

Joe East was from the Home Counties, quiet and well spoken.

"Has to be. Put him on the tackle and she'll run out uneven. We've both our two each side."

Lynch looked at the new man.

"Now, listen. After the gun is loaded, we have to run it out. You'll know that's happening because the tacklemen will be pulling on those ropes to send the gun up to the gunport, that square hole there. When you see that happening, you push, from behind, here."

He pointed to the carriage below the gun's cascabel.

"That's for both of us, both guns. When either is being run out, you push that gun. If a tackleman gets killed, that'll be your job."

He looked at him challengingly.

"Is there anything you don't understand?"

Even in the glim of the tallow light they could see real fear cross the man's face, but East continued.

"Now, when the gun's fully up to the side, we will be firing it and it will come back, leap back, faster than you can move. Make sure that you are out of the way."

East looked at the man, waiting for a reaction, but none came. He returned to his own checking of the tackle pulleys. Morris was also looking.

"Your name?"

"Seth Wyatt."

There was nothing confident nor challenging in the voice. The man was plainly very fearful but Morris was not in the mood to dispense sympathy, he had his own line of questioning.

"B'ain't you one of them as was brought aboard after that skirmish at the Captain's house?"

Wyatt looked up at Morris, then down at the deck.

"Yes."

"Then a word of advice. Say nothin', do as yer told, and keep out of the way!"

On the quarterdeck the light of the new day was slowly building. Argent again looked for Fraser.

"Mr. Fraser. Double the lookouts on each mast. Tell them to keep a weather eye to the South, and over to the South East."

Argent returned to his place, subconsciously opened his Dolland glass and then shut it. He turned to McArdle.

"Sailing Master, where would you judge our position now?"

McArdle was already at his chart board beside the binnacle. He had been taking readings from log and compass every fifteen minutes for almost the whole of the night.

"Just under five miles from the French coast, Sir. I'd say Quessant was fine on our starboard bow."

Argent absentmindedly repeated his action with Dolland.

"Mr. Fentiman. You have the deck. I'm going to the foretopmast crosstrees."

At the high lookout position Argent found Jones and Fenwick. Both were staring South and Fenwick crossed to the starboard side of the mast to join Jones, leaving the larboard weatherside for Argent alone.

"Anything?"

"No Sir."

A hazy line that he took to be the French coast was just visible and Argent swept his telescope along its full length. There was, indeed, nothing. They were either too early or too late and, if too early, they must sit and wait, but close no further to the French coast. However, sat away in the North West of any French arrivals from the South East, they were in the gloom of the early dawn and could count on remaining unseen for some time, but that placed them some way North of the French ships' likely course, which would be as close as they dared to their own friendly coast. He shinned quickly down the foremast ratlines and began shouting back to the stern.

"Mr. Fraser. Get the canvas off her. Mr. Short, up helm."

Ariadne swung into the wind and came to a dead stop. The canvas, a minute earlier drum tight and drawing power from the wind, began to writhe and flog, but every spare able man was aloft, including some waisters and afterguard, to soon secure the canvas back against their spars. Ariadne began to rise and fall with the passing waves, her mastheads swaying against the growing pale light of the cloud covered sky. From pounding on at eleven knots, she was now utterly still in the water. Argent returned to his lookout point, Jones and Fenwick having held it vacant for him. He looked again through his glass, this time carefully studying the far South East, from where those they sought would come. Again, nothing. He judged the wind; still a steady South of East, level and strong, but carrying some fine rain. If the French were yet to arrive, they could appear quickly out of this far mist, but they would see them first, of that he was confident, because they would have sails set that could be seen, whilst Ariadne sat beneath bare poles. Argent planned for them to see him at a particular time, then react, and this reaction would then decide his own course of action.

The time passed in the Morning watch, six bells, then seven, but Argent didn't move, he remained as a lookout. Motivated by impatience he looked Southwest to Quessant; again nothing, but Fenwick was nudging his companion and Jones was nodding his head.

"Sir. There's somethin' comin' down the coast. Just about within view and about four mile off."

Argent yanked the telescope open and focused on the furthest point visible to the Southeast, this being the coastline before the light rain hid all. Through the glass he saw a collection of sails and two hulls, but it was too far to discern if there was a third. He kept them in view then saw enough to make him certain. One of the frigates was under full sail, the other on very little canvas, yet they were keeping pace with each other. One must be towing, so this was they. Argent locked his arms over the spar to make a full study, particularly to judge their pace. He wanted them due South of their position, just out of the weather gauge, but not too far on towards the safety of the Quessant channel. Their progress was painfully slow, but as he carefully examined each frigate, recognition came to him. He was almost certain that they were the two that had allowed them passage after Loctudy; their hulls were the deep purple that he had found so noticeable. His memory of both also told him that each was gunned the equal of Ariadne, probably more. He pushed that thought aside and made his judgement; Ariadne would have to wait an hour, approximately, before they came to due South of him. Towing the heavy La Pomone must be more laborious than McArdle had calculated and he studied again, his eye growing damp from its long enclosure within the eyepiece. The escort frigate moved out a fraction. Had they been seen? Relief came when she resumed station after a minute or so, but the movement had revealed La Pomone. She had but a foremast and that truncated, it carrying two sails, the forecourse and foretopsail, and there were what looked like a staysail and an inner jib between that foremast stump and the bowsprit. Back in August they must have done more damage to her than they thought.

"Jones. Fenwick."

"Yes Sir."

"I want to know when she's due South of us. Clear?"

The reply came in unison.

"Aye, aye, Sir."

At last Argent returned to the quarterdeck and spoke first to his Sailing Master.

"An excellent piece of reckoning, Mr. McArdle. La Pomone has less sail than we assumed, she's little more than a hulk, which has held them back. But we are now placed perfectly, my congratulations to you."

McArdle did no more than slowly lower his head, as though acknowledging some student's accurate interpretation of a difficult

Bible text. He then stood stock still, his role, as he saw it, accomplished. Argent turned to Fentiman.

"I'm going to hold here, until they have passed us, or just about to. I'm bargaining that this far out, and with no canvas aloft, we'll not be seen, but send the men aloft. Get the canvas as tight to the spars as can be, give our friends the Johnnies as little to see as possible."

In a minute all masts were covered in topmen tightening the ropes that held the white canvas to the spars and tucking up any odd corners that remained wayward. With that done, there was little to do but wait, with Ariadne facing into the wind. The running waves passed easily under Ariadne's hull, lifting her elegant bows with its equally elegant image of her Greek namesake, then running on, to lift the neat stern. From time to time, Argent couldn't resist a climb to the foremast crosstrees to check on progress, but that of the three ships was indeed painfully slow. Below the gangways, on the gundecks, the guncrews waited patiently, some chipping shot, some merely talking, discussing some point of gunnery, or ships, or sailors, or whatever came to mind. Many were plainly ill at ease, this would be their first action, or perhaps they remembered too well the experience of the last one. The three Midshipmen met at the mainmast but said little. Wentworth went to each of his eight guns, which included the sternchasers, not being annoyingly inquisitive, but simply gaining opinions on some point or other. The gundeck was tense. Eight bells sounded to end the Morning Watch, therefore, by the regular ship's routine, this was now time for breakfast, but the men had already been fed. Mortimor and his two mates were cleaning down the pots and cauldrons, but Argent decided that, nevertheless, the time should be acknowledged. Fraser was on the quarterdeck.

"Mr. Fraser. "Up spirits", a half ration. Something to warm the men in this chill weather. Go and warn Mortimor."

The "Monkey's Orphan" was called for and the young seaman arranged his drum to his satisfaction then rolled out "Drops of Brandy", the beat being instantly recognised and the men disappeared to the lower deck to obtain their mugs and beakers, the mess cooks to obtain the large jug to obtain the ration for their mess. Soon, under the supervision of Master at Arms Ackroyd, Bosun's Mate Ball was doling out enough for the half tot and soon after that, the men were back at their guns, but almost all now more cheerful as they consumed their grog.

Argent returned to the lookouts, these now being Whiting and Beddows.

"Where away?"

"Almost on due South now, Sir. We was just about to call out."

Argent focused his glass. They were, indeed, now due South. The escort frigate had moved slightly ahead and La Pomone could be seen, her deck a clean sweep up to her foremast, neither mizzen nor mainmast standing above her outline. Argent snapped the glass shut, time to make a start. He climbed down the ratlines, making calculations and, once on the gangway, he immediately looked for Fraser, but he was already stood waiting.

"Mr. Fraser. Are the barrels ready?"

"Yes Sir."

"Drop them down."

"Aye, aye, Sir."

"Mr. Ball."

He was at Fraser's side.

"All plain sail. Lower and topmast staysails. All jibsails. Close hauled, larboard tack, wind one point large."

That said, he took himself back to the quarterdeck.

"Mr. Short. Steer due South. Larboard tack."

As Fraser himself cut the ropes holding the cluster of half filled barrels suspended above each side of the stern, he groaned inwardly as he thought of the press of canvas that Ariadne would soon carry, yet having her speed being severely cut by the barrels straining on both catheads. However, he consoled himself that last time, against La Mouette, it had been an artful and effective ploy. Ariadne came onto due South and picked up speed and the final adjustments to her sail trims were made. Argent climbed back to the foremast crosstrees and as he arrived at the spar he immediately made enquiry.

"Any change?"

There had been and Beddows gave the report, pointing each time to the subject he described, beginning right ahead.

"Yes Sir. They've seen us, Sir. The one as was towin' must've cast off, 'cos she's added sail an' is movin' quicker, an' it looks like she's comin round straight for us."

He changed position to point off to the left.

"T'other, the escort, 'as hauled 'er wind an' is takin' it on the starboard beam. She has now come right round an' is steerin' full off to our larboard, almost goin' back on where she's come from. Sir."

Argent listened to the detailed description, but at the same time he focused his glass. The escort was under a heavy press of sail and was clearly heading far out to Ariadne's left, her larboard. Focusing on the other frigate, which had been towing, he saw her profile narrow then hold. She had changed course and was now sailing directly at Ariadne, almost on the opposite course. He closed the glass.

"These two know their business!"

He returned to the quarterdeck.

"Mr. McArdle, the log if you please."

The log was thrown and, as the minutes passed, Argent impatiently smacked his telescope into the palm of his hand, in between focusing it, alternately, onto each of his manoeuvring opponents. McArdle arrived at his side.

"Nine knots, sir."

Argent looked up at the sails. With that spread of canvas, in this wind, Ariadne was capable of eleven knots and over. He wanted an increase of three when she went to full speed.

He walked the larboard gangway to find Bosun Fraser. He spoke quietly.

"Mr. Fraser."

"Sir?"

"The sails are too well trimmed. I want the wind spilled from each. Not too much as can be seen, but enough to keep way off the ship. We need one knot less. Am I clear?"

"Yes Sir. Aye aye, Sir."

"Right, see to the sheets. You'll know when I want her back up to your best trim."

Fraser saluted, somewhat puzzled, but orders were orders, however Argent, seeing Fraser's puzzlement, took the time to explain, he had too much respect for his thoroughly capable Bosun.

"With all the canvas we're carrying, I want to make the Johnnies think this is our best speed. That's important. Just like with La Mouette, remember?"

"Aye aye, Sir."

They parted company, Fraser to supervise the afterguard, Argent back to his quarterdeck. There he found the whole of his Officer corps, including the Midshipmen and he called these three forward, each a different shade of ghostly pale and in a different state of trepidation. Trenchard was visibly shaking.

"Now, gentlemen. For your information, these are the problems. That facing the French is that they have to stop us getting to La Pomone and probably rake her, easily, as she is so incapable of manoeuvre. Ours is to get past those two and then, indeed, rake her. Now, they could form a line astern in front of her as a kind of screen, but they know that would not serve. We would then sail out to larboard, gain the weather gauge and come across to rake both the last escort and La Pomone. They cannot sail backwards into the wind to stop us. They could stop and allow La Pomone to sail on, and somehow try to block our path, but, with the weather gauge, we could manoeuvre around and one would certainly get raked before we went on to La Pomone. That they know."

He paused for breath and also to assemble his next explanation.

"They could both come on at us directly, as that one on our bows is now doing, but they know we could dodge to one side and use one to mask the other. We would almost certainly get past them. So this is their plan."

He pointed to the manoeuvring escort, now far across their larboard bow.

"You see our friend out there?"

All looked and nodded.

"He is gaining the weather gauge on us. He will turn when he feels that he can circle fully around, then come down upon us, match our course and get onto our larboard. He wishes to time that turn so that he comes onto us just before we cross with his companion there. With one beside us and one passing, they will then have us between two fires, at least for a minute or so. They know that they must have one ship that can follow us on to La Pomone and prevent any attack upon her. That ship will be that one, out there, soon to turn and join our course."

He now pointed down the line of his ship to the second escort, heading straight for them.

"That one, on our bows, would like either to cause some kind of collision and then grapple our hulls together, or hold sufficient distance between us to elevate her guns to disable our sails. Either will enable his companion to sail down upon us and pound either our embraced self, or our disabled self. Our task is to throw out their timing by being able to suddenly increase our speed and then dodge past that fellow in front, who is showing himself to be so keen to halt our progress in some manner."

He allowed all three time to examine their two opponents. It didn't seem to help the feelings within any of them, but Argent continued.

"Now, your role as Gunsection Commanders. Expect to exchange fire with him in front first, then to fire into La Pomone. I look to you all to keep your men well in hand, calm and steady, and to fire fast and accurately. Talk to them; tell them that we are counting on their highest capabilities, that they are right "man o' war's men" and better than any Johnny Frogs afloat!"

The faintest of smiles passed across the face of each.

"I anticipate only three broadsides, perhaps four. Now, to your stations and good luck to you all."

Argent solemnly shook the hand of all three and they left to take charge of their section of guns, but Argent called Bright to a halt.

"Mr. Bright. Please to give Mr. Tucker my compliments and ask him to join me on the quarterdeck."

Bright disappeared and Argent walked slowly to his place at the weatherside, his eyes on the circling escort. She was still sailing far out, still gaining searoom for the turn that Argent anticipated. He turned to his remaining Officers.

"Something less than a fashionable dance this, gentleman! Soon it will be time to open The Ball."

The best reaction was a ghost of a smile from Wentworth as he began his own descent to his section of guns. Within minutes, Master Gunner Tucker appeared up the starboard companionway, came to Argent and saluted.

"Mr. Tucker. I intend to give that Johnny in front a short-range broadside, of sufficient weight to knock him sideways a foot or two. I can't say yet which battery. Double shot, do you think?"

"Yes Sir. At short range?"

"Yes. Double charge?"

Tucker thought.

"I'd say not, Sir. At that range it'll make small difference, and why risk burstin' a gun? Extra half charge."

"Very well. Thank you, Mr. Tucker. Both batteries, load double shot. Extra half charge."

Tucker knuckled his forehead and bustled off. Soon, from his quarterdeck, Argent could see the guns being hauled back for loading, which his guncrews began immediately. He then looked at his opponents. The one upwind to larboard was still moving out to give herself room to make her 180 degree turn; whilst the frigate ahead had moved significantly off to Ariadne's starboard, inviting her to pass on her current course. The distance would be suitable to give the French guncrews sufficient room to elevate their guns and disable Ariadne's sails with chainshot, thus making her easy prey for her companion, who was surely soon to turn and come up to take Ariadne from the opposite side.

"Mr. Short. I want to run down so's we pass that frigate at less than pistol shot. Give her a nudge if you have to, a glancing blow would suit us fine."

Short had no idea which words to use that would adequately acknowledge Argent's order, and so he used just six.

"Aye, aye, Sir. Pistol shot, Sir."

Argent looked again at the frigate far out. Soon she would be making her turn.

"Mr. Fraser! Stand by with your axes and ready your topmen."

Fraser ran off, shouting in all directions, but most importantly to Henry Ball, requiring him to also obtain a boarding axe. Argent checked again on both opponents. The frigate ahead had edged even further over to Ariadne's right in response to Short's change of course, but Short had followed, steering further to starboard and the afterguard made no adjustments, allowing the sail trim to remain poor. Argent looked at the other frigate off to windward and gave her his full attention, one minute, then two, then four, and then her profile began to change, she was turning. Argent seized a speaking trumpet and yelled forward.

"Mr. Fraser. Cut loose!"

He saw both axes rise and fall, then Fraser was running back to supervise the sail trimming but he had little to say. The men were at their places and had begun to trim all sails up to standard as the restraining barrels disappeared astern. Argent felt Ariadne heel to starboard as her hull responded and within a minute the waves were passing her hull at noticeably greater speed. He spoke to himself.

"Right. That's ruined their timing. Now to get past this fellow."

He considered his options, suddenly less sure, but continuing his analysis. If he continued with what was a collision course, the Frenchman could turn downwind as they approached and fire first, giving Ariadne a full starboard broadside. As if in confirmation, he saw this Frenchman turn further downwind to avoid the collision and give himself cannon room. He then looked over at the other Frenchman making his turn, he would be late at Ariadne's crossing with the frigate ahead, but only by minutes and she was now spreading more canvas to make up for the obvious fact that she was going to be late to carry out their plan to take Ariadne on both sides. Argent looked at both, several times, gauging course and speed.

If he changed course and steered left, up to windward, he would pass the Frenchman in front at long range, too far for him to be certain of disabling Ariadne. In fact the Frenchman would have to turn upwind himself to keep Ariadne at optimum range for chainshot and that would turn his threatening starboard guns away from Ariadne, at least for some minutes, before he came back on course.

"Mr. Short. Up helm. Come to South by East."

Short's acknowledgment was drowned by Argent's orders to Fraser.

"Mr. Fraser. Close hauled, larboard tack."

Ariadne's bowsprit swung over the horizon, she was on the edge of the wind but Argent knew that Ariadne could go a little more if needed. She raced on, close hauled, the wind now coming from just forward of beam on but the sail trimming held the wind strong in her sails. The gap that would exist between Ariadne and her immediate opponent forward was widening, to create such a range that would probably enable Ariadne to sail past with minimal damage. The Frenchman responded, he had to, and he turned upwind to close with Ariadne. Argent saw their starboard battery begin to disappear as she swung across to meet them and point harmlessly away. Now it was a question of timing, a crucial question, they were a quarter mile distant and closing rapidly. Argent waited a minute, then two, then another half.

"Mr. Short, down helm. Come to South West. Take us across her bows."

Again the acknowledgment was drowned as Argent yelled to the waiting Fraser.

"Mr. Fraser. Five points large. Wind over the larboard quarter."

The major change from where Ariadne took the wind required a major change in the set of the sheets and braces and, as Ariadne's bowsprit swung over to starboard, the masts were crowded with topmen and the gangways full of waisters and afterguard ready to haul around the braces of the yards and then trim the sheets on the sails. Ariadne's momentum took her around and she regained her speed, it was now a question of relative speeds and angles of geometry, to decide which ship would cross which ship's bows. Argent looked at their opponent and then at Short. He saw him take a better grip on the ship's wheel.

On the gundeck there had been no change for over an hour. The crews, particularly the Gun Captains, could hear the orders changing their course and could see the topmen adjusting the sheets and braces that controlled each sail and they could also see those on the gangways responding to the frantic orders of Fraser, Ball, and the other Bosun's Mates. They felt the deck tilt and then settle, then came the shouted order from Sanders, repeated unnecessarily down the gundeck by the Gun Captains.

"Larboard battery. Converging broadside. All guns train admidships!"

The guns at the stern had to point forward and those at the bows to point back. Their shot would then all pass through one central area, rather than be spread out. The crews furthest from amidships had the furthest to swing their guns around and there was intense activity with their hand spikes to lever over the gun carriages as Bright, commanding the forward section, checked that his guns were trained back aft, onto the centre, and Trenchard checked that his were trained forward. More shouts and orders from above, then Sanders again.

"Aim down one mark."

All along the gundeck the quoins were pushed in to one mark beyond the point at which the guns were level, this to raise the cascabel and lower the muzzles. The Gun Captains crouched, sighting along their barrels, concentrating on an empty sea, but now hearing Sanders again.

"Ready?"

Sixteen right arms were raised in the air.

"Coming up right soon, lads. Hit her larboard bow, fire as you bear."

Soldiers have an early sighting of their enemy, but sailors, beneath their decks, see nothing but empty water through their gunports. Around them all remains as familiar as if they were sat in harbour, they can only wait, until the order comes for them to fire and then the sides of their own ship burst in, the shot and the splinters to kill and maim. The guncrews felt the deck tilt to starboard, lifting their aim, but the call had been to lower their muzzles and now, with the tilt of the deck, their guns were level across the water. A minute filled an hour, then numbers one and two fired together, to be followed by the others, all in quick succession, because they were all on converging aim, therefore they saw their target almost as one. Now smoke was everywhere and they began to reload. Then the enemy's broadside began to come through their own ship's side and the screaming began, source unseen as the smoke came back through their gunports. Then they felt the ship lurch sideways to starboard, the movement from back at the stern, all simultaneous to a crash and then the bellowing of men.

Fraser and his men were immediately up the larboard shrouds, chopping and hacking as men gone mad. The Frenchman's bowsprit had pierced the larboard mizzen shrouds, the ladder-like construction of heavy rope that led up to the mizzentop. The bowsprit had penetrated just under the top and they were now desperate to cut it loose. It had come it at a sharp angle after the Frenchman had turned hard downwind in response to the same from Ariadne and a collision had become inevitable. The hulls of the two ships were now almost together along their full length, the Frenchman's shattered larboardbow touching a quarterway along Ariadne's larboardside, with the gap between growing forward from touching to a final gap of six yards. The Frenchman's first three gunports had been beaten into one long gash. Fraser threw his axe down to the deck; knives were now needed to cut a passage through the shrouds to allow the bowsprit to slide out. Beside him, a man spluttered and slumped through the rope squares, to then hang upside down and lifeless, shot from the Frenchman's foretop. He was pulled clear to fall into the sea and another seaman took his place. The thick, tarred rope was parting but it was slow work. Below him the carronade fired and the Marines, lining the rail, added to the conflict taking place at a range of mere feet. Smoke was everywhere, for which Fraser was grateful. He suddenly found Ball opposite him, he had climbed up the inside of the shrouds and was using his knife on the next section over, where the bowsprit should slide after Fraser had opened the section that still held it fast.

Argent looked up at the feverish activity above him, at the surreal picture of another ship's bowsprit piercing his own rigging. He had no fear of being boarded, his Marines were maintaining an incessant fire onto the Frenchman's forecastle and the quarterdeck carronade was being rapidly reloaded. His fear was of the second French frigate, now chasing up, having made her turn. His ship was held fast. Some grapnels were coming over, but these were quickly severed; however, if the bowsprit was not freed, the second frigate would be up on their starboard side and they would certainly be lost; it would be merely a matter of time. His own guns roared again, they had beaten the French to the second broadside, but that was of no matter if they could not cut themselves free. He looked up, the job was not done; he looked astern, the second frigate was but minutes away. He seized a speaking trumpet and leaned over to see Sanders anxiously peering down the gundeck.

"Mr. Sanders. Starboard battery to train full aft. Fire as they bear. Larboard battery, double shot; wait for my order."

The Frenchman fired again and he felt the shot hit his ship, but the broadside seemed ragged and less potent, his guncrews' two broadsides had inflicted significant damage on their French opponent.

He looked up again, but the righting of the ship's deck confirmed what he could now see. The bowsprit was free and was moving astern, Fraser and Ball, in destructive farewell, axing apart much of the French rigging on the departing bowsprit. All other ropes in its path had been severed, including the vital larboard mizzen backstays, but no matter for now. He leaned over the rail.

"Mr. Sanders. Ladboard battery. As a broadside, fire!"

Obedient to Sanders orders, the guns crashed out as one. Such was the weight of shot hitting the Frenchman that it physically moved him sideways and the gap grew between the hulls. The Marines continued to maintain their fire, calmly encouraged by Breakspeare, although, Argent noted, with a torrent of the vilest language, but Argent had to get his ship moving. Fraser, Ball and a collection of seamen were lashing several splints onto the severed ends of the backstays, holding them together was a vital task if they were to use the sails on the mizzen mast, especially the driver. If it didn't hold, in the strong wind the mast would be over the side and they would be lost. The wind worked on the sails, now more in number, as the topmen, without orders, set everything they could. Ariadne slowly gained way, some sails remaining slack as those of the Frenchman robbed them of their wind, but in succession each slack sail gained the wind as they moved forward of their immediate opponent, and then each began to draw. The French fired again, but this time reduced further. His men had won their duel but now Ariadne had a duel with time, could she gain enough speed quickly enough to remain ahead of the second French frigate? This ship was now up and within cannonshot range if her Captain chose to turn downwind and bring around his larboard broadside, rather than stand on his current course to overtake.

Ariadne was accelerating. Fraser and Ball looked anxiously at their splints as the mizzen sails took the wind. Mizzen topmen were attaching extra ropes from the stays to any fixed point on the quarterdeck. The splints creaked and stretched but they held. Fraser and Ball added more, from further up the stays, and the mizzen topmen were rushing up replacements from the cable locker, but it would take some time to fix in place such heavy cables and then release the old. The French frigate was still gaining, but not so quickly and the exchange began between Ariadne's two sternchasers and the two bowchasers on the Frenchman. Shot hit home from both vessels and Argent drew satisfaction from a shower of splinters flying up from the Frenchman's forecastle rail. She was 50 yards back, almost in line astern, but Ariadne was beginning to match her speed. However, the Frenchman had one more trick which he could play and it seemed that he was going to play it. The frigate suddenly surged off downwind to starboard causing the range to grow rapidly. Ariadne's starboard guns, trained right back, at last got a sight and fired, not as one, but each carefully aimed. The distance was far and the angle difficult, but with the guns remaining double shotted, Argent saw many strike home on the Frenchman's forecastle, but he knew what the Frenchman was about.

"Mr. Short. Up helm, hard! Come due South."

He seized a speaking trumpet and pointed it upwards to his men manning the yardarms.

"Down on deck. Everyman. Now!"

Every topman seized or jumped onto a convenient rope and slid down as Short spun the wheel. The French frigate was bringing around her larboard broadside to fire at Ariadne's masts and sails. If they could bring enough down, they could sail up and fight at an advantage and so, in response, Argent was turning his ship stern on to narrow the target. The Frenchman fired and all heard the buzz and hum of the shot overhead. Many holes appeared in the sails, some rigging jerked apart and the starboard maintopsail yardarm parted in the middle, but Ariadne sailed on. The Frenchman had loaded his guns with ball, anticipating a close exchange. Standing beside McArdle, Argent spoke a short prayer at the French Captain's decision not to load chainshot. McArdle listened and spoke Amen.

The topmen swarmed back aloft to repair the damage, and those on the gangways adjusted the sheets and braces for the new course. Argent now looked further ahead to examine the problem of their next opponent, although this was an over description. La Pomone was a lumbering hulk, barely making way with just four sails making use of her short foremast; nevertheless, her Captain had hauled his wind, realising that continuing on Westward would expose his stern to Ariadne. La Pomone was now steering North, she had no choice but to turn to meet Ariadne and try to regain the protection of her two escorts. Argent immediately realised that, if Ariadne was to do La Pomone any damage it had to be on her bows, eighteen shot into the waterline of her bows should be fatal, but they would have to avoid La Pomone's own very potent broadside.

Ariadne's present course of South was upwind, to the left, of La Pomone, if both held their courses, they would pass at a cable distance, but soon Argent would have all the weather gauge he needed. Argent looked back at the chasing frigate, she had resumed the chase, but it was hopeless. Ariadne would be onto La Pomone far in advance of her, even more so in the case of Ariadne's first opponent which had to turn to join the chase. Argent looked at La Pomone, again judging speed and distance. Soon he would turn Ariadne to starboard in order to cross La Pomone's course, using a curving course that would take her onto her bows, then curve away, away from her larboard guns. The turn must take them close enough to hit La Pomone hard, yet not be so close as to come into the line of fire of her waiting starboard broadside, even if trained fully forward. Argent assumed that, soon, to give his ship a chance, La Pomone's Captain would turn downwind to at least try to present his starboard broadside to the threatening English frigate. He calculated in his mind where that would place La Pomone, she was already turning to do this but at barely any speed, she had no chance of avoiding a swooping Ariadne. Time to turn.

"Mr. Short. Down helm. West Sou'west."

Ariadne's larboard battery would be needed again. He leaned over the quarterdeck rail to see Lieutenant Sanders.

"Mr. Sanders. Soon we will cross La Pomone's bows. Larboard battery, load single ball with extra half charge. Train forward. Assume tilt to larboard and fire at her waterline. Tell the men, they have one shot at her, just one. Four minutes, probably less!"

Sanders ran forward to his three Midshipmen, through a gundeck that resembled a madhouse, full of feverish and chaotic activity after their duel with the French frigate. Bloodstained sand discoloured the deck in many places, but the dead had been pulled back to the masts and the last of the wounded were disappearing below. On the larboard side, three guns had been damaged; one had lost a wheel but another, more seriously had had the fixing of her left breeching rope next to the gunport shot out. If it were fired with just one breeching, the recoil would slew it dangerously across the deck. However, more seriously still, another had had its carriage shattered and the barrel lay totally dismounted on the deck. The three were the centre of manic activity, the first was having its axle replaced from a gun in the starboard battery, the crew of the second were improvising a breech fixing by dropping a length of timber through the shothole and lashing the severed breeching rope onto it, but the third gun, number three, had to be completely replaced. They had practiced it many times and the dismounted barrel was being hauled clear and number three starboard was being hauled over. Orders were unnecessary, such that Bright, feeling wholly superfluous, simply put his shoulder to the guncarriage and pushed alongside the men, with Sam Morris shouting the "two, six, heave!" They felt the deck heel to larboard as Ariadne made her turn, but few heard the shouted orders and the running feet and even less saw the men on the gangways or in the rigging. Sanders stood watching, helpless; he could shout himself hoarse, but to what end? It was now up to the men. He heard Argent call from behind and above.

"Mr. Sanders.

Sanders ran back and looked up.

"Sir?"

"30 yards range, off the larboard side. Two minutes."

Sanders walked forward five paces and shouted at the top of his lungs down the still dishevelled gundeck.

"Load! Extra half charge, single ball. Train forward. Down one mark."

The guncrews immediately began to obey his order. He waited, hoping, then he began, as he knew he must.

"Ready?"

The response came and Sanders swallowed hard, his chin clenched with emotion. Sixteen hands were raised in the air.

"30 yards off. At her bows, on her waterline. As you bear."

Then the moment got the better of him.

"Hit her right, boys, you've one shot, but bloody sink her!"

Each Gun Captain called for the quoin to be adjusted to the elevation for thirty yards range, on La Pomone's waterline. The deck was steady; Argent had set royaltopgallants, whose maximum leverage held the masts steadier at a constant angle. Sam Morris was the stand-in Gun Captain of Number Three, him having been killed when the gun was dismounted, but all the crew stood intent, waiting for orders. Morris looked at the tackleman nearest the gunport on the left.

"Look out through the port. Give me warning when you see him."

Master Gunner Tucker had come up from his magazine, his role now finished, to patrol the gundeck and add his calming presence to the tense gundeck.

"Steady now, lads, steady. Lay it right and fire only when 'tis true."

Morris checked the elevation again. Ariadne, now almost running before the wind, had righted herself slightly, lifting the gunmuzzle.

"Quoin in. Half mark."

Two tacklemen thrust the handles of the handspikes into the spaces either side between the barrel and the carriage and levered up the cascabel just enough for the quoin to be thrust in and lower the muzzle. Morris crouched and tightened the lanyard. The tackleman spoke.

"Coming up, Sam."

A cannonball came in high up, just below the gangway between numbers five and six and three men were felled by splinters, but the waiting guncrews ignored it all. They heard the carronade fire above on the forecastle, then number one fired, then two, then Morris saw the dark, soaked wood of La Pomone's bows, seeming huge in the frame of the gunport. The gunmuzzle was a little high, but Ariadne dipped a little to larboard. The barrel came onto the dark hull at the waterline and Morris jerked the lanyard. Half a second and the gun roared and sprang back, a plume of smoke rising up from the touchhole. Exactly at the moment of firing, Morris had seen his gun trained perfectly on the bowstem. The remaining guns each added their own roar back towards the stern, then there were just the cries of the wounded and the familiar noises from the hull and rigging, whilst the crews stood still and silent, waiting for orders.

Argent had watched the strike of his shot. The extra half charge was needed to penetrate the thick and reinforced timber of La Pomone's bows, but with each discharge he saw a hole appear, on or just above the waterline, or spray rise up as the ball hit water before hitting wood. His own ship had taken two further hits from La Pomone's bowchasers, but he left that to Fentiman. Wentworth should now be there to help and Argent looked around, but he wasn't. He brought his mind back to the next problem, to escape the two frigates. Ariadne had continued her curve around; soon she would be taking the wind over the starboard quarter, for the first time since leaving Falmouth.

"Mr. Fraser. Starboard tack. Wind three points on the quarter!"

He drew back from the rail to speak to the helmsman.

"Steer Nor'west."

The repeat came and Argent went to the taffrail to find the whereabouts of the nearest chasing frigate. She was less than two cables off and her Captain had ordered a turn to chase Ariadne, but Argent paid it little heed, Ariadne had all the speed they now needed to make good their escape, the wind was on her best point of sailing. He trained his glass on La Pomone and noted immediately that she was significantly down at the bows; her crew had taken in her sails, but the pressure of water as she pushed forward through the sea must be surging unstoppably through all eighteen shot holes. She was doomed. Argent saw the chasing frigate suddenly come up into the wind and give up the chase, her priority now was to rescue the crew of the sinking frigate. Argent saw the change and made his own response.

"Mr. Fraser. Take in royals, topgallants, and all staysails. Take in fore and mainsail."

With the large drop in her spread of canvas, Ariadne's speed fell, Argent wanted to keep La Pomone within sight; they had to be certain that La Pomone was gone, therefore they would slow down and wait. Argent trained his telescope over the taffrail and he was soon joined by several others. Through their telescopes they saw that La Pomone's forecastle was awash and her crew were launching their boats. The "chasing" frigate, chasing no more, was launching her own boats and the second frigate was soon to arrive. McArdle lowered his own glass.

"Pray God they get them all off."

Several Amen's were heard across the quarterdeck, including that from Argent. All continued to watch as Ariadne continued on under easy sail and many of her crew were in the rigging, watching the end of their opponent from months back in St. Malo. The weight of her 42 guns and the ballast stones deep in La Pomone's hull, which kept her upright and stiff in a side-on wind, were taking her to the bottom. Now there was little to see but her quarterdeck and the stump of her foremast. Suddenly she slid under, leaving just black shapes, some human, some flotsam, bobbing in the water. Ariadne's crew cheered, Argent let them, but somehow he felt no glory for himself nor for his ship, they had done no more than deliver the coup de grace to a helpless enemy, unable to manoeuvre and defend herself. He turned to McArdle.

"A course for Falmouth, please, Sailing Master."

He consulted the windgauge on the quarterdeck.

"Wind now South East."

He saw Fentiman along the Larboard gangway, examining shot damage.

"Mr. Fentiman. House the guns and stand down. Get some food to the men."

Then Wentworth came up on deck, his head and chin swathed in new bandage, his lower face badly discoloured and swollen, but he did manage an odd-shaped grin in Argent's direction.

* * *

Budgen was looking disconcertingly cheerful. Rolls and coffee were being offered, even pushed, across the wide desk, Argent wasn't sure why, but perhaps it was part of Budgen's plan to keep Argent occupied whilst he devoured the pages in Ariadne's Logbook that described the sinking of La Pomone. Argent sipped his coffee and waited, distracting himself by looking through the window at his ship, now back alongside the Navy mole, with carpenters all over her hull and lumber carts arriving down from the main quayside, but mostly he watched his own men in the rigging, some making repairs, some, quite frankly, skylarking.

Budgen had finished reading. He closed the book and placed his pudgy hand on top, and stared at the embossed title on the cover, his face a round picture of contentment, whilst his round head nodded his satisfaction and he self indulgently spoke, mouthing carefully and repeating several words.

"Hmmm. La Pomone, La Pomone, no less, sunk. Sunk and down with Davey!."

The last three words, the seaman's term for the ocean floor, were spoken slowly and carefully, and Argent grinned at Budgen's use of common seaman's language, from a man usually so punctilious over his representation of himself as a Commanding Officer. Budgen scratched his ear and rested his head in the palm of his left hand, whilst rubbing his right cheek with the other. Suddenly he became decisive.

"A "42" taken out of the French Channel fleet. Who can argue with that?"

He paused.

"And two more damaged! One badly?"

He looked questioningly at Argent.

"Yes, Sir. I'd say so. We wrecked her gundeck."

Budgen nodded some more, his mouth pursed; however, his next words seemed to come reluctantly.

"That was good work, Argent. Good work. Fair's fair and congratulations are due."

Argent sat up at the unexpectedly pleasant tone and replied in like manner.

"Thank you, Sir, but I owe a great deal to my crew. Their seamanship and fighting ability was what turned..."

Budgen held up his hand, dismissively.

"Yes, yes, Argent, yes. Quite so."

Argent fell quiet but so did Budgen. The silence lasted until Budgen changed the subject.

"Now, what of your damage? You gave some numbers in your Log, but I forget."

"To the hull, Sir. 33 hits from shot and two guns disabled, one completely. Ummm..."

Argent worked his head from side to side.

"...you can see through the window that the carpenters are working on the damage now. I must say that was quick work to get them mobilised, Sir, and thank you."

Budgen became almost pleasant.

"Put it down to anticipation, Argent. When do you ever come back into port without something wrecked or broken? I warned the Dockyard Commissariat that you would return with some damage and there they were, waiting for you at the Navy mole. Seeing as you came back in with the crack of the dawn, they had time to meet you as you berthed. And your casualties?"

"Five dead, Sir. Fifteen wounded, ten like to fully recover."

"Are your dead still aboard?"

"Yes Sir. My First Lieutenant is making the arrangements now. My surgeon tells me that the five seriously wounded should be brought ashore and he is making those arrangements."

Argent pondered why Budgen was showing such parental concern over such shipboard details, but Budgen was leaning back and staring at him, his face grave and in no way triumphant. Argent remained quiet and it was Budgen who broke the silence, his earlier compassion now explained.

"There's going to be a Court Martial, Argent."

Argent's face remained blank.

"Yes, Sir. I expected it."

Budgen leaned forward, his face almost sympathetic.

"I'll be candid with you. Grant and myself did not, not expect it, that is. I was angry with you after that slaver, I confess, but what it did for our reputation in these parts, and across all England, when the newssheets got hold of it, did, well, mellow me somewhat. I can't walk down the damn road without someone wanting to shake my hand or somesuch thing, and the Mayor and his crew can't do enough for us."

He was nodding and almost smiling, almost Fatherly.

"Grant was of the opinion, and I shared it, that to convene a Court Martial of the Captain involved in such a rescue would make the Navy a laughing stock, and we felt sure that their Sea Lordships would feel the same, but..."

He sat back and his face became grave again.

"There's politics involved. Dirty politics."

He sat forward again.

"I got this from Admiral Grant. Lord Liverpool's Tory Government is in trouble with their Industry Bill and they need every vote to defeat a Whig amendment. They need Cinch and he's struck a bargain. He's stood up in the House to condemn the, and I quote, if I get it right, "flagrant flouting of Naval discipline, such as to possibly jeopardise the security of the one standing army this country possesses". Liverpool has to arrange a Court Martial to keep Cinch in the fold. Therefore one will be convened."

Budgen's face softened.

"I'm sorry Argent."

Argent deliberately brightened himself up. He was pleasantly surprised at the 'sea change" in Budgen's attitude towards him and felt disposed to respond.

"Not at all, Sir. As I said before, I welcome it. I stand ready to justify the actions I took."

He paused.

"Do you know when, Sir?"

"I don't. I can only guess at late next week, or the week after. It has to be set quickly in train to keep Cinch where Liverpool wants him."

Budgen placed his hands palms down on the top of the desk and looked as though he was about to raise himself up, but he did not. Instead he pushed the Log back towards Argent.

"When I know anything definite, Argent, you'll be the first to know after me. My advice to you now, is to get your story clear and straight, especially witnesses from your own ship. That sort of thing."

"Yes, Sir. I understand."

Argent took the returning of the Log as his cue and stood up, to salute and then leave, but he did not exit immediately, not before exchanging words with Venables along the lines of "up The Marines." His return to his ship was greeted with the now familiar sounds of sawing and hammering, produced by several workgangs all working assiduously on the gangways and gundeck, using new oak planking or carrying that which was shattered up to the gangways and removing it to the quayside. He went straight to his cabin and sent for Fentiman, who entered, carrying the communications addressed to Argent.

Fentiman placed them on the desk, but Argent did not fail to notice that Fentiman's hand dwelt long on the letter on top and, when it did, his hand slid away, in a kind of caress. Argent took the top letter and noticed what he thought was almost certainly a female hand. He slit away the seal and read. He noticed Fentiman studying him intently but he saw the signature and read to the bottom; the letter was from Charlotte Willoughby.

"It's from Charlotte. She has heard what I was just about to tell you, that there is to be a Court Martial over my decision to take the slaver."

He looked up at Fentiman.

"That was why I asked for you to come here. She must have learnt of it from Admiral Grant, who has also told Budgen. She is saying, and this is most magnificent of her, that she has approached the..."

He looked again at the letter

"Society for the Mitigation and Gradual Abolition of Slavery, and she hopes that they may be able to provide some form of support. She has also written a letter to The Times stating her outrage at the absurdity of convening a Court in the first place."

Argent looked at Fentiman and noted immediately that his First Lieutenant seemed wholly depressed and cast down, but Argent finished what he wanted to say.

"I think that is most kind and most supportive. You would agree?"

Fentiman nodded, but there was no change in his demeanor. Argent studied him closely.

"Anything wrong, Henry? Not a family bereavement, I hope, nor anything of that nature?"

Fentiman perked himself up, now realising that his low mood was evident and that he needed to meet the requirement of his duties. However, whilst Argent was reading the letter, he had debated within himself whether or not to tell Argent about his own letter, just received and just read, also from Charlotte, but informing him that, "She was greatly flattered and honoured by his proposal of marriage the last time they had met, but that her heart belonged to another". Now he was further downcast by the notion that Charlotte had written to himself at the same time as writing to Argent, his own now seeming to be merely a routine letter within a routine bout of letter writing.

"No, Sir. Nothing wrong."

He looked at Argent, who, now reassured, had set Charlotte's letter aside and was opening the next.

"What are your orders, Sir?"

Argent looked up, dropping the cover and the opener.

"We can do nothing until the repairs are completed. That will take up the greater part of a week. Between times, ready the ship for sea; supplies and such, but we were only away two days; that cannot be too onerous a task."

"It's not, Sir, but what about the Court Martial? We should make some preparations. Witnesses on your behalf. You have the right to call whomsoever you choose. We should make our selection and, well, brief them, so as to get our story straight. Any discrepancy, they'll seize upon."

Argent smiled inwardly at Fentiman's use of "our" instead of "your". He felt much strengthened by the evidently loyal support of his First Lieutenant, who seemed to be taking the whole thing as a slur against the whole ship. Argent sat back and thought.

"Well, it doesn't take much deduction to say that everything will hang on justifying the decision not to go straight across the Bay, but to instead follow the coast. The first thing they'll jump on, is that going straight would deliver the letter quicker, following the coast put us on the more likely course of the slaver. Who was involved in that?"

Argent paused, and then answered his own question.

"Reece. McArdle, and yourself."

He looked up at Fentiman.

"We'd better get them in."

As Fentiman left, he returned to the half opened cover. He broke the seal and found difficulty in levering open the thick paper. The first thing he noticed as the top fold bent back was the unmistakeable crest of the Admiralty. Beneath, in the body of the letter, there were merely three sentences.

"You are ordered to present yourself and your ship's books at the residence of the Commander in Chief, Plymouth, at 9.00 am of the 24th November 1809, in order to attend a Court Martial of yourself, at 2.00 pm. This has been convened to sit in judgment on your recent conduct pertaining to the conveyance of a despatch from His Majesty's Government to the Commander of His Majesty's Forces in Portugal. The Court will be composed of the Judge Advocate, Charles Manners-Sutton; President of the Court, Vice Admiral Holdsworth; Rear Admiral Grant; Rear Admiral Broke; Captain Henry Blackwood and Captain Sir Digby Cinch."

Argent allowed the heavy vellum to fall to the desk. How many of those could he count on for some sympathy? Grant alone! And what the Hell was Cinch doing there? He must be ex-Navy, not in post but still on the active list, his presence told of the underlying politics. Holdsworth understood nothing but obedience; Cinch and Broke harboured a deep loathing for himself and Blackwood was an unknown quantity to him, save that he had commanded a frigate at the Battle of Trafalgar. He sat back and philosophised; oh, well, what will be, will be!

He opened the other letters and set about the affairs they mentioned, all concerning the ship, all requiring absolute concentration amidst the incessant hammering and sawing. Then again came the knock on the door and those named previously trooped in; Reece wholly apprehensive, McArdle simply obeying his Captain's bidding and Fentiman, last, closing the door.

* * *

For two days he cudgelled his thoughts away from the impending Court Martial, now but five days away. Most often he worked alone in his cabin, where he couldn't resist several re-readings of the blunt, cold, accusing words that afforded no comfort, nor the endless examination of the reaction he could expect from the partially unknown Holdsworth and the wholly unknown Blackwood. On the second morning he had received a letter from The Society for the Mitigation and Gradual Abolition of Slavery pledging their full support, but any help financial was beyond them, but they did promise to mount a campaign to "fully inform the authorities of the public disquiet at the persecution of so evidently humane and valuable a Naval Officer". He had just set the letter down when the Marine Sentry knocked and entered.

"There's a gen'leman at the foot of the gangway, Sir, wishin' to see you."

Argent looked up and pondered, but not for long, for he then gave the only reply possible.

"Ask him to come aboard and please conduct him here, to my cabin."

The "Aye aye Sir", came around an already closing door and Argent sat and waited. Soon he heard footsteps in the corridor outside and the same sentry opened the door and flattened himself against the doorjamb to allow the visitor to enter. Argent stood to make his greetings and soon recognised the distinguished gentlemen who had paid Argent and the ship such compliments at the end of the Lord Mayor's visit. He was dressed in the same identical manner that Argent remembered, his iron grey hair, in light contrast to his dark suit and that itself contrasting to the snow white linen. A folded newspaper, under his arm, stood out in contrast to the dark cloth of his suit. Argent stood waiting as the man crossed the space in the cabin between the door and the desk.

"Thank you for seeing me, Captain. May I introduce myself, as I so remissly failed to do the last time we met? My name is Josiah Meade."

They shook hands, but Meade politely remained standing.

"Please do sit down, Mr. Meade. It's a pleasure to see you again."

"I hope it will be so, Captain Argent, I sincerely hope so."

He placed the newspaper on the desk, it was the latest copy of The Times. It was folded to reveal one particular article, which Meade pointed to. It was not a large article, but its headline read, simply, "Captain

Nathan Argent, HMS Ariadne, to appear before Court Martial." Argent looked at Meade.

"May I?"

Meade pushed the newspaper further towards him as an answer. Argent read the few sentences, noticing the absence this time of any hyperbole, merely stating the fact of the Court Martial for the capture of the slaver rather than deliver the letter at all speed. It finished with Argent's other career events, these being the capture of La Mouette, the raid on St. Malo and the sinking of La Pomone. Meade allowed Argent to finish reading, then he sat forward in his chair.

"Captain. What form do these Court Martials take? Are they similar to a Trial in a Public Court?"

Argent sat back and thought, his brow furrowed as he looked down at his desk.

"Yes, as far as I am aware. Only the Jury is The Bench, if you understand; it is made up of Naval Officers, controlled by a Judge Advocate, him being there to ensure that the affair is conducted properly. He makes no judgement, the others do."

"Are there Lawyers for the defence and for the prosecution?"

"Yes and no, although a defendant can ask for a civilian Lawyer, but he must meet the expense himself. The defence and prosecution are usually conducted by Officers of the defendant's rank, the defence is often described as "a friend", which could be anyone; someone from the defendant's own ship, for example. They interrogate the witnesses, as can Members of The Bench."

"Do you have a Lawyer, or "a friend" to represent you?"

"No. There is no Captain that I can call upon in our part of the world, and the person from my ship, here, whom I could ask, I cannot, because he will almost certainly be called upon to testify on my behalf. It could all get a bit incestuous. However, I can, of course, speak for myself, which is what I intend."

Meade sat back, his decision taken.

"Then it is my wish that I provide a Lawyer for you, Captain."

Argent stared back at him, in shock and astonishment.

"That is most kind of you, Sir, but I cannot possibly accept. The monetary cost to yourself would be immense, I cannot possibly allow you to make such an outlay on my behalf."

The reaction was wholly unexpected and equally strange. Meade held up the backs of his hands for Argent to see.

"Do you see these scars? Do you know where they come from?"

Argent shook his head.

"The mine. Coal, copper, tin; all miners get them. You get a cut, in goes the dust and it never comes out."

He paused to allow that to sink in, but its relevance escaped Argent.

"I'm a rich man. I have mines all over England of all three types, especially tin here in Cornwall, but I started up country with my own hole in the ground as a free miner. I still work alongside my men and they are as important to me as my own family and I saw the impact on them when their relations and friends were taken. You brought them back and to help you, as it now dwells in my power, is what they would want me to do. So, no argument, I'm going to seek out and employ a Lawyer knowledgeable in naval affairs to act on your behalf."

Argent sat back, quelled and resigned.

"I can only say thank you and that I am most grateful."

"Forget the thanks! There's no time."

Meade sprang to his feet.

"Right. I'm off, off to Plymouth, or even Portsmouth, to seek that which we need."

He held out his right hand, that being the most scarred. Argent took it with the firm grip he felt given.

"Good day to you, Captain."

Argent felt buoyed up. The facts were unchanged but at least he now had an experienced legal mind to present his case. He picked up Charlotte's letter, admiring the neat hand, then he reached for a piece of blank vellum from the pile on his desk and began writing, but in mid sentence came a knock on the door and Fentiman entered. Argent looked up.

"Henry. Good, I was just about to send for you. There's been a development which should help our cause."

"That's pleasing, Sir, but there's a problem on the gundeck. A dispute between a carpenter and our Mr. Baines. I think you should attend, Sir."

Argent dropped the quill into the inkwell.

"Oh, very well, I'll go, but you may as well wait here, then I can tell you my news. We've got a Lawyer!"

Argent grinned as he passed Fentiman, who took a seat to wait. As Argent closed the door on his exit, Fentiman's eye fell on the letter Argent had started. Even upside down, the addressee, Charlotte Willoughby, was obvious. He stared at it for a minute, leaned forward, sat back, and then sat fully forward to read the brief beginning, merely half the opening sentence.

"My Dearest Charlotte,

I write to further make known to you my deepest and undying..."

* * *

The coach rumbled over the cobbles past The Tower on its way to the Rear Admiral's residence, through a morning which had not yet realised that it should have blessed the hour with the daylight of dawn, for the morning was bleak and dark, with alternating waves of rain and fog. The coach held five, comprising the four sailors and their lawyer; one Christopher Sampson, young but old enough to have learnt his trade, clean cut and presentable, but not so much as to impress as fresh and inexperienced. It was he who had held the conversation since leaving Falmouth, carefully and precisely going over the testimony of each, patient with mistakes and encouraging a certain nuance here, an emphasis there. It was clear to Argent that he possessed a clear, logical and uncluttered mind, setting a course for them all through the forthcoming examination as he saw it. Eli Reece had given no trouble at all, performing in such circumstances before his superiors was comprehensively within his experience and he soon learnt and understood what was expected of him. Whatever needed saying he would say it, but McArdle was a different matter, he would "speak nae falsehoods, nor bear any false witness". However, Sampson, attending to every detail, had spent the whole of the previous day aboard Ariadne and, laboriously, had finally coached even McArdle's evidence into a form that would best help their cause.

They pulled into the familiar gates and the coach halted. The steps to the portico were almost deserted but for one or two civilian servants and, leaving the other three inside the coach, Argent and Sampson mounted the steps and entered. They were looking for someone who would know something about the forthcoming Court Martial, but no one could be seen. The two exchanged puzzled looks before Argent proceeded on down the entrance hall, to the door to the main hall where the St. Malo enquiry had been held. Sampson followed and when they opened the door, they first saw servants, busy with chairs for the audience, then they saw what they sought, an Officer in full Post Captain's uniform at a long table, which could only be there for the Judge Advocate. Argent walked up to him and saluted, using "Sir", although he had no need to.

"Good morning Sir. I am Captain Argent. I am here early, as requested, to make my Logbook available prior to the hearing."

He held the book out in the Officer's direction and the officer returned a stern, disapproving look, before taking the Log offered.

"Thank you, Captain. The Court is all here, bar Captain Cinch. The Judge Advocate will be grateful for your prompt obedience."

He turned to look at Sampson.

"And this gentleman is?"

"Permit me to introduce Christopher Sampson, Sir. My Lawyer."

A hint of shock crossed the Captain's face, but he soon recovered.

"I am Commodore Makeworthy. I serve as Clerk to the Court."

Sampson spoke up, brightly and pertly.

"Your servant, Sir. But may I point out that the defendant here, my client, has not received his entitlement as a defendant, namely, a copy of the charge sheet, a list of the witnesses that the prosecutor intends to call, accompanied by copies of their statements, and, finally, a list of the exhibits intended to be used in evidence."

Makeworthy listened to the pert, almost disrespectful words, noted the tone in which they were spoken, then he paused to consider his answer.

"The last two, I can answer now, if it will serve, that there will be no prosecution witnesses, save the Captain himself, here, and the only exhibit is the Logbook itself, here, which I now hold."

"Who is conducting the prosecution?"

"A Captain Cheveley."

Sampson looked at Argent, but saw no reaction, however, it was Makeworthy who spoke next.

"If there is nothing else?"

Sampson answered.

"Well, I'm afraid there is. The charge sheet. It should have been lodged with the Captain here some days ago."

Argent winced. He saw no point in being overly aggressive and spoke to mollify Makeworthy.

"Can I assume, Sir, that the charge is worded the same as in the original letter I received last week?"

Makeworthy nodded.

"Then that will perfectly suffice. Thank you for your time."

Makeworthy nodded and left for the door in the corner, the Log under his arm. Argent turned to Sampson.

"Right nothing to do until 2.00 pm. Time to kill."

"Right. And I know how to kill it. Would there be a room we could use, here, do you know?"

"I don't know, but do I know someone who does."

They left the main hall, now fully arranged once again as a Court, and they returned to the entrance hall. Argent knocked on a side door and heard a familiar voice shout for them to enter. Argent opened the door to see the familiar face and uniform of Marine Captain Baker. Dispensing with salutes they both shook hands, each genuinely pleased to see the other.

"Captain Baker, may I present my Lawyer, Christopher Sampson?"

Sampson's face soon matched the good cheer of both Argent and Baker as he shook the Marine's hand.

"Your servant, Sir."

Argent maintained the bonhomie.

"How's the choir?"

"Oh most excellent, everything in perfect harmony, if you get my drift?"

"I believe I do, and I'm pleased to hear it. I expect an invitation, if her parents will countenance such as yourself as a son-in-law and I'm not in some prison hulk."

The last lowered the atmosphere somewhat and changed Baker to his businesslike self.

"How can I help, Sir?"

"Do you have a room we could use, to wait, until this thing begins?"

"We do. One upstairs and I'll lay on some refreshment. How many are you."

"Five."

"Right. I'll take you there now."

They left the office and mounted the stairs, where Baker spoke first.

"You know who you're against?"

"Yes. What's the word?"

"The word on the dinner circuit is that Cheveley can't lose. That's what he's saying and so are many others."

Argent nodded, but Baker continued.

"Cheveley's relishing this opportunity, you know."

"Yes, I can imagine."

"Any thoughts, Sir?"

"If it were not him, it would be someone else. I'm up against it, no matter what. Have you seen who's on the Board! But, whatever, we can do no more than play it out."

They reached the room and all entered. There was some furniture, three chairs and a table and Sampson looked around and pronounced his opinion.

"Perfect."

"For what?"

"Rehearsal. I'll set it up, if you could go and fetch the others? If you'd be so good."

Argent nodded and he and Baker left, leaving Sampson to move furniture. They both descended the staircase.

"I wish you good luck, Sir, but it looks bad."

Argent smiled wanly.

"Yes. But I've had a few good months!"

Baker chuckled.

"I'll say. Dishing it out to the French, putting Broke's and Cheveley's noses thoroughly out of joint, making Ariadne the toast of the country! I'll say. Ariadne's the most favoured girls name, for newborns, as we speak. Did you know?"

Argent looked down and gave a short laugh himself.

"Poor things! Named after a ship."

Baker continued, more sombrely.

"But do watch out, Sir, they'll hit you as hard as they can. They're out to finish you."

"I suspected no less, but thank you for your good wishes. And the warning."

They had reached the entrance hall and Argent returned to the coach where the three had been patiently waiting.

"The thing starts at two, so we've some time. Sampson wants to spend it in rehearsal, as he calls it, and we've a room. Captain Baker laid it on. So, up we go."

On entering the room, all could see immediately that Sampson had arranged the table and chair to resemble the Court downstairs. He looked at all four.

"Right. Seaman Reece, we'll start with you."

Sampson took himself behind the table.

"Able Seaman Reece. Come forward."

Reece took three paces forward, came to the attention and saluted. Sampson looked at Argent.

"Will they allow him to stand at ease, as you call it?"

"Probably not."

"Hmmm. Well, I'm entitled to tell him to stand at ease. So, Reece, stand at ease."

Reece's shoulders dropped an inch and his feet moved to eighteen inches apart, but he remained statue straight, staring over Sampson's left shoulder.

"Hmmm. Reece, I want you to feel at ease, not just stand as such. Stand to make yourself comfortable."

Reece thought, then crossed his left hand to hold his right wrist. Sampson nodded.

"Excellent. Now, when Captain Cheveley comes to ask you questions, you don't move a muscle from that. We're hoisting him up, or lifting his anchor; whatever the nautical term is. Anything that disturbs his mind will be to our good and I'll try to do my bit in that direction, too. Now, relate the conversation you had with Captain Argent here, on the quarterdeck, after you had passed Quessant."

For the intervening hours he rehearsed the four; their stance, speech, tone and testimony, asking each a stream of awkward questions. Food came and was welcome, then, after another hour of intense coaching, came the knock on the door. Argent opened it to reveal Captain Baker.

"They're about to assemble, Sir."

Argent stood up and looked instead at Fentiman, who immediately came forward, extending his hand, but his words were formal.

"My best wishes, Sir.

Reece did the same, but his concern was more evident on his face.

"Good luck from me, Sir, if I may make so bold?"

Argent took his hand and nodded his thanks. McArdle was already stood, and, looking as if all the Angels of the Heavenly Host were at his shoulder and lending him their spiritual power, he simply shook Argent's hand, but the look in his eyes and the grip of his hand conveyed his full sentiment. Argent followed Baker out of the room and onto the landing but at the top of the stairs the whole scene below erupted into a cacophony of shouts at his appearance. The noisiest and most visible, because of their placards, could only be the Society for the Mitigation and Gradual Abolition of Slavery, at least 40 strong, waving their signs and shouting encouragement. Charlotte Willoughby was prominent amongst them, as she would be in any crowd, smiling encouragement upwards at him. Before them were at least a dozen gentlemen of the press all shouting their questions and, behind them, he saw his sisters Enid and Emily furiously waving. It was a bedlam that Argent descended into, but before he reached the crowd Reede and McArdle were before him, forcing a way through. However, he managed to reach out to touch Emily's hand extended to him from a distance. One journalist managed to get close enough to shout a question into Argent's face.

"Captain, how do you feel about being Court Martialled?"

Argent grinned and gave a quick reply before moving on at their best speed.

"As would any other Naval Officer!"

A second question was lost in the noise and jostle behind him, but Reece and McArdle had made a way to the main hall, the door guarded by Marine sentries. They opened the doors and Argent entered, to find it empty, save Makeworthy stood before the Court table. There were three other tables between the one for the Court and the audience seats, one in the centre and one on each side. Makeworthy gestured Argent towards that in the centre, before the place of the Judge Advocate, whilst Sampson went straight to the table on Argent's right and began to arrange his papers. Immediately upon taking his seat, Argent knew, from the bustle and talk that came to him, that the crowd had spilled in behind and were filling the hall.

His pulse was racing. He took three deep breaths and exhaled each slowly. He clasped his hands together and allowed his forearms to fall onto the table, then he looked up at the ancient paintings that himself and Fentiman had examined during the St. Malo enquiry. He flung away the thought that each showed some kind of disaster which presaged his own shipwreck, at which point he noticed Makeworthy stood to his left, looking angry but appearing helpless. Argent turned around to discover the cause of Makeworthy's agitation and quickly saw why. The worthy anti-slavery Society were all ranged at the back, standing, with placards erect, and Argent took the time to read some of them, but they were mostly along the line of "He who frees a slave, frees Christ" and "Freeing the work of God is the finest work of Man". He noticed Charlotte stood amongst them and she waved when she saw him turned towards her and he smiled and gave a small wave in reply. Fentiman occupied himself by twisting front and back in his chair, studying both Charlotte and Argent.

Cheveley arrived at the table on Argent's left and so, following Sampson's strategy of "winding up" their opponent, Argent applied his most insolent grin.

"Afternoon, Cheveley."

Cheveley turned his face just enough to display a mouth twisted somewhere between a sneer and that caused by a bad smell. Argent chuckled and turned away, then Makeworthy drew himself up to his full height and shout above the general hubbub.

"All rise!"

All rose and silence descended. Argent looked to the door that was the entrance for the occasion's notaries and they came forth, three he knew from the previous enquiry; Holdsworth, Grant and Broke, but he could not stop himself from an examination, necessarily brief, of the remaining three. The youngest he took to be Blackwood and he judged him favourably, full faced, fair-haired and with a pleasant demeanour. The figure more fearsome even than Holdsworth he took to be the Adjutant General, dressed in immaculate and sober civilian clothes, the only colour being provided by his sash of office. He walked on with effortless pomp and dignity, which was far more than could be said for the final figure who could only be Cinch. Argent had no way of precisely dating the last time Cinch wore his Captain's uniform, but it must have been a long time before he had settled into very easy living. It was now far too small and many buttons were in grave danger of giving way, and plainly constricting his breathing, now under strain from even the short walk, and only achieved in shallow pants, causing his face to appear unhealthily scarlet. Under any other circumstances Argent would have laughed, but the sight of Holdsworth again and the monumental presence of the Adjutant General, Charles Manners-Sutton, choked any humour at birth. The six claimed their places in the order they had entered and five sat, giving all there gathered a signal that they should sit also, but many stopped in mid descent. Manners-Sutton had remained standing and stood with a gaze plainly fixed on the back of the hall where were ranged the placards and standing members of the Society for the Mitigation and Gradual Abolition of Slavery. The Adjutant General was plainly more that a little concerned at this threat to the due dignity of the proceedings about to take place.

"I have to warn the audience that, whilst Court Martials are open to the public, it is within my power to clear the Court if I feel that good order is in any way prejudiced by unseemly and disturbing behaviour. I expect that the proceedings about to take place will be heard in the silence necessary for a due and balanced judgement."

His reply was silence, bar one or two placards being hoisted up and down. Seemingly satisfied he took his place, as did all others who had halted the lowering of themselves onto their own seats. Once sat, Manners-Sutton clasped his hands, lay his arms on the desk and lifted his heavy head, finally lifting his heavier eyebrows.

"My name is Charles Manners-Sutton. I am the Adjutant General of the Royal Navy. My role in this Court Martial is to ensure that all is conducted in the proper manner and that all proceedings adhere to the requirements as laid down in His Majesty's Regulations as they apply to Court Martials."

He paused to enable his next words to gather weight from the sepulchral silence.

"I do not sit in judgment. My fellow members of the Bench will undertake that role. So, if I may name them from my right; Vice Admiral Broke, Vice Admiral Grant, and Rear Admiral Holdsworth, who is the President of the Court."

He dropped his right hand and raised his left.

"Captain Blackwood and Captain Cinch."

At that point, the worst, at the sound if his name, one of Cinch's buttons finally gave way and he rapidly covered the resultant gap with his arm.

"I will now hand over to the President of the Court."

He looked at Holdsworth who took his cue and looked at Argent.

"Captain Argent."

Argent felt the need to stand and did so. Holdsworth adjusted his pince-nez and carefully read from the charge sheet.

"The charge against you is that on or about the 10th October 1809 you did wilfully disobey your orders. Namely, that, having been ordered to proceed with all possible haste to the port of Figuiera da Foz to deliver a dispatch from His Majesty's Government, you did, alternatively, use your vessel to pursue an action of your own ambition and choosing, namely to seek and take a slaver pirate. To this end you diverted from your best course and took time to take the slaver pirate when you did find him, thus risking your own ship, the communication itself and inevitably causing further delay."

Holdsworth looked over the frames of the aids to his near eyesight.

"How do you plead, Captain?"

"Not guilty, Sir."

"Please surrender your sword."

Argent had suspected the possibility, but he had been uncertain. Now he was relieved that he had chosen to wear it, but the formal words, so significant for any Officers, hit heavily upon him. He unclipped the two slings, walked around the desk and handed it, with both hands, to Holdsworth. He took it and laid the battered and workaday object lengthways along the desk before him. Argent returned to sitting, but the silence was broken by a female sob, which he hoped was not one of his sisters but strongly suspected that it was. Holdsworth gave the sword but the briefest glance before nodding towards Makeworthy.

"You will now be sworn in."

The Commodore approached with a Bible in his hand and Argent stood again and was duly sworn to "tell the truth and nothing but the truth, so help him God!" Holdsworth resumed.

"Captain."

Argent stood, pulse again racing, but he deliberately relaxed his face to deadpan.

"You deny the charge and so, presumably, you have your own story to justify the actions you took."

"Yes Sir,"

"Now is your opportunity to make this known to the Court. At this stage please confine your statement to the question of your chosen course. We will deal with your closing with the slaver later in the proceedings."

Argent took a deep breath and relayed the story. He had read his Logbook so many times that he could quote from it practically word for word, which was just as well, for Holdsworth was following, matching Argent's words against those in the Log, looking for any discrepancy. He stopped after describing the change of wind direction off La Rochelle, saying that it had been a perfect wind for Cape Finisterre. Holdsworth looked at Sampson.

"Mr. Sampson. Do you have any questions?"

"Yes Sir. If I may."

Holdsworth sounded impatient.

"Yes Sir, you may! Now is your time."

Sampson smiled, not at all discomfited.

"Captain. Can we get this clear? A course to cross the Bay of Biscay by the shortest would have been which bearing?"

"South Sou'West".

"But you chose South South East."

"Yes."

"Why?"

"I have, had, very experienced sailors aboard my ship. The information that they offered, gave me great concern that there would be a heavy storm in the centre of The Bay. Steering South Sou'West of Quessant would have placed my ship right in the middle. What I was told by them was based upon their experience, that of each being far longer than my own. I thought it prudent to act upon it."

"So, if I understand you correctly, you took decisions to best safeguard not only your ship, but also the message, the vital communication, that you carried. In steering South South East you lessened the risk of both being lost. Am I correct in saying that?"

"Yes. You are."

"And when the wind became favourable off La Rochelle, what did you do?"

"I set a direct course for Finisterre and clapped on all the sail we could."

"Thank you Captain. I have no further questions."

Holdsworth looked at Cheveley, but he was already on his feet. He came to stand almost before Argent, topping him by some inches. His uniform was in the highest order, buttons, epaulettes and buckles all gleaming and the odd thought crossed Argent's mind that he must have employed half his crew to get it to such a state, but Cheveley soon brought his thoughts back.

"Captain, when you cleared Quessant, what was the wind direction?"

"West to North West."

"A perfect wind for a fast crossing of the Bay. You would agree? A good wind over your starboard quarter, most frigate's best point of sailing."

Argent suddenly felt secure. He had an answer.

"Yes, if that were the only consideration, then, yes, it was a perfect wind to sail directly across The Bay, but any Navy Captain, worthy of his ticket and his title, would know that there are other elements to the decision. The French call The Bay, "The Bay of Storms", for good reason. I had clear information that a storm was imminent out in, "The Bay". I ask you, knowing such, why should I take such a risk? Counting myself a prudent Captain, taking all into consideration, I chose the least risk course. My Ariadne is fast. She could make up the time and she did, and we missed the storm and avoided being wrecked! I mean, after all, how often do we sail a direct course to anywhere? We sail to pick up the Trade Winds and any Captain would sail around a storm, if he thought one were there."

At the back of Cheveley's eyes, he saw the last point strike home, but Cheveley pressed on.

"And there was nothing else on your mind when choosing that course, merely sea-going prudence."

Argent's mind wrestled with the complex truth, but he held to the rehearsed answer agreed with Sampson.

"When the decision was upon me, yes. At that time I chose the least risk course."

"At that time, Captain. At that time, there was nothing else on your mind, bar a safe course to Figuiera da Foz?"

"Yes."

"Then justify your pause to take a look into Quessant Bay."

"The slaver may have been there."

"The slaver may have been there!"

Cheveley voice rose to a shout.

"The slaver may have been there!"

Cheveley let the words echo around the hall.

"But Captain, mere seconds ago you said that a safe course was your only concern."

Argent made himself pause and clamped his jaw shut to think, and he took the few seconds.

"Having found Quessant Bay empty, I set about choosing my course. One came distinctly after the other."

"Was looking into Quessant Bay part of your orders?"

"No."

"Then time was lost in doing so".

"Yes. About one bell."

"So there were other things on your mind when you cleared Quessant?"

"No, its bay was empty. I concerned myself with it no further."

"But you did take the time to look into the bay! Why go there, Captain, in the first place?"

To Argent's relief, Holdsworth intervened.

"Captain Cheveley, I do believe that you are straying onto the second question at issue here, that Captain Argent wasted further time trying to close with the slaver. I wish to hear more regarding his choice of course. I am going to call another witness."

Cheveley bowed and returned to his seat and Holdsworth spoke almost soundlessly to Makeworthy, who then stood.

"Able Seaman Eli Reece."

Reece stood from the front row, smoothed down his duck trousers, tucked his tarred hat under his left arm and marched forward to come to the attention and salute. Makeworthy came forward, thrust The Bible at him whilst regarding him with great suspicion and Reece was sworn in. Holdsworth began the questioning.

"What is your Service Record, Reece?"

Reece took a deep breath and, carefully, with each word thoroughly spoken, he repeated the story as rehearsed with Sampson.

"I joined the Merchant Navy as a ship's boy in 1765. I was in the slave trade for 15 years, workin' The Triangle, before I was pressed into the Antigone whilst comin' back up Channel. Then I was in the Euryalus, then the Glatton, then w'er' I am now, Sir, in the Ariadne."

"Would you say that you were experienced regarding the Bay of Biscay?"

"Yes Sir, I'd say. Crossed it more times than I can remember. Sir."

"And this 'herringbone sky" is a cloud pattern?"

"It is, Sir. Yes."

"And it means a storm in the Bay?"

"Sir."

"And that is your experience?"

"Sir."

"You have sailed across The Bay, under such a cloud pattern, and there been hit by a storm?"

"No, Sir. I never was under a Captain as did. When he saw that sky, he went Sou' Sou' East, or due West, dependin' on the wind. Sir. Never full across."

"And you made that known to Captain Argent?"

"I did Sir. Yes. Me an' my mate Ben Raisey."

A few sniggers were heard, but Holdsworth was now looking at Sampson, who made reply to the silent question conveyed by the enquiring look.

"Thank you, yes."

Sampson stood and approached Reece.

"Stand at ease, please, Reece."

Reece adopted the agreed pose and adjusted his hat under his arm.

"Did Captain Argent seek this knowledge from you?"

"No Sir. He 'eard me an Ben talkin' about it."

"In worried tones? You were talking in worried tones?"

"Yes, Sir. We was much fearful."

"What did Captain Argent do then?"

"He asked us for full details, Sir, then he talked to Sailin' Master McArdle about it."

"So, how did it seem to you, regarding Captain Argent's prior knowledge of this "herring-bone sky"?"

"He knew nothin' about it, Sir."

"And he then made doubly sure by consulting the Sailing Master?"

"Yes Sir. That's what he did?"

"You both saw and heard that?"

"Yes, Sir. We was workin' by the starboard mizzen shrouds. We stayed to finish the job."

"Thank you, Reece. No further questions."

Holdsworth looked at Cheveley, who stood and approached Reece, but stopped to maintain a distinct, distasteful, distance.

"At the attention, Reece!"

Eli Reece placed his hat on his head and came to the attention. Cheveley immediately took umbrage.

"You will remove your hat, Reece, in the presence of a superior Officer."

Reece did so and placed his hat once again under his left arm, but Sampson and Argent noted with satisfaction the look of impatience that came over Holdsworth's face, but Cheveley was continuing, himself annoyed and treating Reece as a criminal defaulter.

"Reece!"

Reece straightened slightly.

"Does your Captain make a habit of seeking advice from his crew regarding the actions of his ship?"

Reece's brows kitted together.

"I wouldn't know Sir. We don't talk together that often!"

More sniggers and Cheveley's face darkened.

"But he did ask for and take your advice. Have you ever served under such a Captain before?"

"No, Sir. But Ariadne's a fine, taught ship, Sir. An' a fightin' ship, Sir."

Sounds of approval came forward, but Holdsworth's impatience had remained thin.

"Captain. I fail to see where this is going. I am of the opinion that we would do better to now hear from the Sailing Master."

Cheveley turned towards his seat without looking at either Reece or Holdsworth.

"No further questions."

Holdsworth looked at Reece.

"Stand down, Reece."

Reece replaced his hat and saluted, which Holdsworth, surprisingly, returned, then he looked at Makeworthy and spoke quietly, for the latter to then speak up.

"Sailing Master McArdle."

McArdle rose and walked slowly forward to be met by The Bible held by Makeworthy, who suddenly himself, looked in no small way reduced, now faced by the baleful gaze of McArdle delivered down from his full height and imparting his deep antipathy at being administered an Oath by no "man o' the cloth." Nevertheless, as before and in the same place, he held The Bible high and repeated the words as though exhorting the whole congregation within earshot to repent and fall onto their knees before a justly vengeful Lord. The memory of his first encounter with McArdle was still lodged with Holdsworth as they exchanged challenging looks.

"Sailing Master McArdle. Did you hear the conversation between your Captain and Seaman Reece."

"I did."

"What happened then?"

"There is little to tell, Sir. Captain Argent asked me if I had heard such and I replied that I had. It was within ma experience. Captain Argent then took his decision, Sir."

Holdsworth looked across.

"Mr. Sampson?"

"Thank you. I have only one question."

He leaned upon his knuckles on the table.

"Mr. McArdle. Would you agree that your Captain sought confirmation from you regarding this item of, er, "naval lore"?"

"I would, aye. He gained two opinions from, if I may judge myself as such, two experienced sailors."

"He did not seek from you an excuse, any excuse, to not set a direct course."

"No, Sir. In so many words, he asked my opinion of the weather we may well encounter."

Sampson sat down as Cheveley rose.

"Sailing Master."

McArdle swung his disapproving gaze towards to Cheveley and, if anything, it intensified.

"What do you think would have happened had you said that you had no knowledge of this cloud pattern presaging a storm?"

McArdle looked at him as though he were an idiot, his air of impatience not being lost on Cheveley, nor Holdsworth, the whole being confirmed by McArdle's tone of voice.

"How can I be expected to divine that, Sir? Ye'll have tae ask the Captain himself. Ye've been told what happened, the exact story. Nae man can do any more!"

Holdsworth joined in as Cheveley plainly angered.

"Answer the question, McArdle."

McArdle took a deep breath and answered angrily himself.

"I think any man who ignored such a thing would be a fool, even if it came from only one source. We had a good wind for South South East, and that's as guid a way to cross The Bay as any I've heard. I can only surmise that, had I expressed my ignorance, our Captain would still have used what he was told and would nae take the chance on the storm. If he did make sae foolish a choice and try tae sail direct, it would be the first time I've seen him act as such a fool! What he did choose was nothing unusual for any ship I've served in, I've never made Finisterre yet, without a tack of some kind."

The forceful words emphasized the silence that followed, but Cheveley had given up the choice of course as a lost cause. It was no longer a stick to beat Argent with, he was now eager to pursue the next part of the charge.

"No further questions."

McArdle was dismissed and Holdsworth looked at Sampson.

"Mr. Sampson. Do you have any more witnesses that could help us with the first issue of the course chosen?"

"Yes, Sir, I do. Captain Cheveley."

Cheveley looked angrily across the Court, but to be met with a blank look from Sampson. Broke spoke immediately.

"This is highly irregular, Adjutant General. Is this allowable?"

Manners-Sutton reached across to a paper that lay before Holdsworth. He picked it up and passed it, unread, to Broke, but accompanied by a cold stare.

"The name's there, on the list of witnesses the Defence wishes to call. Captain Cheveley has received a copy. That makes it allowable."

He looked at Holdsworth and nodded. Makeworthy gave the order.

"Captain Cheveley, please come forward to be sworn in."

Face reddening from a complexion already liverish, Cheveley stood and Makeworthy, with no apparent emotion nor sympathy, spoke the oath, which Cheveley repeated, albeit through clenched teeth. Sampson waited patiently and then spoke as he approached.

"Captain Cheveley. You were dispatched to seek out the slaver, were you not, and you sailed on the seventh, one day before Captain Argent?"

"Yes to both."

"And you attempted a passage directly across The Bay, did you not?"

"Yes."

"And what happened?"

Cheveley took a deep breath and fidgeted, before shooting out his lace cuffs. He answered in a voice as low as he felt acceptable.

"We were severely damaged."

Sampson stepped back and spoke so loud as to be almost shouting.

"You were severely damaged!"

He paused.

"What by?"

"A bad storm."

Sampson stood before him, nodding.

"So, in the event, Captain Argent's choice was a wise one?"

Cheveley nodded, but Holdsworth intervened.

"A spoken answer, please, Captain."

Cheveley clenched his jaw and spoke.

"Yes."

Sampson continued.

"And did you get to Cape Finisterre?"

"No."

Sampson jumped in immediately, so that his first word came as a following rhyme.

"So! Had you been given the despatch, it would never have arrived?"

Cheveley fidgeted some more.

"We'd have got there, somehow."

"Yes, but with great delay surely?"

He paused, no answer came, but he passed on.

"Now, please inform the Court of your Log entry for the day you sustained your damage. What does it say? The gist will suffice, Captain, verbatim is not required."

Cheveley looked blank, so Sampson immediately responded.

"Remember, please, Captain, that I could call your Logbook as evidence. To save us all the great inconvenience of lost time, please respond."

Cheveley cleared his throat.

"Course North East. Damage makes it impossible to tack into a headwind now West South West. Can only run before the wind and return to port."

"So, had Captain Argent followed your course of action, a similar disaster would very likely have befallen him. Yes?"

"It's possible."

"One day behind you, Captain, very probable."

Cheveley made no reply, but Sampson was bent on mischief.

"Captain, you are aware of Ariadne's record with Captain Argent in command?"

"I am."

"How does the record of your own Herodotus compare?"

Sniggers came forward from the audience, but Holdsworth jumped in.

"Mr. Sampson. That is wholly irrelevant to the question we are examining! Either make your questions relevant, or sit down."

"No further questions."

As Sampson and Cheveley returned to their seats, Cheveley working his jaw beneath a very red face, Holdsworth consulted his watch and then showed it to Manners-Sutton. They spoke softly, and then Holdsworth addressed the assembly.

"The Court wishes to withdraw now to consider the evidence so far and decide on the form in which it will proceed during its next session. This Court is adjourned until 10.00 am tomorrow."

All rose as the bench rose and remained respectfully in place as the Court filed out; Cinch in the lead and carefully holding his left forearm over the gap of the missing button. Sampson sorted his papers, then he walked the short way to Argent.

"A good start Captain. I think we've sunk the choice of course issue, but tomorrow's the one."

He grinned at Argent.

"But. A good start!"

"Do we need to meet this evening? To discuss anything?"

"No. I think not. Your seaman Reece and Master McArdle performed very well. I see no reason to over rehearse your First Lieutenant beyond today."

He looked up, still smiling, evidently very pleased.

"I'll see you tomorrow."

As Sampson packed his papers in the satchel and turned away, Enid and Emily arrived at Argent's side, both their faces, Emily's especially, fluctuating rapidly between anxiety and anger, each emotion flashing rapidly between their eyes and mouths. It was Emily who spoke, more than a little angry. Enid nodded vigorously at each appropriate moment.

"Reuben. You sent no word about this. We only found out when Lady Grant sent up a newssheet. Why didn't you tell us?"

"Navy business, Emily. Navy business, nothing to concern you overly. You've had enough worries, I didn't want to add any more."

She pulled at his lapel.

"Nothing to concern us! A Court Martial! Of you!"

Argent held up his hand.

"Be at peace. This will all work out. Now, where are you both staying, or do you intend to go back to Falmouth?"

The question of practicalities seemed to calm her, and confuse her not a little. Enid stood by, listening.

"We thought it would all be done in one day. We don't know."

She chewed her lower lip and looked anxiously at her sister, but Argent placed a hand on the shoulder of each and tried to look reassuring.

"Lady Grant has a property here. I'm sure, if we took you there, they would give you both a bed for the night. If not, we're staying at an Inn. If they have no room, you can have mine and I'll bunk with Fentiman."

At the sound of his name, Fentiman came forward. Argent made the introductions.

"Henry Fentiman, may I present my sisters, Enid Trethewey and Emily Argent?"

Fentiman came to the attention, smiled and bowed, whilst Enid and Emily curtsied. "A great pleasure, Mrs. Trethewey, Miss Argent. I trust I find you both well?"

It was Enid who answered.

"Quite well, Lieutenant Fentiman. I thank you."

Argent intervened, but he noted that Emily, who had said nothing, was staring intently at Fentiman. However, he needed to hurry on and spoke to his First Lieutenant.

"We must find a place for Enid and Emily, or, more accurately, I must. For us four, I anticipated this and I have booked rooms at The Benbow, for us all. At my expense. Please take Reece and McArdle there and await my return. I hope not to be long."

Reece and McArdle, both stood at a respectful distance, came to the attention and saluted as Argent passed, then both removed their hats at the passing of their Captain's sisters. Outside, Captain Baker was overseeing all, including the slow dispersal of the "Anti Slavers". He quickly signaled up a small carriage and Argent, Enid and Emily set off along The Hoe. It was still light outside, but raining, the heavy early winter droplets drumming on the roof. Enid's mood matched the weather.

"What will happen if they find you guilty?"

He looked at her in the half-light.

"You are not to worry. The worse that can happen is that I'll be reduced in rank. Not considered fit for command; something like that."

He tried to sound cheerful and speak with humour.

"I'll not be shot, nor anything like. It's a technical point that may go against me. I'll be alright, I promise."

She gave a half smile and took his hand. She looked at him for some seconds.

"We're all very proud of you!"

Emily joined in.

"Yes!"

He chuckled softly.

"Well, if it helps, I'm quite content with myself."

Enid squeezed his hand and they sat in silence until they reached the modest, but somehow imposing frontage of the Willoughby town house in Plymouth. The rain beat upon them as they alighted the carriage and Argent sheltered his sisters as best he could under his boatcloak as they hurried to the front door. Argent immediately applied the doorknocker to its stud and the door opened almost as quickly. Just behind the servant was Grant himself and it was he that spoke before the servant could.

"In! Come in. Out of the rain!"

The door closed behind them and both stood in the hallway, wider than expected and all within it and around very elegantly furnished, nothing lavish nor ostentatious, but all in the best of taste. Argent began immediately

"Sir, I don't know if you've met my sisters Enid and Emily, but..."

Grant interrupted.

"I have and it is a great pleasure to meet you again, Mrs. Trethewey, I hope that you and your family are quite well, especially that bonny son of yours."

He took her hand and bowed over it, as Enid curtsied and made her reply. Grant then turned to Emily.

"Miss Argent, my same to you."

Emily replied her thanks, then Argent continued.

"Sir. I was hoping to impose upon you to gain a room for my sisters this night. They came for the Court Martial, but were under the impression that it would be over in one day. If that is not possible, then I'm sure that..."

Grant held up his hand.

"No more, Argent. No more! Enid and Emily are most thoroughly welcome under my roof and it is our honour to be of their service."

He turned to the Housekeeper, hovering in the background.

"Mrs. Ringwood. Please conduct Captain Argent's sisters to the sitting room. Tell cook to prepare extra and Johnson to set two extra places. Then prepare rooms."

As Mrs. Ringwood hurried off, Grant motioned for Enid and Emily to follow her. Argent bade his farewells.

"I'll see you both tomorrow, when it's all over."

Enid smiled and Emily gave a little wave, then both were gone, into the gloom of the passage. Argent turned to Grant.

"Sir, I cannot thank you enough for this service. I, we, my family will be eternally grateful."

Grant laughed and threw back his head.

"Eternity's a long time, Captain, but dismiss the thought. Lady Grant would have keelhauled me had I done anything different."

Now it was Argent's turn to laugh, then silence fell between them. Grant broke it.

"You know I cannot discuss the case with you."

"I know, Sir."

"I cannot even wish you luck."

"No, but I can."

The unmistakable voice of Charlotte came down the hallway and she quickly followed it.

"I wish him every good fortune."

Even fresh from a day in a Courtroom holding a placard, then a wet journey home, Charlotte Willoughby looked absolutely radiant as she smiled up at him. Argent could only bow and mumble his thanks.

"My thanks, but I'm afraid I must quickly take my leave of you. I left my men back at The Benbow and I think it right that I re-join them soonest. So..."

He replaced his hat and adjusted his boatcloak.

"...I must bid you good night and thank you once more for your kind hospitality to my family."

Whilst Charlotte stood smiling, it was Grant who opened and held the door.

"It's nothing. Let's hear no more. I'll see you out."

Argent was surprised that Grant followed him out, holding the door slightly ajar, but remaining within the cover of the overhanging ornate porch roof. Argent turned and waited.

"Argent. Now we're out of the hearing of the servants. Broke, Cheveley, and Cinch are planning something. I don't know what, but in the morning of today's session I saw the three gathered in cabal, and, when they saw me, they shut up and moved off. Be on your guard, something's coming and it could be a sinker. Double your lookouts, even after what's been a good day for your side."

Argent thanked him, they shook hands, then the door closed heavily behind him and Argent ran to the coach. The driver soon turned the coach and the horses needed no urging to return to their stable. Argent was dropped off at the Inn and he soon found his room and those of the others. For their evening meal, he insisted that Reece and McArdle join himself and Fentiman, but he did not consult his First Lieutenant over the niceties of such as Reece joining themselves, them being Officers, at table. Argent was too tired and could not bring himself to banish McArdle and Reece to their own table, as they also had distinct distances of both society and rank between them. He motioned all to a table of four and sat himself the last. The atmosphere between them was cool and awkward, but all took a drink, even McArdle, of good ale and, as the plain but wholesome food was consumed, the bond of shipmates asserted itself. Soon, through the conversation, the sea going lives of both Reece and McArdle began to come out and the evening was spent with both sea-going veterans regaling the fascinated Argent and Fentiman of voyages and sea fights, storms and shipwreck. The four broke up in an easier atmosphere than when they had first sat and together they left the bar to disperse to their rooms.

Argent gratefully took off his heavy dress coat and sat on the bed, chin in his hand, thinking. The day had gone well. Sampson was certainly worth his fee and the memory of his rough handling of Cheveley brought an open smile to his face, which did not disappear as he thought of how Reece and McArdle had both conducted themselves, but soon he came to dwell on Grant's warning. "Planning something!" Tomorrow the Court would hear his decision not to sail on past the slaver. That was his Achilles Heel, but what more could be made of that? The prosecution could not go beyond the journey being merely delayed, and then decry the fact of rescuing Christian women and children. That was the salient fact! He sat pondering further, but then he heard voices in the corridor outside and, as they passed his door, he heard distinctly "He's a fool if he doesn't." The voice was definitely Broke's. He opened his door and looked down the corridor to the end that led downstairs. Just reaching the end were the unmistakable figures of Broke, Cinch and Cheveley. When they disappeared he stepped out of his own door and thought, the only room beyond his to the opposite end was Fentiman's, they must have been calling on him! He went to Fentiman's door and knocked. No answer. He tried the door. It was locked.

* * *

The Court was filling up with but minutes to go until the due time of 10.00am. The "Anti-Slavers" were in their place and there were additional placards this time, these carried by a not insignificant delegation from Ruanporth, mostly crude and simple, mostly saying that Argent was innocent, he had done his duty, and such. Sampson was at his desk, looking as though he were about to have a highly enjoyable morning; Reece and McArdle were there, but there was an empty place where Fentiman had sat the previous day. He had not appeared at breakfast, either. Sat in his place, Argent faced the front, hands folded before his mouth, elbows on the table, thinking and analysing. What was the significance of Fentiman's absence? He would almost certainly be called today; Argent was surprised that he had not been called yesterday. Was Fentiman involved with Broke et al in some way? A deal? Or a threat? Was waiting to call him today part of their scheme? Fentiman scheming against him! He found it almost impossible to hold the thought in his head. He looked around and this time saw Fentiman taking his seat, so he turned fully and caught his attention.

"Henry. Are you alright? We missed you at breakfast."
Fentiman looked thoroughly ill at ease, but he did answer.
"No, Sir. I went for a walk, early."
Argent's reply was killed in his throat.
"All rise."

Makeworthy had appeared before the bench table and the Court was now filing in. Argent saw that his sword had appeared on the table that had been bare before, presumably brought in by Makeworthy. The six were in the same order as the previous day and, as they reached their table, Argent couldn't fail to notice that Cinch's uniform had a bright new button, but others, both above and below, were under mortal strain. Stood in their places, both Manners-Sutton and Holdsworth looked stonily at the assembly before them, then they sat, but the gravelike silence remained. Manners-Sutton looked at Holdsworth, nodded, and the latter began.

"This session is to examine Captain Argent's decision to abandon his mission to deliver the official despatch with all possible haste. Namely, to instead, stop and engage the pirate slaver."

Holdsworth, looked directly at Argent.

"Captain, would you care to make a beginning for us by giving us your statement? Please remember that you are still on oath."

The word "abandon" had hit Argent like a hammerblow. The Court, it seemed, was trying him on what was tantamount to rank disobedience of orders and nothing could be much more serious. If it were in the face of the enemy he would be shot! His pulse rate increased as he stood, but he cleared his throat and began, his voice not as steady as he would have wished.

"On the 14th October the wind backed to South East and so I lay a course for Finisterre. The following day we sighted the slaver and I decided to engage him. However, I broke off the attack when they threw a child overboard."

Argent had to pause as the gasps came from the assembly behind.

"It was clear, that if we pressed home our attack, they would kill all the prisoners. So, we tracked her through that night, got over the horizon before dawn, darkened the ship next day, and attacked her the following night, surprising her. We took her and freed all the prisoners, unharmed."

Cheering broke out from the Ruanporths and the anti-Salveries. Argent lowered his head to hide his smile, but Manners-Sutton was on his feet.

"Silence! Silence there. Any repeat of this outrage and I will clear the Court."

He retained his feet as silence did, quickly fall. Whilst lowering himself onto his seat, Sutton-Manners looked at Holdsworth, who then looked at Sampson.

"Mr. Sampson."

He had realised that Argent's statement had been cut off by the cheering and he spoke to Argent.

"Have you anything further to add, Captain?"

"Yes. We reached Figuiera da Foz on 18th October and that evening I placed the letter into the hands of General Hill, Lord Wellington's

Second in Command and he gave me a receipt. We had been ten days out."

"Ten days! That's a good passage as I understand it."

"That's my understanding also."

Sampson returned to his table.

"I have here a letter from General Hill, and, may it please the Court, I would wish this to be added to the evidence. May I please read certain extracts?"

Holdsworth nodded and Sampson cleared his throat.

"This is from General Hill, and he says, "I wish to make it perfectly clear that the delay in Ariadne's passage to capture the slave galley and release the prisoners made not the smallest difference to the plans of His Majesty's Forces in Portugal. In fact there were no plans in any stage of either development nor implementation."

Sampson paused and turned the page of the letter.

"Further General Hill gives his own opinion of Captain Argent's actions. I quote, "Had Captain Argent taken the decision to not engage the slave galley and leave the captives to their most abhorrent fate, it is my opinion that such a failure would have been a dereliction of duty far greater than the slight deviation from his course which delayed the delivery of the despatch in his charge, albeit contrary to his strict orders."

Sampson laid the paper on the desk before Holdsworth, who immediately slid it over to Blackwood on his left. Sampson moved to stand close to Argent, but to one side.

"Now, Captain. We reach the question. Exactly why did you halt the passage of your ship to instead engage the slave galley?"

Argent decided that this momentous question was best answered standing. He rose, leant on the table and then stood at his full height.

"Slavery is against the law in this country. If you count yourself as English or even merely stood on English soil, whatever your nationality, you are free! Under my lee I had a galley filled, for all I knew, with English women and children being taken into slavery. I have never had any cause to doubt that the overarching role of the Royal Navy is the protection of His Majesty's subjects from harm or capture by foreign powers, small or large. I was the Captain on the spot, the decision rested with myself. I elected to uphold the law of our country and act for the protection of her citizens. In that way I justified to myself the deviation from my orders."

A cheer began from the Anti-Slavery Society, but it died in their throats at the sudden raising of Manners-Sutton's head and then the viciously fierce look directed to the back of the hall. Sampson continued.

"So, if we may make this clear. You looked upon yourself as the Officer at the scene and, unable to communicate with superiors, you therefore took it upon yourself and, even though aware of the risk to your own career..."

He allowed the words to hang.

"...you decided it right to rescue the innocent and helpless women and children that had been taken from these shores and others. And you justified this to yourself as being within the prime function of the Royal Navy in which you serve?"

"Yes. It seemed wholly wrong to me that a fighting ship such as mine should pass by and do nothing."

"And there were French women and children also held within the galley."

Sampson had returned to his desk.

"May it please the Court, but this morning I received a letter, believe it or not, from France, more precisely, from the Prefecteur of Brittany. This was the part of France that suffered all raids from the slaver and this Official has somehow heard of this Court Martial and taken the trouble to write, to us here, sitting in judgement on Captain Argent's actions. I would like to make a full translation, but I can only make out the gist of the sentiment, for my French is not fully up to the task, but..."

A female voice came from the back.

"Mine is!"

Manners-Sutton glowered anew at the source, but was mollified on realising that no further disturbance was immediately forthcoming.

"Who spoke?"

"Me. I did. I'll translate it."

It was Charlotte, standing with her hand half held up, smiling incandescently towards the front of the Court. The Adjutant General's expression changed immediately at the sight of Charlotte and, on top, came the realisation that someone of her evident quality presented no threat to the dignity of the Court. He conversed quickly with Holdsworth and the short conversation ended with the latter giving a curt nod.

"Please come forward, Madam, and provide this service for us. We are grateful. Your name, please."

"Charlotte Willoughby."

She immediately began her walk to the front. Cinch looked put out, but Henry Blackwood perked up visibly, suddenly immensely interested. Charlotte took the letter from Sampson, graced Argent with another beaming smile and then began to read. All was silent as she read, but all was not as still in the mind of Henry Fentiman. To the state of high tension generated by his forthcoming turn to give evidence was added a jealousy that he could not suppress. He slumped glumly in his chair. Meanwhile Charlotte had read the whole and she pronounced.

"It is not a long letter, but this is what it says. "It is with some concern that the Council of Brittany learns that the Captain of HMS Ariadne is to be tried for the rescue of several women and children taken from both our countries to become slaves. The Council views the rescue of these captives and their return to their families in both our countries, as an action motivated by the highest humanitarian principles and brings credit and dignity to the Royal Navy, whom we have always regarded as our most courageous and honourable opponent throughout the current hostilities. The Council urges that Captain Argent be released not only with reputation unstained, but with his standing enhanced as a gracious Officer in the forces of your King." The letter ends."

She laid the letter on Sampson's table. Blackwood was grinning openly. Holdsworth offered thanks.

"We thank you, Miss Willoughby. That was well done. Thank you once again."

With a final smile at Argent, Charlotte Willoughby returned to the back of the hall. Meanwhile Sampson had sat down and Holdsworth looked to Cheveley to take his turn. He stood, his face showed his evident anger and he began curtly and abruptly, but Argent was now feeling quite controlled himself and, after the reading of the letter, which was a surprise to him, his spirits were almost buoyant.

"Captain Argent. What is your estimation of the time it took you to capture the slaver galley.

"Two days. Plus a half."

"And at one point your were actually sailing North, away from your destination?"

"Yes."

"And so, recovering that distance also added to your delay."

"Yes."

"You knew what the communication was concerned with, it being from the Prime Minister himself."

"Yes. That the Austrians were soon to be out of the war."

"And you were told the possible consequences of that?"

"Yes, that Wellington could soon be faced with additional French armies."

Cheveley paused, crossed his arms across his chest and regarded Argent coldly.

"So, in the additional time of your delay, Captain, Lord Wellington may well have set in train an action that, with the addition of unknown French forces, could have put in deep jeopardy all the forces under his command, him being ignorant of the new developments, because you had not yet arrived!"

Cheveley leaned forward to add force to his last words, but Argent remained expressionless.

"Perhaps, Captain, yes, but I would wish to make a point of fact, that any army rarely marches more than twenty miles a day. It is very unlikely that the delay would have caused any form of disaster. A fifty mile advance, at most, over the two or three days of my delay could soon be reversed by a fast messenger. That is, if the new information I brought merited it, which, as we have been told, was not the case."

"But you did not know that?"

"No, but sat here now, it doesn't take a great deal of working out for those able to give it some informed thought."

The sarcasm brought sniggers from the audience, which angered Cheveley still further. The audience was on Argent's side, that was plain, but it was time for his main throw of the dice. He stood facing the Bench.

"I wish to return Captain, to examine your attitude to your voyage from the outset."

He suddenly turned to face Argent.

"I put it to you, Captain, that all through, from first setting sail, you fully intended to hunt for that galley. To give that priority and only then fully apply yourself to delivering the message, if you were still afloat!"

"Not true. My orders were clear."

"And the question of the slave galley never entered your head, nor was discussed with your Officers?"

Argent paused and took two long seconds before answering.

"Not so. There was the clear possibility of us encountering the pirate. We had to decide what we would do."

"We?"

"Yes. Myself and my First. Lieutenant Henry Fentiman."

Cheveley turned to Holdsworth.

"I wish to call Lieutenant Fentiman as a witness for the prosecution."

Holdsworth looked at his papers.

"He's not on your list!"

At this point Broke interrupted.

"Captain Cheveley gave the request to me, written, here it is."

He passed the paper along.

"I do beg your pardon. Giving it to you before we began, slipped my mind."

Holdsworth looked angrily at him, then turned to Manners-Sutton, but the latter nodded.

"The request has been presented to the bench. That makes it allowable."

Holdsworth looked to his front.

"Very well. Lieutenant Henry Fentiman. Please come forward."

Fentiman stood, leaving his hat on the chair. He came and stood before Holdsworth, to Argent's left as he sat at his table. He was plainly agitated and in some unrest; whether from nerves or for some other reason, Argent could not decide. Makeworthy swore him in but one phrase had to be repeated. Cheveley stood by his table and began; he looked confident.

"Lieutenant Fentiman. Your Captain, Captain Argent, has just told the Court that he discussed with you the issue of the slaver, namely, what you should do if you found him. What is your recollection of that conversation?"

Fentiman shifted his feet and eased his neck out of his collar.

"We decided that, if we came upon the slaver, we would take him."

"That was decided from the outset?"

"Yes."

"And you would look out for him as you progressed.

"Yes."

"With the same level of effort as if you were actually trying to find him?

"Yes."

Cheveley began to smile; it was evident that he considered this to be a good beginning.

"Exploring this decision to search. Is it your recollection that you agreed between you to anticipate his course back to Africa and follow?"

Fentiman swallowed hard, then seemed to compose himself.

"That was discussed."

Cheveley seemed stalled in the flow of his questioning.

"And what was said?"

Fentiman opened his mouth and took a deep breath. It was some moments before he answered.

"It was decided to look into Quessant Bay. We would be passing quite close and we thought that it may have served as a base for him and he may still be there."

Slight confusion passed quickly across Cheveley's face, but he quickly recovered.

"So you did plan a deviation?"

Again Fentiman paused, as though struggling for an answer.

"Not as such."

It seemed that frustration was building within Cheveley.

"What then?"

"Looking into Quessant Bay was a spur of the moment decision."

This was plainly an answer that Cheveley neither wanted nor even expected.

"Lieutenant, as you crossed The Channel, you established priorities, yes?"

"After a fashion."

"That is no answer, Lieutenant."

But Fentiman made no further reply. Argent looked at Broke and Cinch. Both faces showed concern and another button had surrendered on Cinch's uniform, but it had gone unnoticed. Cheveley was now up close to Fentiman, almost towering over him.

"To which did you give priority?"

A change came over Fentiman. He drew himself up to his full height, the muscles in the side of his face standing out as he closed his jaw tight. His fists opened, then closed. Then he spoke.

"Sir. Our orders were clear, to deliver the letter. We resolved that nothing must put that at risk, but, if we encountered the slaver during that passage, we would stop and take him. Sir."

Cheveley was now visibly angry. He remained forceful, but a hint of desperation had crept in.

"I put it to you, that, as you crossed The Channel you laid plans to go looking for the slaver."

Fentiman answered immediately.

"No."

"You concluded between you, that finding that galley mattered most and should come first."

"Not true."

"That you always intended to follow the coast, the most likely course for a shallow draught galley."

"No."

"And that you would falsify the Log if needs be to hide your true intent and your actions to carry that out."

The last was shouted, almost directly into Fentiman's face.

"Sir. We are Naval Officers. We do not falsify Logbooks."

Cheveley looked at Fentiman as though he were trying to reduce him to ash with the heat of his gaze. Fentiman looked directly back at him, expressionless. The exchange was held for some seconds, then Cheveley turned away.

"No further questions."

Holdsworth looked over at Sampson but he was wearing a contented half smile, sure in himself that something momentous had just happened.

"No questions, Sir."

"Have you any more witnesses?"

"No."

"Captain Cheveley?"

Cheveley was sat sprawling in his chair, clearly out of sorts.

"No."

Holdsworth sat back. He looked at his fellow members, both left and right.

"Has any member of the Court any questions for Captain Argent."

He looked again both left and right, but Captain Blackwood had sat forward.

"Through you, Mr. President."

He leant on his elbows, hands clasped before his chin.

"Captain Argent. I see you wear a bronze Nelson medal."

Argent returned the open, almost friendly, look.

"Yes."

"I do also. Mine is for Trafalgar. And yours?"

"Copenhagen. I was the Fifth on the Ganges. My first Commission."

"Right in the centre. The Ganges took a pounding."

"She did."

"Nelson had orders to withdraw and he ignored them."

Blackwood sat back to pause and look carefully at Argent.

"So what do you think of Nelson?"

Argent paused himself and thought. Silence was held for some seconds.

"If you served under Nelson, he made you believe that anything was possible. And, led by Nelson, you were the men to do it!"

Holdsworth and Grant exchanged glances and sat back in their chairs, faces serious but not disapproving, more showing that they had heard something they would both remember. However, Blackwood was not finished.

"He openly disobeyed an order to withdraw. What should have happened to him?"

"He should have been called to account."

"But he wasn't."

"No. He was made a Viscount and his Commanding Officer dismissed."

Blackwood smiled and sat back, looking at Holdsworth, enough to convey that he was finished. Holdsworth leaned forward.

"Captain Cheveley. Your closing statement, please."

Cheveley lugged himself upright and stood, but did not leave his table.

"Sirs. Captain Argent is guilty of disobeying orders. His orders were quite clear, to deliver a vital communication from the Prime Minister to the Commander of our forces in The Peninsula; to deliver it with the utmost haste. Any delay in arrival could cause those forces to be placed in great peril, of this he was well aware. That peril would have been caused by the lack of vital information concerning momentous developments elsewhere in Europe and days were then lost through Captain Argent ignoring his duty to obey orders, no matter the consequences. Instead he set his ship off on a series of actions to gain personal glory, that of the momentary acclaim for rescuing a small number of civilians, when a whole army could be at risk."

Cheveley rose to his full height, warming to his theme.

"We who serve know we have to make difficult choices, but our choice is directed by our orders, and Captain Argent had his. Instead he lost time searching into Quessant Bay. He even uses the excuse of allowing old seaman's tales gleaned from the common members of his crew, to divert him from his most direct course. He lost almost three days to engage the slaver, at one time sailing directly away from his destination. It is clear, from these actions, that Captain Argent had but one intention when he first set sail, that being to set his orders aside and go seeking public acclaim and approval for his own personal glory and satisfaction. Guilty is the only possible verdict."

To growls from the audience, Cheveley sat down. Holdsworth looked across at Sampson, who stood and placed himself sideways on, to half face the Bench and half face the audience. He seized both lapels and began.

"Captain Argent is Not Guilty. Nothing has been placed before this Court to prove that he did not use all the seamanship, experience and expertise at his disposal to guide his ship the quickest to its destination as ordered. He chose the course that he considered most prudent when threatened by a storm and, when the wind and weather became favourable, he set a direct course and set all possible sail."

He paused and drew himself up, his voice rising correspondingly.

"I put it to the Court that this was an unimpeachable series of actions in order to carry out his orders. That it duplicated what would have been done to intercept the slaver pirate is of no consequence, it was pure coincidence."

He paused and looked at the floor, before raising his head and continuing.

"The slaver was encountered. Let us not say found, let us say encountered, by pure chance. At that point, Captain Argent had under his command a ship of very proven quality, a quality that has been displayed once more, very recently. Just last week, unsupported, his ship engaged three French cruisers, sank one and damaged another."

He paused and adjusted his hands on his lapels, noting with satisfaction the nodding heads around the hall.

"Are we to say, that this good Captain, should sail right past, right past, and do nothing, nothing, to rescue those women and children who were being shipped off to who knows what kind of Hell, as slaves to North African despots and potentates?"

Growls of agreement came from the audience, which Sampson allowed to be heard before he continued.

"To answer that question, we only have to ask, what is the Royal Navy for? Captain Argent himself answered that question, the answer being to keep the citizens of our King George from injury and harm, both themselves and their freedom. And their freedom!"

He paused again.

"Captain Argent was the deciding Officer at the scene and he chose to rescue those people. Not only was that the correct humanitarian act, but, as the letter from Brittany has shown, he has increased the standing of our country and our Navy, even amongst our enemies, as being motivated and guided by the highest ideals of honour and integrity. That he is innocent of both charges is the only possible outcome."

Cheering broke out from certain quarters around the hall but Holdsworth seized his gavel and hammered it into silence. That done, Holdsworth spoke.

"This Court will now withdraw to consider its verdict."

He looked directly at Argent.

"Captain Argent. Whilst the verdict is being considered, we must consider you to be a prisoner. You must remain in your place, there, until we return."

He looked off to the side and three Marines came forward to place themselves around Argent's table, one behind him and one at each side. Argent remained sitting, whilst all others stood as the Bench filed out, with Makeworthy carrying the sword. Sampson came first to his table and Argent stood, checking first that this was allowable with the Sergeant of Marines. Sampson spoke first.

"I think optimism is justified. I feel we've won on both points. Well done."

"Well done to you, Christopher. All arguments well marshalled, I don't think we could have done more. We have good cause to be hopeful."

He smiled at Sampson.

"Now. Don't let me keep you here. They'll be at least two hours and you deserve some refreshment and some fresh air."

At that moment Enid, Emily and Charlotte arrived together. Sampson bowed and took his leave as Emily shouted from yards away.

"You're innocent! It's obvious."

Argent released a deep breath, which terminated in a laugh.

"I very much hope so, but you are not to worry. It's all technical. The worst that can happen is that I'll end up pushing a plough alongside Father."

He laughed at his own joke, but his sisters' faces remained deeply worried. Argent turned to Charlotte.

"My deepest thanks for the support you have brought with you, and your translation of the letter. Did it really say that?"

She screwed up her face.

"Well, yes, sort of. I did my best, but I may have embellished it a bit! "Added in translation" would be my excuse."

All laughed, even Enid and Emily, just!

"Well, I'm grateful. It all helped I'm sure. But..."

He sighed and shrugged his shoulders.

"...I'm afraid I'm ordered remain here."

It was Enid who answered.

"Would you like something to eat? And to drink?"

Argent nodded, vigorously.

"Yes, that would be nice. I am thirsty."

He turned to the Marine Sergeant.

"Is that allowable, Sergeant?"

The reply was growled from behind a coal black chinstrap, from a face more quarried than born of woman.

"If it isn't, Sir, I just made it so."

Argent smiled at Charlotte and his sisters, turning carefully to each, and they disappeared off behind him. He turned in his seat to see what remained of the audience in the hall, but few were there. Fentiman was not, but Reece and McArdle both were, still sitting, solid and stern, a few rows behind their Captain. Argent looked at both, simply to exchange looks, then he nodded and turned away. Enid and Charlotte soon returned, Enid with sandwiches, Charlotte with a bottle of small beer, a pint bottle. She had also obtained a china mug.

"That's good work. Thank you both. Where did it come from?"

Charlotte answered.

"That nice Marine Captain. He found what was needed and told us where to go to get what he couldn't."

Argent grinned inwardly. At the sight of Charlotte, Marine Captain Baker would have been moved to move mountains. He opened the beer.

"Where's Emily?"

Enid looked beyond him.

"At the back there, talking to Lieutenant Fentiman."

Argent nodded.

"Thank you both again, but I'm afraid that I must be left in solitude. At the moment I'm a lowly prisoner."

He turned again to the Marine Sergeant.

"Is that not right, Sergeant?"

"Yes, Sir, I'm afraid it is. Strictly, no one should be speaking to you, bar your lawyer, Sir."

Argent raised his eyebrows and gave a wry grin. He looked finally at Enid and nodded vigorously.

"It's going to be fine. You are not to worry."

Enid immediately became tearful, but she followed Charlotte away. Argent filled the china pot and offered it first to the Sergeant.

"We're alright, Sir, thank you."

Argent relaxed back into his chair, eating and drinking. He felt at ease. All that could be, had been said and done, and so he contented himself that it was all now in the lap of the Gods. He couldn't even bring himself to weigh up the likely verdict of each member of the Court. The minutes passed and then an hour. His sentries remained stock-still and from time to time Argent turned in his seat to view developments in the hall. As time passed, so the hall refilled, first with the placard carrying agitators. After almost another hour all seats were filled and the audience had spilled around to the spaces at the side. He was clearing his table of plate, mug and bottle, when suddenly the hall fell silent.

"All rise!"

Makeworthy had reappeared at the door in the corner, carrying Argent's sword. He walked to the waiting table, followed by the members of the Court. Argent noted that Cinch had lost yet another button. Makeworthy stood with his back to the audience, waiting at the place where Holdsworth would be sat, still holding the sword. The six filed through to their places and all sat, all bar Holdsworth. As the audience sat in response, many poised undecided as to whether they should, Makeworthy handed the sword to Holdsworth and then stood aside. Argent remained standing, his eyes on nothing but the sword, would it be placed on the table, pointing at him, indicating guilt, to whatever extent, or across the table indicating, no guilt? Holdsworth placed the sword on the table, along its length. Argent exhaled a long breath. At least he wasn't going to be shot! Holdsworth sat down and looked at Argent, his face stern, so much so that Argent lost his own ghost of a smile.

"Captain Argent. This Court Martial has found you not guilty."

Loud cheering and clapping broke out all around the room and Holdsworth immediately seized his gavel and pounded the block until silence eventually fell.

"This Court must remain silent!"

His fierce eyes traversed the room to quell any possible repeat. Satisfied that his own superiority had been established, he continued.

"By a majority, three to two, the Court finds you not guilty of disobeying orders, for the major reason that your most primary order was eventually carried out, the letter was delivered into the right hands at the correct place. However, it is plain that the secondary order was not, that being, "with all possible speed." That said, the Court is content that a satisfactory passage was made and the letter delivered after a time that could not be considered as so slow as to cause any disadvantage. However, regarding the taking of the slaver-pirate, that was a significant diversion and it was contrary to your strict orders. That will be placed on your record."

He paused; his expression becoming almost sympathetic.

"However, as Captain Blackwood put it, "often there is little that any Officer can do, other than to deal with what is immediately in front of him.""

He paused again.

"This Court Martial is at an end."

The room exploded with clapping and cheering, this time unconstrained. Argent stood to shake Sampson's hand. He turned around to see a whole cavalcade coming towards him, Josiah Meade, grinning like a child, Charlotte, Enid, Lady Grant, and Emily, now looking her cheerful best, side by side with Henry Fentiman, each sharing the joy of the moment with the other.

Chapter Twelve

A Life More Sedate

"Welcome hame, tae as dreich a morn as any ye'd nae wish ta see!"

Argent's open smile was wholly in opposition to the gravely, Calvinist pulpit tones of the dispiriting observation passed by his Sailing Master. However, he smiled contentedly, secure on his own quarterdeck and secure within his own mind by what he could see before him. All was well! Ariadne was allowing the tide to gently and exactly carry her into Falmouth Harbour, even though the North wind, which had made them work so hard on the last leg of her "Triangle Patrol", still remained and prevailed, fully set against providing any aid to their entry of their homeport. Argent was allowing the tide to achieve his entry, and his ship slowly drifted in, with no sails, but still slowed by the wind, the only aid to her safe arrival being the launch that was out ahead carrying a cable to attach her to a mooring buoy. So prime a task as bringing her to a safe standstill on the last of the tide was under the intense supervision of Bosun Fraser and his blandishments and deprecations to the launch crew could be heard over the still water of the dank December dawn of their homecoming. Ariadne drifted on, the mist that clung to the surface of the sea blurring the distinction between the grey water and her black waterline. Her masts, also showing black with moisture from the clinging mist, pointed up into a grey, overcast sky that frequently took it upon itself to send down thick layers of fine rain to add to the bleak picture that only Ariadne brought life to.

Argent took himself over to the starboard side. Fraser had closed with the buoy and the double cable was being passed through the mooring ring, the loose end to be quickly tossed up to Bosun's Mate Ball. Him, up on the forecastle, had seen all for himself and he checked the run of the slack back to the capstan. All was secure and, as the cable tightened to halt Ariadne's progress, ejected water sprayed both up and down all along its length; thus the ship's slow drift was halted and her bows began to turn as the dying tide worked on her free stern. Soon she came to a halt, her bows facing the harbour entrance, her figurehead fixing her sightless eyes back to follow the winter mist that rolled past, out on the carrying wind, towards the unseen Channel. Ball took command of the Starboard Watch manning the capstan and very few turns brought Ariadne close up to her mooring. Argent leaned on the rail and watched the recovery of the launch and then was not surprised that the first action of Fraser, when he came back over the side, was to check the fastenings of their moorings upon the forecastle. Fraser's turn towards the quarterdeck and his salute told Argent that all was well.

All was also well within himself. During their patrol, they had seen nothing eventful bar three Indiamen beating close hauled up The Channel, as close to the safety of the Cornish Coast as they could, but the Indiamen were fairly safe, the steady North wind was holding any French cruisers within their home ports. However, Ariadne had, nevertheless, seen it as her duty to escort them over the most dangerous miles.

Argent had been grateful to have been sent out on the patrol immediately after the Court Martial. He felt it to be of much benefit to himself, that the removal of his two deep troubles, notwithstanding the question of finding the Will, was allowed to slowly establish itself at the back of his mind, subconsciously, hidden beneath the day to day concerns of conning his ship to the Fastnet Rock, then onto the final two legs of his patrol. Gradually it came that all was healed within Argent's world, the solidity of this slow process finally completing its work after they had left the Fastnet behind. Leaving this barren marker astern had been a salient moment, as though the threat of the rock tangibly represented the threat to his family land and his own career. All aboard had been grateful, the wicked tooth being hid unseen by a moving fog coming from the land, this swirling around them, beneath a bafflingly clear sky. Their Noon Sight and the cacophony of squabbling seagulls told them that they were near enough to The Rock to count the first leg completed and Argent was happy enough to take the North wind fine over the larboard quarter and sail South, all aboard grateful to hear the diminishing sounds of the surf and the birds.

After this salient event, his unburdened mind had taken it upon itself to wander to many places and the proximity of Ireland had re-awakened memories of Sinead Malley, not that they had ever been particularly dormant. Therefore, with the Fastnet now unseen in their wake, he had begun to pen a letter, it quickly becoming an odd and rambling affair, borne from the fact that, really, he knew not what to say and was equally confused over how to say what did present itself at random to his mind. What did come, appeared behind his pen as gauche and disjointed, but the letter, nine days worth of odd anecdotes, news, questions, hopes and fears, now dwelt folded within his pocket.

Now, with his ship safe and doing no more than rocking gently in the ebbing tide, he looked idly at the quayside adjacent to the town and saw that, at least that part of Falmouth was awake, just, with commercial carts and carriages traversing the length of the wet and worn stones, all showing their age, grey and mishaped. He called for his barge and idled on the larboard side of the quarterdeck to await its being readied, his back against the rail, allowing his mind to wander at will. Where it did alight was on the memory of a French bowsprit stuck through his mizzen shrouds; this thought aroused by the new ropework above and around, including a smart new mizzen backstay. As his bargecrew descended he walked along the gangway to the entryport, wrapping his boatcloak tight around himself and his Ship's Books especially, as much to prevent the cloak catching on any projection during his descent, as to keep out the cold.

Whiting called for a slow, leisurely stroke from his crew; there were no girls as yet on the quayside and so it was a relaxed journey for them all. Once on the firm stones of the quayside, Argent regathered up the Ship's Log and Ledger and took himself directly to the Commodore's Office. There he found Sergeant Venables manning his place, but no Budgen.

"The Commodore's not in yet, Sir, but if you leave your books, I'll keep them safe and the Commodore'll take them onto his desk when he arrives, Sir, I'm sure."

Argent did as he was bid and, as the books were carefully placed, Venables reached down and produced a canvas mailbag, this with Ariadne stencilled on the outside.

"Your mail, Sir. Not too much, it being not much more'n two weeks, but there's some there. One dropped off by a Lady, too. Very striking she was; a real head turner! She even brought the Commodore up out of his office, even though his rolls and coffee had just gone down."

Argent laughed and nodded.

"Yes, Sergeant, I think you've painted a vivid enough picture and that one I'll read with interest."

Argent took the mailbag and weighed the contents on his hand.

"No, not much here, but then it depends on who's doing the writing, if you take my meaning."

He reached inside his coat and dropped the letter to Sinead onto the desk, then he reached inside his breeches pocket to extract a shilling piece.

"Could you see that this gets posted, Sergeant? I'd be grateful."

"A pleasure, Sir. Leave it with me."

Customary salutes were exchanged, then Argent left, but once out of the door he met Commodore Budgen, or rather towered over him, but Budgen was in genial enough mood.

"Welcome home, Captain. Anything of note to report?"

"No, Sir. All's quiet out in The Channel, even the weather, but I've left my Logbook with your Sergeant."

Budgen hunched himself against the cold and made for the door.

"Yes, yes, I'll take a look, but for now I'll let you get back to your ship. I bid you good-day."

Argent saluted Budgen's disappearing back, his hand being lowered to a closed door and, with that, he took himself back to the quay steps and his waiting barge. His appearance caused all to empty their pipes against the damp stonework, but, within seconds, they were in their places and waiting for Argent to step into the launch. The light rain had become heavier and Argent turned up his collar to marry with his hat and it was but a few drops that managed to enter and trickle down inside to wet his collar. During the journey back he used a length of line to make a loop through the handle of the mailbag and so, with it slung secure over his shoulder and safe from a fall into the water, he climbed through the entryport and made for his cabin. There he unceremoniously dumped the contents of the bag onto his desk. A dozen or so letters fell to the surface, but two stood out. One, a quality cover of a delicate pastel shade that Argent recognised immediately, and, the other, the plain white, but thick paper, of an Admiralty communication. He looked at both, undecided as to which to deal with first. He chose the latter. He used his paperknife to ease off the seal, but it did not part from the paper, rather it cracked open.

The first item that fell out from the cover was a highly impressive document, which, having read the top line, Argent saw was a Banker's Draft, the imposing heading taking his eye immediately to the amount, which read as "£168,462 10s 9d. Argent's jaw dropped as involuntarily as did the Draft from his stunned fingers. He held his head in his hands as he looked down at the further impressive array of copperplate printing and cultured handwriting, then he collected himself, enough to prise open the accompanying letter and saw immediately that it was from the Admiralty Prize Court. The wording was brief and to the point, stating simply that La Mouette had been condemned at a value of £168,462 10s 9d and was to be purchased into the Royal Navy. The distribution of the prizemoney was left to Argent, but that he was to follow the "1808 Regulations pertaining to the Distribution of Prizemonies". He sat back, still stunned. This was his first prizemoney and he knew little of how to proceed from there. He looked at his closed door.

"Sentry!"

The door opened in a second and one second later the Marine was stood inside, at attention with ordered arms.

"Sir?"

"Send for Mr. Maybank. Please."

"Sir."

The acknowledgement coincided with the salute and then the sentry was gone. Argent looked again at the Banker's Draft and then, with difficulty and a trembling hand, set it aside. He forced his attention towards the other letter, the seal of which broke in much more genteel fashion, but from this also there fell an inclusion, in fact two, both smaller yet heavier. He recognised them as pasteboard invitations. Argent picked one up, turned it the right way and, with it's reading, found himself almost as dumbfounded as he had been with the Banker's Draft. The pasteboard was of the highest quality and held gold embossed writing, apart from one line, which was handwritten, this in a hand that he instantly recognised as the hand of Charlotte Willoughby. He began to read from the top, as he felt obliged to.

> Invitation Sir Matthew and Lady Maude Willoughby request the presence of Lieutenant Henry Fentimanat the wedding of their daughter, Charlotte, to Major Algernon St. John Blake, at All Saint's Church, Falmouth, at 11.00am on the 14th December 1809. Matthew and Maude Willoughby R.S.V.P.

Henry Fentiman's name was handwritten in. He looked at the second card and it contained his name. His first question was whether they would be at sea, but today was 4th December. A ten day stay in port was long, but not overlong, and perhaps Grant would use his influence to prolong their stay. He was musing along those lines when came a knock on the door.

"Enter."

In came the sentry to hold the door open for Purser Merryman Maybank, who edged his way in, then stood nervously, fiddling alternately with his waistcoat buttons and his thin whispy hair, which hung, as wind or gravity dictated, over a head and face of pale complexion, containing wide, watery eyes, this the result of him spending days below decks in candlelight, attending to his ledgers. Nevertheless, his blue Purser's uniform was clean, pressed and up to the mark, as was the white linen at the vee of his waistcoat. Argent stood to greet him; Maybank's evident nervousness motivated Argent to be as welcoming as he could.

"Mr. Maybank. I trust I find you well. Please come forward and take a seat."

Maybank nodded and managed a nervous smile but he did bring himself forward and he did take a seat. Argent did no more than slide the Banker's Draft in front of Maybank. The reaction was a considerable widening of the watery eyes, these below now very elevated, pale lashes and brows.

"That's our prizemoney, Mr. Maybank. From La Mouette!"

Maybank looked up, this time wearing a definite smile that broke into a wide grin.

"Now, Mr. Maybank. This letter, from the Prize Court..."

Argent slid over the thick vellum to place it next to the Draft.

"...states that it must be distributed according to the 1808 Regulations. On this I need your help."

Maybank pulled his eyes away from the sum shown and began to speak, clearly and authoritatively. Argent was re-assured; his Purser knew his trade.

"Sir. The Regulations are quite simple, until it comes to the crew. The Admiral who signed our orders for the voyage, receives one twelfth of the prize money, you, the captain receive one sixth, the wardroom officers one eighth, the standing warrant officers receive one eighth and the remaining half is distributed among the rest of the crew, based on their ranks, but not necessarily evenly. That decision rests with you, Sir."

Argent stared back at him, but already thinking.

"I'd like the Gun Captains, and Top Captains, to have extra. Perhaps a half share extra. That can be done, I presume."

Maybank spoke lucidly and confidently, meeting Argent's gaze, now at home in his world of figures.

"Yes, Sir. Very easily. When we captured La Mouette, our complement was 213, but we had one runner. So that gives 212 men, 424 half shares. Extra half shares for three Top Captains and 38 Gun Captains adds on 41 more half shares. That gives 465 shares for the men, Sir."

Argent looked back, impressed.

"You know how to undertake this?"

"Yes Sir. I have first to take this to a bank. I would appreciate an armed escort, Sir."

"Consider it done."

Argent paused.

"Do you start now?"

"Yes, Sir, if you so choose."

"Good."

He placed the draft back in the cover and handed it over and Maybank took it with both hands and carefully placed it into an inside pocket. He then stood and saluted. It was not to quarterdeck standard, but Argent's informal grin befitted the occasion. Maybank turned and left, but Argent was already reaching for pen and paper. One sixth to himself! A quick division gave him a figure of just over £28,000! A fortune! He was a very rich man! Then he indulged in another gladdening thought, the Admiral who had signed their orders for the La Mouette patrol had not been Broke, but Leadbitter, whom Broke replaced. He must make that known to Maybank, then he did some more calculating. His men would receive half, that being £84,231. Some intricate division gave a half share at £182 15s. Each seaman would receive £365 10s. His "Captains", having an extra half share, would receive £547 5s. They were rich men!

The Warrant Officers were easy. He had ten, which gave over £2,000 each. Heavens! A huge thought. That included Mortimor! Then he could not resist further calculations for his Officers, but paused to think. Should a Midshipman receive the same as a Lieutenant? He thought not, then thought further. When taking La Mouette he had a Wardroom of ten, including McArdle, Maybank, and Surgeon Smallpiece. He thought it right that a Midshipman should receive one share, then he added on from there, up the ranks, counting Ramsey's widow alongside 2nd Lieutenant Bentley, until he came to Fentiman, who would receive four. The total of shares came to 21. More hurried calculations ensued until he sat back thoroughly satisfied. A Midshipman would receive over £1,000, but Fentiman would receive over £4,000! He was a rich man.

* * *

"Henry! I've news, much news!"

Fentiman had arrived within minutes of being bidden and he came forward, his face alternating between the emotion of possible glad tidings and deep apprehension for the possible opposite.

"I've just seen Maybank going off in the launch, with six Marines and a full crew. Is that part of your news?"

"It is, and here it is."

Argent pushed forward the letter from the Prize Court and pointed to the figure.

"That is the value they have placed on La Mouette. They're going to buy her into the Service."

Argent sat back to let the fact sink into his First Lieutenant, but, surprisingly, he saw no change. However, undeterred, he pressed on, his glee almost getting the better of him.

"I've calculated your share. Over 4,000! What do you think of that?"

A half smile crossed Fentiman's face, but then left it.

"Henry? Are you well? All's well at home?"

"Quite well, Sir, thank you."

Argent cleared his throat. Perhaps his First Lieutenant was already possessed of significant private means, unknown to himself, so he pressed on further and pushed across Fentiman's invitation to the wedding. As Fentiman read it, Argent saw a whole gamut of emotions cross his First Lieutenant's face, but it finally settled, sombre and almost at peace. Argent waited for a reaction, but none came.

"I'm going to accept. What about you?"

The answer was immediate and accompanied by a sharp nod of his head,

"Yes, me also. I'll be pleased to attend."

Argent waited for more, but nothing came, bar some turmoil behind Fentiman's eyes, but eventually he did speak.

"Sir. I've something to tell you concerning your recent Court Martial, which I…"

There came a knock on the door and Sanders entered immediately.

"Sir, sorry to barge in, Sir, but Admiral Grant is on his way to us, Sir, and like to arrive in a few minutes."

Argent and Fentiman both stood, Argent reaching for his coat.

"Thank you, Jonathan. You are right to interrupt. Get a side party organized immediately, will you?"

Sanders disappeared and, with Argent still buttoning his coat, both Officers left the cabin; Fentiman, so it seemed to Argent, trying hard to pull himself together, both inside his mind and outside, especially his buttons, both of waistcoat and jacket.

Ten minutes later, a rumour was running all over the ship and it included one of the few times when the men of the maintop were civil to those of the fore. Jack Bilsley, Captain of the Maintop, shouted it forward to Gabriel Whiting and the whole crew of the foretop descended to join the huddle about to swamp Bosun Fraser.

"Now, I don't know no more'n you. All I can say, is, that 'tis a very tidy sum, and that each of us as was there when we took her, is in for a very 'andy amount of coin."

From all around came the same question.

"How much?"

"That's what I've no way of sayin'. But, 'tis arrived, and that Frencher was a fine vessel and worth a fair amount. That's what's comin' our way, as shares, and 'twill arrive all in good time."

"When?"

"All in good time, but 'tis here, and so, all I can say is, 'twon't be long."

More questions arrived, mostly repeats, but Bosun Fraser had had enough.

"Now, back to work, the damn lot of you. I want's this barky ready for a new voyage tomorrow, if asked for. Now move! Shove off! Away!"

But three did not move. Henry Ball, Sam Morris and Gabriel Whiting remained and George Fraser gave no objection. Sam Morris spoke first.

"Well, this is what I know, that when the Caroline took the San Rafael, back in the year seven, each man got nigh on five hundred!"

But it was Gabriel Whiting who answered.

"Ah, but she were a treasure ship. That doubled her value, the same won't be comin' our way."

He looked at George Fraser.

"How's it work, George. You ever had prize money afore?"

"Yes, some, when I was on a Revenuer, an' we took a smuggler full of brandy. We didn't get much for the spirits, but the vessel was a neat package and we each got £95. That brought every doxy, diddykite, and shyster down to the harbour, each with some scheme to part us of the crew from our prizemoney; an' they succeeded with it too, but most went on drink in the pothouses, I'm sorry to say, an' the whores an' the dice. They gives it out as bags of coin, you see. 'Tis so easy to spend."

Sam Morris looked concerned.

"Yours an' all?"

"Some, but most was sent home, an' that's where it still is. I 'as hopes of buyin' a Inn or summat, somewhere. Somewhere a long way from the sea.

Gabriel Whiting smiled.

"This dose of cash, then, just might do it."

"It might, we'll see."

He paused.

"Now, we've all ship's business, but time's soon we'll all know."

With that he turned to mount the companionway and could soon be heard shouting at some waisters about "grasscombing lubber's work."

Meanwhile, Argent and Fentiman were bidding farewell to Admiral Grant. Their time together had been short, enough for report on Ariadne's state of readiness, the La Pomone engagement, a glass of madeira and for Grant to allay Argent's fears that they would be at sea for the wedding. As Grant's barge pulled away, Argent turned to his First Lieutenant.

"We have to talk!"

Down in his cabin, Argent explained his concerns

"Our Purser is in the Mining and Mercantile even as we speak and within days chests full of money will be coming aboard; they won't have enough in coin to meet the £84,000; most will have to arrive from up country. Then Maybank will begin the distribution; bags of coin will be issued to the men. Our lowliest seaman will receive £365! It doesn't take a genius to predict what comes next. If we let them ashore, we'll get heavy desertion, even after they've lost half of it to every cheat and whore in Devon and Cornwall. If we keep them on board they will gamble, then steal, then fight. Where else do they have to keep it, but in their seachests?"

Fentiman remained distant, even distracted, but he did respond.

"It is their money, and that's always how it's been done. What I do agree with, Sir, is that we cannot allow them ashore. A quarter of the crew, more, are pressed men, and those we'll not see again."

Argent looked at him.

"When Maybank returns, send him straight to me.

When Purser Maybank did return, with his heavy Marine escort, he went straight to Argent's cabin and spent sometime closeted there with his Captain. When they were finished Argent came onto his quarterdeck and summoned Bosun Fraser.

"Assemble the men."

The Bosun's whistles blew and, from all parts, the whole crew assembled at the mizzenmast, the Marines parading on the starboard gangway, but stood at ease with ordered arms. Argent walked forward to the quarterdeck rail and waited for silence, which quickly fell.

"Men, the prizemoney from La Mouette has arrived. Those of you on the lowest rate will receive £365 and some, the gun and top Captains will receive close to £550."

He watched the reaction move over their faces, as a gust of wind flows over ripe corn, but none spoke, either from shock or astonishment or the wish to hear further what their Captain had to say.

"You are entitled to receive your money in coin of the realm. But..."

He paused.

"I want to point out to you that such a sum will set you up for life, for the time when the war is over. It could buy you a home or even a small concern."

He paused again. Should he lay bare the fact that he could not take the risk of a mass desertion if they were allowed ashore? He decided no, and moved on.

"It is my strongest advice that you lodge your prizemoney with the Mining and Mercantile Bank, to wait for the end of hostilities, for there it will earn interest. Those of you that choose to hold yours in coin will keep it with you on board ship. Those of you that choose to take my advice will receive a banker's draft from Purser Maybank, made out in your name, drawn on the Mining and Mercantile and you can choose to keep that yourself, or lodge it with Purser Maybank, or have it sent home."

He paused and adjusted his feet and hands.

"I would strongly advise that you lodge your money with the bank, you single men give the note to Purser Maybank, you with families, send it home. Left with them, if you do not return, for as man o' war's men we all know that you may not, your loved ones can still claim the money. The issue will take place the day after tomorrow."

He looked at the expanse of upturned faces, but said no more.

"Dismiss."

The hubbub of discussion came at last, as the men moved away. Few showed the pleasure of the award; almost all were considering their Captain's words. It was a considerable sum, far above their expectations and its future was the subject of serious discussion. It continued in their messes at suppertime and the conversation of number three starboard was typical, the wise Sam Morris speaking in reply to Tom Bearman's wish to have his share in coin.

"And come one year, there'll not be one brass farthing left! It'll be lost, stolen, gambled, or spent in some God forsaken hole at the back of beyond. The Captain's right, what if we sinks and your chest goes down with it? If we sees the end of the war, in one piece, then we'n set up, like the Captain says, for a home and perhaps a little business. And come the end of the war, make no mistake, you'm out, an' lookin' for work, along with 50,000 others, but like as not we'll finish with somethin' missing, and you've seen the one armed, or one legged, or poor blind beggars around Plymouth and Portsmouth; sailors and soldiers. What if that's you, chucked aside to beg a livin'? With that sum tucked away, you'll still be alright. An' if you'm dead, 'tis there for your family, like the Captain said."

He allowed his words to sink in.

"I'm for stowin' it with the bank. I likes what the Captain said."

All looked thoughtful, considering the wisdom of their Gun Captain, but Bearman was adamant.

"You talks about sinkin', but Banks can go down an' all. I'm for coin. That's my right, and that's my choice."

The rest held their council and the subject closed, so they spent the rest of the meal listening to one of Ted Cable's stories about life aboard the slave galley.

The following day, at ten o'clock, four bells of the forenoon watch, two heavy chests were swung aboard, double cable to lift and four more to guide each aboard and provide extra security. Maybank set up his table, but he was not alone, for beside him sat the Manager of Falmouth Mining and Mercantile, with a whole sheaf of blank drafts. For the rest of the day, the crew filed past, some bearing away bags of coin, and some a burden not so very heavy, for many had accepted the new £1 and £2 notes. However, almost all left with only some coin and also a paper receipt to show that their draft was either lodged with Purser Maybank or with the august and trustworthy Manager. The Warrant Officers were finally dealt with, then finally, Maybank and the Manager removed themselves to the Captain's cabin to dispense the prizemoney of the Officers. All accepted a Banker's Draft, bar the Midshipmen, who took some of theirs in notes and coin. With the dying light, the chests were unshipped and, again under heavy Marine escort, they were rowed to the quayside and carefully ensconced once more inside the bank. It was a very contented crew that settled down for the night, but the dice rolled, well for some, but poorly for many.

* * *

Both were stood rigid and stock-still. Bible Mortimor circled each, like a bird of prey, eyes equally intense to spot any blemish. He had a clean rag in his hand, which he flicked at anything suspicious. Finally, he was satisfied; the two would not disgrace the ship.

"Ye are like unto whited sepulchres, which indeed appear beautiful outward. Matthew 23, verse 27."

"Thank you, Mortimor. We'll take that as the highest possible verdict of approval."

Mortimor flicked at a last piece of dust and stepped back, then he made a noise in the back of his throat to signify that he was done. Argent and Fentiman looked for themselves at their new breeches, shoes, and hose, then checked the "shoot" of their quality linen shirtsleeves from beyond their cuffs. Only their dress coats were not recently purchased but Mortimor, with his dark arts, had brought these up to the mark. With all three now satisfied, both Officers passed the Marine Sentry, him fiercely presenting arms, and they emerged out onto the gundeck, where many stopped work to see their Captain and First, and admire the sight of both decked out in full fig. Salutes and smiles were exchanged all round as they made their way to the entry port to be piped over by Fraser and his Mates, then down into the Captain's barge. All involved were in newly heightened states of finery, new duck trousers, jackets, vests and shoes! The last being very black, with a shiny pewter buckle!

Argent and Fentiman settled into the sternsheets and made careful placement of their swords, Fentiman giving the handguard of his an extra polish with his sleeve. The day was kind, the sun a possibility, and light enough, mild and not raining. Whiting stood resplendent at the tiller, "Ariadne" prominent on his hatband and, with his Officers secure, he called for a smart and brisk stroke to take them swiftly to the quayside and finally see their Officers ashore and safely up the steps and on their way. For the bargecrew, this would be, unfailingly, a good day, with many hours of freedom, because their passengers would not return until late afternoon and so their time ashore would be their own. As they had argued on many an occasion, needs must that they remain ashore, for they may be needed for a swift return. They rowed their boat up to the Marine steps, moored it under their supervision, and then disembarked themselves. Whiting walked up to the Marine Sergeant.

"We'd like to leave our Captain's barge up here, mate. Be that alright with you?"

"Good enough, but if you'm needed, where will you be?"

"The Pale Horse."

He felt his crewmates surprise behind him and, when he turned, was not surprised to see it written all over their faces. Able Jones spoke the words.

"The Pale Horse! Now isn't that one up from our deck? What's the matter with The Ship Aground?"

Then he paused and stood with his arms akimbo, realisation growing on his face.

"Or has this got something to do with a certain serving girl?"

"Never you mind about the why's and the wherefore's, Abe Jones. Only one thing I wants to know from you, is where can I buy some flowers?"

Argent and Fentiman now sat secure in their cab; both checking that neither smudge nor stain had adhered anywhere, nor was liable to, from the possibly unclean public compartment. Fentiman consulted his new watch, which agreed with Argent's much older family heirloom. The time was nigh on 10.30 and ten minutes would see them at the church gate. Both sat back, seemingly relaxed, but Argent noticed the fingers of Fentiman's left hand flexing back and forth upon the pommel of his sword.

"My family live just up from the church. It's but a short walk and I'd like you to meet them."

The response was a sudden turn of Fentiman's head, which surprised Argent a little.

"If you've no objection! I mean, if you feel no need to hurry back to the ship."

"N-no. No. I'd be honoured. It'll be a pleasure."

He paused.

"I've already met Enid and Emily, you remember. Most charming, Emily especially."

Argent laughed slightly.

"Well, I'm reassured that you did not name the married one!"

"No, no! Your sister Emily, well, I found her most companionable."

"Well. I wouldn't argue."

However, Argent looked carefully at his first Lieutenant. He was subdued, but somehow also fixed and stern, as though they were about to enter a battle, but he felt able to close the subject.

"Good."

He paused.

"I'm sure there'll be some sort of occasion across the road, at Lady Grant's, then we'll stroll up. It's not far."

Fentiman nodded and gazed out of the window. Argent took the conversation as ended and gazed out of the window of his own side. The watery sun was breaking through.

The cab rattled on, out of the town, but the closer it came to the church, the slower its progress became. The lane to the Willoughby Estate and to his home beyond, became progressively chocked with carriages, well-wishers, and onlookers eager to view a society wedding. After a stop of some minutes, Argent had had enough.

"Come. We'll walk."

They alighted, paid the cabman and began to walk. The lane was thronged, but Argent was grateful that they did not have far to go, the church tower could clearly be seen merely half a cable ahead. However, many from the Willoughby lands and estate were in the lane, many from Ruanporth, several that Argent recognised as rescuees and several that recognised him. These proved to be more of a delay to their correct time of arrival than the traffic, all wanting to greet him, shake his hand, ask after him and show him their children, now growing up well. The Officers progressed on through as best they could, remaining only as long as politeness dictated, then passing on from one family group to the next, none of which could be avoided in the narrow lane, until they finally left behind the last of those who would greet and thank, at the church gate. They had arrived.

In a visual catalogue to fully convey an image of England, a country Parish Church would stand as well worth, even demanding of, its inclusion. Just so, All Saints at Lanbe Barton. The beech and chestnut trees had long shed their leaves, but their shape and stature gave both pomp and dignity to a setting that was not without natural colour, generously bathed in the gentle sun. The overarch of these two classic English trees gave a bower of shelter and seclusion, through which yew trees marched, green and self important, along the path from the lych-gate and on to the church itself. This sat squat, solid and timeless, but its solidity pronounced its status as a cornerstone of close-knit country society, all clasped within by their canon of shared code and belief. Here all met, including generations of Argent's own family, each Sunday, to stand, whatever their rank and status, merely as fragments of a common congregation, gathered together for communal worship. The pale pink granite and the deep purple of the tiling above, gave the church prominence within its winter surroundings, both colours being picked out by the cheering sun, this now glinting in the glass as welcoming eyes within the ancient windows.

Colour also came from the multitude of army uniforms; almost all infantry, red and resplendent, standing out as highpoints amid the summer dresses, despite the chill, resurrected for an occasion such as this; an important wedding. Argent and Fentiman had arrived just in time, all were filing in, and so they presented themselves at the edge of the throng and allowed themselves to be gently carried forward. Inside the door stood four Lieutenants in the uniform that Argent recognised from their white facings and cuffs, as Algernon Blake's Regiment, the 32nd Cornwall Foot. The nearest approached and both held out their invitations.

"Morning Sirs. Bride or groom?"

Fentiman answered, being nearest.

"Bride."

"Anywhere on the left, then Sirs. Thank you."

Both nodded their replies and walked forward. They quickly found two seats, beside the aisle but necessarily close to the back, themselves being amongst the last inside. Thus established, they looked around. The church was a riot of colour, all floral; front, back and sides, whites, reds, pinks, yellows and purple, all offset by the deep green of holly, ivy and laurel. Argent felt the need to remark upon it.

"Lady Grant's gardeners must have worked miracles to keep all this fresh and ready for the occasion."

Fentiman turned surprised.

"What? Sorry, I was miles away."

Argent smiled.

"I was just remarking on the effort needed to produce all this floral decoration in December."

"Oh, yes. Of course. Most laudable."

The final words tailed off and Fentiman said no more. Argent studied the service sheet and then looked forward and was able to see the

Groom, Algernon Blake, recognisable even from the back, his broad shoulders and powerful neck below neat, fair hair. A soldier of equal rank and stature, sat on his right. Behind them, sat what Argent took to be his family, his Mother and an older version of Blake, also in red with the shoulder insignia of a Brigadier. The Grants could just be seen on the opposite side of the aisle, Lady Constance in her full finery, beside the Admiral, both with garments clean and spotless and all decorations brightly polished. The Reverend Guilder added himself to the flowers at the beginning of the Sanctuary, beatified by his coming role in this occasion, himself the archetypal image of a country vicar; medium stature, hands clasped across his small paunch, eyes bright, mouth smiling, all topped by a bald head, defined by a narrow monklike fringe of dark hair, extending back and around from temple to temple.

Argent looked around further, at the familiar massive timbers of the roof, with the barrel ceiling, like an inverted ship, he couldn't help but conclude. Then he looked to the side, at the stainedglass windows and plaques, remembered from his childhood, almost all mentioning Willoughbys from times long past. That done, he sat and daydreamed easily, almost too easily, because the image of Sinead Malley came first into his mind, vividly remembering the last time he had seen her, and held her. Suddenly the organ gave a short wheeze and then the organist began. All stood immediately. Argent did not recognise the music, but someone behind murmured what he took to be its name.

"Ah, Bach! Prelude One in C"

This didn't mean much to him, but it was very pleasant. However, all thoughts of music were swept aside as Charlotte passed forward on the arm of her Father, wearing a dress of cream satin, plain, no ostentation, but displaying the highest quality. Four bridesmaids followed, each in pale yellow. Charlotte reached the Sanctuary where the beaming Reverend Guilder stood waiting, then she was joined by Algernon Blake. The look they exchanged was one of deepest affection and Argent felt Fentiman move at his side. The ceremony progressed, all conducted by the good Reverend, who was plainly in the highest transport of spiritual delight. The hymns were sung politely, if not with gusto, but the tune from the organ, certainly maintained by the Willoughby estate, carried them along. Both Mothers sobbed as the vows were spoken and the rings exchanged, then the Reverend made his ecstatic pronouncement. The Bride and Groom kissed each other with wholehearted enthusiasm and both signed the Register. Then came the time to walk down the aisle as husband and wife.

At the sight of both, Argent was genuinely moved. Both looked more at each other than at any of the nearby guests, who were left to marvel at the image of the deeply happy couple, both radiantly handsome and thoroughly and rightly joined together. Argent and

Fentiman were amongst the few noticed by either and both were treated to a dissolving smile from Charlotte and a nod and a grin from Blake. Then they passed on. Argent looked at Fentiman, remembering that he had once been asked by him, seemingly ages ago, about his own chances with Charlotte if he proposed. He knew nothing of the outcome, other than, plainly, it had been a rejection. His First Lieutenant took a long deep breath, which he exhaled slowly, then he turned and looked at Argent, a look neither resigned nor sad, more a look of "that's that, chapter closed, finished and over." Argent felt better, felt reassured, and smiled back. By this time the emptying of the pews to join the procession up the aisle had reached them and they left their places to follow out into the churchyard.

The air outside felt cold after the body warmth in the church, even though the wan sun still shone clear. Few were standing to talk, almost all had exited through the gate and were crossing the road to pass through the opened gates to the Willoughby Estate, walking slowly and contentedly up the drive. Argent and Fentiman joined them, strolling in similar mood, walking on through a loose audience of Willoughby tenants, many of whom called out, once more, as they recognised them and he greeted them equally. Suddenly, Argent recognised a voice he knew only too well, this confirmed by the words chosen to address them from behind.

"Still pandering to the common herd, then, Argent?"

Argent and Fentiman turned to see Cheveley, with his wife on his arm, she pretty enough, but, by demeanour, a subdued and passive figure. Argent turned away, then felt the need to make some kind of reply, so he turned around to walk a few steps backward.

"Morning Cheveley, I trust I find you well. Quite recovered? A fine wedding, you'd agree?"

Argent hoped that the middle two words, alluding to the Court Martial, would have some impact, but nothing more was said and they reached the entrance to the house. Cloaks were being taken by the servants, but, not having theirs, both Officers carried on down the entrance hall, having surrendered only their hats. At the doors to the great hall, stood the parents of both, then finally Blake and Charlotte. Argent allowed Fentiman to go first and he perfectly offered his thanks and congratulations to both sets of parents, followed by Argent. Fentiman shook hands with the Groom, then came Argent's turn and he was immediately recognised. They looked at each other with knowing smiles, as though old friends being ridiculously required to do something unnecessarily formal. The exchange, at first, was brusque, almost pantomime, spoken in flat, matter o' fact, tones.

"Captain!"

"Major!"

"Thank you for coming."

"Not at all. It's a pleasure.

"Hope you are well?"

"Never better. And congratulations!"

"Thank you. Pleased to see you.

"Same from me."

After the staccato exchange, both relaxed somewhat.

"Its all been a bit of a rush, you'll appreciate."

"How so?"

"Just got back from the Peninsula. A month's leave. So we decided to do a quick job, whilst I was home."

Argent nodded understandingly.

"Well, congratulations once again. I'm sure you'll be very happy."

Blake looked at Argent as he passed on.

"No doubt of it. I am the most fortunate of men."

Argent had no knowledge of what had passed between Charlotte and Fentiman, but now it was his turn to kiss the elated and stunning Bride. She took both his hands in hers and her warmth towards him was genuine, this conveyed by the sincerest of smiles that immediately turned into a little laugh. Argent could only laugh himself at her evident happiness.

"Congratulations, Charlotte. You look wonderful. Algernon's a very lucky man."

"What's that about luck?"

Blake was unoccupied for a second and had overheard, but it was Charlotte who answered.

"Yes you are! Now, keep looking cheerful, as though you've got something right for once, and make sure you say what's proper. And expected."

"As you order, ma'am!"

Argent laughed at the exchange and took one of Charlotte's hands in both his before walking on. He was genuinely moved by the happiness between them. He moved on to enter the door and remembered the last time he had been there, this being the festivity for those of his crew. Along the opposite side from the door was a long run of tables, all crowded with food, wine, plates, glasses and cutlery, the last shining bright in the candlelight from the holders and candelabras above. Waiters circulated with poised silver trays bearing more wine. Argent and Fentiman looked at each other, then at the food; they said nothing, there was no need, agreement came by both moving immediately in that direction. The buffet was sumptuous and the choice, with merely a standard sized plate, almost impossible to make. However, both covered its surface, although regretting what had been left behind. Fentiman was evidently expert at holding both a wineglass and a plate in one hand, whilst eating with the other and so Argent copied his example and suffered no mishaps. Fentiman seemed relaxed and at ease and both talked of what could be expected in the coming weeks.

"Do you expect much time in harbour, Sir?"

"I doubt it. Grant delayed our departure to enable us to attend this. We'll soon be out on "the triangle", if not sent back down to Figuiera, or somesuch."

Argent paused.

"Any problem with the ship?"

"No. But I expect another draft to make up our complement; the great majority convicts and pressmen, no doubt."

Argent frowned, but felt some cause for optimism.

"Well, yes, perhaps, but don't forget, we've just received prizemoney and that news will get around. Perhaps more volunteers than last time."

Fentiman nodded whilst chewing a tasty mouthful. Argent looked around, the Bride and Groom and parents were circulating, but still some way away from themselves, where they were standing. However, both remained concerned with food, both their plates were now empty and much of the buffet table was unoccupied.

"I'm for more."

"The same from me! Should we take some back for the Wardroom? They'll never believe us when we tell them of this."

Argent laughed as they walked forward.

"I very much doubt that we could get it back in the state as presented here. They'll just have to take our word for it, and live in envy!"

At the table they began to fill their plates again, however, as they did so, Argent heard, once more, the harsh voice he recognised very well.

"You know, I do think that society occasions, should be for society people. It's getting as bad as The Service. Sons of tenant farmers being made up to command, which only goes to show that not all change is for the better!"

Argent left the table and began to walk back to where himself and Fentiman had been standing, but he took the time to look sideways at Cheveley who was taking no food but holding an empty wineglass. A waiter passed and he placed his empty glass on the tray and took another. Cheveley was staring pointedly at Argent, whilst those of his party stood with confused, and partly embarrassed, rictus grins. His wife studied her feet. Argent continued to walk slowly on and bestow upon Cheveley an insolent smile that was added to by his own wineglass being raised in a mock toast. Argent then looked away, but from Cheveley there came more.

"The tedious thing about peasant farmers is that they are always suffering some kind of avoidable mishap. Fire and pestilence. Especially fire."

Argent continued walking, but the words had had their effect. Was that just Cheveley being foul; drunken talk and lies, wishing to discomfit by any means, spurred on by his intense dislike and desire for revenge, or something more sinister, and planned? In vino veritas! They regained their place by the wall and Argent thought, rationally, he hoped, as he ate and managed to dismiss the threat as in keeping with the evil, drink fuelled nature of Cheveley. However, he had another concern.

"I think we should leave. Cheveley's going to get more drunk and spark something off, with me, no doubt. This is a wedding and I want no part in spoiling it. We'll finish this, then go."

They ate hurriedly, left the hall and went for their hats arranged on the hall table, but they were spotted by Lady Grant, she hurrying around organising the next stages of the celebration.

"Reuben! Lieutenant Fentiman. Going so soon? But we haven't toasted the Bride and Groom, nor heard any speeches. And there's entertainment."

Argent walked towards her, followed by Fentiman, and bowed.

"Lady Grant. We feel we must go. I fear something unpleasant may happen that would spoil the occasion."

Lady Grant looked astonished.

"Unpleasant?"

"Yes, between myself and Captain Cheveley. It is well known to you the low level of relations between him and myself. He is drinking heavily and has already tried his best to stir up something today, twice in fact, by saying something provocative. It is best that we go and remove any threat to Charlotte and Algernon's special day."

He paused, then spoke emphatically to reinforce his decision.

"We should go. I do think it's for the best. So thank you, for your wonderful hospitality. The food was memorable."

He tried to be lighthearted, but Lady Grant was having none of it.

"Cheveley, being unpleasant and offensive, yes? The Admiral will take a dim view of that, very dim. But, I do see your point, and I thank you for your good sense."

She leaned forward and placed a hand on the sleeve of both.

"You know that you are very welcome here, any time, both of you."

Both bowed again, put on their hats, saluted the Lady and left. Dusk was falling and the driveway was picked out by the lanterns of the waiting carriages, the reflections from the highly polished coachwork and wheels adding to the original light. They walked on and down to the gate, acknowledging the fingers to foreheads of the waiting coachmen, but soon they were on the road up to Argent's family farm, which cheered Argent significantly.

"I hope you'll like them."

He leaned forward and over in the half light.

"Those you haven't yet met, I mean. I'm biased, of course, but I'm sure, sure, you'll get along fine. Both my sisters are excellent cooks, and I'm still hungry!"

But from Fentiman there came only a silence, which Argent couldn't comprehend, but he made no effort to fill it himself. However, eventually it was Fentiman who spoke.

"Sir, there is something that I have to tell you. It concerns your Court Martial, and I tried to make a start some days ago, back on board, but we were interrupted by the arrival of Admiral Grant."

Argent looked at him through the growing gloom, but said nothing, allowing Fentiman the space to continue.

"The evening after the first day of your Court Martial, I was visited in my room, by Admiral Broke, Cheveley, and that toad like man Cinch. They made me an offer."

Argent let the silence hang and Fentiman continued.

"The offer was command of a big Revenue cutter, with myself being made up to Commander. In return I was to say, when cross examined by Cheveley, that I had strongly protested at us not going straight across The Bay, and that we should obey the strict letter of our orders, to make as fast a passage as possible and head directly for Finisterre."

Again a silence.

"I was to tell of your reply."

Another pause.

"Which concoction was, that you had decided to give absolute precedence to finding that slaver. You would do that first, and deliver the dispatch second."

Argent stopped walking and placed his hand on Fentiman's sleeve to halt him. He held out his hand and Fentiman took it.

"I must count myself fortunate, very fortunate, in my First Lieutenant. I have to thank you. There are plenty who would have accepted such an offer."

They shook hands and walked on, in silence. After a minute Fentiman spoke further.

"There's more. I'm saying this now, because I have done you an injustice, in my own mind. I was convinced that it was you to whom Charlotte's affections belonged. "My affections belong to another". Those were the words that she used in her reply to my own proposal and it clouded my own thoughts towards you. I was convinced that you were the object of her affections and you were aware of that when I told you of my thoughts towards making a proposal to her, but you said nothing. I know now that I was very wrong and for that I apologise."

Argent's reply was physical, two light pats on Fentiman's right shoulder blade.

"Love and war, Henry! That's the game we're in. Think no more on it, all is now resolved."

But Fentiman was intent on yet more unburdening.

"The more I think on what they attempted, the angrier I become. That they should view my own integrity as being so shallow! Is there any way that we could take it further. It's corruption!"

"It is, but they'd deny it. I saw them at the end of the corridor of our rooms, presumably after they left you, but they could say anything. They were lost! Anything! Let it go, the matter's closed."

He paused.

"But, frankly, I'm not surprised. But, as I say, it's done and gone. Leave it there."

He smiled and laughed, his teeth white in the near dark.

"That's an order!"

They both laughed.

"And we're here, this is home."

Argent led the way through the yard and, feeling that the presence of a guest required some formality, he knocked on the door, which was opened by Emily.

"Reuben! Why is your coming always a surprise? And this time at night."

Argent ignored the chiding.

"Hello Emily. I've brought a guest. My First Lieutenant Henry Fentiman."

He paused.

"Henry Fentiman, I'd like to re-introduce you to my sister, Emily."

He stood aside and proffered his hand for Fentiman to enter and he stepped forward from the gloom. Emily saw him and something came into her face like happy surprise, then embarrassment. Fentiman was now in the light from the room, but Emily was looking at the floor. Argent, even from the side, could see that something had come over Fentiman's own face, but by now he was making his greetings to Emily, offering to shake hands with her, and she took the hand offered and curtsied.

"How do you do, Miss Argent? It is a pleasure to meet you again, I trust I find you well?"

"How do you do, Sir? You find me very well, I thank you."

There was a pause. Each was definitely looking at the other, a moment of warmth, created by each for the other, but Fentiman was blocking the door. Argent took charge, after wondering what was going on and where it had come from.

"Perhaps we should go fully in. All the heat is escaping."

Fentiman gave a nervous laugh and stepped fully in, still looking at Emily. Argent took charge again.

"Permit me to introduce the other members of my family. This is my Father."

Argent Senior was already advancing around the table, hand extended.

"How do you do, Lieutenant Fentiman? You are very welcome here."

Argent Senior then took over. He gestured first towards Beryan.

"This is my son-in-law, Beryan Trethewey."

The two shook hands, each smiling broadly in greeting.

"And this is my elder daughter, Beryan's wife, Enid. She's holding my grandson Jacob."

Fentiman bowed and Enid curtsied, despite holding Jacob. Argent Senior continued.

"Now, pleased to sit. Would you like something to eat? We always keep spare, what with Reuben, your Captain and my son, likely to pop in through the door at anytime, like some kind of annoying jack-in-the-box."

Fentiman gave a short laugh as they both removed their jackets and sat. Emily had swung the stewpot back over the fire and stood, where she could best see Fentiman and he lost no time in looking back at her. Argent was not blind to what was happening and sat laughing inwardly, smiling outwardly. Emily spoke first, naming no one, but obviously talking to Fentiman.

"Were you with Reuben when he captured La Mouette?"

But Argent answered first.

"He was, but you know that! His name was in the newssheet that you read out!"

"Be quiet! Quiet! I'm being polite, unlike you, who's just being tedious!"

Argent grinned, nodded, surrendered himself deeper down into his chair, and did keep quiet. His sisters had great licence with him, even if they did not often use it, but Fentiman did politely answer."

"Yes, I was there. And at St. Malo and against La Pomone. Was that in a newssheet, La Pomone, that being?"

Emily answered.

"It was. We'll try to find it. But…"

She walked back to the door, pulling a stool, which she stood on to take down the sword lodged over it.

"…this was the Captain's sword from La Mouette. Do you recognise it?"

She placed it on the table before Fentiman. He looked up at her for a long moment before answering.

"Yes I do. It was my first prize also. We were all very proud. And overjoyed, that almost all of us came through that unscathed."

Argent broke in.

" Did you get my letter about the prizemoney?"

Emily replied, not Enid. Her sister could see what was happening and decided to keep right out of it.

"Yes, we did. And we found the Will. It was with Branch, Branch, and whatnot, like Lady Constance said."

She folded her arms and took a deep breath that raised her shoulders.

"So, everything is now "squared away". Is that not how you say it, Lieutenant?"

Fentiman treated himself to a long look before replying.

"Yes, Miss Argent, that's exactly how we say it. "Squared away"; everything as it should be. And my name's Henry."

Emily blushed deeply, then grinned, only a little less awkwardly than before.

"Yes, now, your food must be ready. Here."

She took some plates from the mantle above the cooking fire and placed them before the two, then she spooned out the food. Argent was amazed how any landed accurately onto the plate, Emily spending so much of the time looking at Fentiman. The two Officers fell to eating, spooning the good stew and drinking the small beer. Emily sat opposite and soon the conversation was flowing between herself and Fentiman, she enquiring about his family and him answering in great detail, which held Emily in no small level of fascination and so she felt encouraged to ask more. This continued for ten minutes until she realized that she had been wholly monopolising the evening in her eagerness and suddenly looked around embarrassed at the others in the room, but Argent saw and immediately stepped in.

"What's planted, Father?"

"Winter wheat, in the ground that I know will stay as mine. Enclosures are going through and it's a Court come down from Exeter that are doing the apportioning."

"Not Broke, nor Cinch!"

"No. Local Judges."

Argent nodded.

"Then all should be well!"

"Yes. God willing."

Smiling openly, Argent looked at Enid, then Emily.

"We've just come from Charlotte Willoughby's wedding. Did you know? Did you come down?"

Emily felt it better to remain silent, so it was Enid who answered.

"Yes we knew, and we did go down, but got nowhere near, it was too crowded."

She paused.

"What was it like?"

"Well, as far as I'm any judge of weddings, I'd say it was wonderful, magical! You'd agree Henry?"

Fentiman was looking as cheerful and in good spirits as Argent had seen him in a long time.

"I would, and those are the two exact words I'd choose."

He looked at Enid.

"And this is wonderful stew. My compliments to the cook. I wish you'd come and teach ours a thing or two."

"Emily made it!"

Enid lied, but it was a subterfuge and conspiracy between sisters, well understood by each, but it gave the excuse for a long exchange between the eyes of Emily and Fentiman, but him now familiarly known as Henry.

"It's very good!"

"Thank you, Henry."

With food taken and plates cleared, all sat around the fire, the two Officers bringing dining chairs up close. The talk between them was quiet, leisurely and wide ranging, the newssheet was found and the sinking of La Pomone described and re-enacted using four table knives and a big kitchen knife to show the wind direction. Fentiman did most of the talking and any questions that came from Emily, Argent allowed Fentiman to answer. At the finish Argent decided that they should return to their ship, darkness had long descended. Beryan offered to harness the gig, but Argent would not have him take the trouble, it was but an hour's walk back to the ship, a walk that would do them good.

Argent managed to draw his Father aside for a brief moment and told him of the words spoken by Cheveley. Argent Senior's reply was to place his hand on his son's shoulder and grin up into face.

"Son. You worry too much!"

He let the words sink in. Argent was somewhat taken aback.

"Me and the likes of me have been dealing with the likes of Broke, Cinch and your Cheveley since times now forgotten. They try everything, fire, loose stock, broken fences, buried stones in your fallow, rubbish in your well, everything! Up here, we're a community and we all know what our neighbour Broke is capable of. We look out for each other, and, if it makes you sleep easier, we'll keep buckets of water by the windows. Now you worry about your ship, I'll worry about the farm."

Fond leave was taken and not only of Argent by his family. As the two set out on the easy walk back down the hill and their eyes grew used to the dark, Fentiman soon spoke.

"I think I like your family! Very much."

"Yes. I think I noticed! Anyone in particular?"

"The answer's got to be yes."

* * *

"And what, Mr. Bright, would our Admiral Beaufort make of this?"

Midshipman Bright winced as lumps of spray slammed against his cheek, to leave water to run down his neck inside his tarpaulin cloak. He opened his eyes gingerly and took a long look at the waves over the weatherside, ducking his head as the spray from another shattered wave skimmed across the quarterdeck.

"Force five, Sir. Pushing into six."

Argent grinned as his Senior Midshipman screwed his weather eye against the wind and the possibility of further spray.

"And our sail pattern?"

"I'd be thinking about losing topsails, Sir. But not for the moment."

"And replacing them with staysails?"

"Perhaps, sir, yes. They can spill wind and be adjusted easier, if needs be."

"A good piece of thinking, Mr. Bright. My thoughts entirely, but not just yet."

Then a blanket of spray hit them both, as Ariadne lurched into a trough and then climbed out of it, with such a lift that all on the quarterdeck felt their knees give slightly with the upward pressure.

Ariadne was speeding onto station. As soon as Argent and Fentiman had returned back on board from the farm a messenger was chasing them up the gangplank with orders, even in the dark. They were to join a squadron under the command of Admiral Leadbitter in HMS Foudroyant of 80 guns, along with HMS Scipion, a 74, and the Curacoa, a brand new 36 gun frigate. They had sailed with the tide, at very first light, followed out by Herodotus, whose Captain, Argent assumed, had received the same orders. Those orders spoke of a possible French invasion of Ireland, so Intelligence believed, which would be yet another attempt to stir up trouble in Great Britain's backyard, another attempt to follow the farcical effort of 1796 and the disastrous and brutal affair of 1798.

Herodotus had kept pace with Ariadne through the morning of the first day, each propelled along by a growing South Southwest wind and Argent had studied her quarterdeck through his Dolland glass, but could see nothing of Cheveley, only a succession of Lieutenants, one of which he thought to be the very Honourable Lord Charles Langley, no less than the First of the Herodotus. Argent could only suppose that Cheveley had carried on drinking throughout the post wedding reception and was recovering below decks. The orders gave no mention of proceeding in consort and so Argent set all the prudent sail that would give maximum speed. Herodotus also set sails to match, but fell away and with the first dawn, Ariadne had the ocean to herself, a ragged ocean in a bullying day. That day and another night, brought them to their present position, with the wind now strengthened further, stirring up the sea under a sky bright, but half hidden by ragged, hurrying cloud. The Noon Sight gave their position as almost due South of the Fastnet Rock, Latitude 51-18, Longtitude 9-18, and the class had all agreed with McArdle, although he retained his disapproving expression until all members had dispersed and then there came a single and slow nod of satisfaction in the direction of his Captain as he left the quarterdeck.

Lieutenant Wentworth was on watch, a curious, even comical figure, his jaw bound up both laterally and vertically by leather straps, and a woolly hat overall. He could speak, but only by moving his lips, his teeth were clenched by his bindings. A splinter from La Pomone's bowchasers had broken his jaw and so, understandably, he said little, and what he did say was terse and very much to the point, and he could not shout. Instead he relied on a messenger, today, this being Seaman Wheeler, lately Smallsize, who had remained on the quarterdeck after attending McArdle's class. Argent turned to Wentworth.

"Our squadron should be topsails up very soon, Mr. Wentworth. Please to double the lookouts."

Wentworth looked at Wheeler and nodded, thus the boy ran off to find Bosun Fraser. This worthy's exhortations sent Abel Jones up to join Moses King. The first King knew of this was Jones' weather-beaten face appearing over the edge of the foretop, one spar below. King watched as Jones climbed to his final perch on the topgallant yardarm. King spoke first.

"Doubling of lookouts?"

"Aye. But 'tis better up yer than on that deck, 'part from the wind."

As if to make the point a wave surged up the larboard bow, flooding through the scuppers, and then reaching up to tumble over the rail, where these broken waters were picked up by the wind to skim across the forecastle and soak further the men working there. At the sight, subconsciously, both men pulled closer the collars of their woollen jackets, then the newcomer asked his question.

"What be we lookin' for? An' where away?"

"Anythin' forrard's what the Captain's expectin', but don't expect that gashgilt tub what we left behind yesterday. Wiped his eye; floggin' sod!"

Jones grinned at the happy thought of Ariadne easing away, effortlessly, even under common sail. He looked forward, just to the left of the bowsprit, the tip of which was almost at their height, his head instinctively jutting forward.

"Well, I reckon my arrival's done the job. Is that two, far out, fine on the larboard bow?"

King shielded his eyes, as much from the wind as to shield out the light from the winterlit sky. He studied to form his own opinion, then concluded.

"Two, maybe I'd say, but certainly somethin'. Better call, before one of they grasscombing buggers on the Main sees and shouts."

Jones slid quickly down the outside of the shrouds to the foretop. To shout from their high lookout position would be lost in the wind.

"Deck there. Two sail. Fine on the larboard bow."

Wentworth was the nearest Officer of any rank and he looked up and waved a hand in salute to both acknowledge and reply. Jones grinned at the sight of the leatherbound face, but not derisively, merely a humorous chuckle to himself. Wentworth reached the quarterdeck and spoke through his clenched teeth.

"Forward lookouts, Sir, report two sail, fine on the weather bow."

Argent noted inwardly the lack of any stutter, but decided to make no mention.

"Very good, Mr. Wentworth. Up and join them, if you please, take a glass. The sighting should prove to be two third rates."

Wentworth saluted and soon joined King and Jones, who moved to the lee side of the mast, giving the Officer the weather, larboard, side, where the sightings were. Wentworth's lengthy arms locked him tight to the spar and he studied both through the glass, then he handed the glass to King. Again he spoke through clenched teeth, but King could see the extensive and unsightly discolouring of Wentworth's face from the bruising, only now beginning to fade into peculiar colours. His feelings were only of sympathy, despite Wentworth's comical speech, which he listened to carefully.

"The first, I'd say was a two decker. What about the second?"

King studied through the glass, then passed it onto Jones, who answered.

"First is a two decker alright. For the second, can't tell. She's too far behind, and the seas be reaching too far up her side, to be certain. Makin' too much spray."

Wentworth nodded, and took the glass.

"Thanks to you both. But one is definitely a two decker, so that's our squadron."

He reached for the shrouds, but King felt a question to this Officer would not be out of place.

"When does your frapping come off, Sir?"

"One month."

He paused.

"Then I'm going to have the biggest feed in history. Nothing but soup since La Pomone."

Both foretopmen laughed openly, Jones adding his contribution.

"Plus a drop of spirits, Sir!"

"That too. My single comfort, but both through a reed!"

Both laughed again as Wentworth grew smaller as he quickly descended the shrouds. Each looked at each other, still laughing and shaking their heads, then they resumed their lookout. Wentworth reached the quarterdeck, speaking very briefly.

"One is a two decker, Sir, the other may well be."

"Very good, Mr. Wentworth. What's our speed?"

The two Master's Mates on Watch spared Wentworth the torture of having to speak and immediately broke out the log board. Five minutes work brought the answer; 11 knots. Argent heard and thought of extra sail, a bit of a show would not come amiss, she was Ariadne after all, but prudence won. The pennant above was ruler straight and for a topgallant to carry away would be disaster, however, perhaps there was potential in what they already carried. He leaned over the rail, to save Wentworth the struggle.

"Mr. Fraser. Check your trimming, if you please. I'd like an extra half knot."

Fraser beetled off, taking two trusted Able Seamen with him. Soon all three were looking aloft and altering the set of sheets and braces. The response from Ariadne was to crash even harder into the cross-seas, but Argent was content.

Not so in the Midshipman's Berth, where Midshipman Trenchard just managed to rescue his sliding beaker of extra watered grog.

"My life, but the ship's jumping about, like some kind of nervous filly, just let out."

He carefully replaced the beaker, but did not release it, expecting yet another buck and lurch. Berry reached for a pile of books and strategically placed them to provide support. That done, both felt the beaker secure.

"Why, thank you, Daniel! Most kind."

In the absence of the cheerful Bright, conversation between these two could become somewhat stilted, but Trenchard respected Berry as a good shipmate. Although plainly wanting of the academic level required to achieve an Officer's capabilities, especially in navigation, his instinct for ship handling was the equal of them all and he had shown no shirk when the ship had been in action.

"Any thoughts on what you'll do with your prizemoney?"

Berry's face screwed up in thought, he had only lit upon one possibility and this moment's thinking did not produce another.

"Just one, to get my family out of their rented home, and into a property of their own. More security, you see, and no one able to increase the rent. Nor evict them!"

"You could invest it. The income would pay the rent!"

Berry's face screwed up again, but he made no answer, so Trenchard made his own.

"It's a thought!"

At that point, Bright arrived off Watch, his tarpaulin shedding water everywhere in the cramped berth. Most went on Trenchard, him being seated. By now relations had thoroughly gelled in the Midshipman's Berth.

"I say, William, what do you think you are? Some kind of ornamental fountain? Spray somewhere else, will you, there's a considerate chap?"

"You hope that it's settled down when your Watch comes, that's all I can say. It's pretty brutal out there."

He looked on the table.

"Is that grog? Can I have a swallow?"

Without waiting for an answer, he seized the beaker and took a drink.

"Heavens above, William, you really are the most annoying sort of fellow! Spraying sea water all over a body and then filching his grog!"

But Trenchard had moved over to make room on the bench and allow Bright to get nearest to their small coal heater. Bright warmed his hands.

"Our squadron's topsails up."

"What happens now?"

"Well, if we're all going somewhere, we form line astern and go on our way, wherever that may be. If a picket line, we'll be ordered away to some far out station and spend days just mooching up and down."

He reached again for the grog, but Trenchard beat him to it and clasped the precious beaker to his chest, holding it on the far side from Bright, then looking aghast at the further attempt at thievery. Berry stood quiet and smiling.

On the quarterdeck, Argent knew very well which of the two possibilities lay in the future, but was debating what it would mean. With Ariadne so fast and handy, almost certainly it would mean holding the station furthest out. Wentworth had his glass to his eye, whilst stood on the weatherside carronade. He was studying the two third rates, both on opposite and converging courses in the Southerly wind and closing rapidly.

"There's another some way behind them, Sir."

"That'll be Curacoa."

"The nearest is making her number, Sir."

"Make ours."

The signalmen reacted to Argent's order and soon, with Identification achieved, orders were being received. Again Wentworth relayed the information.

"Signal from flagship, Sir. "Take far West station. Maintain contact with Curacoa."

Argent's suspicions were confirmed.

"Steady as she goes, Quartermaster."

The acknowledgement came, just ahead of more mangled words from Wentworth.

"Another signal, Sir, for us. "Have you seen Herodotus?"

Argent grinned, which was shared all round the quarterdeck, even by Wentworth, although his face looked more like a ventriloquist's dummy.

"Make reply, "Following astern."

Still laughing, the Signalmen bent on the required flags.

Ariadne sped on, past the flagship, Foudroyant, and then the Scipion, a two decker, as she now plainly was. The lee side rails of both warships were crowded with faces, as Ariadne sailed past, her bowave often above her gunports, her hull dipping and rising easily through the irregular waves, sails perfectly trimmed and drawing fully, white ensign proudly out to leeward. Spray from waves, shouldered arrogantly aside, reached up to her main yards and her figurehead, now mysteriously newly painted, stared challengingly at the seas before her. Most amongst those looking on, did so approvingly, especially the more timeserved. She surged on past both, the famed Ariadne, a crack frigate!

"Another signal, Sir, but not our number. To Curacoa "Follow Ariadne onto station. Maintain contact with Scipion and Ariadne."

Argent looked ahead. The new frigate was well within view and, having seen the signal, was hauling her wind to come smartly about and match Ariadne's heading.

"Can you look up Curacoa's Captain, Lieutenant?"

Wentworth disappeared down the companionway to reach the Purser's Room, where such books and their updates were lodged. He came back after five minutes.

"Captain Galsworthy, Sir. Jeremy Galsworthy."

Argent smiled.

"I've got a feeling that there will be no following, if this Captain's the Galsworthy I used to know."

"Sir?"

"When I was Fifth on the Ganges, he was Fourth. If they are the same, of course, but I suspect it will be so."

Curacoa was swooping round in the following wind, a perfect example of the shipwright's art. Clean, white sails, above a sleek hull, this newly painted black, with the hull strakes of the gunports picked out in yellow. Bursts of sunlight played upon the clean black tar of her shrouds, not yet too salt-stained. Ariadne held her course constant and Curacoa took station off her larboard bow, but less than 200 yards, under a cable's length ahead. After a short time, her Captain ordered a reduction in sail, down to that which perfectly matched that of Ariadne; this was to be a trial between the two ships and their crews. It would be decided by the individual ships and the sail handling, so the Ariadnies all checked and re-checked their own settings. Nothing happened for some minutes, then a gust hit Ariadne, just as she topped a wave. The thrust of the wind combined with the force of gravity down the backside of the wave accelerated Ariadne up to within 100 yards, but the gain stopped. Curacoa was now taking Ariadne's wind, her sails falling slack in the broken air, then filling, then slackening. The new frigate took in her topsails for Ariadne to close and soon she did, with but 30 yards between their hulls. Argent took a speaking trumpet and climbed onto the larboard quarterdeck carronade.

"Ahoy! Do I have the pleasure of addressing one Captain Galsworthy?"

A corresponding Captain's figure appeared on the quarterdeck rail, holding the mizzen shrouds.

"You do! Captain Argent, I presume."

"The same, and you are stealing my wind, as you stole my fruit when we were aboard the Ganges."

"And very tasty it was too. As is your ship! My congratulations." Argent laughed.

"And mine to you, she's a lovely vessel!"

"Let's hope we both stay that way on this picket line."

"My thoughts as well. Good luck to us both."

The reply was a wave of the loud hailer and the figure disappeared. She sheared off upwind to give Ariadne a fair wind and Ariadne moved further up, but once back on the same course both kept pace with each other, until Curacoa reached her station, cut her sail and fell behind, Scipion was now on the horizon. There was a wave from Curacoa's quarterdeck as she turned into the wind to halt at her allotted place, whilst Ariadne continued on. From the pressure on his left cheek, Argent thought the wind may have abated slightly, but he called for no increase in sail. After less than an hour Curacoa was "sails only" and, just as she was about to disappear, Argent called for his crew to wear ship and then sail back the way they had come, on much reduced sail. Bosun Fraser, on the forecastle, looked at Bosun's Mate Ball.

"Sentry go! If ever there's a job to wear down a man, this is it."

* * *

The days seemed endless, as monotonous as the drip, drip, of moisture from the sails, all vainly attempting to gather the fickle wind above. The weather turned to murk rather than increased storm and it was clear to all aboard that a fleet could sail past and not be detected if they silenced their bells and were further away than one cable. Argent stepped up the gun practice to twice a day, with exercises that included depleted crews and disabled guns. The topmen did not escape, being required to raise and lower topmasts and set top gallants, all to the pitiless secondhand of Argent's half hunter. All three masts were within ten seconds of each other, not enough to give any mast the bragging rights, but the mizzenmast had been quicker, only because their topmast was shorter; at least this was the verdict according to the other two. The Officer's thoughts dwelled mostly on home and how they would bring Christmas on board, for there was little else to concern them, as each day the ship was at inspection standard in all respects. Every Noon Sight brought a calculation that differed but in minutes around Latitude 51-20, Longtitude 9-53, until the clouds closed over and none were possible. A signal gun was loaded and readied, but each day the charge had to be drawn and replaced, ruined by the damp.

On day ten, the day dawned with the same damp fog that had for days made them feel isolated in their own world on their own ocean. The ship was largely becalmed, bar curious shapes of fog that rose up eerily over the sides and drifted on, unworldly and wraithlike, disturbing to those harbouring the occult, the pale spectres seeming to take their own time to investigate some fitting on the deck, before quitting the ship for the banks of grey beyond, returning to merge with their own kind. The sails hung limp and idle, gathering their own portion of moisture, which quickly coagulated to descend slyly down to the deck and land on the heads of those on Watch, shivering in their warmest jackets with the damp-cold of the winter Atlantic. The Officers frequently checked the ship's many headings against the compass, or looked all around for any sort of wind, or looked over the taffrail to see if Ariadne had any kind of wake. It was hard to detect any in the all enveloping fog.

Suddenly came the kind of change that most frequently occurs in Northern latitudes; post dawn a breeze arrived, more like a breath, not enough to move the ship, but enough to move the fog. This thinned and dispersed and the horizon sprang outwards.

"Sail ho! Fine on the starboard bow."

Silas Beddows had come down to the foretop. Sanders was on Watch and he hurried along the gangway to the foremast shrouds, carrying his glass. Mist still lingered at the surface, albeit far out, and so, from the deck, he could see nothing.

"What ship?"

"Topsail schooner. Two masts."

"What's her heading?"

"Becalmed, like us."

Sanders decided that he must look for himself, so he rapidly climbed the shrouds to the topgallant crosstrees. He locked himself against the mast and locked a leg over the spar to focus on the newcomer, to be immediately surprised at how close she was, a significantly under two cables, he judged. She was at an angle to them, mostly stern on, and the first thing he noticed was, hanging limp but still detectable, the red and white stripes of the flag of the new United States of America. The mist, now no longer achieving the status of fog, cleared further and Sanders could see the detail of the whole vessel and he concluded that she looked built for speed, a sleek hull supporting two tall masts of almost equal height, a "fore and aft" rig, bar two square sails atop each mast. Nothing was moving, both ships were becalmed. Sanders slid down a backstay and hurried back to report.

"Sir. She's an American schooner. Very neat. Two masted, fore and aft rig and topsails. She looks fast, that's all I can say, Sir."

Argent turned to his Sailing Master.

"Mr. McArdle. What would you give as our distance from the Irish coast?"

McArdle pursed his lips, his common reaction before answering to whatever he was not sure of.

"Four miles, Captain. Could be three, could be five. I'll know this Noon."

Argent nodded.

"Which in the fog, could be construed as three; placing us within territorial waters."

He turned back to Sanders

"I want to know what she's about. Ready the longboat. Take yourself, Mr. Berry, and a full crew. Ask her business and what she's carrying."

Sanders moved to the companionway ladder, but Argent said more.

"Go in peace, Mr. Sanders. I'd rather not start an international incident! However, clear the ship for action."

The drums rolled out and Ariadne was readied for combat, but despite the bustle and shortage of idle men, the longboat was soon swung out and the crew embarked. As they pulled away for their journey, Argent studied the schooner from the foretop. His Dolland produced enough detail to enable him to read the name, "James Makepeace", and he could see her Captain, or at least an Officer, studying them through a spyglass. His longboat was covering the distance, but few men could be seen on either the schooner's deck or the quarterdeck. The longboat came to 50 yards when Argent's breath froze within him, a rank of muskets appeared over the schooner's taffrail and opened fire. Argent saw the smoke before he heard the report and whoever was on the longboat's tiller turned the longboat away and called for an increase in the stroke rate, which Argent could see immediately doubled. The crew were pulling for their lives and two oars were already hanging idle. The longboat's bows swung further to point back to Ariadne and then came the second volley. In his telescope, Argent saw one of the blue-coated figures in the stern slump forward to be seized by the other. A third volley came, but the longboat was out of effective range. Argent angered immediately and descended to reach the forecastle, then turned to see him that he wanted.

"Mr. Fraser! I want two guns, mounted up here and able to fire forward. Get Mr. Tucker and Mr. Baines involved. I want that inside an hour, one hour!"

Fraser had seen the incident himself and was as angry as Argent. Within five minutes timber was arriving from the hold to make two platforms that would enable the guns to fire over the forecastle rail. Meanwhile, Argent was waiting anxiously at the entry port as the longboat limped back, a wounded sailor at the tiller and the surviving Officer at an oar. Argent could only see his back and anxious moments passed as the longboat closed. The Officer at the oar looked up, it was Sanders, who wasted no time.

"Two dead, one wounded, Sir. Midshipman Berry, I think he's gone."

A bosun's chair was already being lowered over the side for the wounded. Berry came up first, held in place by a sailor, but when he was lowered to the deck, Argent could see that the wound had been fatal. Surgeon Smallpiece, newly arrived, knelt and shook his head; Berry was dead.

The bosun's chair was employed for the wounded sailor and the other dead man was taken aboard in the same way. The longboat was quickly swung aboard and lodged on its cradle whilst the two bodies were laid out and wrapped in sailcloth. Argent was incensed, a feeling which ran through the whole crew. He spent his time on the forecastle, saying little, but his presence added urgency to the work undertaken there, but within 30 minutes Baines and his mates had constructed two platforms, wide enough for a gun carriage to be trained around for 20 degrees either side. Two loosened cannon, both number three's, waited below on the gundeck, already with lashings that would enable them to be hoisted up and one already connected to the capstan.

Suddenly a sail flapped overhead, showering them with moisture. Argent looked immediately at the pennant, now writhing hopefully out from the masthead and extending back astern. The weather was changing, quickly it would seem, for a North West wind had arrived, strengthening rapidly. Argent hurried back to the quarterdeck and there he saw a very downcast Midshipman Bright, but Argent had no time for commiserations.

"Mr. Bright. Get up the mast. If you can see Curacoa, fire a gun, then signal to Flag. "Smuggler. Large Schooner. Permission to pursue".

Fentiman spoke up.

"That in the Log, Sir?"

"Yes, make it so."

Argent looked at his sail pattern and walked to where he could see Bosun's Mate Ball, stood waiting for orders. Waves, tide and the idleness of no breeze had placed Ariadne pointing directly into the wind, whilst the schooner was perfectly placed to use it immediately. He extended his Dolland and looked at the schooner. What was to be her reaction? Even as he focused he could see sails being trimmed and the square topsails on the high two yards of each mast being set. She was making a move, South, a course giving her best point of sailing, this being on the starboard tack with a wind perfect over her starboard quarter, but as he looked his jaw clenched further. While the schooner rapidly picked up speed, he could see a whole rank of bare backsides displayed over her lee rail, towards them; the crew were delivering their last insult before they made off. Argent spoke aloud.

"We'll see! We'll bloody well see!"

His crew were yelling insults back over the water, but far too far away to be heard by the American. Argent let the wind play on the sails to judge which way to turn to gain the wind, then Ariadne moved astern but her bows swung slightly to starboard.

"Mr. Fraser! Jibsails to larboard!"

All jibsails extending down from the foremast to the bowsprit were pulled across and immediately caught the wind. Ariadne's bows began to rapidly move around and soon she had turned past 90 degrees then further and, at that angle, the headsails lost their leverage.

"Driver to larboard!"

Still boiling angry, Argent seized onto the driver's sheets himself to help haul the huge sail over to catch the wind and push Ariadne's stern further to complete the job begun by the headsails.

"Mr. Fraser! Starboard tack, six points large! Everything she'll carry, stunsails, main and mizzen staysails."

Fraser called "all hands" and the guncrews ran from their positions to attend to the huge increase in sail. The courses and topsails on each mast were already set, but the acreage of her sail was about to almost treble. Argent went to the starboard quarterdeck carronade and climbed, to stop with one foot on the barrel, the other on the rail, then extended his glass. Their quarry had accelerated rapidly, faster then themselves and was a good three-quarter mile, probably more, fine off their starboard bow.

"Mr. McArdle, a loan of a sextant, if you please!"

McArdle went to the quarterdeck locker and produced the instrument permanently stored there. Argent took a sight on the schooner to measure the angle formed between the schooner's waterline and the top of her mast. Measured from Ariadne, the height distance between the schooner's mast and waterline gave an angle of two degrees. If they were gaining that would increase and his rival, ahead on the schooner, was doing the same for Ariadne he was certain, only him hoping for the angle to decrease. He looked aloft, his men were moving around in the rigging like frantic apes, setting the topgallants, the royals, and the most difficult, the stunsails. The afterguard had already set the two lowest staysails, these being the only staysails that would draw the wind; a squaresail sail set above, before and after, would block the wind from them. However, Ariadne was responding and picking up speed rapidly. Argent returned the sextant.

"My thanks, Sailing Master. Throw the log, when you judge all to be in place and ready above, if you please."

Argent's face was fixed and stern as he walked forward along the starboard companionway to the forecastle. The second gun was being swung into place, the breeching ropes and hauling tackles already in place on the first gun, these extending to improvised fixings over the forecastle rail. Gunner Tucker was taking glances ahead at the schooner, whilst supervising the readying of both guns. He did not see his Captain approach as he continued to stare ahead and he spoke aloud.

"Come on, girl, time to take offence! Just get us up to her."

He looked around and was embarrassed to see his Captain, who almost certainly had overheard. He spoke to break the moment.

"Never fear, Sir. We'll get her."

The reply was a curt nod and a look from a face still set and angry. Wheeler came running up, and waited for his Captain's attention before saluting.

"From Mr. McArdle, Sir. Eleven knots and a half. And the wind's strengthening, Sir, now Force Four, gusting to Five."

Argent's face softened slightly.

"Thank you, Seaman Wheeler. Now return to the quarterdeck."

Wheeler gave his best salute and left. Argent looked aloft at the huge spread of canvas. Everything was in place and his topmen were still there checking the holdings of each sail, that being every rope that held the sail to its spar and every sheet and brace that placed the sail to where it would best catch the wind. He returned to his quarterdeck, thinking, "Eleven knots and a half." She was catching all the wind there was, so, for now, no more could be done. He checked again with the sextant: no change. Neither himself nor his opponent would be happy, Argent hoping to gain, the schooner's Captain expecting to move away. He consoled himself that his opponent would be the least content, him surely expecting to show a British frigate a very clean pair of heels. There were still many hours of daylight left, but during one of the shortest days, the gloom of evening would come early. He looked again through his telescope, the schooner was moving from right to left, coming across onto a course more South East.

"What's our course?"

Short gave an immediate reply.

"Sou' sou' east, Sir."

The schooner was heading for France, not the deep Atlantic. If smuggler she was, plainly her Commander remained confident of his escape. McArdle spoke behind him.

"Wind on five, now Sir. Steady."

With this spread of sail, Ariadne could take six, but above that, then her highest sails, the Royals, with their extra leverage from above, would drive her bows too deep into the sea. Also the strain on her masts would be huge and on the borders of good sense. Meanwhile, should he react to the schooner's change, the wind coming six points free was Ariadne's best point of sailing.

"Steady as she goes."

"As she goes, Sir, aye aye."

The wind had risen, all his sails were in place and trimmed, so what was Ariadne's speed now?

"The log, please, Mr. McArdle."

Five minutes of tense waiting.

"Twelve, Sir. And a half."

He reached for the sextant, then stopped, allowing it to fall slowly to the binnacle cabinet next to the motionless compass. Give the ship some time, he thought, and took himself over to the weather quarterdeck rail, where he clasped his hands behind his back and told himself to be patient. All over the companionways, the men were attending to the sails, watching for the slightest shiver that spoke of a bad alignment, whilst beneath their feet they could feel their ship rise and fall smoothly, responding eagerly to the needs of the chase, surging on over each long wave. Thus were the crew occupied for the next hour, all making tiny adjustments to better harness the wind, but Argent barely took his eyes of the American ahead. He reached for the sextant and sighted it, his pulse rate increasing. Two degrees and 20 minutes, they were gaining. He hurried forward to the two guns.

"Mr. Tucker. What do you think?"

"We've made on her, Sir, but too far as yet."

"What's your judgment? The range you need, I mean?"

"On him, what we need, Sir, with our long eighteens, is 300 yards. As we look at it, we're now on the quarter mile. It won't be too much longer."

As if in reply, the schooner moved further East. Was she trying to rob Ariadne of her best point of sailing? With their fore and aft rig, they could harness the wind with no slackening of speed from a wider range of angles, but Ariadne was plainly faster than the schooner's Captain had bargained for, seriously faster. Argent placed himself in the mind of the schooner's Captain. To him, Ariadne was gaining; she must look like a mountain of canvas, very determined, and the threat from her was growing with every hour passing. As things were, he would be caught, what to do? His only option was to turn and sail close to the wind, as Ariadne had done with La Mouette and, with a fore and aft rig, she would be able to sail closer than the square rigged Ariadne, and faster. If he did choose to turn, which way? Impossible to tell, as yet, so Argent stood, opening and closing his hands. What would I do?

He thought further. The wind is North West, over the starboard quarter of us both. For the American, fore and aft rigged, turning fully East meant making a tack, losing speed, but with France still possible. Turning West was an easy haul of his wind, but a course away from France. He could do either. Argent left the problem alone, consoling himself with the thought that the schooner's commander must be easily the more worried of them both. His schooner, which he evidently thought so highly of, so much so that they felt safe enough to send deep insults in Ariadne's direction, had now been run down. Argent finally answered Tucker's comment.

"I'll leave it to you, Mr. Tucker. Whenever you think it worth the powder."

Argent returned to the quarterdeck.

"Mr. Bright. Did you get a signal off to Curacao?"

Bright took a deep breath.

"No Sir. We never saw her through the mist."

Argent nodded and picked up the sextant again; three degrees and just over. His ship was winning the race, therefore the schooner would have to make a move soon, if she was to escape and it would have to be done outside the effective range of Ariadne's guns. Any damage to her sails would be fatal and her Captain would well know the range of a British frigate's long eighteen!

The last of the sand in the glass fell aimlessly, issuing through the neck and making odd patterns on the pile beneath. Argent watched, equally aimlessly, until a Master's Mate turned the glass and rang six bells of the Forenoon Watch. Two more until the Noon Sight, if there was enough sun. Prudently, he took a look at the weather and saw solid grey cloud lowered over all, therefore nothing new over any horizon. Argent turned to his First Lieutenant.

"Try to get the men some food. If only some biscuit and a mug of coffee."

Fentimen descended the companionway and Argent studied the sails and watched the falling sand some more.

"Wind strength, please, Mr. McArdle?"

A pause before the Highland tones replied.

"Just touching six, Sir."

Argent looked up at the sails, then took himself over to the mizzen mast backstay, the new one on the larboard side. He placed his hand on it and whatever was transferred, between his ship and her Captain, his ship was telling him that all was yet well.

"Just a wee under thirteen knots, Sir."

McArdle had decided himself that another throw of the log was called for and, at that moment, came the double report of both cannon firing ahead. Argent had his telescope instantly to his eye, just in time to see the fall of shot, at what looked like 20 to 30 yards astern of the schooner. Argent hurried forward.

"Extra half charge, Mr. Tucker?"

"Already using that, Sir."

As they spoke Argent could see the schooner's profile change. Her Captain had decided that the time had come and was tacking his ship, turning fully East, to make France still possible. A bad choice, Argent thought, he's probably rattled, even panicked, his trusted schooner now having been thoroughly bested. The schooner's speed fell before the two huge drivers could cross his deck and then be sheeted home, whilst his pursuer, Ariadne, had only to follow around and wear ship, holding the wind favourable for much of the turn. She being square rigged the reduction in speed would be negligible. From behind he heard the voice he needed and fully recognised.

"Orders? Sir."

"Mr. Fraser, wear ship, larboard tack, wind six points free, full on our quarter. I leave you to inform Mr. Short."

As Fraser ran off, Argent turned back to Tucker.

"As he turns, we'll see more of him, and I don't think he's judged it too well."

As if to confirm, the two guns fired again. A long second, then came the waterspouts, both just short and one each side. Argent gave himself some seconds of thought.

"Mr. Tucker. How many of those shrapnel shells have we left?"

The light of inspiration came into Tucker's face.

"Quite a few, Sir."

"Then I think this to be just the occasion when we use them up! You'd agree?"

Tucker was already hurrying off the forecastle and Argent went to the starboard gun, commonly number three of the starboard side. Sam Morris came to the attention as his crew sponged out for the next reload.

"Belay the reload, Morris. You are going to fire a six-pound ball at our friend yonder. How much powder?"

Morris thought, then answered.

"Normal charge, Sir, but well packed with guncotton. A six-pound ball leaves a great deal of windage, Sir. Wastes the push, Sir."

"You mean the gap between the ball and the inside of the barrel?"

"Aye Sir. Yes."

"Right, I understand. Mr. Tucker is on his way, load as you say."

Morris nodded to his crew and the other gun followed the same. Tucker appeared with four seamen carrying the box marked "shrapnel shell" and he had had the same thoughts as Morris, two more seamen were carrying bales of guncotton. As they loaded, Argent looked at the schooner. She was full in line with their bowsprit, as Short curved Ariadne around East to follow the schooner's turn and Fraser organised the sails as they wore ship. Tucker looked up and made his judgement.

"One second fuse."

He poured powder into his measure and then tipped all into the fuse hole of the shell held by Morris. The powder was poured in and tamped down, then a repeat for a second shell. Both guns were loaded and Morris and the other Guncaptain, Jem Bates, crouched down over their barrels, giving instructions. Morris fired first, immediately followed by Bates. The smoke cleared quickly in the wind and they saw the shells explode, in line, but short and slightly low. The guns were rapidly reloaded and Morris primed his flintlock.

"Let's see you stick yer backsides over the rail now!"

Tucker retained one second; the range was falling as they closed, the schooner trying to turn into the wind to lose Ariadne; the frigate holding her turn. Bates called to his crew.

"Up a half."

As Bate's crew responded, Morris' crew looked at him and he nodded. Both quoins were withdrawn a half mark, then, once more, both Morris and Bates crouched behind their guns. Both fired together, as did the shells explode, almost in the same place, that being alongside the schooner's mainsail. In an instant, the canvas, under massive strain, was in rags and shreds, streaming away in the wind. Argent saw her hull slump into the water, as the forward drive that had been lifting her up and out, fell by a half.

"Good shooting, Morris, Bates. Give her more, until she heaves to."

Two more exploded on the schooner, this time one above and one just short, but sufficiently over her hull for the shrapnel to reach. Immediately they saw that her Captain had had enough, he turned into the wind and the way fell off his ship. Ariadne's crew began cheering, loud enough to carry over on the wind, but Fraser soon put a stop to all.

"Belay that! Get the canvas away, or we'll be on past her!."

In an instant the ratlines were full of topmen, also any waister and afterguard who could make the main spars. As the sheets were loosened Ariadne's speed slackened, and through the busy scene Argent walked aft, carefully avoiding the two bodies.

"Mr. Short. Bring her into the wind, with yon Yankee under our starboard broadside."

"Into the wind, starboard broadside to bear. Aye aye, Sir."

As if they had an audience, as indeed they did, for the schooner's crew were all lining their rail, Ariadne's topmen furled sails and struck down their stunsails and all else, bar the main and fore courses. It must have been close to a naval record time. Silas Beddows looked across at the schooner, as he clamped down the last reef line to secure the foretopgallantsail neatly to its yard. His mates grinned as he vented his spleen towards the crew over the water.

"That's how it's done, you pieces of shite! Who did you think you was dealin' with? An Essex coalbarge?"

Argent was issuing his orders.

"Captain Breakspeare. I'm sending both the launch and the longboat. I will be in the launch, I'd like you in the longboat. Your Marines spread over both. Lieutenant Sanders will be in your boat."

Breakspeare saluted and ran off to pass on the orders to Sergeant Ackroyd. Argent then heard Fentiman below on the gundeck.

"Run out!"

The port lids thumped back against the sides and then he heard the squeal of the gun trucks as they emerged through their gunports. He gave a satisfied nod to himself, then looked to the boats about to be sent over the side, his own barge crew helping, for they would be amongst those manning the launch. Argent looked again at the motionless schooner. She had not struck her colours.

* * *

The entryport had no handropes, but at least it was open. There were no faces to be seen. Coxswain Whiting brought the launch around parallel to the side of the schooner that rose up sheer, black and glossy, above them. Argent stood up, amidst the erect oars and erect bayonets all around him and he looked at Abel Jones in the bows.

"Jones. Hand me that grapnel."

The grapnel with its rope was passed back and Argent lobbed it gently to stick on the rail to the right of the ladder that led up. He pulled it taut and placed his right foot on the first rung.

"Marines first after me, then the rest of you follow up. Jones you remain, keep the boat secure against her side."

He climbed, using the single rope of his grapnel, hand over hand. Soon he was looking along the deck at eye level, it looked dishevelled, then he was stood in the entryport. Facing him were the crew, about two dozen men, three in some type of uniform, but not military, more merchant marine. He looked at the rail under his right hand, noting it to be pock marked and torn, presumably from the shrapnel and so, as a gesture of possession, which was how he felt, he brushed away some lose splinters.

"Who's in command here?"

A tallish and angular man, early middle-aged, stepped forward, plainly very angry, but at that moment Brakespeare's Marines came up and over the rail behind. The crew looked around at the bayonets, muskets, black shakoes and angry faces, these followed by the hated red uniform. More Marines were also arriving from Argent's route and the Americans' apprehension grew, whilst the commander resumed his angry look at Argent.

"This is piracy!"

"Hardly! We've not taken your ship from you and locked you below, nor taken any of your property. Not yet, that is. You, on the other hand, have killed two of my men and injured a third. That was an unprovoked attack on an unarmed longboat that was despatched to simply ask your business in British Territorial Waters. If there is any piracy, it lies with you. Perhaps you had designs to capture our longboat?"

The Commander ignored the question.

"We were not in Territorial Waters. We were on the High Seas!"

"You can't be sure, neither could we, either way. We haven't taken a Sight for days, neither could you."

He paused. There was no answer.

"We are going to search your ship."

The Commander drew himself up to his full height.

"My Government will hear of this!"

"After this, you can do as you choose, but I repeat, you fired on an unarmed boat's crew. Because of that, I now have dead to bury!"

Argent took a deep breath, his mood suddenly becoming very belligerent and it showed.

"I'd like you to be aware, that from my point of view, I'd like nothing better than to quit your deck, now, go back to my ship and then blow you out of the water! Then, whom of you would be alive to tell the story to any Government?"

He saw the Commander's face change with apprehension, as did those of the crew, lined up behind him. Was this Captain cold-hearted enough to carry out such a threat?

"My best advice to you, now, is to shut up and allow the search; then it's possible that you may sail on your way. I acknowledge that, at first sight, you are a foreign ship, under a foreign flag, but that remains to be proven."

The Commander exploded in anger. Argent's threat had not done enough to fully subdue him. He delivered his speech.

"This is an American vessel, on the High Seas, going about legitimate business of trade. I demand that you quit this deck!"

"You surprise me. Legitimate business of trade? On a course for France, with whom my country is at war? If you are legitimate, as you say, you will have a Ship's Manifest, and a Bill of Lading. If you would be so good as to show those, our search will be much shortened."

Silence, but the American's face grew in concern.

"Did you load in Ireland?"

A nod.

"At which port? If your trade is legitimate, I should say that you would be able to name the safe harbour that you loaded at and sailed from."

Silence. Argent now delivered his speech.

"It is my strong suspicion that you are a smuggler taking goods from Ireland for sale in France. My men will now search your ship. And you. And your men."

He nodded to his sailors and Marines, who both spread themselves all over the ship to disappear through doors and down companionways. Some sailors began to loosen the covers on the main hatchway. The Commander started shouting.

"This is an American ship. We are American sailors. You have no right!"

"The events of the past few hours give me the right."

He turned to King, Beddows and Whiting, waiting just behind.

"Search them."

The three sailors, two very large, walked menacingly forward, their movements covered by six Marines with levelled muskets and threatening bayonets. Whiting went to the Commander, King and Beddows began with the rest, starting from opposite ends. Whiting looked at the Commander as though he would dearly like to hit him.

"Turn out your pockets. Onto the deck."

The same was repeated by King and Beddows. One sailor protested loudly, to then receive a precise punch on the jaw from King.

"Bare your arse to me, would thee? I d'reckon you'm lucky to not end up sunk an' down to the "old place" You an' this mongrel barky!"

Whiting was satisfied with the response he had received and pointed to the Commander's possessions, after he had fully spread them around with his foot.

"Pick them up!"

The Commander went red in the face, but Whiting glared right back, equally challenging. It was Beddows who broke the moment.

"I d'reckon this one here to be very familiar!"

He turned to Argent

"Sir? Didn't we see this one back in Kilannan?"

Argent walked forward to confront the stocky figure indicated by Beddows. All he could see was the top of his head, his face being lowered fully down to stare at the deck.

"Who are you?"

No response and the head was not raised. Argent lost patience and reached forward himself to seize the head under the chin. His first thoughts were the feel of the coarse stubble; the next was one of recognition.

"Michael!"

The face was unmistakable, confirmed by the horseshoe scar.

"Michael, what are you doing here, on board?"

No reply, bar a look growing increasingly terrified.

"Michael. You are onboard a ship that has just fired on British sailors, killing two. You are very liable to hang!"

The look of terror increased. Argent turned to the nearest two Marines.

"Take him to the Captain's cabin. Hold him there, until I arrive."

At that point Brakespeare looked up from leaning over the now uncovered hold.

"Irish linen, Sir. Bales of it. Way upwards of one hundred, pushing two, perhaps."

Argent turned to the Commander.

"Now, Captain. Let me tell you what I see here. I am dealing with a ship that was very confident that she could escape on a course to France, which she takes. I have two dead crew, killed by you. You can provide no Bill of Lading nor Manifest. You cannot name the port you sailed from. I am of the strong opinion that your flag, up there, is a mere ruse. You may be Americans, but I think that you are Americans in an American built ship, but a ship no longer American. She was bought by someone French or Irish, for her speed, and crewed by you, to engage in the very lucrative smuggling trade between Ireland and France."

Argent paused to gauge the reaction in the Commander. What he saw was apprehension behind the front of anger.

"Tell me I'm wrong. But if you do, you'll have to prove it."

The reply was simple, but now weaker.

"This is an American ship. We are American sailors. We defended ourselves against being boarded."

Argent looked at the Commander quizzically, tilting his head slightly to the right.

"I'd like to see your Identification Document showing Port of Registration. This applies to all British shipping, perhaps also to yours?"

"We are from the United States. That does not apply."

Argent clasped his hands behind his back and rose up onto his toes.

"Oh dear!"

He turned to Sergeant Ackroyd.

"We'll have these sat on the deck, Sergeant, whilst I talk to Michael."

Argent then turned his back on the scene of the whole crew and their Officers being forced to the deck, but it was neither a quiet nor a dignified process, much being accomplished by musket butts.

"Lieutenant Sanders. Please accompany me."

In the Captain's cabin, Argent found Michael, sat on the deck in a corner of a small, but well furnished and tidy cabin, him with two bayonet points not one foot from his chest.

"You two, on sentry, outside the door."

As the two Marines left, Argent turned to Sanders.

"Jonathan, search the cabin. Any papers that may help us find out what's going on. The Logbook first."

Argent found a chair for Michael and motioned him to sit in it, whilst Argent brought around the Commander's chair from behind the desk to give Sanders space for his searching. Soon, one was sat opposite the other and Argent looked at Michael for several seconds and Michael's mouth began to twitch and his eyes to swivel violently.

"Michael. You are going to hang. You have been found on a smuggler that has killed two British seaman. But…"

He left the word poised. There was no change in the level of terror in Michael's face, but Argent certainly had his full attention.

"You have one route of escape. As yet you have not been found guilty and you are a British citizen. I can press you out of this ship and you will be signed on as a seaman of my crew. I can classify you as a British citizen serving aboard a foreign ship found in British national waters, which means I can press you into mine"

The response was a vigorous nodding of Michael's head, but Argent was shaking his.

"It's not that simple, Michael. You must tell me all that you know about this crew, this vessel, her cargo, and who owns the linen. Miss out anything and you'll hang, it'll be the gallows dance for sure, and it's a God awful way to die, Michael, hauled up to jerk and choke before a gleeful crowd!"

Terror crossed his face but then Michael took a deep breath, released it, swivelled his eyes, and then took another.

"'Tis Fallows!"

Argent jumped straight in, Michael's reply had not surprised him.

"Now understand this Michael, very clearly. Either he hangs, or you!"

The result was another deep breath and Michael's hands twisting agonisingly together.

"This is his cargo. Loaded at a bay up from Killannan, on his ground still."

More finger twisting.

"Heading for France."

"And this ship?"

"Hired in France. She works up and down the French coast, she's a Yankee alright, but not been home in years."

"So, Fallows hires an American schooner to do his smuggling of linen from Ireland to France. Is that the story?"

The finger mangling had lessened.

"It is."

"And where's Fallows now? Remember, it's your neck or his."

"On board."

"On board?"

"Yes."

Argent made no reply, silently requiring Michael to say more.

"There's a hidey hole, in the bows, under the deck up front. He went there as soon as it was obvious that we was going to be caught."

Argent sprang up out of his chair.

"Jonathan!"

Sanders ceased his search of the ship's papers.

"Nothing here, Sir, and I'd say the Logbook was false."

"Belay that. Get written down all that Michael has said and get him to sign it. Teach him to write his own name if you have to."

Before the sentence had finished Argent was heading for the door. Outside he gathered the two Marines and went out onto the weather deck. There he gained four more, and he hurried, with the six in tow, down below the forecastle to what were the crew's quarters. He found a lamp and stooped low to find his way forward and there he ordered three Marines to search for any kind of door, the remaining three to find a way further down below, then to search there. He joined the upper search himself, pulling away stores of canvas, ropes and unidentified boxes. Nothing was found. They obtained another lamp and searched the seams of the planking minutely, still nothing that would show a door. Suddenly, they heard shouts and foul words from beneath their feet. Using the lamps, they went back astern to find their way down into what was the ship's bilges, the whole keel covered in ballast stones, all showing a sickly grey-green in the yellow light of the lanterns. Ahead, in the gloom, Argent's three Marines were dragging a struggling figure across the uneven surface of the ballast and Argent recognised the voice before he recognised the figure. Fallows was bellowing to be released, between streams of evil language.

"Shut him up."

A Marine took this literally, so, very simply and not even considering finding cloth for a gag, he punched Fallows in the mouth. The result was a marked reduction in the volume of words, but cries and moans replaced the protests and oaths.

"Get him above, tied up and into a boat."

The still struggling Fallows, half walking, half being dragged, was hauled up to the crew's deck, then to the weather deck above. Immediately he was pushed roughly to fall into the longboat where his hands and feet were tied. Argent walked past the seated Commander and his crew, but none met his gaze. They had well realised that the discovery of Fallows, the smuggler in chief, had made their position even less secure. Back in the cabin he found Sanders teaching Michael how to hold a pen.

"Has he signed?"

"Just about to, Sir."

Sanders looked at Michael, who, with intense concentration and hard labour, signed his name to a short document.

"Now Michael. There is one last thing before you become an Ariadne, rather than a dead man on a rope! I still haven't signed you on, and remember, you were part of a crew that killed our shipmates. If you join our crew to save your neck, and after that still wake up in your hammock wholly alive, you must now point out those who fired the muskets. How many were there, Lieutenant?"

"Six, Sir, and I can recognise two."

"Very well. The others are for you, Michael."

As Sanders rolled up Michael's statement, Argent pushed Michael out onto the weather deck. Sanders soon followed and immediately pointed to two of the crew.

"Those two."

Argent turned to Ackroyd.

"Sergeant. Those two fired on our longboat and killed our men. Get them over the side with the other prisoner."

As the pair were roughly dragged out and thrown down to land alongside Fallows, four others could see what was coming and it showed in their faces, which twisted with pure hatred as Michael pointed them out. Then they, which included an Officer, were roughly seized, punched silent, hauled to their feet and sent over the side. Argent then approached the Commander, who rose to his feet.

"Your cargo is contraband and you and your ship have been hired to engage in the smuggling trade out of Ireland."

He took a deep breath.

"However, I am convinced that you are American and that this is an American ship. I am going to release you, but I am taking the men who killed mine. I am also taking your cargo. Your men will be handed over to the authorities, who will decide what is to be done, with them."

Argent let that sink in.

"You now have two choices. After we have relieved you of the linen, you can sail away. Or you can sail back with me, to find my commanding Admiral. With him you can plead your case to have your men released. He may do that, or he may impound your whole ship, and you!"

The answer was almost instant.

"I'll sail, what kind of choice is that?"

His brow furrowed.

"I'll be short handed!"

The reply was curt and contemptuous.

"Then shorten sail!"

Leaving Sanders and the Marines on the schooner, the latter with loaded and lowered muskets and fixed bayonets, both boats rowed back to Ariadne. Soon, by spreading both headsails and driver, Ariadne drifted down onto the schooner. As the sun Westered, the linen was swung aboard the frigate, the task finishing by lantern light. With the arrival of the last cargo net, Argent ordered topsails and courses on the larboard tack and he spoke no more to anyone on the schooner's deck. He did not even look, as the vessel's elegant masts slid past, the depleted crew bending on another mainsail by lantern light.

* * *

James Fallows looked a much diminished man; clothes filthy, smelling of the bilges, bald and blotchy head now shorn of the elegance provided by the usual wig and his mouth split, bloody and swollen. All that remained of his previous stature was the ingrained attitude of superiority, built up over years of total hegemony over his wide estates.

"I'm saying nothing!"

Argent looked at him from the other side of the desk, head to one side, hands folded above forearms supported on the desk, his face contemptuous. He sighed.

"Nothing! You've nothing to say? And you think that will make any difference? That'll help you? You've commissioned an American ship to smuggle Irish linen to our country's enemy, and the ship you hire kills two British seamen and wounds a third. And we find you on board! It's my opinion that there's no point in you saying anything, nor do we need to hear anything. It's an open and shut case, with you off to the gallows."

Argent paused to watch Fallows' eyes shift from side to side and his mouth open and shut.

"They're going to hang you, Fallows. No mercy. They'll brand you a thief, a smuggler, and a murderer. And a coward, after your non performance when the slaver came to call. They're going to hang you, and I may just well come to watch!"

This seemed to be Fallows moment of realisation. His shoulders sagged, his hands came together and he looked at the deck. After some seconds, his head came back up, his face fearful, but still yet showing anger.

"I know things."

Argent's face grew even more contemptuous.

"Things that will do what? Help your case? Set all this at nought?"

Fallows angered at Argent's dismissive reaction.

"I've been smuggling for years. How do you think I've always been able to get past your Fastnet frigate, and never got caught?"

Argent sat up and leaned forward, but he let the silence hang.

"I always knew when your ship would show up and then sail off."

Argent looked at Fallows as though he wished his eyes would bore holes in him.

"How?"

"Not how, who! Broke and Cheveley, that's who. Taking a fat share of the profits for the information."

The words hit Argent like a hammer, but he held his mouth closed, then he looked calmly and levelly at Fallows.

"Too easy to say, you can say that easily, too easily. They'll deny it and condemn it as a story you've dreamed up to save your own neck."

Argent paused and leaned forward, his voice heavy with sarcasm.

"Is that what this is, Fallows? The smearing of two Royal Navy Officers? Some spatchcock story to bargain with and save you from the long haul up?"

"It's no story, and there's proof!"

"Where?"

"In my castle at Killannan."

"In what form?"

"Letters from Broke and Cheveley both, telling me when their boat will be coming along and then going."

Expressionless, Argent looked at Fallows for a long moment. He then reached down to open a drawer and pull out some paper. This, with the inkstand, he pushed across the desk in Fallows direction.

"Every detail, Fallows. Details, and instructions. Someone will be going to your castle and searching for these letters and if they cannot find them, your story is a sculpture in smoke, it'll disappear with the first puff of wind. The wind that'll swing you on the gallows!"

He reached down and produced another piece of paper.

"In fact, were I you, I would produce a letter of instruction to one of your servants, someone who knows, to hand over the whole box or whatever that contains them, to the Servant of the Crown. He will most certainly come to call and him leaving with that box is the only hope you have of saving your neck."

He paused.

"And I'd hurry up if I were you. That Yankee may just double back and fire your house, to rid all concerned of any inconvenient evidence. He's no cause now to go to France."

Fallows pulled one of the pieces of paper over in front of him and began writing furiously.

* * *

In the event, Fallows letter to a servant had not been required. Three days later Argent had the box open before him on his cabin desk and was methodically sifting through each paper there contained.

They had returned to the squadron position and, in the good visibility had seen nothing of their fellows. Argent could only conclude that the squadron was either fighting a running battle with a French invasion force, or it was returning to port and he suspected more the latter. In the circumstances of time on his hands and the possibility of corruption at Admiral level, Argent thought it justifiable to take the small detour to Killannan. Using a beam wind, they had arrived out of the January mist, encountering first a fishing boat, just off shore. Both had idled together to allow Maybank to buy their small catch, while the longboat with a dozen Marines, Argent, Fentiman and Fallows pulled for the shingle. Argent had been apprehensive for another reason beyond Fallows box and so, it was with both relief and disappointment that he learned from Patrick that "herself was away on business, up country." Fallows had been escorted, hands tied, up to his residence and, closely supervised, he had taken himself immediately to an office room and found the box. Argent had found the interior of "Fallows Castle" to be gloomy, odorous and oppressive, a strange throwback to late medieval times, the furniture thick, sturdy and crude. Whether from choice or from inheritance, he had not bothered to enquire, he had been glad to leave and the journey back down had been more eventful, almost enjoyable. The word had spread of Fallows obvious arrest and the Marines were needed to keep back the growing crowd, all eager to make clear their hatred of their life's master and their glee at his "proper come down."

Now Argent had the incriminating notes available at his leisure. He noted that none of the letters were signed. He had not expected it, but two styles of handwriting were present, both very distinctive from the other. He thought a moment, then he went to his own files to find the order given to send them to Figuiera da Foz, he remembered that it had been Broke that had drafted it, in the absence of Grant. He found the order, opened it and took it back to his desk, then he compared the handwriting to some of the notes in Fallows' box. The writing style of his Order matched that of over half the notes within.

Come the next day, Ariadne was idling off the entrance to Kinsale, gently rubbing sides with a another fishing boat, whose Captain was now drinking Navy rum whilst sat on the opposite side of Argent's desk. The fisherman was in some state of cheerfulness, caused by his piece of good fortune, his whole catch was being bought and now, lined up before him were three objects; a full glass of rum, a letter, and a purse containing eight sovereigns, seven for his catch and one for the errand he was about to undertake. His rough and disfigured hands could not decide which to touch first, but the drink won, half was swallowed and then he gathered up the other two. He grinned from a tanned face, exposing surprisingly white teeth, as he waved the letter before Argent.

"You've no need to fear, Captain. This'll go straight to Commodore Harper, so it will. Fallows is no friend of mine, nor anyone in these parts. Tight landlord, so he is, scrimpin' landlord, of the worst kind, not an ounce of human kindness in his whole scrimpin' body. Evil to his tenants and he lifted not one finger when that pirate came to call. That story spread, I can tell you, and, on top, we know of the way that you, yourself, gathered testimony of it all from his sufferin' tenants. That gained him a pile of trouble, so it did. So, you can count on my help with this, Captain, so you can, as God's my judge!"

He drained the last and slammed the empty glass onto the desk, as though this somehow sealed a bargain.

"Now, I'll away. And make no worry; this'll get where it needs to go."

Minutes later, Argent saw the diminishing keel leaving a wake that pointed straight into Kinsale harbour. A letter of explanation from Argent was heading into Ireland with all speed, informing Commodore Harper of the smuggling so far discovered, and the need to occupy Fallows residence to prevent harm, both to it and to any possible extra evidence. All was either in place or in train, time now to head for home.

Chapter Thirteen

Just Conclusions

Argent sought reassurance that Admiral Grant was there and, indeed, his unmistakable figure did become clear as he focused his telescope at the quayside; the Admiral could be seen waiting with a squad of Marines. Evidently he had responded with due gravity to the signal "important prisoner need Admiral Grant"; this being sent on their first sight of the Lizard signal station. The signalmen must have sent on their request and he was much re-assured to see that what he had asked for had not been denied. The launch was already in the water before, even, Ariadne had been drawn up to her usual mooring buoy and now he could see Fallows being tied to a strong rope from which he would be lowered into the readied vessel. He looked a thoroughly dejected and dishevelled figure, much reduced from the all-powerful Master of the Estate that he had been in Killannan. There were holes in his clothing over both knees and elbows, he was filthy and unshaven, the whole made even more incongruous by the odd tufts of hair that grew from his dirty, bare and balding head. His evident misery covered all, his dire plight having finally lodged itself firmly in his troubled mind. A bleak December day further depressed both him and the occasion, this as solemn as Argent himself, him now stood with dour expression, wrapped in his boatcloak, the sharp corner of a box conspicuous front right.

Argent waited until Fallows was safely lodged on the bottom boards and then chained down by the neck to a stretcher bar; there was to be no repeat of what happened with Kalil Al'Ahbim. With Argent in place and all ready, Whiting called "give way all" and Silas Beddows set a brisk stroke which, with an Admiral viewing all, quickly brought the barge to the foot of the quayside steps. The landing was flawlessly executed and Argent ascended the steps first.

"Good afternoon, Sir. Thank you for acceding to my request. Might I further ask that we take ourselves immediately to Commodore Budgen's office? I feel that what I have to say should only be discussed behind closed doors."

Grant's brow furrowed, as much in surprise as in concern.

"As you choose, Captain, as you think best.

However, Argent did not yet walk on, because Fallows was arriving at the top of the steps. Argent turned to the Marine Lieutenant nearby.

"I leave this man in your charge, Lieutenant. Lock him up, feed him, but keep him secure. And he talks to no one."

The answer was a brisk salute and, as Argent began his walk with Grant, Fallows was seized by two Marines and frogmarched into their guardhouse.

For some paces Grant and Argent exchanged no words, until Argent looked at Grant and the latter responded with a question.

"This is serious?"

"It is. Very!"

Small talk seemed wholly out of place in view of the gravity of those few words and so they both kept step together and their silence, until they entered Budgen's Office. Marine Sergeant Venables immediately sprang to his feet at the sight of both and, with the downward movement from his salute, gathered up their hats. Grant asked the question.

"Is Commodore Budgen still here?"

"Yes Sir. Has been since you came on the quayside, Sir."

"Very good. We are not to be disturbed. Clear?"

Venables saluted.

"Yes, Sir."

Grant went straight through the door and Argent followed. Two chairs were before the desk and Budgen sat waiting behind it, the desk clear of all his "consumables", but Budgen was plainly apprehensive. Grant chose his seat and spoke first, this being to Argent.

"We are your audience, Captain."

Argent opened the box and took out Fallows confession, his letter of authority and Michael's statement. He lined them all up on the desk and then placed his finger on the confession, the largest of the three.

"That is the confession of an Irish smuggler, James Fallows, whom you just saw, Admiral. He owns extensive estates in Southern Ireland. We captured him aboard an American schooner, which tried to escape after killing two of my men. I took off the six who fired the muskets and found the schooner full of Irish linen. She was bound for France."

Argent paused.

"As if that wasn't serious enough! He says he's been smuggling for years, regularly sending boats to France loaded with linen, their usual cargo. He says that he escapes our patrol of the coast to the Fastnet, "the Plymouth Picket", because he is informed when our frigate will not be at sea."

Argent sat up to his full height. On hearing his words, so did the other two.

"Here is the bombshell. He states in his confession that he is informed by letter from either Admiral Broke or Captain Cheveley of the dates when Herodotus will definitely be in port. Thus safe, that's when he sails, and Broke and Cheveley take a share of the profits."

The words hung, suspended on the shock they had caused. Grant's face grew very grave as he picked up Fallows confession and began to read, fully some parts, scanning others. Budgen looked as though he had seen a ghost. The other two gave Grant time, and then he spoke.

"And the other documents?"

Argent pointed.

"A letter from Fallows, instructing a servant to give the box containing the letters from Broke and Cheveley to a Servant of the Crown. I saved anyone the trouble by calling at Killannan myself and I took Fallows into his residence and he brought out the box. I sent a letter into Kinsale suggesting that Commodore Harper take possession of Fallows' residence, in case there is any more evidence there."

He pointed at the remaining document.

"That is a confession of Michael Regan, Fallows servant, implicating Fallows."

Grant looked at him.

"And the box?"

Argent held it open and placed it on the desk, the contents visible.

"Those are the letters Fallows alludes to. Their contents support what Fallows says, but none are signed. However, I compared the handwriting with that of an order from Admiral Broke's which I have on board, and it matches at least half the letters. Quite distinctively."

Grant looked at Budgen then at Argent. He was decisive, but his expression was tired and matter-of-fact, almost resigned. He looked at Argent.

"Fallows' place is in the hands of the authorities, you say?"

"Yes, Sir. My letter into Kinsale asked for exactly that to happen."

Grant took a deep breath, then released it slowly through his nose.

"We'd better get someone off to Kinsale on the next mail packet. This may go deeper, I'll trust no one there, so I'll send Baker with a letter of authorisation from me, to make a thorough search. We'll give him Fallows' letter also."

He looked at Budgen.

"Can I use your office, here, now?"

"Yes Sir. Of course."

Grant nodded.

"I feel I need to write the two letters suspending Broke and Cheveley immediately."

Budgen looked overwhelmed.

"What will happen, then, Sir? After the suspensions?"

"Probably a full trial, but that is in the hands of their Admiralty Lordships. This is criminal, so, if they do go down that route, it will be the King's Bench and these letters from Fallows' residence and the other three documents will undoubtedly be used in evidence."

"Will they be gaoled in the meantime?"

"I think not. That is up to the local Magistrate, and I suspect that, for now, he'll give both the benefit of the doubt, until all this has been thoroughly examined. If it stands up as you describe, then gaol it will be, but until then, well? They do have connections!"

He paused and took another deep breath.

"Now, Argent. What else?"

"I have six Americans held prisoner, Sir. They fired on my longboat and killed two of my crew. We let the rest go, and their ship."

"Heavens be thanked for that! As for the six, send them to the town gaol and I'll send them to London. That's for the Admiralty, no, it's probably beyond that, it's for the politicians. Much too complex for the likes of us. Anything else?"

"Yes Sir. Michael Regan, Fallows servant, was on the American schooner. He did not fire on us, and so I pressed him onto Ariadne. Strictly, he is a smuggler and crewed the vessel that fired on a King's ship, but he gave us Fallows who was hidden on the schooner and he identified four of the six."

He placed his finger on his statement.

"As I have said, that is his statement implicating Fallows, which then forced Fallows to implicate Admiral Broke and Captain Cheveley. Should I also send him ashore?"

Grant furrowed his brow and screwed his lips. After a moment he answered.

"No. Let it go. Were he arrested, as a smuggler the Magistrate would sentence him to time on a warship anyway. I'll get that cleared. If this Michael wants a full trial he can have one, but he'd be a damn fool were he to insist on that."

He allowed his fingers to fall onto the desk edge, as a gesture of finality.

"Right. Commodore, I need to use your desk. Argent, send Venables down with paper, ink and sealing wax."

However, Argent was not finished.

"Sir, do you know, I don't know if you do, but what will happen to Fallows estate?"

"If memory serves; the property of felons, judged to be the result of their criminality, becomes Crown Property and is invariably sold off, usually at auction."

Argent grinned and nodded.

"Yes Sir. Thank you. I'll send Venables down now, on my way out.

However, he did not make an immediate exit. He made full use of the goodwill of Sergeant Venables to dash off a quick letter to Sinead, telling her of Fallows arrest for smuggling and that she was to keep a look out, maintain a "weather eye" he added, for any notice of the sale of Fallow's estate. An ambition had emerged within him, new born, but almost fully grown.

Back on board, Argent issued his orders, then went straight to his cabin and so he saw nothing of the longboat being loaded with the six American prisoners and a Marine escort for each. On his final exit from Budgen's office, Venables had given him the ship's mail and, once at his desk, Argent tipped the contents onto the empty surface. One he recognised; it being the same as the letter from the Admiralty Prize Court, another was of a new form, addressed in a businesslike, but feminine hand. He felt duty bound to deal with the former first and had difficulty bending it to break the seal, but, that done, he prized it all open and found the Banker's Draft which confirmed his thoughts. It said £16,533, 9s, 8d, this for the smuggler they had taken in the Autumn. He could not bring himself to bother with the calculations as for La Mouette, his thoughts were too preoccupied with the other letter, so instead he called for Purser Maybank. The Prize Court letter summarily placed aside, he looked at the second.

He read his name and the name of his ship several times, then he broke the seal and folded back the paper. The first line hit him like a hammer blow and brought a huge grin to his face. "My special Captain. It means much to me that you are still thinking of me." The rest was a jumble of ideas, events and observations, as much as Argent's letter to her had been, but it was signed "Your Sinead." He read every word, some carefully, some quickly, then he re-read the whole, four pages of it, and was still reading when Purser Maybank arrived. Argent did little more than raise his head at his entry and, whilst still reading, he pushed the Prize Court documents towards Maybank's side of the desk. He did manage some words of greeting and instruction.

"Purser Maybank! Joy of the afternoon to you. Please to take care of this, it's more prize money. Distribution as for La Mouette."

Maybank took this as both the commencement and the termination of his time in his Captain's presence and he carefully gathered the documents and took himself away, leaving his superior Officer to lean back in his chair and begin at the beginning once more. Later, having almost committed the whole to memory, he placed the letter in his inside pocket and took himself up on deck, to the quarterdeck. There he observed the Quarterdeck Afterguard about their business, the Watch about their's on the gangways, some topmen in the rigging and so, thus fully absorbed, he decided to take a turn around the ship. With his hands clasped behind his back, smiling all round and describing the occasional jig, he took himself along the starboard companionway and up to the forecastle. He passed Bosun Fraser, who followed Argent with his eyes, then observed to his companion, Bosun's Mate Ball.

"Somethin's put a spring in his step!"

* * *

The days were pushing onto Christmas. With Ariadne still at her mooring, on the 22nd December, Herodotus sailed past, making her exit for the open sea and to begin her duty on the "Plymouth picket".

Argent and all his Officers could not resist going to the rail and observing who was on her quarterdeck. The rumour mill had been at work and all had some inkling of what had befallen Broke and Cheveley, therefore, would Cheveley be on his quarterdeck? He was not, in his place was an unknown figure who had the courtesy to raise his hat as the tide took his ship on past. All Ariadne Officers raised their's in reply and not a few amongst both crews waved in both greeting and farewell. None of the Ariadne's could bring themselves to view those of the Herodotus as the bitter rivals that they would the crew of any other frigate.

Argent drew his own thoughts towards the subject of Christmas. With Herodotus out, it would seem that Ariadne would not be at sea, bar some emergency and, in addition, she was due a thorough overhaul, just short of a refit. This would involve striking down the spars and topmasts to repair and replace, also thoroughly renewing, where needed, both the running and standing rigging. In the event of an overhaul, he had decided that a Christmas meal for the whole crew and Officers would be very much in order, especially with the extra prize money.

Argent felt secure in assuming the refit and Maybank was, therefore, ordered to place a "voluntary" tax on the extra prizemoney, to pay for the festivity. Thus, the following day, Argent sought Budgen's permission to begin the overhaul, but he dropped into the conversation, outwardly as a mere aside, but tactically as a cunning bribe, that he was organising a Christmas feast for the whole crew. The overhaul was granted, unsurprisingly, on the understanding that Budgen would receive an invitation, and the extra supplies were bought in for the feast and carefully stowed where neither damp nor rodent could do them harm. However, for the good Commodore, a surprise awaited.

On Christmas Eve the lowerdeck was prepared, this being looked forward to by all aboard as being rations a "cut above the usual", but Budgen found himself part of an occasion when the Officers served the men, an Argent innovation. To remain sitting alone at the Officer's table even he could condemn as churlish and so he grudgingly, but eventually with good grace, provided an extra pair of hands, finding the men both cheerful and respectful. There was one other notable occurrence, in that "Smallsize" had become Midshipman Wheeler, him now elevated to fill the vacancy in that Mess, sponsored by Argent. It was he that, as chance would have it, came to serve the mess of number three starboard. Morris sat back with folded arms and, in a Fatherly fashion, looked approvingly upon his, now uniformed, ex-powdermonkey, as he placed the dish of roast pork and the bucket of bread onto the table, to go with the pot of peas and the jug of beer brought earlier.

"Nothing new about you bringin' such as that 'ere for us. Eh? Sir!"

All at the table knuckled their foreheads in the presence of their ne Midshipman, humorously but respectfully and Wheeler departed smiling. The Officers ate with the men, then Argent made a short speech which finished with a toast to Ariadne. The eagerness with which the men sprang to their feet and the gusto in the shout to repeat the name of their ship was not lost on Budgen nor on the Marine sentries on the quayside who turned their heads as the name came echoing across the chill, grey water. The meal finished, the Officers remained to watch, and sometimes to join in, the post prandial entertainment. This took the form of all types of formation dancing and most modes of singing, bar that of concert standard, but the fiddles and squeezeboxes gave no one the choice of remaining silent. Argent and Fentiman slipped away, feeling the need to take Budgen with them, him now being well in his cups and swaying markedly. After the departure of Budgen, Argent and Fentiman were alone in the main cabin, both were happily intoxicated and Argent enquired of Fentiman the possibility of him spending some time with his own family. The reply came as a surprise.

"It is my dearest wish, but I fear that the East coast, King's Lynn that being, is too far a journey."

"Not so! Within two days, this ship will not be fit for sea and the refurbishment will take several days, possibly a week. On the day that begins, you must go."

He refilled the glasses of both.

"Right, that leaves tomorrow, Christmas Day. You must come with me, to the farm. As my guest. I insist!"

He paused and looked fully at his First Lieutenant.

"I've arranged it all anyway!"

The light that came into Fentiman's face showed that any form of insisting was wholly unnecessary; plainly, it was a notion that he welcomed as fully as a warm fire on a wet night, plus a comfy chair!

"Nothing would give me more pleasure, I would be delighted to accept."

Argent emptied his glass and set it back down on the table, a little too heavily.

"Right, that's settled. I'm for returning to the men. I am very much in the right mood for a bit of a sing song!"

The next day, Christmas Day found them standing at the farm door, Argent again formally knocking. The door was opened, unsurprisingly, by Emily, in her best dress and the pleasure of both her and Fentiman to, once again, be in each other's presence was unmistakable. Fentiman felt he now had sufficient licence to take Emily's hand and kiss it and, whilst Emily blushed and studied the floor, Argent passed judgment.

"Hmmm. Lady's man!"

"Be quiet! Out of the way!"

This time from Enid and Argent allowed himself to be pushed to the table and around to the place at his Father's right hand and then be forced down into a chair. When their plates were filled, all stood for a solemn grace, said by Father, but the others standing with heads bowed were unaware that Emily and Fentiman spent the short time stealing glances at each other. The meal was excellent, plain food properly cooked, plain, apart from roast potatoes, which added much to Argent's enjoyment. The meal finished, all fell to talking, all sated and content. After some minutes the conversation split, then Fentiman and Emily rose and he helped her on with her cloak and without a word they left through the front door. Argent and Argent Senior, being at the opposite end of the table from their now empty places, looked querulously at Enid.

"Some fresh air."

Then she pointed an arresting finger at Argent.

"Nothing from you!"

Argent shrank down and back into his chair much to the amusement of his Father and Beryan, but then tea arrived, the cups being carefully placed before these two, but slammed down in front of Argent. The message was very clear and so, as much to avoid the ire of his elder sister, he changed the subject, turning to his Father.

"My warning, or worry, as you termed it, that I mentioned last time; has anything happened?"

His Father sat back in his chair, then looked at Beryan.

"Not sure. One of Broke's estate workers tipped us the word of a few strangers arriving at his place back week before last. A few neighbours and I kept watch at his gate and outside here, but nothing happened, bar a handful walking down the hill, one evening. Since then, all's been very quiet. Not much happening at Higher Barton at all, few lights even, but I hear that Broke's got extra troubles of his own."

Argent looked at his Father, old, yes, but solid, craggy, and in the best spirits he had seen in him for some time.

"Yes, Broke's been suspended from duty. Stood down, him and Cheveley."

"That I'd heard but had no confirmation. Something to do with smuggling."

"Correct. And it was me as broke the news."

Argent Senior nodded, eyebrows elevated.

"Well Blessings Be!"

What that meant was submerged in the re-appearance of Fentiman and Emily. Argent lifted up his head and began to grin, Enid saw all the signs and a commanding finger was once more thrust in his direction, backed up by a fierce frown. Argent understood its dire threat and her knitted brow correctly and he wisely saw the need to hold his peace. With the meal finished all sat by the fire, talking happily, mostly about Jacob, all save Emily and Fentiman who sat at the table, hands just touching. However, they came over to the fire when presents were exchanged, but not opened; that would be for Boxing Day, the Argent family held to the day when the alms box would be opened for the poor in the church down the hill.

The moving shadow through the window told of the failing daylight and so farewells were made. Whilst Argent did the rounds of his family, Fentiman and Emily's hands lingered together just a little overlong, thus she was the last to kiss her brother good-bye. On the hill down Fentiman began laughing out loud. Argent turned to look at him

"Something you ate, Henry?"

Fentiman did not reply immediately

"I've asked Emily if I may write to her. She said yes!"

There was a pause whilst he laughed some more.

"Do you think your Father will give his consent?"

Argent stopped, as did Fentiman. Argent seized his right hand in both his.

"Nothing more certain, my dear fellow, I'd safely say that you can assume it. I'm pleased with that, for you both, more than I can say."

He paused to grin at him full in the face, then face his own front to walk jauntily on down the hill.

At the same time Argent's barge crew were emerging from the Pale Horse, Captain of the Foretop, Gabriel Whiting most prominent in all his finery as a "right man o' war's man."

"Well, that's me sorted."

"Gettin' spliced strikes me as more like gettin' sunk"

"That's enough from you, Able Jones. I now sees myself as a man of substance an' property an' I needs a wife to go with it. My Molly's come along at just the right time, an' you'm right, I may truly be sunk, but not in the way you means."

The giant Moses King understood perfectly and clapped his dinnerplate hand in full support on Whiting's shoulder, then Whiting turned to his crewmates.

"All you lot have got to come! An' lookin' ready for an Admiral's inspection!"

"You fixed a time? When?"

"Captain permittin', day after tomorrow!"

Beddows, a native Northerner, made his own observation.

"Things moves quick in these parts."

The day after tomorrow Whiting stood with his bride before an understanding Vicar, this understanding having been obtained in the form of a Bishop's licence, negating the need for the Banns. Molly's brother had hired a fast horse for the vital journey to Truro. The final required permission had come with Argent airily and cheerfully waving his assent from behind his desk to allow them all ashore, this time wholly on their own account. The church was largely devoid of colour, bar the variegated greens of ivy, holly, and laurel gathered by the bride's family the day before to add to the Christmas decorations remaining in place. Molly's family added a white spray of hellebore, the "Christmas Rose, but all was clean and polished and truly "done proper".

Truly "done proper" was, indeed, the correct term, for all suspicions and traditions had been thoroughly observed and allowed for. On their way to the altar, Molly wore her best dress, the blue trimming at the hem having been just not quite completed the night before, this omission there to give her something to sew up immediately prior to leaving her house. All mirrors were hid away, she had walked out over smashed crockery to be proceeded by a fiddler and at the church gate was a chimney sweep who tipped a black cat out of a bag for it to immediately run up a tree. Whiting stood at the altar wearing a shirt that Molly had hastily made, but almost all was hidden under his Captain of the Foretop jacket. Able Jones stood by to hold his hat, newly tarred and sparkling, but more importantly, the ring. On the Groom's side were his fellow foretopmen; Fraser and his Mates, plus a few others, who could be trusted not to "run". Argent, Fentiman, and Sanders provided the Officer's presence at the back. Wentworth was still too frightening.

The reception back at the Pale Horse was just short of a riot. After the breaking of the bride's pie, Molly danced the wreath dance, surrounded by some married women, which was sedate enough, until some from amongst her side grew very irritated at the inhibition of their drinking time and, before due time, they broke into the circle to steal the wreath. At least then tradition took over when her brother broke up the wreath and scattered it to the assembly. Molly then put on a matron's cap to symbolise the end of her "spinster days". The three Officers had long taken themselves away, which was just as well for then the serious drinking and the roughneck games began and went on, to be terminated with Able Jones and a cousin of Molly having a fight out the back. After three rounds they forgot what the fight was all about so each downed a quart in honour of the other. Then it began to snow, which was a sign of great good fortune, and perhaps Molly and Whiting did take the time to look out of their upstairs window to see it, but this was viewed with some doubt. In every way, it had been the most perfect wedding.

* * *

Argent, as was dictated by his disposition these days, was impatient for the mail and often went ashore to fetch it for himself. It was now 4th January, so, just days previously, New Year's Eve had arrived and this had been celebrated in much the same way as Christmas, the only difference being that the crew were not served by their Officers. However, a good meal had been consumed and then, as for Christmas, came the drinking, necessarily constrained aboard a serving warship, but not the dancing, at which each Watch did their best to outdo the other. At five to midnight, Eli Reece, as the oldest, had been carried around in a hammock, suitably robed and bearded, to resemble old Father Time. A boarding pike had to serve as his scythe. At the vital moment, he disappeared and in came the youngest ship's boy, bound up like a babe, carried on a bosun's chair, a white sheet around his loins and a carved dummy stuck in his anxious mouth. Argent still smiled at the memory of both festive affairs, but now he was carrying the mail sack back to his cabin, taken from the hands of Marine Sergeant Ackroyd. The shouts of the men making the last additions to complete the overhaul, were shut out by the closed door and he was alone. The sack was tipped onto the desk and there, at last, was a letter he both recognised and was eager for.

He broke the seal and read. His pulse rate increased at the greeting; "My Dearest Reuben", but then she wrote as a conspirator, writing of a secret plot, known only to themselves. Fallows estate was coming up for auction 10th January and the auction was to be at Kinsale. Argent thought quickly; today was the fourth. Even if they sailed on the next tide to arrive ideally on the ninth, five days would be a fast passage with the wind fixed due West and wholly unfavourable and also, on top, he had no permission to leave port. He read her signing off, "Your own Sinead", looking at this for a full minute, then he cudgelled his thoughts back to the immediate. He opened the rest of the mail and found, to his relief, nothing vital and so he piled them on a corner of the desk for Fentiman and Maybank. Grabbing his hat on the run he left his cabin, calling for Bosun Fraser.

Up on deck Fraser came immediately, to be told to prepare his barge. Fraser moved off to obey, but Argent was not finished.

"The overhaul?"

"Last jobs just finishin' now, Sir."

"How many are we down on our complement?"

"Twenty-two, Sir."

"The most for some time."

"Yes Sir."

"Injuries and such, plus illness?"

"All those, Sir, plus old age."

"Yes, of course. Thank you Bosun."

Fraser saluted and made off to oversee the last of the operations to lower the barge. Soon Argent was on his way to the quayside, steered by a very happy Gabriel Whiting, who knew that he may be granted some time to visit his new wife, whom he had set up, using his prizemoney, in a small but well appointed cottage just up from the harbour. All kinds of anticipations ran through his mind and his hopes were high, for his Captain rarely returned within the hour. As for Argent, he had forced himself to be calm, it would be some while before they could sail, even if permission was granted, for the tide was on the make and with some way to run in, having just turned three hours before from complete ebb. Suddenly he felt cold and realised he had, in his haste, forgotten his boatcloak and so was grateful to step out of the boat, mount the steps and begin his journey, but at this point Whiting asked his question.

"Permission to go into town, Sir?"

Argent looked at Whiting, well knowing his circumstances.

"One hour, Whiting. No more."

Whiting saluted and turned to check the moorings as Argent turned away to be about his own business. This took him rapidly to the office of Commodore Budgen and, thankfully, Venables sent him straight down to see the unpredictable Commodore. Argent got straight to the point, even before he was sat in one of the two visitor chairs placed before the desk in the warm office. The desk was strategically placed to benefit its occupant most from the fire; Budgen cared for his creature comforts in more ways than one.

"Sir, Herodotus is due back soon and I assume that we will be sent to replace her?"

Budgen sat back and poised his fingers together, his elbows comfortably on the comfortable arms of his chair. He nodded slowly.

"Well, Sir, I'd like to request to go out early. We are refitted, but my complement is significantly down, twenty-two in fact. I'd like to call in at some Southern Irish ports, perhaps to gain some volunteers and press a few more besides. I have several Irish in my crew and they have proven to be the right sort of recruit. Some more of their ilk will not come amiss, so if we leave early, I will have time to perhaps make up my complement and yet not be late on station. Sir."

Budgen looked at him head on one side, he was suspicious, but also puzzled.

"And your last draft from the Courts was insufficient?"

"Just five, Sir, and one was medically unfit."

"No volunteers?"

"Five, Sir, but injuries, disease, and old age have taken us to where we are. Twenty-two is the number, Sir, and I was hoping to gain a few more, as I say, from Ireland, which gained us three recruits when we were first there without us even trying."

Budgen parted his fingers three times, then held them together, his pudgy face impassive. He gave the impression that he would like to say no, but could think of no reason to be negative. Finally, he sat forward, nodding his head.

"Very well. What you say makes sense, therefore I can raise no objection."

He shifted his bulk sideways; his arms were too short to reach the paper as he sat upright. Argent helped him with the inkwell.

"I'll draft the order now, and Venables will make it formal."

He began writing.

"Come back in an hour."

Argent stood and saluted the bald spot on the top of Budgen's head. On his way out he saluted Venables' beaming face, but outside waited a world of impatience. He walked the quayside, looked into some shops, drank two cups of coffee and looked at his watch every five minutes. After fifty-five minutes he was back outside the office door, just in time to cross over with Whiting who was hurrying back down to the quayside. Argent was grateful for the coincidence.

"Ready the boat. I'll be five minutes."

Inside he found Venables just folding the thick paper.

"No need for a seal, Sergeant. I'll take it as it is."

Venables stood, to hand over the orders, which Argent immediately tucked down into an inside pocket. Venables saluted.

"Good luck, Sir."

"Some will not come amiss on this mission, so thank you Sergeant."

Once at the steps, Argent descended immediately, to step into his barge, now ready and waiting. Whiting sensed his Captain's urgency and upped the rate. Back on board, Argent found Fraser and issued his orders.

"Is all now finished, Mr. Fraser?"

"Sir."

"We sail as soon as we can head the tide. Make preparations."

"Aye, aye, Sir, but it's just a question of droppin' the sails, Sir. As you order."

Argent looked carefully at his Bosun, impressed despite his own impatience.

"Very good, Mr. Fraser. Have the Watch stand by."

However, the next hour was one of intense frustration. The tide poured in, strong and constant, pieces of flotsam coming in at ten knots, even eleven. The wind was fresh but not strong enough to even hold Ariadne constant in such a flow, even with all sail set. Argent could only stand, impatient and ill-tempered, watching the tide run around a straining buoy, the strength of the tide such as to send it under, to quickly bob back up, then to be sent down again, by the push of the incoming water. He turned away to find Fraser and Fentiman stood awaiting orders.

"Is all ready?"

The 'Yes Sir' and the "Aye aye Sir" tangled with each other. Argent took a turn round the deck, forcing himself to pay attention to the new rigging, which, even in his heightened state, he had to admire, Fraser had supervised a very good job. Then back to the rail to study the buoy and, eventually, at last, it showed mere turbulence around its bulbous shape, flotsam now merely drifting by. Argent looked at the pennant and found it out to larboard with strength; that was enough.

"Mr. Fraser. Starboard tack. All courses and topsails. Driver and jibsails. All upper staysails. We'll sail out over our mooring."

Fraser hurried away, calling for his Mates. Fentiman looked just short of amazed, Ariadne would be sailing out with canvas enough for her to get urgently into an engagement. Argent looked back, with raised eyebrows, suddenly in better mood.

"No time to lose, Mr. Fentiman!"

Fentiman smiled back, still somewhat bemused.

"No, Sir."

Argent walked back to lean against the taffrail and watched the squaresails falling and the staysails rising, as their lifts hauled them up to their top pulleys. As the sails were sheeted home and began to draw, Ariadne began to free herself from the grip of the still incoming tide. She began to move in relation to the land, then her mooring rope, once iron hard, now slackened to become limp and Fraser and Ball themselves judged when to cast free and haul in. Ariadne picked up momentum, defying the slackening tide to begin her exit, slowly at first, then with gathering speed. She sailed powerfully into the harbour channel, then, within half an hour, she had all the sea room she needed and at this point Argent could be found in his cabin with Mr. McArdle, plotting their course into a Westerly wind, calculating the angles and the point where she would make her first tack.

* * *

Argent finished writing the Log.

"7th January. Noon position North 51 – 58, West 6 – 56. Wind unfavourable, due West and Force Two. Sighted Southern coast of Ireland, believed to be coast of Waterford, then onto starboard tack, now heading South West by South."

Argent allowed the ink to dry and then closed the Log. He took himself along the corridor to the gundeck, finding his way automatically, thinking of the two sailing days left to make Kinsale. Would he have the morning of the 10th? As things stood, he would need it. He mounted the steps to the quarterdeck to see the end of an unseasonably bright January day, the sun dying in an explosion of red and orange, all changing very slowly with the dying sun as he looked into the execrable West wind, useless for his passage, yet too weak to move any cloud to deaden the glory of a sunset at the point of the compass it claimed its name from. McArdle was on the quarterdeck, himself feeling his Captain's need and anxious, therefore, to meet his requirement of as fast a passage as possible.

"Sir. As things stand, come the Morning Watch, I'd say we can come to North West."

"What log?'

"Three knots, Sir, the last time, one bell ago."

The unusual lilting cheerfulness in McArdle's voice did little to raise his spirits. In the Force Two wind, Ariadne was barely making enough headway to combat the wallow from the endless troughs and peaks that rolled against her out of the sunset. Ariadne was on all fore and aft sail, plus all topsails. Argent considered setting the courses, which would just draw, but they would only rob wind from the staysails and the sailor in him told him that this was the Irish Sea and an evil squall could arrive from no-where. He had no choice but to sit it out, batten down his impatience and trust the ship and his crew.

With the dark, the wind died further, giving Ariadne almost no momentum to achieve her chosen tack point. Argent asked himself, was the weather changing? It certainly felt colder.

"The weather, Mr. McArdle, do you have an opinion?"

There was a silence as McArdle formed his answer.

"It's the North wind as brings a chill, Sir, but it's strength, well, nae man can tell."

Argent formed his own thoughts, but they brought no answer, only a question.

"Kinsale is due West of us, yes?"

"Some South of West, Sir."

Argent nodded in the dark, a North wind would be almost perfect, he could but hope, but for now some sleep. In his cabin he slept better than he had hoped, but the dawn saw the lantern above his desk swaying and swinging this way and then the other. The wind direction repeater from the quarterdeck told of a North wind, but he could feel Ariadne's hull moving solely with the motion of the waves. She was becalmed. He dressed and took himself on deck and there a study of the sails confirmed his fears, they slapped and banged against the masts, this not being caused by the wind, but by Ariadne's rocking motion as a regular sea passed obliquely under her hull, starboard bow to larboard quarter. He had come on deck at six bells of the morning watch, the time of "up all hammocks" and so he idly watched as the crew brought their rolled hammocks to the Bosun's Mates to test if they were tight enough to pass through his measuring hoop, then to be stowed carefully in the hammock nettings. Seth Wyatt's did not and so, using a starter, Henry Ball sent him back below to try again.

Argent had no need of anyone to tell him that this day was the eighth. With everything as he would wish, tomorrow they should be sailing into Kinsale, but with the growing of the day the skies cleared and the temperature dropped to give frosty, wintry, weather, chill and still, no kind of weather for any kind of sailing. Through the day Ariadne's hull turned with the tide; at five bells of the Forenoon Watch, the North point on the compass pointed straight along her deck, directed on her bowsprit, at five bells of the Afternoon, it pointed directly out to starboard. Argent occupied the crew with extra gundrill by rowing targets 100 yards out, these being empty barrels with a pennant and allowing the crews to achieve three shots at their best speed. Number five starboard just recoiled into its breeching ropes before all the others. On the larboard it was number ten. The topmen were allowed a turn, being given nine guns, three for each mast. Bragging rights went to Gabriel Whiting's crew, who were just the fastest, although slower than the regular crews, but the most accurate of the topmen. Whiting had been a Number Two on a 24 lb gun before he became a topman and they had the advantage of the giants King and Fenwick as tacklemen for a fast hauling out.

None of this helped Argent at all. The men went down to their supper in good spirits, as were his Officers at theirs and, at this meal, Argent presided, but contributed little. Most of the entertainment came from Brakespeare, from his endless fund of stories, and when he thought he had spoke enough, Sanders took over, from his experience before the mast on the Defiance. With the subdued disposition of their Captain, the diners broke up early and went about their business, that of securing the ship for the night, securing all sail and hoisting the riding lights, although where another ship could find enough wind to cause a collision, was a question left both unasked and unanswered.

Argent slept fitfully that night and his mood was not improved when, as he climbed the companionway in the morning to the quarterdeck, he heard McArdle exchanging opinions with Short.

"Aye, 'tis weather that can lock itself in, if ye tak' ma meanin'. Hold itself over ye for days!"

When Argent mounted the last step, Short was nodding and polishing the brass circumference of the wheel, both sides, there was no speed on the ship such that would require any handling of the spokes. Argent looked at the sky to see high, wispy cloud strung itself out in long tendrils, an unchanging pattern that reminded Argent of a ploughed field. He walked to the taffrail to disappointingly observe, as he nevertheless expected, no wake showing; then to the quarterdeck rail, to see all neatly stowed and clean, bright clean, enhanced by the weak sunlight. Even the sails were symmetricaly stowed on their yards either side of the mast. Argent took a deep breath, sighed, and went below. What to do? What could he do? Nothing was the answer. It was fate, his luck had run out. He returned to his Cabin and Mortimor brought in some coffee, unbidden, but he had recognised the depth of his Captain's mood.

"The wind bloweth where it listeth, and thou hearest the sound thereof, but canst not tell whence it cometh, and whither it goeth. John 3, verse 8."

Argent looked at Mortimor as though he could cheerfully have heaved him out of the cabin window. Mortimor recognised the black look.

"But, perhaps not, Sir. Eli Reece is sure of a wind, come Noon. He saw the signs in the sky, so he says. We are saved by hope, Romans 8, 24. Reece is right, Sir, more often as he is wrong."

Hope grew but little in Argent's mind.

"Then we place our faith in Reece's divination of the sky!"

The words on where Faith should be placed gave Mortimor his turn to take umbrage and it brought a look of thunder onto his face, which Argent quickly reacted to.

"I know, I know, the home of our Faith remains constant with the Lord! I know."

Slightly appeased, Mortimor gave his parting shot.

"Is any thing too hard for the Lord? Genesis 18, verse 14."

He then left, leaving Argent stretched on his cot, hoping for some rest to compensate for his poor night of worry. If he slept, he knew not; subconsciously the Watch bells from above broke in, especially the long chimes of eight bells for the Noon Sight. He opened his eyes and thought to himself.

"Noon on the day before. Little chance now, still 100 miles off Kinsale."

He rose and stamped his foot on the deck, then slapped his hand against the huge hull rib beside his cot.

"You didn't let me down, old girl. 'Twas just the weather and a run of luck, mostly bad. Not your fault.

He looked at the deck between his shoes.

"Reece and his damn skies. Did they get me into trouble, or out of it?"

He dismissed the question and sat more upright on his cot, rubbing his face then chasing an irritation in his ear. A movement above caught his eye; the wind repeater had swung decisively South East. Was it caused by a lurch of the hull? He studied it further, waiting for it to move; it didn't. Then the lantern above his desk took on an angle that it held. In a minute he was on deck, but Fentiman had set all in train, and McArdle was plotting a course, or more like checking the one he had already calculated. Ariadne's bows lay West and so Short had little to do bar wait for the ship to gain way across the gentle sea. Canvas was appearing on the yards as if by a magician's wand, but the seaman in Argent felt the need to check Fentiman's decision.

"What have you ordered, Lieutenant?"

"Courses and topsails, Sir. Driver and all staysails."

Argent nodded.

"Plus outer and flying jib."

"Aye, aye, Sir."

"This wind may strengthen. We must stay the right side of caution."

"Yes, Sir."

"So you add more sail" Fentiman thought.

* * *

But the wind didn't strengthen. From force three it fell to a poor force two, but Ariadne used the wind well and held a speed of six knots and, with the throwing of the log, Argent did the maths, Noon to Noon Ariadne would cover over 100 miles. Adding the topgallants helped and extra lookouts were sent aloft to keep watch on the weather. A Southerly wind was warmer, but it carried squalls, an extra worry with so much spread across the masts.

As the day died behind thick but broken cloud, McArdle calculated their position.

"51- 40. 7 - 45, Sir. Fifty miles tae go, would be my answer."

The question had not been asked, but McArdle answered it anyway. Argent nodded.

"I'll take this Watch."

"As ye wish, Sir. Aye, aye."

Argent peered through the gloom at his lugubrious Sailing Master, his clifflike face impassive as he returned his Captain's gaze.

"I've never thanked you properly, Mr. McArdle, for the good work you do aboard this ship."

McArdle's head shifted backwards slightly, almost dismissive.

"Nae need, Sir. We all do our job. Yon's a good crew, and that's what being what we like tae call a good crew is all aboot!"

Argent managed to disentangle the sentence, but left it at that and then he studied the sails in the last of the light. All were drawing, but few were tight, and this state changed from sail to sail, each changing from tight to slack and back, with an angry slap. The wind was becoming unsteady, so Argent called for the log to be thrown and five knots was the answer. He stood his quarterdeck until dawn, keeping the Watch busy with small adjustments, but the dawn still found them on an open sea. Hammocks and breakfast came and went, but the wind strengthened and their speed went back to six knots.

Argent was studying his watch as much as the draw of the sails. It said 9.30, this confirmed by three bells of the Forenoon. 9.30 on the 10th.

"Land ho! Full ahead."

Several telescopes were raised on the quarterdeck to view what resembled no more than discoloured mist, but, if land it was, it did stretch far on either side so, surely, this was the coast of Ireland. Argent gauged the wind on his left cheek, deciding there was no change from that of the night. He concluded that he was being too cautious.

"Set Royals."

With the extra sail, their speed increased by half a knot and slowly the features grew. Argent was at the foremast topgallant crosstrees, looking through the winter haze for the telltale hillock island that they had seen back in the fair weather of late July, which heralded the entrance to Kinsale harbour. The coast could now be seen through the naked eye, but what of the island? This required a telescope and Argent trained his own back and forth, praying that he would see the telltale lump downwind and not up, which would require a tack back out to sea. He sighed with relief, it was there, off their starboard beam, McArdle had plotted true and their landfall was better than it had been back then. He slid down a backstay, staining his breeches, but not noticing, instead shouting back to the quarterdeck.

"Mr. Short. Steer Nor'nor'east."

As Ariadne turned onto her new course and his crew placed themselves where best to wait for orders, Argent again consulted his watch, 10.30. He looked for Fraser and found him, but it was more that Fraser had come to him, appreciating the new course meant changes that would soon be his to oversee.

"Starboard tack, Mr. Fraser. Close hauled, wind one point on the quarter. Down all staysails, set all plain sail."

"It's already aloft, Sir! All plain sail."

The reply brought home to Argent how distracted he was. He rebuked himself thoroughly, he had a job to do that was not receiving his fullest attention.

"My apologies Mr. Fraser. I think the main staysail will draw and so will both spritsails."

Fraser knuckled his forehead and took himself off, shaking his head. The Watch busied themselves to carry out the new orders, the topmen and those remaining on deck working in close conjunction to set the ship for the new tack. However, the wind was now almost astern and Argent was disappointed, but not surprised, that there was no appreciable change in speed. However, they had made a good landfall and the island at the mouth of the harbour grew steadily in size. Argent looked at his watch, it was now gone eleven. If the auction was not late afternoon, he would be too late, but he became resigned. He was powerless, he told to himself, and then he brought his attention back to what he should be about, that being entering a harbour with the purpose of gaining recruits for his undermanned ship. The former was in hand for the moment; time to see about the latter. He returned to the quarterdeck and found Fentiman.

"Mr. Fentiman. I will be going ashore in my barge, but we are here to try to find volunteers, or even a few "hard bargains" in the town gaol. I'd like you to accompany me in the longboat, with a party that can put on a show, but also press a few if needs be, come evening. A bit of finery and a few tales of adventure and prizemoney will not come amiss. Guncaptains and Topcaptains should best fit that bill, and my own bargecrew could well add to the theatre, and muscle for the press. Can I leave that with you?"

Fentiman saluted.

"Yes, Sir."

Argent returned to the job in hand.

"What tide, Mr. McArdle?"

The Sailing Master had already addressed the matter.

"Top o' the tide, Sir. Just. Ye'll have plenty o' room!"

"First bit of luck for too long a while!"

"As ye say, Sir, aye aye."

Argent looked at his Sailing Master, but found him staring impassively ahead and so he concerned himself with the affairs of the ship. They were passing the island and Kinsale Roads were opening up, due North. The last time they had anchored outside and gone in by small boat, but, he reasoned, the sight of Ariadne may induce a few extra recruits. With all plain sail and more, Ariadne was on six knots, approximately running pace, therefore, a few more minutes, he concluded, and they would reduce to topsails and courses. However, the few minutes extended out to almost half an hour, before they hauled their wind onto the larboard tack to turn Westwards into Kinsale, the houses of which could just be seen at the end of the long arm of the harbour, picked out in bright and cheery colour, even on so dank a day. Holding to the right hand side of the channel, they held the wind that now swept down off the hills to their left, this good breeze taking them between Charles' Fort on the mainland and James' Fort far up on the headland, this amazing landform created by the sharp left turn of the estuary further inland. Both ship and stone respectfully dipped their colours to the other. They had reached the turn, which at sea would require a full tack, but Argent decided that a bit of a show would not come amiss, especially as a crowd was gathering along the nearest quayside.

"Mr. Fraser. In all plain sail, set all fore and aft."

Fraser turned to run down the larboard gangway, but Argent had more to say.

"We have an audience, Mr. Fraser. Sharp and lively will do no harm."

Fraser ran down the larboard gangway, shouting first for "all hands" and "all Bosuns". As the rigging became black with men, Fraser issued his final instructions.

"I wants it smart, you bastards! Smart! Smart as paint!"

Smart it was. The square sails were gone in minutes to be replaced by the staysails that flew up to their top pulleys. The extra time of them holding the wind for the final yards took Ariadne perfectly to a prominent mooring buoy and, with the staysails holding her against the slow ebb of the tide, George Fraser himself commanded the gig that was waiting to take the cable to the buoy. A double loop through the ring brought the ship to her mooring and the tail end thrown up to Henry Ball for the final securing completed the job. All sails were furled. Ariadne had arrived.

* * *

Both boats pulled purposefully for the quayside, their oars not only in time within their own crews, but in time boat with boat; the display of Naval class and style was to begin from the very outset. All were in their best finery, including a squad of Marines, sat red and upright in the bows of the longboat, but Argent sat in the stern of his barge, looking glumly at his watch. The mournful single bell of the clock on the quayside told of one o' clock, as confirmed by his own timepiece, if the auction was in the morning, he was now too late; but perhaps it would be in the afternoon, or even the evening. He could only hope.

On the quayside, formalities had to be performed. There stood the same Port Commodore Harper, perhaps with a little more flesh on his bones, but his face the same as July, showing a formal yet kindly welcome, but plainly curious. He stepped forward as Argent mounted the top step to the quayside.

"Captain Argent! Again you surprise us, and this time you have brought in your whole ship."

He let the silence hang.

"You have orders?"

Argent handed over Budgen's order. Harper read it, and then studied the signature.

"Budgen again. Still in place, I see. Is he well?"

"When I left him, Sir, yes, tolerably well."

"Well now, let's see. He signs himself per pro Admiral Grant, so I suppose we must jump about to obtain you some recruits."

He allowed his arm holding the paper to fall. His speech was sharp and clipped.

"You're not the first surprise. We had a Marine Captain Baker through here, some days prior to Christmas. Came through and went away, in a fast cutter, quick as a flash, carrying a bag of some form of stuff, and left me with the job of putting a garrison into Fallows place, Grant's orders again. He never took a bite nor a drink in my eyesight; first Marine to refuse a good feed that I've heard of."

Argent smiled inwardly, but Harper looked again at the orders and then spoke directly to Argent.

"You are welcome to set up your show, of course. I would advise the square, half a cable up that street there."

He indicated with a pointed finger.

"We have some in the gaol, I feel sure, and I'll contact the Magistrate, to meet you there, or whoever you delegate."

He grinned, the humour not mislaid on his face.

"There'll be more than one who'll regret the extra pints and quarts of last night, eh, Argent?"

Argent managed a half smile, then looked behind to gratefully see Fentiman approaching, having climbed his own set of steps to the quayside.

"Absolutely, Sir, but may I introduce my First, Lieutenant Henry Fentiman. I would wish to leave the recruiting business to him, Sir. I have some affairs here of my own, which I would like to take this opportunity to deal with. If that falls in with your own needs, Sir?"

Harper looked from one Officer to the other, then stretched forward to shake Fentiman's hand.

"Certainly, Captain. Please to be our guest. Pleasurable I hope? A little of that added to business does not come amiss here. This is Ireland after all!"

"Yes Sir."

Argent paused.

"So, if we may?"

"Of course. But please to call in before you sail. There are the usual formalities that are unavoidable."

Argent saluted, as did Fentiman, and the Port Commodore turned and walked at leisurely pace through the crowd, now significantly grown, of curious onlookers. Argent took a deep breath and let it out.

"Henry. The Commodore recommends starting in the square, up that street there."

Argent indicated with an inclination of his head.

"But, with this crowd, I can see no harm in a bit of a bellow, here, on the quayside. Can I leave that with you?"

Fentiman looked at his recruiting party; they had already begun, led by Fraser. He was proclaiming, with his topmast voice, the wonders and rewards of a life in the Royal Navy, much backed up by the grinning, bedecked "Captains", all nodding in agreement. Sanders was present and despite the dignity of his Officer's uniform, he also was all smiles and gentle bonhomie.

"I'll take the Marines to the gaol, Sir, and see what's there. Will a Magistrate confirm my choice, do you think?"

"Almost certain. According to Harper, him just left, a Magistrate should meet you there, but first you must find it."

Argent's patience had run out.

"As must I, find a certain place. I'll find you in the square or here, agreed?"

"Yes, Sir."

But this to Argent's back. He was gone, into the crowd, heading, as was his best guess, towards the busiest street that would lead to the most important part of town. Argent entered into its crowded and narrow confines and, as a statement of faith, joined the stream of people moving up to what must be the Town Hall or somesuch. He saw two Militiamen coming down the other way and he moved across to stand in front of them. They immediately came to a very passable full attention.

"I'm looking for the building where today's auction was, is, held. I'd be obliged for your help."

The shorter of the two took the initiative.

"Yes Sir. It's my belief that such is held in the rooms of Stanhope and Murphy, Sir. I know that 'cos me Mother's a sweeper there, Sir."

Nothing more was forthcoming. Argent moved the conversation on.

"And this place is where?"

The Militiaman thought, then looked at his companion, as if for confirmation.

"On up, past the Town Hall, you'll know that by it's clock above the door, then, on the left, the second, no third, turning, on the left. Joe, am I right?"

Both Militiamen nodded at each other. The shorter one continued.

"Yes, that'll be right, Sir. Third left, after the clock."

Argent nodded, whilst finding two single shillings in his pocket. He handed one to each.

"Have a drink on me. I'm obliged."

The shorter replied.

"Obliged we are to you, your Honour, now. We hope that you find it easy, as ye should."

Both saluted smartly and Argent returned the salute and hurried on. The clock soon appeared above and ahead and, once past, Argent counted the streets on his left. At the third he found the need to check his bearings, so he asked a passerby.

"Excuse me, Stanhope and Murphy?"

The first reply was the finger, pointed down the street, this then confirmed by the second form of indication.

"Down there. You'll see it on your right. The place has a big overhang."

Argent nodded his thanks and hurried on. He saw the overhang immediately, but, after a few steps more, his spirits sank. A servant was carrying in a big auction sign and there were very few people around, merely one or two either going in or out or merely standing. Then he pulled hope back up within himself, "Perhaps that's because all is still in session." He continued on and entered the double doors, then his spirits did wholly deflate. Once inside he could see into the auction hall and it was empty, save a few servants removing chairs and two important looking characters at the top table. He went in and approached these. His uniform captured their attention.

"Excuse me, but may I enquire? Was the Fallows estate sold?"

The one in the biggest chair answered.

"It was."

Then he continued, with feeling.

"And at a scrawny price, too, even for the deadalive hole that it is, but sure, it's gone."

Argent's shoulders sank, then he heard the voice.

"You're late!"

He turned around and it was Sinead, her face turned up to him, bathing him in her own sunshine; bright and happy, even in the gloomy room.

"I'm late."

"Yes. Late! Y'are!"

But she was now holding the buttons on his left cuff and all kinds of things were going through his mind, but he held to the point and blurted out the question.

"Fallows' estate, who got it? Plainly it wasn't me, perhaps I could buy it off them. I've heard that the price was low."

She looked at his face and grinned, her mouth and eyes in pure harmony.

"Then, sure, you'd be buying it off yourself!"

Argent's eyebrows knitted together in confusion, but Sinead was moving on.

"Sure, now just how much of a fool d'you think I am? It was as plain as can be that you wanted the place, so I bid for you. Acted as your agent, sort of thing."

"But you had no authorization, no paper."

"Didn't I now?"

She pulled him away from the top table and whispered, so close that his chin touched her hair.

"Your signature isn't so very hard to copy, you know. You should do something about that."

Then she held a piece of paper between their faces. It clearly stated "This paper gives one Sinead Malley, the authorisation to act as the agent of Captain Reuben Argent, RN for the purchase of the Killannan Estate" At the bottom was a very good likeness of his signature. He leaned back.

"How much did I pay?"

"£9,520."

"And that's cheap?"

She pulled his cuff in rebuke.

"Why, ye've got a whole village, a castle, a road and acres and acres off over the hills! All fertile or good grazing and, and, prosperous! Ten years and ye'll get most back in rent and such. And profits! If ye've a good Estate Manger."

She looked at him very knowingly and Argent looked at her, head to one side, then pointed to the auctioneers over his shoulder.

"He said it was a deadalive hole!"

"And sure what does he know? Never even been there is my guess. Sure, I've never seen him there, not that I'd want to, miserable squint!"

Argent laughed.

"So I've got something worthwhile. And the buildings? And the use of the road?"

She swung her hips coquettishly and inclined her head.

"Well, I was hoping we could come to some arrangement over those."

Argent nodded, resignedly, but then his face cheered up.

"And I've got a castle!"

"So ye have, but ye can't live there! It's all taken."

"Taken?"

"Yes. There's a perfect building for a school! And a bothy for foundlings."

"A school? And a bothy?"

"Yes. And an infirnary, away off, There's a perfect building there for that, too, on the side where it's quiet. But the castle proper is for some more looms, driven by a steam engine!"

She allowed the surprise to register on Argent's face.

"I've been finding out all about them. They're the future."

She looped both her arms into his left arm and held it tight against her side, then led him out of the hall.

"A man called James Watt, Scottish, not English, couldn't possibly be, invented one, way back.

Argent answered, in mock impatience, spoken in a slow drawl.

"Yes, I am aware."

But Sinead was continuing

"Well, his engines are being hooked up to mills all over King George's kingdom, and I've got just the same plan."

"Your plan! In my castle!"

"Yes, and a good plan. There's water, and coal! On your own estate, for free! Sure, a steam engine's just the thing, but you can't live close to one. No. All noise and steam and smoke and smells.

"So, I'm being thrown out of my castle by a steam engine?"

She ran to stand in front of him and took both his hands in hers. The look on her face left him dissolved.

"And just think now, what good's a castle to you, you on your own, rattling about in such a place? You need somewhere more cosy."

He replied softly and gently, gazing down at who, suddenly, was the only person, speaking of the only things, that mattered in the whole wide world.

"And you have a plan about that, too?"

"Oh, yes, but you'll have to bring your ship around and have a look. It involves the pair of us both, you see."